**Published by Kensington Publishing Corporation**

# RUTHLESS

## LISA JACKSON

**ZEBRA BOOKS**
**KENSINGTON PUBLISHING CORP.**
http://www.kensingtonbooks.com

ZEBRA BOOKS are published by

Kensington Publishing Corp.
119 West 40th Street
New York, NY 10018

All Kensington titles, imprints, and distributed lines are available at
special quantity discounts for bulk purchases for sales promotion,
premiums, fund-raising, educational, or institutional use.

Special book excerpts or customized printings can also be created
to fit specific needs. For details, write or phone the office of the
Kensington Sales Manager: Attn.: Sales Department. Kensington
Publishing Corp., 119 West 40th Street, New York, NY 10018.
Phone: 1-800-221-2647.

Zebra and the Z logo Reg. U.S. Pat. & TM Off.

First Zebra Books Mass-Market Paperback Printing: March 2018
ISBN-13: 978-1-4201-4640-0
ISBN-10: 1-4201-4640-8

eISBN-13: 978-1-4201-4641-7
eISBN-10: 1-4201-4641-6

10 9 8 7 6 5 4 3 2 1

Printed in the United States of America

# CONTENTS

# WITH NO REGRETS

# CHAPTER ONE

"You can't do this to me!" Kimberly Bennett's fingers curled around the smooth oak arms of her chair. She stared, dumbfounded, at her attorney.

"And here I thought you'd be the first to offer congratulations!" Diane Welby, petite and blond, leaned her chin on her clasped hands. Her elbows were planted firmly on the top of her wide desk, and her eyes fairly sparkled. "I'm getting married, for God's sake!"

"I know, I know, but why *now*?" Kimberly asked, seeing all her plans go down the proverbial drain.

"Because Scott asked me." Diane had been widowed for seven years.

Kimberly's brows drew together in vexation. "Fine. Congratulations. I'm glad you're getting married, Diane, really, but do you have to move out of the state?"

"Scott's job is in L.A."

"But your practice is here and I need you!"

Diane sighed. "You don't need *me*—you need a good lawyer."

"You *are* a good lawyer. The best," Kimberly said, a slow

panic spreading through her when she thought of her ex-husband and his most recent demands. She shivered. There was a side to Robert she hated to think about—a deadly side. "Robert's not kidding. He's threatened to take Lindsay away."

Diane grew sober. She tapped her pen on her desk. "Look, Kim, he doesn't have much of a leg to stand on. The court already decided to grant you custody."

"But that was before he cared," Kimberly pointed out, feeling her hands begin to sweat. As soon as the divorce had become final, Robert had married his mistress, a gorgeous woman who was blind to Robert's flaws—just as Kimberly had been, years before.

"And now he cares?" Obviously Diane didn't believe it.

"Apparently!"

"Why?"

Kimberly's throat felt tight. "I guess Stella can't give him a son, either."

"And now he'll settle for a daughter?" Diane asked dryly.

Hot injustice swept through Kimberly's veins. "So it seems."

Diane's mouth clamped together thoughtfully. "You know, I wouldn't just abandon you. I know Robert and how . . . determined he can be. The man who bought my practice is a lawyer—the best—and he's agreed to either take my pending cases or refer them to someone else."

"I don't want some man I've never met." Kimberly insisted, trying to hang on to her rapidly escaping calm. "I want you." Unnerved, she stood, folded her arms across her chest and walked past Diane's desk to the window. She watched a few dying maple leaves fall to the wet asphalt of the parking lot. In the past few years Robert had changed, and his reputation had become black as ink. No court would give him custody—or would it? She couldn't trust fate. "Maybe it's crazy, but I'd rather have a woman represent me."

"Why?"

Kimberly shrugged.

"Let me guess. You think a woman can better understand your maternal feelings?"

"Yeah." She glanced over the shoulder of her black suit. "A man might sympathize with Robert."

Diane scowled. "I doubt it. And as for Jake—"

"Who?"

"Jake McGowan, the lawyer who bought me out."

"Oh."

"He can help you. And he'll do a damn good job." Diane's voice was filled with admiration.

"He works on custody cases?" Kimberly asked without much interest.

"He used to."

"Used to?" Kimberly whirled, her blue-green gaze pinned on Diane's face. "What's that supposed to mean?"

Diane lifted a shoulder and slid her gaze away from Kimberly's. "He concentrates on corporate law now. You know— taxes, mergers, that sort of thing."

"Yeah, I know," Kimberly said, thinking of the bevy of lawyers who were retained by the bank for which she worked. And then there were the attorneys who had worked for Robert. It seemed as if half the lawyers in Portland had been on her ex-husband's payroll at one time or another. She worried her lip. The name McGowan was familiar—but not as one of Robert's gophers. No . . . but there was something . . .

"At one time Jake McGowan was the best domestic relations attorney in Portland."

"'Was' seems to be the operative word," Kimberly challenged.

Diane twisted in her chair so that she could stare up at Kimberly and hold her with her frank blue gaze. Her forehead creased thoughtfully. "I wouldn't refer you to him unless I had absolute faith. He's the best. The man you need. There was a time when he hadn't lost a case."

"And what happened?"

Diane hesitated. "He had a few personal problems."

"Oh great."

"But they're in the past. Listen, Kim, would I refer you to him if he weren't the best? He'll go up against anyone Robert hires and come out on top."

"You're sure"

"As sure as I am about anything."

Kimberly felt Diane was holding something back—something important. "What is it you're not telling me?"

"Nothing. As I said, at one time he was the best in the business. He still could be."

"If . . ." Kimberly prodded.

Diane's mouth tightened. "If he were properly motivated."

"'If he were motivated.'" Kimberly repeated with more than a trace of cynicism. "This isn't some case in one of your textbooks, you know. This is my life, *and* Lindsay's."

"That's why you need Jake."

Kimberly wasn't convinced but forced a thin smile and raked her fingers through her long hair. A headache was building behind her eyes. "You know, I think it's wonderful that you're getting married again. Really."

"You have a funny way of showing it."

"Maybe I'm just envious."

"You? The woman who's sworn off men for life?"

Kimberly managed a thin smile. "Yeah, but Scott's a great guy, and I'm sure you'll be happy breathing all that smog in L.A.—"

Diane laughed.

"I'm just disappointed, that's all. I was counting on you."

"So, count on McGowan. Believe me, he can help you. Better than I can. I'll leave a note with Sarah—she's staying on—and she'll set up an appointment for you in the next couple of weeks." Diane touched Kimberly on the shoulder, "Trust me."

"I guess I have to," she said, feeling as if she had no other choice.

"You'll like him, I guarantee it."

"And if I don't?"

"You'll be the first woman who didn't."

"Oh great. A lady-killer." Kimberly wasn't impressed. Robert had cured her of that.

Diane shook her head. "It's not intentional," she said.

"Good. Not that it matters. He wouldn't get to me."

"Oh?"

Kimberly skewered the lawyer with a suspicious look. "I'm not in the market for a man—any man. If Robert taught me one thing, it's that I can only depend on myself." She offered Diane a small smile. "I'm just interested in McGowan if he can help me keep my daughter."

"He can." Diane was firm.

Kimberly's answer was a skeptical smile. She glanced out the window, noticing that the ominous sky had opened up and rain was pounding the horizon in furious, windblown waves. Raindrops drizzled in jagged rivulets across the windows. The gutters of the old cottage-turned-office gurgled. Ever-widening puddles appeared on the uneven asphalt of the parking lot. Kimberly's thoughts were as dark as the slate colored sky. Could anyone really help her if Robert decided to follow through on his demands? Or worse yet, would Robert ignore the law, as she suspected he had in the past, and just steal Lindsay away? Kimberly's fist clenched. *Over my dead body.*

If it was the last thing she ever did, she'd keep Lindsay safe with her. And if it took Jake McGowan or an act of God to do so, then so be it.

Robert, whether he knew it or not, was in for the fight of his miserable life!

She left Diane's office and headed home, stopping for groceries before driving through the dark, rain-slickened streets to her neighborhood, an older section in the southeast section of Portland known as Sellwood.

Her house, built in the early twenties, was a story and a half, painted white, trimmed in beet red and mortgage free. Though a little cramped inside, the rooms were cozy and big enough to accommodate a single mother and an energetic five-year-old. The fenced yard was surrounded by a laurel hedge and was equipped with a sandbox, picnic table and swing set. True, the house wasn't nearly as grand as the massive brick colonial she'd shared with Robert during their marriage, but the little cottage would do. And do nicely. If only Robert would leave things as they were.

As if expecting Robert or one of his shady underlings to be watching, she glanced nervously over her shoulder, then shook off her case of nerves. She couldn't afford paranoia—not now.

She locked the car, then, balancing two grocery sacks, ducked under a dripping clematis and hurried up the cracked concrete walk to the back door.

"I'm home," she called as she stepped into the kitchen and shook the rain from her hair. She heard a high-pitched squeal and the scamper of excited feet as Lindsay clambered through the hardwood halls to the kitchen.

"Mommy!" Two blond pigtails, their ribbons long gone, streamed behind an impish face and sparkling blue eyes. Lindsay flung herself at her mother.

"How're ya, pumpkin?" Kimberly asked, scooping her daughter into her arms and kissing Lindsay's flushed cheek.

"Hungry!"

"Oh, don't tell me, Arlene doesn't feed you?" Kimberly guessed, laughing as she pointed to the stains from lunch on the front of Lindsay's sweatshirt.

Lindsay's lower lip protruded. "She doesn't feed me enough!"

With a chuckle Arlene Henderson, a neighbor who took

care of Lindsay while Kimberly worked, entered the room. An energetic, whip-thin woman of fifty-five, Arlene seemed taller than her five feet two inches. With frizzy, steel-gray hair and twinkling brown eyes, she winked broadly at Lindsay. "She's just mad 'cause I won't let her have a cookie until after supper. We made pumpkin cookies today, didn't we?" she asked a still-pouting Lindsay. "Even though Halloween's long over and Christmas is just around the corner."

Kimberly chuckled, but Lindsay's brow pulled into deep furrows. "I'm starving," she complained, rubbing her stomach theatrically.

"You'll survive," Kimberly predicted. "We're going to have hamburgers in less than a half an hour."

"At McDonald's!"

"No, here."

Lindsay frowned again, then squirmed out of her mother's arms. "I like McDonald's better," she pronounced, sneaking a sly look up at Kimberly.

"I know you do."

"And they've got fries and McNuggets and—and fruit pies!"

"We'll go on Saturday," Kimberly promised.

"Tonight!"

"Then not at all."

"Saturday!" Lindsay cried.

"Fair enough."

Mollified, Lindsay cast a suspicious look over her shoulder and wandered back into the living room. Once there, she began assembling Legos in front of the television.

"Robert stopped by today," Arlene said when the child was out of earshot.

Kimberly felt a cold knot settle in the pit of her stomach.

"What did he want?"

"To talk to Lindsay, which he did." Arlene scowled as she slipped her arms through the sleeves of her oversized jacket. "Of course I didn't leave the room. I don't trust him."

Kimberly fought down the panic that crawled up her spine. "What did he want?"

"Well, actually he asked about you."

"He knows I work—"

"I know, but he stopped by the bank and you weren't there, so he assumed . . ." Arlene shrugged.

"I was with Diane."

"I didn't mention you had a lawyer."

"Good—because I don't," Kimberly said, kicking off her heels.

"No lawyer? And why in heaven's name not?"

"It's a long story—I'll fill you in later. Just tell me about Robert."

"Well, the pixie was glad to see him."

"She should be—he's her father," Kimberly said woodenly.

Arlene rolled her eyes. "If you can call him that. Anyway, he didn't stay long, just said hello, hugged her and asked about you."

"Was anyone with him?"

"Two men. But they waited in the car."

His bodyguard and chauffer. In recent years, Robert was never without either man.

"Lindsay wasn't upset?"

"No," Arlene admitted grudgingly. "And I guess he does have the right to see his daughter, but . . ." She shrugged her slim shoulders.

"Of course he does," Kimberly said, ignoring the ridiculous panic that chilled her to the very bone. She'd been married to Robert for less than two years, and he'd been a stranger. She hadn't known him at all. The marriage had been a mistake from day one. They both knew it. And now, suddenly he wanted Lindsay. Ignoring the tightness in her chest, she reached for one of the cookies still cooling on racks near the window.

"Well he isn't much of a father, and don't you stand up for

him!" Arlene didn't even try to hide her dislike. "You and I both know he walks on the dark side of the law."

"It's never been proven," Kimberly said, defending him instinctively, as she had for years. She couldn't believe some of the stories she'd heard about him—wouldn't. And yet . . .

"No, but then he didn't do right by you. Carrying on with that Stella woman while you two were married."

"That Stella woman's his wife now."

"And now she wants *your* daughter."

"She won't get her," Kimberly said, though she felt the familiar fear knot in her stomach.

"Diane tell you that?"

Kimberly frowned. "No," she admitted, explaining about her visit with her attorney.

"So Diane's remarrying—that's good," Arlene said, scratching her head. "But what do you know about this McGowan character?"

"Not much, except that Diane's sure he's the man for the job."

In the living room Lindsay giggled loudly, and Kimberly's heart turned over. She glanced down the hall and spied her daughter. Lindsay, tired of her building blocks, was trying to do headstands on the couch. She tossed her legs into the air, tried to balance against the wall and ended up flopping back on the couch only to start the process all over again.

"Things'll work out," Arlene predicted with a steadfast smile. "The Lord will look after you."

"I hope so," Kimberly said.

"I *know* so!" Arlene snatched her umbrella from the floor. "Don't you worry, and if you take Lindsay outside, you bundle her up good. There's already a foot of snow in the mountains. Winter's coming early this year."

"I'll remember that," Kimberly replied.

"Good. I'll see you tomorrow." Waving, she hurried down the hall and called a quick goodbye to Lindsay.

As Arlene shut the door behind her, Kimberly snapped the blinds shut and thought ahead to meeting with Jake McGowan. Why did she feel there was something she should know about him? What was it?

"Come on, Mommy! Let's cut paper dolls!" Lindsay gave up her balancing act, turned off the television and, dragging one tattered, fuzzy pink bunny, dashed over to her mother. "Please, now!"

"I thought you couldn't wait to eat."

"We can do both!"

Kimberly laughed, forgetting about Jake McGowan for the moment. "I don't think so," she said. "I might get confused and cut my hamburger with the scissors and pour ketchup all over the dollies."

Lindsay giggled. "That's silly!"

"So are you pumpkin," Kimberly said, poking a finger in Lindsay's belly.

"No way!" Jake growled, disgusted. His shirtsleeves rolled over his forearms, his tie strung loosely over the back of his chair, he sat amid boxes, pictures and framed awards that had been stacked against Diane Welby's desk. With a flourish he signed the contract for the house and grounds Diane had owned. A second document took care of the legal practice. "You know how I feel about custody cases."

"She needs your help," Diane insisted.

"She doesn't need me. There are several dozen lawyers in the yellow pages."

"Humor me, Jake—meet with her." Diane skimmed her copies of the agreement, deed and contract before stuffing all the papers into a file and jamming them into her briefcase. Satisfied, she snapped the black leather case closed. "The movers will take care of all this—" she motioned to the office debris she was shipping to Los Angeles "—on Thursday."

"Good."

"Now, about Kimberly—give it a shot, okay?"

Jake's lips compressed, and he grew thoughtful. "Oh, I get it," he drawled. "This is a 'special client,' right? Maybe a friend or a friend of a friend, and she's upset you're abandoning her."

"Something like that."

Shaking his head, Jake said, "Find someone else."

"Just meet with her. If it doesn't work out, refer her to Dennis Briggs or Tyler Patton."

"They're both good."

"Not as good as you are—"

"As I *was*."

"You could be again if you'd stop wallowing in self-pity."

"Is that what I'm doing?" Jake asked, feeling his lips curve downward. He really didn't give a damn.

"Yes. And it's such a waste. You could've been—could still be—the best!"

"Maybe I don't want to be," he said, scowling darkly.

"Suit yourself. But this time someone *needs* you."

"Humph."

Diane slid her case off the desk and walked to the door. Her hand rested on the knob. "Do yourself and me a favor— meet Kimberly Bennett. I'll have Sarah set up an appointment next week."

"I'm going skiing next week."

"Then the next."

"It's a waste of time."

"I don't know why I bother with you."

"Neither do I."

Diane sighed, opened the door, then closed it again and,

holding her briefcase in both hands, said, "Fine, consider it calling in my markers—okay?"

Jake's jaw clenched, and the knot in his stomach twisted. Diane Welby had helped him pick up the pieces of his life when he needed her most. Again the horrid grief seared his soul. There was no period in his life he'd rather forget more. The days and nights had seemed to run together in pitch darkness. And the pain! God, the pain had been so intense—so all consuming. He would have given up and accepted a fate of living in his own hell, had it not been for Diane.

At the time, Jake and Diane had worked at a large firm in Portland. Diane had covered for him at the office—given him the time he needed—and comforted him when he didn't want anyone around. She'd even helped him make the move from domestic to corporate law just so he could function again. Finally he'd managed to pull himself back together to the point where he could go on with his life. And he owed Diane Welby.

A grim smile tightened his lips. He shoved his hands deep into his pockets. "I guess I owe you one, *Dr.* Welby."

Shaking her head, she laughed. "More than one, but who's counting?" Opening the door again, she glanced over her shoulder. "And it won't be Dr. Welby much longer."

He laughed. The pet name he'd given her when she'd cared for him would always stick. "Dr. Donaldson just doesn't have the same ring."

"Work on it. I'll see you at the wedding next week."

"I wouldn't miss it for the world," Jake said with a cynicism too ingrained for his thirty-five years. Through the window he watched Diane slide into her bronze Mustang, and he wondered if she had any idea what she was getting herself into.

*Marriage,* he thought with the same stygian anger that always consumed him when he thought of his own tragic, short-lived union, *who needs it?*

# CHAPTER TWO

He was late. Checking his watch and frowning, Jake drove his pickup into the parking lot of his new office building. Tall maple and fir trees separated the lot from the main road, and the building itself, a pasty-colored stucco cottage with sloped roof, gables, moss-green shutters and several chimney stacks, reminded him of country homes he'd seen in Europe. Without the wooden sign swinging in the front yard, no one would guess this quaint little retreat to be a lawyer's office.

Perversely the office appealed to him, though he'd bought Diane Welby's practice on a whim because he was tired of the run-as-fast-as-you-can pace of downtown Portland.

He parked the pickup near the door and climbed out. Rain lashed at his neck and tossed his hair away from his face. Hiking the collar of his denim jacket against the wind, he lowered the tailgate and pulled out the first box of books he could reach.

Despite a plastic tarp, the box was wet. The cardboard sagged as he carried the awkward crate through the lot and down a mossy brick path to the door. Cursing as the box began to split, Jake shouldered his way into the building.

He dropped the box on his desk and rubbed the crick from the small of his back. As he surveyed the spacious room with its mullioned windows, fawn-colored carpet, any use fireplace and plaster walls, he wondered if he'd made a mistake.

But he'd been bored with the rat race of the city and was sick of the high-rises, chrome, glass and crisp white shirts beneath neatly buttoned wool vests. He'd had it. If he never saw an athletic club again, or walked into a boardroom of self-important executives surrounding a hardwood table and puffing on cigars, or spent hours reading through the latest books on tax loopholes, it would be too soon.

"So, here you are, McGowan," he muttered as he spied a half-full bottle of Scotch shoved into his soggy box. His lips curled into a sardonic smile. Ignoring the fact that it wasn't quite noon, he dusted off the bottle, twisted off the top and, mentally toasting this new turn of his career, muttered, "Cheers."

He took a long pull right from the bottle. As the liquor hit the back of his throat and burned a path to his stomach, he grimaced. Without bothering to recap the bottle, he strode outside.

Sooty gray clouds moved restlessly across the sky. The wind whistled through the fir boughs, and rain peppered the ground. Growling to himself, Jake climbed into the rear of the pickup, threw back the tarp and yanked on a heavy crate. He'd overslept, got a late start packing these final boxes and now he couldn't possibly drive to Mt. Bachelor by nightfall.

Hearing the purr of an engine, he glanced over his shoulder.

A sleek black Mercedes wheeled into the lot. The driver, a woman, yanked on the emergency brake, cut the engine and climbed out. Clasping a billowing black jacket around her, she headed straight for the cottage. She didn't even glance his way, but sidestepped the puddles and walked crisply along the path. Once inside the open door, she stopped dead in her tracks. "Hello?" she called in a voice so low he could barely hear it. "Sarah? Are you here?"

Jake vaulted from the bed of the pickup. His eyes narrowed on the rich woman and her raven-black coat and matching boots. He hauled the box off the back of the truck and followed her path just as she, perplexed, walked back outside. Statuesque, with high cheekbones, skin flush from the cold and mahogany-colored hair dark with the rain, she stared at him through the most intense blue-green eyes he'd ever seen. "Excuse me, I'm looking for Jake McGowan," she said, offering a tentative smile.

"I'm McGowan."

"You?" she repeated as if she didn't believe him. Her gaze moved from his wind-tossed hair to his scuffed boots. "But I thought—the man I'm looking for is a lawyer. . . ."

"As I said, I'm Jake McGowan," he repeated flatly.

Kimberly didn't know whether to laugh or cry. *This* was the hotshot attorney Diane had told her about? This man dressed in worn denim, in desperate need of a shave and smelling slightly of alcohol? "There—there must be some mistake."

"If you say so." He shifted a huge box full of books and desk paraphernalia and carried it down a short hallway—to Diane's office, or what had been Diane's office.

Wary, half-expecting him to own up to the fact that he was the groundskeeper, Kimberly followed a few steps behind, noting the man's broad shoulders stretching taut a cotton T shirt, his lean hips, low-slung, extremely faded jeans and well-worn leather boots.

He dropped the crate in the one empty corner of the office, then turned to face her, resting his hips on a large walnut desk and crossing his arms insolently across his chest. "What can I do for you, Ms.—?"

"Bennett. Kimberly Bennett. I have an appointment with Mr. Mc—you—this morning."

Something flashed in his eyes. "So, you're Kimberly Bennett," he drawled as if her name were distasteful. His gaze moved slowly from her head to her feet, then he glanced through the window to the parking lot at her car.

"Diane told you about me?"

"A little. But your appointment is *next* Monday."

"This is the second—"

"Sarah told me the ninth."

"Oh, no." Kimberly thought ahead to her schedule at the bank. Next week was overbooked with trust clients starting to put together their year-end information. "I don't know if I can make it then . . . look, I'm here now. Can't you just see if this is going to work?" she asked. "I don't know if I can get away next week."

He smiled as if at some private joke.

Kimberly plunged on. "Diane must've mentioned how desperate I am," she said nervously. "I don't want to lose my daughter."

"Not even to her father?"

Why did he sound so bitter? "Not to anyone. Lindsay's only five. The divorce was hard enough on her, and Robert and I agreed that I should have full custody."

Jake's brows shot up.

"But he's changed his mind."

"Why?" His strong, chiseled features were taut beneath his tanned skin.

Kimberly's shoulders squared at the antagonism charging the air. He hadn't said as much, but she felt as if he didn't trust her, didn't believe her, though they'd barely met. "He claims it's because he remarried and his new wife can't conceive children." Her lips twisted at the irony of it all. Robert, the man who had once thought she should consider abortion as the solution to her surprise pregnancy, now wanted his daughter all to himself. "Robert claims Stella doesn't want to adopt."

"He *claims*?" Jake repeated. "You don't believe him?"

"It's difficult—with Robert."

"Why?"

Kimberly bristled. Damn, these questions were personal. *What did you expect?* "He, uh, was less than honest while we were married."

Jake's mouth twitched. "And now he wants full custody?"

"That's what he says." She felt herself shaking inside, shaking with the rage that gnawed at her often during the nights when she couldn't sleep. "He told me he'd go to any lengths, even if it meant proving me unfit."

"Could he?"

"Prove me unfit? No! Of course not." Her cheeks flushed angrily. "I mean—it's not true. He has no proof, no evidence— and I don't even think he'd go through with it, but I don't know. He's been obsessive about Lindsay lately."

"Lindsay's your daughter?"

"Yes."

"And Stella's his wife—have I got it straight?"

"Right."

His silvery eyes were cold, his gaze intense. "Wasn't Robert 'obsessed' with your daughter while you were married?"

"No—not at all." She cleared her throat. "At times he acted as if she didn't exist."

"And yet, now that he's changed his mind, he'd go as far as to claim you're unfit?"

Was this man baiting her? "I believe him."

"Because of his track record?"

That did it. "Look, I'm just telling you what he told me— okay? That's what he's threatened."

Scowling to himself, Jake plowed one hand through his wet, near-black hair. Then, noticing the condition of the room for the first time, he muttered something under his breath, cleared a dusty stack of files from a nearby chair and waved her onto the cushion.

Kimberly perched on the edge of the chair.

"I wouldn't worry about the unfit business," he said, rubbing the back of his neck.

"Why not?"

"If there's no proof, your husband's attorney won't go along with it."

"His attorney would jump off a cliff if Robert told him to."

Jake actually grinned—a crooked smile twisted by derision. Kimberly smiled back. "Will you take my case?"

"I don't usually handle custody or domestic problems—"

"You did once. Diane said you were the best in Portland."

"She's stretching the truth."

Kimberly's eyebrows raised. "And why would she do that?"

"I don't know. Maybe to satisfy you."

"I don't think so, Mr. McGowan. She seemed to think you could help me."

"Any attorney can help you," he replied evenly.

"I want the best."

"Then try Ben Kesler," he suggested coldly, feeling the irony of the situation. The bastard had been Jake's wife's lawyer. "He's gained quite a reputation for himself as a divorce attorney."

"Can't do it," she said softly as all the color drained from her face and her voice threatened to give out.

"And why not?"

"Kesler's my husband's lawyer."

Jake froze. His shoulders bunched, and pain flickered across his angular features before he looked away quickly, through the window to a flock of geese flying south in an uneven V. "Then we've got problems."

"That much I already know," she snapped. "Listen, this wasn't my idea. But Diane seems to think you're the best attorney around. I don't know you from Adam, but I trust Diane." Kimberly rose to her feet and took two steps closer to him. The pointed toes of her boots nearly brushed the worn leather of his. "I'll do anything I have to do for my child," she said in a low, determined voice. Her chin angled upward mutinously. "Do you have any children, Mr. McGowan?"

His breath hissed between his teeth. "No," he replied. He knew his expression was giving too much away, and he pressed his lips together.

"Then you can't possibly understand what I'm going through. Until you've experienced the vulnerability of having a child—"

"I understand," he said swiftly.

"Do you? Do you know what it's like to think you'll never see your child laugh again? Do you know how you'd feel if your daughter were scared at night? Can you imagine how much it hurts to think you've inadvertently caused your child some pain—"

"I get the picture," he cut in.

"What I'm trying to tell you, Mr. McGowan, is that I'm afraid—terrified—that I'll lose my daughter."

"To her father," he whispered.

Kimberly drew herself up to her full five feet six inches, then pinned him with her sea-green eyes. "I have the right to be afraid. Robert doesn't like to lose."

"No one does."

"But it's deeper than that."

"Meaning?"

Kimberly hesitated, thought for a moment and then said with forced calm, "Robert accused me of being unfaithful to him. He claimed he knew who my lover was, had a private detective follow us and could name places and times when we'd met."

"I'm not interested in your love life," he said flatly.

Kimberly wasn't about to stop. Not now.

"There's nothing to be interested in, Mr. McGowan. That's the point. I never cheated on him. But the fact is he had the gall to accuse me, and could bring it up in court, then pay off someone to lie. To put it frankly, Robert put the fear of God in me."

"Nice guy, your ex."

She clamped her lips shut and glared at him. "Obviously this is a waste of my time."

"I didn't say that. But you paint him as an ogre."

Smiling bitterly, she ran shaking fingers through her hair. "I didn't know him—at least not well enough. And he changed . . ." She stopped, knowing it sounded trite, though it was true enough. During the course of their short marriage, Robert's business connections had taken a different direction, had turned a corner that frightened her. She swallowed against a suddenly dry throat.

"And now he's going to create a phony case against you, then perjure himself to get his kid back, is that right?"

"Yes." It did sound bizarre, even to Kimberly.

"Who *is* this guy? If he's lying, it's easy enough to prove." He crossed his arms over his chest and stared at her long and hard.

She was ashamed of the weak little wife she'd once been— the girl with her head in the clouds. She'd been blind and foolish. But no more. "My marriage was a mistake, and the only good thing that came from it is Lindsay. And I assure you, Mr. McGowan, I don't intend to lose her," she vowed, her fingers curling in conviction. "He can drag me through hell and back, but this time I intend to fight him every step of the way. Now, either you can help me, or I can find someone else."

Jake stared straight at her, and though subconsciously he knew that he should hear her out, trust her wide-eyed innocence, he didn't listen. He wasn't about to be dragged into this mess, whatever it was. Maybe she was a liar, maybe her husband wasn't such a bad guy—and maybe she was telling the truth. Whatever the case, it didn't concern him. "I'm sorry, Ms. Bennett," he said levelly, "but I think you'd be better off with someone else. Tyler Patton—"

"Has worked for my husband."

Jake's brows pulled together. Something in the back of his brain clicked together. "What's your ex-husband's name? Robert Bennett?"

"Fisher," she said. "I took back my maiden name when the divorce was final."

Jake didn't move, but just stared at her. His eyes narrowed suspiciously, and he felt every muscle in his body go stiff. When he finally spoke, his voice was low. "Just one question."

"Shoot."

"Why did you marry him?"

"Because I was young and stupid," she answered. "He represented everything I didn't have as a child—money, power, looks, sophistication. What I didn't realize is that all those things don't add up to love." As if she were suddenly embarrassed, she looked away, glanced pointedly at her watch and frowned. "I've got to go, Mr. McGowan. . . ." She handed him her card and met his gaze squarely. "Can you help me?"

His expression was intense. "I don't know."

She let out an exasperated breath and headed for the door. "I'm sorry I wasted my breath and your time. I guess Diane was wrong about you. Just send me a bill for—" she gestured with one hand "—this." At that, she swept out of the room.

She shoved open the door, and a blast of damp wind blew into the room, snatching at the hem of her cloak and tangling her hair. Without looking back, she marched determinedly across the puddled parking lot.

Jake caught up with her at the car and grabbed the crook of her arm. "Wait." He tugged, whirling her around until she was face-to-face with him again, her eyes level with his chin. "Look, I said I didn't know if I could help you, but I told Diane I'd try and I will. If—if it doesn't work out, I'll find you someone else."

"Don't bother. I'm tired of being passed around like yesterday's trash. Diane said you were the best, and that's why

I'm here. If you can't handle the job, I'm perfectly capable of finding someone who is."

His throat worked, and the crook of her arm tightened. "Diane didn't have all the facts."

"Meaning?"

Scowling, he said, "Meaning that there are other people more qualified."

"She didn't seem to think so."

"As I said, I'll look over your file, make a few inquiries when I get back into town next week—"

"Don't bother," she muttered, jerking her arm free and sliding into the interior of her car. "I'll find someone myself." She slammed the car door shut and turned on the ignition.

Surprised, Jake stepped back and watched as she threw the car into gear. She glanced back once. Intense blue-green eyes focused on him without blinking, and Jake, who'd sworn never to trust another beautiful woman again, especially a beautiful *rich* woman, realized with fatal dismay that he wanted to help her. Kimberly Bennett with her black Mercedes, expensive coat, rain-dampened hair and high cheekbones now flushed from the cold, had gotten to him. Even though she'd fairly oozed money.

Robert Fisher's money.

Money made from Fisher's illegitimate business deals. Drugs, smuggling, you name it—Fisher was reported to be into it these days. Somehow, though, he managed to keep his distance from the actual crimes. And no one in his organization would talk. At least no one had. But maybe that could change.

Jake's gut tightened as he watched the sleek car roll onto the main road and disappear. His fists clenched impotently, and he shoved them into the pockets of his jacket.

Kimberly's Mercedes and her expensive clothes made sense. Robert Fisher was one of the wealthiest men in Portland. He owned real estate in the West Hills, several restaurants downtown, held the majority interest in three lumber mills outside the city and was allegedly one of the kingpins of organized crime in the Pacific Northwest.

Nothing had ever been proven, of course. Fisher was too slippery, his attorneys too slick. No, Robert Fisher always managed to keep one step ahead of the law—even when the law had been Jake's half-brother, Daniel Stevens.

Rain drizzled down Jake's neck and slid beneath his collar. He didn't notice.

So, Diane's friend, Fisher's ex-wife, wanted to battle Robert Fisher. For that, Kimberly Bennett had Jake's grudging approval. And she was willing to fight not only Fisher, but his attorney, Ben Kesler, a man Jake would personally nominate for bastard-of-the-century.

Well, more power to her. If nothing else, Kimberly Bennett had guts. And if she were going to take on Fisher, she'd need all of them.

Shoving wet hair from his eyes, he walked back to the pickup, unloaded another crate of files and headed inside. Once in his new office, he dropped the crate and pawed through Diane's files until he found one marked, BENNETT, KIMBERLY L. He noticed the bottle of Scotch and a glass tumbler. Well, why not? he thought with one glance at the rain outside. He poured himself another drink and smiled grimly.

Leaning back in his chair, wet boots propped on the top of his desk, he began to read all about Robert Fisher's intriguing ex-wife. He probably couldn't help her, but he'd make a stab at it, for Diane if nothing else. After all, he'd promised.

And the prospect of nailing Robert Fisher's hide to the wall was appealing—if purely selfish and vengeful.

The only problem was the child. She was an innocent in all this. She shouldn't have to suffer. He eyed his drink. He had a few days to think about Kimberly Bennett and he could run a check on her. In the meantime he had other plans. As soon as he was unpacked, he was going to take a short skiing vacation to clear his mind. When he came back, he'd have a decision on the Bennett/Fisher custody case.

Taking a long swallow from his glass, he felt the liquor burn the back of his throat. He glanced down at the open file folder and began to read all about Ms. Kimberly Bennett.


Kimberly wheeled into the parking garage of the bank where she worked and slid the Mercedes into her spot. "Idiot," she muttered, cutting the engine. She took a minute to compose herself. There were other attorneys, she told herself, hundreds of them in Portland alone. She'd find one who would help her, someone who would care, someone who didn't seem to be prejudiced against divorced mothers and someone who wouldn't be cowed by the thought of riding roughshod over Robert Fisher.

She winced a little at that and glanced around the parking lot of the bank where Robert still did business. Hadn't she gotten her job here because of Robert? Didn't the bank's president consider Robert his personal friend? Weren't Robert's companies the biggest depositors at First Cascade?

"So get another job," she told herself for what had to be the thousandth time. She glanced at her reflection in the rearview mirror. Worried sea-green eyes stared back at her. "There are other banks . . . and other lawyers."

Frowning at the thought of Jake McGowan again, Kimberly quickly finger-combed her hair, hoping to tame her wayward auburn curls. Then she grabbed her briefcase and made a bee-line for the elevator

In the trust department on the third floor, Kimberly weaved her way through a maze of desks. Computers hummed, telephones rang and snatches of conversation floated in the air. The walls were polished cherry wood, the carpet plush forest green, and brass lamps and fixtures added to the image of money the bank tried so hard to preserve.

Kimberly's secretary, Marcie, was typing frantically at her desk. A black headset creased her perfect, honey-blonde locks.

She glanced up at Kimberly's approach and ripped off the headpiece. "Thank God you're back!"

"That sounds ominous," Kimberly remarked.

"No kidding."

"What happened?" Kimberly picked up a stack of messages on the corner of Marcie's desk. "Miss me?" she asked

"*Everything!*" Marcie stage-whispered, "It's been a *zoo*— I mean an honest-to-God zoo around here. Zealander's on the warpath again, claims you're stealing *his* clients."

Kimberly smothered a smile. Bill Zealander was always worried that Kimberly was climbing the corporate ladder a little more quickly than he. He blamed it on her looks, women's rights and the fact that their boss, Eric Compton, had asked Kimberly out several times since her divorce. "I can handle Bill," she said, hoping to calm Marcie down.

But Marcie was in no mood for calming. "And then there's Mrs. Pendergraft," she rattled on. "She fell and broke her hip and is in a nursing home. The trust has to pay her expenses . . ." Marcie went on and on, filling Kimberly in on office gossip as well as client problems. When she'd finished, she sighed loudly.

"Why don't you take a break?" Kimberly suggested, glancing around and spying Bill's secretary. "Heather and I can hold the fort."

"If you're sure . . ." But Marcie was already reaching for her purse.

"Positive. And when you get back, send Mrs. Pendergraft some flowers with a note from the bank, and whatever you do, *don't* charge her account for it!"

"Will do," Marcie promised.

Smiling, Kimberly walked into her office. She hung her coat on the brass hall tree near the window just as Marcie popped in and set a steaming cup of coffee on the desk.

"I thought you might need fortification."

Kimberly sighed gratefully. "I think I needed this two hours ago, before I went out."

"So, the meeting with the new lawyer didn't go well?"

"That might be the understatement of the century," she said wryly.

"Can I help?"

Kimberly took a sip from the hot coffee and thought aloud. "Can you find out all the attorneys who work directly or indirectly for the bank?" she asked. "Anyone who's on the board, or done real estate work or that sort of thing?"

"I suppose so. But it'll take time."

"That's okay," Kimberly said, frowning a little. "I just don't want anyone even loosely connected with First Cascade."

"Will do." Marcie said. "I'll get on it the minute I get back from break." With a wave she hurried out of the office, and Kimberly was left holding her steaming cup of coffee between her hands. McGowan hadn't said he wouldn't represent her, but Kimberly wasn't certain she wanted him. She needed someone dedicated, someone who had Lindsay's best interest in mind, someone committed.

And that left Jake McGowan, with his unconventional good looks and cynical disposition, out of the running.

# CHAPTER THREE

Jake wiped the dabs of shaving cream from his jaw and told himself he was the worst kind of fool.

The past three hours he'd done nothing but dwell on Kimberly Bennett and her custody case. He'd even given up unpacking his office and had driven home to shave and shower before he caught up with Kimberly again. And that was just plain nuts. If he had any brains at all, he'd leave Ms. Bennett and her problems alone. But he couldn't. Maybe it was because she'd been married to Robert Fisher, a man Jake had sworn vengeance against, or maybe it was because it had been long enough to bury his own personal demons and practice the kind of law he loved again. Or, he thought, frowning at his reflection, maybe it was because she was the most beautiful woman he'd seen in a long, long while.

Whatever the reason, he was back in his little cottage on the shores of Lake Oswego, shaving and dressing as if he cared what she thought.

Muttering to himself, he slid a cream-colored sweater over his head, then started for the door. He ignored the open suitcase on his bed and the stack of ski clothes he intended to pack.

Tonight he would call Kimberly Bennett's bluff—find out just what her game was. He'd read all the typewritten pages in her file, even deciphered Diane's illegible notes to herself, but there were still a lot of holes in Ms. Bennett's case.

Why was Fisher interested in his daughter now? Some latent paternal feelings? Jake's lips twisted, and his stomach tightened as it always did when he thought about Robert Fisher. Fisher was capable of only one motive—greed.

If he'd wanted his daughter, why had Fisher let his wife have full custody over three years ago? What had changed his mind?

Stuffing his arms through his battered leather jacket, he reached for his keys and tried not to dwell on Robert Fisher. A part of him knew it was best to let sleeping dogs lie and let the police department handle Fisher. Eventually they'd catch him, and there wouldn't be a loophole big enough for him to slip through.

Unfortunately patience wasn't Jake's long suit. And the thought of nailing Fisher's hide to the wall was more than appealing. It had been too long already.

Hiking his collar against the wind, he strode across the wet grass to his Bronco, parked near the pickup he'd use in the move. He climbed into the cabin and shoved the rig into reverse, sending up a spray of gravel as he pulled out of the driveway and headed north to the winking lights of Portland.

Kimberly. The thought that she had been Fisher's wife bothered Jake—much more than it should have. Although he shouldn't have been surprised. He'd known of Fisher's interest in younger, beautiful women. Kimberly Bennett was no exception.

Or was she?

Slowing for a red light, he snapped on the radio and tried to concentrate on the news. But his thoughts were already ahead, on the one woman who could help him bring down Robert Fisher.

He felt an unexpected pang of guilt for hiding the fact that he knew all about Fisher—knew of his cruelty the hard way. He should come clean with her, but he couldn't. Not yet. Kimberly Bennett, despite her beauty and obvious charm, had been involved with Fisher—had been the man's wife, for God's sake—and therefore she was fair game. Besides, he rationalized as he traveled in a path parallel to the dark waters of the Willamette River, this was a trade. Even up. He'd help her if she'd help him. Tit for tat.

So, why did his conscience twinge? And why did he feel as if he was using her?

"Because you're a fool," he said again, glancing at his eyes in the rearview mirror. "A damn fool."


Kimberly spent the remainder of the afternoon trying not to think about Jake McGowan. Instead she filled out reports, made phone calls, dictated letters and dealt with the investment department. She finally looked up from her desk at six and realized she'd be late again.

"Great," she mumbled, dialing her home phone quickly and waiting impatiently until Arlene answered.

"Hello?"

"Hi," she said. "Take a guess where I am."

Arlene chuckled. "Oh, I don't know, trapped behind a stack of tax forms or files or whatever you've got down there."

"Right. Still at the bank. But I'll be home in twenty minutes."

"Don't worry about it." Arlene's voice was full of mirth, and Kimberly sent up a silent prayer for her good nature. "I'll just take Lindsay home with me. She can help with dinner for Lyle. He'd love it if you let her stay and eat with us."

"I couldn't."

"He doesn't see her very often," Arlene added. "You know she's the granddaughter he never had."

Kimberly sighed. "I shouldn't do this."

"Sure you should. Slow down and enjoy life a little," Arlene advised. "Go out with a friend tonight. Leave Lindsay to me."

"I don't have any plans—"

"So make some. Don't you have a friend or two down at the bank?"

"I suppose."

"Then go on. We'll be fine."

"Okay, but I'll pick her up by seven-thirty," Kimberly promised, thanking her and hanging up. She did have a couple of errands to run, she remembered, snatching up her purse, briefcase and coat as she headed out of her office. After she'd run to the pharmacy, dry cleaners and grocery store, she'd collect Lindsay.

She slapped the call button on the elevator and rode down to the basement parking lot. A few other employees straggled to their cars as she crossed the dimly lit lot and headed for her Mercedes. Just as she reached the car, she stopped short. There, one hip resting insolently against a sleek black fender, was Jake McGowan.

He'd replaced his faded jeans and work shirt with a pair of gray cords, a cream-colored sweater and beat-up leather jacket. His hair, though still on the wild side, wasn't quite so rumpled, and some of the antagonism had left his face. Nonetheless, he still possessed that earthy sensuality she'd noticed when she'd first met him.

She ignored his charm and walked quickly to the car. "What're you doing here?"

"Waiting for you."

She lifted a brow. "Why?"

"I thought we should talk. About your case."

Tossing her briefcase and purse inside the Mercedes, she said, "We talked earlier. You made it perfectly clear you aren't interested in helping me or my daughter." For effect, she planted her hands on her hips and stared him down. "I don't think we have anything further to discuss."

His eyes didn't flicker. "Maybe you're right," he agreed, "but I've done a lot of thinking this afternoon and I read your file."

"Would you like a round of applause? You shouldn't have bothered."

His jaw clenched. "Look, I'm just here trying to help, that's all. I thought we could talk things out a little. It's no big commitment. But I told Diane I'd help you."

"Listen, Mr. McGowan—"

"Jake."

"Jake, then. You don't owe me any favors. As far as I'm concerned, you're off the hook. As for whatever obligation you have toward Diane, just forget it. I'll tell her it didn't work out and I found someone else."

"Who?"

*Good question.* She tossed her hair over her shoulder. "I don't know yet. But when I find her, I'll tell Diane."

"*Her?* Find her?" he repeated.

"Yes, her. I think I'd work better with a woman."

He smiled at that, and she couldn't figure out what he found so damn amusing. What kind of game was he playing, telling her to go jump in a lake this afternoon and chasing her down tonight? The man was a bastard.

"It might look better to the judge if a man represented you," he thought aloud.

"I doubt it." Why was she even bothering with him?

"Your ex might insinuate you can't get along with men. . . ."

She felt the blood surge to her face. "No judge would buy anything so ridiculous."

"Maybe. Maybe not. Your husband—"

"*Ex*-husband," she corrected.

"—is a very powerful man. You already said he knows just about every attorney in town. What about judges? Does he have any 'friends' on the bench?"

Her legs felt suddenly shaky, but she tilted her chin up and stared him down. "And I suppose you know who'll be assigned?" she baited. What was it about this man that agitated her to no end?

"No."

"Of course not. No one does."

"But Robert—I have the feeling he'd like to tilt the odds in his favor a little."

"How would you know?"

His jaw clenched. "I read the papers."

Of course. Robert's had more than his share of trouble with the law lately—or at least his name had been linked to a couple police cases.

"It wouldn't surprise me if Fisher somehow ended up with a judge who was lenient where fathers' rights are concerned."

She swallowed hard and leaned against the car. She knew Robert had friends in high places, including the courts. "You don't have much faith in our judicial system."

"There are flaws."

"Surely no one who knows Robert would accept the case. . . ." Her voice trailed off. She'd thought of it before, of course, had considered the possibility of Robert buying a judge, but it seemed so bizarre and unlikely, something out of a made-for-television movie.

"All I'm saying," Jake said, his expression suddenly kind, "is there's a chance I can help you—or at the very least find someone who can do the best job."

"That's quite a turnaround. Why would you bother?"

"Because I do owe Diane Welby a lot and because I know a little about Robert Fisher."

"Oh, I remember. The papers, right?"

He grimaced. "Right."

She looked into his eyes. McGowan. Had Robert ever said that name before? She couldn't remember. But there was something about Jake McGowan that touched her. Beneath his crusty, cynical exterior, she saw honesty in his flinty gray eyes that drew her like a magnet. So, what would it hurt to find out what he had to say? She still didn't have to hire him.

"It goes without saying that Fisher isn't one of my favorite people," Jake was saying, "and if Ben Kesler's going to represent him, we'd better get cracking."

"Tonight?"

"Tonight." His smile was hard. "I'm going out of town for a few days."

"So it's now or never, right?" she asked, feeling more than a little prickly.

His eyes flashed in the darkened lot. "No, it's now or late next week."

She almost smiled. He was clever, and that was good. She was tempted to listen to what he had to say, but she had to clear the air first. "Look, McGowan, let's be honest, I didn't like the way you treated me this afternoon. I came to you for help, and you immediately started baiting me."

"That's what'll happen in court," Jake replied.

"Fine. I don't need it from my attorney."

His sensual lips tightened. "Let's just get one thing straight. If we come to some sort of agreement and I take your case, we'll play this my way."

She bit back a sharp response. This new side of Jake McGowan, slightly threatening and authoritative, caused her temper to flare, but maybe his arrogance was an attribute. She certainly didn't want a wimp representing her, and right now, glaring at her in the shadowy parking lot, McGowan looked far from wimpy. In fact, he was downright imposing. He'd be perfect against the likes of Kesler. For the first time since she'd met him, she felt a ray of hope.

She checked her watch. "I promised my babysitter I'd be home by seven-thirty."

"We could start there—at your place."

The thought of him inside her home was more than a tad threatening. It made her feel naked and vulnerable. But what choice did she have? She needed a lawyer, McGowan might just be the best man for the job and she wanted to get home to Lindsay. "My place'll be fine," she said with more calm than she felt. "I live—"

"I know your address," he cut in. "Remember, I read your file this afternoon."

"Oh." For the first time since meeting him, Kimberly was tongue-tied. The thought of his going through her private life, reading between the lines as he reviewed her relationship with Robert, was unnerving. She hated the thought of baring her soul to him, of sharing her innermost feelings. And yet she didn't have much of a choice. If he were going to represent her, he'd have to know everything.

"I'll meet you there later," he suggested.

"Right." She watched as he climbed into a silver Bronco. Tall and slim, with dark hair and expressive eyes, he walked with an innate sensuality that caused her breath to stop somewhere between her lungs and lips. She noticed the casual movement of his hips, and when he unlocked the door of the Bronco and reached across the front seat, his sweater lifted, showing just the hint of tight skin across his abdomen.

Swallowing hard, Kimberly slid into her own car. She couldn't think of Jake McGowan as a man. He was her attorney—nothing more. And he wasn't even that, yet, she reminded herself as she jammed her key into the ignition. He hadn't said he'd take her case—just that he'd help her. And she wasn't all that convinced he was the man for the job. Not yet. But at least he was offering to help.

"Well, it's a step in the right direction," she told herself as she pulled out of the lot.

\* \* \*

Jake pulled out his phone, noticed his battery was starting to wear, and placed another call—his third in the past two hours. On the fourth ring voicemail picked up and Ron Koski's voice rasped in his ear, telling him to leave his name and number.

"It's McGowan again," Jake started, just as he saw Ron's number pop up on call waiting.

"Ron."

"I got your message earlier," Ron said, his voice gravelly from too few hours' sleep and too many cigarettes. "I thought you'd given up on Fisher."

Jake grimaced, turning up the collar of his coat against the cold. "I guess I can't."

"Maybe you should give it a rest, man. Nothin' you can do will bring Dan back."

Jake had told himself the same thing for the past few years. "I know, but I got caught in something else, and Fisher's name came up." He had pulled over to make the call and he glanced out his windshield to the dark night and the few people walking briskly along the wet streets, making sure no one was watching him.

"So you want me to reopen the investigation?"

"Immediately. And send me a copy of everything you have on Fisher."

Ron laughed. "It'll fill an encyclopedia. But nothing can be proved. There's no hard evidence."

"I know, but send it anyway—and that friend of yours in the police department?"

"Brecken?"

"Yeah. See what he knows about Fisher, his organization and his wife."

"His *wife*?"

"Yeah. Both wives, actually. The first one's name is Bennett—Kimberly Bennett. She's the mother of his only child. The current wife is a woman named Stella Cross Fisher."

"What do his wives have to do with anything?"

"Probably nothing," Jake admitted, surprised he cared. He found himself hoping Kimberly was just a naïve innocent—a woman who really didn't know her husband was Portland's answer to the *Godfather*. "But check them out anyway."

"It's your money," Ron said.

*No*, Jake thought as he hung up, it's *Kimberly Bennett's money and it probably comes right from the source—Robert Fisher*. No doubt Kimberly made out like a bandit when she divorced Fisher, though nothing in her file suggested a huge settlement: just the house, which was a piece of rental property Fisher had owned, the car, college education for the kid and a few dollars a month in child support.

He hopped back into his Bronco and took off, threading the rig through the city traffic that still, though it was nearly seven, crawled at a snail's pace.

He felt the sting of guilt when he considered that he'd been less than honest with Ms. Bennett, but he rationalized his deception as a necessity. Until he knew just how far he could trust her, he needed to keep some things close to the vest—especially anything to do with Daniel.

He headed south through the wet, shimmering streets and across the Sellwood Bridge. Lights from the houseboats on the east side of the river were reflected in the dark water. On the east side of the Willamette, he rounded several corners and wondered at her choice of neighborhoods. Sellwood had its points, but it was hardly prestigious enough to attract a woman of Kimberly's means.

But then much about Robert Fisher's beautiful ex-wife didn't make sense. The woman worked—held down a nine-to-five at First Cascade and had for a few years. No, he decided as he wheeled into the rutted driveway of the small cottage that was her home, there were things about Kimberly Bennett that just didn't fit the rich-bitch image.

He strode up a cracked concrete path that was littered with gold-and-brown maple leaves. On the front porch he punched the bell and the door opened almost immediately.

Kimberly, dressed in a soft plum sweater and stone-washed jeans, looked nervous and younger than she had in her stark black coat and business suit. Her cheeks were flushed, her eyes wide. "Come on in," she invited, moving out of the doorway to let him pass. She leaned back against the door to shut it. "I think you should know that I'm not used to baring my soul to strangers."

He smiled. "No one is."

"I know, but I don't want you to get the wrong impression. I don't like talking about my marriage or my ex-husband. As far as I'm concerned, it's all ancient history. Dredging it up again is . . . difficult. And if it weren't for the fact that I'll do *anything* to keep Lindsay, I wouldn't talk about my marriage— or the rest of my private life—at all."

"Fair enough."

She took in a deep breath and rubbed her hands together. "Well, now that that's over with, maybe we should start over. I'll take your coat. . . ."

"Thanks." He shrugged out of the jacket and watched as she hung it in a nearby closet.

She managed an anxious smile. "If you light the fire, I'll make coffee."

"It's a deal." He walked into a small room lighted only by table lamps placed strategically in the corners. An old sofa filled the wall opposite the fireplace, and there was an antique rocker near the archway leading to the dining room. Wicker baskets filled with greenery and dried flowers added color to the rather sparse room. A few sketches, drawn by a young child, were framed and hung on the walls.

"It's nothing fancy," she explained, "but it's home."

Jake tried to hide his surprise. The house was cozy, filled

with a scent of spice, lemon and last night's fire, but it lacked the feel of wealth he expected. Aside from a few antique faded Persian rugs, nothing inside the small rooms seemed of any value.

Then he reminded himself of the sleek black Mercedes in the garage. And the expensive coat and boots—he hadn't imagined them.

So, what was it with Ms. Bennett?

Kimberly disappeared through the dining room and called over her shoulder, "There's kindling in the basket and matches on the mantelpiece."

Jake found the necessities, leaned over the grate, adjusted a few musty oak logs and struck a match to the cedar kindling. The fire caught and crackled, adding flickering light in the room.

He dusted his hands and rocked back on his heels, spreading his palms to the gentle warmth of the first few flames. Feeling someone's gaze on his back, he glanced over her shoulder and saw Kimberly standing in the doorway to the kitchen, her wary blue-green eyes transfixed on him. "Something wrong?"

She licked her lips, and something deep inside Jake stirred—something dangerous and very, very primal.

"No—yes . . . well, everything," she said with a small smile. "If things were going great, you wouldn't be here, would you?"

"I guess not."

"The coffee's about ready. Do you want sugar or cream?"

"Black's fine. I'm a purist."

"It's decaf."

His lips twisted. "Well, I've never claimed to be all that pure."

Kimberly knew then that she'd made a colossal mistake by inviting him into her home. He was too masculine, too irreverent, too damn sexy. Maybe it was just that she hadn't been with a man for years—hadn't dated much since the divorce, but Jake's presence seemed to fill the entire house.

Forcing a smile she didn't feel, she retreated to the kitchen and tried to calm her nerves. He was just a man—an attractive man, yes, but she met attractive men every day. Still, her hand shook a little as she poured the coffee, and she silently berated herself for being such a ninny.

By the time she returned to the living room, Jake had already opened his briefcase and withdrawn a pad, paper and digital recorder. He sat on a corner of the couch, the yellow pad resting on one knee.

He looked up as she entered. "I think we'd better get started. You ready?"

*Never.* "As ready as I'll ever be." She set both steaming mugs on the table.

"Okay, let's start at the beginning. How you met Fisher, how long you dated, when you got married and how it fell apart."

"Diane knows most of this," she said.

"I know. But I'd like to hear it from you."

She should have expected this, she supposed, but still it was difficult. "I was barely twenty, still going to school. I transferred up here from U.C.L.A.—"

"Why?"

"Why what?"

"Why the transfer?"

"Scholarship. My mother didn't have any money to send me to school, and I worked part-time, but the scholarship up here was a godsend." She took a sip from her cup and frowned.

"And you met Fisher at school?"

She shook her head. "No. I was working part-time at First Cascade as a loan clerk. He met me there." With difficulty she went on to explain about those first few magic months when she'd dated one of the bank's wealthiest customers and how, because of Robert's sophistication, charm and money, he'd swept her off her feet. She glanced up at him. "I know this all sounds ridiculous now. But that's how I felt."

"You didn't know about his reputation?"

Kimberly swallowed a sip of coffee. "I'd heard a few rumors while I was dating him, of course, but I chalked them up to office gossip and jealousy. When he asked me to marry him, I jumped at the chance."

"He's quite a bit older than you are."

"Fifteen years," she admitted.

"That didn't bother you?"

Kimberly sighed, but lifted her eyes to meet the question in Jake's. "It bothered me a little. But not enough. I'd convinced myself that I loved him."

He quit writing. The fire burned softly. The clock on the mantel ticked. Shadows flickered across his face. "Did you?"

Compressing her lips, she struggled with an answer. "I—uh, I don't think so. I don't know how I could have."

"Why not?"

"The rumors . . . I couldn't ignore them and all those lawsuits. I thought they were all part of his business until a few years ago when a man was killed—or committed suicide." She shuddered and noticed Jake's face had become tense, his eyes narrowing.

"Go on," he urged.

"The man's name was . . . Daniel . . . Stevens, I think."

"You don't remember?"

She snapped her head up. "I try not to. Anyway, from that point on, things were worse, much worse. Robert became secretive, and he changed, grew colder." She bit her lip as painful, frightening memories enveloped her.

"What do you know about Daniel Stevens?"

"Nothing. Only what I read in the papers," she said.

"Robert never said anything?"

"We didn't discuss anything remotely connected with his business."

"And you think Steven's death was connected to your husband's business?"

"I didn't say that. He was a police officer. And I understand he was investigating Robert. That's all I know." She took a sip of her coffee and asked, "What's this got to do with my divorce?"

Jake's eyes were dark. Tiny lines bracketed his mouth. "I just need to know all the facts."

"Well, I don't know anything more about Daniel Stevens."

He hesitated a second, his gaze hard and assessing. "So, even after all Robert's bad press, his shady business ties, the fact that he may have been involved with Daniel—"

"No—he wasn't. It was suicide, I think."

"Despite all that, you still stayed married to him?" he asked, his voice filled with disbelief.

"You have to understand that I grew up believing in marriage, and vows, and loyalty."

"Oh, until death do you part?" he said caustically.

"Yes."

"And I—I didn't want the stigma of divorce."

"It's not a stigma."

"But it was to me. My parents had a wonderful marriage—never a fight until the day my father died. And I thought—I hoped—that Robert would . . . That he'd see that he was on the wrong path."

"But he didn't?"

"No."

"So, what changed your mind about divorcing him?"

Kimberly frowned. "Robert was unfaithful—had been all along, I guess. But then he met a woman and he fell in love with her."

"Stella?"

"Yes." Kimberly let out a long sigh. Why Robert's affair with

Stella hurt, she didn't know. She didn't love him, probably never had, but Robert's betrayal had cut deep into her pride. And then there were all those accusations . . . all those late nights. Had he been trysting with Stella—or had it been much worse? She shivered, then went on to explain that Robert was so anxious to be rid of her that he'd agreed to give her full custody of Lindsay. She demanded nothing else of him—the support she received she stuck into a trust fund for Lindsay. He'd given her the small house and car.

Jake asked a few more questions, less personal but difficult just the same. Kimberly answered as honestly as possible, but didn't meet his eyes. Instead she concentrated on her coffee, or watched the fire burn down and tried not to notice the scent of his aftershave.

Suddenly the front door burst open, sending in a blast of chill air. Lindsay, blonde hair flying behind, bounced into the room. "Mommy!" she cried, stopping dead in her tracks when she spied Jake. "Who're you?"

Kimberly stood, held her arms open and was rewarded by Lindsay flinging herself against her. She swung her daughter up into the air and squeezed her. "This is Mr. McGowan, he's . . . a friend of mine," she said as Arlene bustled inside.

"I'm Jake," he said, his face softening as he stared at the tiny blonde bundle of energy.

"I told her to slow down," Arlene complained good-naturedly, sending Lindsay a knowing look, "but she was just too excited."

"It's all right," Kimberly said. Lindsay's chubby arms surrounded her neck, and she smelled of lilac soap.

"She's all ready for bed. Just take off her coat and boots," Arlene explained, though her gaze wandered to Jake.

Still holding Lindsay, Kimberly made quick introductions, and Arlene's dark eyes regarded Jake with more than a little interest. "Glad to meet you," she said, then added quickly,

"I've got to run. Lyle will worry if I don't hightail it back." She adjusted her jacket's hood over her gray frizz.

"Thanks a bunch," Kimberly said.

"No problem." Arlene glanced again at Jake. "Any time. You know we love to have her." With a quick wave she hurried out the door.

Jake shoved his notes and pens inside his briefcase and snapped the leather case shut. "I think it's time I shoved off, too."

"Good." Lindsay regarded him suspiciously, her lower lip thrust out.

"I'll call you when I get back into town," he said, his lips twitching in response to Lindsay's outright hostility. "We'll get together and sort this all out."

Kimberly's heartbeat accelerated. Suddenly she wanted him as her attorney. She'd seen a hard edge to him, felt his intensity. If he represented her, he'd give it his best shot. "Then you'll take my case?"

He rubbed the back of his neck and frowned. "I'll take it on two conditions. The first, you already know—we do things my way."

"And the second?"

"That you don't hold anything back from me," he said solemnly. "There are things you might not want to talk about, but if we're going to win the case, I'll need all the facts. Painful as they may be."

"Of course," she said quickly, though his gaze seemed to read her mind. She tilted her chin up and squared her shoulders. "I have a couple of conditions myself."

"Shoot."

"I want you to keep me abreast of the case at all times. No surprises."

"Fair enough."

"And if you ever think, even for a second, that Robert's got the upper hand, I want to know about it."

"Why?" he asked.

"I just want to know where I stand," she said, lying a little. Already she was beginning to trust Jake, and if he thought Robert had a chance of taking Lindsay away from her, then she'd do what she had to do to keep her daughter with her. Even if it meant running away from Robert—and the law.

# CHAPTER FOUR

Jake sat in the bar and glared out the window to the snow-covered slopes of Mt. Bachelor. Grey clouds hovered over the craggy peaks of the Cascades, and a fine, misting rain drizzled from the sky, melting the snow. The temperature was nearly forty degrees, and the extended forecast called for a warming trend.

"Wonderful," Jake muttered sarcastically, signaling to the bartender for another drink. He sipped his beer slowly, and his mood deteriorated with the weather. The raucous noise from the bar's sound system didn't interest him, and he couldn't care less about the skiing exhibition on the big screen.

Other patrons of the bar, drenched skiers in wet jackets and sopping wool hats, seemed to find solace in grumbling together, drinking and even laughing about the rain.

Jake didn't. He'd spent too many weeks planning this trip. He was anxious and coiled tight as a spring. And, though he was loath to admit it, his thoughts kept turning to Kimberly.

Her image had been with him ever since he'd left her two nights before, lingering with him like the evocative scent of an expensive perfume. Try as he might, he couldn't forget her wise blue-green eyes, gently curving lips or the sweet seduction of her voice. He couldn't help feeling he should've stayed in Portland and started working on the mess with her ex-husband.

At the thought of Fisher, he pulled his eyebrows together. Glancing outside to the dismal day, he wondered if God were getting even with him and the rest of the noisy crowd in the smoky bar.

He swore pointedly under his breath, finished his drink, left some bills on the polished bar and strode through the throng that had gathered as fast as his ski boots would allow.

Outside, the weather was miserable. Melting icicles dripping in tempo with the soft fall of the rain. Ignoring the conditions, he stomped into his ski bindings and jabbed his poles into the ground. His right ski caught in the slush, but he made it to the four-man lift and, without a word to the other souls braving the rain, let the chair carry him over the tops of the drooping pine trees to the summit.

Once there, he skied down the ramp and stopped, surveying the lower slopes. Partially hidden by low-hanging clouds, the run was wet and slushy.

Cold rain ran down his neck and settled into his bones. He blew on his wet gloves, but his fingers were frigid. Glowering furiously at the dark heavens, he found no relief in the ominous sky.

There was no reason on earth to stay here any longer. He thought again of Kimberly, shoved his poles into the snow and took off, nearly flying down the run. He may as well return to Portland, he decided fatalistically as he headed for the lodge. At least in the city he could do something worthwhile.

*And he would see her again*. For the first time that miserable afternoon, Jake smiled.

* * *

Kimberly placed a set of statements for the Juniper account on the security cashier's desk in the operations section of the trust department. "If you could just double-check the dividends—make sure that everything was posted last quarter," she said to Charlene, who handled all the bond and stock transfers.

"Anything wrong?" Charlene asked. Red-haired and quick, she hardly ever made a mistake.

"Nothing that I know of, but Mr. Juniper has some questions. He's sure the dividends and interest were down for the quarter. I looked it over and it seems fine, but if you'd double-check it, I'd appreciate it."

"You got it," Charlene said as the phone in her office started ringing.

Kimberly headed back to the administrative offices and nearly bumped into Marcie. "Oh, good, I was looking for you," Marcie said. "Mr. Compton's scheduled a meeting for all of the officers at four-thirty in the boardroom."

Checking her watch, Kimberly said, "I'll be there."

"Good. Oh, and that list of attorneys you wanted? The ones associated with this bank? I left it on your desk."

"Thanks, Marcie," Kimberly said as she turned the corner and came face-to-face with Robert. Her footsteps faltered, but she managed to keep walking.

Robert glanced lazily her way, then turned back to the cluster of men he was with. Tall and distinguished-looking, he was surrounded by a group of bank bigwigs. Eric Compton, vice president for the trust department, Bill Zealander, Aaron Thornburn, president of the bank, and Earl Kellerman, advisor to the board, were gathered together near the elevator doors.

Robert's blue eyes flicked back to Kimberly's quickly again before returning to Thornburn. A cold needle of dread stabbing her.

"I'll be in my office," she said to Marcie.

She'd just settled into her chair when Robert slid into the room and closed the door quietly behind him.

For the first time since the divorce, Kimberly was alone with him. "Hello, Kimberly." His voice was just as melodic as she remembered.

"What do you want?" she asked. She leaned back in her chair to stare up at him.

He slung one leg over the corner of her desk. "Now that's a silly question."

Her heart began to pound. "I mean, what're you doing here?"

"Oh—" he waved and frowned "—nothing important. Just a little bank business."

"And it's finished? Then you can leave."

"In a minute." He folded his hands over his knee. "I thought you and I should talk—and not through our attorneys." He smiled warmly, and Kimberly saw a glimpse of the man she'd married—charming and sophisticated.

"Talk about what?"

"Our daughter."

Kimberly braced herself. "What about her?" she asked, feigning innocence.

"You know she's better off with me."

"I don't think so."

"Kimberly," he whispered in a way he thought was seductive. It made her furious.

"Just say what you have to say, Robert."

He looked perturbed. "I want my daughter, Kim. She needs a father."

"And a mother."

"Stella—"

"Isn't her mother. I don't want to hear about Stella. I'm Lindsay's mother."

His color began to rise, and he arched an imperious brow.

"There comes a time when a man needs to know he's not . . . so mortal, I guess."

"You should have thought of that before."

His eyes blazed, and he bit out, "I won't rest until she's with me, y'know."

The arrogance of the man! "So, what is this—some kind of threat?"

"No," he said, his smooth brow creasing. "Threats don't seem to work with you."

"Then what?" Dear Lord, she hoped he couldn't hear her heart pounding.

"I want you to reconsider. Think what's best for the child. Stella and I can offer her anything money can buy."

"Maybe that's not enough. I give her love, Robert. I'm the one who wanted her, remember? You weren't too interested in having children. Especially a daughter."

"I know, I know," he said with maddening calm. "But things have changed."

"You mean since Stella can't give you a son?"

"That's a cold way of putting it."

"Too bad. It's the truth. It doesn't change things. We had an agreement, Robert." She stood, hoping to gain some advantage from the added inches in height. "And I expect you to honor it. Lindsay stays with me."

"You know, Kimberly, you're too stubborn for your own good."

"I don't think so."

"I could make it worth your while."

"What's this?" she asked, incredulous. "A bribe? Get real, Robert! I don't want your money. If I had, I would have made claims during the divorce."

He clucked his tongue. "Kimberly, Kimberly," he said, rising to his feet and towering over her. "You just don't get it, do you? I want my daughter."

"Do you? Well, why is it that never once have I heard you say you love her?"

His mouth clamped shut, and all the friendliness left his eyes. "You know, you might be singing a different tune if you lost your job."

She thought about his influence with the bank. "I'd get another one."

"It might not be that easy," he said.

"Your scare tactics don't work with me, Robert. You said so yourself." She leaned across her desk, propping herself up with her hands, and forced her features to remain calm while deep inside she was quaking to her very soul. "If you care anything for Lindsay, don't do anything that might hurt her. Consider her first."

"Oh, like you've done."

"Yes!"

A sharp rap interrupted them, and Robert's bodyguard, a burly blond man with a ponytail, poked his head into the room. "You said to remind you of the meeting with Schuster," he said, almost bowing.

Kimberly thought she might get sick.

"I'll be right there," Robert told him. He glanced down at Kimberly's hands on the desktop, and for the first time she noticed the document on her desk—the list of attorneys connected to the bank and therefore to Robert.

She didn't even bother being sly; she just turned the page over before he could read too much.

His cold eyes held hers. "I guess I'll see you in court."

She didn't flinch. "I guess so."

"And you'll lose, you know. You'll lose big."

"I don't think so."

"We'll see."

She couldn't resist one parting shot. "At least I don't have to travel with a bodyguard."

"Maybe you should." With a tight smile he left the room. The second the door closed, Kimberly collapsed into her chair. What was he planning? How could he be so self-assured? No court would grant him custody—right?

Biting her lip, she flipped the paper over and scanned the list of names, searching for one. But Jake McGowan wasn't listed.

She felt a tiny sense of relief, but it was short-lived. She knew she'd heard Jake's name before. Diane had mentioned him, of course, but someone else had, as well. If she hadn't heard Jake's name from someone in the bank, then where? Certainly not from Robert. Or had she?

Her throat went dry with dread. She sensed that Jake had run across Robert before, though he hadn't said as much. He seemed to have a knowledge and interest in Robert that went beyond the usual curiosity derived from reading the paper. Had Jake been Robert's attorney? Had Robert double-crossed him?

"Oh, stop it," she whispered, angry with herself. Shuddering, she rubbed her arms. Robert meant business. And she was scared. More scared than she'd ever been in her life.

The intercom buzzed. Marcie said, "It's Mr. Juniper on line two again. Should I, uh, tell him to call back?"

"No . . ." Kimberly shook her head as if Marcie could see through the walls. "I'll get it." She picked up the phone, glad for the distraction. "Hello?"

"She's at it again!" Henry Juniper exclaimed.

"Who's at what?"

"Carole's going for blood, I tell you. She's going to contest the entire will—claims she needs an additional three hundred thousand for taking care of Dad during the last couple of years. And then she wants her legal fees paid on top of that! It's positively ludicrous."

"Please, slow down, Mr. Juniper," Kimberly said evenly,

though she was still distracted. "Why don't you start at the beginning?"

As Henry Juniper launched into his tale of woe, she listened, but her gaze was fixed on the picture of Lindsay propped on the corner of her desk. Her fingers curled tightly around the telephone, and her jaw set. For the first time in his life, Robert wouldn't win. The stakes were just too damn high.

Hours later she'd calmed down. The evening with Lindsay had been special, and she'd tucked the child into bed later than usual, enjoying every waking moment with her.

Only when Lindsay had yawned and repeatedly rubbed her eyes had Kimberly done her motherly duty and turned out the lights in Lindsay's sleeping loft.

Now, her back propped against the couch, an old quilt tossed over her shoulders, Kimberly sat on the floor in the front of the fire. She tried to concentrate on the magazines spread open on her lap but couldn't. Her mind was working overtime—with thoughts of Robert and Jake. Robert's threats kept pounding in her brain, and she kept them at bay by hoping Jake could help her. At the thought of him she smiled, though the situation was far from happy.

"Mommy?" Lindsay's voice filtered down from the loft.

Kimberly was on her feet in an instant. "What is it, honey?" she called, climbing the stairs two at a time.

Sitting up in her bed rubbing her eyes, Lindsay complained, "I had another bad dream."

"It's over now, sweetheart."

"But it was scary." Tears gathered in Lindsay's eyes.

"I know." Kimberly sat on the edge of Lindsay's twin mattress and smoothed her tousled hair. Wrapping her arms around Lindsay's shoulders, Kimberly whispered, "Just think happy thoughts like rainbows and dinosaurs and snow and puppies—"

"Can I have one?" Lindsay asked, her tears forgotten.

*The great debate*, Kimberly thought. "Someday."

"When?"

"I don't know. When you're older."

"Like tomorrow?"

"Like in a few years when you're old enough to feed it, walk it and clean up after it."

"I just want to love it," Lindsay argued, her lower lip protruding in a tired pout. "Daddy said he'd give me a puppy."

Kimberly's heart froze. Every muscle in her body went rigid. "He did?"

"Mm-hmm." Lindsay was nodding off again. "When he called me."

"He called you? Here? Again?" Kimberly repeated, trying not to sound alarmed, though cold panic was taking hold. All of his threats echoed through her head. Would he try something as foolish as kidnapping his own daughter? Certainly not unless the custody battle went against him. Her throat was suddenly tight, the words hard to form. "Did Arlene talk to him?"

Lindsay skidded lower under the covers. "No. She was in the basement." Turning her face into her pillow, Lindsay yawned.

"Has Daddy called before when I'm not here?"

But Lindsay didn't answer. Breathing softly, she snuggled deeper between the sheets and drifted to sleep. Kimberly stared at the sleeping child and wanted to cry. She'd always wanted children, but even that overpowering desire to become a mother hadn't prepared her for the depth of her feelings for this sometimes spoiled, often precocious, but always precious daughter.

After dropping a kiss on Lindsay's tangled crown, she silently walked downstairs. So Robert had called. So what? He had every right to talk to his daughter. There was no need to panic. But the memory of her own conversation with Robert left her chilled to the bone.

She poured herself a glass of water, then set the teakettle on the stove. Gazing out the window, she wondered if she should just give up the fight, grab Lindsay and a few of her belongings and flee. And run where? California? Canada? Mexico? Her head began to throb. She pressed the cold glass to her forehead.

The kettle shrilled loudly, and Kimberly switched off the stove and reached for it just as the doorbell rang.

She glanced at the clock. It was after nine. Who would be braving the rain and wind at this time of night?

*Robert!*

And his entourage of bodyguards . . .

Her heart dropped like a stone, then she managed to pull herself together. Robert was in for the fight of his life. Steeling herself, she set the kettle down and marched back through the living room, ready to lambast the man.

She peeked through the arched window carved in the front door, and her knees threatened to collapse as she saw Jake standing in the protection of the porch, his breath fogging in the cold air. Dressed in faded denim jeans, a steel-gray sweater and blue ski jacket, Jake reached for the bell again, then glanced at the window, where his gaze touched hers.

A smile warm as a southern breeze slashed across his chin.

Kimberly fumbled with the lock, then threw the door open. "Thank God it's you," she said, clinging to the knob so she wouldn't impulsively rush into his arms like an idiot.

He actually chuckled. "You missed me?"

"A little," she lied. "Well, maybe more than a little." Her throat grew thick, and she felt hot tears of relief well in the corners of her eyes.

Jake's smile faded. "What is it?"

For a second she didn't trust her voice. She closed the door and leaned heavily against the cool wood panels. "It's Robert," she admitted, clearing her throat. "I saw him today—he was . . . pretty determined."

"To get his daughter back?"

"Right." Her throat swelled again. "He wasn't too subtle."

"He *threatened* you?" Jake demanded. His face became a hard mask.

"Warned me, I think, would be more like it. When the doorbell rang, I thought you were him. I'd even gone so far as to think he'd just bulldoze his way in here, grab Lindsay and disappear in the night, so . . ." She glanced up at him and managed a tremulous smile. "Just give me a minute to pull myself together, okay?"

"Sure." To her surprise, he reached forward and surrounded her with his arms, drawing her close against his wet jacket. His strength and warmth seemed to permeate his clothes and flow into her. She didn't think twice, just rested her cheek against the steadying wall of his chest. His scent enveloped her, an earthy smell that reminded her of pine forests and clean skin.

Listening to the steadying sound of his breathing, she wouldn't acknowledge that he interested her as a man. Being attracted to him was just too complicated. And dangerous. Still, being held and comforted, feeling his breath stir her hair, caused her skin to tingle.

"You okay?" he asked gently.

She nodded against his jacket, wondering why she saw this roguish, cynical man as some kind of knight in shining armor. The fantasy made her smile. He'd die a thousand deaths if he knew.

She lifted her head and slowly stepped out of his embrace. "I, uh, thought you were out of town," she said, embarrassed that she'd let down her reserve, that he'd caught sight of a vulnerable side of her.

"I'm back."

"Obviously," she said dryly. "Look, I didn't mean to fall apart on you—"

"You didn't."

"Yeah, I did." She nodded.

He grinned again, and she felt the stupid urge to smile back at him. "Okay, you did. Now, tell me what happened."

"Can we wait a little on the heavy stuff?" she said, still trying to calm down. "I'll be okay, but I need a few minutes."

"Sure." He turned his palms up. "Whatever you want."

For the first time, she really looked at him, noticing the water spots on his shoulders and his wet hair. "No umbrella?"

His grin twisted. "I'm an Oregonian. We don't use those things. The rain and I are well acquainted, I just spent a couple of days wiping off my goggles up at Mt. Bachelor."

"Oh, so you're a skier?"

His eyes flashed devilishly. "You wouldn't have guessed it this week." He glanced around the room and shoved his hands in the pockets of his jeans. "When the weather report said 'more of the same,' I decided to pack it in. I have plenty of work, and I thought we could pick up where we left off."

"Now?"

"No time like the present." Bending one knee against the hearth, he rubbed his hands together, then placed his palms near the flames. Firelight caught in his hair, reflecting on the dark strands and casting golden shadows over his angular features. Glancing over his shoulder, he said, "Relax, I won't bite."

"Is that a promise?"

"Yes." His eyes twinkled. "Are you sure you're all right?"

"I think so."

"Can we get started?"

She nodded, rubbing her hands together. "It's going to be difficult, you know. Telling you my life story."

He snorted. "You'd better get used to the idea. We'll be spending a lot of time together."

Somehow that was, comforting.

"I'll have to know about you—and Robert—and anything

you think is important, no matter how 'difficult' it is to talk about."

"I see."

"You want to back out?"

"No," she said sharply. "We've got a deal. Remember?"

"Right."

Despite her uneasiness, she felt the corners of her mouth lift. There was something about him that made her want to smile, and yet there was a part of him, a dark, sensual side that touched her deep inside. "So . . . would you like something warm—a cup of coffee or tea, or maybe something stronger? I think I've got . . . eh, I don't really know," she said with a shrug. "Maybe vodka?"

"Anything."

He followed her down the short, scarred wooden floor of the hallway leading to a tiny kitchen.

"Is Lindsay already in bed?" he asked as she poured hot water into mugs.

"For the second time." She told him about Lindsay's nightmares and sighed. "They began last summer, a couple of months before she started kindergarten. Coffee or tea?"

"Coffee—so she goes to school every day?" he asked.

"Half days. Arlene picks Lindsay up after lunch and brings her home for her nap. They spend their time here unless Arlene decides to run errands or take Lindsay to the park to feed the ducks."

"And Lindsay likes Arlene."

"Adores her."

"You're sure?"

"Mm-hmm."

"And school. Does she like it?"

"Yes—and her teacher is a dream. What is this, the third degree?" she asked as she handed him a steaming mug.

"Not yet. Just the preliminaries." He took an experimental sip from the cup. "Believe me, it gets worse."

"That's what I was afraid of," she murmured, motioning toward a small round table with two chairs. "Please, sit down."

Jake twisted a cane-backed chair around and straddled it, leaning forward. "So, tell me about Arlene."

"Why?"

"She's Lindsay's babysitter. That might be a sore point with Robert. He might bring up something about your work and leaving his daughter in the care of an elderly woman."

Kimberly sipped her tea. "I wouldn't call Arlene elderly to her face if I valued my life," she said.

Jake grinned. "I'll remember that. You trust her?"

Kimberly almost laughed. "I've known her all my life. She's a friend of my mother's. They grew up together in the Midwest before Mom and Dad moved to California."

"She's married?"

Nodding, Kimberly set her tea bag in a saucer. "Lyle's her husband. He was a longshoreman, but he retired a couple years ago when he hurt his back."

"So Arlene watches Lindsay for the money?"

Kimberly bristled at the implication. "The money really doesn't matter. Arlene loves my daughter. Lindsay is the granddaughter she never had." She set her cup on the table and forced her eyes to Jake's. "You met her the other night— what do you think?"

"Just showing you a preview of what the courtroom will be like," he said, his face growing sober. "If it gets that far. Believe me, it's not going to be a picnic. Not for you. Or Lindsay."

"I know." She felt the same nervous jitters in her stomach she always did when she thought about the court date looming ahead. "I wish I could avoid it. I don't like the thought of fighting over Lindsay, or hanging my dirty laundry out where everyone can see it. Robert's name is in the paper enough."

A dark cloud seemed to shadow Jake's eyes. But it passed quickly. "Maybe we can avoid that," he suggested.

"How?"

"If we can convince Robert to drop the case—"

Kimberly laughed bitterly. "Impossible. I've tried. When it comes to Lindsay, we don't see eye to eye."

"But he gave you custody once."

"Yeah," she said, sighing. "When he wanted the divorce so that he could marry Stella. That was before he knew she couldn't bear children. It's ironic," she added sadly. "He didn't want a child, and the fact that Lindsay was a girl only made it worse. But suddenly, now that Stella can't conceive, he's interested in Lindsay again." She explained about seeing Robert at the bank and recounted the meeting to an entranced Jake. Kimberly saw the tensing of his muscles, the wariness in his eyes.

"Wonderful man," he said finally.

"I thought so once," she admitted, wondering how she could have been so naïve. Feeling suddenly cold, she rubbed her arms and asked, "Have you ever been married?"

He frowned into his palm and his jaw tightened. "It didn't last long. Probably a mistake from the beginning."

Surprised, she glanced up and saw pain flicker in his eyes. A cold spot settled in her heart. Jake obviously loved his wife very much.

"She's gone now," he said, clipping the words out, his voice husky. "Killed in a car accident a few years ago. It happened not long after the divorce."

Her heart went out to him. "I'm sorry," she whispered.

"Don't be. It wasn't your fault."

"I know, but—"

"I'd rather not talk about it," he said darkly. Shifting uncomfortably in his chair, he added, "Besides, I didn't come here to discuss my personal life."

"No, you're here for mine."

"Right. So, what about yours? Let's start with Robert."

Kimberly's stomach twisted.

"Do you still love him?"

Her gaze flew to his. "What kind of question is that? He's remarried and—"

"Do you still love him?"

"Of course not."

He lifted a dark brow.

Instantly outraged, she said, "Would I be fighting him so hard if I still cared about him?"

"I don't know. Sometimes relationships are complicated. I just thought we should start with the basics."

"And I thought I told you I'm not sure I ever loved him."

His gaze didn't falter. "Okay. Now, the other side of the coin. Do you hate him?"

"No."

"Why not?"

"He's Lindsay's father—I can't forget that."

Jake snorted. "A man comes by and threatens to take your child away and you can't forget he's the kid's father."

Her fists clenched impotently.

"This isn't going to be a walk in the park, you know," he said kindly. "It could get pretty bloody."

"I realize that."

"Then tell me, what kind of a man is Fisher?"

"Relentless," she said quickly, "and single-minded. When he wants something, he goes after it."

He tented his fingers under his chin. "Tell me about him—this relentless side of his nature."

Her hands shook a little as she picked up her cup. She sipped her tea, found it tepid and set the cup back on the table. "For example, if he wanted your law practice, he'd find a way to get it. He's incredibly patient, and he'd do whatever he had to do, wait however long it took to make you see that it was in *your* best interests to sell to him, whether you wanted to or not."

The lines near the corner of Jake's mouth tightened.

"So, now that he's zeroed in on having Lindsay come live with him, he won't back down. Diane already told me he doesn't have a chance, and yet I don't believe it. Robert's like a cat—he always lands on his feet." She bit her lower lip. "And sometimes his claws are extended."

Jake surveyed her thoughtfully. "What was it like being married to him?"

She frowned, feeling all the old pain. "At first it was wonderful—at least I thought it was—but that all changed fairly quickly."

"Why?"

She lifted a shoulder. "I don't know. I suppose I began to bore him."

One side of his mouth lifted, and his gaze softened. "I find it hard to think of you as boring."

"Well, he lost interest, and then there were all those stories about him. You know, rumors tying him to everything that's wrong in the city."

Jake's stare grew stern. "You don't believe he's part of organized crime in Portland."

"No."

"But you're not sure."

"He's Lindsay's father," she said automatically.

"What does that have to do with my question?"

Kimberly tossed her hair away from her face and thought long and hard. For years she'd heard the rumors about Robert, but never would believe he was as horrible as he'd been painted. "Maybe I'm incredibly naïve, but I lived with the man. I won't dispute he walks a thin line with the law, and he's probably even bent it on occasion. But I can't believe he's a part of anything as sinister as the mob."

Jake scowled. "You're right on one count. You *are* incredibly naïve."

She bit at the inside of her lip. "Well, it's hard to think that the man you married . . ." She shuddered.

"Go on."

"As I said, I don't know what all he's involved in, but he did change about the time of that police investigation."

"Change? How?"

She couldn't really explain it. "He grew more secretive, and some of his business acquaintances changed."

Jake was staring at her so hard that his gaze seemed to cut through to her soul. She rubbed her fingers together nervously.

"What acquaintances?" he asked so quietly she barely heard the question.

"I didn't know them, never really met them, but I got the feeling . . ." She lifted her eyes to his. "That Robert's business interests had shifted. Maybe it was all in my mind, but, I swear, he changed."

Jake rubbed his chin. "You never heard any new names?"

"No—he didn't confide in me."

The seconds ticked by, and Jake didn't take his eyes off her. The fire popping and the hum of the furnace provided the only sounds.

"You know, Kimberly, if we could prove Fisher is a part of something—anything—illegal, it'll weaken his case considerably."

"I know."

He touched her lightly on the arm. "Would you be willing to testify against him?"

She remembered the cold fury in Robert's eyes that afternoon. Taking a bracing breath, she nodded. "I would, but believe me, I don't know anything."

"Just think about it." Then, as if dismissing the subject, he waved and glanced at his watch. "It's late. I'd better shove off." Standing, he returned his chair to the table. "I'll call you next week after I've talked with Kesler. There's a chance he and I can work something out that you and Robert will both agree to."

"I doubt it."

He flashed a cocky smile as they started down the hall to the living room. He grabbed his coat off the back of the couch. "You never know until you try."

She shook her head. "Obviously you haven't come up against Robert."

His features tightened almost imperceptibly. "There's always a way," he said calmly, his voice turning strangely dangerous as he slipped his arms through the sleeves of his jacket. "I'll call you next week."

As he opened the door, a rush of damp air filled the room, billowing the curtains and causing the dying flames within the grate to leap brilliantly. Running quickly down the steps, Jake disappeared into the night. A few seconds later, the interior light of his Bronco flickered, and Kimberly watched him slide easily behind the steering wheel.

She shut the front door and wondered why the house seemed so suddenly empty without him. "Don't be a fool," she said, but smiled nonetheless.

In the kitchen she poured herself a fresh cup of hot tea and had just sat down with a magazine when the phone rang. Smiling, she picked it up on the third ring. "Hello?"

"Hi!" Diane Welby's voice sounded over the wire.

Kimberly glanced out the window. "Well, how's the bride-to-be? Cold feet yet?"

"Never! In fact I'm not even nervous."

"Sure."

From the window, she could see the shimmering dark streets. Beneath the street lamp, she noticed a man lingering, drawing deeply on his cigarette as he gazed steadily at her house. Her heart began to pound.

Diane was saying, "I just called to see how things were going with Jake. He's taking your case, right?"

"Why—oh, yeah, he is."

"Good."

Kimberly snapped off the kitchen light so that she could watch the man, but it was too dark to see his features. He was tall, wore a raincoat and hat—nothing out of the ordinary. She thought about confiding in Diane, but what could she say? It wasn't against the law to smoke on the street corner.

"And are you two getting along?"

The man on the street started walking away, around the corner and out of her line of vision.

"Kimberly?" Diane said, bringing Kimberly's focus back to the conversation.

"Oh, yes. Well, we got off to a pretty rough start," she admitted, still looking out the window as she filled Diane in on the particulars. ". . . He just left about fifteen minutes ago."

"Good, good. I'm not kidding about the fact that he's the best."

"Best or not, he wasn't all that crazy about representing me," Kimberly said, shifting the phone to her other ear. "But he won't say why."

There was a long silence on the other end of the line, and finally she heard Diane let out her breath. "Jake had a difficult time a few years back. A messy divorce."

"He mentioned it."

"Did he?" Diane sounded delighted.

"He didn't go into it much."

"He wouldn't," Diane said, but didn't elaborate.

There was a click on the line, and Diane muttered, "I've got another call. I just wanted to know everything's okay and that you'll be coming to the wedding."

"I'll be there," Kimberly promised. "See you then." She

hung up and stared out the window. But other than the normal evening traffic, nothing seemed out of the ordinary. "You're losing it, Bennett," she told herself as she snapped the shade shut. "Definitely losing it."

Nonetheless, she looked in on Lindsay again, double-checked the deadbolts and window latching and knew she wouldn't get much sleep.

Jake paid little attention to the speed limit. Putting his Bronco through its paces, he steered through the puddled streets of Sellwood, across the Willamette River and on to Lake Oswego. His house, a bungalow that had once been a cabin retreat for wealthy Portlanders in the early nineteen hundreds, was located on the south side of the lake.

The drive home took twenty minutes, but Jake didn't remember any of it. His thoughts hadn't strayed from Kimberly.

In the driveway, he braked to a gravel-spinning stop and switched off the engine. Rain continued to beat on the roof as the cooling engine ticked in counterpoint. Jake stared through the blurred windshield and wrestled with his conscience.

Inwardly he sensed that Kimberly Bennett was a woman with whom he could enjoy a lasting relationship. But now, because he'd agreed to see her professionally, she was, at least in the broadest sense of the word, his client. And she'd been married to the man who Jake was sure had been responsible for Daniel's death. Getting involved with Kimberly would only spell trouble.

And then there was her daughter—cute as a button, but Jake didn't want to get too close. Nope, he had enough pain to last him a lifetime, and if he could help Kimberly out and put Fisher away at the same time, that's all he could ask for. So, why couldn't he forget her?

His fingers curled over the steering wheel, and he had to beat down the urge to drive back to her home and offer to take her out. Or to bed, he silently added, furious with himself for a physical attraction that was so damn compelling he couldn't think straight.

"Get real," he muttered to himself as he climbed out of his car and slammed the door shut. Lupus, his white shepherd, barked loudly. Tail whipping at a furious tempo, Lupus leapt from beneath the dirty branches of a rhododendron. Jake bent down and scratched the old dog's wet ears. But his mind hadn't left Kimberly.

Starting an affair was out of the question, he told himself for the hundredth time as he headed to the door. He couldn't see her socially, and there was no point in even thinking about it. She was his client, Robert Fisher's ex, and that was that.

Why, then, he wondered, kicking angrily at a stone in his path, was making love to her lodged so firmly in his mind?

# CHAPTER FIVE

Two nights later Jake stood and stretched. His back ached from sitting at the desk in his living room, where he'd been reading everything he could on the most current custody cases.

Lupus, curled on the rug near the window, growled low in his throat. His snow-white hair bristled at the sound of footsteps on the porch.

"Relax," Jake chided the dog as he opened the door. "It's only Ron."

Ron Koski grinned, displaying slightly yellowed teeth. "*Only* Ron? Tough crowd, especially after what I went through for you." He wiped his ratty old Nikes on the mat and stepped inside. A draft of cold winter air seeped in with him. "As a matter of fact, you owe me a beer. It's *definitely* Miller time."

"You're on."

Lupus curled up beside the fire, and Ron took a chair at the small table in Jake's dining alcove.

"So, you got something on Fisher?" Jake called over his

shoulder as he wandered into the kitchen, opened the refrigerator and yanked out two bottles.

"I don't know if you'd call it 'something.' You know how slippery Fisher is."

"Yeah, I know." Probably better than most people, he thought, twisting off the caps and thinking of Daniel.

Returning to the dining alcove, he found Ron with one foot propped on another chair and a thick file spread on the table. "Here's what I got on Fisher," he said, accepting the offered bottle with a grin. "Mostly news clippings, a couple of police reports I managed to get from Brecken and some information from the surveillance job I did on him a few years ago."

"I remember." Jake pulled up a chair and eyed neatly typed reports, yellowed newspaper articles and snapshots. Robert Fisher always seemed to photograph well. A large man with thick, jet-black hair, intelligent brown eyes and a heavy-boned face, he cut an imposing figure—even in yellowed black-and-white clippings. Jake skimmed the report on Daniel's suicide, and his stomach tightened. Daniel had been an investigator for the Portland police. He'd been assigned to the narcotics detail and had eventually followed a lead to Robert Fisher.

From what Jake learned later, Daniel had hoped to make a huge drug bust and expose Fisher, but it hadn't worked out. Daniel had been found dead, from what appeared to be a self-inflicted overdose. Several kilos of cocaine, stolen from the police department's evidence warehouse, had been found at his apartment along with a typed suicide note.

The ensuing scandal had rocked the very foundation of the police department.

Jake stared at the copy of the note included in Ron's file, and hot rage burned in his gut. Daniel was clean. He'd never used drugs in his life. His body was clean—no needle marks. On top of all that, he wouldn't have taken his own life.

There had been an investigation, of course, but it had been short and inconclusive and swept under the rug with the rest of the dirt that couldn't be explained.

Jake had never bought the suicide theory. It just didn't wash.

Ron ran a hand through his short blonde hair. "There's no reason to dredge all this up again. It's over, man."

"Maybe not." Jake flipped through the first few reports, his eyes scanned the sheets.

"What're you on to?"

"Nothing as sordid as all this," he replied, disgusted at the pile of dead ends that should have led to Fisher. "It's a custody case. Fisher's daughter."

"What about her?"

"He's making noise about wanting custody. His ex-wife doesn't like the idea."

"Don't blame her." He finished his beer, then took a final drag of his cigarette and crushed it in the ashtray. "Fisher doesn't seem like the fatherly type," he said in a cloud of blue smoke.

"He wasn't. But for some reason he's changed his mind."

"Can he do that?"

Jake's mouth turned into a thin, determined line. "Not if I can help it," he said, sifting through the documents. The opportunity to thwart Robert Fisher was a stroke of luck, and the chance to help Kimberly made it all the more tantalizing.

He started to smile at the thought of her. Though he barely knew her, he hadn't been able to get her out of his mind for the past couple of days.

"So, what's she like?" Ron asked, lighting another cigarette and letting it burn neglected in the ashtray.

"Who?"

"Fisher's ex." Ron's eyebrows elevated a fraction. "Young? Beautiful? Built?"

Jake's gut tightened. "I suppose," he evaded, refusing to think about Kimberly with the likes of Robert Fisher.

"Probably took him to the cleaners—if that's possible."

"Maybe, but I'm not sure about that." Her car and some of her clothes were expensive, her house was little more than a cottage, vintage 1920 or so. And the documents he'd seen indicated she hadn't stiffed Fisher for half of his vast property holdings or alimony. It appeared as if Kimberly had wanted out of the marriage—period. Unless she had a Swiss bank account or a stock portfolio hidden away somewhere, she seemed relatively middle-class.

Jake rolled his sleeves over his forearms, aware that he'd been lost in thought, and Ron was staring at him curiously. "She seems to think that Fisher was clean until Daniel started poking around."

"No way." Koski narrowed his eyes a fraction. "But it does seem that until then, he wasn't in quite so deep. It's been since Dan's death that Fisher's risen in the organization."

"How do you figure that?"

Koski thought. "My guess is that someone killed Daniel and Fisher owed some big favors to keep his name out of it." He glanced sharply at his friend. "I doubt that Fisher did the dirty work. He likes to keep his hands clean."

Jake's chest grew tight, and his mind wandered back to dangerous territory. "Doesn't matter," he said without much conviction. "Daniel's dead."

"And now you're helping out Fisher's wife."

"Ex," Jake reminded him. "There's a big difference."

Ron shrugged. "Have you met the kid?"

Jake nodded. "Five-year-old girl."

"Too bad she's caught up in all this."

"Yeah," Jake said, thinking of Lindsay's laughing blue eyes and pixieish expression. She was beguiling, no doubt about it, but he wasn't about to get too close to Robert Fisher's child. Nor his ex-wife. "Come on," he said gruffly. "Let's get to work."

"Some of us already have been," Ron said with a good-natured chuckle. "You know, when I talked to Brecken at the department, I got the feeling he wasn't telling me everything."

"He's supposed to be discreet."

Ron drew thoughtfully on his cigarette. "No, it was more than that," he said. "I think he was being evasive."

Jake's head snapped up. "Meaning?"

Ron grinned. "I've known Brecken a long time. When he clams up, something's going down. And I'll bet you it has to do with our friend here." He tapped a thick finger on the picture of Robert. "Ten to one, the police are on to him again."

"You think he's about to be nabbed?"

"Nah." Ron stubbed out his cigarette. "I bet the police think they're going to nail him again. There's a big difference."

*Amen*, Jake thought. Scowling, he sorted the information into stacks. It would take days to sift through everything, but he'd take the time. He owed it to himself and to Daniel. *And to Kimberly*, he told himself, surprised at the turn in his thoughts.


"You may kiss the bride!" The preacher's words rang happily through the little chapel.

From the back pew Kimberly swallowed the lump in her throat. She watched Scott Donaldson lift the ivory-colored veil, uncovering Diane's flushed face. Diane's eyes were bright and blue, her cheeks rosy as she tilted her head back. Scott entwined his fingers in her blond, wreath-covered hair and lowered his head, taking her lips possessively with his.

A whisper of approval swept through the tiny chapel, and teary-eyed guests smiled.

Kimberly felt close to tears herself. It was obvious these people loved each other—Diane, nearly angelic in ivory silk, and Scott, tall and lean in his black tuxedo.

Jake sat at the far end of the pew in the back. He looked the part of the courtroom attorney in his stiff white shirt and dark tie.

His gaze shifted, and his steely eyes clashed with hers.

Then he smiled—a lazy, off-center grin that caused her heart to beat double-time.

The organist pounded on the keys, and the bridal march filled the chapel. The bride and groom strolled from the pulpit down a long wine-colored carpet and through the exterior doors. The guests followed suit.

Outside, mist gathered in the cool air, clinging to the blackened branches of the bare oak and maple trees that flanked the church.

Diane and Scott received guests on the chapel steps. Kimberly stood in line, waiting, and saw Jake, detached from the crowd, hands in his pockets, on the brick path leading to an ancient cemetery. He was studying her intensely, not bothering to hide the fact that he was staring. One cocky black brow rising in expectation as she moved closer. Kimberly met his gaze, forcing a thin smile and hoped to God that her accelerated pulse wasn't visible in the hollow of her throat.

Storm clouds gathered overhead, and the wind picked up, catching in her skirt. Kimberly barely noticed, her attention was solely on Jake.

Suddenly she felt Diane's hand on hers and forced her gaze back to the laughing eyes of her friend. "Congratulations," Kimberly whispered, hugging her. "It was a wonderful ceremony."

"Can you forgive me for bailing out on you?" Diane teased.

"No, but I've learned to live with that." Kimberly felt her

cheeks dimple. "But if there's any way I can talk you and Scott into staying . . ."

The groom, overhearing her, laughed. "Not a prayer."

"What can I say?" Diane rolled her eyes. "L.A. born and bred."

Kimberly sighed. "Well, if you ever get tired of the warm weather, sunshine and beaches . . ."

"Don't count on it," Scott said with a chuckle.

"So, how're things with you?" Diane asked, her smile replaced by sudden concern.

"Same as ever."

"And Jake?" She motioned to the path where Jake was standing.

"He's very concerned," Kimberly allowed. "I think he'll do a good job."

"I know he will," Diane said, squeezing her arm. Then she smiled again. "And admit it, he's not too hard on the eyes."

"Who isn't? Me?" Scott asked, picking up on the tail end of the conversation.

"Only you, darling," Diane deadpanned.

"Come on, you've got to meet Frankie and Paul. . . ."

The thunder rumbled over the hills, and Kimberly moved on, allowing other guests access to the bride and groom.

Kimberly glanced back to the path, but Jake had moved, had walked farther up the cracked old bricks to the cemetery. He stood, shoulder propped against the rough bark of an ancient cedar, his face trained toward the sea of weathered white tombstones. Hesitating only a second, she took off up the path, gathering her skirts in one hand so that they wouldn't drag in the pools of standing water and mud.

His back to her, Jake shoved a hand through his hair. The wind played havoc with the branches overhead and tossed his hair back across his face.

Kimberly stopped behind him. "The rest of the party's going on inside," she said.

"What?" He turned quickly, and his expression was grim, his eyes dark and remote, as if he were caught in some private hell.

"I'm sorry—I didn't mean to intrude—"

"You didn't." He forced a smile. His lips, thin and sensual, curved wryly, and his eyes glinted with silvery interest. Lightning sizzled across the dark sky.

"It's not safe out here." With a large hand on her shoulder, he drew her away from the protection of the leafy branches of the cedar tree until they stood beneath a weathered arbor, where rose vines, now only skeletal brambles, still clung to the latticework.

"Maybe we should go inside," she whispered, suddenly breathless. She was all too aware of the warm palm against her shoulder, the tips of his fingers leaving hot impressions on her bare skin.

He glanced to the heavens as thunder rumbled again and electricity charged the air. It was late afternoon, but the day had turned suddenly dark as midnight. Rain started to fall, thick drops splattering against the ground. Instinctively he held her closer. One arm slid around her waist, offering the slight protection of his jacket. She was pressed against his body, hard and lean, and the scent of aftershave mingled with the fresh, rain-washed air.

His expression grew tender. Absurdly protective, and his eyes turned to quicksilver. Intuitively she knew he was about to kiss her, and she swallowed hard. Her hammering heart nearly fell to the rain-spattered bricks, and her breath was lost somewhere between her throat and lungs. She could see her own reflection in his eyes as he lowered his head, pulling her to him, crushing her against him. His lips slanted over hers for such possession, she couldn't think, could do nothing but feel—the strength of him, the warmth of his mouth on hers, the sensual touch of his hands splayed across her back.

Her pulse skyrocketed. She closed her eyes and kissed him back. A few solitary raindrops slid down her neck to tingle already electrified skin.

Her lips parted willingly, and he kissed them, causing a shudder to pass through her. Her knees went weak.

Groaning, he lifted his head. His heavy-lidded gaze delved deep into her. "Oh, God, Kimberly," he whispered against her hair. "I shouldn't have—"

"No, don't." She couldn't stand an apology. Not now. She didn't want to think about a kiss filled with so much passion that her fingers still trembled in its aftermath. She forced a smile. "A few nights ago, you helped me."

His mouth quirked. "So it's payback time?"

"You looked like you could use a friend."

"Thank you." The sadness in his eyes disappeared. "I do. Is this how you treat all your friends, Ms. Bennett?" he asked.

Laughing, she shook her head. "Only very special friends."

Thunder cracked again, and the rain began in earnest, slanting persistently downward. Jake grabbed her hand and started back to the reception hall just off the chapel. Half-running to keep up with him, her skirt bunched in one hand, she dashed down the brick path to the reception hall.

Inside, the party was in full swing. Most of the guests had already convened in the softly lighted room. Candles, their flames quivering, graced long linen-clad tables, and flowers filled the hall with the delicate fragrances of rose and carnation. Floor-to-ceiling windows glowed with the reflection of the candlelight as bejeweled guests clustered in small groups.

Jake poured them each some champagne. She watched the raindrops bead in his hair. She couldn't deny the physical attraction she felt for him and wondered what she could do about it. She wasn't in the market for a man, and this man, the man representing her, was the last person she could get involved with. Whatever happened, it was important that she keep his objectivity in the custody case.

He offered her a glass. "To Diane and Scott?" he said, holding his glass aloft.

Kimberly nodded, glad he hadn't said "To us." There could be no "us." She clinked the rim of her tall glass to his, then stared through the paned windows to the murky Willamette River as it rolled slowly northward.

The door burst open, and Diane and Scott stepped into the room. Laughing gaily, they shook rain from their hair and suffered good-naturedly through the rites of the newly married. Together they managed to slice the three-tiered cake, feed each other a gooey, frosting-laden piece and, with arms entwined, drink champagne from the engraved silver cups.

"Barbaric ritual, isn't it?" Jake joked.

Kimberly laughed, relaxing a little as Diane tossed her bouquet of roses, baby's breath and carnations high into the air. The beribboned flowers landed squarely in a young girl's hands, and she squealed in delight.

"You should have tried to catch it," Jake said. "It's lucky."

"Or unlucky, depending on how you look at it," Kimberly replied.

"Uh-oh, that sounds a little cynical, Ms. Bennett."

"Just judging from experience."

"So, don't tell me you've given up on the institution of marriage."

"Not for everyone," she replied. "Just for me." She eyed him over the rim of her champagne glass. "And what about you?"

"Once is more than enough," he agreed.

"No need to have a wife serve your every whim—wash your floors, scratch your back, clean your Porsche?"

His eyes flashed. "You applying for the job?"

"No."

"Good, 'cause I don't have a Porsche. But I think you deserve a consolation prize."

"For what?"

"Not catching the bouquet. Here . . ." Reaching with his free hand, he plucked a long-stemmed white rose from a basket overflowing with blue and white flowers. "For you," he said, his voice husky, his eyes bright.

"Don't you think Diane will mind?"

"Diane owes me."

"Funny, that's what she says about you."

"Ha! But I'm paying off my debt." His eyes glinted. "Besides, I think Diane's too wrapped up in Scott to notice one flower."

Kimberly accepted the fragile flower.

From a corner near a broad bank of windows, tuxedoed musicians tuned up. As the soft notes of the anniversary waltz filled the room, Mr. and Mrs. Scott Donaldson danced together for the first time as man and wife.

"Shall we join them?" Jake asked, cocking his head toward the dance floor. Flickering candlelight reflected in his sable-brown hair.

She glanced at her watch. "I really should be going . . ." But she felt the glass being lifted from her fingers, and then she was swung gracefully onto the shiny patina of the dance floor, joining Scott and Diane and a few of the braver guests.

She hadn't danced in years, but Jake made following the strains of the waltz easy. His strong arms wrapped comfortably around her waist, and his body, hard and lean, pressed intimately against hers.

He gazed down at her, his eyes sparkling from the candlelight, his breath whispering through her hair.

Though the room was filled with guests, she didn't notice anyone or anything but Jake and the central power of his embrace. He pulled her even closer, so close that her breasts were crushed against his chest and her thighs pressed intimately against his. One of his hands splayed possessively across the small of her back.

The fragrance of rose and carnations filled her nostrils

as she closed her eyes to sway still closer to him. Though a thousand voices in her mind screamed "beware," she didn't heed one of them.

His gaze, dark with passion, drove deep into hers, and she shivered, not from cold, but from the tingle of electricity that swept up her spine.

This couldn't be happening. It *couldn't*. She was feeling like a teenager again, thrilling to this man's touch when he was the last man in the world she should be attracted to.

The dance ended and she stepped out of his arms. "I really have to go," she said, reaffirming the notion to herself.

"The party's just begun, and I think we could have fun," he persuaded.

She was tempted, but knew in her heart she couldn't get entangled with him. "Really. I have to get back. Arlene's got Lindsay and she's probably already waiting for me." Forcing a smile and still holding the single white rose, she turned to leave before she did something brash like change her mind and stay with him.

His brow knit in frustration, Jake stared after her, watching her escape—for that's what it seemed to be. Her mahogany-colored hair billowed away from her face, and her silky gown shimmered as she dashed through the door.

*Just like Cinderella at the stroke of midnight*, he thought furiously, his fists clenched as he shoved them into his pockets.

He wanted to follow her. There was something about her that challenged him—something that touched him in a way he'd never been touched before. "You're imagining it," he told himself as the band started playing a lively pop tune.

He stared through the windows, saw her sidestep the puddles of the parking lot, her slim legs moving quickly, the wind catching in her hair. A jagged flash of lightning illuminated her face—a beautiful face that was fierce with determination one second, only to melt into sensual invitation the next.

He wondered if there was another man in her life, but

discarded the idea. He'd felt her respond when he'd kissed her so impulsively. That was a decided mistake. Kissing Robert Fisher's ex-wife, for God's sake. *What's gotten into you, McGowan?*

She drove out of the lot, and another car, a white station wagon, pulled away from the curb at the same time. Jake had caught only a glance of the driver when Diane nudged him on the shoulder.

"So—I see you're getting along well with your new client?" She tried to hide a smile and failed. Her blue eyes danced, and Jake felt as if he'd been conned.

A waiter carrying a silver tray passed by, and Jake reached for another glass of champagne. "Don't tell me this is another one of your feeble attempts at matchmaking, Dr. Welby."

"It's Donaldson now—remember that," she warned. "And it didn't look so feeble to me. Besides, she needs your help."

"Both of you keep saying that."

Diane's eyes lost their mischievous sparkle, and she grew serious. "I shouldn't have to explain to you about the fear of losing a child."

Jake stiffened as if to protect himself.

"And you could help her, you know, and get back at Robert Fisher at the same time. Kill two birds with one stone."

Jake's head snapped up. "You told her about Daniel?"

Diane shook her head. "Of course not. It's not my business." Her blue eyes clouded, and she touched the side of his face. "But I wish there were a way you could lay him to rest."

"*I will*," Jake bit out as Diane, spying Scott across the room, threaded her way back to her groom.

Eventually, he supposed, he'd have to tell Kimberly about his relationship with Daniel. And he'd have to do it before he lost his head and got involved with her.

He took a long swallow of champagne and stared out the window, wondering what to do about her. If he were scrupulous, he'd lay his cards on the table, tell her everything that was going on, admit that he was Daniel Steven's half-brother and that he didn't want to get involved emotionally with any woman—especially a woman who had a child and had once been married to Robert Fisher. He'd also have to tell her that he wanted her.

Unfortunately it seemed lately that scruples weren't his long suit.

# CHAPTER SIX

Kimberly hardly dared breathe until she had driven several blocks away from Pioneer Chapel and Jake McGowan. Why had she followed him to the cemetery? Why had she let his bleak look disturb her? And why, dear God, had she let him kiss her?

Sighing, she glanced at the single white rose, now dewy with rainwater, lying on the passenger seat.

Smiling wryly at the bedraggled flower, she flicked on the wipers, then licked her lips anxiously, only to be reminded of Jake and his overpowering kiss. Deep inside her there was a yearning—a yearning she didn't want to acknowledge.

"Get a grip on yourself," she warned, glancing at her reflection in the rearview mirror. Her hair was a mess, her cheeks flushed, her eyes unnaturally bright. "Oh, Kimberly, you *are* an idiot," she whispered, barely noticing the car trailing after.

Compressing her lips, imagining the feel of Jake's mouth against hers, she cranked on the steering wheel and ferried her car into the puddle-strewn driveway of her cottage near the park.

Steadfastly Kimberly pushed aside her fantasies of Jake. They were out of the question. He was her lawyer, for God's sake. He had to remain objective in order to help her keep Lindsay!

Scooping up her purse and the rose, she climbed out of the car and ducked under the dripping clematis clinging to the eaves of the back porch.

The door banged shut behind her.

"Mommy!" Footsteps echoed in the hallway, and Lindsay, her cheeks rosy, her blond hair streaming behind her, nearly slipped as she ran across the kitchen floor and threw herself into Kimberly's waiting arms.

"Hi, honey!" Kimberly hugged her daughter fiercely, as if in so doing she could erase the black cloud that hung over them.

Lindsay squirmed, squealing happily in her arms. "Oooh. You look beautiful!" Blue eyes studied Kimberly's dress and the single strand of pearls encircling her throat.

"Where'd you go?"

"To a wedding. And look—here's something for you!" Kimberly handed Lindsay the white bud.

"I wanted to go, too." Lindsay pouted, her lower lip protruding in vexation as she took the flower and contemplated the ivory-colored petals.

Kimberly kissed her daughter's forehead. "Maybe next time," she promised as she heard Arlene's brisk footsteps in the hall.

"How was the wedding?" Arlene asked, entering the kitchen.

"Just like the ending of a fairytale. Diane was working her way past cloud nine and headed for ten."

"Good for her. You could take a lesson, you know."

"On love?"

"Yes—on love. All men aren't the same," she said meaningfully as she untied her apron.

*Don't I know it*, Kimberly thought. Lindsay climbed away from her mother and headed down the hall.

Kimberly shook the rain from her hair. "So, how'd it go today? How was Lindsay?"

"An angel, as usual."

"Sure." Kimberly laughed.

"Well, maybe her halo tilts once in a while, but she wouldn't be normal if it didn't."

"I suppose you're right." Kimberly found a cup in the cupboard and poured coffee from the glass pot in the coffee maker. She held up the pot to Arlene, but the older woman shook her head.

"Had enough. My back teeth are already floating. Now, tell me every last detail of the wedding."

Kimberly went through the entire ceremony, and Arlene's eyes twinkled. "Well, I'm glad you went. You need to go out and have yourself a good time once in a while."

"I don't know if I'd call a wedding a 'good time.'"

"You know what I mean. You need to live a little and kick up your heels. And going out sure beats sitting around here worrying about what—" Arlene glanced nervously at Lindsay, but the little girl was already in the living room searching for her blanket "—that ex-husband of yours has up his sleeve. I tell you, if I ever see him again face-to-face . . ." She let her warning trail off, but her sharp birdlike eyes blazed with indignation.

Despite her fears, Kimberly laughed at Arlene's militancy. "If Robert only knew, he'd be shaking in his boots!"

"He'd better be! Now, listen, I made a big pot of lentil soup. It's on the stove. And there are fresh chocolate macaroons in the cookie jar."

"Oh, thanks. But take some home to Lyle," Kimberly insisted, thinking of Arlene's crippled husband.

"Another time, maybe, but not tonight. The last thing we need is something more to nibble on." She reached for a plaid jacket hanging on a peg near the back door. "Okay, I'll be back in the morning. If the weather clears up, I'll take Lindsay over to the park—just to see if there are any ducks who haven't figured out that they should be in Palm Beach." With a wave she stepped outside.

Kimberly watched her leave, then lifted the lid of the soup kettle. Tangy, spice-laden steam curled upward in a soft cloud.

"Hey—lookie at me!" Lindsay stumbled into the kitchen. She was wearing a rhinestone tiara in her hair, a long strand of beads around her neck, one of Kimberly's lace slips and a pair of Kimberly's satin pumps. "I'm a bride," she proclaimed proudly, her large eyes meeting her mother's.

"And a beautiful one," Kimberly said, laughing as she twirled her daughter off her feet. One of the high heels dropped with a clank to the floor. "So, who's the lucky guy?"

"Guy?"

Kimberly couldn't help grinning. "You know—the man you're going to marry."

"No one!" Lindsay said emphatically. "Like you."

"Like me," Kimberly said as she held Lindsay close. "Well, pumpkin, it's hard to have a wedding without a groom—but if that's the way you want it, it's okay by me."

"Good." Lindsay smiled slyly and eyed the ceramic teddy bear jar on the counter just out of her reach. "Now can I have a cookie?"

"Later. First, we'll have some soup."

Lindsay made a face, crinkling up her nose. "I like macaroons better."

"Most of us do," Kimberly admitted as she placed her daughter on the floor. Lindsay concentrated on balancing in the high heels again.

Kimberly padded Lindsay's pale curls. "I've got to get changed, and then we'll have dinner."

She hurried down the short hall to her bedroom, and Lindsay followed, the shoes clumping noisily.

"Who was the bride today?" Lindsay asked.

"Diane—remember?"

"Oh."

Lindsay turned and marched out of the bedroom and down the hall, singing loudly, "Here comes the bride."

Kimberly tugged the dress over her head and stared at her reflection in the oval mirror above her bureau. Small creases lined her brow, but her blue-green eyes sparkled. Thoughts of Jake skittered through her mind.

She felt an annoying flush climb slowly from the swell of her breasts to her throat. Smiling to herself, she brushed the tangles from her wet, bedraggled hair. Her feelings concerning Jake McGowan were in a jumble. Professionalism had to overcome this ludicrous joy she felt at the mere thought of him. Suddenly annoyed, she flung her brush onto the bureau and kicked off her shoes.

She should never have followed him to the cemetery, she never should have allowed herself to be charmed by Jake McGowan. Glancing at the mirror again, she frowned. "You've made a mess of things this time," she chided her reflection. Wearing only her satin slip, her hair shining from the recent brushing, she sank onto the mattress of her double bed.

No matter what happened she still had to approach Jake as a professional. Damn it, she needed him. "You've got no choice," she whispered into the empty room. With that, she leaned back against the pillows and closed her eyes, only to see the mocking image of Jake's face.

His thoughts all tangled in Kimberly, Jake drove home from the wedding reception. His senses still reeled, and he wondered what kind of fool he'd been, kissing Kimberly impulsively, then dancing so close to her. Caught in the fragrant cloud of her perfume and the yielding warmth of her body pressed tantalizingly to his, he hadn't been able to think clearly.

Even now his palms began to sweat around the steering wheel as he remembered looking down at her when they'd danced. She'd tossed her head back, her hair brushing his arm, her gaze touching a forbidden part of his soul.

She hadn't seemed to mind that her dress was stained by the rain, nor that her hair had been tossed in the wind. He'd wanted to bury himself in those long, rain-darkened strands, and he'd had trouble dragging his gaze away from the pink pout of her lips.

Overwhelmed, Jake had felt a crazy desire to sweep her off her feet and steal her away so that he could get lost in her body and soul. But he hadn't. Common sense had prevailed.

Staring at the dark streets. He realized he hadn't been so fascinated with a woman in years. Though his mind screamed that he was making an irrevocable mistake, he couldn't fight the jolt of possession that ripped through him.

That she had been Robert Fisher's wife was unthinkable. She was warm and soft, and erotic thoughts still fired his blood, pounding with the same driving beat of his heart.

Tail lights glowed in front of him, and he stomped on the brakes. The Bronco fishtailed. "Forget her," he growled at himself. But as the words passed his lips, he knew he never would.


Three days later Jake winced against the morning sunlight. His eyes burned from too little sleep and too many hours poring over every scrap of information in the Robert Fisher file. He hoped to come up with something he could pin on Fisher, something concrete he could use as a bargaining tool to get him to drop the custody case.

Of course, he'd hoped for even more than that. Some shred

of overlooked evidence that would put Fisher away for good. No such luck.

But early this morning, when he'd finally given up and closed the Fisher file, he'd dropped onto the bed, only to stare at the clock and listen to the sounds of the night while his mind wandered back to Kimberly—over and over again. No matter how many times he forced his thoughts away from her, they always crept back to her soft smile and dark-fringed eyes.

Muttering an oath to himself, he shoved open the office door and was greeted by the sound of classical music and the smell of warm coffee.

Sarah, the plump secretary he'd inherited from Diane, was at her desk, diligently working on her computer, her fingers moving skillfully.

She glanced up at him and smiled. "Good morning, Mr. McGowan."

"It's Jake. Remember? Unless we're dealing with stuffy clients, let's keep things informal."

"You got it. Coffee's on. You want a cup?"

He forced a smile. "I can get it myself."

"I'd be glad to—"

He held up a palm. "Relax, Sarah. This isn't the Dark Ages. You're liberated now, remember?"

She snorted, but smiled and went back to her work.

Jake headed down the hall. In the kitchen he poured a mug of dark coffee and warmed his hands on the side of the cup. He had several client appointments this morning, but his concentration wasn't on property line disputes, patent infringement or tax loopholes—or anything other than Robert Fisher.

And Kimberly Bennett.

"You're obsessed," he muttered, crossing through the reception area and picking up the stack of phone messages from the corner of Sarah's desk. He flipped through them quickly, hoping to spot Kimberly's name, but stopped at the final note. Ben Kesler had finally returned his call.

Jake McGowan's mood improved. "Now we're getting somewhere," he said as he kicked his office door closed and plopped down in his chair.

He hadn't noticed that Sarah had rearranged his desk, not until he picked up the receiver and saw the picture. His hand paused in midair as he stared onto the face of a small, two-year-old boy. A boy with dark hair and blue eyes. A boy holding a stuffed yellow duck and wearing a wide smile. A boy he loved with all his heart. A boy he'd called his son.

Jake let the telephone receiver drop. His throat nodded, and he picked up the picture, staring at the lifeless photograph. Steeling himself as he always did, he took the framed photo and placed it behind him on the credenza.

His forehead creased, and he waited until he was composed again. Then he reached for the phone and punched Kesler's number.

Kesler was in a meeting and would call back. Without really thinking, Jake dialed Ron Koski's number and left a message. Ron called back half an hour later.

"How're you doing?" he asked, his gravelly voice needing no introduction.

Jake got right to the point. "I didn't find much in the Fisher file," he said, "in fact, just about nothing I didn't know already. So I want you to get back to Brecken. See if you can find out anything."

"What's up?"

"Nothing, probably," Jake thought aloud, leaning back in his chair. "But if the police are getting close to Fisher, he'll know it. Someone will leak the information to him for the right price. If that's the case, maybe he's getting ready for a long vacation."

Koski let out a low whistle. "You think that's why he's interested in his kid all of a sudden."

"I don't know," Jake admitted, hating to think what would happen to Kimberly if she lost her child. "I just want to cover all the bases. See what you can dig up."

"Will do. But Brecken's become pretty tight-lipped."

"I know," Jake said, rubbing his jaw. "That's what worries me."


At five o'clock Bill Zealander stormed into Kimberly's office. His ruddy face was set in a scowl, and his eyes, behind wire-rimmed glasses, were nearly black. "What's the meaning of this?" he demanded, slapping down a file folder with a memo clipped to it.

"Of what?"

His eyes narrowed as he read the memo. "Eric's reassigned the Juniper trust to you. Why?"

"Because the heirs requested me."

His nostrils flared. "Which heirs?"

"Henry and Carole—the children."

"That's preposterous! You know them?" he challenged.

"Not personally, no," she said calmly. "But I helped Henry secure a building loan when I worked in mortgage trust, and I helped Carole set up a custodial account."

"And that's all?" he asked, concealing his disbelief.

"Other than the couple of weeks I've worked with them on the estate. Why?"

"You know why." He leaned over her desk. "The Juniper trust is well over five million dollars—one of the largest in the department." His mouth set in a tight grimace. "Don't think I won't talk to Eric about this!"

Kimberly smiled, but her eyes met his levelly. "I wouldn't dream of it, Bill. Go right ahead. Talk all you want."

"I will." Snapping the folder up, he strode out the door as quickly as he'd marched in. Kimberly dropped her forehead into her hands. "Men," she muttered under her breath.

"Ms. Bennett?" Marcie's voice buzzed over the intercom. "Call for you on line two. Mr. McGowan."

Kimberly's heart jumped. "Thanks," she said into the intercom, she picked up the phone. "Kimberly Bennett."

Jake got right to the point. "I'd like to meet with you. As soon as possible. I just got off the phone with Kesler."

Kimberly's breath stilled. "And?"

"And it looks like you were right. Robert is hell-bent to gain full custody."

She closed her eyes, and her fingers tightened around the receiver, holding it in a death grip. "I knew it," she said, seriously. "I just knew it!"

"I think we'd better get together."

"Absolutely."

"I'll pick you up at the bank right after closing. We'll go to dinner, then get down to brass tacks."

She didn't even think about arguing. She was too shaken. So, Robert was going through with it. Just as he'd threatened. "Can he take her away from me?" she asked, bracing herself.

"Not if I can help it."

Still numb, she hung up the phone. At least she had Jake on her side. That was good. Jake McGowan, she decided, thinking back to the jut of his chin and the anger that would spark in his flinty eyes, would be a dangerous enemy.

True to his word, Jake arrived less than forty-five minutes later. Marcy, who showed the man to Kimberly's office, winked at Kimberly from behind his back, then made a quick escape.

Kimberly glanced up from her desk, saw the concern in his eyes and felt her heart flutter uncontrollably.

"What did Kesler say?" she demanded, shutting the door behind him.

"You want to talk here?" he asked.

She glanced around the cherry-paneled walls and bit her lip. "Probably not. This might sound paranoid, but there's too much of Robert here. He's a major client with the bank."

"And the walls have ears?" One side of his mouth tilted upward.

"I just don't like to take any chances." Kimberly licked her lips. "I'm scared, Jake," she admitted. "Really scared."

"Don't be. Nothing's happened yet."

"I can't lose her. I can't." He wrapped his arms around her, and she leaned against him. The strength of his body felt so right—so natural. She didn't even consider pulling out of his embrace, but clung to him. The soft texture of his jacket rubbed against her cheek, and the smell of leather and after-shave filled her nostrils. "Lindsay—"

"Shh. Didn't I tell you I wouldn't let that happen?"

She nodded, her crown brushing his chin. "But you don't know Robert."

His muscles tensed. "I know him."

"He can be so . . ."

"Ruthless?"

"Yes," she admitted, shivering. "Ruthless."

He tilted her chin up with one finger and forced her frightened gaze to meet the calm depth of his. "Then I guess I'll just have to be more ruthless, won't I?"

"You'd stoop to his level?"

His mouth twisted sardonically. "Let's just say I'll do whatever's necessary. Now, come on, let's go."

She didn't argue. Slipping reluctantly from the security of his embrace, she stuffed some files in her briefcase, snapped the leather case closed and grabbed her cape. "Where to?"

"Some place close?"

"No." The after-work crowd hung out during happy hour in some of the local bars and restaurants nearby, and Kimberly didn't want to risk being overheard by anyone at the bank.

"Bollinger's, then?" he suggested.

Bollinger's was a restaurant perched high on the hills in Northwest Portland. She couldn't have suggested anywhere that was more out of the way. And, as far as she knew, Bollinger's wasn't one of Robert's regular haunts. "I'll meet you there."

"I could drive you."

She felt suddenly silly for the way she'd nearly fallen apart. Tossing her hair from her face, she said, "I can drive myself. Really. It's just easier that way."

"If that's the way you want it."

She walked with him to the elevators. In the parking garage she watched as he unlocked his Bronco, then she slid into her Mercedes and headed west.

Within twenty minutes she was seated across a small table from him. The restaurant was housed in an old Victorian structure, complete with turrets and gables. It clung to a forested hill in Northwest Portland and had been remodeled several times since the turn of the twentieth century. Filled with paraphernalia of bygone years, Bollinger's was an eclectic blend of antiques—Army recruiting posters from the World Wars, artifacts from the forties and fifties, record jackets from the sixties and Tiffany lamps with hanging prisms and classic movie posters.

Kimberly barely noticed. "Tell me everything Ben Kesler said."

Jake sat on the other side of the small table. His knees nearly brushed hers, and candlelight flickered over the stern set of his features. "It's pretty simple, really. They're planning on trying to wrest custody from you because Robert's convinced you're unfit."

"Oh, God."

"Saying it and proving it are two different matters," Jake pointed out.

A waiter dropped by the table, and Jake ordered them a bottle of wine. When she started to protest, he wouldn't hear of it, and without consulting her, ordered for them both.

Kimberly didn't care. She wasn't interested in food. She was only concerned about Lindsay.

The waiter returned with the wine, and Jake poured them each a glass. "Now, tell me about your life," he suggested.

"What about it?"

"What do you do all day?"

"You mean in my free time—between being a mother and a full-time bank officer."

His eyes twinkled in the reflection of the candles. "Right."

"I sleep—exercise a little. Watch some TV and read. Pretty interesting stuff, eh?" she asked, sipping from her glass.

The waiter deposited crisp salads and a crusty loaf of Viennese bread on their table.

"What about the men in your life?"

"Men? Plural?" she responded, feeling a little defensive.

"Okay, tell me about the *man* in your life."

She dropped her eyes and tried to stem the rage that boiled up by pounding a tomato slice on her salad plate. "I hate this, y'know."

"What?"

"This—accountability. My life dissected under a micro-scope."

"I know." He reached across the table, and his hand covered hers. "But I have to ask."

The tender gesture tore at her heart. She withdrew her hand and lifted her eyes to his. "There is no man." *Except maybe you.*

Jake stared at her for a second, then blinked and turned his attention to cutting the loaf of bread on the board between them. "Surely you've dated since the divorce."

He placed a thick slice onto her plate.

"Not much."

"So, tell me about the dates."

She wasn't used to sharing her personal life with a man— any man. And Jake was different. Baring her soul to him took courage. She had to remind herself that she hired him to probe into her personal life. "There's nothing much to tell," she said as the waiter removed the salad plates and placed steaming platters of pasta and vegetables on the table. "The first man was an old family friend—nothing romantic. And the second— well, it was a mistake."

"Why?"

"The man was Eric Compton. My boss at First Cascade. He's the vice president in charge of the trust department, only one step down from Aaron Thornburn, the president. It was only one date, but it caused all kinds of problems."

"Such as?"

"Other employees, one in particular, thought I was trying to sleep my way to the top."

He stared at her for a second. "Were you?"

Her mouth nearly dropped open, but she clamped it firmly shut. Did he think so little of her? "What do you think?"

His mouth curved into a lazy smile. "It doesn't seem your style."

"It isn't. I wish I'd never gone out with Eric. Things would've been much simpler." She frowned at the memory. Eric had hoped to start something that night, had expected her to fall at his feet. He'd even gone so far as to suggest she spend the night at his place, and she'd nearly choked on her drink. In many ways the evening had been a disaster.

"And you've never gone out with him again?"

"No." She sipped from her water glass.

"Why not?"

"No reason to fan the fires of gossip. I've got enough problems being the only woman trust officer without having to be known as the boss's 'woman.'"

"And Compton—he's accepted this?"

"He doesn't have much of a choice."

Jake stared at her. "Anyone else?"

"No one serious."

Silence stretched uncomfortably between them, and Kimberly wished she'd never agreed to meet him here. The small table was too intimate, and Jake was too close, his stare too intense. She could feel his gaze on her as he sipped his wine. She watched his throat work as he swallowed. That small motion, so natural, was sensual in the dark room. She dragged her gaze away from his throat and stared through the window. The lights of Portland twinkled in the distance.

"Tell me about Lindsay," Jake whispered.

Kimberly's head snapped up. "What about her?"

"Everything. She's what? Five?"

"Yes. Robert and I had been married a little over a year when she was born." Kimberly felt suddenly self-conscious. "When I found out I was pregnant, I was ecstatic."

"And Robert?"

"Suggested an abortion." That had been the start of the end, she knew now. "I wouldn't hear of it, and we argued a lot. During the last part of the pregnancy, he seemed to change his mind and became interested until she was born."

Jake's eyes were penetrating, the hard angles of his face illuminated by the single flickering candle. "What went wrong?"

"He wanted a boy." She smiled sourly. "Archaic, right?"

A shadow passed over his eyes. "Very."

She pushed the remains of her meal around on her plate, then let her fork drop. "He never seemed to care about her.

Don't get me wrong—he was never cruel or anything, just inattentive. And he lost interest in me, too."

"So you wanted out—"

"Oh, no." Surprised that it was so important that he understand, Kimberly said, "He wanted the divorce. I fought it at first."

"Why?"

"Because we were parents. We had this wonderful baby, and I wanted to create this perfect little family unit." Her lips twisted cynically. "You know the image, right off the front pages of the old *Saturday Evening Post.*"

"And he didn't feel that way?"

"By that time he'd found someone else," she said, the pain as real and cold as it had been the night he'd explained about Stella. "And then I started paying more attention to the rumors and innuendos in the papers."

"And believing them?"

"No—yes—I don't know. I believe where there's smoke there's fire, but I never saw or heard anything that would confirm all the speculation about him."

She finished what she could of the dinner and pushed aside any lingering thoughts of Robert and their short, unhappy marriage. Jake turned the conversation away from the painful subject, and soon he had taken care of the bill and escorted her through the double doors.

"You know," he said once they were outside and darkness surrounded them, "we've got a problem."

"Just one?" she teased, flashing a smile in the clear night air.

"Believe me, it's enough." He took her hand in his, and his fingers were warm. A thrill raced up her arm.

Her heart began to beat against her ribs. "What is it?"

"You and me."

"What about us?"

"I'd like to see more of you, Kimberly," he said, the admission obviously difficult.

"I think we'll see a lot of each other in the next couple weeks."

He plowed stiff fingers through his hair. "I know. But the trouble is, I want more. More than just a business relationship. I know it's crazy and off-limits, but that's the way it is." His eyes darkened with the night, and her pulse was pounding in her head.

"I don't think it's wise—"

"I *know* it isn't. But we can't deny what we feel."

"Oh, Jake, don't—"

He cut her off. "Don't deny it, Kimberly."

Her throat tightened as he drew her close.

"I asked you those questions in the restaurant for two reasons. One was for the case. The other was for me."

Her pulse quickened. Unconsciously she licked her lips, and his gaze drifted down to her mouth. "I—I think we'd better keep this professional," she said, her voice unfamiliarly husky.

"I agree—but I don't think I can." He stared at her with such honesty, she nearly melted inside.

"I have a daughter to think about."

"I know."

"And . . ." She slowly pulled her hand from his. "And sometimes I feel you're holding back. That you're not being completely honest."

His expression turned guarded. If he were going to share any secrets with her, it wouldn't be tonight.

Disappointed, she turned away, only to feel his fingers clamp on her shoulders and turn her quickly. "I know it's crazy, but I can't help it," he grounded out before his lips descended on hers and he kissed her with that same raging fire she'd felt before. She couldn't stop him, and kissed him back. Swept away in a rising storm of passion, she clung to him.

When at last he lifted his head, he stared at her with a hint of amusement. "Now, just how're we going to ignore this, Ms. Bennett?"

"I'll find a way," she teased back, her equilibrium shattered.

"You think so?" His grin slashed white in the night. "I wouldn't count on it if I were you." He dropped his arms to let her go, but she lingered a second.

"I just don't think I can get involved with anyone right now. Not until this is all over."

"I wonder if that's possible."

"I don't know," she whispered, turning to her car, not trusting herself alone with him another minute. She climbed into the Mercedes and took off.

She drove home automatically, guiding the car by instinct. Though she tried not to think of Jake's handsome face or enigmatic, off-center smile, his image seemed to loom in her mind's eye. He was her lawyer, for crying out loud. She'd convinced him to help her, and that was that. She touched her mouth softly, remembering the firm lines of Jake's lips as they had covered hers with a possession so demanding, so vibrant that she could still feel the pulsing desire that had swept from his body to hers.

"Stop it," she muttered, cranking on the wheel as she turned into the driveway. Angry with her wayward fantasies, she cut the engine and dashed up the back steps.

Stepping into the kitchen, she spied a pajama-clad Lindsay standing on a chair. Her heart wrenched at the thought of a future without Lindsay's precocious remarks and bright eyes.

A huge lump filled her throat. Lindsay was watching Arlene as the older woman bent over a bowl and stirred slowly. The scent of lemon filled the room.

"Baking again?" Kimberly asked as she dropped her purse onto the table.

"Mommy!" Lindsay scrambled out of her chair and to Kimberly's waiting arms. "You're late!"

"I know, I'm sorry."

"I missed you," Lindsay pouted.

Arlene clucked her tongue. "Don't you fuss," she warned, glancing fondly at Lindsay. "I told you she called." Arlene resumed her stirring and nodded in Kimberly's direction. "Just give me a minute. Lindsay wanted lemon pie."

"But we still have cookies!"

"So eat 'em."

Kimberly slid out of her coat. "Really, Arlene, you didn't have to go through the trouble—"

"No trouble at all," Arlene said, chuckling. "It kept her busy, and lemon's my favorite, too."

"Arlene says I can stay overnight with her."

"Oh?" Still balancing her daughter on her hip, Kimberly crossed the kitchen and peeked into the kettle of simmering lemon pudding.

"Next weekend, if it's all right with you," Arlene verified.

"Are you sure?"

"Positive. Besides, it'll do Lyle a world of good to watch this little one."

Lindsay clapped her hands together. "We are going to make you a Christmas—"

"Shh!" Arlene said, grinning. "It's a surprise. Remember?"

"Oh!" The child looked positively stricken.

Kimberly touched her blond curls fondly. "Okay. You can spend the night, *if* you promise to be good, brush your teeth and go right to sleep when Mrs. Henderson tells you to."

"I'm always good," Lindsay proclaimed, crossing her little arms over her flannel-covered chest.

"An absolute angel," Arlene said, smothering a smile. "Okay, here we go." She poured the lemon filling into a warm piecrust, then spoon fed globs of shiny meringue on top. Lindsay couldn't stand not being part of the action. She squirmed from Kimberly's arms, climbed back on her chair and promptly stuck a finger in the cloudlike meringue.

Kimberly tried to stop her daughter. "Don't—"

"It's all right," Arlene said. "Half the fun of baking is testing, isn't it, sweetheart?"

Lindsay cast Kimberly an I-told-you-so look over her small shoulder. A dot of meringue stuck to the tip of her nose, and Kimberly had to laugh.

"I think we better wash you up and get ready for bed."

"Not yet—"

"Come on," Kimberly insisted. "It's after eight."

"But I'm not tired."

"I don't believe that for a second," Kimberly remarked, noting the blue smudges beneath Lindsay's bright eyes and the fact that her thumb kept slipping between her small lips. "Come on, angel, I'll read you a story."

"But I want—"

"Shh." Kimberly carried her protesting daughter to the loft, which served as Lindsay's bedroom. Tucking the child between the covers, she lay beside her, opened a book of favorite nursery rhymes and began reading. Within minutes Lindsay drifted to sleep, her lips moving slightly, her blond head resting on a plump pillow, while she clutched her favorite stuffed animal, a fuzzy raccoon.

Kimberly's throat constricted as she stared at her sleeping child. No matter what, she couldn't lose Lindsay.

Listening to the sound of the rain drumming against the roof, she placed her arm around her daughter's waist and Kimberly closed her eyes. Somehow, she vowed silently, she'd find a way to keep Lindsay with her. And Jacob McGowan would help.

# CHAPTER SEVEN

Eric Compton knocked twice, then shoved open the door of Kimberly's office. A tall, striking man with thinning black hair, straight nose and brown eyes, he offered her his well-practiced smile. "Glad I caught you," he said, glancing at his watch. "I thought you might need the tax file on the Juniper estate." He dropped a manila folder onto the corner of her desk.

"Thanks." She took the file and tossed it into her basket. "Have you got a minute?"

"For you? At least one—maybe even ten."

She grinned. "Good."

He dropped into a chair near the desk. "Shoot."

"Okay. I got a little flack about this one," she said, tapping the closed file with a fingernail.

"From Zealander. I heard." Eric frowned and ran his fingers through his receding hair. "Bill came flying into my office the other day. He thinks I favor you."

"Do you?"

Eric smiled. "I'd like to. But not by giving you plums in the office. I've always tried to keep my private and professional lives separate."

"Good. So have I," she said.

"I told Bill the same thing." He plucked at the crease of his slacks. "However, I'm not sure he believed me. But—" placing his hands on the arms of his chair, he pushed himself up, "—that's his problem. Now, anything else?" he asked without the usual double entendre.

"Not that I can think of."

His well-oiled smile faltered a little. "Good. You know, Kim, I'd like to take you out. I've got tickets to the symphony next Friday."

Kimberly sighed and shook her head. "I don't think so."

"Another time?"

"Maybe," she said, then winced when she recognized a gleam of hope in his eye. "But probably not. As long as I'm working here, I think it would be better not to date bank employees."

"Even the boss?"

"Especially the boss," she said, offering a dimpled smile.

He shrugged. "Okay, but this is a warning. I'm not giving up. Just let me know when you change your mind." He started for the door, then paused and glanced over his shoulder. "By the way, I saw a man hanging around the parking lot late last night. Be careful, will you? There'll be a memo sent to all the employees, but I'm telling everyone in my department personally."

"You think he's dangerous?"

"Probably not, but we can't be too careful," Compton said as he closed the door firmly behind him.

Kimberly stared at the closed door. She thought about the man she'd seen lingering at the lamppost near her house and shivered. Though she'd nearly forgotten the incident, Eric's warning brought it all back into sharp focus.

She tapped her pencil on her desk as the intercom buzzed.

"Ms. Bennett? Mr. Juniper's here to see you," Marcie announced just as the door to her office burst open again and Henry Juniper, a small, round man with a red face, strode up to Kimberly's desk. She started to rise.

"My sister's trying to cut me out of the estate, isn't she?"

Kimberly was dumbstruck. "There's no way she could. I thought I explained all that."

"Oh, sure," Henry said, his blue eyes flaming. "Where there's a will, there's a way. Especially if you get a greedy lawyer involved."

"Why don't you slow down and tell me what you're talking about."

"It's Carole," he said in exasperation. "She's hired some hotshot attorney and now she wants more money! This guy— what's his name—Kesler—he's out to bleed me dry!"

Kimberly's heart dropped to the floor. "Ben Kesler?"

"The shark himself. I've heard he's a barracuda, that he never gives up. Just keeps biting at you!"

Kimberly, shaking inside, held up a hand. "The terms of your father's will were very clear. There is nothing Mr. Kesler can do to change that. Anything he tries will just be smoke and mirrors. The will is cut and dried."

He calmed a little and nearly fell into the chair recently vacated by Eric Compton. His fingers tapped nervously together. "You're sure about this?"

"Positive."

"And there's never been a case where one heir has been able to squeeze out a little more?"

"I didn't say that. It depends upon the circumstances, of course—"

"Aha! I knew it." His hands flew into the air. "Father lived with Carole for a while, you know, while he was convalescing after his hospital stay. I suggested a nursing home, but oh, no, she wouldn't hear of it. Wouldn't hear of it, I tell you!" He leaned closer. "Wanted to get on his good side, don't you know. I think she was trying to get him to change his will the entire time he was with her. It didn't work, and now she's going to charge the estate for his care—and then there's Kesler's attorney fees and God-only-knows what else!"

"Slow down, Mr. Juniper," she said. "The head of our department, Mr. Compton, is an attorney himself, and he's worked very closely with the attorney for the estate. I assure you that everything's in order."

"Oh, great, just what we need! A couple more attorneys involved. That's what got us into this mess in the first place!"

She spent the next half hour going over the account and settling him down. By the time six o'clock rolled around, all she could think about was going home to dinner with Lindsay, a hot bath and a good book.

She tossed a few files into her briefcase and frowned at the pink memo in her in-basket—the memo reminding everyone to be careful in the parking garage.

As she swiped her coat from the hall tree, the phone rang. Balancing purse, case and coat in one arm, she grabbed the receiver quickly. "Kimberly Bennett."

"Jake McGowan."

At the sound of his voice, her heart somersaulted.

"I know it's late, but I thought we could catch a movie, then have a late dinner."

"I thought we had an agreement."

"No, lady, you had an agreement."

"Jake, this isn't going to work—"

"What if I told you we have work to do?"

She smiled, forgetting about the hot bath and book. "I still can't go out. Arlene's busy tonight."

"You don't have another sitter?"

"None that I can count on." She was surprised at how her heart seemed to drop to the floor in disappointment.

"Then I guess we'll have to forgo the movie and get right to it. I could drop by your place, and you could make me dinner."

She laughed and threw caution to the wind. What could one night hurt? "All right, counselor, you're on. I owe you that much."

There was a long, nerve-wracking silence on the other end of the line. "You don't *owe* me anything." His tone was dead sober.

"Okay, don't consider it a debt. In fact, you can bring the wine."

"White or red?"

"Surprise me."

"I'd love to," he said silkily.

Kimberly's heart tripped.

"I'll see you between seven-thirty and eight."

Kimberly stood rooted to the spot until she heard him hang up. Then she dropped the receiver. Clutching her bag, briefcase and coat to her breast, she muttered, "You'd better get moving."

She took the elevator to the basement lot, which was as poorly lighted as ever. The hairs on the back of her neck raised a little and she felt as if unseen eyes were boring into her back. "Don't be paranoid," she chided herself, but nearly jumped out of her skin when she heard the scrape of a shoe behind her.

Her heart leaped to her throat as she remembered Eric Compton's warning. Spinning, she surveyed the lot, but saw nothing out of the ordinary, just a few other employees walking to their vehicles.

Behind the wheel, her hands began to sweat, and she locked all the doors before pulling out of her parking space. As she drove through the gate, she caught a glimpse of a shadowy figure huddled behind a post, but it disappeared as quickly as it had appeared. "It's just your imagination," she said, hoping to calm her jittery nerves. "Nothing else." But she couldn't shake the feeling that she was being watched as she drove across the river to Sellwood.

The drive home, including a stop for groceries, took less than thirty minutes.

Kimberly juggled two sacks as she unlocked the back door and hurried inside. Arlene and Lindsay were in the kitchen.

"Did you get anything for me?" Lindsay asked, eyeing the sacks from her vantage point under the table, where she was carefully stacking building blocks.

"Everything," Kimberly replied with a sly grin. "It's dinner. And we're having company."

Arlene's brows inched upward.

"What company?" Lindsay demanded. She scooted out of her hiding place and eyed her mother. "Who's coming over here?"

"Jake—you met him earlier."

Lindsay's lower lip protruded, and her pudgy face clouded suspiciously. "I don't like him!"

"Why not?"

Lindsay shrugged. "He's too big."

Arlene smothered a smile.

"Tell him to go home!"

"Wonderful," Kimberly whispered sarcastically. "This is shaping up to be a barrel of laughs."

"Come on, you," Arlene said fondly, taking Lindsay's hand. "I'll help you get cleaned up."

While Arlene and Lindsay were upstairs, Kimberly unpacked the groceries she'd bought, put a kettle of water on the stove and raced into the bedroom. She changed into a pair of black jeans and an aqua-blue sweater, then hurried back to the kitchen and tossed the lasagna noodles into the steaming kettle. After starting another can of tomato paste simmering, she yanked out vegetables, cheese and the remains of a baked chicken, then started grating mozzarella cheese.

Arlene returned to the kitchen. "Lindsay wanted to finish dressing herself. She'll be down in a minute." She studied the boiling pot on the stove. "What're you making?"

"Chicken lasagna."

"Need some help?" Arlene snatched her favorite apron from a hook near the back door and tied the strings around her thin waist.

"I'll manage," Kimberly said wryly. She glanced nervously at the clock mounted over the stove and started working double-time on the cheese.

"Then let me," Arlene offered. Without waiting for a reply, she found a sharp knife and began expertly separating bones from meat. "Tell me about this McGowan character," she said, casting Kimberly a sly glance.

"Well, he's my lawyer."

"That much I know. I met him already. I assume he's single?"

"You assume correctly," Kimberly said, remembering how pained Jake had appeared when he'd talked of marriage. "But he was married once. His wife's dead. They were divorced."

"What about children? Does he have any?"

"No." She filled Arlene in, surprised at how little she knew about Jake.

"Sounds like a bit of a mystery man to me," Arlene observed as she stripped off her apron.

"He is," she admitted, frowning. "I keep thinking I've heard of him before, but I don't know where."

"Does it matter?"

Kimberly lifted a shoulder. "Probably not." She layered the lasagna and stuffed it into the oven.

Lindsay barreled into the room. Wearing lavender stretch pants and a T-shirt with mint-green bears tumbling across its front, she handed her mother a wrinkled ribbon. "I did my ponytail myself!"

"So I see."

"But I can't tie the ribbon."

"I'll help."

"And I've got to scoot," Arlene said, pressing a kiss onto Lindsay's forehead. "I'll see you in the morning."

Lindsay cried, "What about the tree?"

"Tree?" Kimberly asked.

"The Christmas tree!"

Arlene's hand was poised over the doorknob, but she stopped. "Oh, right. Maybe tomorrow." She explained to Kimberly, "I've got a little Douglas fir I promised Lindsay. Lyle's brother brought us a couple of firs from his tree farm by Estacada. We only need one, so I left the other in a corner on your back porch."

And we're s'posed to put the lights on it!" Lindsay said.

"Tomorrow—"

"Now!" Lindsay cried.

Rolling her eyes toward the ceiling, Arlene said, "I'll see you in the morning, angel. Don't forget you're staying overnight with me Friday night."

The tree momentarily forgotten, Lindsay grinned.

"And you," Arlene said to Kimberly as she opened the door, "take my advice and go out."

"I'll think about it," Kimberly said to the door as it shut.

"Go out where?" Lindsay demanded.

"I don't think it matters." Kimberly laughed, wiping her hands and then tying the ribbon around Lindsay's ponytail. "As long as I go. Come on, you can help me." She reached into the drawer and pulled out three settings of silver—part of a wedding gift from her grandmother. "Put these and the red placemats around the table in the dining room."

"Candles?" Lindsay asked, "and fancy glasses?"

"Silver, china, candles, the works," Kimberly said, laughing.

Lindsay's face brightened. She tore into the dining room and started her task with a vengeance.

Twenty minutes later the doorbell peeled, and Kimberly nearly jumped out of her skin.

"I'll get it!" Lindsay said, sprinting into the living room.

"Be sure to look out the window first—"

But Lindsay had already yanked the door wide open. Jake was standing on the porch, two bottles of wine tucked under his arm. Cold air swept across the porch, swirling the few dry leaves that had collected near the railing.

At the sight of Jake, Kimberly's heart did an unexpected flip, but Lindsay eyed him suspiciously.

"Come in," Kimberly said, closing the door and taking Jake's jacket. "Dinner'll be a while."

Inhaling dramatically, Jake said, "It smells great."

"Let's just hope it tastes as good as it smells."

"Here." He handed her the two bottles of wine, his fingers grazing hers. "Red or white—whichever you prefer."

"I want red!" Lindsay announced.

Kimberly laughed. "But you'll get white—the kind that comes from cows."

Jake uncorked the wine and poured them each a glass. "To success," he said, nodding in Lindsay's direction.

"Success," she agreed, wondering if it were possible as she touched her glass to his.

"Now, which do you want first—the good news or the bad?"

She froze. So this is why he'd wanted to go out. To prepare her. She felt her face pale a little. "I hate good news-bad news jokes," she said softly.

"This is no joke."

She sucked in her breath. "I was afraid of that. Okay, let's start with the good."

"Robert's attorney petitioned for a change of custody, and we have a court date. January twentieth."

"That's good news?" she asked, her heart nearly stopped.

"It gives us time to work."

"I hate to ask what the bad news is."

Jake touched her arm. "The judge assigned to the case is Ken Monaghan."

Kimberly nearly dropped her wine glass. "Monaghan? But he and Robert . . ."

Jake's lips thinned. ". . . have known each other for years."

"Surely he couldn't take the case."

"I objected and made a lot of noise at city hall, but Monaghan was assigned the case."

Kimberly rested a hip against the counter. All her fears settled in her heart. She'd been kidding herself, of course; there was no way to fight a man as powerful as Robert.

"Don't worry," Jake said, reaching forward, his hand cupping her shoulder.

"But he could take her away." Tears stung her eyes, and she had to fight from breaking down completely.

Jake drew her close. "Hey, I told you I wouldn't let that happen, didn't I?"

"But—"

"You asked me to keep you informed, to let you know everything that's going on. That's why I told you. But we've got to work fast."

"How—?"

"By proving that Robert isn't fit to be a father."

The room seemed to close in on her. Going to court against Robert was one thing. Trying to publicly rebuke him was another. "But I couldn't—"

Jake's expression turned stern. "You promised," he reminded her, "that we would do this my way or no way. We both know that Fisher has been involved in a lot of shady deals, some of which have been downright illegal. You've suspected as much for a long time. All we have to do is connect him to the crimes."

Kimberly stiffened. "Crimes?" she repeated. It sounded so harsh. Her insides quaked.

"You don't have to play innocent," Jake said, all kindness gone from his features. His gaze drilled into hers. "You were his wife. You lived with the man. You saw things no policeman has ever seen."

"So you want me to play spy, is that it?" she asked bitterly.

"I want you to do everything possible to keep your child with you."

Kimberly leaned heavily against the counter. She knew it would come to this, of course. Jake had been dogged in leading up to Robert and his questionable connections. She sipped her wine but didn't taste it. Jake, like so many others, believed the worst of Robert. Not that she didn't think he had his faults. But a criminal? A crime lord? A man involved in drugs and prostitution and smuggling? She didn't believe it, though she'd noticed the change in him. "I just don't have any proof," she said. "I told you that already."

Jake's face grew taut. "You're the only one who was close enough to him to know of anything incriminating."

"We've been over this before. He never discussed his business with me while we were married, and we've barely spoken since."

Jake's eyes grew cold and calculating. Kimberly shuddered as he insisted, "Maybe you saw or heard something you don't think is important," he prodded, pressuring her.

With a great amount of effort she concentrated, her thoughts returning to that bleak, lonely time that was her marriage to Robert Fisher. She remembered many things she'd rather forget, but nothing to do with his business.

"He," she began on a sigh, "was cold. Not interested much in the family. He spent a lot of nights away from the house."

"Did anyone visit him?"

"No." She chewed on her lower lip. "We had only a couple of parties while we were married, and most of the people who came were wealthy businessmen and their wives."

Jake's jaw split the side. "What about after Daniel Steven's death?" he asked quietly.

She shook her head. "Nothing."

"It *wasn't* suicide, you know," Jake said, his gaze never leaving her.

"You don't know that."

"I do. Believe me, it just didn't happen that way."

Kimberly finally understood. "You knew him, didn't you?" she asked gently.

"Yes."

"And you didn't tell me before?" she asked, staring at him as if he were a stranger—for in many ways he was. "Why not?"

"I didn't want to color your judgment."

"Or you didn't trust me with the truth." She felt anger swell up inside her. "That's it, isn't it? Even though you told me you'd tell me everything."

"Daniel's death doesn't have anything to do with your case."

"Then why do you keep bringing it up? You lied to me."

He grabbed her wrist in an iron-like grip. "I didn't lie to you. I just didn't mention my friend."

"Why not?"

"What would be the point?" They eyed each other for several seconds, and Kimberly was sure he would feel the quick beat of her pulse on his fingertips at her wrist.

"Let's just start out being honest with each other, okay?"

His mouth tightened. "Of course." Then, explaining, he said, "Daniel investigated a man who's been known to associate with the less desirable elements of society, including your ex-husband. And Dan ends up dead." Jake's nostrils flared slightly. "Now, Kim, just what conclusion would you draw from that?" His eyes were dark with an inner, raging fire.

"I don't know," she said, swallowing hard, unable to believe that Robert would be involved in drugs and murder. Her throat worked, and her voice was barely a whisper. "I—I'm sorry about your friend."

"So am I," he said, dropping his arm. He finished his wine and set his glass in the sink. "Let's not think about Dan," he said under his breath. He shoved his fists into his pockets and closed his eyes. Slowly the tension in his features relaxed. "At least, let's not think about him tonight." He stared for a few long seconds through the kitchen window to the black night beyond. "Enough for now," he said quietly, "but if you think of anything—*anything*—that might tie your ex-husband to organized crime, you'll let me know."

"Organized crime?" she choked out, but his stern expression cut off any further protests.

"Yes."

"All right," she agreed, mentally crossing her fingers. Fighting Robert for custody of Lindsay was one thing; trying to prove him a hardened criminal—perhaps a murderer—was beyond her comprehension. And she couldn't forget that Jake, if he hadn't actually lied to her, had kept the truth to himself.

The timer buzzed. Kimberly started, then getting a grip on herself, motioned toward the dining room. "Sit—and pour us each some more wine. The red. Lindsay and I'll serve."

Jake settled into a chair at the table. The hard anger in his face disappeared, and he actually managed a thin smile. Oddly, despite his mood swings, Kimberly sensed that he belonged in this house, that his presence filled an empty void that she hadn't known existed until she'd met him.

"Lindsay," Kimberly called to the girl in the next room, "can you put your toys away and come in here, please."

Rustling could be heard outside the kitchen, followed by Lindsay's jovial voice. "Coming!" she proclaimed.

With Lindsay's help Jake lighted the cream-colored tapers. Candlelight gleamed in his dark hair and in the ruby-red claret as he poured.

Kimberly placed the thick Portland phonebook on a chair and hoisted Lindsay on top of it. Once Lindsay was settled, she set the platter of lasagna on the table and took the chair opposite Jake's. His gaze touched hers as she sat down. His sensual lips curved into a smile, and Kimberly's chest constricted against a wayward rush of emotion.

They could be friends, she thought, maybe even lovers, if circumstances were different. Jake McGowan was a fascinating, mysterious man and she liked him—more than liked him. That was the problem. Whether she wanted to admit it or not, she was falling in love with him. And yet there was so much she had yet to learn. Why hadn't he told her about Daniel Stevens being his friend? And why did she feel he was still holding something back?

Later, after the dinner dishes had been cleared and Kimberly had tucked Lindsay into bed, Jake tried to tell himself to go home, that he had no business being here. He couldn't afford to fall for Kimberly, and he certainly didn't want to form any attachment to her daughter. Yet he lingered, watching Kimberly with a growing fascination that was dangerous and wanting to please the little blond girl.

"Coffee?" she asked, pouring water into the coffee maker.

"Maybe later." He motioned toward the back porch, where he'd seen what appeared to be a bedraggled fir tree. "Let's put up the tree and surprise Lindsay."

"You'd do that?" she asked, setting the plates in the sink.

He lifted his shoulder. "Why not?" Jake noticed the proud set of her spine, the graceful way her hair fell between her shoulder blades and the nip of her waist, visible when she reached into a high cupboard for the sugar jar. Her sweater slid up a bit, exposing creamy white skin. Jake felt a stirring deep within and glanced away, swallowing hard against a suddenly dry throat.

While he wrestled with the tree, Kimberly opened the closet under the stairs and began pulling out boxes of lights, tissue paper and ornaments. Finally she found the stand. After wiping off the dust and moving the old rocker, she placed the stand by the window and watched Jake struggle with the fir.

Dark needled branches swiped at Jake's face as he attempted to place the sawed-off trunk squarely in the stand. The house filled with the scent of fresh air and pitch. Unaware of needles caught in his hair or that his muscles moved fluidly beneath his sweater, he adjusted the brace and asked Kimberly to hold the tree straight.

"I think it leans a little," Kimberly said, eyeing the listing Douglas fir.

"Which way?"

"Right—no, left."

Jake laughed. "Make up your mind."

"I will, when you quit moving it."

Swearing under his breath, Jake gave the tree a shake.

"That's better."

Jake's deep, rumbling chuckle erupted from beneath the lowest branches. "This could take all night."

Through the branches, he saw her grin. She was beautiful. Her hair was mussed, red-brown and framing her face in tangled curls, and her eyes, wide and intelligent, were the most seductive shade of blue he'd ever seen. She didn't want to get involved with him—he'd made no bones about it— and he knew getting romantically entangled with the ex-Mrs. Fisher was an irrevocable mistake. Yet he couldn't shake the hope that maybe she would change her mind.

"Okay—let's take a look," he announced, climbing from beneath the branches and shoving his hair from his eyes. The poor tree was drooping, fighting a losing battle with gravity. "Just a few minor adjustments," he said, delving beneath the lowest branches again. Extracting a pocket knife from his pants, he worked on the trunk, trimming off a few unnecessary limbs. His voice was muffled when he said, "how about a hand—can you straighten this thing?"

"I can try." Kimberly tugged on the tree, and finally stood upright as Jake adjusted the brace.

"That's better," he said, leaning back on his heels to check the angle of the fir. Satisfied, he stood, dusting his hands.

He was so close to Kimberly she could see the streaks of dark gray in his eyes, feel his breath against her hair, smell the scent of musky aftershave mingled with the odor of fresh fir boughs surrounding him.

"Now, the lights!"

She laughed. "You're as bad as Lindsay!"

"Doesn't everybody love Christmas?" he asked, grinning.

"Not everybody. Remember Scrooge and the Grinch and—"

Without a word he swept her into his arms so suddenly, her breath rushed out in a gasp. "Enough, already." His lips molded over her so intimately that Kimberly's knees went weak.

"I—thought we had an agreement," she rasped when he finally lifted his head.

"We do."

"Then what—?"

"Hang on." Eyes twinkling, he reached into his pocket and held up a sprig of mistletoe. "This cancels any rash promises we've made."

"That's not fair," she said, giggling. "Isn't it supposed to be dangling from the ceiling or something?"

"Something," he murmured, holding the sprig over her head and kissing her soundly again. This time Kimberly was ready, and despite the doubts crowding her thoughts, she returned the fever of his kiss, delighting in the feel of his lips, tasting the wine-flavored sweetness of forbidden passion.

His tongue prodded her lips, and she opened her mouth eagerly, her arms twining around his neck and his fingers gently scraped the bottom of her sweater, where the soft skin of her abdomen stretched enticingly.

Desire burned like wildfire in her veins. She felt his hips press intimately to hers, an erotic swelling beneath his slacks moving sensually against her. Slowly he lifted his head. "I can't get enough of you," he rasped.

Liquid inside, she opened her eyes. She was tingling all over, and she felt the bittersweet ache coiling deep within.

"This can't happen," he said as if trying to convince himself. "Shit, it just can't." He stepped away from her and forced stiff fingers through his hair. "It's unfair what you do to me."

Bereft, Kimberly tried to slow the pounding of her heart, but hot desire still ran wantonly through her limbs. "That works two ways, counselor."

He smiled, a self-mocking grin that lifted one corner of his mouth. "I hope to God it does," he said.

"Believe me." Taking deep breaths to steady herself, she found the string of lights and began untangling the green wires. "After we finish with these, maybe we should get back to business," she said, wishing she didn't have to bring up the custody hearing.

"What's the matter, Kimberly? Are you scared of what might happen if we don't keep things strictly business?"

She couldn't ignore his challenge. "No way."

He cocked a defiant dark brow. "You're worried that things might get out of hand."

She met the mockery in his gaze with her own. "Are you?"

"Hell, yes!" he whispered, stringing the lights.

Together they wound several strings of lights through the branches. Jake shoved the plug into the socket. The tree sparkled in a blaze of red, green and gold.

Kimberly crossed her arms under her breasts and nodded. "Good job."

"Not bad, if I do say so myself," he admitted, observing the tree.

"I guess I'm in the majority that loves Christmas," she admitted.

"That doesn't surprise me." He stared straight at Kimberly,

then brushed some needles from her hair. Kimberly's pulse jumped at the seductive glint in his eyes. "This year is going to be special."

"Oh, wow!" Lindsay chimed from the stairs. Her eyes were wide, and she flew down the stairs, her tattered blanket billowing behind her. "It's *beautiful*!" She clasped chubby hands together and dropped the blanket.

Kimberly grinned and picked her up. "What're you doing up?"

"Couldn't sleep," Lindsay said, then looked at Jake and added, "my daddy's giving me a puppy for Christmas!"

The magic of the moment shattered. Kimberly drew in a sharp breath, detesting Robert for his promise. "Oh, no, honey, I don't think—"

"He is, he told me." Lindsay folded her arms across her chest defiantly.

"We'll see."

"He is. He said so!"

Kimberly's brows drew together. "I just don't want you to be disappointed."

"Daddy doesn't do that."

"If you say so." Kimberly carried her daughter and the blanket up the stairs. Silently praying that Lindsay hadn't seen Jake kissing her, Kimberly said, "Come on, sweetheart, let's get you back in bed."

"Daddy promised!"

"He and I have to talk," Kimberly decided. "But right now it's time for bed."

"No—"

"Shh. It's late. Come on." She tucked Lindsay under the covers. "Good night, precious," Kimberly said as her daughter yawned and snuggled under the comforter. A few minutes later Lindsay was snoring softly. Kimberly kissed Lindsay's curly crown before sneaking quietly downstairs.

Jake was leaning over the fireplace, stacking chunks of fir in the grate. His shoulders bunched beneath his sweater as he worked, and Kimberly could imagine the rippling strength of his muscles hidden beneath the soft wool.

He glanced over his shoulder at the sound of her footsteps. "You don't mind, do you?" he asked.

"No, by all means—" she motioned toward the grate "—a fire would be nice." The room had become cozy, the colored lights of the tree glowing softly against the raindrops drizzling on the windowpanes.

"I thought it might make things more comfortable before we begin."

"Begin?"

Then she noticed the coffee table. Mugs of coffee were steaming next to a yellow legal pad. Her heart sank. She didn't want to think about Robert any longer. Tired of his promises to Lindsay, his fight for custody, his dark business dealings and his damn lies she wanted to block out of her mind forever. But, of course, she couldn't. She sat on the arm of the couch, staring at the fire while twisting her fingers in her lap. "Let's get it over with."

He smiled, displaying the same crooked grin that touched her heart. "It's not an execution, you know." Stepping across the carpet until he was standing above her, he stared down at her, his gray eyes filled with kindness and understanding.

He lifted her chin with one finger. "Relax. This is gonna be a piece of cake."

"I hope so." She forced a wobbly smile and tried not to concentrate on the warmth of his skin against hers. She swallowed hard, and, as if he'd seen her reaction, he quickly withdrew his hand, picking up his pen and snapping off the cap with his teeth.

Pressing a button on his recorder, he sat on the edge of the table, disturbingly close as he faced her. "Okay. We'll start out slow. Tell me about your family life as a child. Would you say it was happy?"

"Yes."

"How?"

She shrugged. "I don't know. We lived on a farm in Illinois before moving to California. Mom and Dad worked hard, and we never had a lot, but we didn't go without either. It was a, oh, what's the right word?" she said, looking to the ceiling. "Carefree. Yeah, it was a carefree existence. At least to me," she finished.

"What about your folks?"

"Well, they worried a lot. About the weather and the crops and the price of grain. That sort of thing. Mom gave piano lessons to some of the neighborhood kids for extra money."

"So, all in all you were content?"

"As much as any kid," she replied, surprised at how easily she explained her life on the farm. She entwined her fingers around one knee and thought back to the rolling hills of sweet-smelling hay, the apple trees in bloom, the sound of the windmill clicking as a breeze picked up. Telling him about helping with the haying in summer, harvesting and canning in the fall, she recounted her early years and smiled. The memories of life on the farm wrapped around her like a coat she'd outgrown but had missed. She went on to describe moving to California and eventually the loss of her father.

Jake brought the conversation back to Robert and her marriage. Folding her arms around herself as if against a sudden chill, she stared at the yellow flames of the fire. She could feel Jake's eyes on her and knew he was searching her face for some trace of emotion, but she refused to look at him. Thinking about Robert and all the hope she'd foolishly held in her heart saddened her.

She couldn't tell him anything she hadn't already. And eventually Jake snapped off the recorder and leaned back on the couch.

"Is that it?" she asked, finding her voice. It sounded weak, and she knew her skin was pale.

"For now."

"Thank God." She was still caught in the storm of feelings that had surrounded her marriage, was still staring blindly at the fire when she felt his fingers surround her wrist.

"If it's any consolation," he said slowly, "I think your husband is the biggest fool I've ever heard of. He was crazy to let you get away." Grabbing her wrist, he drew her forward, off the arm of the couch, so that she fell against him. Her hair tumbled around her face, and her hands pressed against the soft fabric of his sweater.

His arms surrounded her. "And just for the record," he said, his voice low, "I think you're the prettiest, sexiest and most intelligent woman I've ever met."

Surprised, she had to suck in her breath.

Her face was only inches from his, and his eyes, a luminous gray, reflected the scarlet embers of the fire. "I also think you're the most intriguing woman I've known in a long time."

She could barely breathe.

The brackets near the corners of his sensual mouth deepened. His gaze shifted to her lips, lingering as if he were lost in their promise. His fingers spread lazily across the small of her back, moving gently.

"I—I don't think this is such a good idea," she whispered, but already her blood was throbbing through her veins.

"Neither do I." But he didn't release her. If anything, his grip seemed to tighten.

"Is this a test?" she wondered aloud, trying to think.

"A what?"

"You know—for the hearing—to see if I'm promiscuous?"

He chuckled. "If this is a test, it's a test of my self-control." His face was flushed, his eyes beginning to glaze.

Kimberly's heart was pounding so loudly she was sure he could hear it over the hiss of the fire, and she thought she heard a separate cadence, as if he, too, was having trouble slowing his heartbeat.

She knew he was going to kiss her again and she felt his fingers move lazily upward to tangle in her hair. She didn't stop him, because she couldn't. She wanted him as desperately as he wanted her.

All the reasons for her to get up, keep their relationship strictly business, crossed her mind, but still she didn't struggle for freedom. When his lips finally caressed hers, she melted inside. Her lips parted of their own accord, and her arms wound around his neck.

She relished the delicate pressure of his tongue rimming her lips before slipping between her teeth and exploring the velvet-soft recess of her mouth. A feminine ache, starting deep in her soul and spreading outward, throbbed for release as the pressure of his lips increased. He sank deeper into the soft cushions of the couch, taking her with him.

Her fingers settled around his neck. She felt the fringe of his hair brush against the back of her hand.

Groaning, he kissed her harder, his lips molding over hers as one hand twisted in the fiery strands of her hair, pulling her head backward, exposing the creamy column of her throat.

"Kim . . ." he whispered, pressing hot kisses against her skin, ". . . why are you doing this to me?"

"I'm—not doing anything," she murmured, barely able to think as his hot lips seared the length of her neck and lingered at the small circle of bone surrounding the base of her throat.

She felt his leg rub against hers as he held her closer still, until she was lying above him, her hair falling like a shimmering curtain to his shoulders, brushing against his chest.

"This shouldn't be happening," he groaned.

She stared into his eyes then and read the torment of conflict and emotion in his gaze.

"Then—then stop."

"I can't, dammit," he growled, swearing under his breath before cupping the back of her head with his hands. Pulling her forward, he forced her lips to crash against his in a kiss that forced the breath from her lungs and sent her dizzy mind reeling faster and faster until she couldn't think, couldn't reason, could only feel.

"Mommy?"

Kimberly froze. Swallowing hard, she heard Lindsay's feet hit the floor.

"Again?" Jake asked, dazed.

"I told you about the nightmares."

"Because of the custody battle?" Jake asked, his brows drawing down in concern.

"I don't know. I hope not." Kimberly sat up and calmed her hair with her fingers as she heard the patter of feet.

Lindsay, blanket in tow, stood at the top step, rubbing her eyes.

"I had a bad dream."

"Oh, pumpkin." On her feet in an instant, Kimberly dashed up the stairs, scooped her daughter in her arms and held her close, glad that Lindsay wouldn't understand the flush climbing up her neck or the side of her heart. "Let's get you a glass of water, hmm?"

Lindsay buried her face in Kimberly's neck. "I was scared."

"I know, sweetie, but nothing's wrong. I'm here with you and I always will be." Glancing down the stairs, she spied Jake staring up at her.

Still half-sprawled on the couch, his hair tousled over his eyes, he caught her gaze and winked suggestively. Kimberly's heart turned over as she carried Lindsay into the bathroom, gave her daughter a drink, then helped her back in bed.

"I'll leave the bathroom light on for you," she said softly. Pressing her swollen lips against Lindsay's blond curls, she asked, "Will you be all right?"

"Stay with me," Lindsay pleaded, and Kimberly couldn't resist.

"Okay." She climbed into the bed, holding her daughter's head against her breast, stroking her baby-fine hair, and feeling the heat of Lindsay's breath as her daughter snuggled against her. "Go to sleep, honey," she whispered, watching the steady rise and fall of Lindsay's chest as she tried to calm her own breathing.

As Lindsay fell asleep, Kimberly thought about Jake and her violent reaction to him. Startled at the intensity of her feelings for a man she'd known only a few weeks, she cradled her daughter closer, shut her eyes and wondered how she would get through the coming court battle. She couldn't imagine being near Jake and still being able to keep her distance.

A quiet cough caught her attention. Her eyes flew open, and she found Jake leaning against the rail of the loft. He had already donned his jacket. He was leaving! Every emotion deep inside broke free, and she almost begged him to stay.

But before she could form a protest, he blew her a kiss and winked, letting her know he didn't begrudge her closeness with Lindsay. Then he disappeared from view. She heard the front door open and close while a gust of icy wind danced up the stairs. From the living room below, the glow of colored lights seeped into the loft, and Kimberly smiled to herself. No matter what the future brought, it included Jake, and that thought alone was comforting.

# CHAPTER EIGHT

By the end of the week, Kimberly couldn't wait to leave the bank. She hadn't heard from Jake in two days, and she was surprised how often she thought of him, how much she longed to hear from him. And it wasn't only because of the custody hearing looming in her future.

Sighing, she slapped a few papers in her briefcase and snapped it closed.

Outside, winter had landed full force on Portland. A storm had dropped six inches of snow on the city, tangling traffic and causing delays. Electrical outages caused commuter tie-ups and fender benders on the frozen streets. The bank's messenger service had been crippled, and everyone's nerves were at the breaking point.

Bill Zealander was the worst. Since the transfer of the Juniper account to Kimberly, he'd first complained loudly to Eric Compton, and when all his arguments hadn't changed Compton's decision, Zealander had begun to ignore her completely. Fortunately Kimberly had been kept busy dealing with Henry Juniper's paranoia, and she couldn't worry about

Bill's fragile ego. Not when Henry was convinced his sister Carole was getting into Daddy's funds.

She'd deal with Zealander next week, she decided, yanking her briefcase from the desk. Maybe he'd cool down over the weekend. Then again, maybe he'd only be worse.

"Don't borrow trouble," she told herself as she joined the exodus to the elevators. The doors parted, and Jake sauntered through. His warm gray gaze landed on her, and her heartbeat instantly quickened. "Well, counselor," she drawled with a smile, "what brings you here?"

"One guess," he teased.

"I give."

"You."

Her spirits soared. What was it about him that touched her so? Wearing a ski jacket, sweater, insulated pants and Cheshire-cat grin, he took hold of her arm. "Taking off early?" he mocked.

"I pulled the early shift." She grinned up at him. "And it's been a loooong week."

"Good."

"I don't know what's 'good' about it."

He propelled her toward the elevators, along with the crush of other employees. "I have a proposition for you," he whispered in her ear as elevator doors whispered shut.

"That sounds interesting," she murmured.

"It is, believe me."

The elevator groaned to a stop at the bottom floor, and the doors opened. Jostled by the tightly packed crowd, Kimberly let Jake guide her to the corner of the garage where his Bronco was parked next to her car.

"Okay, McGowan. Spit it out," she said, her mood lightened just because she was with him. "What's the proposition?"

"How about going skiing with me?"

"Tonight?" Kimberly asked, shivering from the cold and the unheated garage.

"Why not?"

"Well, because it's dark and cold and a blizzard."

"Sounds perfect for night skiing to me," he said, a lazy smile slashing insolently across his face.

"I've never been night skiing in my life—"

"You haven't been living then. You do ski, don't you?"

"Once upon a time. But it's been years."

"You have gear?"

"Somewhere. But I really can't. Lindsay's—"

"Staying with Arlene and Lyle," he finished for her. "She said so the other night. So, unless you have any other excuses . . ."

She wanted to find some. But Arlene's advice rang in her ears as clearly as silver bells. *Kick up your heels—live a little.*

Glancing up at him, she asked, "And what's in it for me? You said a proposition, right? Both parties benefit."

"Why, you, Ms. Bennett, get my time and attention for the next six to eight hours."

"How can I say no?" she quipped sarcastically.

"You can't." His gray eyes caught in the dim light and fairly twinkled.

"I must be out of my mind," she muttered.

"I'll take that as a yes."

"A reluctant yes," she qualified.

"Then let's get going. I'll follow you to your place."

Wondering if she'd truly lost her senses, Kimberly climbed behind the wheel of her Mercedes and watched as Jake moved to his Bronco. Smiling, she started the engine of her car and backed out of her parking space, glancing toward the elevator shaft where Bill Zealander, *Wall Street Journal* and black umbrella tucked under his arm, stood glaring at her.

No doubt he'd watched the entire exchange. There was a chance he may have heard snatches of their conversation.

Kimberly shuddered. The expression on his face was cruel and calculating.

*You've done nothing wrong*, she reminded herself as she put the car in gear, forced a smile and waved to Zealander, though he didn't acknowledge her wave.

The drive home was a nightmare. Added to the normal congestion of Friday afternoon rush hour was the anxiety caused by the snow and slush turning to ice as night fell. Cars crept along at a snail's pace. Though the houseboats on the river glowed with colorful Christmas lights reflected on the inky water, the spirit of the coming season seemed lost in the chaos of traffic forcing its way across the Sellwood Bridge.

By the time Kimberly pulled into her driveway, she was a nervous wreck. She told herself it was because of the weather and didn't have anything to do with Jake McGowan or the fact that she'd agreed to spend the evening with him. But even as the thought drifted through her mind, she knew she was lying to herself. She was excited at the prospect of being alone with him.

As she turned off the engine, she heard his car roar down the street and saw the flash of headlights in her rearview mirror.

He climbed out of his car at the same moment she did, following her to the back door, their boots crunching in the heavy snow. The eaves were hung with icicles. Dead leaves of the clematis had been trapped in the crystal-like prisons.

"This isn't a smart thing to do," Kimberly said, shivering as she unlocked the door.

"What isn't?"

"Driving in this mess. The road to the mountain must be treacherous."

"I checked. It's been plowed and sanded."

"When?" She glanced pointedly at the shower of snowflakes still drifting to the ground before she shoved open the door and stepped into the relative warmth of the kitchen. "It's been snowing all day."

"No problem," he assured her. "I've got four-wheel drive. This'll be a walk in the park."

"Sure."

His gaze scanned the kitchen, eyeing the coffee pot. "You got a thermos?"

"Under the sink."

"You don't mind if I heat this up and bring it along?" he asked, lifting the pot. The cold coffee sloshing the glass container.

"Be my guest." She hung her coat and then spied a large envelope with her name scrawled crudely across the white surface. Opening it, she found a piece of tablet paper cut into the shape of a snowflake. Around the cut out diamonds and triangles Lindsay had written "I love you" in uneven, oversized letters. Kimberly's heart turned over. She reached for her phone and quickly punched out a number.

Arlene finally answered on the fifth ring. "Hello?"

"Hi. How's it going?"

"Just fine," Arlene said with a hearty chuckle. "We've already built a snowman, pulled out the Christmas candles and arranged the Nativity scene on the mantel. Now Lindsay's insisting we put up our tree."

"I know the feeling," Kimberly said, resting her hips against the hall table and staring at the paper snowflake.

"You want to talk to her?"

"Can I? For just a second."

"I'll see if I can wrestle her away from the tree."

Kimberly waited impatiently as Jake stepped into the hall. "Trouble?" he asked, suddenly concerned.

"No—"

"Mommy?" Lindsay said as she took the phone from Arlene. Kimberly's heart melted. "Hi, honey."

"Did you get my surprise?" Lindsay asked, her voice lifting.

"I sure did. That's why I called—to thank you. I'm going to take it to work on Monday and hang it in my office."

"Are you *really*?"

"You bet. Now, are you being good?"

"Good as an angel," Lindsay said emphatically. "That's what they call me over here."

"So I've heard," she laughed. "I'll see you in the morning, then. I love you."

"Me, too."

"Let me talk to Arlene again."

"'Kay."

With Arlene back on the line, Kimberly explained that she was planning to go skiing and would pick up Lindsay the next morning at ten.

"Just don't rush over here," Arlene remarked. "Lindsay's doin' a world of good for Lyle."

"Thanks."

After hanging up, she found Jake still lounging in the doorway between the hallway and kitchen. "How's it going over there?" he asked.

"Good. I think I'll have to pry Lindsay out of there with a crowbar tomorrow."

Jake glanced down at the paper snowflake. "I doubt it," he whispered, and the timbre of his voice touched a special spot in her heart. "It seems as if your daughter's pretty stuck on you." His eyes turned introspective.

"I hope so." Kimberly met his eyes, lost for a minute in his silvery gaze, then cleared her throat and passed him in the hallway. "It'll just take me a little while to find everything."

"No hurry. As long as you can manage it in fifteen minutes."

"Don't hold your breath," she said, grinning as she walked into her bedroom and closed the door. Then, to make up for lost time, she yanked off her leather boots and scrounged through her closet until she found the old ski bag. She'd shoved it into a dark corner years before. "How about that?" she murmured, tossing the bag onto the bed and unzipping it. Inside were insulated ski pants in a deep violet color, goggles, hat, sweater and long underwear.

Stripping out of her black suit, blouse and stockings, she crossed her fingers and hoped her outfit would fit. She hadn't worn any of her ski clothes since long before Lindsay had been born. Though she weighed less than before her pregnancy, some of her weight seemed to have shifted.

However, a few minutes later she stood in front of the oval mirror on the bureau, her bibs and sweater were snug but not too tight.

Quickly she braided her hair away from her face and ignored the blush that colored her cheeks. Excited about the evening ahead, she couldn't hide the sparkle in her eyes or keep herself from smiling.

By the time she found her ski boots and jacket in the front closet, Jake had reheated the coffee and filled her thermos. "My skis are in the garage," she said, a bag of dry clothes slung over her arm.

His gaze slid over her before landing on her eyes. "Then what're we waiting for?"

"A break in the storm? Reason to overcome insanity?"

"Trust me," he said.

And she did. Whether it was foolish or not, she trusted this man with his slashing, enigmatic smile, his wise-beyond-his-years expression and observant eyes.

They found her skis, snapped them into the rack on his vehicle, and, still brushing snow from their hair and shoulders, climbed into the Bronco.

Through the slushy streets, beneath bare trees, past houses glowing in rainbows of Christmas lights, Jake guided the rig, heading east to the slopes of Mt. Hood. The wipers slapped away the falling snow, and quiet strains of holiday music sounded over the grind of the engine.

While Jake drove the Bronco through the darkened roads, Kimberly poured them each a cup of coffee. Handing him a cup, she asked, "Have you lived in Portland long?"

"Most of my life."

"And your family?"

His jaw tightened a fraction as he switched lanes. "My folks died a few years ago."

"No sisters or brothers?"

"Nope."

She longed to ask for more, especially about his wife. She wanted to know so much about him, but he seemed to keep much of himself from her. Glancing through the foggy windshield, she wondered whether he had secrets he would ever share with her. "So, you've known Diane a long time?"

"Since law school."

"And then?"

"We worked together downtown in a big firm." A muscle pumped in his jaw. "She helped me through a few rough years. Got me into corporate law."

"Why?" she asked.

"Why what?"

"Why the move from domestic relations?"

He pressed his lips together hard and downshifted quickly. "It seemed the thing to do," he evaded, sliding her a glance. They headed out of the city, past rolling acres of farmland. Snow, adding quiet illumination to the night, drifted against fences and buildings.

"You were supposed to be one of the best family lawyers in the city," Kimberly persisted.

He lifted a shoulder. "That's a matter of opinion."

"And you weren't that crazy about taking my case."

He slid a glance her way. "What is this? Twenty questions?"

Leaning against the door, she eyed him, his handsome,

chiseled features, large eyes, strong chin now covered with a faint shadow. "Well, it's only fair, since you seem to know everything about me."

"Not yet."

"But soon. I figured it was my turn, that I should know a little about you."

"Not much to know."

She thought for a minute, then asked the one question that had been on her mind for a long while. "Why haven't you ever remarried?"

"Does the statement 'I never met the right woman' sound too cliché?"

"Yes."

"Well, it's true. That, and the fact that I'm not sure the institution of marriage is such a good idea."

Kimberly's brow inched up. "Why not?"

"Probably for the same reason you've given up on it."

She had given up on marriage—that much was true. But since Jake had entered her life, she hadn't found the idea of tying herself to one man so difficult to accept. But then, she didn't allow herself to fantasize.

Jake continued. "Let's just say my experience wasn't so great. My wife wasn't happy with me, and it didn't last. As for my parents, they hung together, but it was a war zone most of the time." He glanced her way. "Surely you feel the same."

She shook her head and thought about the loving years she'd spent with her own family. "No, I think marriage can be perfect."

He snorted. "You've changed your tune since Diane's wedding."

"I guess I did sound a little cynical."

"A lot cynical."

"Well, obviously you have to find the right person." She frowned into her cup. "In my case, Robert wasn't the one."

"I'll buy that," he said dryly, but didn't comment further.

Had his ex-wife wanted him so badly? Had he loved her so much that she'd soured him on marriage when she'd wanted a divorce? They drove in silence for a while, and the snow-covered farmland gave way to steeper hills. The road began to climb, winding through the foothills of the Cascade Mountains, past small towns decorated with lights, and tinsel and brightly lighted trees before the solitude of the forest closed around them.

Traffic slowed. The pavement was covered with packed snow and ice. Several cars pulled over, their drivers frantically chaining up.

Though Kimberly was white-knuckled whenever the Bronco slid on the icy pavement. Jake remained calm, and before seven o'clock he pulled into the crowded parking lot near the lodge. "We made it," he said, patting her knee.

"Thank God." Ignoring the warmth of his hand on her leg, she gulped the rest of her coffee. Jake opened the Bronco's door and stepped into the eight inches of powdery snow.

Following his lead, she donned ski boots, mask and goggles before tromping, skis balanced on her shoulders, to the lodge.

"You hungry?" Jake asked as they clipped on their lift tickets.

"A little."

"Want to eat now?"

She shook her head and surveyed the mountain. Stretched under the glow of colored lamps, the slopes gleamed in pristine invitation. "Let's take a couple runs first."

"I won't argue with that."

They skated to the left and after a short wait climbed onto icy chairs. Snowflakes caught in the few strands of hair that had escaped from Kimberly's hat and lingered against her cheeks.

"Warm enough?" Jake asked. He draped one arm around her shoulders, giving her a hug.

"Yes."

They were carried slowly up the hill, above the tops of majestic firs and hemlocks. Leafy branches, now laden with snow, moved slowly in the breeze. The sky was black, but lights illuminated the side of the mountain, showing off the white runs and craggy rocks of the higher elevations.

"It's beautiful up here," Kimberly breathed. "I'd forgotten."

"And quiet. Sometimes I think it's the solitude that's so special," he said. "Not many people here at night."

He was right. She'd remembered weekend skiing, when the lift lines had taken longer than the run. But tonight, a week before the holiday break, the mountain wasn't crowded. It seemed as if they were alone.

Jake's arm tightened around her, and she felt a warmth deep inside stretching itself throughout her body. Relaxed and content, she wondered how much time she could spend with Jake and still feel this fascination for him.

He was the first man who had interested her since her divorce, and the intensity of her feelings was overwhelming. She'd never expected to fall in love again, but here, swinging over the treetops, feeling the serenity of the snow-draped forest, she felt a kinship with him that went far beyond the bounds of mere friendship or, she thought ruefully, a professional relationship with her lawyer. The thought that she was falling in love nagged at her, but she ignored it. She couldn't afford to fall in love. Not now. Not until Lindsay's future with her was secure.

"Here we go." Taking her gloved hand in his, he helped her ski down the ramp at the top of the run. "Ready?" he asked, stopping at a ridge.

"As I'll ever be."

"Okay. Show me your stuff."

Trying her best to muster some self-confidence, she plunged her poles into the powder and pushed forward, feeling the exhilaration of the frigid air against her face as she skied down the hill. At first her legs were uncomfortable and awkward, and she was careful. But slowly, as she made her way down a wide, tiered bowl, she became more confident.

She saw Jake ski past her, then wait at the next ridge near a rustic wooden structure with a huge stone fireplace. Smoke curled from the chimney, and lights glowed through the misty, paned windows.

Breathless, Kimberly caught up with him. She could feel the color in her cheeks.

"You're good," he said in admiration.

"I've taken more than my share of lessons—and spills."

"So, why'd you give it up?"

Kimberly wiped the snow from her goggles. "I got pregnant and didn't want to fall, then Lindsay came along and I was caught up in diapers, rattles and bottles." Thinking back to those years when her marriage had turned to ashes, she frowned and glanced toward the weathered, barn-like building. "What's this?" she asked.

"The warming hut," he said. "You can stop in here to get a drink or a doughnut and warm up."

"Up here?" She gazed down the hill, where skiers, gliding along the snow far below, were barely visible. Groups in pairs and singles wound around the mountain. One man, dressed in navy blue from ski mask to boots, slid to a stop beside them and bent over to adjust his bindings. Kimberly didn't pay much attention to him.

Jake was still explaining. "The warming hut can take the chill out of the lift ride. Sometimes it's a blizzard up here."

She believed him. Not far from the timberline above them, the ski run was long and steep. Smiling mischievously, she adjusted her goggles and said, "Come on, I'll race you to the bottom."

"You're joking . . ."

But she took off, flying down the hill, the wind screaming past her face as she sliced through the snow.

Jake caught her midway down, waved and left her to maneuver expertly down a narrow part of the run to the lift below. "You cheated," he exclaimed, laughing as she slid to a stop, spraying snow all over his pants.

She giggled. "Just a little head start. Besides, it didn't help. How about a rematch?"

"You're on."

The next run ended same as the first, with Jake flying by her expertly, despite the fact that she was skiing better than she remembered. At the bottom of the hill, she flipped off her goggles and held up her hands in mock surrender. "I give up," she said, laughing and seeing her breath fog in the air.

Jake hugged her. "Just to prove that I'm not an obnoxious winner, I'll buy you dinner."

"You're on," Kimberly agreed. Together they skied back to the lodge, and she was only vaguely aware of the tall, ski-masked figure in navy blue gliding effortlessly down the slopes.

Once inside, stripped of goggles and gloves, they found a table near a floor-to-ceiling stone fireplace. In a far corner stood a bushy Douglas fir decorated with silver bells, scarlet ribbons and winking lights.

"Until last night," Kimberly said, cradling a cup of Irish coffee Jake had ordered, "I'd almost forgotten about Christmas."

"Is that possible with a five-year-old?"

"Not really. But I was so wrapped up in this custody thing I hadn't really felt much Christmas spirit." Her eyes sparkled with the reflection of the lighted tree. "Thanks for bringing me up here."

"Believe me, it's my pleasure." He toasted her before resting both elbows on the table, his coffee cup cradled between his palms. His eyes were warm and flinty, and when his gaze found hers, a spreading awareness—like an early-morning mist—filled every corner of her soul.

They ate in relative silence, devouring grilled salmon and wild rice until Kimberly was stuffed. "If I eat another bite," she groaned, motioning with her fork at the remains of the pink, flaky salmon on her plate, "I won't be able to ski anymore."

Jake's lips twitched. "You're not getting out of another run that easily."

"I wasn't trying to."

"Good. Let's get back out there. Double or nothing." Reaching down, he snapped the buckles on his boots, then left some money on the table.

"Hey—whoa. What're you talking about?"

"Let's race again. The bet's double or nothing."

"But we didn't bet the first time!"

"So, let's bet now," he suggested, his eyes glinting like liquid silver as they walked outside.

"For what? A dollar? A drink?"

"Come on, you can be more imaginative than that."

She rolled her eyes. "Don't tell me—just like junior high, right? The one who loses is the other's slave for a week?"

Laughing, he shook his head. Snowflakes collected in his dark hair. "Now, *that* would be interesting, but how about something not quite that bizarre?"

"What?" she asked suspiciously.

"The one who loses has to spend one entire day helping the other one around his or her house."

"Meaning . . . ?"

"Well, for example, I've got some clothes that need mending, windows washed, that sort of thing."

"Oh, great," she murmured, but thought of the busted back door lock, the paint peeling off the swing set, the faucet that wouldn't quit dripping and the rotten front steps that had needed to be replaced for over a year.

"I'll give you a head start," he encouraged, eyes dancing.

"How far?"

"Two slopes. I won't take off until you pass the warming hut."

"But that's nearly a third of the way down."

"I know," he taunted, grinning with the self-assurance of one who assumes he'll win.

Kimberly thought she had an even chance and would have dearly loved to wipe that cocky smile right off his face. "You're on, counselor. But let's up the bet. Whoever wins gets two days of free labor."

"And how many nights?" he asked.

She lifted a brow coyly. "That depends."

"On?"

"How much I win by."

His white teeth flashed in the night. "So, what're we waiting for?"

He won, of course.

Just when Kimberly had thought victory was within her grasp, Jake swooshed past her in a blinding spray of snow.

Awestruck and furious, she skied the remainder of the run, asking herself why she'd been so stupid as to go along with the bet. Even though she'd sped down the hill at the top of her game, he'd passed her as if she were standing still.

"Idiot," she chided herself under her breath as she struggled up the hill by the lodge. He'd already taken off his goggles and hat and was trying nobly to wipe the smirk from his face.

"I'd like to accuse you of cheating," she charged, "but I can't."

His teeth gleamed. "What about double or nothing now?"

"No way!" she caught the teasing glimmer in his eyes and

tried to remain stern. But her traitorous heart began to pound, and she could feel a dimple creasing her cheek.

Laughing, he linked his arm with hers. "For starters, I need all my shirts ironed, and the curtains could be cleaned and pressed. Then there's dinner. I'll expect three courses, no less—"

"I get the picture," she said dryly. "We are back to a slave-for-a-day."

"Two days," he corrected. "Starting tomorrow."

"*This* weekend?"

"Right."

Why not? she thought, glad for any excuse to spend more time with him. "Okay, then this weekend," she agreed, refusing to listen to the doubts crowding her mind, the doubts that reminded her he was her lawyer and she should keep her relationship professional.

Laughing, they trudged back to the parking lot, and Kimberly noticed the solitary skier in navy blue carrying his skis to a white station wagon. He stopped at the car and wiped his goggles, but his back was to her and she couldn't get a glimpse of his face. She felt as if she should know the car— or the driver—but before she had a chance to say something, Jake clipped their skis into the rack and helped her climb into the Bronco.

Jake noticed Kimberly's fascination with the man in the white wagon, and it bothered him. Did she know him? Why didn't she stop and say hello? Looking back, it seemed as if the man had been dogging them, following them down the slopes.

"Let's go," he said a trifle impatiently as he slid behind the steering wheel. Kimberly's expression was clouded, and he wondered what she was thinking.

"Someone you know?" he asked, nodding toward the car with its wheels spinning in the snow.

"No—at least I don't think so." She flashed a smile toward Jake and that caught him unaware. Her fiery brown hair fell past her shoulders in tangled curls, and snowflakes, now melted, sparkled like tiny diamonds nestled in the vibrant strands.

The interior of the Bronco was foggy as the car idled, and ice slowly began to melt on the windshield.

"Warm enough?" he asked.

"Mm-hmm." She shivered, her cheeks rosy, her eyes luminous as the snow-globe world they were entrenched in. Damn, she was the most fascinating woman he'd met in years.

"Coffee?" she held up the thermos.

"Great idea." He watched as she poured.

"You should take all the credit," she murmured, sipping from the red plastic mug, then made a face as if the coffee was hot and strong—too strong. "Here—if you want this, it's yours."

"I'll pass," he said, seeing her grimace.

She poured the dregs back into the thermos, then tightened the lid. Slanting a glance in his direction, she said, "Thanks for tonight. I've enjoyed myself."

"Me, too." Her eyes were hypnotizing as they stared up at him through the sweep of dark, curling lashes, and seemed to cut right into his soul.

"We'll do it again," he promised, wondering why he would make such a rash statement. Knowing in his heart he couldn't get involved with her, that she didn't want emotional entanglement any more than he did, he rammed the Bronco into gear and he picked his way through the other cars, trying not to think ahead to the night stretching long before him.

Had the situation been different, he would have begun

planning his seduction right now. He couldn't help it. Desire had flared hotly as the hours with Kimberly had passed.

Lapsing into silence, he tried to ignore the gentle curve of her knee so close to his hand on the gearshift, willed himself not to notice the soft rise and fall of her breasts as she breathed or the soft power of her lips.

She rested her head against the far window and closed her eyes, seeming all the more seductive with her hair falling over her cheek.

He felt a tenderness for her that went far beyond reason. Without thinking, he pushed the wayward lock of hair from her face with one finger.

Her eyes blinked open, and she smiled, a soft grin bored quickly into his heart. "Are we home yet?" she asked, yawning.

"Just a few more miles. Go back to sleep," he whispered gently, touched by the slumber still clouding her gaze.

His throat felt raw, and the burning deep within him didn't let up. Swallowing with difficulty, he attempted to concentrate on the road before him and the lights of Portland stretching endlessly beneath the inky sky. The asphalt was icy. Snow still fell, but Jake had trouble keeping his eyes on the highway ahead. As if having a mind of its own, his gaze wandered back to her perfect face.

Never had he wanted a woman more. In all his years, including a stretch of regrettable lust during his teens, he had never burned with a passion so hot as when he burned for Kimberly Bennett.

The Bronco slid a little, and Kimberly moaned softly. Jake eased down on the brakes, forcing himself to concentrate on the road and the trip home.

# CHAPTER NINE

Kimberly stretched and worked the crick from her neck. She wasn't yet ready to give up on the dream—a dream that promised the happy family she had worked so hard for. . . .

Opening her eyes, she watched as Jake slowed and wheeled into her driveway.

"Finally wake up?" he asked as he switched off the engine.

"I think so." She yawned. "Sorry I fell asleep."

"It must've been all my sparkling, intelligent conversation."

"Must've been," she repeated dryly as she shoved the door open and a blast of icy wind knifed through the Bronco's cozy interior.

Snow fell silently, and her yard was covered with a thick, white blanket. Street lamps cast an ethereal glow over the whiteness, and some houses still displayed colorful lights, brilliant points of green and red reflected in the icy white powder.

She grabbed her boots and bag from the back of the Bronco as Jake unstrapped her skis and shouldered them. "You want these back in the garage?"

"That would be great."

Hunched against the wind, she carried her bag to the back door, then stomped the snow from her boots on the porch.

Inside, the house was dark and cold. Kimberly fumbled with the switches, turning on the lights and adjusting the thermostat before plugging in the coffee maker.

She tossed her jacket over the foot of her bed, then, on impulse, dashed into the living room and flipped the switch that was connected to the Christmas tree. Red, yellow and green lights winked in the shadowy room.

It was suddenly important that Jake see the house as she saw it—warm and cheerful. *And seductive?* She swallowed hard and leaned over the grate, striking a match to the logs in the fireplace, unable to find a suitable answer.

The dry kindling caught, popping and hissing. Flames licked the mossy trunks of oak. She heard the back door creak open, felt the chill of a breeze seep through the room. "Come on in," she called over her shoulder. "I'll make us something hot in a few minutes—but don't expect anything as fancy as the drinks up at the lodge."

Jake chuckled, a deep, throaty sound that filled an aching void within her—a void that had been empty for so very long.

"I don't care what it is," he said, his voice nearer. Her heart began to pound. "Just as long as it's warm and liquid."

"That, I can promise." She felt his arms circle her waist, his chin balance gently on her crown, his warmth envelop her.

"You've been driving me crazy all night," he admitted with a heartfelt sigh. The fire crackled.

"Me? Drive you crazy?" But she, too, had felt a special warmth at his touch. And she'd seen the naked sensuality in his gaze.

"You know things have changed between us."

Her throat worked. "Have they?"

His hands splayed across her abdomen, one thumb tucked

beneath her breast, and his breath whispered through her hair. "I want you, Kimberly," he conceded, his voice low. "I want you more than I've wanted a woman in a long time. Maybe ever."

Her heart soared. It was pounding so loudly, it echoed in her ears. Or was that thundering the sound of his heart beating out of control? She tried to reason, to be calm and rational and clear thinking. But emotion clouded all her thoughts, and when his hands drew her closer still, surrounding her with his arms, all she could feel was the wonder of him, the sheer maleness demanding of him, the hard evidence of his desire planted firmly against her hips. A thrill of anticipation darted up her spine.

"Tell me this'll never work," he whispered.

"We both know it won't." But she entwined her fingers in his and felt his lips brush against her hair. The shadowed corners of the room closed in around them, and she felt that being with him could never be wrong.

"Tell me I should stop."

"You—you should."

His hands moved upward, one thumb tracing the weight of her breast as his lips covered invitingly over her neck.

"Tell me you don't want me."

"I can't," she admitted, her throat catching. There was no need to lie. They both knew the power of desire, the galloping, thoughtless heat of passion stirring deep in their souls. Slowly he turned her so that she was forced to look into the depths of his silvery eyes. Lost in the erotic gaze, she wound her arms around his neck.

"I thought we had a deal."

A smile tugged at the corners of his mouth. "Nothing on paper," he murmured. "Remember who you're dealing with—if it isn't signed, it isn't valid."

"You should have warned me."

He laughed quietly. "You should have warned *me*. I wasn't ready for this."

"Neither was I."

He stared at her for a few heart-stopping seconds, then his lips claimed hers with a fire as hungry as the flames burning in the grate, a passion as hot as the red embers beginning to glow in the fireplace.

His tongue probed her lips, and she parted them willingly, unafraid. Despite her doubts, she responded, arching her back, pressing her breasts as close to him as possible. Her tongue embraced his, eagerly meeting the delicate thrusts and teasing retreats.

Her fingers ran through the hair, felt the drops of melting snow still lingering in the dark strands as slowly, with his weight, he pushed them both to the couch where they had nearly made love before.

Lying over her, his eyes delving deep into hers, he felt his throat constrict. "Don't say no," he whispered, his hands deftly removing her jacket and finding the hem of her sweater.

"Don't worry," she promised, her voice as breathless as the soothing whisper of the fire.

He lifted her sweater over her head, and once the heavy garment was removed, stared down at her, gazing at her right breast peaking delicately over the sculpted lace of her bra, her firm nipples straining through the sheer fabric, dark, dusty circles that invited him . . . tantalized . . .

"Kim," he whispered hoarsely, then, taking her lips in his, he kissed her with the fever burning deep in his heart. Her lips, full and red, parted in invitation.

As his hands moved upward, skimming over her ribs to toy with the edge of her bra, Kimberly's breath seemed to stop somewhere between her throat and lungs. Sensations as warm and seductive as a summer breeze enveloped her.

He kissed her breasts, his tongue lazily caressing first

one nipple, then the other. Against the wet fabric, dark buds blossomed.

"Please . . ."

"Please what?" His breath fanned the wet lace, fueling fires of passion sweeping through her blood.

*Make me yours*, she thought wildly, her words trapped deep within as her fingers worked feverishly on his jacket, sweater and shirt to discard them on the floor. When his dark chest was exposed, gilded by the flickering light of the fire, he unclasped her bra, dropping the tiny scrap of lace onto his clothes.

"Make love to me," he whispered, his eyes locking with hers.

She couldn't help herself. Lost in the wonder he created, she felt his fingertips skim beneath her ski pants, grazing the soft flesh of her abdomen. Moaning, she heard the rustle of her bibs as they glided easily down the length of her legs.

After kicking off his ski pants, he lay over her, the soft down on his legs pressing intimately to hers. His lips found hers again, and his hands spread over her shoulders, lifting her up to meet him, a satiny glow spread across her skin.

"I don't want to hurt you," he whispered.

"You won't."

"And I don't want us to make any mistakes."

She tried to think, but his hands against her skin were playing havoc with her reasoning skills. "Mistakes?"

"I don't want to get you pregnant." The words sounded harsh, though he'd spoken them gently.

She tried to think straight—tried to consider the days of the month, but they blurred together as he caressed her. Pregnancy was the last thing on her mind. "You—you won't."

"You're sure?"

"We're good," she said dreamily, mentally calculating the days, then gasping as his thumb toyed with her nipple.

"You're positive?" Deep creases lined his brow.

"Yeah," she whispered huskily. He never quit tormenting

her. Kimberly was swimming in that timeless sea of passion. Lightly touching his shoulders and forearms, sleek back and buttocks, she tingled at each sensual curve of his body. She tasted him, the salt of his skin welcome on her lips.

He kissed her hard and Kimberly eagerly accepted his tongue and lips, weaving her fingers through the hair on the back of his head, pulling him closer. She could feel his desire throbbing against her. He pulled away from her mouth and as she took a deep breath, she felt his tongue make circles against her neck, his lips caressing the sensitive skin above her collarbone. She let out a gasp, completely at the mercy of the pleasure she felt. His hands were working in complement to his mouth, massaging her breasts, teasing her nipples. Moaning, she pressed against him, begging for more.

Jake's mouth did not disappoint, moving slowly from her throat to her breast, making smaller and smaller circles around her nipple until he finally took it in his mouth. The warmth of his tongue was euphoric.

"Please . . . don't . . . stop," was all she could think to say, her mind lost to the feeling of his every touch.

At that, he took his hand and brushed the soft curls at the apex of her legs before stroking a finger softly against her inner thigh. She parted her legs for him, exposing herself, feeling completely safe, excited for Jake to have all of her. Jake slid his hand against her opening, feeling her wetness.

"Oh, Jake . . ." she managed to say, lost in the intoxication of his touch, positioning him between her legs. She could see his erection, knew that for as much as she was turned on, the feeling was reciprocated. He rubbed his manhood against her, teasing her before entering slowly, his hardness setting off a burst of ecstasy as it filled her. She knew there was no turning back, his eyes holding her gaze as he started to rhythmically thrust, pulling out only to delve again, deeper and faster.

She moved with him, finding his tempo and feeling the earth shake beneath them. Every sense aware, she kissed his chest, flicking his small nipples with her tongue and running her fingers through the hair of his firm chest. His body was fluid, his muscles rippling beneath his skin as he moved faster and faster. Kimberly closed her eyes, wanting to feel every inch of him against her, engulfed in the bliss of their love-making.

She felt as if she were spinning, faster and faster, higher and higher, entrapped in the mounting pressure inside her as he moved skillfully. Every nerve ending was tingling as her pleasure built, she could feel Jake trying to control himself and knew he was close. She dug her fingers into his back, her hips bucking, and let out a cry of joy as primal as any winter wind as all her tension released, waves of pleasure overtaking her body.

As she climaxed, she felt Jake complete himself inside her, his essence touching her deepest parts, filling her with warmth. "Kim!" he choked out, collapsing on top of her, placing his head just above her shoulder. His warm breath was soothing, his hard body reassuring. He breathed deep, taking in her scent, and kissed the downy skin of her shoulder, tasting her sweetness.

They laid there in silence for a few moments, still fused as one.

She breathed a long sigh, feeling a sea of emotions churn within her.

He looked up then softly touched her cheek, stroking the soft skin.

"Regrets?" he asked gently.

"No—"

"Then, what?"

She sniffed, blinking rapidly. Self-conscious, she laughed nervously. "It's—been a long time," she said, and silently added, *and it's never been like this. I've never felt so turned inside out—so completely at someone else's mercy.*

"You know you can trust me."

"I do," she admitted, smiling. "That's the problem."

Jake's eyes were filled with compassion, and he pushed a burnished curl off her forehead before placing his lips against her brow. "How did Robert hurt you so badly?"

"I let him," she admitted. "But it's over." She didn't want to think of Robert. Not tonight. Tonight she had only room for Jake, and he filled her very essence, her thoughts, her mind, her body.

"You're sure?" His gaze sought conviction in hers. A log in the fire split, falling into pieces.

"Positive."

"Good—because I intend to make you forget him." Hard lines of conviction surrounding his mouth, Jake twisted his fingers in her hair.

She sighed. "If only you could."

"Let me try," he suggested, his voice low as he kissed her again with the same breathtaking passion of just a few minutes before. Then he lifted her off the couch and carried her into the bedroom.

"What're you doing?"

He cocked a jaunty dark brow and grinned devilishly. "Having my way with you."

"Wrong," Kimberly clipped, winding her arms around his neck. "I'm having *my* way with you."

He tossed his head back and laughed. "I'll try to remember that."

"Good." Caught up in the wonder of this man, Kimberly decided that come what may, she would have this one night to flirt with danger without a thought to the future.

He crossed the threshold to her room, kicked the door shut and dropped her onto the cool coverlet of her bed. He was on top of her in an instant, the mattress sagging with his weight. "So have your way," he growled against her ear. Delicious shivers raced up her spine and he took her hand in his and guided it to touch him, to stroke his growing member until he was at his full length again. It was thrilling, to have him harden at her touch, to feel his body react to her, his muscles contracting and relaxing with her every movement.

"You're wicked," she chuckled.

"Only with you, love," he whispered.


Stretching lazily, Kimberly rolled over in bed. She opened her eyes slowly and felt a strong arm pin her to the sheets.

Jake grinned devilishly, his jaw shadowed. Propped on one elbow, his bare chest covered with a fine mat of dark hair, he stared down at her with silvery, erotic eyes. "Good morning, lazybones," he drawled.

Passionate images flashed through her mind. Their love-making had been glorious, crazy and perfect. "Lazybones?" she whispered, her cheeks coloring as she shoved a tangled handful of hair from her eyes and glanced at the clock. It was nearly ten. Groaning, she flopped back on the pillow. "I've got to pick up Lindsay."

"I already took care of it."

"You did *what*?" she cried, sitting bolt upright in the bed. Then, as his gaze drifted lower to her uncovered breasts, she clasped the sheets to her bosom.

His grin stretched. "I called Arlene—she's very nice, by the way, very understanding."

"I'll bet." Kimberly moaned. Arlene would be doing hand-springs if she thought Kimberly was involved with a man, es-pecially a man like Jake.

"Anyway, I told her I was going to buy you brunch and we would pick up Lindsay around noon."

"You had no right—"

"I know." Leaning forward, he pulled the sheet to expose one dark nipple. To his delight, it puckered instantly beneath his stare.

"Jake, really . . ."

Taking the dark bud in his lips, he slowly tugged.

Kimberly melted inside, and all her concentration centered on that one aching breast. "Don't you think . . . ?"

But he obviously didn't. With a groan he rolled over her, his lips finding hers, his tongue tracing the edges of her mouth as he moved familiarly on top of her and spread her legs apart. "Just one more time," he whispered against her hair.

Already her heart was pounding, the blood rushing wantonly through her veins. "We—we really should be getting up," she murmured, but his fingers caressed her, found that spot that was so vulnerable, and then his mouth lowered hungrily to suckle at her breast.

She couldn't stop him. Her fingers coiled in the sheets of her old four-poster as he wet each delicate nipple and breathed across their dampened tautness.

He left a trail of kisses as his mouth went lower, tasting the soft skin below her waist, tracing the contours of her hipbone before brushing his lips across her tuft of hair. He parted her legs and his tongue swirled against her, making her gasp every time it brushed her peak of sensitivity. As she grew comfortable with his intimate touch, he grew bolder, fluttering his tongue against her, and softly suckling until she couldn't stand the build up any longer.

She pulled his head up to her, and staring into his eyes, kissed him as she found his manhood and positioned it at her entrance. Arching upward, desire raging in her core, she welcomed him, rejoicing in their union.

Jake moved slowly at first, gaining speed as pressure built inside Kimberly. He brought her time after time to the brink until he could resist no longer.

Convulsing, she cried low in her throat, and his voice joined hers, resounding in the tiny room, bouncing off the ice-covered windowpanes and echoing in her heart. She felt him spill into her as she clung to him, legs entwined, their bodies dewy with perspiration. Dear Lord, she'd fallen in love with him, fallen so fast her head was spinning. Loving Jake was crazy, ludicrous—the one emotion she shouldn't allow herself to feel. But there it was. Big as life.

His breath, ragged and shallow, fanned across her naked breasts, and she sighed in contentment.

"As I said last night," Jake finally rasped, "you're driving me out of my mind." He thought about the night before and how he'd made love to her over and over again, as if in so doing he could satiate himself with her.

But the lovemaking had proved true just the opposite. The more he had her, the more he wanted, a deep thirst that couldn't be quenched.

"I don't think we should talk about sanity," she said, her thoughts turning black as she considered the court battle in front of her. "At least not this morning."

"I agree," he said, a triumphant smile stretching mischievously over his jaw. "Because for the next two days, you're in my debt."

"Don't remind me," she groaned, then suddenly smelled the scent of coffee drifting through the rooms. Casting him a suspicious look, she asked, "How long have you been awake?"

"Hours," he drawled.

"I don't believe it."

"How about long enough to make coffee and a phone call?"

"That's more likely." She reached to the foot of her bed, where her robe usually laid. During the night it had slipped to the floor unnoticed. With a wry grin, she scooped it up and slid her arms through the sleeves. "I'll start my indentured servitude by making you breakfast."

"I like my eggs over-easy with waffles and homemade peach jam," he said.

"Dreamer," she tossed back at him as she scrambled off the bed.

"You know, I could get used to this," he teased. His grey

eyes sparkled, and Kimberly couldn't help but notice the way his shoulder muscles rippled as he shifted.

"I don't think that's such a good idea," she said, but she didn't mean it. Waking up in Jake's arms, sharing breakfast with him, spending every day with him sounded like heaven. As she walked out the door, she felt the pillow land with a thump against her rear end.

Laughing, still thinking about what it would be like to be married to him, she made her way down the hall. "You're fantasizing again, Bennett," she told herself as she breezed into the kitchen, the linoleum cold beneath her bare feet.

"What's that?" Jake asked, walking up behind her.

"Nothing—maybe you'd like to fetch the paper."

"Oh, yeah, that's just what I'd like." Grumbling good-naturedly, he slid into his ski pants and sweater, then walked outside.

Kimberly watched through the frosted window as he broke a path in the six inches of snow.

The sun was high in a winter-blue sky, and golden rays reflected off December's thick white mantle.

If not for the custody hearing and Robert's threats, Kimberly thought, her life would be perfect. But those were a couple of pretty big ifs.

She watched as Jake reached into the paper's box. He glanced back. Catching sight of her in the window, he smiled and gave her a crisp military salute. She laughed, and her stupid heart soared. Just the sight of him caused a thickening in her throat that she couldn't explain.

He stopped at his car, took out a huge bag and returned, stomping his boots in the back porch. "Mind if I change?" he asked as he passed through the kitchen and pressed cool lips to the back of her neck.

She was breaking eggs into a skillet as one strong arm

surrounded her waist and he pressed his face into her hair. "As long as I get to watch."

She turned back to the stove. So he'd packed a change of clothes. Doubts crowded her thoughts, and she pinched her lip in her teeth.

*And what about you?* Her mind nagged. *With the soft lights, fire and zero resistance. Just who was seducing whom?*

A few minutes later she heard the water running in the bathroom and the muffled sound of his off-key singing. Kimberly tried to convince herself that being with Jake was a mistake, that spending any time with him other than in his office was dangerous, but she couldn't believe it. How could anything that felt so right be wrong? she wondered as she scrambled eggs and prodded sizzling strips of bacon with her fork.

She heard the shower stop. Her heart began to pound all over again, and a few seconds later Jake, wearing only boxer-briefs slung low over his hips, a white towel draped around his neck and a knowing smile, entered the kitchen. "This smells great, and to think I'd suggested eating out," he said, winking and talking as if to himself. "Not only beautiful, but she can cook, too. You're a lucky man, McGowan."

She had to do a double-take when she turned to look at him. The hard lines of his abdomen and sparse clothing took her breath away. Regaining her stature, she said, "We may never make it to Arlene's if you don't put some clothes on."

"I think Arlene could handle another day—"

Kimberly's playfully stern look stopped him short.

With a sheepish grin he grabbed a shirt out of his bag. "If you insist," Jake murmured, pulling his head through the shirt's opening.

"Good. Now sit down and eat," she ordered, but felt the complement warm her cheeks.

They ate and talked, read the paper and sipped coffee, even

cleared the table together. It was strange, Kimberly thought, as she stacked the dishes in the dishwasher, how easily she could slip into a life with him.

After she'd showered and changed, they walked to Arlene's house and found Lindsay already shaping the third in a family of snow people. "Hi, Mommy," Lindsay called energetically, waving a mittened hand. "Wanna help?"

"Sure," Kimberly said, bending on one knee to sculpt the rotund sides of the snowman.

"That's Daddy," Lindsay said proudly, finding two sticks and stuffing them into the snowman's sides.

Kimberly's throat went raw.

"And that's you, and this is me." She indicated the other two snow people. "Now all we have to do is make a puppy!"

"Then what?" Kimberly asked, glancing up at Jake. His expression was unreadable as he leaned over and rolled another snowball.

"Then the family's done," Lindsay answered.

"I see." Kimberly's heart ached. Lindsay stated everything in a matter-of-fact voice, Kimberly wondered just how much pain the divorce had already caused her child. What would happen to Lindsay if there were a court battle?

"Here we go," Jake said, shaping a lumpy snowball.

"What's that?" Lindsay asked.

"The dog."

She eyed his four-legged sculpture suspiciously. "What kind?"

"A mutt."

If he felt uncomfortable about working on the perfect family, Jake didn't show it. Kimberly, despite her worries, almost laughed at his pathetic attempt.

"I've never seen a dog like that before," Lindsay said, wrinkling her nose and eyeing the creature that looked more like a Saturday-morning cartoon character than anything remotely canine.

Jake glanced at the statue of the rotund snowwoman. "Well, if it won't do, we'll start over. Because that—" he pointed to the icy figure "—is the spitting image of your mother."

"Oooh!" Kimberly cried, grinning. "Harsh words, counselor." She scooped up a handful of snow and hurled it at him. It smashed against his jacket, and he let out a whoop. "Those are fighting words."

Jake's silvery eyes gleamed. "Oh, yeah? Come on, Lindsay, let's teach your mom a lesson."

Before she could duck behind a nearby tree, Jake pelted her with three snowballs and Lindsay tossed another that landed at her feet.

Giggling, Lindsay grabbed another handful of snow before Jake lifted the child to his shoulders and they chased Kimberly around the yard. Laughing and breathing hard, Kimberly finally had to beg for mercy near the front steps.

"Give?" Jake asked, his smile a satisfied slash.

"Yes—I give," she gasped, her eyes sparkling.

"More, more!" Lindsay insisted just as the front door opened with a bang.

"Lindsay—what's going on out here?" Arlene asked. Still wearing an oversized terry robe and slippers, she chuckled as she saw Lindsay riding on Jake's broad shoulders.

"They're trying to kill me," Kimberly mocked.

"Exact our punishment," Jake corrected.

"Good point," he drawled.

"Details, details," Kimberly murmured.

"Well, come in and have a cup of coffee before all three of you catch your death." Arlene's eyes were bright behind her glasses. She stood back from the door to let them pass.

Kimberly stomped the snow from her boots and followed

Jake and Lindsay inside. She introduced Jake to Lyle, then hung her coat on the hall tree.

"We made you a surprise!" Lindsay announced.

They were sitting around a small maple table in Arlene's roomy kitchen, warming their frozen fingers around steaming cups of coffee and cocoa.

"What is it?" Kimberly asked.

Lindsay's face clouded. "I can't tell—otherwise it won't be a surprise. It's for Christmas!" She glanced at Lyle for support. "That's right, isn't it?"

Lyle nodded from his wheelchair. "That's right, angel. Maybe you'd better leave it over here for safekeeping until Christmas. Your mom might sneak a peek otherwise."

Lindsay's eyes rounded. "Would you?"

"Of course not," Kimberly laughed, tousling her daughter's silky hair.

"Good." Lindsay scampered into the spare bedroom and returned, carrying a crudely wrapped bundle that was half as big as she was.

"This is for me?" Kimberly asked, astounded.

"At Christmastime."

"I can't wait," Kimberly murmured, eyeing the package and feeling as if her heart might burst.

After coffee and cinnamon rolls, Jake shoved his chair away from the table. "I've got to get going."

"But you just got here," Arlene protested.

Jake grinned. "I know, but I've got a dog who probably thinks I've abandoned him, and there's the matter of a bet that has to be settled."

Kimberly felt her cheeks flame. "I guess we'd better be on our way, too," she said hastily before anyone could question Jake about his bet.

"No reason to rush off," Lyle interjected, but his wife, as

if reading the signals between Jake and Kimberly, put a hand on Lyle's arm.

"We'll see you later," she said, her bright eyes shining. "Monday morning."

After donning their coats and gloves, Jake, Kimberly and Lindsay, carrying her ungainly present, trudged past the melting snow-family to Kimberly's house. Jake insisted on carrying Lindsay's overnight bag over one shoulder while he held tightly to Kimberly's hand.

Lindsay slid on her boots down a small hill. She whooped with delight as she landed on her rear.

"Looks like she's a skier already," Jake remarked, laughing.

"Will you take me some time?" Lindsay asked eagerly.

Jake glanced to Kimberly. "I suppose we could arrange that."

"At nighttime?"

"Maybe," Kimberly said cautiously.

"Arlene said you went night skiing," Lindsay explained.

"Oh, she did, did she?" Kimberly asked.

"Uh-hum."

"What else did she say?"

"Just that you and me and Jake would probably be doing a lot of skiing."

"Once a matchmaker, always a matchmaker," Kimberly murmured.

"She told me all about you, too," Lindsay said, eyeing Jake. "You're a . . . turn key."

Jake smothered a laugh.

"An attorney," her mother corrected.

Lindsay's eyes were filled with questions, her cheeks rosy from the cold. "What's that?"

Kimberly struggled for the right words. "He's a man who's going to help us, honey," she said.

"We don't need help."

"Sometimes everyone needs help."

"Not me!" Lindsay said, then squealed when Kimberly pulled her daughter to her and kissed her soundly on the cheek.

"Do it again!" Lindsay commanded, but Kimberly shook her head.

"That's enough for now."

Lindsay didn't seem convinced, but didn't argue.

Once they were inside Kimberly's house and Lindsay had placed her package under the tree, Jake lingered near the door. "You're coming over, aren't you?" he asked.

"I promised, didn't I?" she quipped, though her stomach did a nervous flip. After the passion of the night before, she chided herself for her anxiety, but the thought of spending most of the weekend at his place was unnerving.

"You could catch a ride with me."

"I know, but I think I'll bring my own car. Most of the streets are plowed."

"You're not having second thoughts, are you?"

"No way."

"Good." He reached into his wallet, found a business card, then wrote his home address on the backside. "Call if you get lost."

"In Lake Oswego?"

"It can be confusing."

"Don't send a search party out for a while."

Flashing her a smile, he glanced at his watch. "You've got two hours."

"And if I'm late?"

Grinning wickedly, he slid a glance over her body that made her pulse leap. "Then I'll exact my punishment in ways too numerous to count."

"You *are* a dreamer," she retorted as he opened the door and strode briskly outside. A few minutes later she heard his Bronco roar down the driveway.

Still considering the night before and all the ramifications of a love affair with Jake McGowan, she carried Lindsay's overnight bag to the loft and unpacked.

She heard Lindsay's footsteps rush up the stairs. A few minutes later, blue eyes gleaming, Lindsay peeked around the rail. She stared at her bag.

"Are we going somewhere?"

"To Jake's house."

Lindsay eyed the bag suspiciously. "Overnight?"

"Oh—no." Laughing, Kimberly tossed Lindsay's dirty clothes into a hamper. "I was just unpacking from *last* night."

"Oh." Lindsay worried her lower lip in her teeth. "I like him," she announced. "Even if he's a . . . whatever it's called."

Kimberly felt a surprising sense of relief. "I like him, too," she agreed. *I like him far too much.*

"Do you like him more than Daddy?"

Sighing, Kimberly sat on the edge of Lindsay's bed, hauled her daughter onto her lap and hugged her close. "I like him differently than I like your dad," she said slowly. "Your dad and I . . . we just don't get along."

"You don't love him."

That was true.

"And he doesn't love you," Lindsay said soberly.

Kimberly sighed again, surprised at the wisdom of her child. "No, he doesn't, not like he used to. But he loves you very much," she said, cringing as she considered her life. She was certain Robert didn't know the meaning of the word "love," not even where his daughter was concerned. She squeezed Lindsay and planted a kiss on her forehead. "And I love you so much I could burst!"

"I know that."

*Thank goodness!*

"Do you love Jake?" Lindsay asked, twisting around so that she could stare straight into Kimberly's eyes.

"I like him a lot," Kimberly hedged.

"I know, but do you love him?"

"Can't I just like him—you know, as a special friend?"

Lindsay frowned as she considered. Finally she shook her blond curls. "I don't think so," she murmured.

*I don't, either,* Kimberly silently agreed.

"So—do you love him or not?"

"I guess I do," Kimberly admitted, not wanting to lie again. "I love him, but it's a different kind of love."

"Oh, I know. All that mushy stuff."

Kimberly rolled her eyes as she set Lindsay back on the floor. "Let's just think of him as a good friend. And keep this to yourself, will you?"

Wrinkling her nose, Lindsay grinned. "I won't tell anybody!"

Kimberly hoped her daughter could keep a secret. "Good, I'll hold you to it."

"I promise," Lindsay vowed. "Are you gonna marry him?"

"No!" she nearly shouted, then seeing Lindsay's vexed expression, added, "love is complicated."

"No, it isn't. If you love someone, you marry them. That's what Shawna Briggs says."

"Oh, does she?" Kimberly said with a smile as she thought of Kimberly's friend in kindergarten.

"Yep. And she loves Josh Barton and she's gonna marry him."

"Well, I hope you get invited to the wedding."

"I will," Lindsay announced with all the self-confidence of her five years.

As Kimberly unpacked, she tried not to think of anything as foolish as marriage to Jake, yet the idea refused to go away. Jake wasn't the marrying kind, she told herself. He'd gone as far as saying so. And there was still so much to learn about him.

"Come on, let's get changed," she said to Lindsay when the last of her clothes were placed in the drawer. "Then, if you want, we can go visit Jake at his place. Would that be all right?"

Lindsay grinned from ear to ear. "He has a puppy, doesn't he?"

\* \* \*

Jake did indeed have a dog. A big, bounding, white wolf-like creature that barked and whined as Kimberly eased her car down the slippery drive.

Jake's house was small, little more than a cottage. Pearl gray and nestled in a thicket of tall Douglas fir trees, his home looked like the vacation property it had originally been. Snow was piled in droves against the windowpanes. A blanket of white weighted the drooping fir boughs and covered the ground.

Smoke curled from a river-rock chimney, dispersing in a cloudless blue sky.

"Oh, look!" Lindsay cried happily as Lupus placed his paws on the passenger side of the Mercedes, his nose against the glass.

"Lupus!" Jake was standing in the doorway, waiting.

Kimberly's heart soared at the sight of him. He'd changed into a plaid wool shirt, tan cords and running shoes. Without a thought to jacket or boots, he loped down a path that had been made through the snow.

"I'd about given up," he said, helping Kimberly out of the car.

"You said two hours."

"And you pushed it."

"It took us a while."

Lindsay scrambled over the handbrake and out the door on the driver's side. Lupus scurried around the car, discovered her, wiped her face with his tongue and barked excitedly. Lindsay squealed with delight, and the chase was on. Through the drifting unplowed powder, dog and child bounced, laughing and yipping.

"Soulmates," Jake observed dryly.

Kimberly was laughing so hard, tears sprang to her eyes. "He's beautiful," Lindsay called, and Kimberly laughed again.

"That's the first time he's ever heard that," Jake said, taking her hand. "Come on, I'll show you around."

While Lindsay and Lupus cavorted, Jake took Kimberly's arm and led her down a snow-crested path through the trees.

Behind the house, the ground sloped down to the shore of Lake Oswego. Icicles clung to the docking, and the icy water of the lake lapped against the bleached wood. The water was calm and stretched far to the opposite bank.

"It's gorgeous here," Kimberly said, her breath misting in the cold air. The privacy of Jake's backyard was insured by the trees, a fence and, of course, the lake.

"You should see it in the summer."

From the front of the house, Kimberly heard Lindsay's laugh and Lupus's loud yip.

Though the temperature was below freezing, she felt warm inside and didn't protest when he folded his arms around her and pressed chilled lips to hers. She responded immediately. The fire within her needed little stoking. The pressure of his mouth moving sensually over hers was all it took to turn her liquid inside.

Willingly she wound her arms around his neck and felt his hands, bare and cold, slip beneath her jacket to rub anxiously against her sweater.

"I missed you." His voice was low and rough, and though he whispered, the words seemed to ring in the still air.

"It only took me a couple of hours to get here."

"Too long," he groaned, his mouth fitting perfectly over hers. She felt the pads of his fingers through her sweater, his warmth permeating the thick weave.

Lifting his head with a ragged sigh, he stared into her eyes. His hand slid from under her jacket to entwine in her hair. "Promise me when this is all over, you'll go away with me."

"What?" She didn't understand, but stared deep into his eyes, mesmerized by his gaze.

"When the custody battle's over, I want to take you away

from here. Maybe we'll go to Mexico, or the Caribbean. Someplace we can be alone for a long time."

"And . . . what about Lindsay?"

"She can come, too."

"So much for being alone," she said, but her voice sounded breathless. He was moving too fast. Kimberly couldn't think straight. "I don't know. Maybe that's not such a good idea."

"Think about it."

Lindsay and Lupus plowed through the snow toward them.

"Come on inside," Jake offered. "I've got a surprise for you."

Lindsay, already flushed in the face, positively beamed. "What is it?"

"You'll see."

She raced to the back door.

"Take off your boots—" but it was too late. Kimberly's command was lost in the winter air as the screen door banged shut. Lindsay let out a cry of delight, and Lupus whined pitifully at the back door.

"You didn't!" Kimberly cried, glancing at Jake as if he'd lost his mind. But he was grinning from ear to ear as they mounted the back steps and walked into the kitchen. "Look, she can keep it here, if you'd prefer."

"And you'll keep it for her?"

Kimberly was prepared to see Lindsay clinging to the neck of a puppy and was ready to give Jake a piece of her mind. But instead Lindsay was entranced with a furry brown-and-white guinea pig huddled in one corner of the cage.

"Can I pick him up?" Lindsay asked, her eyes as bright as the frightened rodent's.

"If you're careful."

"I will be." She reached into the cage, scooped up the nervous animal and held him close to her.

"A guinea pig? You bought her a guinea pig?" Kimberly couldn't believe it. "Why?"

"It was cheaper than a cocker spaniel," he deadpanned.

"Thank God."

"Every kid needs a pet."

"I suppose."

Lupus was whining and scratching at the back door. Once the guinea pig could be pried from Lindsay's hands and was safely back in his cage, Jake let the dog inside. He scrambled across the linoleum and leaped up, trying to lick Lindsay's face.

"He's jealous," Jake said with a laugh. "Now, how about some mint cocoa?"

A few minutes later, while Lindsay was dividing her time between dog and rodent, Jake and Kimberly sipped hot chocolate in front of the fire. Leaning next to him on the couch, her feet stretched out to the warmth of the flames, she felt as if she'd finally come home.

"So, when do I start paying?" she asked.

"You are," he said and slipped one arm comfortably around her shoulders.

She leaned her head into the crook of his neck and closed her eyes. Being with Jake was perfect. Listening to the sound of Lindsay's muted chatter, soft Christmas music, the crackling fire and the steady beat of Jake's heart, she felt more content and safe than she had in a long, long while.

# Chapter Ten

Lindsay fell asleep on a blanket near the fire. Her thumb slid between her lips, and she sighed.

The guinea pig came to life, digging in the shavings and his cage on the desk, and Lupus, ever vigilant, kept his eyes trained on the furry little creature.

"I think I'd better take Lindsay home," Kimberly said quietly. "She's had a long day."

Jake grinned. "Very long."

Snuggled with Jake on the couch, sipping the last of mulled wine, she didn't want to move, couldn't imagine returning to her own house without him.

He brushed his lips across her cheek. Touching the underside of her chin, he forced her to look at him. "Stay," he whispered, and his silvery eyes wouldn't let her go. "Spend the night with me. I mean, that was part of our bargain—two days and . . . as many nights as you want." His voice was low and velvety. "I'll make it worth your while."

She giggled. "Has anyone ever told you that you have an incredible ego, Mr. McGowan?"

"Too many to count," he said with a teasing grin. "Come on, live a little."

"I—shouldn't."

"Sure you should." His eyes gleamed. "I've got plenty of room for both of you."

"You mean all three of us," Kimberly teased, motioning to Lindsay's new pet. The guinea pig found his exercise wheel and started running.

Jake chuckled, but he wouldn't take no for an answer. He disappeared into the back bedrooms, only to return with a quilted baby blanket in which he gently wrapped the sleeping Lindsay.

Bemused, Kimberly followed him down the hall to a small bedroom where L-shaped bunk beds fitted into one corner and a matching dresser was pushed against the wall. The room, painted white, was stark and bare except for the two pieces of furniture, and Kimberly guessed no one had ever occupied it. And yet it stood ready for a child. What child? Certainly not Lindsay.

Tenderly Jake laid Lindsay on the bottom bunk, brushing a strand of her hair from her face and pulling the blanket close around her chin. Kimberly's heart turned over. Never had she seen Robert deal with Lindsay with such care—such obvious love. This man treated her as if she were his own. If only . . . she thought, projecting ahead. But she couldn't let herself think of a future in which she and Jake and Lindsay became a family. There were too many hurdles to vault first. And there were things about Jake, secrets he hadn't confided to her.

Jake reached to the dresser and snapped off the light. "See," he said, standing, his voice husky. "She'll be fine." Lupus trotted into the room, curled in a ball near the foot of the bed and, placing his nose between his front paws, sighed loudly. Jake chuckled. "She's even got a guard dog." He patted the white shepherd fondly, and Lupus's tail thumped the floor.

Kimberly smiled inwardly as they walked back to the living room in silence. The fire had nearly died. Jake busied himself rearranging logs in the grate while Kimberly stared for the first time at the bookshelves lining the wall. Law books, textbooks, computer manuals and a collection of science fiction and mystery paperbacks filled the overflowing shelves.

In frames on the walls were Jake's diplomas and a graduation picture. But the photograph that caught her eye was a small snapshot in a handmade frame on a corner of the mantel. A dark-haired boy, around three years old and dressed in a blue jogging suit, a football tucked under his chubby arm, smiled back at her. His blue eyes were serious, his grin a little forced. She didn't have to be told he was related to Jake.

Jake had stopped fiddling with the fire. Still squatting, he'd rocked back on his heels and stared up at her with an expression that could only be described as bleak. "That's Sam," he said gruffly. "My son." His eyes grew distant and unreadable.

"He's very handsome," she said, slightly bewildered. Hadn't Jake said he was childless?

"Thanks."

Standing, Jake shoved his hands into the back pockets of his jeans, and pain lingered in his eyes. "I told you I didn't have any children, but that wasn't the truth. I had a child for nearly three years. Sam was killed shortly after that picture was taken." Jake's throat worked, and he had to clear it.

Kimberly felt numb inside. *To lose a child*. Her heart went out to him. "Oh, Jake . . ."

He held up a palm and shook his head. "Don't say you're sorry, okay. I just don't want to hear it."

She bit her lower lip and wished there were some words of

comfort, some tender endearment that she could whisper to ease his pain. Of course, there was none. "I—I didn't know."

He picked up the picture and held it in his palm. Staring at the photograph, he blinked rapidly. "Some things just never go away," he said, "no matter how hard you try to forget them."

Taking a deep breath, he turned the picture facedown on the mantel, then stood near the window, bracing one hand against the casing as he gazed outside. "It happened years ago, but it's with me every day."

She ached to touch him—to offer some comfort. "Is Lindsay sleeping in his room?"

He shook his head but didn't look back at her. "No. His furniture. But not his room. I—we—lived in the city then, a big house in Dunthorpe." Turning, he tried to smile, failed and pursed his lips. "Lydia, Sam's mother, wasn't happy. Thought I should be working harder to become a partner in the firm. She expected me to climb the success ladder a little more quickly than I was. Anyway, after Sam was born, she was really dissatisfied—claimed life was passing her by." He shoved the dark thatch of hair from his eyes. "So she found someone else, another attorney in town, a man really going places. A man with expensive cars, a boat, a private plane." His lips curled. "A man who had the right connections."

Kimberly felt cold to the center of her soul.

Jake's eyes narrowed, and he walked to the bar, where he poured himself a stiff shot of Scotch.

"Who?" Kimberly asked, shaking inside. She wasn't sure she wanted to know the answer.

He tossed back his drink. "Your friend and mine. Ben Kesler."

"Holy shit," she whispered, her fingers clenching together. Ben was more than Robert's attorney—they were partners in some business ventures. Even Ben's plane, which was kept in Mulino, miles out of the city, was partially owned by Robert.

The seconds ticked by as Jake stared gloomily into his

glass. "Yep. She intended to take Sam, make sure I never saw him again and marry Kesler." He glanced at Kimberly. His mouth twisted wryly. "Now, that was her side of the story, mind you. I don't know if Kesler had any intentions of marching down the aisle with her. He was just her divorce attorney and lover at that point—but it doesn't matter. Right after the divorce was final, Lydia and Sam were in an automobile accident. Neither survived." He took in a long bracing breath, and Kimberly crossed the room and took his face between her hands.

"I *am* sorry," she said feeling him tremble beneath her touch. "And I won't say I know how you feel, because I don't. I can't imagine losing a child."

"It's hell," he whispered, his eyes dark with agony. "Pure hell. I swear to you here and now, I'll never go through it again."

Her throat closed and she had to whisper. "The joy of having a child is worth the risk."

He knocked her hands away and turned his back to her. "As you said, you can't know how I feel. No one can." He reached for the bottle of Scotch again, grabbed it by the neck, discovered it was nearly empty and, swearing under his breath, hurled it into the fire. The bottle crashed, splintering into a hundred shards, and flames roared and flared as alcohol splattered against the wood.

"Jake . . ."

He didn't answer her, wouldn't look her way.

"Don't shut me out," Kimberly whispered.

The muscles of his shoulders bunched.

Kimberly felt helpless. "Please, Jake. I care too much for you. Let me help."

When he turned to look at her, agony was in every line of his strained features.

Suddenly she understood far more than he'd admitted. His divorce and the loss of this child had happened while he'd worked with Diane. He didn't have to say it. Kimberly knew. Diane had helped pull him from the abyss his life had become after Sam's death. She'd pushed him in a new direction—into corporate law—when he couldn't stand to deal with custody or adoption or divorce cases any longer.

How difficult it must have been for Jake to take her case. Tears filled her eyes. "I'd like to help."

His eyes held hers. "No one can bring Sam back."

Her heart breaking, she reached for him and wrapped her arms around his waist. She settled her head against his chest and fought tears. Slowly she felt his strong, tense arms folded around her. She tilted her face to his and pressed wet, tear-stained kisses to his lips.

He groaned loudly, his tall body stretched against hers.

"Trust me, Jake," she whispered as his lips, hot and hungry, slanted over hers again. He was everywhere. His tall frame molded hard around her, his hands moving anxiously against her skin, his mouth and tongue seeking solace in hers.

She opened up to him as a flower to the sun, hoping to ease his pain.

His hands were tangled in her hair, and he pulled them both down to the thick carpet in front of the fire. He stripped them of their clothes and lay upon her, his long, hard muscles firm against her yielding flesh. Staring into her eyes, kissing her neck, cheeks, breasts and abdomen, Jake lost control.

In front of the fire, with golden shadows playing upon their skin, Kimberly helped him forget. If only for a little while.

The next morning Jake blinked rapidly. His head pounded, and he was disoriented. Finally his blurry eyes focused on the bright room—his room. Sunlight, reflecting on the snow outside, was streaming in blinding rays through the windows. He stretched lazily and stared down at the woman sharing his bed.

Her dark, red-brown hair, was mussed, tossed around her face in a fiery cloud. Dark lashes lay against creamy-white skin, and her expression was peaceful and still, her nostrils barely moving as she breathed.

The sheet, twisted and wrinkled, covered one of her breasts. The other was bare, the dark bud of her nipple protruding beguilingly upward. Memories of wild, savage lovemaking slipped into his conscience, and he grinned wickedly. He'd spent the night purging the past in fierce union with this beautiful woman, and she'd met his wild passion with a wanton abandon that he'd never before experienced.

He twisted a lock of her hair in his fingers and wondered about her. She was kind and caring, but could turn into a seductress so intense that he still ached for more of her.

His memory ablaze with desire, he stared again at her breast—so perfect, so enticing. Unable to stop himself, he leaned over to kiss the rosy seductive point. Immediately he felt a tightening inside and a heated response in his loins.

To his delight the nipple hardened, and Kimberly moaned softly, shifting closer. He threw a leg across her, and she sighed. Still kissing her breasts, he reached under the covers, to the apex of her legs, to touch her sweet essence and delve his fingers within.

She was ready—moist and waiting, letting out soft moans as he moved his fingers inside her. He stroked the bundle of nerves on her top wall, making her hips buck against his hand.

His gut tightened, and the ache between his own legs begged for release. He nibbled her nipple again and glanced up at her face as her eyes fluttered open. Two slumberous blue-green eyes looked up at him with such erotic adoration that he nearly stopped.

She smiled, and that did him in. Sliding up the length of her, he kissed her face, laid himself atop her and buried himself deep within that warm, inviting spot that tore his soul from his body.

"Wh—what are you doing, counselor?"

"Saying 'Good morning,'" he drawled.

"I like the way you say it . . ."

He thrust deep inside.

She tried to say something, but when she opened her mouth, no words came out.

With the flat of his hand he felt her heartbeat pound erratically, saw the shallow breathing and the rise and fall of her beautiful breasts. "You're gorgeous," he reminded her, taking in her flat stomach and toned legs.

Slowly he moved, so lazily that she lifted up to meet him, grabbing his buttocks in frustration, pulling him against her.

"Be patient," he whispered, kneading her breasts and gritting back the urge to claim her as fiercely as he had only hours earlier.

While last night was lust to cure sexual abandon, a cleansing of all the pain in his past, this morning he paced himself. Giving and receiving, he watched for her response, enjoying himself as she reached peak after peak until at last she, not he, was spent. "Oh, Jake," she sighed.

Only then did he satisfy himself, losing his self-control as he stared down into an angelic face relaxed in afterglow.

They laid together afterward, Jake holding her close. Her face was pressed to his bare chest, and the clean scent of her hair filled his nostrils.

"We failed, you know," she finally said, glancing up at him and offering an impish smile.

"Failed? And here I thought we'd scored perfect tens last night."

She blushed, then laughed. "I wasn't talking about that."

"I hope not!"

"But we didn't manage to stay uninvolved."

"No kidding," he agreed. How could he ever live without her? How had he survived such a lonely past?

She looked over to the bedside clock and groaned, throwing

an arm over her forehead theatrically. "I'd better get up before Lindsay comes running in here with all kinds of questions."

Jake grinned boyishly. "You're ashamed of me."

"No, counselor," she said, rolling her tongue in the corner of her cheek, "but I'm not up to explaining the situation to a curious five-year-old. However, if you'd like to fill her in on the facts of life—" she waved the fingers of one hand "—be my guest."

"I think I'll pass on that one."

"I thought so."

Stretching, he finally released her and watched as she slid out of bed, then snatched her clothes from the chair near the closet. He loved the length of her thighs, the round curve of her hips, the nip of her waist, the way her breasts swung free. Unconsciously seductive as she pulled her sweater over her head, shook her hair free and slid into her jeans, Kimberly finished dressing, and Jake finally closed his eyes so that he could resist the urge to jump out of bed, grab her and throw her back across the rumpled sheets again.

What was the matter with him? He'd been with more than his share of women in his life. But never had he felt this insatiable urge to claim one again and again. He'd gotten bored before. He knew that this woman with her quick wit and dimpled smile would always interest him. And he realized, with a shock that rocked him to his bones, that he wanted to spend the rest of his life with her. With Robert Fisher's ex-wife.

Groaning, he covered his face with a pillow. What had gotten into him?

He tossed off the pillow just to catch the movement of her backside as she walked out of the room.

Springing from the bed, he headed straight for the cool, healing spray of the shower. He considered calling her into the bathroom and stripping her beneath the misting rivulets of hot, running water, but discarded the idea. Though he could imagine her giggling with delight, he could also picture Lindsay waking up and walking in at just the wrong moment. Frowning, he twisted on the water.

Nope, he wasn't ready to explain his personal sexual fantasies to an inquisitive five-year-old. He stepped into the shower and felt the needles of water against his back.

And what about Lindsay? If he wanted Kimberly, he'd end up with her daughter as well. They were a package deal. He, who'd sworn never to become a parent again, he, who would do just about anything to avoid the inevitable pain of fatherhood, was considering changing all his convictions and opening himself up to being a husband and father again.

"God dammit," he muttered to himself, frustrated by his predicament. Maybe all these feelings would go away. When Fisher was caught and Lindsay was secure with Kimberly, Jake might have a chance to live his life the way he had before she'd shown up at his office, her black coat billowing around her, her gorgeous blue-green eyes searching his very soul.

A few minutes later, while buckling his belt, he heard the sound of footsteps padding across the oak floor of the bedroom. Glancing over his bare shoulder, he spied Lindsay staring at him curiously from the doorway.

"Good morning," he said as she gave him the once-over.

"Mornin'."

"You hungry?"

"Why're we still here?"

"What?"

Her little brows drew together, and she stuck out her lower lip. "I thought we were going home last night."

"It was too late."

She looked as if she didn't believe him, but she thought about it and changed the subject. "Why don't you have a Christmas tree?" she demanded.

Jake's jaw grew rock hard. He hadn't put up a tree since Sam had died. The trappings and festivities associated with the holidays had seemed frivolous and pointless without

Sam's bright eyes and laughter. "I guess I just haven't gotten around to it," he evaded.

She tilted her little chin upward. "I'll help."

"Will you?" Jake grinned, charmed despite his own warnings not to get too close to this little blond imp. "Sounds like a plan to me!"

"We can do it right now. Mommy's making breakfast." With that, she took off down the hall, and Jake, dumbfounded, wiped the remainder of the shaving cream from his face.

Lindsay was right. Kimberly was making breakfast. Her hair pulled back in a ponytail, she moved around his kitchen as if she'd done it for years.

Jake crossed his arms over his chest, propping a shoulder against the wall and watched her work. Waffles browned in the waffle iron, coffee perked on the stove and sausage simmered in a frying pan. The kitchen was filled with a sense that tantalized and brought back memories he'd tried to keep in the back of his mind. As he stared at Kimberly cracking eggs into another frying pan, he remembered his wife.

There had been a time when Lydia had taken time for the family and cooked a large Sunday breakfast. But that time, when she'd loved him and wanted to deal with Sam, had been brief.

"Come on!" Lindsay cried. She'd found her coat and boots and was heading for the back door.

Kimberly smiled as she looked over her shoulder. "Don't tell me," she said, "you've been drafted into hunting down a tree."

"I already have one," Jake replied.

"Where?" Lindsay stared pointedly at the barren living room.

"Out here." He opened the door to the back porch, and Lupus dashed through, startling a cat creeping under the rhododendron bushes flanking the house and giving loud chase. The cat sprinted to the nearest maple tree and scrambled upward while Lupus pawed and barked at the trunk, his tail whipping behind him, his paws sliding on the rough bark.

"He's silly!" Lindsay proclaimed.

"Very," Jake agreed, calling to the dog. "Lupus, here!" He slapped his leg loudly, but the shepherd wouldn't be distracted and whined loudly. "He'll give up," Jake confided to Lindsay.

"When?"

Jake considered. "Probably by the spring thaw. Come on, let's tackle that tree."

While Kimberly finished making breakfast, Jake pulled the little potted pine tree from his back porch into the living room. He found an old string of lights with only a few burned-out bulbs and a box of ornaments, and though the decorations were a little worn, the tree did add a festive touch to the room.

Lindsay wasn't convinced the tree would do. "You need new stuff," she said, eyeing a broken decoration. "Lots of it. And a bigger tree."

"Next year," he said, swinging her off her feet. She squealed happily, then slid to the floor.

"Arlene will get you one," Lindsay exclaimed.

"Maybe we should ask her before you go making promises," he said, moving back to the kitchen.

"Here, you deserve this," Kimberly said, handing him an enamel mug filled with coffee. Her eyes were the color of a tropical sea, and her lips puckered into a little grin.

He took a sip, nearly burned his tongue and asked, "So, what's gotten into you? Why are you Ms. Domesticity?"

"Merely paying off my debt, Mr. McGowan," she said. "Remember? This is the weekend I work for you. After that, it's all over."

Jake grinned wickedly. "In that case I'll have to see that you don't waste a second."

She laughed. "Go ahead. I'm sure I can handle anything you dish out."

His eyes sparkled. "We'll see about that."

"I hate to admit it, but I'm not worried in the least bit," she said, plucking a long pine needle from his freshly washed hair. "You and Lindsay better sit and eat before breakfast gets cold. Oh—and by the way—while you were in the shower—"

"Yes." He took a swallow from his cup.

"The phone rang and I answered it. Some man—Koski, I think his name was—wants you to call him back."

Jake's muscles tensed. "Ron Koski?"

"That was it," she said, nodding. "He seemed rather insistent. Said he might be taking off for a few days. I left the message on your desk."

Jake glanced at his phone. His fingers tightened over the handle of the cup. "I'll call him later," he said, hoping his expression didn't give him away. For the time being, he didn't want Kimberly to know about Ron or the investigation, if there was one, on Robert. He wasn't yet ready to explain completely about Daniel, though he felt guilty that he hadn't placed all his cards on the table.

*In time*, he told himself as he slid into a chair and watched her take a seat across from him, *when things have settled down*. Then we'll destroy all the ghosts from the past and concentrate on the future.

The weekend flew by. Kimberly spent every second with Jake and, true to her word, mended a couple of his shirts, organized his kitchen, did two loads of laundry and even dusted and vacuumed his house.

He protested vehemently, but she didn't slack off, and in the end he contented himself by helping out and amusing Lindsay.

* * *

Kimberly couldn't remember when she'd been happier, and that worried her as she walked into the offices of First Cascade on Monday morning. Christmas music murmured through the speakers, and the lobby of the bank was decorated for the holidays with strings of lights. Red and green letters spelling out Happy Holidays hung over the teller windows.

In the trust department, Marcie was already busy at her computer. She looked up and smiled at Kimberly, but her fingers never left the keyboard.

Kimberly hung up her coat, then walked back through the reception area to the cafeteria, where she poured herself a cup of hot water and dumped a teabag into it. Several women from the mortgage banking department were clustered around a couple of Formica-topped tables. They drank coffee and nibbled on doughnuts as they talked and laughed before they had to head downstairs.

Kimberly spoke to Kelly and Annie, women she'd worked with in the mortgage department, then turned to head back to her office. She didn't get far. Bill Zealander, his face flushed, marched stiffly into the room. "I need to talk to you," he announced.

Kimberly refused to be cowed. "So talk."

He glanced at the women gossiping at the roundtable. "Not here."

"Why not?"

His lips compressed, and behind his glasses his eyes slitted. "Because this is private. Okay?"

"Fine, Bill." Kimberly wasn't in the mood to argue. She left her teacup, followed Bill out of the cafeteria, explained where she'd be to Marcie, then strode through the door of Bill's office. "Okay, what's up?" she asked, trying to keep the irritation out of her voice. She didn't like his high-handed attitude, and she didn't bother sitting down. Instead she crossed her arms impatiently and waited for the storm that was sure to hit.

Bill stood on the other side of the desk, his back to a bank of windows as he fiddled with the knot of his tie. "I want to know what's going on with the Juniper trust."

"I thought you said this was personal."

"It is." He slid her a glance that was meant to cut her to the quick. It didn't. "You and I both know that you're mishandling the account."

"I'm what?" she demanded, floored.

"Oh, for Pete's sake, Kimberly, admit it. You can't even handle the heirs. Every other day Henry Juniper's crying on your shoulder. And from what I understand, Carole is planning to contest the will. You've had to ask for extra help from operations to make sure all the dividends were paid. And you can barely keep your mind on business."

"What're you talking about?"

He yanked off his glasses and polished them with a tissue. "The custody hearing for your daughter."

Kimberly crossed the room and leaned over his desk. "What do *you* know about that?"

He gestured with the hand holding his wire-rimmed glasses. "It's common knowledge, Kim. Robert Fisher's a biggie around here. And it's no secret that you've hired some has-been attorney with a vendetta to get to Fisher. If you ask me, you're playing with fire."

"No one's asking you anything," she said, stung. It took all of her strength to stay calm. "And what I do with my personal life is none of your business."

"I know. But you're obviously under strain. You've got more important things to think about than business."

"You're way out of line, Bill," she said. He shrugged and polished the lenses of his glasses again. Seeing him in a dark suit, in relief against the windows, set off a memory of another tall man—a man dressed in dark blue, a man polishing his goggles after night skiing. She didn't move, couldn't believe that her mind was leaping to such conclusions. And yet. . . . Her mouth went dry.

"Now, look, I'm just trying to help you out," he was saying. He smiled benignly and slipped the glasses onto his nose. "I could handle the Juniper trust, get Henry and Carole working together rather than at cross-purposes, at least for a while, until you get your personal life back on track."

"My life is on track."

"Get real, Kim."

"Do you ski, Bill?" she asked suddenly, deciding she'd had enough of his arrogant insinuations.

"Do I what?" he asked, taken aback.

"Ski."

"Yes, but what—" he stopped suddenly, and a red flush climbed steadily up his neck.

She couldn't believe his reaction. "Have you been following me?"

"Are you out of your mind?"

"I don't think so." So furious she was shaking, she said, "I've just had this feeling lately that someone was watching me. And I thought I saw you up on the mountain night skiing."

He laughed nervously and reached into his suit pocket for a piece of nicotine gum. "Now you've really gone off the deep end."

"Have I?"

"Kimberly—"

"I don't know what the fuck you're up to, Bill, but I don't like it. Stay the hell out of my life." Spinning on her heel, she strode straight into her office and resisted the urge to slam the door.

Her temples throbbed. Taking deep breaths, she tried to think straight. Had Bill Zealander, in his efforts to further himself, actually taken to following her? But why? And what were all those cracks about Robert being an important client at the bank? She felt a cold lump settle in her heart. Did

Zealander's spying have something to do with the custody hearing? "Oh, God," she whispered prayerfully.

Her headache pounded behind her eyes.

She thought about talking to Eric Compton, but discarded the idea. Compton hated office in-fighting and petty jealousy, and she didn't blame him. Besides, she had no proof. No, she'd keep this to herself. At least until she saw Jake again.

Bill Zealander had known she'd hired an attorney—presumably Jake. So, why the remark about a has-been lawyer with a vendetta?

She went back to the cafeteria, found her now-tepid cup of tea and reheated it. Then she stormed back to her office, located a small bottle of aspirin in her purse and swallowed two of the bitter tablets.

"Forget about Zealander," she told herself as she clicked open her briefcase and pulled out several thick files. She didn't have time to deal with penny-ante personality problems.

The intercom buzzed and Marcie announced that Henry Juniper was on line one. Kimberly smiled, grateful for once for the distraction. Things were back to normal.

Jake finally connected with Ron Koski Monday afternoon. He stopped by Ron's office, a small three-room suite tucked between a maid service and a travel agency in Oregon City.

Ron's furniture consisted of a desk, two chairs, a small table and a credenza. A plate-glass window offered a view of Willamette Falls, a railroad crossing and smokestacks from a nearby paper mill. White clouds of steam rose over the city, melding with the gray sky.

Ron, in need of a shave, looked up when Jake strode in. "About time you showed up." Seated at his desk, his blond crew cut on the longish side, he offered Jake his hand.

"I've called you three times since yesterday." Jake clasped Ron's hand and shook it firmly. They'd been friends since high school. And Ron was one of two people Jake trusted with his life. Diane Welby was the other. And now, of course, there was Kimberly Bennett.

Ron waved him into one of the side chairs. "I've been on a stakeout. But I thought you'd want to know that the police are definitely on to Fisher." He reached behind him, found a thermos of coffee and poured two cups.

Jake took the cup he was offered and dropped into a chair near the desk. "The police have been on to him before."

"I know, and there's always the chance he'll get away." Ron shrugged. "But the D.A. won't go for anything less than an open-and-shut case. He can't afford to go after Fisher without anything else. Too much public embarrassment."

"How do you know all this?"

"I've got my sources." Ron grinned and suddenly slammed his hand down on the desk. "Sorry, I hate spiders," he said, grabbing a tissue and cleaning up the remnants of the bug, tossing it into the trash.

"Brecken? Is he talking again?" Jake took a sip of coffee. Bitter and hot, it burned all the way down his throat.

"Nope, Brecken's been tightlipped, but trust me, this source is good."

"When will it go down?"

"Don't know."

Jake was worried. The timing and the set-up were all wrong. "Why hasn't Fisher gotten wind of it?"

Ron frowned. "Maybe he has."

"Will he run?"

"Your guess is as good as mine. He's got a lot of ties here in Portland—it would be hard to pull up stakes."

*That it would*, Jake thought gloomily. Especially if Fisher intended to hang around long enough to fight Kimberly in court. Unless, of course, Fisher took the law into his own hands.

Cold certainty settled in the small of his back. Of course

Fisher would run. His gut twisted, and it took all his self-control not to run out of the office, grab Kimberly and Lindsay and hide them somewhere safe. Robert Fisher was running scared and if he really wanted his daughter with him, he'd just take her. "Give me all the details," he said to Ron, his voice short.

"I don't have many."

"What?"

"My source gave me a little information, but she didn't blow the whole operation."

"She?"

Ron smiled slyly. "Okay . . . this is what I know. . . ."

The last person Kimberly expected to run into on her way out of the bank that night was Robert. But there he was, big as life, surrounded by bank bigwigs again. And Bill Zealander within the group.

Dread crept up her spine.

She hadn't seen Robert in the offices of First Cascade for a while, and now he seemed to be there every other day. He saw her approach, but didn't bother to smile. In fact his face seemed strained, his lips a little white, and his eyes were so cold she actually shivered.

Robert and entourage disappeared into the elevator. Marcie was wrapping a wool scarf around her neck and had already slung the strap of her purse over her shoulder. "Wait," Kimberly called as the elevator doors closed.

"Sorry, boss, I'm outta here," Marcie teased.

"No, I don't need anything, just some information."

Marcie grinned. "You've got five minutes. I'm meeting Glen downstairs."

"Do you know what's going on with Bill and Robert Fisher?"

Marcie, who always had an ear open to office gossip, shrugged and swept her bangs under the red scarf. "Nothing specific, but I do know that Bill's been busy lately. A lot of closed-door meetings."

"With Robert?"

Marcie nodded. "Once in a while."

Kimberly gulped and tried not to panic.

"As for Fisher, I think he's moving some money around."

"Within the bank?"

"I guess. Or maybe he's transferring it to another branch or something." She pulled out her compact and checked her makeup, then brushed a fleck of mascara from her cheek.

Kimberly's mouth went dry. Something was going on. Something big. "How do you know this?"

Marcie grinned. "From Heather. She knows everything."

And Heather was Bill Zealander's secretary. Images flashed through Kimberly's mind, pictures of Bill trotting after Robert when he was in the bank, a lone skier watching her with Jake, a man lingering near the lamppost across her street.

"Is something wrong?" Marcie asked, staring at her as she clicked her compact shut and stuffed it back into her purse.

Kimberly forced a tight smile. "I don't know. But thanks."

"Any time. And I'll check with Heather, see if she knows anything else." She waved as she walked to the elevators.

Kimberly picked up the phone on Marcie's desk. With quaking fingers, she dialed her home. The phone rang three times before Lindsay's voice called, "Hello?"

Kimberly's knees went weak. She sank against the desk. "Oh, hi, honey, how're you? Was school okay today?"

"It was crummy. Bobby Hendricks kicked me. I got him back, though. I pinched him in the neck!" Lindsay launched into a blow-by-blow account of her day at school while Kimberly battled against sudden tears.

"Well, you certainly had an interesting day," Kimberly said before Arlene took over the phone and assured her that nothing was out of the ordinary and she was, as usual, watching Lindsay like a hawk.

"Now, don't you change your plans," Arlene admonished. "You go along and do some shopping before you come home."

Christmas shopping! She'd forgotten all about it. "I think I'd better come straight home."

"Hogwash! Lindsay and I are knee-deep in a project here, anyway. We'll see you in a couple of hours."

"All right, just be careful," Kimberly replied.

"I always am."

After hanging up, she took the elevator downstairs to the lobby and walked out the main doors of the bank. The Santas on every street corner rang bells, shoppers trooped along the ice-glazed streets and store windows glowed with elegant Christmas displays.

The night air was crisp and cold, and Kimberly determined that for the next few hours she'd get lost in the dizzying, light-hearted spirit of Christmas shopping and leave her worries behind.

She glanced over her shoulder twice, just to make sure no one was following her, then she ducked into a department store and headed straight for the toy department.

Tonight she'd find the perfect gift for Lindsay and maybe something special for Jake, as well.

Jake. Thank God he was on her side.

# CHAPTER ELEVEN

Ben Kesler's smile said it all: smug, self-confident and pleased with himself. Dressed in an expensive wool suit, he leaned back in his desk chair and tented his hands under the beginning of a double chin. A Rolex peaked from beneath his starched white cuff, while diamonds glittered in his tight clasp and cufflinks. Yep, Ben had money and he wore it, Jake thought, eyeing the attorney with distaste.

His hair was thick and blond, trimmed neatly, his skin copper brown and his eyes a watery shade of blue. He looked as if he worked with weights and spent his extra hours inside a tanning booth.

Jake didn't mince words. "You said you wanted to work out a deal."

"That's right. On the Fisher case."

Jake crossed his arms over his chest and waited. He noticed the mirrored bar recessed behind teak doors. The thick gray carpet, the coiled paneling and various objects of art placed strategically around the room on the twenty-eighth floor. The office smelled of interior design, and Jake's lips twisted at the thought of his tiny office in West Linn.

Ben leaned forward. "I don't have to tell you that Mr. Fisher wants custody of his daughter very badly. He's willing to go to great lengths to have her with him."

"What lengths?"

"Five hundred thousand dollars."

Jake raised an eyebrow. "Half a million dollars? He wants to *buy* custody?"

Ben sat up and grinned even wider. "Mr. Fisher knows that Ms. Bennett has had to struggle. Working long hours, hiring an elderly woman as a babysitter to make ends meet. He thinks now that he should have been fairer with her during the divorce." Kesler drummed his ringed fingers. "He's willing to make it up to her."

"As I understand it, he didn't want custody then."

"He's changed his mind." Ben lifted a palm, and his eyes grew sharp. "You know how it is, Jake. During a divorce emotions run high, tempers flare—sometimes the best or most equitable decisions are passed by."

"So I've heard," Jake mentioned dryly as a secretary, tall and dark-haired with a trim figure and green eyes, stepped into the room. Quietly she left a tray of coffee on the corner of Kesler's desk.

"Anything else?" she asked, glancing quickly at Jake before turning back to Kesler.

"Not now." He waved her away, and she slid obediently out of the room. Jake half expected her to bow in the doorway. He felt sick.

"Anyway," Kesler continued, offering Jake a cup and picking up a mug with his initials engraved on it, "Fisher thinks he was hasty. He wants Kimberly to have all of the creature comforts she was used to when she was married to him."

"In exchange for custody."

Ben smiled as if to say, "What could be fairer?"

"She won't go for it."

"You don't know—"

"I know."

"But half a million dollars is nothing to sneeze at."

"Neither is a child." Jake got to his feet, looking down his nose at Kesler. The man, and his Rolex and gold rings, was pathetic. How had he ever been jealous of him?

"Robert Fisher isn't used to taking no for an answer," Ben reminded.

"Maybe it's time he got used to it." Jake started for the door, and Kesler sighed heavily.

"Fisher will up the ante."

"No dice."

"But—"

"I'll see you in court, Kesler." Jake strode through the door and let it slam shut behind him. As he did, he heard Ben swear loudly—a stream of expletives that would have made a truck driver blush. Maybe Kesler wasn't so bad after all. With a smile Jake sauntered down the hallway, nodded to the dark-haired secretary and took the elevator to the first floor. It felt good to get under Kesler's skin. Damn good. Now, if only he could best him at his own game.

On the first floor he zipped up his jacket and walked outside. The city was ablaze with light, the sky was black and the wind, whistling down from the Columbia River Gorge, was bitterly cold. Ice glazed the streets. Patches of snow, piled against the curb from the plow, contrasted with the black asphalt.

Jake's Bronco was parked two streets over. He stopped beneath the street lamp to pull on a pair of gloves when he noticed a silver Mercedes idling at the curb.

Robert Fisher climbed out of the back seat, straightened the lapels of his black overcoat and, head bent against the wind, started for the building.

Jake's diaphragm tightened. He didn't breathe for a minute as the man snaked his way through the revolving doors. It was hard to imagine Robert Fisher as Kimberly's husband . . . her lover.

And now he was trying to buy Lindsay.

Jake stretched his gloves over his fingers and walked briskly to his Bronco. Obviously Fisher didn't understand Kimberly at all, or he wouldn't have made his ridiculous offer. Half a million dollars for a child, was he kidding?

Climbing into the cool interior of his Bronco, he thought of Sam. No amount of money could replace him. Nor could it buy Fisher custody of Kimberly's daughter.

He jammed his key into the ignition, and the Bronco's cold engine sputtered twice, finally firing on the third try. Shoving the truck into gear, he guided it through the thick evening traffic and turned south. He started for Sellwood, but changed his mind and headed home.

With a cold sense of certainty, Jake knew Fisher was beginning to panic. And there was a good chance he would try to bolt—with Lindsay. Gritting his teeth, Jake suffered through the traffic delays and finally, nearly half an hour later, pulled into the driveway of his house in Lake Oswego.

With Lupus on his heels, he raced into the house, packed a bag and set his plan into motion by calling Ron Koski. Then, whistling to the dog, he headed back outside. "You've got a job to do," he said as Lupus bounded into the passenger side of the Bronco. He scratched the white shepherd behind the ears. "Be on your toes tonight, okay?"

The dog whined and pricked his ears forward.

Jaw set, Jake backed out of the drive. Tonight or tomorrow or whenever Fisher decided to stray, Jake intended to beat him at his own game.

Kimberly wheeled around the corner of her street and noticed Jake's Bronco parked at the curb near the house. Despite her long day at work and fighting the Christmas shopping crowd, she smiled as she pulled into the driveway.

Stashing her packages—a small bike, two games, a book

and a stuffed animal—in the garage beneath an old blanket, she tried to keep her heartbeat under control.

She hurried inside and found Jake, Arlene and Lindsay diligently packing cookies into tins. The kitchen was covered with cooling racks and cookies shaped like trees, dusted with sugar or decorated with green frosting and red cinnamon candies.

"Hi, mommy," Lindsay said, looking up from her work. She and Jake were struggling with a red bow on a round tin decorated with a reprint of a Currier and Ives Yuletide lithograph.

"We don't already have enough cookies? Or do we need another twenty dozen?" Kimberly deadpanned.

"These are for all Lyle's relatives," Arlene explained.

Kimberly surveyed the kitchen slowly. "He must have an incredible family tree."

"Oh, we give them to friends, too. And there's always the church bazaar in the nursing home."

"And a few left over?" Kimberly teased.

"Just a few," Arlene admitted, her eyes twinkling.

"Arlene says we can keep some!" Lindsay shouted excitedly.

"But not many. What was it—ten, or twelve dozen?" Jake asked, giving up on the bow and straightening. He grabbed Kimberly's hand and squeezed it.

"Very funny," Arlene remarked, but she chuckled. "You three just run along, and I'll finish up here."

"Run along?"

Lindsay tied the bow, but it slipped off the tin. She gave up and trotted over to her mother. "They're singing Christmas songs—"

"Carols," Arlene corrected.

"—carols in the park. Jake said he'd take us."

"When?"

Jake glanced at his watch. "Ten minutes ago. We were just about to give up on you."

Kimberly grinned. "So, what're we waiting for?" She

helped Lindsay into her coat, boots and mittens, and prodded Arlene into joining them, but Arlene would have none of it.

"I'm too busy here. Besides, I don't want to go out and freeze my tail off just to hear some kids singin'. Now, go on—it'll just take me a few minutes to finish up."

Lindsay bounded for the front door and opened it. Lupus, waiting patiently outside, started to run in, but Jake caught him on the porch and snapped a leash on his collar.

Kimberly eyed the dog. "The whole family, eh?"

"It's almost Christmas," Jake explained. "I didn't want to leave him alone." He smiled, but his eyes didn't warm as they usually did, and for the first time, Kimberly noticed a small duffel bag in the corner of the porch. Jake's duffel bag. He intended to spend the night. One part of her was thrilled, until she saw again the wariness in his eyes. "Come on, we're late."

They hustled across the street to the park. Lindsay, holding hands with both of them, skipped as she hurried along the snow-crusted path. Lupus strained against the leash, sniffing the ground and leading the way.

Evergreens, their branches drooping from the weight of the snow, flanked the walkway. Soft light from street lamps glistened against the white snow, and a few flakes fell from the sky. The sound of Christmas carols drifted through the trees, growing louder as Kimberly, Jake and Lindsay approached a clearing near the pond. "*God rest ye merry gentlemen, let nothing ye dismay . . .*"

The carolers, fourth-graders from a local church, sang from the risers placed near the lake. A crowd had gathered nearby.

"I can't see," Lindsay said, frustrated by the tall people in front of her.

"We can take care of that." Jake handed Kimberly the leash, then swung the little girl onto his shoulders, giving her a birds-eye view of the singers. "How's that?" he asked.

She held his head for dear life. Her mittened fingers clutched his hair. "It's good," she said, enthralled.

Kimberly's heart felt as if it had lodged permanently in her throat. Jake, the man who never wanted any more children, who wouldn't let himself get that emotionally strapped again, and Lindsay, a child whose father considered her an imposition, something to own—together they were laughing and as happy as if they were father and daughter.

*Stop it*, she told herself, angry at the romantic turn of her thoughts. How could she even project to a future that was so uncertain?

Jake brushed a snowflake from her nose, and her heart twisted.

We all belong together, she thought. Jake closed his fingers over her hand. He stared at her, and she wondered if he could read her mind. Did he know that she imagined them a perfect little family, without the problems of their past, with the future as silver lined as the moon-washed snow?

How ridiculous. But the vision wouldn't fade.

"*Hark the herald angels sing . . .*"

Lindsay giggled. "That's what Lyle calls me," she said. "An angel."

Jake, his left hand wrapped firmly around both of Lindsay's ankles, winked at Kimberly. "Is that so? Where are your halo and wings?"

"Tell him they're at the cleaners," Kimberly put in.

"That's silly!" Lindsay laughed gaily, and Kimberly thought she couldn't be happier. Snuggled close to Jake, listening to the sounds of Christmas music punctuated by Lindsay's childish giggles, she felt the magic of the season and the wonder of this one very special man.

"*Silver bells. Silver bells. It's Christmastime in the city . . .*"

Lupus's ears pricked forward. Restless, he pulled on the leash and walked behind her. "Come here," Kimberly whispered, but the white dog padded back and forth, sniffing the air, his eyes trained on the thicket of trees that divided one edge of the park from the noise and traffic of the street.

"I see a car like Daddy's," Lindsay proclaimed from her perch. She stretched a chubby arm toward the street.

Kimberly tried not to panic. "It's probably just one that looks like his."

Shaking her head, Lindsay said, "I don't think so."

Jake's lips compressed, and his eyes narrowed as he stared over the heads in front of him, looking in the direction of Lindsay's outstretched arm, her eyes squinting against the darkness and falling flakes.

Kimberly's chest constricted. "Is it—"

"I don't see anything," he said.

Lupus whined, tugging on the leash.

"He must smell a squirrel," Kimberly said, trying to push all thoughts of Robert aside.

"Or a rat." Jake, too, was watching the dog. His fingers tightened around Lindsay's ankles.

The carolers broke into "We Wish You a Merry Christmas" and ended the program. Jake helped Lindsay to the ground, but didn't let go of her hand.

Kimberly shivered, but not from the cold. A chill settled in her bones. There was something Jake wasn't telling her, something he'd learned today, something about the custody hearing. . . . Something that wasn't good. That's why he'd shown up with Lupus and his overnight bag.

As the crowd splintered in different directions, Jake, Kimberly and Lindsay trudged to the house. Inside, Lindsay demanded hot chocolate and popcorn, which they devoured along with several of Arlene's sugar-dusted cookies.

"Okay, kiddo, it's time for bed," Kimberly said, wiping the colored sugar crystals from Lindsay's cheek.

"Not yet." Lindsay protested loudly, but Kimberly managed to carry her upstairs, bathe her, read her a story and turn out the lights by nine-fifteen. "I love you, Mommy," Lindsay whispered as Kimberly kissed her cheek.

"I love you, too, sweetheart."

When Lindsay nestled deep between the covers, Kimberly padded quietly downstairs. She found Jake in the living room, staring out the front window. He snapped the blinds shut on all the windows as she reached the bottom step.

"There's something you should know," she said, taking a seat on the arm of the over-stuffed couch. "I think Bill Zealander, a man I work with, is involved with Robert."

Jake's jaw clenched. He leaned his back against the fireplace. "Go on."

She explained about her conversation with Zealander and the times she'd seen him with Robert.

Jake's face grew hard, his expression brooding. "Why didn't you tell me you thought you were being watched?"

"Because it sounded so paranoid." She shoved her hair out of her face. "I thought I was being overly sensitive, hysterical about nothing."

"And now?"

"Now I don't know," she admitted.

"Does Bill Zealander drive a white station wagon?"

"I—I don't know."

"I saw a wagon follow you out of the parking lot after Diane's wedding," he said, thinking aloud. "It could've been the same car up on the mountain."

Kimberly felt numb inside.

"Is there anything else?"

"I'm not sure," she admitted with a sigh. "But there's some gossip about Robert at the bank. He's moving money around."

"Where?"

"I don't know, but I'll find out."

"No!" He shoved himself upright and leaned over her, his

face only inches from hers. "I don't think you should take the chance."

"What chance?"

"If Fisher's really going to blow town, he might try to grab Lindsay."

"Blow town?" she repeated, dumbstruck. "You think he's leaving?"

"I don't know." He strode into the bedroom, opened her closet and found her suitcase. He flung it on the bed and snapped it open. "You've got to leave."

"Leave?"

"Yes. I know a place—a beach house of a friend of mine. You and Lindsay'll be safe there."

Her heart chilled and she licked her lips nervously as she found her courage. "Okay, McGowan," she said softly, her hands clutching the bedpost in a death grip, "what happened today?"

Jake leaned one knee on the bed. "I saw Ben Kesler. He seems to think Robert will go to any lengths to get his daughter."

"I already told you that." She eyed him closely, and a cold fear settled in the pit of her stomach. "There's something more, isn't there—something you're not telling me?"

He hesitated.

"Look, we had a deal. Remember? You keep me informed on everything, and I do what you say. So far I've kept my end of the bargain."

He straightened. "I've got a hunch that Fisher's not going to wait around for any court date to try to win his daughter."

She was shaking inside. "Why?"

Raking his fingers through his hair in frustration, he turned and faced her. "Because it's only a matter of time before the police link him to organized crime in Portland."

"I've heard this all before . . ." She started out the bedroom door, but Jake grabbed her arm and spun her around so quickly the breath escaped from her lungs in a gasp.

"I'm serious," he said calmly. "I don't think you should take any chances."

"You've talked to the police?" she said, guessing, her throat so dry it barely worked.

"No, but I know someone who has. And my guess is that Fisher knows what's going down, too." His jaw clenched tight. "I talked to Ben Kesler today. Robert's willing to pay you five hundred thousand dollars for custody."

"*What?!*"

"I told him you weren't interested."

"And?" she whispered.

"He said Fisher would up the ante."

Sick inside, she said, "But that doesn't mean—"

He grabbed hold of her arm. "You just told me he's moving money around. The way I see it, there's a damn good chance he's gonna run. And if he does, my guess is he'll try to take Lindsay." His fingers dug deep into her arm. "He was your husband, Kim. You told me yourself that he'd stop at nothing to get what he wanted, and right now, for God-only-knows-what reason, he wants Lindsay."

She didn't want to believe him, but she saw the earnestness on his features. "What did you mean when you said Robert knows what's going on?"

"That the police are going to bust him."

"You're sure?"

"No." But his eyes were cold and convincing.

She sagged against the bed, and he sat beside her, holding her shoulders, supporting her.

"Now, tell me more about Bill Zealander."

Heart pounding with dread, she told him everything she could think of, including Bill's jealousy over the Juniper account and her friendship with Eric Compton. "And I'm sure he was the man who was following us on the ski slopes that day," she said, rubbing her arms feeling cold to the bone.

"Then you've got to go away."

"You mean hide out, don't you?" she tossed back at him.

"However you want to look at it."

She glanced through the bedroom door and down the hall to the Christmas tree shining brightly in the cozy little room. Tilting her chin up beautifully, she said, "I'm not going to run away," she said, realizing that as many times as she thought of it, she couldn't run, wouldn't hide. She wasn't going to let Robert or any other man force her into being a coward. "Lindsay's my daughter, and unless he goes to court for her, he has no claim—"

"But he might not have the option of waiting around for the courts or his friend Monaghan to make that decision." Jake clenched his teeth together. "Look, you said once you'd do anything to save your child."

"I will."

"And you promised to do things my way."

"But—"

He placed a finger to her lips. "Just listen, will you? Tonight we'll pack, and then tomorrow you'll pretend everything's normal. Head for the bank as usual, have Arlene come over, but take Lindsay with you and go straight through Portland. About the time you should be at the bank, you'll call your boss and tell him you're sick. Then you'll drive to the coast." He reached into the pocket of his jeans and extracted a key. "I'll meet you there later."

"You've got it all worked out, haven't you?" she asked, appalled. Things were moving too quickly. Trying to think, she walked into the living room.

"I hope so."

"But I can't leave. Not without some notice."

His face turned back. "You hired me for one reason—

Lindsay's safety. Right? And even though you've been denying that your ex-husband is involved in organized crime, we both know you're kidding yourself. So, unless you want to take the chance that Robert will take her from you, you'd better face the facts—you'll have to hide out for a while."

"But my job—"

"You've got a choice, Kimberly. The bank or Lindsay. Personally I think First Cascade will stumble along without you for a few days, but what about your daughter? How will she do without a mother?"

"Stop," she hissed. "Lindsay's more important to me than any job—"

"Is she?" he taunted. "Then prove it and do the smart thing."

She plopped down in a rocker and tucked her knees beneath her chin. "I hate to be bossed around."

"I know, but you hired me," he pointed out. "Not the other way around."

He was right and she knew it. But she despised the thought of being manipulated by Robert. And all of Jake's talk about organized crime—she hated to face it. Deep in her heart she knew Robert was involved in something dark and sinister. She couldn't hide her head in the sand and expect to protect herself and Lindsay.

Squeezing her eyes shut, she tried to block out images of dark figures involved in drug deals or worse. . . . Though she'd finally accepted that his business dealings were shady, what Jake seemed so sure of was much more evil than she'd ever believed possible.

She felt Jake's finger under her chin. He lifted her face. "It's going to be all right," he said. "I guarantee it."

Her stomach jerked as he leaned down to kiss her with such warmth and tenderness she thought her heart would break.

"You're sure about this?"

"Positive," he said with conviction. "Now, tomorrow morning we'll pretend everything is normal, okay?"

"Okay," she whispered, but as he lifted her from her feet and carried her back into the bedroom, she had a sinking sensation that her life would never be normal again.

# CHAPTER TWELVE

Click.

Jake stirred, one eye opening. Had he heard something? Quietly, so as not to disturb Kimberly, he rolled out of bed and yanked on his jeans.

From the living room Lupus growled low in his throat.

The warning hairs on the back of Jake's neck stood on end as he moved barefoot through the darkness to the hallway. The floor was cold, the house silent. His ears strained, and his eyes, growing accustomed to the half-light, searched the shadowy house.

Lupus padded up to him, his ears cocked toward the kitchen. He growled again, then started barking wildly.

"Jake?" Kimberly's voice caught his attention, and he turned. From the corner of his eye he saw a movement, darker than the house—the black figure of an intruder.

Jake scrambled for the light switch, but his hand was yanked hard behind him and something crashed down on his head. Lights exploded behind his eyes. Pain ripped through his body. His legs gave way, and he fell to his knees. Think, McGowan, think!

"Jake?"

"Get out of here!" he yelled, but it was too late.

Kimberly found the switch, and the kitchen was flooded with intense blinding white. Her eyes moved from Jake to the intruder, a big burly blond man with a ponytail. "Jake . . . Oh, God!"

Lupus leaped into the air, lunging for the intruder's throat.

"Run!" Jake yelled, and was rewarded with a swift kick that knocked the air from his lungs. "Kimberly, run!" His face crashed against the cold floor. He blinked, trying to keep unconsciousness at bay. The overhead light in the kitchen was blinding, and he couldn't focus. But Lupus had the intruder down, his jaws clamped around the burly, blond man's arm.

"You damn bastard," the man yelled, trying to beat Lupus off. But the shepherd wouldn't let go.

Kimberly ran from the room. He heard her footsteps on the stairs leading to Lindsay's room.

Staggering, Jake jumped on the blond man, and his fist crashed into a stubbled jaw, sending pain jarring up his arm. Bones cracked, and the big man groaned. Jake wouldn't let up. They struggled, each pounding the other.

Breathing hard, Jake found his feet just as Burly did the same.

The man took a swing at Jake and missed, and Lupus attacked again, lunging for the intruder's rubbery legs while Jake connected with a left hook.

"Who the hell are you?" Jake growled, feeling hot, sticky liquid running down his face as the man stumbled backward. Jake curled his fingers around the bigger man's jacket and lifted him back to his feet. "Don't tell me, you're one of Fisher's goons!"

"He's Robert's bodyguard," Kimberly said, returning to

the kitchen with a wide-eyed, frightened Lindsay huddled against her.

Jake's nostrils flared, and he pulled the man closer, meeting him face-to-face. "Call 911," he yelled to Kimberly, though his eyes didn't leave the beefy man. "Talk to Detective Brecken. Tell him to send a squad car on the double."

"Don't bother," a cool voice said from behind his head.

Jake realized with sickening certainty that his worst fear was being realized. Fisher was there, for Lindsay!

"Let him go," Robert commanded.

Jake's fingers tamed the denim clenched between his fingers. He wasn't about to release the man, not yet. He turned and eyed the man who was his sworn enemy. Robert, standing in the doorway, seemed calm, but his eyes were slitted, and the raincoat he'd tossed over his shoulders didn't hide the barrel of a small pistol he was pointing directly at Jake's chest.

"I said, let him go." Fisher repeated.

"Daddy?" Lindsay's small voice asked.

Robert flicked a glance her way and he actually smiled, not the cold, calculating grin that Jake associated with Fisher, but a warm smile. "I'm sorry, honey," he said, adjusting the coat to hide his pistol. "This'll be over in a little while, and we'll go for a ride."

Lindsay clung tightly to her mother. "I don't want a ride."

"Sure you do. That'll be fun." His gaze moved to Kimberly. "Pack her clothes."

"No," Kimberly cried. "Get out of here, Robert, before I call the police! You have no right—"

"Do it, Kim!" he commanded again, momentarily distracted.

Lupus, who had been quelled at Kimberly's feet, sprang. "No!" Jake cried.

Fisher reacted, shooting blindly. The shot blasted through the house, and Lupus's body flinched. The dog yipped pitifully and fell to the floor. Blood stained the shepherd's white coat near his hip.

"You bastard!" Jake dropped the bodyguard and took a step forward, but Robert waved the gun in his face.

"Back off, McGowan."

"No! No!" Lindsay cried, her face twisted as she tried to climb from her mother's arms and reach Lupus.

"Shh, honey, shh," Kimberly whispered.

"Lupus!" Lindsay wailed.

"Let him be," Fisher ordered, forcing Jake away from the dog. His gaze shifted back to Kimberly. "I mean it, Kim. Move it!"

"Daddy, oh, Daddy, you shot Lupus . . . You shot him dead. I hate you!" Lindsay cried, big, fat tears rolling down her cheeks. "I hate you forever!"

Robert's composure cracked a little. Regret darkened his eyes. "I didn't mean to—"

"You're not taking her anywhere," Kimberly said, sounding much stronger than she felt.

His expression turned ugly. "You've got no choice in the matter," he said, his teeth clenching together.

Lindsay buried her face in her mother's neck, and Jake moved slowly, positioning himself between Fisher and Kimberly. He glanced pointedly at the blond man huddled in the corner. Old Ponytail was holding his jaw and breathing hard. Blood oozed from his mouth.

"You'd better find yourself another bodyguard, Fisher," Jake baited. "This one's about dead on his feet."

Lupus whimpered pitifully.

"Hang in there," Jake whispered, his heart twisting, fury firing his blood.

"All those stories are true, aren't they?" Kimberly asked, eyeing the man who had been her husband. Her throat worked, and tears stood in her gorgeous eyes.

Robert didn't bother to answer. He tried to shoulder past

Jake to get to Lindsay, but Jake blocked his path. "It's all over, Fisher," he said, his pulse throbbing in his brain.

Fisher barked out a cruel laugh. "It's not over until I get my daughter. Get out of the way, McGowan."

But Jake didn't budge. He noticed Kimberly inching backward toward the hall. "If I were you, I'd leave now, before the police get here. Someone's bound to have heard the shot, and there just may be people outside waiting for you. People who may have already contacted the cops."

Robert's eyes narrowed. "What do you mean? Who?"

But Jake didn't answer.

Robert motioned to his bodyguard. The burly man stepped forward and reached for Lindsay. Jake attacked, hitting the man squarely in the midsection as the front door burst open.

"Hold it! Police!" A harsh male voice boomed through the house.

Robert whirled, heading for the back door, but another policeman was on the back porch. His gun aimed at Robert's chest. "Don't even think about it," he warned.

Robert dropped his gun, and Kimberly, still clutching Lindsay, fell into Jake's arms. A few minutes later Detective Brecken appeared. With a grin at Jake he snapped handcuffs on Robert and instructed the younger policeman to read Fisher his rights. But Fisher wasn't finished. He glared at Jake, and his gaze oozed pure hatred. "I'm not talking until I speak with my lawyer," he clipped, then his eyes turned to Kimberly. "You know, Kim, you don't have a very good track record of taking lovers. Your boy here—" he motioned to Jake "—isn't interested in you as much as he wanted to get at me."

"Shut up, Fisher," Brecken warned.

But Robert was picking up speed. "He's only involved with you because he's on some wild-goose chase, a vendetta for his brother. He's got the crazy notion I was involved in his death. Well, I wasn't. The man did himself in. And as for caring for you, get real. McGowan's a loner. Only cares about himself and, of course, vengeance. Daniel Stevens killed himself, McGowan. Face it."

"Can it, Fisher," the younger policeman said.

Kimberly sagged against the wall and held her daughter close. Her heart was thudding in her brain. Robert's wild accusations didn't make any sense.

But it was over. Thank God, it was over.

Her arms tightened around Lindsay, and she fought back the urge to break into tears of relief.

"You okay?" Jake asked, touching her on the arm. His warmth filled her with an inner strength, and she nodded weakly, still using the wall for support.

Jake snatched a clean dish towel and bent over Lupus as Ron Koski sauntered in. "I'm glad you called," Koski said. "Even if it did mean freezing my tail off."

"Thanks," Jake replied, "I owe you one."

"Make it a draught."

Jake nodded, his face white beneath his tan as he tended Lupus's wound.

Kimberly glanced from Ron to Jake, who was trying to stem the flow of blood from Lupus's midsection.

"This is my friend, the private investigator," Jake muttered, wincing as the dog whimpered. "Ron Koski—Kimberly Bennett and Lindsay. Ron staked out the place and had told the police what he was doing. He alerted Detective Brecken the minute Fisher pulled up."

Kimberly was stunned. So that's how the police had arrived so quickly. Jake had known Robert would show up?

"Will Lupus be all right?" Lindsay whispered.

Kimberly's heart stuck in her throat. "I hope so, honey."

Ron leaned over the dog. "I'll take this old boy to the vet," he offered. "You take care of the ladies."

"We'll be okay," Kimberly said, seeing the pain in Jake's

eyes, the emotions he was trying to keep at bay. Her own eyes filled with tears, and rage burned deep inside.

She looked at the man who had been her husband and felt sick. "Don't you ever, *ever* come into my house again," she said through clenched teeth. "And stay away from my daughter!"

"She's my daughter, too," Robert reminded her.

Lindsay shook her head and cried. Kimberly carried her into the living room, away from the bleeding dog and the sight of her father being led, swearing and cuffed, to the squad car outside.

Still holding her daughter, Kimberly dropped into a rocker, barely listening to the sounds of voices and feet shuffling in the kitchen. She switched on the Christmas tree and stared at the light, singing softly to her child, hoping the nightmare would go away. But Lindsay continued to sob, crying for Lupus.

Kimberly didn't even hear Jake approach. "We both have to go down to the station," he said softly.

She glanced up, seeing his bloodied face and loving him. "I know."

Detective Brecken entered the room. "It's just a formality."

"And my daughter?" Kimberly finally asked.

"She's been through enough tonight," Brecken replied. "If you have some place she'd be comfortable . . ."

Kimberly nodded. "I'll only be a minute."

"No!" Lindsay wailed. "Please, mommy, don't leave me."

"Oh, I won't, precious." Kimberly said, her throat tight. She looked at Jake and swallowed hard. "She'll come with us," she said firmly. "I'll call Arlene and ask her to go with us."

"Good idea."

Kimberly reached for the phone.

It wasn't until they were in the police station, giving their accounts of Robert's kidnap attempt on Lindsay, that Kimberly started piecing all the facts together. And she didn't like the conclusions she was drawing.

She and Jake had finished giving their statements and were drinking bitter coffee from white cups. Detective Brecken had told them to go home for the night.

"Who was Daniel Stevens?" she asked as she crumpled her cup and threw it in the trash.

Jake's jaw hardened. His grey eyes grew cold. "When we get home," he said, "and Lindsay's asleep—we'll talk. I have a lot to explain."

Kimberly's stomach twisted painfully, and she barely heard anything Arlene or Lindsay said all the way back to Sellwood. They dropped Arlene off, then returned to the house. Shivering, Kimberly carried Lindsay inside.

Jake dialed the emergency veterinarian clinic for a report on Lupus, and Kimberly carried Lindsay upstairs to her bed. "No!" Lindsay whispered, refusing to let go of her mother's neck as Kimberly tried to lay her down. "Mommy, please, can I sleep with you?"

Kimberly smiled sadly. "Of course you can, sweetheart." She wished she'd thought of it herself. Lindsay had just gotten over her nightmares, and now she'd witnessed her father shooting a favorite pet, threatening her mother and then being handcuffed and taken away in a police car. Lindsay would need time and patience to understand everything that had happened tonight. And so, Kimberly thought, would she.

"Come on, we'll take your blanket and Sebastian." She scooped up Lindsay's pink elephant and wrapped the faded blanket around Lindsay's shoulders.

Downstairs Jake had cleaned up the kitchen, but his face was grim and set. He watched as she carried Lindsay into the bedroom.

"You sleep now, too," Lindsay whispered as Kimberly settled her into the bed.

"Of course I will," Kimberly said. "It's late and I'm tired."

That was a lie. She was so keyed up, she couldn't imagine falling asleep. A thousand unanswered questions raced through her mind. How had Robert got in? Why had he come this night? How had Jake known? What did Robert's crazy comment about Jake's brother mean? Jake didn't have a brother—or did he?

Confused, she snapped off the light and climbed into bed beside her daughter. Lindsay instinctively cuddled closer. Kimberly knew she'd never sleep; she heard Jake in the kitchen, talking on the phone in a low voice, cleaning up, trying to be quiet and failing.

She stared out the window, watching snowflakes fall against the panes. Lindsay's breathing evened out, and Kimberly forced her eyes closed. In the morning, she thought, finally drifting off. In the morning Jake will explain everything, and it will be all right. She'd never have to worry about losing Lindsay again.

Jake hung up and shoved his hair from his eyes. He felt the matted blood on his scalp and wondered if he should have had the wound looked at. Hell, what did it matter? He was alive, wasn't he? Fisher was behind bars. Lindsay was safely with her mother for the rest of her life.

Lupus, unfortunately, wasn't doing too well. The bullet had ripped through his flank and done some internal damage. The vet had performed surgery, but it would be touch and go for a little while.

He poured himself a cup of coffee and stared unseeingly through the kitchen window to the black night beyond. Robert Fisher was finally where he should be. So, why didn't Jake feel an intense satisfaction, a lifting of the weight that had been on his shoulders for years?

He glanced to the short hallway in the bedroom beyond.

Now he'd have to tell her everything and admit that he'd lied, and, yes, in the beginning, used her.

And there was Lindsay to think about, a child, for Pete's sake. A child he cared about, a child he was willing to claim as his own.

And the dog—whether he wanted to face it or not—Lupus might not make it.

*Damn Robert Fisher and damn this whole mess!*

He finished his coffee, threw the dregs down the sink and snapped out the lights. Snatching an old quilt from the back of the couch, he headed toward Kimberly's bedroom and cracked the door quietly open.

The scene before his eyes tore at his soul. Kimberly and Lindsay, close together, their faces washed by pale light filtering through the window, were both asleep. Their expressions were calm and peaceful. Outside, the snow was falling again, promising a white Christmas, and the house was silent except for the soft ticking of a clock in the living room.

He sat in the rocker near the corner and stared at the two people he'd come to think of as his family. At least they were his for a little longer. Until Kimberly discovered the truth. He wrapped a blanket around him and waited.


Kimberly's head pounded. She had to force her eyes open against the gray light of dawn. A warm lump cuddled close to her, and she instinctively touched Lindsay's tangled crown.

Yawning, she noticed Jake seated in the rocker near the foot of the bed. His eyes, a little bloodshot, were open and staring at her. His hair had been freshly washed; beads of water still shown in his dark strands. He hadn't bothered shaving, and the dark shadow of his beard added to his innate sexuality. She smiled because she loved him so much.

At the sight of her, his lips parted in a smile and despite his injuries, he was beautiful. God, how she'd love to wake up to his cocky, irreverent smile every morning.

"Been up long?" she asked, pulling on her robe.

"About an hour."

"Short night," she observed, cinching the belt.

"Long enough."

Lindsay stirred, and they walked from the bedroom to the kitchen. Fresh coffee had already brewed, and the kitchen was clean, all evidence of the night before washed away. "How's Lupus?" she asked as she poured them each a cup.

"Still hanging in there."

She noticed the signs of strain, the lines around his mouth and eyes. "I'm sorry."

His jaw clenched, and he swallowed hard. "So am I." He kicked out a chair from the kitchen table and cocked his head toward it. "Sit down," he said. "There's something I've got to tell you."

His voice was low, his gaze short. It wasn't over yet, Kimberly realized with a sickening sense of dread. She wrapped her fingers around her cup for warmth and dropped into the chair.

"First of all, you were right about Bill Zealander. I called Brecken at the police department, and he had already picked him up. Zealander was new to Fisher's organization, but he was in it up to his button-down collar. He was unhappy at the bank, felt he'd been passed over time and time again in favor of you. When Fisher approached him, he was ready."

Her hands were shaking, and she swallowed hard. "Jesus Christ," she whispered.

"That last account Compton gave you—"

"The Juniper trust."

"Right. That was the last straw."

Setting her cup on the table, Kimberly licked her lips. She sensed this was just the start, that there was much more to come. She wasn't sure she wanted to hear it.

"It looks like Zealander lifted your keys and had a duplicate set made."

"When?"

"I don't know. But probably while you were out of your office or something. Do you keep your purse locked?"

"No, it's usually in my desk drawer. He had plenty of opportunity, I suppose." She shivered and rubbed her arms.

"Bill Zealander seemed to think you were the single reason he wasn't advancing in the trust department. Fisher not only provided him with more money than he'd ever be able to earn at the bank, but he'd also given him an opportunity to get back at you."

Kimberly tried to sort it all out. "But why didn't Robert wait until the custody hearing? He might have persuaded Monaghan to give him Lindsay. Why risk a kidnap attempt?"

"There wasn't enough time. The police were on to him. He found out that he was being set up and he panicked." Jake smiled coldly. "And he even had his escape route planned—with Kesler's plane."

"In Mulino?"

"Right. No one would think of him flying out of there, especially using Ben's name."

She blew her hair from her eyes. This was all too much to absorb, but she wanted to know everything. Raising her eyes to meet his, she asked, "And what about you, Jake? How do you fit into this?"

"You came to me, remember?" His eyes slid away from hers.

"But there's more."

"Daniel Stevens was my half brother."

She braced herself, but her insides began to turn. Hadn't Robert said as much? Her chest constricted, and she had trouble breathing as she realized that Jake had lied to her . . . used her. And she loved him, Lord, how she loved him. But at the dawning realization that he had never cared for her, had only agreed to be her attorney to get back at Robert, she dropped her cup. Hot tea sloshed across the table. She didn't bother wiping it up. It didn't matter—nothing did. Jake, her precious Jake, was, in his own way, as bad as Robert. She closed her eyes, squeezing them shut against the truth.

"When I saw the opportunity to go after Fisher. I couldn't resist."

"So, that's what all the questions were about—why you wanted to know about his business," she asked, dread giving way to anger. How could she have been so stupid—so fooled by his easy seduction?

"Partially," he admitted, reaching for her hand. She pulled back. "But I wanted to help you, too."

"Help me, or hurt Robert?" she snapped, her eyes flying open. She was unable to stop the tide of rage roiling through her. "Is that why you slept with me?" she asked, her cheeks flaming, her throat so tight she could barely speak.

"No—"

"Did you want to know what it was like to bed Robert Fisher's ex-wife?"

"Don't be ridiculous."

"Am I?" She scraped her chair back and walked to the far side of the tiny kitchen. Ugly thoughts crept into her mind. "Was it Bill Zealander who was following me?"

"Yes."

"And what about Ron Koski? Isn't he a friend of yours— a private investigator? He was lurking about the house last night, wasn't he? That's why he showed up here so quickly."

"I thought we needed backup."

"And what about before?" she demanded, then felt the blood drain from her face. "You had *me* spied upon, didn't you? You were investigating *me*, weren't you—trying to find out if I was involved in any of Robert's business deals."

"No—"

"Oh, God, Jake, don't tell me you had Ron watching me, checking into my personal life!" Her insides churned, her entire life turned inside out. She'd trusted him, loved him and he'd repaid her by using her.

Jake's jaw grew rock hard. "I was trying to help you."

She shook her head. "That wasn't it. It was your need for vengeance, wasn't it? You know, I thought I should've known your name, but I never connected it with Daniel Stevens until now. I saw your name in the newspaper account of his death—as the surviving relative!" She felt as if she might throw up.

"And that's why you seduced me," she concluded, tears burning the backs of her eyes. "To get back at Robert by getting close to me and digging up anything you could on him. Well, I hope you had a good time, Jake, because it's over. I hope to high heaven that your investigator 'friend' didn't take any pictures of you and me in a compromising position."

"Enough," he bellowed, crossing the kitchen and placing strong, possessive fingers around her shoulders.

"What's wrong?" she went on, her emotions raw. "Have I offended your delicate sensibilities?"

He actually shook her. His fingers dug into her shoulders, and he gave her two hard shakes. "I love you," he vowed, his face twisted and pained.

"Love?" she repeated, nearly laughing hysterically. "You don't know the meaning of the word."

"I know that I was willing to try with you. To take you and your daughter as part of my family. To try all over again."

She wrestled free of his painful grip. "Why? To salve your guilty conscience? Well, don't bother!"

"We're good together."

"'We' never existed. It was all a lie, McGowan. Your lie!"

"That's not the way it was," he thundered, his eyes flashing. He placed warm hands on her cheeks and tilted her face upward. "Look at me, Kimberly," he commanded, his eyes drilling into hers. "Look at me, dammit!"

She forced her eyes to his and saw the agony deep in his

soul. "You should be proud of yourself," she whispered sarcastically. "All you had to do was dance with me, buy me dinner, take me to bed—and I told you everything you wanted to know, to help you set-up my ex-husband."

"And you're sorry?"

"About Robert? No." She shook her head and swallowed against the hot dryness in her throat. "I'm sorry for you and me and all the lies . . . all the bullshit."

"Are you finished?"

"Just about." She braced herself, ripping away from his grip, ignoring the pain shadowing his eyes and finally forcing the words past her tongue. "I think you should be, Jake," she said softly, bleakly. "Send me a bill for your services, and get the hell out of my life."

"I can't do that."

"Sure you can—it's easy. Just walk out the door."

"And what about Lindsay?"

"She'll survive," Kimberly predicted sadly. "Besides, I would never want her to know that all the affection you showed for her was a lie.

"I never lied to Lindsay."

Kimberly forced a brittle smile. "You lied to her every time you walked through that door and pretended she was special. The guinea pig, placing her on your shoulders, making snowmen with her—those were all lies, because they led her to believe that you thought of her as a daughter, or at the very least a special niece—when you and I both know you'll never be tied down to a child again, that you don't have room or time in your life for the pain and vulnerability a child can bring. Now, before you hurt me or my child any more, please leave."

Jake growled an oath and started for the door as the phone rang. Kimberly reached for the receiver automatically, and someone asked for Jake. She handed him the phone without really caring who it was. She felt dead inside—beaten down by a love so vital and now gone.

He took the call quietly, not saying much. When he replaced the receiver, he sighed. "Lupus didn't make it," he muttered, then walked out the back door.

Kimberly's knees gave out, and she slid to the floor. Tears welled in her eyes. Tears for a failed marriage, for a love affair based on lies and for a brave white dog who gave up his life for her and her child. She dropped her head into her knees and felt the soft threads of her terry robe brush her cheek and absorb her tears.

She knew she should be pulling herself together, but she couldn't stop sobbing uncontrollably. Lindsay would be up soon and Arlene would be here, and then back to the bank—as if nothing had happened? Pick up the pieces and go on? Without Jake?

She had to forget him, but would it ever be possible? She sat huddled on the kitchen floor for several minutes until she forced the sobs back.

The front door opened, and Arlene's voice sounded through the house. "Kimberly?"

"In here," she sniffed, struggling to her feet and brushing away any lingering traces of her tears.

Arlene, newspaper tucked under her arm, entered the kitchen. She took one look at Kimberly and wrapped her thin arms around her. "I know, I know," she whispered, patting Kimberly's shoulder. "Now, you sit down and tell me all about it while I make some tea."

As Arlene fussed around the kitchen, Kimberly haltingly admitted that she'd thrown Jake out.

"But why?" Arlene asked as if Kimberly were out of her mind.

Battling tears, Kimberly told Arlene the entire story.

"And you think he betrayed you?" Arlene asked, dunking teabags into two cups of steaming water.

"Betrayed, lied, deceived. You name it, he did it."

"But I've seen the way he looks at you, how he acts around Lindsay. Kimberly, that man's in love with you."

Kimberly let out a bitter laugh. "Sure he is." She sipped from her cup and burned the tip of her tongue. "That's why he was spying on me, and using me."

"You're twisting this all around."

"No, Arlene," she said sadly, "for once I'm seeing things all too clearly."

"Well, if I were you, I'd hightail it out of here and run after him. Find him, admit you were wrong and that you love him and never intend to let him go."

"Arlene, that's crazy."

"It's the soundest advice you'll ever get."

Lindsay, her battered blanket in tow, stumbled into the room. "Mommy?" she whispered, climbing into Kimberly's lap. "You been crying?"

"I'm just tired, sweetheart."

"Where's Jake?" She glanced around the room.

"He had to leave, honey."

"Did he go get Lupus?" Lindsay asked, yawning. From the corner of her eye Kimberly saw Arlene's lips tighten.

Kimberly's chest constricted. She couldn't tell Lindsay about the dog, not yet. But Arlene's eyes pinned her, and she said, "Lupus is in heaven, honey."

Lindsay started to cry, but Kimberly assured her that the white shepherd was happy now. "Come on, let's get you some breakfast, okay?"

"'Kay," Lindsay mumbled, her face red.

"I'll do this," Arlene said, reaching for the instant oatmeal and a bowl.

"Good, I should get ready."

"For work?" The older woman looked stricken. "Today?"

"It's a work day, isn't it?"

"Yes, but you should take some time off."

"I can't."

"Well, think about it. Work won't be easy—you made the front page." Arlene spread the newspaper on the counter, and Kimberly cringed. A huge, grainy picture of Robert dominated the top half of the front page. She skimmed the story, seeing her name and Lindsay's interspersed in the article.

It was a wonder reporters hadn't started calling. "I'll call in today," she said, deciding that her place was here, with Lindsay. "I'll turn the ringer off, too."

"Good idea," Arlene agreed as she stirred oatmeal into hot water. "And we can all go down to my place. That way we won't be bothered."

Kimberly offered the older woman a grateful smile. "I'd appreciate it. Thanks, Arlene. You're a godsend."

"I wish," Arlene said. "Now, go on, get dressed. I'll take care of Lindsay."

Kimberly didn't argue. She walked to the bathroom, stripped out of her robe and nightgown, then twisted on the faucets.

As she stepped under the hot jets of water, she tried to pull herself together. She couldn't let Robert, Jake, the newspaper or the police determine the course of her life. And she couldn't sit around the house moping for Jake and a love that had never existed. No, today she'd take the day off, take Lindsay Christmas shopping and have her daughter's picture taken with Santa. Once things had settled down, she'd get back to business as usual. And somehow she'd forget Jake McGowan had ever existed.

If she could.

# CHAPTER THIRTEEN

Two days later the bank was still a madhouse, the cafeteria buzzing with gossip. Kimberly answered most questions put to her in a very matter-of-fact and straightforward manner. And she tried to ignore the speculative glances cast her way by interested bank employees.

"You were right about Robert," Marcie said, dropping a stack of mail onto the corner of Kimberly's desk. "Heather said he was moving money out of the bank so fast she could barely keep up."

"I thought so," Kimberly replied, managing a wan smile though she found the entire subject depressing.

"And Bill! Can you believe he was involved?" Marcie threw her hands into the air and shook her head. "I thought he was a real nose-to-the-grindstone type."

"I guess we all make judgment errors," she said, thinking of Jake as she had for the past four hours. Why couldn't she stop dwelling on him? It was barely eleven, and she couldn't wait to make tracks home. She'd already been grilled by Eric Compton and Aaron Thornburn, who in turn had been interrogated by the police, FBI, and an auditor from the FDIC, who'd called for a special audit of the bank's books to check for money laundering and all sorts of other crimes involving one of the bank's wealthiest customers.

"Henry Juniper's coming in today," Marcie said.

"Wonderful," Kimberly muttered cynically. The day was getting better and better.

"Oh, and Mrs. Pendergraft called to thank you for the flowers the bank sent her a few weeks ago. She said they were 'gorgeous.'"

The first good news of the day. "Anything else?"

Marcie nodded. "Jake McGowan called again."

"I don't want to talk to him."

"I know. But I thought I should tell you."

Jake. Why couldn't he just take "no" for an answer?

Two hours later Henry Juniper was seated on the other side of her desk, worrying the brim of his hat in his hands, blowing off steam and, in general, not listening to any kind of reason.

Marcie buzzed in. "Ms. Juniper is here," she called.

Henry's face went white. "Carole's here?"

"I asked her to stop by."

"With that snake of an attorney of hers—that Kesler fellow?" Henry demanded, his voice rising an octave.

"I don't think so." The paper had reported that Ben was having a few problems of his own—all because of his association with Robert Fisher.

Marcie led Carole into the room, and the middle-aged woman took the only available chair next to her brother. They glanced at each other once, then stared stonily ahead at Kimberly.

"I'm glad you're here, Carole," Kimberly said, picking up the document file on the Juniper estate. "I wanted to go over the terms of your father's will again, so that each of you see exactly what is in the estate and what share you are entitled to."

Henry's head was bobbing up and down.

Carole's lips pursed.

Kimberly started reading and silently hoped she could find a way to settle the mess between brother and sister without the problem of a lawsuit.

By the time she finished reading, Henry and Carole were exchanging glances. A few minutes later they argued a few points, but eventually agreed to let the bank handle all the bills of the estate, including reasonable bills presented by Carole for her father's care during his convalescence.

"I guess she's entitled to something for all her time," Henry grumbled, stuffing a hat on his head and saying, "I'll see you after the New Year."

"Thanks, Kim," Carole said, "and Merry Christmas."

"Same to you," Kimberly replied. She glanced at the calendar and felt a pang of regret. Soon it would be Christmas Day. And she and Lindsay would spend it alone.


She didn't see Jake again until Christmas Eve. She and Lindsay were drinking hot chocolate, eating popcorn and listening to Christmas carols while the guinea pig exercised on his wheel, the metal cage clicking in time to the song.

"Can't we open just one present now?" Lindsay begged, her gaze on the little tree.

"Santa doesn't come until later."

"I know, but there's some presents under the tree already."

That there were. Half a dozen brightly wrapped packages skirted the Douglas fir.

"Besides," Lindsay prodded, climbing into Kimberly's lap, "I want you to open my package."

"And I want to wait until tomorrow morning."

"Please . . ."

"Okay," Kimberly replied, not having the heart to disappoint her.

Lindsay retrieved the huge package, and Kimberly pulled

off the paper. Inside was a large birdhouse made from scraps of lumber nailed together. The house could hold six nests. "Lyle and I made it," Lindsay said proudly.

"And it's beautiful," Kimberly whispered, admiring it. "You're quite a carpenter."

"I know," Lindsay replied solemnly.

"Thank you very much." She kissed Lindsay's crown.

"Now, can I open one?"

Kimberly sighed. "Just one."

Lindsay hurled herself back under the tree, found a package and tore open a holiday puzzle. "I like it! I do! I do!" She beamed at her mother. "Now, your turn again."

"Oh, no."

"Just one more."

"I can't. Really."

Lindsay nodded. "Open Jake's!"

"Jake's?" Kimberly's insides turned cold. "There isn't a present from Jake."

"Oh, yes, there is!" Lindsay said, scrambling off Kimberly's lap and reaching into the thick branches of the Christmas tree. She hunted a while and withdrew a small box wrapped in silver foil.

"When did this get here?"

Lindsay shrugged. "A long time ago."

"How long?"

"When we heard the singers in the park," Lindsay said, forcing it into her hands.

Kimberly's chest constricted. She didn't want to think about Jake—nor about his present. "I don't think I should open it."

"It's okay. He told me that it had to be a secret until Christmas Eve. And that's now!"

"So it is," Kimberly said, fingering the card while her heart pounded. She opened the envelope, and her throat constricted with tears. "To Kimberly, a woman who has brought happiness and light to my life. I'll love you forever. This was my mother's. No one has ever worn it since she gave it to me."

"Oh, no," she whispered, remembering all the ugly words she'd said. Taking in a deep breath, she untied the small red ribbon and split open the foil. The shiny paper gave way to a tiny jewelry box, and as Kimberly lifted the lid, she felt tears building behind her eyes. There, on a faded cushion of red velvet, was an antique ring. A diamond sparkled brightly in the box.

"Oooh!" Lindsay cried. "It's *beautiful*."

"That it is," Kimberly admitted, feeling awful. Had she judged Jake too harshly? If he'd left the ring before the ordeal with Robert, didn't that mean that he loved her? She had to find out. Stuffing the ring and box in her pocket, she jumped to her feet.

"Come on, Lindsay, we've got work to do."

"But I want to open a present—"

"When we get home." Kimberly found her daughter's coat, boots, mittens and hat. Then, retrieving her coat, she herded Lindsay out the door.

"Where're we going?" Lindsay asked.

"You'll see." Kimberly strapped Lindsay into her car seat, then slid behind the wheel. Tonight, she decided, she'd have it out with Jake. Once and for all. She'd crawl back on her hands and knees to find out if he'd really meant it when he'd said that he loved her. If so, she'd be the happiest woman on the earth. If not . . . She shuddered.

She wheeled into the parking lot of her favorite mall and smiled when she saw that the store was still open. "Come on, Lindsay. You're going to enjoy this. I guarantee it."

Jake whirled his drink, glanced in the mirror and growled, "Merry Christmas," at his reflection. He'd spent the better part of the week trying to forget it was Christmas, that he'd hoped to marry Kimberly Bennett and that his life was empty. He'd failed on every count. Losing Lupus had hurt horribly; losing Kimberly had been a deathblow.

He threw the remains of his drink in the fire, snagged his leather jacket off the back of his couch and started for the door. He was going to have it out with her once and for all. And this time, dammit, he'd force her to believe just how much he loved her.

The doorbell chimed, and he swore. He wasn't in the mood for carolers, shining faces or Christmas cheer. Scowling, he yanked open the door and there, standing in the middle of the porch, was Lindsay, her blue eyes shining, her hair in two lopsided pigtails. She was carrying a box that was nearly as big as she was.

"Merry Christmas!" she sang out.

Jake's heart lurched almost painfully. "Hi!" he said, filled with wonder that this little girl could burrow so deep in his soul.

"Hi."

"Come in, come in." He stood outside of the door, letting her pass. "Your mom with you?"

"Mm-hmm." She set the box on the floor in front of the fire, and Jake was sure it moved, but his attention was diverted when Kimberly, dressed in her familiar black coat, swept into the room.

"Merry Christmas," she said breezily, her eyes deep with mischief, her mahogany-colored hair swirling behind her in a tangled red-brown cloud.

"Well, I guess we saved you a trip." She swung her coat off, and Lindsay giggled, not for a minute leaving the huge box.

To his surprise Kimberly sauntered up, wrapped her arms around his neck and kissed him long and hard.

Jake couldn't help but respond. He wrapped his arms

around her waist. "I'd like to ask you what's going on, but I'm afraid to disturb the fantasy."

Winking broadly, she plucked a sprig of mistletoe from her pocket. "This guy I know convinced me that mistletoe didn't need to be hung."

"A wise man," Jake drawled.

"And I wanted to thank you for my Christmas present."

He grinned, then glanced over to Lindsay. "I thought I said Christmas morning."

"I couldn't wait," Lindsay said.

"And neither could I." Kimberly slid out of his arms and tugged on his hand. "Lindsay and I went shopping tonight . . . for you. And we hope you like what we got. We had trouble deciding on the color."

Jake eyed the box suspiciously. "You want me to open it now?"

"Yes."

"Maybe we should wait 'til morning."

Kimberly laughed merrily. "Oh, I don't think that would be such a good idea."

"All right," he agreed, untying the big green bow and lifting the lid. As he did, an excited yip escaped, and a bright-eyed black puppy leaped up and washed his face with its long pink tongue.

"Hey, slow down," Jake cried, but the pup, a lab-shepherd mix, Jake guessed, jumped on him ecstatically.

Lindsay clapped in joy. "He's perfect, isn't he?"

"Perfect," Jake agreed, smiling as the puppy made three mad dashes around the room and finally landed on Lindsay's belly. The little girl screamed and laughed, her giggles rising to the ceiling. "In fact I think we'll name him that."

"What—Perfect?" Kimberly asked.

Lindsay shook her head. "I like Snowball better."

"But he's black," Kimberly said, laughing.

"Doesn't matter," Lindsay argued.

Jake grinned, staring at Kimberly. Her blue-green eyes were bright, and as she stood near the fireplace, she seemed to fill his house with a warmth and happiness that had been missing for a long, long time. God, how he loved her. It was frightening, yet caused his spirits to soar.

Winking seductively at him, she cocked her head toward the backyard and turned to her daughter. "Come on, Lindsay, let's see if Perfect or Snowball or Perfect Snowball needs to go outside." She helped her daughter back into her coat, mittens and boots.

Jake opened the back door, and the puppy shot through, straining against the leash and pulling Lindsay outside. Jake and Kimberly followed.

The night was quiet. The ghost of a moon dusted the snow-covered ground with the pale light, and beyond the yard the dark waters of the lake lapped quietly. Kimberly took hold of his hand. "I guess I owe you an apology," she said, taking in a deep breath. "I said awful things to you."

"You were upset."

"And I was wrong." Tilting her chin up, she stared at him with wide eyes. "I love you, Jake. I have for a long time. I came here because I want to marry you."

Jake felt the corners of his lips twist. His heart thudded, and love surged through his veins. "Is this a proposal?"

"Oh, yes," she said, her breath misting in the cold winter air. She took his face between her mittened hands and pressed a gentle kiss to his lips.

Jake's lips twisted cynically. "You know, I think maybe I should be asking."

"So, ask already," she teased.

"Will you marry me?"

"Only if we can have a Christmas wedding."

"But that's—"

"Tomorrow."

"You think you can find a preacher on such short notice?"

Kimberly giggled. "It just so happens that Arlene has connections with a little church. The preacher is a personal friend of hers. I bet I could get her to twist his arm. The only problem will be Diane. She'll kill us both if we get married while she's not around."

"I guess that's just a chance we'll have to take," Jake said, wrapping his arms around her and kissing her long and hard.

Lindsay and the puppy dashed by, powdery snow flying, giggles and sharp barking filling the clear night air.

"I love you," Jake whispered against her hair, "and if you think I'm waiting until tomorrow to start the honeymoon, guess again."

Kimberly tossed back her hair. Her expression turned impish as she reached into her pocket. "No reason to wait," she said, holding up the sprig of mistletoe. "As far as I'm concerned, tonight is the first night of our life together."

"Then let's make it count."

"I'm all yours, counselor."

"And I'm yours. Forever."

"I don't think that's going to be long enough," she teased, and was rewarded with a kiss that promised her a lifetime of love. In the distance, from across the lake, she heard the sound of Christmas bells ringing, sending clear notes into the wintry air as Jake lifted her off her feet and carried her back inside their home.

# DOUBLE EXPOSURE

# PROLOGUE

*Taylor's Crossing, Oregon*

The wipers slapped the snow away and the windshield fogged with the cold, but Melanie Walker barely noticed. She drove by rote, unseeing as the miles from the clinic downtown slipped beneath the old truck's tires.

One of her favorite songs was playing on the radio, fighting a losing war with static, but she didn't concentrate on the melody. She couldn't. Her mind wouldn't focus on anything but Gavin and the last time she'd seen him, three weeks before.

His naked body had been the only heat in the hayloft, and his legs and arms had been entwined with hers. The smell of musty hay and animals had filled the air.

"Wait for me, Melanie," he'd whispered against the curve of her neck. His breath had been as warm as a summer wind, his tawny eyes seductive in the half-light of the barn. "Say you'll wait for me."

"You know I will," she had foolishly vowed, unaware that fate was against her. At the time she'd known only that she loved him with all of her young heart. And that was all that mattered.

Until today.

She swallowed a hard lump in her throat and shoved the gearshift into third. Her rendezvous with Gavin had taken place three weeks ago and she hadn't seen him since. And now, all their plans and her entire future had changed.

As she drove through the snow-packed roads, she forced her wobbling chin up and clamped hard on her teeth. She wasn't going to cry, no matter what.

Gavin was over a thousand miles away, chasing a dream, and she was alone in a small Oregon town—two months pregnant.

Her hands clenched over the wheel as she struggled with the right words to explain to her father that she was carrying Gavin Doel's child.

Snowflakes drifted from a gray sky and melted against the windshield as the pickup rumbled along the slippery highway. To the west, the town of Taylor's Crossing nearly bordered Walker land. To the east, fields and pine forest covered the foothills of the Cascades.

Melanie snapped off the radio and glanced into the rear-view mirror. Worried hazel eyes stared back at her.

Pregnant. Unmarried. And seventeen. Even in the cold, her hands began to sweat.

The fact that her father had let Melanie see Gavin had been a miracle. He despised Gavin's father, and heaven only knew why he'd allowed Melanie to go out with "that kid from the wrong side of town," the boy who had the misfortune of being Jim Doel's son.

"Help me," she whispered, feeling entirely alone and knowing she had no option but to tell her father the truth.

*If only Gavin were still here,* she thought selfishly, then whispered to herself, "You can handle this, Melanie. You have to!"

She shifted down and turned into the short lane near the house. The truck slid to a halt.

All Melanie's newfound convictions died on her tongue when she saw her father, axe propped over one shoulder, trudging through the snow toward the barn. The pup, Sassafras, bounded at his heels.

Hearing the rumble of the pickup's engine, Adam Walker turned and grinned. He yanked his baseball cap from his head and tipped it her way, exposing his receding hairline to the elements.

Melanie's mouth went dry. She cut the engine, pocketed the keys and sent up a silent prayer for strength. As she opened the truck's door, a blast of chill winter wind swirled inside. "It's now or never," she told herself, and wished she could choose never.

Stuffing her hands into the pockets of her fleece-lined jacket, she plowed through a blanket of snow. Four inches of powder covered the frozen ground of the small ranch—the ranch that had been her home for as long as she could remember. Though the town of Taylor's Crossing was steadily encroaching, her father had refused to sell—even after his wife's death.

Melanie shivered from the vague memory of losing her mother—and the sorry reasons behind Brenda Walker's death. Her father still held Jim Doel responsible.

Oh, Lord, why did it seem that her entire life had been tangled up with the Doels?

"I'd about given up on you." Her father squared his favorite old Dodgers cap back onto his head, then brushed the snow from the shoulders of his jean jacket.

Melanie wanted to die.

"Go into the house and warm up some coffee. I'll be

back as soon as I feed the stock and split a little kindling."
Whistling, he turned and started for the barn.

"Dad?" Her voice sounded tiny.

"Yeah?"

"I'm going to have a baby."

Time seemed to stand still. The wind, raw with the breath
of winter, soughed through the pines and cut through her
suede jacket. Her father stopped dead in his tracks and turned
to face her again. His jaw dropped, and denial crept over his
strong features.

"You're pregnant?" he whispered.

Nodding, Melanie wrapped her arms around her middle.
"No!"

She shifted from one foot to the other and tried to ignore
the sudden bow in her father's shoulders. All expression left
his face, and he looked older than his forty-seven years. His
throat worked and his brown gaze drilled into hers. "Doel?"
he asked in a voice barely audible over the wind.

She nodded, listening to the painful drum of her heart.

His face turned white. "Oh—Mellie."

"Dad—"

"That black-hearted son of a bitch!" he suddenly growled,
wincing as if physically wounded. The small lines around his
mouth turned white.

Melanie didn't have to be reminded of the hatred that still
simmered between the two families. And she hadn't meant to
fall in love with Jim Doel's son. But Gavin, with his warm
eyes, enigmatic smile, lean, athletic body and razor-sharp wit,
had been irresistible. She'd fallen head-over-heels in love with
him. And she'd thought, foolishly perhaps, that the love they
shared would bridge the painful gap between their families—
the gap that had been created by that horrible accident.

"You're sure about this?" her father whispered, his gloved
fingers opening and closing over the smooth wood of the
axe handle.

"I saw the doctor this afternoon."

"Jesus Christ!" Adam's teeth clenched. He took up the axe and swung it hard into the gnarly bark of a huge ponderosa pine. "He's just like his old man!" An angry flush crept up his neck, and he muttered an oath under his breath. Kicking the toe of his boot into the base of the tree, he grappled with his rage. "I should never have let you see him—never have listened to that stupid brother of mine!" he raged. "But your damned uncle convinced me that if I'd forbidden it, you'd have started sneaking behind my back!"

"Dad, I love Gavin—"

"Love? *Love!* You're only seventeen!" he bellowed, placing both hands on the fence. He breathed deeply, as he always did when he tried to regain his composure. His breath fogged in the air. "I don't have to tell you about the pain Jim Doel has caused this family." His face twisted in agony, and he leaned heavily against the tree.

"I—I know."

"He's a bastard, Mellie, a drunken, useless—" His voice cracked.

"Gavin's not like his father!"

"Cut from the same cloth."

"No—I mean, Dad, I *love* him. I—I want to marry him."

"Oh, God." Setting his jaw, he said more quietly, "And Gavin—how does he feel?"

"He loves me, too."

Snorting, Adam Walker ran a shaky hand over his lip. "He only loves one thing, Melanie, and that's skiing. Downhill racing's his ticket out of Taylor's Crossing and believe me, he's going to use it to stay away."

Melanie's heart wrenched. Some of what her father was saying was true—she'd told herself that the death-defying runs down the face of a rugged mountain were and always would be Gavin's first love, his mistress—but she didn't want to believe it.

Her father glanced through the trees to the snow-laden mountains in the distance. Absently he rubbed his chest. "I guess I can't really blame him on that one."

"But, when he gets back from Colorado . . ." she protested as the wind tossed her hair in front of her face.

"He won't be coming back. He's gonna make the Olympic team." Her father's gaze returned to hers. The sadness in his eyes was so profound it cut to her soul. "Sweet Mary, you're just a child."

"I'm—"

"Seventeen, for God's sake!" His breath whistled through his teeth.

"It doesn't matter."

"Life hasn't begun at seventeen." He reached into the pocket of his work shirt for his cigarettes, then swore when he discovered the pack was missing. He'd quit smoking nearly three years before.

Walking on numb legs, Melanie crossed the yard and propped her elbows on the top rail of the fence. Through the pines she could see the spiny ridge of the Cascade Mountains. The highest peak, Mount Prosperity, loomed over the valley.

Her father's throat worked as he followed her. He touched her gently on the shoulder. "Doc Thompson at the clinic, he can—"

"No!" she cried, pounding her fist against the weathered top rail. "I'm having this baby!" She turned, appalled that he would suggest anything so vile. "This is *my* child," she said, tossing her black hair from her eyes. "My child and Gavin's, and I'm going to keep him and raise him and love him!"

"And where does Gavin figure into all this? Does he know?"

She shook her head. "Not yet. I just found out this afternoon."

Adam Walker looked suddenly tired. He said softly, "He may not want it, you know."

"He does!" Her fists clenched so hard that her hands ached.

"He might consider a wife and baby extra baggage."

She'd thought of that, of course. And it worried her. Gavin, if his dreams were realized and he made the Olympic team, might not be back for months. Unless he felt duty bound to give up everything he'd worked for and return to support a teenage wife and child. Nervously, she chewed on the inside of her lip.

"What do you think he'll do when he finds out?"

"Come back here," she said weakly.

"And give up skiing?"

Though she felt like crying, she nodded.

He sighed loudly. "And that's what you want?"

"No. Yes! Oh, Dad, yes!" She threw up her hands. How could anything so wonderful as Gavin's child make life so complicated? She loved Gavin, he loved her, and they would have a baby. It was simple, wasn't it? Deep in her heart, she knew she was wrong, but she didn't want to face the truth.

"You want the man you love to give up a huge part of his life, something his world revolves around?" her father asked, bringing to light some of Melanie's immaturity.

She felt her father's hand on her shoulder. "I'll see you through this, Melanie. You just tell me what you want."

Melanie smiled, though her eyes burned with tears. "I want Gavin," she said.

Her father's hand stiffened, and when she glanced up at him, she saw that his face had turned ashen. He measured his words carefully. "You didn't plan this, did you?"

"Plan what?" she asked before she realized the turn of his thoughts. She felt the color drain from her face. "No!"

"Some women work out these things ahead of time—"

"No!" She shook her head. "The baby was an accident. *A glorious, wonderful accident!*

"Good." He pressed his lips together. "'Cause no man wants to feel trapped."

"I—I know," she whispered.

He touched her chin with a gloved finger, and his expression became tender. "You've got a lot going for you. Finish high school and go to college. Become a photographer like you wanted—or anything else. You can do it. With or without Gavin."

"Can I?" she asked.

"'Course you can. And Gavin's not the only fish in the sea, you know. Neil Brooks is still interested."

Melanie was horrified. "Dad, I'm pregnant! This is for real!"

"Some men don't mind raising another man's child and some men don't even know they've done it."

"What's that supposed to mean?" she demanded, but a sick feeling grew inside her as she grasped his meaning.

"Only that you're not out of options."

She thought about Neil Brooks, a boy her father approved of. At twenty-two, he was already through college and working full-time in his father's lumber brokerage. Neil Brooks came from the right side of the tracks. Gavin Doel didn't.

"I'm not going to lie to Neil," she said.

"Of course you're not," her father agreed, but his eyes narrowed just a fraction. "Go on now, you go into the house and change. I'll take you into town and we'll celebrate."

"Celebrate what?" she asked.

He rolled his eyes to the cloud-covered heavens. "I suppose the fact that I'm going to be a grandfather, though I'll have you know I'm *much* too young." He was trying to cheer her up—she knew that—but she still saw pain flicker in his eyes. She'd wounded him more than he'd ever admit.

Gritting his teeth and flexing his muscles, he walked back to the ancient pine and wiggled the axe blade free, leaving a fresh, ugly gash in the rough bark.

He headed for the barn with Sassafras on his heels again. But he was no longer whistling.

Melanie shoved her hands into her pockets and trudged into the old log house that had been in her family for three generations. Inside, the kitchen was warm and cheery, a fire burning in the wood stove. She rubbed her hands near the stovetop, but deep inside she was cold—as cold as the winter wind that ripped through the valley.

She knew what she had to do, of course. Her father was right. And, in her heart, she'd come to the same agonizing conclusion. She couldn't burden Gavin with a wife and child—not now. *Not ever,* a voice inside her head nagged.

Climbing the stairs to her room, she decided that she would never stand between Gavin and his dream. He'd found a way to unshackle himself from a life of poverty and the ridicule of being the town drunk's son. And she wouldn't stop him. She couldn't. She loved him too much.

On his way to Olympic stardom as a downhill skier, Gavin couldn't be tied down to a wife and child. Though he might gladly give up skiing to support her and the baby, one day he would resent them both. Unconsciously, Melanie rubbed her flat abdomen with her free hand. She smiled sadly. If nothing else, she'd have a special part of Gavin forever.

Her pine-paneled room was filled with pictures of Gavin— snapshots she'd taken whenever they were together. Slowly, looking lovingly at each photograph of his laughing gold-colored eyes, strong jaw and wind-tossed blond hair, she removed every memento that reminded her of Gavin.

She closed her eyes and, once again, remembered the last time she'd seen him. His tanned skin had been smooth and supple beneath her fingers. His pervasive male scent had mingled with the fragrance of hay in the loft.

"Wait for me," he'd whispered. He had cupped her face in

his hands, pressed warm kisses to her eyelids, touched a part of her no other man would ever find.

She remembered, too, how he had traced the slope of her jaw with one long finger, then pressed hard, urgent lips to hers. "Say you'll wait for me."

"You know I will," she'd vowed, her fingers tangling in his thick blond hair, her cheeks, wet from tears, pressed to his.

His smile had slashed white in the darkened hayloft. "I'll always love you, Melanie," he'd sworn as he'd kissed her and settled his hard, sensual body over hers.

*And I'll love you,* she thought now, as she found a pen and paper and began the letter that would set him free.

# CHAPTER ONE

*Taylor's Crossing, Oregon*
*Eight Years Later*

Flags snapped in the breeze. Barkers chanted from their booths. An old merry-go-round resplendent with glistening painted stallions pumped blue diesel smoke and music into the clear mountain air. Children laughed and scampered through the trampled dry grass of Broadacres Fairgrounds.

Long hair flying behind her, Melanie hurried between the hastily assembled tents to the rodeo grounds of the annual fair. She ducked between paddocks until she spied her Uncle Bart, who was holding tight to a lead rope. On the other end was the apple of his eye and the pride of this year's fair—a feisty Appaloosa colt appropriately named Big Money.

Whip thin and pushing sixty, Bart strained to keep the lead rope taut. His skin had become leathery with age, his hair snow-white, but Melanie remembered him as a younger man, before her father's death, when Bart had been Adam Walker's best friend as well as his older brother.

"Thought you might have forgotten us," Bart muttered

out of the corner of his mouth. His eyes were trained on the obstinate colt.

"Me?" She looked up and offered him a smile. "Forget you? Nah!" Opening her camera bag, she pulled out her Canon EOS and removed the lens cap. "I just got caught up taking pictures of the fortune teller and weight lifter." Her eyes twinkling, she glanced up at Bart and wrinkled her nose. "If you ask me, Mr. Muscle hasn't got a thing on you."

"That's what all the ladies say," he teased back.

"I bet. So this is your star?" She motioned to the fidgeting Appaloosa.

"In the flesh."

Melanie concentrated as she gazed through the lens of her camera. *Okay,* she thought, focusing on the horse, *don't move.* But the prizewinning colt, a mean-spirited creature who knew he was the crowning glory of the fair, tossed his head and snorted menacingly.

Melanie smothered a grin. She snapped off three quick shots as the horse reared suddenly, tearing the lead rope from Bart's grip.

"You blasted hellion," Bart muttered.

Melanie clicked off several more pictures of the colt prancing, nostrils flared, gray coat catching the late afternoon sunlight.

"You devil," Bart muttered, advancing on the wild-eyed Big Money, who, snorting, wheeled and bolted to the far side of the paddock. "You know you're something', don't ya?"

The horse pawed the dry ground, and his white-speckled rump shifted as Bart advanced. "Now, calm down. Melanie here just wants to take a few pictures for the *Tribune.*"

"It's all right," Melanie called. "I've got all I need."

"You sure?" He grabbed the lead rope and pulled hard. The colt, eyes blazing mischievously, followed reluctantly behind.

"Mmm-hmm. In next week's edition. This is the twenty-second annual fair. It's big news at the *Trib,*" Melanie teased.

"And here I thought all the news was the reopening of Ridge Lodge," Bart observed. "And Gavin Doel's broken leg."

Melanie stiffened. "Not *all* the news," she replied quickly. She didn't want to think about Gavin, nor the fact that a skiing accident may have ended his career prematurely, bringing about his return to Taylor's Crossing.

Uncle Bart wound the rope around the top rail of the fence and slipped through the gate after Melanie. "You been up to the lodge lately?"

Melanie slid him a glance and hid the fact that her lips tightened a little. "It's still closed."

"But not for long." Bart reached into his breast pocket for his pack of cigarettes. "I figured since you were with the paper and all, you'd have some inside information."

"Nothing official," she said, somehow managing to keep her composure. "But the rumors are flying."

"They always are," Bart agreed, shaking out a cigarette. Big Money pulled on the rope. "And, from what I hear, Doel thinks he can pull it off—turn the ski resort into a profit-making operation."

Melanie's heart skipped a beat. "That's the latest," she agreed.

"Gavin tell you that himself?" he asked, lighting up and blowing out a thin stream of smoke.

"I haven't seen Gavin in years."

"Maybe it's time you did."

"I don't think so," Melanie replied, replacing the lens cap and fitting the camera back into its case.

Bart reached forward and touched her arm. "You know, Mellie, when your dad died, all the bad blood between Gavin's family and ours dried up. Maybe it's time you buried the past."

*Oh, I've done that,* she thought sadly, but said, "Meaning?"

"Go see Gavin," he suggested.

"Why?"

"You and he were close once. I remember seeing you up at

the lodge together." He slanted her a sly glance. "Some fires are tough to put out."

*Amen!* "I'm a grown woman, Bart. I'm twenty-five and have a B.A., work for the *Trib* and even moonlight on the side. What would be the point?"

He studied her through the curling smoke of his cigarette. "You could square things up with Jim Doel. Whether your dad ever believed it or not, Jim paid his dues."

Melanie didn't want to think about Jim Doel or the fact that the man had suffered, just as she had, for that horrid night so long ago. Though she'd been only seven at the time, she remembered that night as vividly as any in her life—the night Jim Doel had lost control of his car, the night she'd lost her mother forever.

"As for Gavin," Uncle Bart went on, "he's back and unmarried. Seeing him again might do you a world of good."

Melanie shot him a suspicious glance. "A world of good?" she repeated. "I didn't know I was hurting so bad."

Bart chuckled.

"Believe it or not, I've got everything I want."

"Do you?"

"Yes."

"What about a husband and a house full of kids?"

She felt the color drain from her face. Somehow, she managed a thin smile. She still couldn't think about children without an incredible pain. "I had a husband."

"Not the right one."

"Could be that they're all the same."

"Don't tell your Aunt Lila that."

"Okay, so you're different."

Bart scratched his head. "Everyone is, and you're too smart not to know it. Comparing Neil Brooks to Gavin Doel is like matching up a mule to a thoroughbred."

Despite the constriction in her throat Melanie had to laugh. "Don't tell Neil," she warned.

"I don't even talk to the man—not even when he shows up here. Thank God, it's not too often. But it's a shame you didn't have a passel of kids."

Her insides were shaking by now. "It didn't work out," she said, refusing to admit that she and Neil could never have children, though they'd tried—at least at first. She and Neil had remained childless, and maybe, considering how things had turned out, it had been for the best. But still she grieved for the one child she'd conceived and lost.

Clearing her throat, she caught her uncle staring at her. "I—I guess it's a good thing we never had any children. Especially since the marriage didn't work." The lie still hurt. She would have loved children—especially Gavin's child.

Uncle Bart scowled. "Brooks is and always was a number-one bastard."

Melanie didn't want to dwell on her ex-husband, nor the reasons she'd married him.

"But Gavin," Bart continued, "he was never as good on paper, but no one can deny his passion."

With that, Melanie felt that the conversation was heading back in the wrong direction. With a sigh, she said, "Look, Bart, I really can make my own decisions."

"If you say so." He didn't seem the least bit convinced.

She said, "Not many people in town know or remember that Gavin and I had ever dated. I'd like to keep it that way."

"Don't see why—"

She touched his arm. "Please."

Deep furrows lined his brow as he dropped his cigarette and ground it out under the heel of his scruffy boot. "You know I can keep a secret when I have to."

"Good," she said, deciding to change the subject as quickly as possible. "Now, if you want to see Big Money's picture in the *Tribune* next week, I've got to run. Give Lila my love." With a wave she was off, trudging back through the dry grass, ignoring the noise and excitement of the carnival as she headed toward her battered old Volkswagen, determined not to think about Gavin Doel again for the rest of the day.


Unfortunately, Gavin was the hottest gossip the town of Taylor's Crossing had experienced in years.

Back at the newspaper office, Melanie pulled up the pictures on her desktop and was and had just procured a fresh cup of coffee when Jan Freemont, a reporter for the paper, slammed the receiver of her phone down and announced, "I got it, folks—the interview of the year!"

Melanie cocked a brow in her direction. "Of the year?"

"Maybe of the decade! Barbara Walters, move over!"

Constance Rava, the society page editor, whose desk was near Melanie's work area, looked up from her word processor. A small woman with short, curly black hair and brown eyes hidden by thick reading glasses, she studied Jan dubiously. "What've you got?"

"An interview with Gavin Doel!"

Melanie nearly choked on her coffee. She leaned her hips against her cluttered desk and hoped she didn't look as apoplectic as she felt.

"Get out of here!" Constance exclaimed.

"That's right!" Jan said, tossing her strawberry blond hair away from her face and grinning ear to ear. "He hasn't granted an interview in years—and it's going to happen tomorrow morning!"

Every face in the small room turned toward Jan's desk.

"So he's really here—in Oregon?" asked Guy Reardon, a curly-haired stringer and part-time movie critic for the paper.

"Yes indeedy." Jan leaned back in her chair, basking in her yet-to-be-fulfilled glory.

"Why didn't we know about it until now?"

"You know Doel," Constance put in. She rolled her eyes

expressively. "He's become one of those Hollywood types who demand their privacy."

Melanie had to bite her tongue to keep from saying something she'd probably regret. Her hands trembled as she set down her cup. Gavin had always created a sensation, probably always would. She'd have to get used to it. And she'd have to forget that there had ever been anything between them.

But the fact that he was back—*here*—caused her heart to thump crazily. Not that it mattered, she told herself. What Gavin did with his life was his business. Period. Except, of course, when it came to news. And though she was loath to admit it, Gavin Doel was news—big news—in Taylor's Crossing. The epitome of "local boy does good."

Sidestepping the tightly packed desks in the newsroom, Jan threaded her way to Melanie's work area. "Can you believe it?"

"Hard to, isn't it?" she murmured, wishing the subject of Gavin Doel would just go away.

"Oh, come on. This is big, Mel. A real coup!"

"I know. But we've heard this all before. Someone's always going to reopen the resort."

"This is a done deal."

Melanie's heart sank. She'd hoped that, once again, the rumors surrounding Ridge Lodge were nothing more than idle speculation—at least as far as Gavin was concerned. Melanie welcomed the thought of the lodge opening, but why did Gavin have to be involved?

Jan wrinkled her nose thoughtfully. "I just got off the phone with Doel's partner, what's his name—" she glanced at her notes "—Rich Johanson. He said Doel would meet me tomorrow at nine at the main lodge!" Opening her hands in front of her, she added dramatically, "I can see it now, a full-page spread on the lodge, interviews with Gavin Doel and maybe a series of articles about the man, his personal and professional life—"

"Don't you think you're pushing things a bit?" Melanie cut in a little desperately. Few people had been with the paper long enough to know about her romance with Gavin, and she intended to keep it that way. "Constance just told us how private he is—"

"But he'll need the publicity if the ski lodge is to reopen for the season. And we all know how Brian feels about this story—he can't wait!"

Brian Michaels was the editor-in-chief of the paper.

"He'll want to run with this one. Now," Jan said, chewing on her lower lip, "we'll need background information and photos. Then, tomorrow, when we're at the lodge—"

*"We're?"* Melanie repeated, reaching for her Garfield coffee cup again. She took a sip of lukewarm coffee as her heart kicked into double time.

"Yes—us," Jan replied as if Melanie had developed some sort of hearing problem. "You and me. I need you for the shoot."

This was too much. Despite her professionalism, Melanie wasn't ready to come face-to-face with Gavin. Not after the way they'd parted. He'd asked her to wait for him and she'd vowed that she would. But she hadn't. In fact, within the month she'd married Neil Brooks. "Can't Geri do the shoot?" she asked.

"She starts vacation tomorrow, remember?" Jan shoved a stack of photographs out of the way and plopped onto the corner of Melanie's desk. Crossing her legs, she leaned over Melanie's in-basket. "Don't you want a chance to photograph one of the most gorgeous men in skiing history?"

"No."

"Why not?"

Melanie dodged that one. There wasn't any reason to tell Jan all about her past—a past she'd rather forget. At least not yet. "I've heard he's not too friendly with photographers."

"Too many paparazzi," Jan surmised, waving off the

statement as if it were a bothersome mosquito. "But that's what he gets for going out with all those famous models. It comes with the territory." She leaned closer. "Confidentially, this paper needs the kind of shot in the arm that Gavin Doel's fame and notoriety could give it. I don't have to tell you that the *Trib*'s in a world of hurt."

Guy, who had wandered over from the copy machine, glanced over his shoulder. "Do you think he brought any of his girlfriends back with him? I'd love to meet Gillian Sentra or Aimee LaRoux."

"You and the rest of the male population," Jan replied dryly.

Melanie's heart wrenched, but she ignored the familiar pain.

"I don't think there'll be any women with him," Constance said from her desk. "He hasn't been seen with anyone since he broke his leg in that fall last spring. The way I understand it, he's become a recluse."

"But not a monk, I'll bet," Guy joked. "Doel's always surrounded by gorgeous women. Anyway, Melanie's right—the guy's just not all that friendly with the press. I can't believe he's going along with the interview."

"Well," Jan said, "I didn't actually talk to Doel himself. But Johanson says he'll be there." Jan checked her watch and glowered at the display. "Look, I've got to run. I want to tell Brian about the interview."

"He'll be ecstatic," Melanie predicted sarcastically. Since the rumors had sprung up that Ridge Lodge was reopening, the editor-in-chief had been busy coming up with articles about the lodge—its economic impact on the community, the environmental issues, the fad; that one of the most famous skiers in America had returned to his small home town. Yes, Gavin was big news, and the *Tribune* needed all the big news it could get.

Jan's brown eyes slitted suspiciously. "You know, Melanie,

everyone in Taylor's Crossing's thrilled about this—except for you, maybe."

"I'm all in favor of Ridge reopening," Melanie said, taking another gulp of her coffee and frowning at the bitter taste. She shoved her cup aside, sloshing coffee on some papers scattered across her desk. Sopping the mess with a tissue, she muttered, "Smooth move," under her breath and avoided Jan's curious gaze.

"So what's the problem?" Jan persisted.

"No problem," Melanie lied, tossing the soppy paper towel into her wastebasket. "I just hope that it all works out. It would be a shame if Ridge Lodge reopened only to close again in a year or two."

"No way—not if Doel's behind it! I swear, that man has the Midas touch." Jan slung the strap of her bag over her shoulder just as Brian Michaels shoved open the door to his glassed-in editor's office and made a beeline for her desk. A short, lean man with prematurely gray hair and contacts that tinted his eyes a darker shade of blue, he dodged desks, glowing computers and overflowing wastebaskets on his way toward the photography section.

"You got the Doel interview?" he asked Jan.

"Yep." Jan explained about her conversation with Gavin's partner, and Brian was so pleased he managed a nervous smile.

"Good. Good. We'll do a story in next week's issue, then follow up with articles between now and ski season." Tugging thoughtfully at his tie, he glanced at Melanie. "Dig out any old pictures we have of Doel. Go back ten years or so—when he was on the ski team for the high school, then the Olympic team. And find everything you can on his professional career and personal life. And I mean everything." He swung his gaze back to Jan. "And you talk to the sports page editor, see what he's got on file and double-check with Constance, see if he's up to anything interesting personally. It doesn't really matter if it's now or in the past. Don't forget to rehash the accident where he broke his leg—poor son of a bitch probably lost his career on that run."

For a split second, Melanie thought she saw a glimmer of satisfaction in Brian's tinted eyes. But it quickly disappeared as he continued. "And check into his love life before he left town, that sort of thing."

Melanie's heart turned stone-cold.

"Will do," Jan said, then frowned at Melanie, who was standing stock-still. Jan pursed her lips as she glanced at her watch again. "I've really got to get moving—the park dedication's in less than an hour. I'll meet you up at the lodge tomorrow morning."

*Unless I chicken out,* Melanie thought grimly as Brian and Jan went their separate ways. So she had to face Gavin again. She felt a premonition of disaster but squared her shoulders. The past was ancient history. There wasn't any reason Gavin would drag it up.

Even so, her stomach tightened at the thought. How could she ever explain why she'd left him so suddenly? Why she'd married Neil? Even if she could say all the right words, it was better he never knew.

She wasn't looking forward to tomorrow in the least, she thought grimly. The last person she wanted to see was Gavin Doel.


"I want it off. Today!" Gavin thundered, glaring darkly at the cast surrounding the lower half of his left leg.

"Just another couple of days." Dr. Hodges, who looked barely out of his teens, tented his hands under his chin and shook his head. He sat behind a bleached oak desk in his Portland sports clinic, trying to look fatherly while gently rebuffing Gavin as if he were a recalcitrant child. "If you want to race professionally again—"

"I do."

"Then let's not push it, shall we?"

Gavin clamped his mouth shut. He wanted to scream—to rant and rave—but knew there was no reason. The young sandy-haired doctor knew his business. "I've got work to do."

"The lodge?"

"The lodge," Gavin agreed.

"Even when you get the cast off, you'll have to be careful."

"I'm tired of being careful."

"I know."

Gavin rubbed an impatient hand around his neck. He hated being idle, hated worse the fact that he'd been sidelined from the sport he loved, but at least he had the resort to keep him busy. Though his feelings about returning to Taylor's Crossing were ambivalent, he was committed to making Ridge Resort the premier ski resort in the Pacific Northwest.

"Come back in on Friday. I'll check the X rays again and then, if the fracture has healed, you can go to a walking cast and no crutches. With physical therapy, you should be back on the slopes by December."

"This is September. It's already been over six months."

"That's because you rushed it before," Hodges said with measured patience. "That hairline fracture above your ankle happened during the spring season and you reinjured it early this summer when you wouldn't slow down. So now you have to pay the price."

Gavin didn't need to be reminded. He shoved his hands through his hair in frustration. "Shit," he muttered to himself. Then, more loudly, "Okay, you've made your point."

"Friday, then?"

"Friday." Helping himself up with his crutches, he started for the door. He made his way through the white labyrinthine corridors to the reception area. He passed by posters of the skeletal system, the neurological system, the human eye and heart, but he barely noticed. He was too wrapped up with the fragility of the human ankle—his damned ankle.

And now he had to drive nearly three hundred miles back to Taylor's Crossing, a town he despised. He would have picked any other location in the Cascades for his resort, but Taylor's Crossing, his partner had assured him, was perfect. The price was right, the location ideal. If only Gavin could get over his past and everything the town represented.

*Melanie.*

Uttering an oath at himself, he shouldered open the door and hobbled across the parking lot to his truck. He shoved his crutches inside and climbed behind the wheel. As he flicked on the ignition, he told himself yet again to forget her. She was out of his life—had been for eight or nine years.

She was married to wealth and probably had a couple of kids by now. Scowling, he threw the truck into reverse, then peeled out of the lot. He didn't want to drive back to Taylor's Crossing tonight, would rather stay in Portland until Friday, when the cast had better come off.

Portland held no bittersweet memories for him. Taylor's Crossing was packed with them. Nonetheless, he headed east, back to Mount Prosperity, where so many memories of Melanie still lingered in the shadowy corners of Ridge Lodge.


At five-thirty, Melanie ignored the headache pounding behind her eyes, stuffed her camera into her bag, snagged her jacket from the closet and headed out of the newsroom. The afternoon had flown by and she hadn't had a chance to dig through the files of past issues and dredge up pictures and information on Gavin. She was glad. She'd heard enough about him for one day, been reminded of him more times than she wanted to count, An invisible, bittersweet cloud of nostalgia had been her companion all afternoon. Seeing pictures of him would only intensify those feelings.

She would save the thrilling task of wading through Gavin's award-strewn past for tomorrow.

Tomorrow. She hardly dared think about it. What would she say to Gavin again? What would she do? How could she possibly focus a camera on his handsome features and not feel a pang of regret for a past they hadn't shared, a future they would never face together, a baby who had never been born?

"Stop it," she chastised herself angrily, shoving open the door.

A wall of late summer heat met her as she walked out onto the dusty streets. A few dry leaves skittered between the parking meters lining the sidewalk. Melanie climbed into the sunbaked interior of her old Volkswagen, rolled down the window and headed east, through the heart of town, past a hodgepodge of shops toward the outskirts, where she lived in the log cabin her great-grandfather had built nearly a hundred years before, the home she'd left eight years ago.

She might not have returned except that her father's illness coincided with her divorce. She'd come back then and hadn't bothered to move. There was no reason to—until now. If she could part with the home that was part of her heritage.

The log house had originally been the center of a ranch, but Taylor's Crossing, barely a fork in the road in her great-grandfather's time, had steadily encroached and now street lamps and concrete sidewalks covered what had once been acres of sagebrush and barbed wire. In the past few years there had been big changes in the place. Acre by acre the ranch had been sold, and now the property surrounding the house was little more than two fields and a weathered old barn. The log cabin itself, upgraded over the years, now boasted electricity, central heating, plumbing and a new addition that housed her small photography studio.

She parked her car near the garage, stopped off at the mailbox and winced at the stack of bills tucked inside. "Great," she muttered as Sassafras, her father's collie whom she'd inherited along with the house, barked excitedly. Wiggling, he bounded ahead to the door. "Miss me?" she asked, and the dog swept the back porch with his tail. She petted his head. "Yeah, me too."

Inside, she tossed the mail and camera on the kitchen table, refilled Sassafras's water bowl and poured herself a tall glass of iced tea. Her headache subsided a little, and she glanced out the window to the Cascade Mountains. The craggy peak of Mount Prosperity, whereon Ridge Resort had been built years before, jutted jaggedly against the blue sky. She wondered if Gavin was there now. Did he live at the resort? Was he planning to stay after it opened? Or would he, once his ankle had healed, resume his downhill racing career?

"What does it matter?" she asked herself, her headache returning to pound full force.

Tomorrow she'd get all her answers and more. Tomorrow she'd meet Gavin again. And what in the world could she possibly say to him?

The next morning, as shafts of early sunlight pierced through thick stands of pine, Melanie drove up the series of switchbacks to the ski resort.

A few clouds drifted around the craggy upper slopes of Mount Prosperity, but otherwise the sky was clear, the air crisp with the fading of summer.

Located just below the timberline, Ridge Lodge, a rambling cedar and stone resort that had been built a few years before the Great Depression, rose four stories in some places, with steep gables and dormers. The building had been remodeled several times but still held an early-twentieth-century charm that blended into the cathedral-like mountains of the central Oregon Cascades.

Melanie had always loved the lodge. Its sloped roofs,

massive fireplaces and weathered exterior appealed to her as much today as it had when she was a child. She'd lived in Taylor's Crossing most of her life, except for the six years she'd been married to Neil and resided in Seattle. Ridge Lodge had been an important part of her youth—a special part that had included Gavin.

As she parked her battered old Volkswagen in the empty lot, her pulse fairly leaped, her skin was covered in goose bumps. The thought of seeing Gavin again brought sweat to her palms.

"Don't be a fool," she berated herself, climbing out of the car and grabbing her heavy camera bag. *He's long forgotten you.* Shading her eyes, she looked over the pockmarked parking lot and noted that Jan's sports car wasn't in sight. "Terrific."

She started up the path, noticing the bulldozers and snow-plows standing like silent sentinels near huge sheds. Behind the lodge, ski lifts—black chairs strung together with cables—marched up the bare mountainside.

"It's now or never," she told herself. Keyed up inside, her senses all too aware, Melanie swallowed back any lingering fear of coming face-to-face with Gavin.

She pounded on the front doors, and they creaked open against her fist. "Hello?" she called into the darkened interior.

No one answered.

Hiking her bag higher, she squared her shoulders and strode inside. The main desk was empty, the lodge still, almost creepy. "Hello?" she yelled again, and her voice echoed to the rafters high overhead. Summoning all her courage, she said, "Gavin?"

The sound of his name, from her own voice, seemed strange. Her nerves, already strung tight, stretched to the breaking point. Where was Jan?

Maybe Gavin had changed his mind. Or, more likely, maybe Rich Johanson had spoken out of turn. Probably Gavin wasn't even here. Disgusted, she turned, thinking she'd wait for Jan outside, then stopped, her breath catching in her throat.

Blocking the doorway, crutches wedged under his arms, eyes hidden behind mirrored aviator glasses, Gavin Doel glared at her.

Melanie's heart nearly dropped through the floor. She tried to step forward but couldn't move.

He was more handsome than before, all boyishness long driven from the bladed angles and planes of his face. His expression was frozen, his thin lips tight. The nostrils of his twice-broken nose flared contemptuously at the sight of her.

In those few heart-stopping seconds Melanie felt the urge to run, get away from him as fast as she could. The once-dead atmosphere in the lodge came to life, charged and dangerous.

Gavin shifted on his crutches, his jaw sliding to the side. "Well, *Mrs.* Brooks," he drawled in a cold voice that disintegrated the remnants of her foolish dreams—dreams she hadn't even realized she'd kept until now, "just what the hell are *you* doing here?"

# CHAPTER TWO

Gavin ripped off his sunglasses and impaled her with his icy gaze. "Well?" he demanded, his eyes slitting dangerously. His jaw thrust forward impatiently. Undercurrents of long-dead emotions charged the air.

"I was waiting for you."

"For me?" His mouth tightened. "Well, now, isn't that a switch?"

The words bit.

"You know, Melanie, you were the last person I expected to run into up here." He dug in his crutches and hobbled past her to the bar.

"I was waiting for you because—"

"I don't want to hear it. In fact," he said, glancing over his shoulder, "I don't think we have anything to say to each other."

Melanie was stunned. This cold, bitter man was Gavin—the boy she'd loved so passionately. Where was the tenderness, the kindness, the laughter she remembered so vividly? "Let's just get through this, okay?"

"What? Get through what? Oh, hell, it doesn't matter." He turned his attention to the dusty mirrored bar.

"Of course it matters! I've got a job to do—"

He frowned, his eyes narrowing on her camera case. "A job?"

"Yes—"

"Just get out."

"Pardon me?"

"I said, 'Get out,' Melanie. Leave. I don't want to talk to you."

"But you agreed—"

"Agreed?" he roared, his fist banging the bar. "Unless memory fails me, the last time we agreed to anything, I was going to Colorado and you *agreed to* wait for me."

"Oh, God." This was worse than she'd imagined. "I couldn't—"

"And guess what? The minute I'm out of town, you left me high and dry."

"That's not exactly how it was," she snapped back.

"Oh, no? Then you tell me, how was it?"

"You were in Colorado—"

"Oh, right, I left you. Look, it doesn't matter. It's over. Period. I shouldn't have brought it up. So just go." Swearing under his breath, he propped himself up with his crutches and scrounged around behind the oak and brass bar, searching the lower cupboards.

From her vantage point, Melanie saw his reflection in the dusty full-length mirror. He was wearing cutoff jeans, and the muscles of his thighs, covered with downy gold hair, strained as he leaned over.

"You did leave me," she pointed out, refusing to back down.

"And you said you'd wait. Stupid me, I believed you."

"I meant it."

"Oh, I get it," he said, glaring at her again. "I just didn't put a time limit on the waiting, is that it? I assumed you meant you'd wait more than a few weeks before you eloped with someone else."

The hackles on the back of her neck rose as he turned his attention back to the cupboard. "You don't understand—"

"No, damn it, I don't. I—" he hooked a thumb at his chest "—wasn't there, was I? I didn't have the advantage of seeing you moving in on Brooks."

"I didn't move in on—"

"Okay, so he moved in on you. Doesn't matter."

"Then what're we arguing about?" she demanded, the heat rushing to her cheeks.

He let out his breath slowly, as if trying to control a temper that was rapidly climbing out of control. "What're you doing here, Melanie? I thought you lived in Seattle and probably owned a Mercedes and had a couple of kids by now."

"Sometimes things don't turn out the way you want them to," she said.

He glanced over the top of the bar, his brows pulled together. "Philosophy? Or real life?"

"Both," she replied, holding up her chin. "I'm here with the *Tribune*."

"The what?" he asked without much interest.

"The *Tribune*. You know, the local newspaper."

"Oh, right." He snorted, returning his attention to the contents of the bar. "So you're a reporter these days? What's that got to do with me?"

"I'm a photographer," she replied quickly. "Not a reporter, but I'm supposed to take pictures of you for the interview."

"I don't give interviews."

Melanie's temper began to simmer. "But yesterday your partner said you'd talk to us—"

His head snapped up, and the look he sent her over the bar was positively furious. "Rich said *what?*"

"That you'd grant an interview to the *Trib*—"

"No way!"

"But—"

"Hey, don't argue with me," he bit out. "You, of all people, should understand why I don't talk to the press. It has to do with privacy and the fact that there are some details of my life I'd rather keep to myself."

"Why me 'of all people?'" she flung back at him.

His lips thinned. "As I remember it, there's still some bad blood between our families and a whole closet full of skeletons that are better left locked away."

She couldn't argue with that, but she wanted to. Damn the man, he still had a way of getting under her skin—even if it was only to irritate her. But he did have a point, she thought grudgingly. She didn't want anyone dredging up their affair or the scandal concerning her mother and his father.

"I'll make sure this is strictly professional."

"You can guarantee that?"

"I can try."

"Not good enough. The *Tribune* doesn't have the greatest reputation around."

"I know, but—"

"Then no interview. Period," he growled, rattling glasses until he found a bottle, yanked it out and blew the dust from its label.

"Let's start over."

He didn't move, but his gaze drilled into hers. "Start over," he repeated. "I wish I could. I would've done a whole lotta things differently."

A lump jammed her throat. Her voice, when she found it, was soft. "I—uh, that's not what I meant. I think we should start the interview over."

"Like hell!" Wincing as he straightened his leg, he rained a drop-dead glance her direction.

Her temper flared. "Look, Gavin, I don't want to be here any more than you want me here!"

"Then leave!" He cleaned the bottom of a short glass with the tail of his shirt, then uncapped the bottle.

"I have a job to do."

"Oh, yeah. Pictures for the *Trib*. I forgot." He poured three fingers of whiskey into the glass and tossed back the entire drink, grimacing as the liquor hit the back of his throat.

"A little early, don't ya—"

"I don't need any advice," he cut in. "Especially from you." A sardonic smile twisted his lips, and he leaned across the bar, holding the bottle in one hand. "Excuse my manners," he bit out, obviously intending to bait her. "Would you like to join me?"

Melanie narrowed her eyes, rising to the challenge. Why not? She'd taken all the flak she intended to, so she'd beat him at his own game. "Sure. And make it a double."

A spark of humor flashed in his tawny eyes. "The lady wants a double." He twisted off the cap. "You never did anything halfway, did ya, Mel? All or nothing."

"That's me," she mocked, but her pulse jumped as he looked her way again, and she remembered him as he had been—younger, more boyish, his hard edges not yet formed. He'd always been striking and arrogant and fiercely competitive, but there had been a gentle side to him. A loving side that she'd never quite forgotten. Now it seemed that tenderness was well hidden under layers of cynicism.

She felt a stab of guilt. How could their wonderful love have turned so bitter?

Forcing a smile, she fought the urge to whisper that she was sorry. Instead she took the glass he offered and sipped the fiery liquor. "Ah . . ." she said, remembering the words her grandfather had used when tasting expensive Scotch, "smooth."

"Right . . . smooth," he challenged, his eyes glinting again. "Good ol' rotgut whiskey. I'll give you a clue, Melanie, it's not smooth. In fact it burns like a son of a bitch."

He was right. The whiskey seared a trail down her throat. She pushed her glass aside and met his gaze squarely. "If you say so."

"I do."

"Then that must be the way it is," she replied smartly, wishing he wasn't so damned handsome. If only she didn't notice the way his dark lashes ringed his eyes, the cut of his cheekbones, the dark hair of his forearms. "Now that we've gotten past going for each other's jugular—maybe we can quit sniping at each other long enough to get down to business."

"Which is?"

"The interview. And pictures for it."

His mouth tightened, and he shoved a wayward lock of blond hair from his eyes before taking another long, slow sip from his glass.

Several seconds ticked by, and he didn't move a muscle. The subject of the interview was obviously closed.

"Right. Well, I tried." With the tips of her fingers Melanie nudged her business card across the bar. "In case you change your mind. And when Jan gets here, would you tell her I went back to the office?"

"Who's Jan?"

"The reporter. The one from the *Tribune* who planned to write a stunning article about your lodge. As I pointed out earlier, I'm just the photographer and I don't care whether you want to be photographed or not. But Jan might see things differently. She's under the false impression that you agreed to an interview."

"She's wrong."

"You can tell her." She started for the door and said sarcastically over her shoulder, "Thanks for the drink."

Shoving his crutches forward, Gavin hobbled around the bar and placed himself squarely in her path to the door. "What're you really doing here?" he asked.

A surge of anger swept through her. "You think I'm lying?"

"I don't know." His lips twisted cynically. "But then, you've had a lot of practice, haven't you?"

That did it! She slung her bag over her shoulder. "For your information, I don't want to be here. If I could, I'd be anywhere on God's green earth rather than here with you!" She spun, but quick as a striking snake his hand shot out, steely fingers curled over her wrist and he whirled her back to face him.

"Before you leave," he said so quietly she could barely hear him, "just answer one question."

Melanie's heart thumped, and her wrist, where his fingers wrapped possessively over her pulse, throbbed. Her throat was suddenly dry. "Shoot."

"Where's your husband?"

"I don't have a husband anymore."

*Where the hell is Jan?* Melanie thought as she grew more uncomfortable the longer her interaction with Gavin continued.

His eyes narrowed as if he expected everything she said to be a lie. She turned back to the door, but he wouldn't release her. "So what happened to good ol' Neil?"

She swallowed hard. "We're divorced."

Something flashed in his eyes. Regret? "I guess I should say I'm sorry."

"No need to lie."

His face softened slightly. "Believe it or not, Melanie, I only wanted the best for you," he said suddenly. "I just didn't think Neil Brooks could make you happy."

"I guess it's a moot point now."

"Is it?" Again the pressure on her arm, the spark in his eyes.

Nervously she licked her lips, and his attention was drawn for a second to her mouth.

His jaw worked, and he said softly, "You know, Melanie, I think it would be best if you didn't come back."

"I only came here because of my job."

"Oh?" he said, eyebrows lifting, the fingers on the inside

of her wrist pressing slightly against her bare skin. "So you weren't curious about me?"

"Not in the least."

"And you didn't think because you rid yourself of your husband that we could pick up where we left off?" His voice had grown husky, his pupils dilating in the darkened lodge.

"That would be crazy," But her heart was pumping madly, slamming against her ribs, and she could barely concentrate on the conversation as his fingers moved on her inner wrist.

"Probably—"

The huge double doors were flung open, and Jan, her briefcase swinging at her side, strode into the lobby. "So here you are! God, I've had a terrible time getting here—" She took one look at Gavin and Melanie, and her train of thought seemed to evaporate.

Self-consciously, Melanie yanked her arm away from Gavin.

"Well," Jan said, as if walking in on an intimate scene between one of her co-workers and an internationally famous skier were an everyday occurrence, "I see you've already started."

"Not quite," Melanie replied, but Jan plunged on, walking up to Gavin and flashing her businesslike smile.

"I'm Jan Freemont. With the Taylor's Crossing *Tribune*." She flicked a confused glance at Melanie, "But I suppose you already guessed."

"I assumed."

Jan dug into her heavy canvas bag. She withdrew a card and handed it to him. "So, you've already met Melanie."

Gavin's mouth quirked. "Years ago."

"Oh?" Jan's brows lifted in interest, and Melanie could have throttled Gavin right then and there.

Instead, she managed a cool smile. "Gavin and I both grew up around here," she explained, hoping that would end this turn in the conversation. She was probably wrong. Jan wasn't one to let the subject drop. Her reporter instincts were probably going crazy already.

"Sorry I'm late," Jan apologized. "I had trouble with my car again."

"I don't think it matters," Melanie said.

Jan was busy extracting a recorder and pad of paper.

Melanie threw Gavin a look that dared him to disagree as she said, "Mr. Doel and I were just discussing the interview."

"Mmm?" Jan asked, searching through her large black shoulder bag.

"There isn't going to be one," Gavin said.

Melanie lifted a shoulder. "Apparently he didn't know about it."

"I didn't," Gavin clarified.

Melanie charged on. "And he's not interested in going through with it."

"You're kidding, right?" Jan asked.

"'Fraid not," Gavin drawled.

"But I spoke with your partner, Mr.—" she flipped open the note pad "—Johanson. He said you'd be glad to talk to us."

"Oh, he did, did he?" Gavin seemed faintly amused. "Well, he was wrong."

*Oh, this is just wonderful,* Melanie thought, wishing she could disappear. She'd known this session would be a disaster, but neither Brian Michaels, the *Trib*'s editor-in-chief, nor Jan, the paper's phenom reporter, had listened to her. Jan saw herself as a new Barbara Walters and Brian was hoping he could turn the *Tribune* into the *Washington Post*. Never mind that the *Tribune* was a small newspaper in central Oregon with a steadily declining readership.

Jan wasn't about to be thwarted. She explained about her phone call to Gavin's partner. She also went into an animated dissertation about how she wanted to write a "local boy does good then returns home" type of story.

Gavin wasn't buying it. He listened to all her arguments, but his hard expression didn't alter and his gaze drilled into her. "If you want information on the lodge, you'll have to get it from Rich," he finally said.

"But our readers will want to know all about you and your injury—"

"My personal life is off limits," Gavin muttered, and Melanie felt a tremor of relief.

"But you're a celebrity," Jan cooed, trying desperately to win him over. "You have fans who are interested—"

"Then they can read all about it in some cheap rag at the checkout counter of their local market. It might not be true, but it's guaranteed to be sensational."

"Now, wait a minute." Jan wasn't about to take this lying down. "Reopening Ridge Lodge is a big story around here! People will be interested and it's great publicity for you—"

"I don't want publicity," he said, glancing icily at Melanie. "I think I've had enough." He hobbled to the door. "If you want to do an article on the lodge reopening, that's fine with me, but I want my name kept out of it as much as possible."

Jan's smile was frozen. "But doesn't that defeat the point? It's your name that's going to bring people here, Mr. Doel. Your face in the paper that will make people interested. You're an international skier. You've endorsed everything from skis to lip balm. Your face will guarantee public interest, and that's what you need to reopen the lodge successfully." She gestured expansively to the inside of the resort. "I know I can convince my editor to do a series of articles about the lodge that will keep public interest up. I'll also freelance stories to ski magazines that are distributed everywhere in the country, so by the time the snow hits and the season is here, you're guaranteed cars in the parking lot, skiers on the runs and people in the bar."

Melanie expected Gavin to say "Bully for you" or something along those lines, but he kept silent.

Jan pressed her point home. "My guess is you need all the publicity you can get."

"I've given you my answer. Rich'll be back here this afternoon. Since he's the one who agreed to this damned interview in the first place, you can talk to him."

He shoved his crutches in front of him and moved awkwardly through the front door.

"That man is something else!" Jan whispered, letting out her breath. "You know, he almost acts like he's got something to hide."

"Constance said he doesn't talk to the press," Melanie reminded her.

"Yeah, but she didn't say why." Jan's lips thinned as she turned to Melanie. "And what was going on between you two when I first got here? You looked like you were deciding whether to kill each other or make love."

Melanie's stomach tightened. "You're exaggerating."

"Nope. And you didn't tell me that you knew him."

Lifting a shoulder, Melanie replied, "It didn't seem important."

Jan's expression clouded with suspicion. "Baloney! That's like saying storm warnings aren't important when you're heading out to sea in a small boat."

Slinging the strap of her camera bag over her shoulder, Melanie said, "Look, I've got another shoot in twenty minutes, so I'm not going to waste my time here."

"But you'll fill me in later?"

"Sure," Melanie replied, wondering just how much she could tell Jan about Gavin as she shoved open the door and stepped into the warm mountain air.

Across the parking lot, near the equipment shed, she spied Gavin leaning hard on his crutches, talking to a man in an orange pickup. A sign on the pickup's door read Gamble Construction.

The two men were engrossed in conversation. Gavin's

reflective aviator glasses were back in place, and the late morning sunlight glinted in his hair. His cast-covered leg looked awkward on his toned, athletic body

Melanie wondered if the rumors were true that his career was over.

He didn't glance her way as she unlocked her car, and she didn't bother trying to get his attention. The less she had to do with him, the better.

Gavin watched the little car speed out of the lot and felt the tension between his shoulder blades relax. He hadn't counted on seeing Melanie again. What was she doing back in Taylor's Crossing, working at that rag of a paper? And why had she and Neil split? Maybe Brooks wasn't making enough money for her now.

But would she give up the good life of luxury to work on a small-time newspaper? Nope, it didn't make sense.

". . . so the crew will be here at the beginning of the week, and I think we can make up for some of the time lost by the strike," Seth Gamble, owner of Gamble Construction, was saying as he leaned out the window of his pickup. Gavin forced his attention back to the conversation.

"Good. I'll see you then." Gavin thumped the dusty hood of the truck with his hand, and Seth, grinning, rammed the pickup into gear and took off.

Shoving the damned crutches under his arms, Gavin started back for the lodge and found Jan whatever-her-name-was, the blond reporter, sweeping toward him. Her expression had turned hard, and he was reminded why he didn't trust reporters. They didn't give a damn about the subject—just that they got the story.

"Mr. Doel!" she said, striding up to him and trying her best to appear hard-edged and tough. "My editor expects a story on the lodge—the story we were promised."

"As I said, you can talk to my partner."

"Is he here?"

"No," Gavin admitted.

"When do you expect him?"

"I don't know. This afternoon, probably."

"Then it looks like we're left with you for the time being if we want to make next week's edition." When Gavin didn't reply, she said, "I'm sorry if we inconvenienced you, Mr. Doel, but what's going on here—" she made a sweeping gesture to the lodge "—is big news. And so, unfortunately, are you. You can't expect the *Tribune* to ignore it, nor, I would think, would you want it ignored."

She stood waiting, cool green eyes staring up at him, firm jaw set, and he couldn't fault her logic. Besides, he wanted to get rid of her. "All right," he finally agreed. "When Rich gets back. Tomorrow. He and I will tell you all about our plans for the resort, but I want my private life kept out of it."

"But not your professional life," Jan said quickly. "People will need to know why you're involved. Some people, believe it or not, might not be familiar with your name."

"My professional life is a matter of record."

"Good. Then we understand each other." She offered her hand, shook his and marched to a red sports car, which coughed and sputtered before sparking to life and tearing through the dusty lot.

"Now you've done it, Doel," he muttered. Inviting the reporter back was probably a mistake. No doubt Melanie would accompany her. His fingers tightened over the handholds on his crutches. Seeing Melanie again wasn't in his plans. Just the sight of her brought back memories he'd rather forget forever, and touching her—good God, why had he done such a foolish thing? Just the feel of her skin made his blood race.

Leveling an oath at himself, he plunged the tips of his crutches into the pavement and headed back for the lodge, intending to throttle Rich Johanson when he showed up.

They'd had an agreement: Rich would handle all the publicity, the legal work and financial information; Gavin would supervise the reconstruction of the lodge and the runs. Gavin had made it clear from the onset that he wasn't going to have a passel of nosy reporters poking around, digging into his personal life.

He hadn't lied to Melanie when he'd mentioned skeletons in the closet. There were just too damned many. Unfortunately, Melanie knew about a lot of them. Her family and his could provide enough scandal to keep the gossip mill in Taylor's Crossing busy for years.

Gavin opened the door to the lodge. There on the bar was the bottle of whiskey. And two glasses—his and Melanie's.

Just what in the hell was she doing back in town?

Melanie, finished her afternoon shoot, headed back to the *Tribune*'s office. Almost serendipitously, Jan pulled into the parking lot as Melanie was climbing out of her car, and in a second, Jan was upon her. "Let me handle Brian," Jan expelled as a greeting, following Melanie through the office's door.

"Good to see you again, too," Melanie responded with a hint of humor in her voice. "He's not going to be thrilled about losing the interview."

Jan flashed her a grin and winked. "All is not yet lost."

Melanie stopped short. "What?"

"I think I've convinced the arrogant Mr. Doel to see things our way."

Melanie couldn't believe her ears. Gavin had been adamant. "How'd you do that?"

"Well, I did have to make a few concessions."

"I bet."

Constance, a worried expression crowding her features, was scanning the society and gossip columns of other papers.

Looking up, she waved two fingers at Melanie, beckoning her over.

Jan made a beeline for the editor's office, but Melanie paused at Constance's desk.

"How'd it go?" Constance asked, once Melanie was in earshot.

"Not so good. You were right. Doel refused."

"Privacy is that man's middle name. So you got nothing?"

"Not so much as one shot," Melanie said, tapping her camera bag, "but Jan's convinced that he's changed his mind."

"I hope so." Constance's wide mouth pinched at the corners. "Brian's on a real tear. Geri called in and said she wanted to extend her vacation by a couple of days—and he told her not to bother coming back."

Geri was Melanie's backup—the only other photographer for the *Tribune*. Suddenly Melanie felt cold inside. "You mean—"

"I mean she's gone, kaput, outta here!" Constance sliced a finger theatrically across her throat.

"But why?"

"I don't know, but my guess is he's getting pressure from the owners of the paper." Her voice lowered. "We all know that sales haven't been so hot lately. Brian's counting on the interest in Ridge Resort to drum up business."

"Oh, great," Melanie said with a sigh. "In that case I'd better go help bail Jan out when she drops the bomb that we came up empty today."

She left her camera at her desk, then marched to Brian's office and knocked softly on the door.

"It's open!" Brian barked angrily.

Melanie slipped into the room as Jan coughed nervously. She was seated in a chair near the desk, notebook open, pencil ready. "I was just explaining that getting an interview with

Gavin Doel was tantamount to gaining an audience with God himself."

Melanie took a chair and nodded, swallowing a smile. "She's right."

"But somehow," Brian said, "she's managed to change his mind."

"Not somehow—I used my exceptional powers of persuasion," Jan remarked. "We're going back up there tomorrow. You know what they say about the mountain and Muhammad."

"He really agreed?" Melanie asked, dumfounded.

"Of course he did," Brian said with a sneer. He rubbed his chin with his hand. "No matter what else he is, Doel's no fool. And he can't snake his way out of this one. I've already devoted half the front page for the story."

Melanie couldn't believe it. What had made Gavin change his mind? And why was Brian so edgy?

"There is a catch," Jan explained.

Brian's lips turned down at the corners.

"Doel only wants his name used professionally. He doesn't want any part of his private life included."

Brian snorted. "That's impossible."

"But that's the deal," Jan insisted.

"Can't we hedge a little?"

Melanie shook her head. "I don't think that would be a good idea."

"Why not? As long as everything we print is true, he can't sue us," Brian argued. "And the way I see it, publicity will only help Ridge Lodge, of which he owns a large percent"

Melanie squirmed. She wasn't afraid to speak her mind— she and Brian had locked horns more often than not, but when it came to Gavin, her emotions were still tangled in the past. "Gavin Doel won't take kindly to us digging through his private life. And I think we should keep good relations with him—at least as long as he owns and runs the resort."

Jan scribbled a note to herself. "Don't worry about it, Melanie, I'll handle the interview. Just get me some shots of the lodge, a few of the ski runs and the mountain and some close-ups of Doel."

Brian tugged at his tie. "I'm counting on this article, men," he said, and Melanie laughed a little. Ever since she and the rest of the female staff had objected to being called girls, Brian had responded by referring to all reporters, photographers, secretaries and receptionists as men, female or male.

Melanie noticed the lines of worry etching Brian's forehead and the pinch of his lips. His complexion was pale, and she wondered, not for the first time, if he were ill. A bottle of antacids sat on the corner of his desk, next to his coffee cup and a crumpled hamburger wrapper.

Brian's phone jangled, and he reached for it. "Okay, that's everything. Let's get on it," he said, lifting the receiver as he dismissed them.

"I want to talk to you," Jan whispered to Melanie as they walked back to the newsroom.

*Here it comes,* Melanie thought, but fortunately Constance waved Jan to her desk and Melanie escaped an inquisition on Gavin, at least for the time being.

She spent the rest of the afternoon sorting through the prints she'd taken of the fair the day before, picking out the shots of children riding the roller coaster and eating cotton candy. She worked on the shots of Uncle Bart's colt, as well, choosing a photograph of Big Money standing calmly by Bart for the next edition. She sorted through the shots again, found one she thought Bart would like and placed it in an envelope. She'd enlarge it later.

When she could no longer put off digging up pictures of Gavin, she set about looking through the files, sorting through old pictures and archived editions, rereading all about Gavin Doel. The photographs brought back memories of Gavin as a young man so full of life and expectation.

His skiing had been remarkable, gaining him a berth on the Olympic team and taking him on a road to fame and fortune. He'd been tough, fearless, and had attacked the most severe runs with a vengeance. His natural grace and balance had been God-given, but his fierce determination and pride had pushed him, driven him, to become the best.

Melanie stared wistfully at the photographs, noting the hard angle of his jaw and the blaze of competitive fire in his eyes before each race—and his smile of satisfaction after a win.

The most recent photographs were of Gavin losing that blissful God-given balance, tumbling on an icy mountainside and finally being carried off in a stretcher, his skin taut over his nose and cheekbones, his mouth pulled in a grimace of pain.

"Oh, Gavin," she whispered, overcome by old feelings of love. "What happened to us?"

Hearing herself, she pulled away from her desk and closed her mind to any of the long-dead emotions that had torn her apart ever since she'd heard he'd returned to Ridge Lodge. "Don't be a fool."

Stuffing the pictures she thought would be most useful into an envelope, she returned the rest of the documents. While sliding Gavin's file into its proper slot she noticed the other slim file marked Doel, James.

Melanie's mouth went dry as she pulled Jim Doel's file from its slot and looked inside. She cringed at the first photograph of Gavin's father. Jim's eyes seemed vacant and haunted. His hands were shackled by handcuffs, and he was escorted by two policemen. In the background a frightened boy of twelve, his blond hair mussed, his pale eyes wide with fear, watched in horror. Restrained by a matronly social worker, Gavin was reaching around her, trying to get to his father as Jim was led to the waiting police car.

"Oh, God," she whispered. Her throat grew hot, and she pitied Gavin—an emotion he would abhor.

Chewing on her lower lip, she slipped the photograph from the file and tucked it quickly into her purse. No, that wasn't good enough. Jan or Brian would just dig deeper. Stomach knotted, she pulled the entire file from the drawer then took anything damaging from Gavin's file as well. There was no reason for Brian or anyone else from the *Tribune* to lay open Jim Doel's life and persecute him again. Nor, she thought, did she want to be reminded of her mother's death. She'd just take the file home and keep it locked away until all the interest in Gavin Doel faded.

She slammed the drawer quickly, and for the first time since returning to Taylor's Crossing two years before, Melanie wondered if coming home had been a mistake.

Gavin rammed his crutches into a corner of his office and glared at his partner. "A reporter and photographer from the *Tribune* were here today," he said. "Seems you gave them the okay for an interview."

Rich shoved a beefy hand through his graying hair and sighed loudly. Tall and heavyset, he looked more like a retired guard for a professional football team than an attorney. "Don't tell me, you threw them out."

"You could have had the decency to let me know about it."

"Yeah. But I thought we agreed that we should start publicity as soon as possible."

"Not with personal interviews!"

Rich was irritated. "For God's sake, what've you got to hide?"

Gavin's jaw began to ache, and only then did he realize he'd clenched it. "I just don't want this to turn into a three-ring circus."

"Four rings would be better," Rich said, dropping into a

chair. "The more interest and excitement we can generate, the better for everyone."

Gavin snorted. Ever since seeing Melanie again, he'd felt restless and caged and he'd been out of sorts. "Look, I'm all for publicity about the resort. But that's as far as it goes. I like my privacy."

"Then you chose the wrong profession." Rich stuffed his hands in his pockets and jangled his keys nervously. "I know you don't want to hear this, but I think public interest in you is healthy."

"Meaning?" Gavin asked suspiciously.

"Meaning that people aren't really all that interested in your professional life. Hell, the Olympics were eons ago. And only a few dyed-in-the-wool fans will care about the ski clinics you developed." His pale blue eyes lighted, and he wagged a finger at Gavin. "But the fact that you jetted all over the continent, skiing with famous celebrities, dating gorgeous women, partying with glamorous Hollywood types—now *that* will get their attention!"

"The wrong kind."

"Any kind will help."

Gavin scowled. "The tabloids made more of it than there was," he said slowly.

"Doesn't matter. The public sees you as an athletic playboy—a guy who plays with the rich and beds the beautiful."

Gavin grimaced. "The public would be disappointed if it knew the truth."

"Let's not allow that to happen," Rich suggested slyly. "What does it hurt to keep the myth alive?"

"Just my reputation."

Rich chuckled as he crossed the room and poured himself a cup of coffee. "Don't you know most men would kill for a reputation like yours?"

"Then they're fools," Gavin grumbled, hobbling over to

the window and staring at the windswept slopes of the mountain rising high behind the lodge. Without snow, the ragged slopes of Mount Prosperity seemed empty and barren.

He thought of Melanie, and his frown deepened. No doubt she'd be back tomorrow, along with that pushy reporter. It didn't matter that he didn't want to see her again.

"Just one more session," he muttered to himself.

"What?" Rich asked.

"Nothing," Gavin replied. "I was just thinking about the interview tomorrow."

"What about it?" Rich blew across his coffee cup.

"I can't wait for it to be over," he declared vehemently. Maybe then he could close his mind to Melanie. Even now, eight years later, her betrayal burned painfully in his gut. Maybe he'd get lucky and they'd send someone else. But more likely he'd have to face her again and find some way of being civil. He doubted he was up to it.

# CHAPTER THREE

The morning sun gilded the steep slopes of Mount Prosperity as Melanie again met Jan at Ridge Lodge Resort. She turned from the view of the mountain to the old rambling cedar and shake lodge. She wished she could be anywhere other than here.

"It'll be over soon," she muttered under her breath.

"What will?" Jan asked, approaching her car.

"This interview."

"You want it over? But why? This has to be the most interesting story we've done all year!"

"Is it?" Melanie asked, leaning inside her warm Volkswagen and snatching her camera case and tripod.

"What is it with you?"

"I don't like Doel's attitude," she replied, starting across the path leading to the front door of the lodge.

"Give him a chance. My bet is he'll grow on you."

"You'll lose your money," Melanie predicted.

They started towards the building, but Jan suddenly stopped short. "Okay, Melanie, are you going to hold out on me forever or are you going to tell me what's going on between you and—" she cocked her head toward the lodge "—our infamous new neighbor?"

"There's nothing going on."

"Didn't look that way yesterday."

"We got into an argument, that's all."

"And it looked like a doozy," Jan exclaimed. "You know you're going to have to tell me the truth about all this. You grew up with him."

"It wasn't all that interesting," Melanie lied, but Jan simply smiled as they headed up the path leading to the main doors.

Gavin was waiting for them.

Lounging at one of the tables near the bar, his leg and cast propped on the seat of another chair, he looked up as they entered but didn't bother trying to stand.

"So you didn't change your mind," he said, his tawny eyes moving from Jan to Melanie.

"Nope," Melanie replied.

"News in Taylor's Crossing must be slow." The weight of his gaze landed full force on Melanie, but she tossed her bag onto the table and unzipped the padded canvas, pretending she didn't care one way or the other that he was staring at her.

Jan slid into a chair opposite him. "Ready?" she asked.

"As I'll ever be." He glanced down at his stiff leg and the plaster cast surrounding his ankle. Grimacing, his jaw rock hard, he added irritably, "Rich isn't here right now."

"But he'll be back?" Jan asked.

"He'd better be," Gavin growled.

Jan looked smug. "We can manage without him."

Melanie set up her tripod near the bar and adjusted its height, then double-checked the camera's settings.

Frowning, Gavin muttered, "Let's get the damned thing over with."

"That's a healthy attitude," Melanie shot back, and Jan stared at her as if she'd lost her mind.

Scowling, Gavin reached behind him, grabbed his crutches, stood and made his way to the other side of the bar. Rock-solid muscles supported him, though he slouched to fit the tops of the crutches under his arms. "What do you want to know?"

"Everything," Jan replied brightly, reaching into her over-sized bag for her pocket recorder, notepad and pen. "The reopening of Ridge Lodge is big news. But then, everything you do is news."

"If that's true, then the world's in worse shape than I thought," Gavin remarked, setting out two glasses and his favorite bottle on the top of the bar. "Join Melanie and me for a drink?" he asked.

"A drink?" Jan's brows rose. "At eleven in the morning?"

"Right. Kind of a celebration, eh, Melanie?"

"Don't ask," Melanie advised Jan as she set her camera onto the tripod.

Gavin was already searching for another glass, but Jan held up her hand. "It's too early for me," she said, curiosity filling her gaze.

"Melanie?" he asked, motioning to the two glasses already placed on the bar. "Another *smooth* one?"

Jan shot her a look that said more clearly than words, *what's he talking about?*

Shrugging, Melanie found the lens she wanted and screwed it onto the camera. Then she checked the light with a meter. "Not today," she replied.

"Too early?" he mocked, pouring himself a hefty shot.

"I'm working." She moved to the windows with her light meter.

"All work and no play?"

"Oh, you know me, nose to the grindstone all the time," she flung back, unable to help herself. Why was he baiting her?

Jan eyed them both. "You two *do* know each other," she

said speculatively while casting Melanie a look that could cut through steel.

"You could say that," Gavin answered evasively.

"How well?" Jan's eyes were full of questions when she turned them on Melanie.

"Gavin and I went to school together—grade school," Melanie replied quickly, silently cursing Gavin. What was he doing firing up Jan's reporter instincts? He was the one who wanted his damned privacy.

Gavin's jaw grew tight. "Small world, isn't it?"

Jan reached for her pen and paper. "Then you're family friends?"

Melanie's heart began to thud, and she felt sweat gather along her spine.

Gavin didn't answer, and the silence stretched long. "Not exactly," he finally said.

"Then 'exactly' what?"

"Acquaintances," he clipped. "Nothing more."

Melanie, wounded, nodded. "That's right. Acquaintances. Mr. Doel is—"

"Gavin, please," Gavin drawled. "No reason to be so formal."

Melanie bristled. "He's a few years older than I am." Jan lifted a brow as Melanie suggested, "Maybe we should just get started."

Gavin forced a cold smile. "I can't wait."

"So you went to school at Taylor High?" Jan began, but Gavin cut her off.

"Nothing personal, remember?"

*You started it,* Melanie thought.

"Okay, okay," Jan said amiably. "We can begin with the lodge. When is it going to reopen? Is it going to be changed in any way? And tell me why you think you and your partner can make it work when the last operation went bankrupt?"

Jan's questions were fair, Melanie decided. Her ear tuned to the conversation, she busied herself with her equipment.

Now that Gavin had steered Jan to safe territory, she was sticking to questions Gavin could answer without much thought. Leaning on the bar for support, he ignored his drink and answered each question carefully. No more spontaneous remarks—just the facts.

Melanie focused the camera on Gavin. He didn't seem to notice, and the lens only magnified his innate sexuality, the hard slope of his jaw, the bladed features of his face, the glint of his straight white teeth and the depth of his eyes, cautious now and sober.

She clicked off a few shots, and he glanced her way. Her heartbeat accelerated as he smiled—that irreverent slash of white against his tanned skin that had always caused her heart to trip.

"You want a tour?" he asked, flicking his gaze back to Jan.

"That would be great!"

Melanie watched him maneuver to the main lobby. Beneath his shirt his shoulders flexed, straining the seams of the white cotton while his hips shifted beneath his shorts and his tanned thighs and one exposed calf strained.

Even though Gavin was on crutches, Jan had to hurry to keep pace with him. Melanie grabbed another camera, double-checked it's battery and switched on the flash as she followed.

Gavin moved quickly across the main lobby, gesturing to the three-storied rock fireplace, scuffed wooden floors and soaring ceiling. Around three sides of the cavernous room, two tiers of balconies opened to private guest rooms. The other wall was solid glass, with a breathtaking view of Mount Prosperity. Now the ski runs were bare, the lifts still, the pine trees towering out of sheer rock. Dry grass and wildflowers covered the slopes.

Showing off the office, kitchen, exercise room and pool room, Gavin explained how the lodge was set up, when it was built and how he planned to restore it. Eventually they returned to the main lobby, and Gavin stopped at a group of tables with chairs overturned on their polished oak surfaces. Balancing on his good leg, he yanked three chairs down and shoved them around a battered table.

Jan plopped down immediately. Gavin kicked a chair Melanie's way, but rather than sit so close to him, she said, "I think I'll look around."

"Not interested in hearing about the lodge?" Gavin baited.

"I can read about it," she tossed back. "Fascinating as it is, I've got work to do."

Jan, sensing the changed atmosphere, said, "Melanie's the best photographer on the paper."

Melanie shot Jan a warning glance. "Right now I think I'm the *only* photographer." *Just let me get through this,* she prayed silently, wishing she could be aloof and uncaring when it came to Gavin Doel. She unzipped her bag and sorted through the lenses, cameras, light meters and memory cards.

Jan leaned across the table to Gavin and turned the questions in a different direction. Writing swiftly in her own fashion of shorthand, she asked about his career as an international skier, his bronze medal from the Olympics nearly eight years before, his interest in the lodge itself. Gavin answered quickly and succinctly, never offering more than a simple, straightforward answer.

*He's used to this,* Melanie realized, wondering how many reporters had tried to pin him down, how many other newspapers had tried to dig into his personal life. Even though the *Tribune* had been known to downplay scandal in the past, especially about a local hero, there were other newspapers that wouldn't have been so kind.

Seeing this as her chance to escape, Melanie wandered through the old rooms, and memories washed over her. She'd been here often, of course, before the last owners had filed for bankruptcy and closed the runs and the lodge for good. She'd even skied here with Gavin, but that had been ages ago. She'd been seventeen, sure of her love of him, happy beyond her wildest dreams. And he'd been on his way to fame and fortune. She sighed. How foolish it all seemed now.

Measuring the light through the large glass windows, she caught sight of her own pale reflection and wondered what Gavin thought about her. Gone was her straight black hair, replaced by crumpled curls that fell past her shoulders. Her eyes were still hazel, her cheekbones more exposed and gaunt following her divorce from Neil. She'd lost weight since Gavin had known her. But it didn't matter. What had happened between Gavin and her was long over. Dead. She'd killed whatever feelings he'd had for her, and she'd destroyed those emotions intentionally when she'd eloped with Neil Brooks.

She glanced back to the table. Gavin was leaning back in his chair, answering Jan's questions, but his eyes followed her as she moved from one bank of windows to the next.

She snapped off a few shots of the interior of the lodge, then, as much to get away from the weight of Gavin's gaze as anything else, wandered down the hallways to the spaces where the shops and restaurant had been housed in years past.

In the tiny shops the shelves and racks were empty. Dust collected on display windows, and the carpet was worn and faded where ski boots had once trod throughout the winter. Bleached-out "Clearance" signs were stacked haphazardly against the walls.

The interior seemed gloomy—too dark for the kind of pictures Brian wanted for the layout. Maybe exterior shots would be better. Even though there wasn't a flake of snow on the mountain, shots of the lodge, the craggy ridge looming behind its gabled roofline, would give the article the right atmosphere.

Outside, she snapped several quick shots of the lodge, a few more of the empty lifts and others of the grassy ski runs.

The mountain air was clear and warm, and a late September breeze cooled her skin and tangled her hair. The scents of pine and dust, fresh lumber and wildflowers mingled, lingering in the autumn afternoon.

"Get what you wanted?" Gavin's voice boomed, startling her.

"What?" Whipping around, she squinted up and found him seated on the rail of a deck, his cast propped on a chair, his eyes shaded by reflective glasses. The deck, because of the lack of snow, was some five feet in the air and he stared down at her.

"What I wanted?" she repeated, shading her eyes with one hand and attempting to hide the fact that at that height he was incredibly intimidating.

"The pictures."

"Oh." Of course that's what he'd meant. For a moment she thought he'd been asking about her life. *You're too sensitive, Melanie. He doesn't give a damn.* "Enough to start with." She noticed his mouth turn down at the edges. "But you never can tell. If these—" she patted her camera fondly "—aren't what Brian had in mind, then I'll be back."

Gavin's jaw clenched even tighter. "So when did you take up photography?"

"I've always been interested in it." *You know that.*

"But as a career?"

"It started out as a hobby. I just kept working at it," she replied, not wanting to go into the fact that after she'd married Neil, she'd taken photography courses. She'd had time on her hands and empty hours to fill without the baby. . . . Neil's money had provided her with the best equipment and classes with some of the Northwest's most highly regarded instructors, and she'd spent hour upon hour learning, focusing on her craft. When she'd landed her first job, Neil had been livid. It was ironic, she supposed, that her hours of idleness and Neil's money had provided her with her escape from a marriage that had been doomed from the start.

Clearing her throat, she looked up and found Gavin staring at her, looking intently, as if he could read her thoughts. "So you took your 'hobby' and started working for the *Tribune*."

"In short, I suppose." Why explain further? "Where's Jan?" she asked, changing the subject as she packed her camera back in its case.

"She took off."

Melanie was surprised. "Already?"

Gavin's lips twitched as she started to climb onto the deck. "She asked one too many personal questions, and when I objected, I guess she thought I was being rude."

Melanie skewered him with a knowing look as she crossed the deck. "Were you?"

"Undoubtedly. She asked for it." Wincing, Gavin swung his leg back to the decking and balanced on his good foot while he scrabbled for his crutches. "Shit," he growled when one crutch clattered to the cedar planks. He twisted, and his face grew white.

"I'll get it."

Melanie started to pick up the offending crutch, but Gavin bent over and, swearing, yanked it out of her hands. "Leave it!"

Melanie's temper flared. "I was only trying to help."

"I don't need any *help*." He didn't say it, but from the flare of his nostrils she expected him to add, "Especially from you." A few beads of sweat collected on his upper lip, but his skin darkened to its normal shade.

"You know, Gavin, you could relax a little. It wouldn't kill you to let someone lend you a hand once in a while."

His lips thinned. "I learned a long time ago not to depend on anyone but myself. That way I'm never disappointed."

Her throat went dry and she felt as if he'd slapped her, but he wasn't finished.

"As for these," he said, shaking a crutch, "I can handle them myself. And I don't need your advice, or your help, or any goddamn pity!" By this time he was standing, leaning on his crutches and breathing hard as he glared at her through his mirrored glasses.

"Then I'm out of here," she said, forcing an icy smile. "If you don't want my help or my advice or my pity, then there's no reason for me to stay."

"No reason at all."

"And I'm sure the shots I've taken will be good enough for the paper. You won't have to worry about me intruding again."

"Good."

"Goodbye, Gavin," she said, swinging her camera case over her shoulder, "and good luck with the lodge."

"Luck has nothing to do with it."

"I'll remember that if we don't get any snow until next February," she said sweetly, turning on her heel and marching through the lodge to the main doors. Her footsteps rang loudly on the weathered flooring, and her fists were clenched so tightly her fingers began to ache. How could she have loved him? *How?* The man was an arrogant SOB and carried around a chip on his shoulder the size of a California sequoia! Muttering under her breath, she shoved open the doors and escaped into the hot parking lot. Heat rose from the dusty asphalt in shimmering waves, only adding to the fire burning in her cheeks.

How could he have changed so drastically? He was unbearable! She unlocked her car door and climbed into the suffocatingly hot interior. Rolling down the windows, she wondered if somehow she were to blame for this new cynical, horrible beast named Gavin Doel. Had she wounded him so badly by marrying Neil—or had he, at last, shown his true colors?

Her father had always warned her that Gavin was cut from

the same cloth as Jim Doel, but she'd never believed him.
Now she wasn't so sure, and it worried her. Twice in two days
Gavin had poured himself healthy doses of Scotch before
noon.

But she hadn't seen him drink any this morning. It had just
been a game. He'd been baiting her again.

"Well, he can drown in his liquor for all I care!" she grumbled as she rammed a pair of sunglasses onto the bridge of her
nose and glanced in the side-view mirror. In the reflection she
saw Gavin standing in the doorway of the lodge, leaning hard
on his crutches and frowning darkly.

She ground the gears of her battered old car and sped out
of the lot. Maybe, if she were lucky, she'd never have to deal
with him again.


Gavin swore roundly and stared after the car. "You're a
fool, Doel," he growled, furious with himself for noting that
Melanie was more beautiful than he remembered. Her black
hair shimmered blue in the sunlight, and her eyes were round
and wide, a fascinating shade hovering between gray and
green.

So what? Her beauty meant nothing. He'd loved her more
than any other woman and she'd betrayed him as callously as
if his feelings hadn't existed. So why should he care?

"Why now?" he muttered. He didn't want to deal with any
latent feelings he might still harbor for her. And he wouldn't.
Just because she was in the same neck of the proverbial
woods didn't mean he had to fall all over himself chasing
after her.

No, he decided, his lips compressing thoughtfully as the
dust from her car settled back onto the asphalt, this time he'd
be in control. This time Melanie Walker Brooks wouldn't get
close to him. No matter what.

* * *

". . . he might be the rudest man I've ever met!" Jan charged. Her eyes were bright, her cheeks flushed at the memory of her interview with Gavin. "And, unfortunately, maybe the best looking."

Melanie couldn't agree more. She'd heard the tail end of the conversation between Jan and Guy as she returned to the office. "I take it you're talking about the new owner of Ridge Resort?"

"You got it," Jan said. "And I'm not kidding. I've met some jerks in my time—good God, I've dated more than my share—but this guy takes the cake!"

"What exactly did he say?"

Jan puffed up like a peacock. "I just mentioned that he'd been linked to several famous models and I brought up Aimee LaRoux's name."

"And?" Guy prodded.

"And he asked me who I'd been linked to. I, uh, said, it was none of his business and he said, 'Precisely.'"

"That doesn't sound so bad to me."

"It gets worse," Jan assured them. "I kept bringing it up and he finally asked me why, if I was so interested in Aimee LaRoux's love life, I just didn't call her and ask her out. Then he had the audacity to scribble a phone number on a book of matches and toss it to me."

Despite her foul mood, Melanie laughed. "You're right," she said. "Doel's obnoxious."

Jan glared at her. "He's got one dismal sense of humor!"

"You think it's really Aimee's number?" Guy asked, his eyes bright.

"No, I don't!" Jan snapped. "Quit drooling."

Guy made a face. "Is it that obvious?"

"Very."

Melanie said, "Just be glad the interview's over. We won't have to deal with Doel again."

"Oh, I wouldn't be so sure of that," Guy disagreed. "Brian seems to think that stories about Gavin Doel and Ridge Lodge can only increase circulation. I think he's planning a series of articles about Mount Prosperity and the lodge and guess who?"

"Goddammit," Jan said, grimacing.

Melanie sighed inwardly. She didn't think she could face Gavin again. And the thought of Gavin's personal life being ripped open put her on edge. "I think Brian's putting too much emphasis on Doel."

"Yeah, it's almost as if he has an axe to grind with him," Guy agreed.

"An axe? What're you talking about?"

Guy shook his head. "Just a feeling I have. I don't think there's any love lost between Brian and Doel."

"Do they know each other?" Melanie asked.

"Beats me."

Jan's purse landed on her desk with a thump. "Well, Brian better get himself another reporter," she declared flatly. "I'm not going to put myself through that ringer again. Doel guards his privacy as if there's something dark and dangerous in his past."

"Maybe there is," Guy said, throwing a leg over Jan's desk and tapping the side of his face with the eraser end of his pencil. "After all, what do we know about the guy—really?"

Jan turned thoughtful eyes on Melanie. "We know more than most," she said, her mouth curving thoughtfully upward.

Melanie steeled herself. Obviously Jan thought she could get information on Gavin through her. Well, she could guess again. For now Melanie's lips were sealed.

"He grew up around here," Jan told Guy. "Melanie went to school with him."

"Did you?" Guy was impressed.

"Well, not really. He's five years older than I am," Melanie countered. "He was out of high school before I entered."

"But you said you knew him," Jan persisted, "and he

concurred. In fact, I'd be willing to bet you two knew each other better than you're letting on."

"Oh really?" Guy asked, his lips forming a slight smile.

Melanie decided it was time for evasive tactics, at least until she knew just how far Jan was willing to dig. "Jan's exaggerating. I knew of him," she corrected, her palms beginning to sweat. "Everyone in town did."

She should probably just tell Jan part of the truth right now and get it over with, but she couldn't. Where would she stop? How would she explain that she married Neil to protect Gavin from the burden of a wife and child? Gavin didn't even know that she'd been pregnant. She certainly wasn't going to tell Jan or Guy or anyone else.

And beyond that, she didn't want the scandal of her mother's death raked up all over again.

"What was Gavin like as a kid? Doesn't he have a deadbeat father?" Jan asked, the wheels turning in her mind.

"I thought you weren't interested in interviewing him again?" Melanie said.

Jan shook her head. "You know me. I was just mad. I let the guy get to me. It was my problem, not his. But it won't happen again. Besides, Barbara Walters wouldn't have let Doel intimidate her, would she? Nope, I've just got to fight fire with fire. So, what was Gavin Doel like before he became famous?"

Melanie thought for a moment, remembering Gavin as he had been. "He was . . . determined and ambitious. Dedicated to being the best skier in the world."

Jan sighed and blew her bangs out of her eyes. "I know all that. But what about the man behind the image? Did you know him?"

*Better than anyone.* Melanie lifted a shoulder. "Not well enough to be quoted. Besides, the way he is about his private life, I think the *Tribune* would be better off if we asked him. That way there's a chance we won't get sued."

"He won't sue us," Jan said.

"Why not?"

"Bad publicity. He can't afford it. But right now he won't tell me anything." She smiled slyly. "This is going to call for some research. What's in the files?"

"I checked yesterday," Melanie said, walking briskly to her desk and knowing there was nothing the least bit damaging in the envelope she snatched from her cluttered in-basket. She tossed the packet on Jan's desk and waited while Jan quickly flipped through the stack of photos as if it were a deck of cards. "Nothing else?" she asked, looking disappointed.

"Nothing interesting."

"You checked the copies that went along with these?"

"Yep."

"Damn!" She pursed her lips and eyed the photographs again. "Well, these are good—" She picked up a glossy black and white of Gavin poised at the top of a ski run. His face was set, his body tight, gloved hands wrapped around his poles, every muscle ready to spring forward at the drop of a flag. "But I think it would give some dimension to our story if we knew a little more about him." Tapping a long fingernail on the photograph, she said, "Privacy or no privacy, I think we should dig up *everything* we can find on Mr. Gavin Doel. We can check with the high school, find out who he dated, if he was ever employed around town."

"I think most of his relatives moved away a long time ago. And as for his employment, he worked at the lodge before it closed down," Melanie offered, hoping to steer Jan away from Gavin's love life.

"Well that doesn't do us a lot of good. Unless he bought the damned thing for sentimental reasons. But we'll find out. The next time I interview him, I'll be ready with a little personal ammunition to get him to talk."

"It's your funeral," Guy said, straightening from the desk.

*And just possibly mine,* Melanie thought inwardly. "I'll do the research," she offered, hoping that she could circumvent any old news story that might prove uncomfortable for Gavin or herself.

"Good." Jan checked her watch. "Look, I've got to run over to the school and talk to the principal about the new gym. Melanie, you coming with me?"

"No, I've already got the pictures. They'll be on your desk tomorrow."

"Good. Thanks." Jan grabbed her bag and headed out of the office.

Melanie was left with the sinking sensation that Gavin's personal life—as well as her own—was about to be splashed all over the front page of the Taylor's Crossing *Tribune*.

# CHAPTER FOUR

Brian Michaels did indeed want to do a series of articles on Ridge Lodge and he wasn't the least bit concerned with Gavin's desire for privacy. In fact, he had his own reasons for wanting to see Gavin's life plastered all over the newspaper. But he kept those to himself.

"He's a public figure, for crying out loud," Brian said the next afternoon as he shook a cigarette from his pack. Jan and Melanie were seated on two worn plastic chairs near his desk. "And on top of that, he's rebuilding a lodge that will turn the economy of this town around. Doel's a fool if he expects to have a private life."

"A man who's made several million dollars in five years isn't a fool," Jan argued.

Brian ran his fingers through his hair, letting his head rest in his palm. "Look, I want to do several articles, one every other week until snow season. Front page stuff." He glanced at Melanie. "I want to see the workers rebuilding the lodge, the furniture being moved in.

"I need photos of the lifts beginning to run, the first snowfall, that sort of thing. Then, find out about the ski school programs and add some schmaltzy stuff, you know, five-year-old kids on skis with their dads helping them."

"Then you don't really need anything on Doel." she ventured.

"Wrong!" Brian was just warming to his subject. "He's going to open that lodge with a huge celebration of some kind. I want a copy of the guest list. Find out if any of the skiers he's competed against are invited and check to see who will be his personal date. If any of his old flames are going to show up, we have to know about it ahead of time." He stared straight at Melanie, waving his hands for emphasis. "And I'll want you at that grand opening with your camera. We'll want every bit of glitz on our front page!"

Melanie's throat went dry as Brian kept talking. "That's not all. I want to know everything about Doel—inside out. His old man's a drunk—why? Didn't he do some time years ago? What happened, and where is he now?"

Evenly, Melanie replied, "I don't see that Jim Doel's tragedies have anything to do with the lodge reopening."

"Like hell. The man raised Gavin alone, didn't he? He shaped the kid. What happened to his mother? Is she still alive? Remarried? Does he have sisters or brothers or an aunt or uncle or cousin around here? You'd be surprised how easy it is to get people to talk about their famous relative. It makes them feel important, as if a little of that fame will rub off on them."

"This series is starting to sound like something you'd find at the checkout counter," Melanie said.

"Why?"

"Because you're more interested in finding out any dirt there is on Doel than reporting about the lodge."

Beside her, Jan drew her breath in sharply, but Brian didn't miss a beat. "I'm not interested in anything of the sort. I just want to sell papers. Period."

"No matter the standards?"

"I didn't say that, but listen, don't knock the tabloids. They make plenty!"

"And they're trashy. They're always getting sued."

"Hey—we won't print anything false. But we've got to generate interest in the lodge, interest in Doel, interest in the *Tribune!* You may as well know that the owners are putting pressure on us. Circulation's down, and we've got to do something about it."

"And that something is throwing Gavin Doel's life open for public inspection?" Melanie challenged.

"You bet." Brian took in a breath before continuing. "Look, he's the one who decided to come back to the small town where he was raised and reopen a resort that had gone bankrupt—a resort that represents a lot to the economy of this town. I can't help it that he's news—in fact, I'm thrilled that he jet-setted around the world and hung out with the rich and famous. All the better for the *Tribune.*"

"How would you feel if it were you?"

"Listen, if I had Doel's money and his fame and I was interested in selling lift tickets, you can bet I'd grab all the press I could get my hands on!"

"No matter what?" Melanie asked.

"No matter what! Do you have a problem with that?"

Melanie could feel her color rising. "I'd just like to think that we were working with the man rather than against him."

"His choice. The way I see it, we're doing him a favor." Clasping his hands behind his head, Brian leaned back in his chair and squinted his aquamarine eyes. "So, let's not let Doel's sensitivity about his privacy bother us too much and get down to business. I'll call his partner, get the go-ahead for the articles and we'll take it from there."

Melanie left the meeting with a sense of impending doom. Brian could whitewash his intentions all he wanted, but Gavin, when he discovered that his life was going to be thrown open and displayed for every reader of the *Tribune,*

would be livid. And Melanie didn't blame him. It occurred to
her that she could tell him what was happening, but he'd probably lay the blame at her feet. Besides, nothing had been
written yet. Maybe she could help edit the story. Crossing her
fingers, she hoped Brian would have a change of heart.

"Let me get this straight," Gavin said, eyeing his partner
angrily. "You agreed to do a *series* of articles about the
lodge."

"Sure. Why not?" Rich shrugged, opened the small refrigerator in the office and pulled out a bottle of beer. "I thought
we agreed that we could use all the publicity we could get."
He shoved the bottle across the coffee table and yanked out
another.

"We did," Gavin said, trying to tamp down the restless
feeling in his gut. "And I thought you were going to hang
around and handle them. Instead you bailed out on me."

"I already apologized. Besides, I had to be at the
courthouse—"

"Yeah, yeah, I know," Gavin said grumpily. "I guess I'm
just suspicious of reporters."

"They're not all out for blood."

"No—just big stories." He twisted off the cap of the bottle
and took a long swallow.

"So?"

"I've been burned before."

"The *Tribune* isn't exactly a national tabloid. It's just a
little local paper with ties to the *Portland Daily*. And those
ties—" he held up his beer to make his point "—are exactly
what we need right now. We have to stir up public awareness
and interest in Ridge Resort from Seattle all the way to L.A."

Gavin scowled. There was a chance that Rich was right, of
course, but in Gavin's opinion, it was a slim chance at best. In
the course of his career, he'd dealt with more than his share of

reporters and photographers, but he'd never had to deal with Melanie before.

He took another long swallow and shoved all thoughts of Melanie aside. She'd showed her true colors long ago, and it was just too damned bad that he'd had the bad luck to run into her again.

"So when's the next session?" he asked Rich.

"Next week. They want some pictures of the crew working on the lodge."

He clenched his teeth. "So they're sending up a photographer."

"Mmm-hmm."

Chest tightening, he asked slowly, "Which one?"

"As far as 1 know they only have one."

"I think we should have our own photos taken."

Rich's brows shot up. "Why?"

"We'll get what we want. No surprises."

"You're the one who wants to stay within budget, remember?" Rich shook his head. "Relax a little and enjoy the free publicity, will ya? This is the best thing that's happened to us so far."

"I doubt it," Gavin growled, feeling suddenly as if he couldn't breathe. Swearing, he reached for his crutches and struggled to his feet. Only one more day of these wretched tools—then, at least, he wouldn't feel like an invalid. Shoving the padded supports under his arms, he moved with surprising agility to the door.

"You know," Rich's voice taunted from behind, "if I didn't know better, I'd say you were all worked up over some woman."

"Well, you don't know better, do you?" Gavin flung over his shoulder, and Rich laughed. Balancing on his good foot, Gavin unlocked the back door and hobbled onto the deck.

Rays of afternoon sunlight filtered through the trees, and the warm air touched the back of his neck where beads of sweat had collected. His hands were slippery on the grips of his crutches and his heart pumped at the thought of coming face-to-face with Melanie again. *Melanie*. He squeezed his eyes shut and willed her gorgeous, lying Jezebel face from his mind.

Melanie spent the rest of the afternoon going through the pictures she'd taken at Ridge Resort. Most of the shots were of the lodge itself, but a few of the photographs were of Gavin, his jaw hard and set, his mouth tight, his eyes intense as he studiously avoided looking at the camera.

"These are perfect," Jan said, pointing to the most provocative shot of the bunch—a profile of Gavin, his hair falling over his face, his features taut, his mouth a thin, sexy line above a thrusting jaw. "Can you blow this one up?"

"Don't you think a shot of the lodge would be better?"

Jan tapped her finger to the side of her mouth and shook her head. "Nope—at least not for the female readers."

"And the male?"

Jan chewed on her lower lip, and her eyes narrowed thoughtfully. "I think even they would be interested in seeing what the enigmatic Mr. Doel looks like up close."

"Maybe we should use an overview of the lodge and a smaller inset of Gavin."

"Maybe," Jan said, but the pucker between her brows didn't go away, and Melanie realized she'd already made up her mind. "Or we could do it the other way around—a large profile of the man behind the lodge and a smaller shot of the resort itself."

"This isn't *People* magazine," Melanie pointed out. "The focus of the story is on the lodge, right?"

"Oh, come on, we'll have plenty of pictures of the construction. Let's focus on Doel. He's the public interest."

"He'll have a fit," Melanie predicted.

Jan smiled. "And won't that be interesting?"

"Interesting? In the same way hurricanes and earthquakes are 'interesting.'"

Jan eyed Melanie thoughtfully. "Just how well did you know Gavin? The truth, now."

"I met him a few times."

"So why're you so defensive about him?"

Melanie toyed with the idea of confiding in Jan, but the phone shrilled and Molly, the receptionist, flagged Jan down.

"It's that call you've been waiting for from the mayor's office," Molly whispered loudly.

"I've got it," she said, before turning back to Melanie. "Has anyone ever told you you worry too much?"

"Not for a while."

"Well, you do. Everything's going to work out. For us and for Doel and his resort."

*I hope you're right,* Melanie thought, but couldn't shake the feeling that the *Tribune* and everyone on its staff were asking for trouble.

Hours later, she drove home and was greeted at the back door by a thoroughly dusty and burr-covered Sassafras.

"Oh no you don't," she said, wedging herself through the door, effectively blocking Sassafras's dodge from the porch into the kitchen. She left her camera case and purse in the kitchen, changed into her faded jeans and an old T-shirt, then squeezed through the door to the porch.

Sassafras whined loudly, scratching at the door.

Melanie plopped onto a small stool. "So, tell me, where've you been?" She laughed, reaching for an old currycomb and ignoring his protests as she combed out his fur. He tried to wriggle free and even clamped his mouth around her wrist when she tugged at a particularly stubborn burr. "Okay, okay, *I* can take a hint," she said, tossing down the currycomb. She brushed the dog hair from her jeans and held open the door. "Now, Mr. Sassafras, you may enter," she teased.

The old collie dashed inside before she could change her mind, and she followed him. She changed clothes again, throwing on a clean skirt and a cotton sweater before returning to the kitchen. She barely had poured herself a glass of iced tea when the doorbell pealed and Sassafras began to bark loudly.

Glancing at her watch, Melanie groaned inwardly at the thought of the next hour and the Anderson children she was supposed to photograph—four of the most rambunctious kids she'd ever met.

Sassafras growled, then settled in his favorite spot under the kitchen table,

"Coming!" Melanie called, hurrying through the cool rooms of the old log house.

Cynthia Anderson and children were huddled on the wide front porch when Melanie opened the door. In matching red crew-neck sweaters and khaki slacks, the wheat-blond boys, ages two through eleven, dashed past Melanie, down the hall and through wide double doors to her studio.

"Boys! Wait!" Casting Melanie an apologetic look, Cynthia Anderson took off after her brood.

By the time Melanie reached the studio, the boys were already jockeying for position around the single wicker chair Melanie used for inside portraits.

"Maybe we should have this picture taken outdoors," Cynthia suggested as Melanie tried to arrange the siblings—oldest with the youngest on his lap, two middle children standing on either side.

Melanie straightened the two-year-old's sweater, then glanced over her shoulder. "If you want exterior shots, we'll have to schedule another appointment. Right now there's not enough light."

Cynthia rolled her eyes. "No way. They're finally back in the swing of school and soccer practice is just about every night. I barely got them together to come today. Believe me, it's now or never."

Melanie was relieved. Though she loved children, one session with these four was all she could handle. "Okay. Sean, you hold Tim on your knee."

"And turn his face to the right," their mother insisted. "He fell yesterday and he's got a black eye. . . ." She rattled on, talking nonstop about the boys as Melanie worked with them. For the next hour Melanie positioned and repositioned the children, adjusted the light, changed lenses and cameras and took as many pictures as she could before all four boys started squirming and pushing and shoving.

"Brian kicked me!" Randy cried, fist curled to retaliate.

"Did not!" Brian replied indignantly. "It was Sean!"

Sean was smothering a sly smile, and Melanie wished she could have caught the act on film.

"Boys, stop that!" Cynthia said. "Sean—you and Brian quit it right now! Ms. Walker is trying to take your picture. The least you could do is behave!"

"I think that'll do it," Melanie said, snapping the final shot.

"Good!" Sean, the oldest, pushed Tim from his lap. "I'm outta here!" He took off down the hall with his brothers following close behind.

"Thanks a bunch," Cynthia said, hastily writing a check for the sitting fee and handing it to Melanie. She shoved her wallet back into her handbag. "You know, I just heard today that Gavin Doel's back in town."

Melanie managed a smile she didn't feel. "Yeah."

"Well, I, for one, am glad someone's doing something with Ridge Resort. This town's been dead ever since it closed."

That much was true. But Melanie wasn't sure that Gavin could bring it back to life.

"Mom!" Outside a horn blared.

"Got to run," Cynthia said, starting for the door. "The natives are restless!"

Later, after uploading the photos and touching up some of the red-eye, making the Anderson boys look less devilish, Melanie soaked in a hot bath, poured herself a cup of tea and relaxed on the couch with a couple of cookies. Sassafras curled on the braided rug at her feet, his ears pricked forward, his eyes on her, hoping for a morsel.

Smiling, she offered the dog a corner of one cookie and he swallowed it without chewing. "You're just a glutton," she teased, and he lifted a paw, scratching her knee for more. "These aren't exactly on your diet." But she let him snatch the remainder of the final cookie from her palm. "Let's not tell the vet—he wouldn't understand."

She picked up the paperback spy thriller she'd been reading for the past week but couldn't concentrate on the intricate plot. Her mind kept wandering. To Gavin.

"Forget him," she chastised herself. "He's obviously forgotten you." Frowning, she tossed down the book, grabbed the remote control and snapped on the television.

A local newscaster, a young dark-haired woman with intelligent blue eyes, was smiling into the camera. ". . . and good news for central Oregon," she said. "All those rumors proved true. Gavin Doel and his partner, Rich Johanson, made a public announcement that they plan to reopen Ridge Resort on Mount Prosperity in time for the winter ski season. Our reporter was at Ridge Resort this afternoon."

The screen changed to footage of Gavin, reflective aviator sunglasses perched on his tanned face, crutches tucked under his arms, standing behind a hefty, steely-haired man whom Melanie assumed was Rich Johanson.

The camera focused on Gavin's features, and Melanie's throat constricted. His face was lean, nearly haggard, partially hidden by the oversized sunglasses. Thin, sensual lips, frozen in an expression of indifference, accentuated his strong, square jaw.

His light brown hair was nearly blond, streaked by days

spent bareheaded in the sun. His angled face was as rugged as the slopes he tackled so effortlessly, and there was a reserve to him evident even on the television screen.

Whereas Richard Johanson was dressed in a business suit and couldn't quit answering questions posed by the media, Gavin seemed bored and remote, as if he wanted only for the whole damn thing to be over with.

The screen flickered again, and the image changed to a steep mountain slope in France. A brightly dressed crowd gathered at the bottom of a ski run, and one woman, red-haired and gorgeous international model Aimee LaRoux, glanced at the camera before training her gaze up the hill.

The camera angle changed. Melanie's lungs constricted as another camera singled out a downhill racer. She'd seen this footage over and over again. Her throat went dry as Gavin, tucked low, streaked down the mountain. Seconds passed before one ski caught, flipping him high into the air. Skis and poles exploded. Gavin, in a bone-shattering fall, spun like a ragdoll end over end down the icy slope.

Melanie's heart went cold, and she snapped the television off. Her hands trembled so badly she stuffed them into the pockets of her terry robe. She didn't need to be reminded of the accident that may have cost Gavin his career—the accident that had fatefully thrown him back to Taylor's Crossing—the accident that had shoved him back into her life.

No, that wasn't right. He wasn't back in her life. She wouldn't let him! Not even if he wanted back in, which, of course, he didn't.

*Let's just keep our distance* she thought to herself, as if by thinking it she could convince herself.


Gavin rotated his foot, wincing as the muscles stretched. His leg was pale, thinner than the other and not much to look at. Several scars around his knee and ankle gave evidence to the wonders of medical science, though, according to his doctor, he still had weeks of physical therapy before he could hope to step into a pair of skis.

"Give it time," he told himself as he struggled into his favorite jeans and stood tentatively, placing only part of his weight on the injured leg. "Easy does it." He saw the cane sitting near his bed and ignored it, taking a few tentative steps around the small suite he'd claimed as his.

Located near the office on the first floor of the lodge, the suite boasted worn furniture he'd found in the basement, a small refrigerator, an oven, a fireplace and two closets. He had private access outside to a small deck. He'd added a microwave and coffee maker.

"All the comforts of home," he said with a sarcastic smile as he steadied himself by placing his hands on the bureau. He'd never been one for carrying around extra baggage, never stayed in one place long enough to collect furniture, paintings or memorabilia. Aside from a few special awards, medals and trophies, he didn't keep much, was always ready to move on. Until now, moving along had been easy. But that was before the accident.

And what now?

Settle down? He made a sound of disgust. He'd given up those dreams long ago, when Melanie had showed him the value of love. His finger curled around the edge of the bureau top, and when he glanced in the mirror, he scowled at his half-dressed reflection.

He remembered all too vividly falling in love with Melanie, as if the years of trying to forget her had only etched her more deeply into his mind. Their affair had been short and passionate and filled with dreams that had turned out to be one-sided. Oh, he'd been good enough to experiment with, make love to, whisper meaningless promises to, but as his old man had predicted, in the end she'd decided he wasn't good enough for her. She'd married a wealthy boy from a socially prominent family rather than gamble on a ski bum.

"All for the best," he grumbled, reaching for a T-shirt he'd tossed over the back of a nearby chair and sliding his arms through the cotton sleeves. Just below the knee his leg began to throb, and he sucked in a breath between his teeth. Tucking the shirt into the waistband of his jeans, his wayward mind wandered back to Melanie.

She'd given him some very valuable lessons, though he doubted she realized that she was the single reason he'd become so self-reliant. Her betrayal had taught him and taught him well. Never would he depend upon anyone but himself, and as for women—well, he'd had a few affairs. They hadn't lasted and he didn't care, though it bothered him a little that he'd gained a reputation as a womanizer in some of the tabloids. The rumors of his sizzling one-night-stands stemmed more from the overly active imaginations of the press than anything else.

He slid into beat-up Nikes and, with the aid of the cane, walked carefully to the office, where he expected to find Rich.

Instead, rounding the corner and shouldering open the door, he ran smack-dab into the one person he wanted out of his life.

But there she was, in beautiful 3-D. Melanie Walker Brooks.

# CHAPTER FIVE

Melanie, who had been waiting impatiently in the office of Ridge Resort, reached for the doorknob, only to have the door thrown open in her face. Startled, she drew back just as Gavin, walking with the aid of a cane, pulled up short. A flicker of surprise lighted his eyes, and he drew in a quick breath.

Muttering ungraciously, he glanced rapidly around the room. "You're here—again?" he demanded.

"Didn't you miss me?" she said, beaming a smile.

His mouth pinched at the corners, and a vein throbbed at his temple. She expected an insult, but he only asked, "Where's Rich?"

"I don't know."

"Are you waiting for him?" His eyes narrowed suspiciously.

"He told me to meet him here."

"When?"

"Today at eleven."

Gavin cast an irritated glance down at his watch, and Melanie had to smother another smile at his obvious frustration. He plowed rigid fingers through his hair, though the rebellious golden strands fell forward again, covering the creases marring his forehead. "What do you want?"

"I don't want anything. But, according to my editor, Brian Michaels, the article on Ridge Lodge has been expanded to a series."

"So I heard."

"Brian talked to Rich and sent me up here for more pictures. I was supposed to meet with your partner, that's all. It's no big mystery."

"So now you're my problem."

"I'm no one's problem, Gavin," she replied, surprised at how easily his name rolled off her tongue and how quickly she could be drawn into an argument with him. "And I suspect whatever problems you do have are of your own making."

"Not all of 'em." Gavin shifted, and his face, beneath his tan, blanched. Instinctively she glanced down at his leg, and he leaned against the doorframe for support, effectively blocking all chance of escape. Not that she wanted to, she reminded herself. She could deal with Gavin one-on-one if need be.

"Didn't you get enough pictures the other day?"

"Not quite. But don't worry, I'll try not to get in the way." He pressed his lips together.

"So why're you so camera shy?" she asked bluntly. "You've been photographed all over the world. But now, when you can use the publicity, you're backpedaling."

"Maybe I don't like yellow journalism."

"But the *Tribune*—"

"Peddles sleaze."

"No way!" she sputtered. "It's a small local paper—"

"With big ambitions. Oh, yeah, the *Trib*, isn't that what you call it—" at her nod he continued "—is subtle and wraps all its smut in a cozy, folksy format."

"That's ridiculous," she said, but she was still nervous with the memory of her last meeting with Brian and Jan.

"Is it?" Gavin asked, shaking his head. "I don't think so. I've dealt with Brian Michaels before."

Melanie caught her breath. "You have?"

"That's right."

This was news. Brian had never mentioned knowing Gavin. "When?" she asked suspiciously.

"Years ago. In Colorado."

She wanted to know more, but the conversation was getting too intense. Gavin was bound to blow up any second. She started through the door, but Gavin thrust out an arm, stopping her before she crossed the threshold. "What were you doing in here?"

"Rich said to meet him in the office. He wants to discuss some other work, I think. Anyway, that's what Brian said."

"What other work?"

"Your guess is as good as mine."

He frowned, the lines around his mouth tightening. "So when he wasn't here, what did you do?"

Melanie's heart began to pound. What did he think? "I waited."

"And while you were waiting?" he prodded.

Suddenly she understood. He thought she'd been snooping! She could see it in his eyes.

"While I was waiting, which has been all of eight or nine minutes, I sat in that chair—" she hooked a thumb at an overstuffed chair near the window "—and thought about the shots I'll need." Lifting her chin an inch, she said, "Oh, and I did snoop around a little—dug through your things, hoping to come up with some trashy dirt I can use in the paper and maybe sell to the tabloids for a few bucks—"

"I didn't accuse you of—"

"Bullshit, Gavin!" she cut in, unable to stop herself. "For your information, I didn't poke around your desk. I came here to take pictures and talk with your partner. I'm sorry to disappoint you but I don't have any devious plans!"

Gavin, using a cane for support, made his way past her and eyed the top of his desk. He frowned. "I bet your friend would have searched the room, if given the opportunity."

"My friend?"

"The reporter—what's her name? Jane?"

"Jan."

"I didn't like her."

"You don't like much, do you?"

He looked up sharply, and a golden flame leapt in his eyes. "Oh, I like some things," he admitted, his voice low.

"What? Just what is it you like these days?"

"I like expensive Scotch, steep mountains and women who don't ask a lot of questions."

"Dumb and beautiful, right?"

"Right," he said with a sarcastic smile. "It just keeps everything so much simpler."

"And that way you don't have to deal with a real woman, a person with a mind of her own, someone who might not deify you because you're some macho athletic jock!"

Stiffly, he dropped into the desk chair. "Seems to me you didn't mind too much."

"That was a long time ago," she shot back, closing her mind to the fact that she'd loved him. Now he was a stranger, a stranger with a biting cynicism that had the ability to slice deep. "And you've changed."

He leaned back in his chair, and his lips twisted. "I wonder why? It couldn't be because I trusted the wrong person, could it?"

Stunned, she swallowed hard. Pain welled up as if he'd struck her. "It doesn't matter," she replied, refusing to let him know he'd wounded her. "I'm here to do a job. That's all. What you think happened in the past really doesn't matter, does it?"

"You bet it matters!"

"Not anymore."

One of his golden brows lifted, challenging her, but she ignored it. Instead she picked up her camera case and said, "If you'll excuse me, I'll get to work. When Mr. Johanson shows up, point him in my direction. I'll be outside." Opening the door to the back deck, she flung over her shoulder, "I'll be at the blue chair."

Slamming the door shut, she marched across the deck, rested her palms on the thick weathered plank of the rail and took in three deep breaths.

*Damn him, damn him, damn him,* she thought, shaking inside.

She brushed her hair from her face and tried to calm down. The mountain air was clear and crisp with the promise of winter. Sunlight dazzled over the rocky cliffs and pine trees while dry grass and wildflowers added the fresh scent of a summer that hadn't quite disappeared. High overhead, against a backdrop of diaphanous clouds, a lonely hawk circled.

Melanie heard the door open behind her and braced herself.

"We don't have a blue chair anymore," he said, his voice soft and caressing. She dug her fingers into the weather-beaten railing but didn't turn to face him.

"Well, then, whatever you call it. You know the one I mean!"

"The Barbary Coast."

"The what?" Slowly she looked over her shoulder and caught him smiling, his eyes dancing with amusement at her bewilderment. But as quickly as it appeared, that fleeting hint of humor fled. "The runs have been named by the colors of their chairs for as long as there have been lifts."

"Then it's time for a change." He walked up to her and propped his injured leg on the lower rail.

What did she care? She wasn't about to argue with him. He could rename the whole damn mountain for all it mattered to her. She turned again, heading for the Barbary Coast chair.

"So where is that partner of yours?" he asked.

"I don't have one."

"The reporter who was here the other day."

Melanie shrugged. "I'm not Jan's keeper. I told her I'd get the shots we needed and she could arrange for another session with you. I didn't see that I needed to be involved."

His lips twisted. "How long is this going to take?"

She'd had enough of his foul mood. "I guess that depends on you," she said sarcastically. "If you're a good boy and answer all Jan's questions, it'll be over quickly, but if you start baiting her like you're doing with me right now, I guarantee you it'll be long and drawn-out."

"And what about you? How long do you plan to be here?"

"Believe me, I want it over as soon as possible. I plan to take some pictures now, a few more when the reconstruction really gets into swing and then, of course, more when the first snow hits and there are actually skiers up here. We'll probably end with a big spread when the lodge opens. That is," she added, "if you don't disapprove."

"Would it matter?"

"I don't know."

Suddenly she was staring at him as she had years ago—full of honesty and integrity. And she felt a very vital, private need to explain. "You're big-time, Gavin. Whether you want to admit it or not. Of course the press is interested. And it's not just your career, you know. It's your lifestyle."

His eyes darkened a fraction.

"You've been seen all over the world, in the glitziest resorts with the most gorgeous women, with a very fast, exciting crowd—actors, actresses, models, artists. You know, the beautiful crowd, the people middle-class America has an affair with."

His jaw clamped tight, and for a few long seconds he stared at her.

"Your name will become synonymous with Ridge Lodge

Resort. It's only natural that the public will be curious. And face it, you and that partner of yours are counting on it. So why don't you quit fighting me every step of the way and enjoy it?"

"Enjoy it," he repeated on a short laugh.

"Most men would love your fame."

"I'm not most men,"

"Lord, don't I know it," she said, hurrying across the deck, down the steps and through the tufts of dry grass. "I still need a few pictures of the interior of the lodge, you, your partner and . . . I don't know . . . something spectacular." She was thinking aloud, staring at the chair lift. "Something like a view from the top of the mountain." Her gaze landed at the hut at the base of the Barbary Coast lift. Twin cables, supported by huge black pillars, swept up the rocky terrain. Blue-backed chairs hung from the strong cable.

He followed her gaze. "You're not going up on that thing."

"Is it unsafe?"

"No, but—"

"It would be such a breathtaking view," she said, her mind already spinning ahead to the panorama that would be visible from the top of the lift. She'd been up there many times in winter, but never had she seen the mountains from that height before the snow season. "Oh, Gavin, it would be perfect!"

Gavin shook his head. "No way."

"Why not?"

"Too risky."

She cocked a disbelieving brow. "I never thought I'd hear you say that." She started for the hut at the base of the lift and motioned to the cables. "Can't you turn this thing on?"

"Yes, but I don't think it would be a good idea."

"That's no surprise. You haven't thought anything about the *Tribune*'s interest in the resort has been a good idea." She was already climbing down the steps of the deck and heading for the chair.

Gavin, using his cane, was right on her heels. "What're you trying to prove?"

"Nothing. I just want to get my job done. Then I won't bother you for a while."

"Promise?"

Spinning, eyes narrowed, she said, "I'll swear in blood if I have to!"

He almost smiled. She could see it in his eyes. But quickly the shutters on his eyes lowered and no hint of emotion showed through.

"Then let's go!"

"You don't have to come with me—"

"Like hell."

"Really—"

"Look, Mrs. Brooks, I don't know what kind of liability I have here, but I'm going with you to make sure you don't do something asinine and end up falling off the lift and killing yourself."

"Thanks for your concern," she mocked.

"It's not concern. It's simply covering my backside."

"And what can you do . . . ?" She motioned to his injured leg and wished she hadn't.

His face tightened. "It's with me or not at all," he muttered, turning away from her and mulishly crossing the remaining distance to the chair lift.

Telling herself she was about to make a grave error, she tucked the strap of her camera over one shoulder, pocketed an extra memory stick and followed him. "I must be out of my mind," she muttered under her breath but decided he was more crass than she as he struggled up the slight incline.

Gavin walked stiffly, jabbing his cane into the dry earth until he reached the hut, which was little more than a huge metal A-frame, open at one end to allow the chairs of the lift to enter, revolve around a huge post, then, after picking up skiers, start back up the hillside. He went into a private glassed-in operator's booth that was positioned on one side of the hut. Inside, visible through the glass, he picked up the receiver of a telephone and punched out a number, then waited, his fingers drumming impatiently on the window.

She watched as he spoke tersely into the phone for a few seconds, then slammed the receiver back into its cradle.

"We're all set," he said, meeting Melanie in the shade of the hut.

"You don't have to—"

"Of course I do," he clipped. "All part of our policy up here at Ridge Lodge to keep the public and the press happy."

"I bet."

A wiry, red-haired man shouted from the lodge, then dashed across the rough ground to the hut.

"This is Erik Link. He's in charge of maintenance of all the equipment," Gavin said as the freckle-faced operator entered the hut. "Erik—Melanie Brooks—"

"Walker," Melanie corrected, extending her hand.

"Nice to meet you," Erik replied.

"Melanie's a photographer for the local paper and she wants some pictures from the summit of the lift." He turned back to Melanie. "Erik will make sure we get up and down in one piece."

"That's encouraging." Melanie said dryly.

Erik grinned. "Piece of cake." He withdrew a key ring from his pocket and went into the lodge.

Sighing, she glanced down at his cane. "Really, Gavin, I can handle this alone. You're still laid up—"

"Temporarily."

"Unless you do something stupid and injure yourself again," she pointed out. "I bet your doctor would have a fit."

He smiled then, that same blinding flash of white that had always trapped the breath in her lungs. "My doctor'll never know." He leaned forward on his cane and surveyed her through inquisitive eyes. "You've changed, Mel," he said quietly. "There was a time when you'd do anything on a dare. Including being alone with me."

"This has nothing to do with being alone with you."

"Doesn't it?" One eyebrow arched dubiously. "You're the one who wanted the best pictures for that damned paper of yours. I'm just giving you what you wanted."

She was tempted. Lord, it would be great knocking the wind from his sails. She eyed the lift with its tall black poles and hesitated.

"Come on, Melanie. I won't bite. I'll even try to keep a rein on my temper."

"I won't hold my breath."

"We'll see." He motioned to Erik, who positioned himself at the station in the hut. A few seconds later, with a rumbling clang and a groan the chairs started moving slowly up the face of the mountain. Erik, smiling, stood at the attendant's box. "Any time," he yelled over the grind of machinery.

Melanie second-guessed herself. "What if we get stuck?"

"We won't."

"How will you get off?" she asked, eyeing his leg and cane. At the top of the lift, the platform had to be several feet below the chair to allow for snowfall. He couldn't possibly jump off the lift without reinjuring himself, and then there was the problem of climbing back on.

"I won't," he said, edging toward the moving chairs. "You'll have to take your pictures from the chair." Before she could argue, he shoved his cane into one hand, grabbed her fingers tightly, moved in front of the next chair and let the lift sweep them off their feet. Within seconds they were airborne.

"Nothing to it," he said, flicking her a satisfied glance.

"Right," she said, still steaming. "You always were bull-headed."

He frowned. "When I want to do something, I just do it."

"That could be dangerous."

"For me—or you?"

"Give me a break," she murmured, angry at being bullied into the chair but feeling a sense of exhilaration nonetheless. A rush of adrenaline swept through her veins as the chair began its ascent. The mountain air was clear, the sky a brilliant shade of autumn blue, broken only by high, thin clouds. A playful breeze was cool against her neck and cheeks and carried with it the fresh, earthy scent of pine.

Melanie slid a glance at Gavin and told herself firmly that the fact that her heart was beating as rapidly as a hummingbird's had nothing to do with the fact that his shoulder brushed hers or that his thigh was only inches from her leg.

Her throat grew tight, and she forced her gaze back to the view. Uncapping the lens from her camera, she stared through the viewfinder, adjusted the focus and clicked off several quick shots of the mountain looming straight ahead.

The peak was dusted with snow, but the rest of the mountain above the timberline was sheer, craggy rock.

"Why'd you come back to Taylor's Crossing?" she asked as the chair climbed up the final steep grade of bare rock.

"Because the deal was right on the resort and because of this." He kicked up his injured foot and frowned at his leg.

"But that's only temporary."

"Maybe."

"Will you be able to race again?"

"It all depends," he admitted, "on how I've healed." His lips tightened. "Maybe it's time to retire."

"At thirty?"

He laughed, but the sound didn't carry any mirth as it bounced off the mountain face. "Looks that way."

The chair rounded the top of the lift and started downward. Melanie had to grit her teeth. Riding the chair up was one thing, but staring down the sheer mountain was quite another. Her hands began to sweat as she lifted the camera again.

Gavin's fingers clamped over her upper arm. "Be careful."

Melanie's concentration centered on those five strong fingers warm against her bare skin, heating her flesh.

She knew he could feel her pulse, hoped it wouldn't betray her as she forced the camera to her eyes and found breathtaking shots of the mountaintops. With her wide-angled lens, she caught the broken ridge of the Cascades. Thin, lazy clouds drifted between the blue peaks, and tall spires of snow pierced the wispy layer.

As the chair moved downward, past the timberline, she caught rays of morning sunlight. Golden beams sifted through the pine trees to dapple the needle-strewn forest floor.

Lower still, she focused the camera on the lodge, snapping off aerial shots of the weathered shake roof and sprawling wings.

"It's beautiful up here," she admitted, hazarding a glance at Gavin. Their gazes locked, and for a breathless instant Melanie was transported back to a place where things were simple and all that mattered was their love. He felt it, too; she could read it in his gold-colored eyes—a tenderness and love so special it still burned bright.

He swallowed and turned quickly to focus on the pines. His voice, when he spoke, was rough. "Look, Mel, I think we should get some things straight. I didn't know you'd be in Taylor's Crossing when I came back."

"Would it have changed your mind?"

"Probably—I don't know. Rich was hell-bent to reopen this lodge, but . . ." His voice drifted off, lost in the gentle rush of the breeze and the steady whir of the lift. "I—you—we made a lot of mistakes, didn't we?"

Her heart wrenched as she thought of their child—a child who hadn't even had a chance to be born. "More than you know."

"And I was wrong about a lot of things," he said, still avoiding her gaze. "And one of those things was you."

Bracing herself, she decided to try to bridge the horrible

abyss that loomed between them, to tell him the truth. She placed her hand on his arm and said, "Look, Gavin, as long as we're talking about the past, there's something you should know—"

"All I know is it's over!" His face grew dark. "The past was just a means to an end. A way to get what I wanted." He stared straight at her. "And what happened didn't really matter. You and I—we were just a couple of kids playing around!"

"And that's why you're carrying this chip the size of Mount Everest on your shoulder," she mocked, "because it 'didn't matter'? Who're you trying to kid?"

He smiled then, slowly and lazily. "If it makes you feel better to think you're the cause of my discontent, go right ahead. But that's making yourself pretty damned self-important, if you ask me."

"Why wouldn't I think it?" she challenged, angry again. "The minute you set eyes on me again, you went for my throat. There has to be a reason you hate me, Gavin."

A muscle worked in his jaw, and his voice, when he spoke, was barely a whisper. "I've never hated you, Melanie."

Her heart turned over. *Don't,* she thought desperately. *Whatever you do, Gavin, don't be kind!*

She opened her mouth, wanting to say something clever, but couldn't find the words. Besides, what good would it do, dredging it all up again? Instead, she fiddled with her camera, pretended interest in a few more shots and wished the ride would end. Being this close to Gavin, tangled up in old and new emotions, was just too difficult. "You're right," she agreed, forcing a cool, disinterested smile. "We were just a couple of kids. We didn't know what we wanted."

"Oh, I knew what I wanted," he said. "I wanted to be the best damn skier in the world."

"And nothing else?"

"Nothing else really mattered, did it?"

"No, I guess you're right," she replied tightly. "Skiing is all there is in life!"

His shoulders tensed, and the corners of his mouth tightened. At the bottom of the lift he motioned to Erik. The lift slowed, and Gavin helped her off, hopping nimbly on his good leg and swinging her to her feet as the lift stopped.

Leaning heavily on his cane, Gavin started hobbling back to the lodge, and she knew she couldn't leave things unsettled. Not if they were going to work together.

"Gavin . . ." Reaching forward, she touched his forearm again, and he spun around quickly, his expression stern, his eyes blazing.

"Go home, Melanie. You've got your pictures, though why you're taking them for that rag's beyond me."

"'That rag' is the paper I work for."

He stopped dead in his tracks. "Couldn't you find a better one in Seattle?"

"I moved back here," she said, inching her chin up a fraction. "After the divorce."

He didn't respond as he propelled himself back to the lodge.

"Fool," she muttered, when he'd slammed into the building. "Why do you try?" *Because he has the right to know what really happened eight years ago.*

Drawing in a deep breath, she walked into the lodge and found Jan in the main lobby, chatting with Rich Johanson.

". . . then we'll be back in a couple days," Jan was saying.

Gavin was nowhere in sight. Slowly Melanie let out her breath, and Jan, spying her, waved her over and made hasty introductions.

"Sorry I was late," Rich apologized. "I got held up in court."

"No problem," Melanie said, hearing uneven footsteps approach. She stiffened.

"I took care of Ms. Brooks," Gavin said.

"Walker," Melanie corrected. "My name's Walker now."

"Again," he said.

"Yes, again." She forced a cool smile in Gavin's direction, though her fists were clenched so tight they ached.

Jan, delighted to find Gavin available, suggested they continue their interview.

He clenched his jaw but didn't disagree, and they settled into a table in a corner of the main lobby.

"Looks like he's in a great mood," Rich observed.

"One of his best," Melanie remarked.

"With Gavin it's hard to tell." Rich shoved his hands through his hair. "Did you get everything you need?"

"I think so."

"Good. Good. Let's go outside." He motioned her into one of the chairs on the deck. "I've heard that you're the best photographer in town."

Melanie sat with her back to the sun. "You must've been talking to my Uncle Bart," she said, laughing.

Rich waved off her modesty. "I've seen your pictures in the paper and looked over the work you did for the Conestoga Hotel. The manager couldn't say enough good things about you."

Melanie was pleased. She'd worked long and hard on the brochures for the Conestoga.

"And you did the photographs in the lobby of the hotel, right?"

Melanie nodded.

"Mmm. Look, I talked to several people in town because I need a photographer for the lodge, not only for pamphlets, brochures and posters but also to hang on the walls. We're reopening the resort with a Gold Rush theme and we'll need old pictures, blown up and colored brown—you know what I mean?"

"Sepia tones on old tintypes and daguerreotypes," she said.

"If you say so," he said a little sheepishly. "I don't know all the technical terms, but I do know what I want. We'll need between twenty and thirty for the lobby. Let me show you what I mean." He opened a side door to the main gathering room in the lodge and held it open while Melanie got to her feet and walked inside.

Jan and Gavin were still seated at the table, and from Gavin's body language Melanie guessed the interview wasn't going all that well.

Rich didn't seem to notice. He pointed to the walls where he wanted to hang the old photos. "Over here," he said with a sweeping gesture, "I'd like several mining shots and on the far wall, pictures of the mountain."

Rich rattled on and on. Though she listened to him, she was aware of Gavin talking reluctantly to Jan. She could feel the weight of his gaze on her back, knew he was glowering.

Eventually Rich guided her into the office where she was supposed to have met him two hours before and offered her a cup of coffee. Once they were seated, he said, "Besides the pictures for the lobby, we'll need photographs for brochures and posters. And we'll be selling artwork in one of the shops downstairs. We'd like some of your photographs on consignment." He opened up his palms. "So, if you're interested, I'd like you to become the photographer for Ridge Resort."

"Have you talked this over with Gavin?" she asked. Though a part of her would like to take the job and let Gavin rant and rave all he liked, the sensible side of her nature prevented her from jumping into a situation that was bound to spell trouble.

"I don't have to talk to him," Rich replied with a grin. "This is my decision."

"Maybe you should say something to him," she suggested, gathering her things.

"Look, Ms. Walker, I don't have much time. We plan to open in two months. I need brochures ASAP."

He offered her a generous flat fee and a percentage on all the posters sold, plus extra money for extra work. The job at Ridge Lodge, should she take it, would help establish her studio as well as pay off some of the debts she'd incurred since her divorce and give her a little cushion so that she wasn't quite so dependent on the *Tribune*. In short, Rich Johanson's offer was too good to pass up.

She cast a nervous glance in Gavin's direction, noted the hard, immovable line of his jaw and knew he would hit the roof. But it didn't matter. She needed all the work she could get. "I'd be glad to work for you," she said, feeling a perverse sense of satisfaction.

Rich grinned and clasped her hand. "Good. I'll draw up a contract and we can get started as soon as it's convenient for you."

"I can work evenings and weekends."

"Will you have enough time?"

She shot another look in Gavin's direction. "Don't worry," she said, ignoring the tight corners of Gavin's mouth and the repressed fury that fairly radiated from him, "I'll make the time." She scrounged in her wallet, handed him her card and added, "Give me a call as things firm up and we can go from there."

"Thanks." Rich stuffed the card in his wallet. "I'll be seeing you soon then." They shook hands again before Melanie, refusing to glance at Gavin one last time, gathered her things and headed for the front doors.

As she made her way down the asphalt path, she heard Jan's quick footsteps behind her. "Hey, Melanie, wait up!"

Melanie turned, watched Jan hurrying to catch her and noticed Gavin, hands braced on the porch rails of the lodge, glaring at her. She couldn't imagine what he'd think when he found out Rich had hired her. With a satisfied grin, she waved at him before turning her attention to a breathless Jan. "How'd it go?" Melanie asked.

"With Doel?" Jan sighed loudly and whispered, "I think

it would be easier to interview a monk who's taken a vow of silence."

"Oh?"

Jan glanced over her shoulder, then said softly, "I want details, Melanie, details."

"About what?"

"You and Doel. I saw the looks he sent you. They were positively sizzling! And when we were up here before, I could've sworn there was something going on between you two. What gives?"

"You're imagining things."

"And you're holding out on me. There's more to it than the fact that you guys went to school together." She reached her car and unlocked the door. "I mean it, Melanie. I want to know everything."

"It's not an interesting story," Melanie replied, though she knew sooner or later Jan would find out the truth—or part of it.

"Anything about Doel is interesting."

"Later," Melanie promised, needing time to sort out just how much she could confide. There was no getting around at least part of the truth. Jan would only discover the information somewhere else, and unfortunately, Taylor's Crossing was a small town. If Jan set her mind to finding out the truth, it wouldn't be too hard to dig up someone who would willingly remember. Only a handful of people had known that she and Gavin had been seeing each other—fewer still guessed they'd been lovers—but the townspeople in Taylor's Crossing had long memories when it came to gossip.

Frowning, Melanie slid into her sunbaked car. She glanced through the dusty windshield to the lodge. Gavin's eyes were narrowed against the sun, his jaw set in granite. How would she ever begin to explain the depth and complexity of her feelings for him? She'd been only seventeen at the time. No one, including Jan, would believe that her romance had been anything but puppy love.

But she knew better. As she slid a pair of sunglasses onto the bridge of her nose and drove out of the lot, she wished she could forget that she'd ever loved him.

# CHAPTER SIX

"You did *what?!*" Gavin roared, eyeing his partner as if he'd lost his mind.

"I hired Melanie Walker."

"You've got to be kidding!" Gavin growled.

"What've you got against her?" Rich asked, his brows drawing together.

"I knew her years ago."

"So?" Sitting at his desk, pen in one hand, Rich stared up at Gavin as if he were the one who had gone mad.

"We dated."

Rich still wasn't getting the point. "I don't understand—"

"While I was gone, she married a guy by the name of Neil Brooks eight years ago."

"Neil Brooks—the lumber broker?"

"You know him?" Gavin growled, rolling his eyes and tossing his hands out as if in supplication to the heavens. "This just gets better and better."

"Of course I know him. Brooks Lumber is our major supplier for the renovation."

"No fucking way," Gavin whispered harshly as he thought

of Melanie's ex-husband—the man who had, in a few short weeks, stolen Melanie from him. He told himself he couldn't really blame Brooks. It had been Melanie who had betrayed him. Nonetheless, he loathed anything to do with Neil Brooks. "Find another lumber company."

"No can do," Rich said, assuming a totally innocent air. "Brooks Lumber is one of the few firms that'll service this area."

"There must be someone else! We're not in Timbuktu, for crying out loud!"

"Brooks offers the best quality for the lowest price."

"I don't give a damn." This was turning into a nightmare. First Melanie and now Neil. Gavin's throat felt suddenly dry. He needed a drink. A double. But he didn't give in to the urge.

"Well, I do. I give a big damn. We don't have a lot of extra cash to throw around. Besides, we had a deal. I handle this end of the business—you help design the runs, bring in the investors and provide the skiing expertise."

"That's exactly what I'm doing. Providing expertise. Don't use Brooks. He's as slippery as a rattler and twice as deadly."

"Are you speaking from personal experience?"

"Yes, damn it!" Gavin crashed his fist against the corner of Rich's desk, sloshing coffee on a few papers.

"Hey, watch it." Rich, perturbed, grabbed his handkerchief and mopped up the mess. "Look, even if I wanted to change lumber companies—which I don't—I can't. It's too late. We've already placed our order. Some of it has already been shipped and paid for. We don't have much time, Gavin, so whatever particular personal gripe you've got with Neil Brooks, you may as well shove it aside. And as for Neil's wife—or ex-wife or whatever she is—she's working for us. We both agreed that we'd employ as many local people as we could, remember? It's just good business sense to keep the locals happy!"

"I didn't know Melanie was back in town."

Rich grinned. "You've always had an eye for good-looking women, and that one—she's a knockout."

Gavin clenched his fist, but this time he did no more than shove it into his pocket. "I'm just not too crazy about some of your choices," Gavin muttered. He didn't want Melanie here, couldn't stand the thought of seeing her every day. He'd told himself he was long over her, but now he wasn't so sure. There was a moment up on the lift when he could've sworn that nothing had changed between them. But, of course, that was pure male ego. Everything had changed. "Was working for the lodge her idea?" he asked.

Rich shook his head. "Nope. In fact, I had to do some hard and fast talking to get her to take the job."

"You should have consulted with me first."

"That's what she said."

Gavin was surprised. "But you didn't listen?"

"No, I didn't. I wanted her. And as for consulting with you, that works both ways."

Gavin's jaw began to work, and he crossed to the window and stared out at the cool late summer day. A few workers dotted the hillside, and down the hall, in the lounge, the pounding of hammers jarred the old building.

"There's something else bothering you," Rich guessed, shoving back his chair and rounding the desk. Crossing his thick arms over his chest, fingers drumming impatiently, he stared at Gavin and waited.

"We don't need any adverse publicity," Gavin said flatly.

"And you think Melanie's going to give us some?"

Gavin hesitated, but only for a second. He trusted Rich, and they were partners. As his business partner, Rich had the right to know the whole story. He probably should have leveled with Rich before. But then, he'd had no idea he would run into Melanie again. If he had guessed she was back in Taylor's Crossing, he might have balked at the project.

"Well?" Rich was waiting.

"You know that I grew up here," Gavin said, seeing Rich's eyes narrow. "And you know that my father had his problems."

"So you said."

Gavin's muscles tightened as he remembered his youth. "Dad's an alcoholic," he said finally, the words still difficult.

"I know."

"And he spent some time in prison."

"You said something about it—an accident that was his fault."

"An accident that killed the driver of the other car," he said quietly. "A woman, Brenda Walker. Melanie's mother."

Rich didn't move.

"Dad was legally drunk at the time."

Frowning, Rich said, "I'm sorry."

"So am I, and so was Dad—when he sobered up enough to understand what had happened. He came away with only a few scrapes and bruises, but Melanie's mother's car was forced off the road and down a steep embankment." Gavin relived the nightmare as if it had happened just yesterday. He'd been twelve at the time when the policemen had knocked on the door, the blue and red lights of their cars casting colored shadows on the sides of the trailer that he and his father had called home. He'd thought for certain his father was dead but had been relieved when he'd found out Jim Doel had survived.

However, that night had been just the tip of the iceberg, the start of a life of living with an aunt and uncle who hadn't given a damn about him.

Through it all, Gavin had escaped by testing himself. From the time he could handle a paper route, he'd spent every dime on the thrill of sliding downhill on skis. He'd landed odd jobs—eventually at Ridge Resort itself—and fed his unending appetite for the heart-pounding excitement of racing headlong down a steep mountain at breakneck speed.

In all the years since the night his father had been taken to jail, Gavin's only distraction from the sport he loved had been Melanie.

The only daughter of the woman his father had killed.

Rich asked, "And you think Melanie still holds a grudge?"

"I don't know," Gavin answered. "I thought I knew her, but I didn't. Ten years after the accident, against her father's better judgment, Melanie and I dated for a while." Gavin's gut wrenched at the vivid memories. "But then I had the opportunity to train for the Olympics."

"So you left her."

"I guess that's the way she saw it. I asked her to wait . . ." Gavin's lips twisted at his own naiveté.

"But she didn't."

Gavin felt again the glacial sting of her rejection. His nostrils flared slightly. "Adam Walker—Melanie's father—never approved of me or my old man. And while I was gone, Melanie married Neil Brooks. My guess is that her old man finally convinced her she'd be better off with the son of a wealthy lumber broker than a ski bum whose father was a drunk."

"And now?"

Gavin looked up sharply. "And now what?"

"Melanie and you?"

Gavin let out a short, ugly laugh. "There is no Melanie and me." His insides turned frigid. "There really never was."

Rich let out a sigh. "You should've told me this earlier, you know."

"Didn't see a reason. As far as I knew she was still living the good life up in Seattle."

"She's already agreed to the job, you know," Rich said, rubbing his temple. "I don't see how we can get out of this without causing a lot of hard feelings. I didn't sign a contract, but if it gets out that we're not good on our word—"

"Don't worry about it. Keep Melanie Walker," Gavin decided suddenly. He could find ways to avoid her. The lodge was large; the resort covered thousands of acres. Besides, he'd be too busy to run into her often. "Just as long as she does the job," he muttered, *and added silently, and doesn't get in my way.*

Jan wouldn't let up. She'd camped out at Melanie's desk when they returned from the resort and wasn't taking no for an answer. "I saw the way he looked at you. You can't convince me there's nothing going on between you and Gavin," she said, checking her reflection in her compact mirror and touching up her lipstick.

"I haven't seen him in years." Melanie walked into the darkroom and picked up the enlarged photograph of Uncle Bart and his prize colt, Big Money. She slipped the black-and-white photo into an envelope and, returning to her desk, pretended she wasn't really interested in Jan's observations about Gavin.

Sighing in exasperation, Jan tossed her hands into the air. "Okay, okay, I believe that you haven't seen him," she said, ignoring Melanie's efforts at nonchalance. "But what happened all those years ago? The looks he sent you today were hot—I mean, scorching, burning, torrid, you name it!"

Tucking the envelope into her purse, Melanie chuckled. "You're overdramatizing."

"I'm a reporter. I don't go in for melodrama. Just the facts. And the fact is he couldn't keep his eyes off you."

"You're exaggerating, then." Melanie walked to the coffeepot and poured two cups.

"Am not! Now, what gives?"

Melanie handed Jan one of the cups, took a sip herself and grimaced at the bitter taste. She opened a small packet of sugar and poured it into her cup. "Well, I guess you're going to find out sooner or later, but this is just between you and me."

"Absolutely!" Jan took a sip of her coffee, but over the rim her eyes were bright, eager.

Haltingly, Melanie explained that she and Gavin had dated

in high school, glossing over how deep her emotions had run. "And so, when he went to train for the Olympics, we lost touch and I married Neil."

Jan shook her head. "You chose Neil Brooks over Gavin Doel?" she asked incredulously. "No offense, Mel, but there's just no comparison."

"Well, that's what happened."

"And nothing else?"

"Nothing," Melanie lied easily. "But what I told you is strictly off the record, right?"

"Absolutely." Jan looked positively stricken. "Besides, no one's going to care whom he dated in high school."

Jan slid a look at her watch and frowned. "I gotta run," she said, "but I'll see you tomorrow. When will the photos of the lodge be ready?"

"I'll have them on your desk first thing in the morning."

"You're a doll. Thanks." With a wave, Jan bustled out of the building.

Melanie spent the next few hours going over the photographs she'd taken at the lodge, toying with the colors and contrast. The shots from the chair were spectacular, vistas of the rugged Cascade Mountains. A few pictures of the workers, too, showed the manpower needed to give the lodge its new look. But the photographs that took her breath away were the close-ups of Gavin that she changed to black-and-white.

His features seemed more chiseled and angular—as earthy and formidable as the mountains he challenged, his eyes more deeply set, his expression innately sexy and masculine. And though she'd seen little evidence of humor in the time she'd spent with him, the photographs belied his harshness by exposing the tiny beginnings of laugh lines near his mouth and tiny crinkles near the corners of his eyes. She wondered vaguely who had been lucky enough to make him laugh.

She noted the best shots, stuffed them in an envelope and left the packet in Jan's in-basket. By the time she was finished, most of the staff had left. Walking into the fading sunlight, she took the time to lock the door behind her, then noticed the cool evening breeze that chilled her bare arms.

The mountain nights had begun to grow cold.

She stopped at the grocery store on the way home and finally turned into her drive a little after seven. The sky was dusky with the coming twilight, shadows stretched across the dry grass of her yard, and a truck she didn't recognize was parked near the garage. Gavin sat behind the wheel.

She stood on the brakes. The Volkswagen screeched to a stop.

Surely he wasn't here.

But as she stared at the truck, her heart slammed into overdrive. Gavin stretched slowly from the cab. *Now what?* she wondered, her throat suddenly dry as she forced herself to appear calm and steeled herself for the upcoming confrontation. It had to be about Rich's offer.

Wearing faded jeans, a black T-shirt, a beat-up leather jacket and scruffy running shoes, he reminded her of the boy she'd once known, the kid from the wrong side of the tracks. No designer labels or fancy ski clothes stated the fact that he was a downhill legend.

Deciding that the best defense was a quick offense, she juggled purse, groceries and camera case as she climbed out of the Volkswagen. "Don't tell me," she said, shoving the car door closed with her hip and forcing a dazzling smile on slightly frozen lips. "You've come racing over here to congratulate me on my new job at the resort."

His jaw slid to the side, and he shoved his sunglasses onto his head. "Not exactly."

She lifted a disdainful eyebrow. "And I thought you'd be thrilled!"

"Rich handles that end of the business,"

"Does he? So you didn't come over here to tell me that I'm relieved of my newfound duties?"

"I considered it," he admitted with maddening calm.

"Look, Gavin, let's get one thing straight," she said. "I'm not going to get into a power struggle with you. If you want me to do the job, fine. If not, believe me, I won't starve. So you don't have to feel guilty. If you want someone else to do the work, just say so."

"Rich seems set on you."

"And you?"

Brackets pinched the corners of his mouth, "I don't know. I haven't seen your work. At least, not for a few years."

She ignored that little jab and marched across the side yard to the back door. She kept her back rigid, pretended that she didn't care in the least that he'd shown up at her doorstep. Over her shoulder she called, "Well, if you're interested, come inside. But if you're just here to give me a bad time, then you may as well leave. I'm not in the mood."

Shifting the groceries and camera case, she unlocked the back door. Sassafras, barking and growling, snapping teeth bared, hurtled through. He didn't even pause for a pet but headed straight for Gavin.

"Don't worry," she called to Gavin over her shoulder, "he's all bark—no bite."

But Gavin didn't appear the least bit concerned about Sassafras's exposed fangs or throaty warnings. He flashed a quick glance at the dog and commanded, "Stop!"

Sassafras skidded on the dry grass but the hairs on the back of his neck rose threateningly.

"That's better," Gavin said, slowly following Melanie up the steps. "Damned leg," he grumbled, pausing in the doorway.

"Come on in," Melanie invited. "I don't bite, either—at least, not usually." She placed the bag on the counter. "Just give me a minute to get things organized." She kicked her shoes into a corner near the table and stuffed a few sacks of vegetables and a package of meat into the refrigerator.

She felt him watching her, but she didn't even glance in his direction. She pretended not to be aware that he was in the room, managing a fake calm expression that she hoped countered her jackhammering heart and suddenly sweating palms. Now that he was in the house, what was she going to do with him? The house seemed suddenly small, more intimate than ever before.

The fact that he was in her house, alone with her, brought back too many reminders of the past. The rooms felt hot and suffocating, though she expected the temperature couldn't be more than sixty-five degrees.

"Come on, my studio's down the hall," she said, opening the door for Sassafras. Cool mountain air streamed in with the old dog as he eyed Gavin warily, growling and dropping onto his favorite spot beneath the kitchen table. "See, he likes you already," Melanie quipped, suppressing a smile at Sassafras's low growl.

"I'd hate to think how he reacts to someone he doesn't like."

"Just about the same." Melanie led Gavin to the front of the house and down a short corridor to her studio. He didn't remark on the changes in the house, but maybe he didn't remember. He'd been over only a few times while they'd dated and he hadn't stayed long because of her father's hostility.

As she opened the studio door, Gavin caught her wrist. "I didn't come here to see your work," he said, spinning her around so that she was only inches from him, her upturned face nearly colliding with his chest.

"But I thought—"

"That was just a ruse." He swallowed, his Adam's apple moving slowly up and down in his throat. Melanie forced her eyes to his. "I came here because I wanted to lay out the ground rules, talk some things out."

"What 'things'?" His hand was still wrapped around her wrist, his fingertips hot against the inside of her arm. No doubt he could feel her thundering pulse. The small, dark hallway felt close. It was all she could do to pull her arm from his grasp.

"I just want you to know that I don't want any trouble."

"And you think I'll give it to you?"

"I think that rag you work for might."

She bristled. "The *Tribune*—"

"We've been over this before," he said, cutting her off as she found the doorknob and backed into the studio. She needed some breathing room. With a flick of her wrist she snapped on the overhead light. "I have a feeling that reporter friend of yours would print anything if she thought it would get her a byline."

"Not true."

"If you say so." He didn't seem convinced. Glancing quickly around the studio, he slung his injured leg over a corner of her desk. "But she gets pretty personal."

"You don't have to worry about Jan," Melanie said, instantly defensive. "I told her a little of our history."

"You did *what?*" he thundered, gold eyes suddenly ice-cold.

"It's all off the record."

"You trust her?"

"Of course I trust her. We work together and she's my friend."

He snorted. "I suppose you trust Michaels, too."

"Yeah," she replied indignantly.

Gavin muttered something unintelligible. "He hasn't been your boss for long has he?"

"No," she conceded. "The paper changed hands about a year ago. Brian was hired to take charge."

"From where?"

"Chicago, I think. He's worked in publishing for years. Before Chicago, there was a paper in Atlanta."

"Right. Never planted his feet down for long, has he? And I wouldn't think Taylor's Crossing, Oregon is the next natural step up on the ladder of success. Atlanta, Chicago, Taylor's Crossing? Doesn't seem likely, does it?"

"What're you trying to say, Gavin?" she asked, bristling at the unspoken innuendos.

"I've met Michaels before. He was a reporter in Vail. I didn't like him then and I don't trust him now."

Folding her arms across her chest, she said, "You are the most suspicious person I know. You don't trust anyone, do you?"

"I wonder why," he said quietly, his features drawn.

Her heart stopped. "So you're blaming me?"

"No, Melanie, I'm blaming myself," he replied, his words cutting sharply. "I was young and foolish when I met you—naive. But you taught me how stupid it is to have blind trust. It's a lesson I needed to learn. It's gotten me through some tough times."

"So you're here to thank me, is that it?" she tossed out, though she was dying inside.

"I'm here to make sure that you and I see eye to eye. I want our past to remain buried, and for that to happen, you'd better quit talking to Jan or anyone else at the *Tribune*."

"Is that so?"

"For both our sakes as well as my father's. No matter what happens, I want Dad's name kept out of the paper."

Melanie bit her lower lip. "I don't know if that's possible."

"Well, use your influence."

"I will, of course I will, but I'm only the photographer."

"And the bottom line is Brian Michaels doesn't give a damn whose life he turns inside out." He stood then, towering over her, his eyes blazing. "My father's paid for what happened over and over again. We all have. There is no reason to dredge it all up again."

"I agree. I just don't know what I can do."

Gavin sighed, raking his fingers through his hair. "Dad's

moving back to Taylor's Crossing and I want to see to it that he can start fresh."

"I doubt anyone'll be interested."

"Aren't you naive! You just don't know what kind of an industry you work for, do you?"

"We report the news—"

"And the gossip and the speculation—anything as long as it sells papers!"

"I'm not going to stand here and argue about it with you," she retorted, wishing she felt a little more conviction. "If you're finished—"

"Not quite. Now that we understand each other—"

"I don't think we ever did."

"Doesn't matter. You stay out of my way and I'll stay out of yours. If you have any questions while you're working up at the lodge, you can ask Rich."

"And if he's not there?"

"Then I'll help you."

"But, don't go chasing after you, is that what you're telling me?" she mocked, simmering fury starting to boil deep inside her.

"I just think it's better if you and I keep our distance."

"Don't worry, Gavin," she remarked, her voice edged in cynicism. "Your virtue is safe with me."

He flushed from the back of his neck. "Don't push me, Melanie."

"Wouldn't dream of it," she threw back at him. "I'm not afraid of you, Gavin."

His gaze shifted to her mouth. "Well, maybe you should be," he whispered hoarsely.

"Why?"

He swallowed hard. His expression tightened in his attempt at self-control. "Because, damn it, even though I know it's crazy, even though I tell myself this'll never work, I just can't help . . . Oh, to hell with it."

His arms surrounded her, and his lips covered hers.

Surprised, Melanie gasped, and his tongue slipped easily between her teeth, tasting and exploring.

She knew she should push him aside, shove with all her might, and she tried—dear Lord, she tried—but as her hands came up against his chest they seemed powerless, and all she could do was close her eyes and remember, in painful detail, the other kisses they'd shared. He still tasted the same, felt as strong and passionate as before.

Her lips softened, and she kissed him back. All the lies and the accusations died away. She was lost in the smell and feel of him, in the power of his embrace, the thundering beat of her heart.

Slowly, his tongue stopped its wonderful exploration, and a low groan escaped from him. "Melanie . . ." he whispered against her hair, his arms strong bands holding her close. "Why?"

She tried to find her voice, but words failed her.

Slowly he released her, stepping backward and shoving shaking fingers through his hair. She watched as he visibly strained for control.

"Gavin, I think we should talk."

"We've said everything that has to be said," he replied. "This isn't going to work, you know."

"We'll make it work."

His gaze slid to her lips again, and she swallowed with difficulty. "No."

"I need to explain about Neil," she said.

His features hardened. "You don't have to explain about anything, Melanie. Let's just forget this ever happened."

"I don't think I can."

"Well, try," he said, turning on his heel and striding out the door.

She didn't move for a full minute, and only after she heard

his pickup spark to life, tires squeal and gravel spray, did she sag against the door.

The next few weeks promised to be hell.

"Jesus Christ!" Gavin pounded on the steering wheel with his fist. What had gotten into him? He'd kissed her! *Kissed* her—and she'd responded. Suddenly, in those few moments, time and space had disappeared, and Gavin was left with the naked truth that she wasn't out of his blood.

He cranked on the wheel and gunned the accelerator as he left the city lights behind and his truck started climbing the dark road leading to the mountain.

He couldn't hide from her. Not now. As a photographer for the resort, she'd be at the lodge more often than not. And then what? Would he kiss her again? Seduce her next time? Delicious possibilities filled his mind, and he remembered how the curve of her spine fit so neatly against his abdomen, or the way her breasts, young and firm, had nestled so softly into his hands, or how her hips had brushed eagerly against his in the dim light of the hayloft.

"Stop it!" he commanded, as if he could will her image out of his mind. He flicked on the radio and tried to concentrate on the weather report. Temperatures were due to drop in the area, a weatherman reported, but Gavin's lips curved cynically. He decided that in the next month or two, his temperature would probably be soaring. All because of Melanie.

# CHAPTER SEVEN

R idge Lodge and Gavin were plastered over the front page of the *Tribune*. There were several pictures of the resort, including a panoramic shot Melanie had taken from the lift, showing the lodge sprawling at the base of the runs, and there was one photograph of Gavin—a thoughtful pose that showed off his hard-edged profile as he talked with the reporter.

He didn't like the picture. It showed too much of his personality and captured the fact that he felt uncomfortable and suspicious while being interviewed. Melanie obviously had a photographer's knack for making a two dimensional picture show character and depth.

"Damn her," he muttered, forcing his eyes to the story. Bold headlines proclaimed: DOEL TO REOPEN RIDGE RESORT. The byline credited Jan Freemont with the story.

Gavin's jaw clenched as he scanned the columns. But the article was straightforward, and aside from mentioning the fact that Gavin had grown up around Taylor's Crossing, his personal life wasn't included. His skiing awards and professional life were touched on, but the focus of the article was the resort.

So maybe Brian Michaels was playing by the rules this

time. Perhaps the *Tribune* was a local newspaper that wasn't interested in trashing everyone's personal life.

Gavin didn't believe it for a minute. He'd met Michaels before. The man's instincts usually centered on gossip and speculation. Unless Michaels had mellowed or developed some sense of conscience.

"No way," Gavin told himself as Rich, several newspapers tucked under his arm, a wide grin stretched across his jaw, strode into the office.

He dropped the papers onto Gavin's desk. "Looks like you were worried for nothing," he said, thumping a finger on the front page.

"We'll see."

"I told you, this is the best source of free publicity, and the story's been picked up by the *Portland Daily* as well as several papers in Washington, Idaho and northern California."

"If you say so," Gavin said, unable to concede the fact that he was wrong.

"And now the *Tribune* is doing a series on the resort with a final full-page article scheduled for the grand opening. What could be better?"

"Can't think of a thing," Gavin drawled, sarcasm heavy in his words.

"Neither can I." Rich stuffed his hands into his pockets and walked to the windows, looking out at a cloudy afternoon sky. "So, you be good to the reporters who start showing up."

"Wouldn't dream of anything else."

Rich sighed theatrically. "I know you gave Ms. Freemont a bad time."

"I was good as gold," Gavin mocked.

"It's your attitude, Doel. It's beyond bad."

"I'll get right on fixing it."

"Do that."

"Thank God you're handling the press from now on."

"I know, I know. But I'm not always here. In fact, I'm

taking off for Portland today, hopefully to settle a case. I need to check on my practice for a couple of days—make sure that legal assistant I hired is handling everything. I'll be back by the weekend."

"And in the meantime, you expect me to deal with—" he glanced at the byline again "—Jan Freemont."

"And anyone else who strolls in here looking for a story or pictures—and that includes Melanie Walker."

Gavin frowned. He'd already decided to try to work things out with Melanie. Bury the past. Forget it. Just treat her like anyone else. If that were possible. After kissing her, he wasn't convinced he could pull it off. One kiss and he'd been spinning—just like a horny high school kid. Disgusting. "I'll do my best," he told Rich, and flashed a cynical smile.

"Try harder than that," Rich said with a laugh as he stuffed some papers into his briefcase.

"Not funny, Johanson."

"Sure it was. That's your problem, you know. No sense of humor."

"As long as I've only got one problem, I guess I'm doing all right. Now, get outta here."

Rich snapped his briefcase closed. "Seriously, Gavin, try not to antagonize too many people—especially reporters— while I'm gone."

Gavin assumed his most innocent expression. "You've got my word. Unless the questions get too personal or way out of line, I'll be—"

"I know, 'good as gold.' God help us," Rich muttered, waving a quick goodbye as he left.

Gavin glanced again at the opened newspaper, his gaze landing on his profile. No doubt Melanie would return within the next couple of days. Well, he'd find a way to be nice to her. Even if it killed him.

* * *

Melanie had every intention of dealing with Rich Johanson and staying clear of Gavin. She'd already spent three sleepless nights thinking of Gavin and how easily she'd responded to him.

And he'd responded, too. Whether he admitted it or not. Her foolish heart soared at the thought, but she quickly brought it back to the ground. No matter how Gavin responded to her, that response was purely sexual. His emotions were far different from hers. He'd kissed her as he'd kissed a dozen women in the past year. She'd kissed him as she'd kissed only him. No other man, including Neil, had ever been able to cause her blood to thunder, her pulse to race out of control.

And that's why Gavin was off-limits, she told herself as she shoved open the door of Ridge Lodge three days after Gavin's visit.

Unfortunately, the first person she ran into was Gavin.

Thankfully, they weren't alone. A work crew was busy hammering and sawing, stripping old wood and refinishing. Men with sagging leather belts filled with hammers, chisels, nails, planers and files moved throughout the interior and scrambled up scaffolding that reached to the joists and beams of the ceiling three stories overhead. Though it was late afternoon, the lodge wasn't dark or intimate because of the huge lights the construction workers had mounted to aid them in their restoration of the rustic inn.

Blueprints, anchored by half-filled bottles, were spread upon the bar while power saws screamed and dust swirled in pale clouds. A radio blared country music, but Melanie was sure no one could hear it over the din.

"I'm, uh, looking for Rich," she shouted over the noise, aware that a blush had stained her neck. Gavin was standing near the bar, eyeing the ceiling. Wearing jeans and a loose Notre Dame sweatshirt, he seemed to be supervising the restoration.

He frowned, dusted off his hands and moved closer, pulling her to him and talking into her ear so he didn't have to shout. "Rich isn't here. He left me in charge."

Gavin's warm breath sent a shiver up Melanie's spine. Great, she thought, bracing herself for an inevitable confrontation.

"And I promised I'd be on my best behavior."

"I wasn't aware you had one."

His lips twitched. "It's buried deep. But you're in luck today. I'm going to try my level best to be charming and helpful."

"Bull," she replied, caught up in his teasing banter.

"Hey." He opened his palms. "Either you deal with me or you come back later."

"I thought you didn't want anything to do with me?"

His eyes darkened. "Sometimes fate works against us."

*Amen,* she thought, but held her tongue. No reason to antagonize him. At least, not while he was trying to be affable.

"Rich left a contract for you on his desk," Gavin was saying, as if the other night hadn't existed—as if nothing had changed. "I'll get it for you. Come on."

Wondering how long his gracious manner would last, she followed him down a short hall and into the office.

Slamming the door behind him, he actually grinned. "Sorry about the mess."

"Doesn't bother me. In fact, I'd like to take a few pictures."

Nodding, he rummaged through the papers on the desk, found the contract and handed it to her.

Taking the document, she observed, "You're in a better mood today."

"Why not?" he tossed back, leaning over the desk. A few pale rays of afternoon sunlight streamed through the window to catch in the golden strands of his hair. Melanie's heart flipped over. "You and I got everything straight the other night, right?"

"Right," she agreed, not sure she was any more comfortable with this affable Gavin than she had been with the jaded, cynical man who had left her only three nights before—a man who had kissed her with a passion that had cut to her soul.

Gavin shoved his hands into the back pockets of his jeans. "And now that the construction's moving along, I feel that I'm not just spinning my wheels any longer."

"And so now everything is just dandy?" she asked, unable to keep the disbelief from her voice.

He glanced up sharply, but a practiced smile curved his lips. "Until something goes wrong."

She didn't believe him for a minute. This was all just an act, but she didn't argue with him. If he were going to be agreeable, it would make her job that much easier.

"Here's the contract. Take it home, look it over, have a lawyer look at it if you want to, but Rich wants it signed by the end of the week."

"No problem," she said as he handed her a stiff white envelope with the name and address of Rich's legal firm printed in the upper left-hand corner. She tucked the envelope into her purse, then settled down to business. "I've got some ideas for the brochure, but what I'd like are old pictures of the lodge and of you for background."

"I don't see why—" He stopped himself short. His sunny disposition clouded for a minute, and small lines etched his forehead. For the first time she understood how difficult it was for him to appear easygoing. "Sure. Why not?" he said. "Everything you'll need is in my suite." With a muttered oath, he grabbed his cane. "Come on. Walk this way."

"Okay Igor," she said, holding back a chuckle.

She followed him down a narrow hallway to a door near the back of the lodge.

Twisting the knob, he said with more than a trace of cynicism, "Home sweet home." He held the door open for her, and she walked into his living quarters.

She'd expected a grand suite with lavish furnishings for a man as wealthy and famous as Gavin, a man who had desperately wanted to shed his poor roots.

Instead, she found the suite comfortable and sparse. A rock fireplace filled one wall. Nearby a bookcase was crammed with books, magazines, a stereo and a television. A faded rug covered the worn wood floor, and a few pieces of furniture were grouped haphazardly around the room.

Wincing, Gavin bent down to the bottom shelf of the bookcase, rummaged around and pulled out a couple of battered photo albums and a box. He tossed everything onto a nearby table. "I think that should do it," he said, forcing a smile as he straightened. "If you need anything else, just holler. I'll be supervising the renovation or working out in the weight room." He cast an impatient glance at his injured leg. "Physical therapy."

"It shouldn't take long," Melanie replied, trying to be polite, though her voice sounded strained.

"Good."

"I'll try not to bother you."

*If you only knew,* Gavin thought, trying his damnedest to be civil. But every time he looked at her, gazed into her wide hazel eyes, he was reminded of how much he'd loved her, how deeply she'd touched his soul.

"Fool," he muttered, leaving the room as quickly as he could. Just being around her made him restless. And though he knew rationally that he was through with her forever, there was a wayward side of his nature that wanted to flirt with danger, a wayward side that kept reminding him of their last kiss and the feel and smell of her yielding against him. What would it hurt to spend time with her—get a little back? Now that he was over her, he could handle any situation that arose—right? The other night hadn't gone exactly as planned. However, he was trying to keep the promise he'd made to Rich and himself, trying not to antagonize her. But it was hell.

In the lobby, he spent nearly an hour with the foreman and was relieved the remodeling, though only a few days old, was still on schedule. Then, because he didn't want to run into

Melanie again, he hobbled down the short flight of steps to the pool and the weight room.

Fortunately, this area needed very little work, and the long, rectangular pool was operational.

He stripped out of his work clothes, stepped into a pair of swim trunks and took a position at the weight machine. Slowly, he started working his leg, stretching the muscles with only a little resistance and weight and adding more pounds as he began to work up a sweat.

"Take it easy," Dr. Hodges had said. "Don't push yourself." Yet that was exactly what he felt compelled to do. Cooped up in this damned lodge with Melanie poking through old photographs upstairs while the upcoming ski season, which could make or break the resort, loomed ahead, Gavin had no choice but to push himself to release tension and nervous energy.

He pressed relentlessly on the foot bar of the thigh machine. Sweat trickled down his back.

The pain in his leg started to burn. He ignored it, pushing again on the weight, stretching out his knee and calf only to release the tension and hear the weights clang down. Gritting his teeth, he shoved again. Sweat dripped from his temples to his chin.

How the hell would he get through the next few weeks, unable to participate in the sport he loved, unable to trust a woman he'd treasured?

"Don't even think about it," he growled to himself, his muscles bulging as he pressed relentlessly on the weights, his thigh muscles quivering. He slammed his eyes shut, but even in his concentration, Melanie appeared—a vision with a gorgeous body and seductive smile. She was older now, a little jaded in her own way. Yet he found her sarcastic remarks and sense of humor refreshing. The fact that she had the nerve to stand up to him was beguiling—or would have been if it weren't so damned maddening. The nerve of her actually baiting him when she'd left him high and dry all those years before.

He wondered if she ever thought of him—of those nights they'd shared. God, with his eyes closed, he could still smell the scent of hay on her skin, see the seductive light in her hazel eyes, hear the sound of her pleasured cries as he . . .

He dropped the weights, and they slammed together, the noise ringing to the rafters. Climbing off the damned machine, he shoved his sweaty hair from his eyes and noticed he felt an uncomfortable swelling between his legs. "Damn it, Doel," he said, swearing beneath his breath.

Embarrassed at a reaction he would have expected from a teenager, he dove into the warm water of the pool and began swimming laps. Stroke after stroke, he knifed through the water, determined to push Melanie from his mind. With supreme concentration he counted his laps, losing track somewhere after thirty and not really caring. The water was refreshing, loosening his muscles, and he stopped only when he felt his ankle begin to throb. He glanced at the clock on the wall. Six-thirty. Nearly three hours had passed since she'd shown up. Surely she was long gone.

Dripping water across the aggregate floor, he snapped a clean towel from the closet and wiped his face. He was still breathing deeply, but at least his ridiculous state of sexual arousal had passed and he felt near exhaustion.

Towel drying his hair, he headed upstairs. The lodge was quiet and nearly dark. He'd go back to his room, change, then head into town for dinner.

*With Melanie?* a voice inside his head suggested.

"Not a chance." The only way he was safe from her was to keep his distance.

Melanie lost all track of time. Poring over the photographs of Ridge Lodge was fascinating. The old pictures created a visual and unique history of the lodge and Taylor's Crossing. She spent hours choosing photographs she thought might enhance the brochure, and she'd had trouble deciding which shots she wanted to enlarge for the lobby and restaurant. She finally picked thirty pictures that had the right feel as well as clarity. She would let Rich and Gavin choose from these.

She should have quit then, but she picked up the second photograph album. The pages fell open to a picture of Gavin barely out of his teens, poised on the crest of a snow-covered hill. His face was tanned, his skin unlined, his hair blowing in the wind, his smile as brilliantly white as the snow surrounding him. She swallowed hard. She recognized the picture. She'd taken it herself on the upper slopes of Mount Prosperity.

Gavin had been an instructor at the time, paying for his skiing by earning his keep at the resort. And she'd spent every minute she could with him.

Her throat ached, and she pressed her lips together as she stared at the image. Memory after memory flashed in her mind, colliding in vital, soul-jarring images that she'd kept buried for eight years.

"Don't do this," she whispered, but she couldn't help herself and she slowly turned the pages, each photograph a chronicle of Gavin's professional life. She saw pictures of breath-stoppingly steep runs, dazzling snow-covered canyons cut into narrow runs that sliced through the rugged slopes, and always Gavin, tucked tightly, skimming across the snow, throwing a wake of powder behind him.

And there were other photographs, as well: pictures of Gavin accepting awards or trophies or standing beside any number of gorgeous women, the most often photographed being Aimee LaRoux.

Melanie had composed herself and her heartbeat had nearly slowed to normal when she lifted the album and a single picture fluttered facedown to the table.

She flipped it over, and time seemed to stand still as she stared at a picture of herself with Gavin, laughing gaily into the camera. Seated at a booth near the huge fireplace in this very lodge, snuggled together, their faces flushed from the last run of the day, their hair mussed, their eyes bright with love for each other. Gavin's arm was thrown carelessly across her shoulders, and he looked as if he had the world on a string. And he did. It was the night he'd learned that he was to train for the Olympic team.

Melanie took in a shuddering breath and released it slowly. "Oh, Lord," she whispered when she heard the creak of old floorboards and looked up to find Gavin standing woodenly in the doorway.

Wearing only swimming trunks and a towel looped casually around his neck, he didn't say a word. But his eyes were filled with a thousand questions.

She tried not to notice the corded muscles of his shoulders or the provocative way his golden hair swirled over his chest. Lowering her eyes, she noticed the thick, muscular thighs and a series of thin scars around his ankle.

"I thought you'd be gone," he finally said.

Oh, God, he'd caught her looking at the picture! Wishing she could slam the album shut, she forced her eyes upward again. He was already crossing the room, and his gaze was focused on the desk and the photograph still clutched in her fingers.

She searched for the right words, but they wouldn't form in her cotton-dry throat.

Stopping at the table, he stared at the photograph, and his lips curved down at the corners. "Reliving the past?" he growled.

"No, I—" She dropped the picture as if it were hot, then was instantly furious with herself for being so self-conscious. Inching her chin upward, she said, "It fell out of the album. I was just putting it back."

"Don't bother."

"Huh?"

"Just toss it."

To her horror, he snatched the picture from her fingers, crumpled it and dropped it into a wastebasket.

"No!" she cried, feeling as if a part of her past had just been wrenched from her soul.

"You want it?"

"No, but—"

"Then let's just leave it where it belongs, okay? It was just an oversight. I got rid of all those pictures a long time ago."

Inside, she was shaking. From rage? Or something else, a deeper, more primal emotion? She didn't know and she didn't care. But her voice was steady as she stood. "You can't just erase what happened between us, Gavin."

"*Nothing* happened."

"We loved each other."

"I thought you agreed we were just two kids fooling around."

"I lied."

His eyes narrowed. "Not the first time, is it?"

She sucked in her breath, feeling as if she'd been slapped. "I think I'd better go."

"Good idea."

She started gathering her things, picking out the photographs she needed and scooping them into a pocket of her case, but he grabbed her arm, forcing her to spin around and face him again.

She swallowed hard.

"Just explain one thing," he ground out.

"Name it."

"If you loved me," he said quietly, every feature on his face tense, "then why didn't you wait for me?"

"I didn't want to be a burden," she said quickly, thinking

for a second that the truth was better than the lies they'd both been living with for years.

"A burden?"

"You had a future—a chance for a berth on an Olympic team. You didn't need a wife tying you down."

His eyes narrowed suspiciously and his nostrils flared, but his hard mouth relaxed slightly. "We could have waited until the Olympics were over and I had started my career."

She licked her lips. Could she tell him about the baby? Now, when honesty seemed so vital? Would he understand? Instinctively, she reached for his forearms, her fingers touching rock-hard muscles. "There's something else—"

But before she could finish, he lowered his head and his mouth slanted over hers in a kiss as familiar as a soft summer breeze. His arms surrounded her, crushing her against him. He tasted of chlorine and salt and whiskey, and she felt his thighs press intimately into the folds of her skirt.

She offered no resistance and kissed him back. Being held by him seemed so natural and right, and all the wasted years between then and now melted away. Once again she was seventeen, caught in the embrace of the man she loved.

Groaning, he shifted, his wet trunks dampening her dress, his fingers catching in the long strands of her hair. Her head lolled back, and her mouth opened to the insistent pressure of his tongue. Quick, moist touches of his tongue against the inside of her mouth caused her blood to boil, her knees to weaken.

He kissed her lips, her cheeks and her throat. Closing her eyes, she ignored the warning bells clanging wildly in her head. His touch was erotic, the hand against the small of her back moving deliciously.

"Melanie," he whispered hoarsely. With his weight, he lowered her to the floor and pinned her against the carpet.

Still kissing her, he found the buttons of her blouse, and the thin fabric gave way to expose her breasts covered in lace.

*Stop him! Stop him now!* But when his palm glided over her breast, she could only moan and writhe as his fingers dipped beneath the lace, gently prodding, touching and withdrawing until her nipple strained tight against the bra and her breasts ached for more.

With agonizing slowness his tongue moved along her cheek and neck and rimmed the circle of bones at the base of her throat. Her own hands were busy touching and exploring the corded strength of his chest and the fine mat of hair that covered suntanned skin. His shoulder muscles were hard as she reached around him, and her fingers dug into his back as he continued to kiss her, moving downward.

"Gavin," she cried as his mouth fit hot and wet over her nipple. His tongue touched her in supple, sure strokes that caused her blood to burn and wiped out any further thoughts she had of stopping him.

He suckled through the lace and moved one free hand to cup her buttocks, bringing her body so close to his that she could feel his thighs and hips straining against the fabric that separated him from her.

Lord, how she wanted him. Nothing else mattered but the smell, taste and feel of him.

Finally, he unhooked her bra; the lace gave way, and she felt cool air against her bare skin before his mouth covered one breast and teased and laved the taut nipple.

She cradled his head against her, wanting more, knowing that only he could fill the ache that was beginning to yearn deep inside.

"Oh, God," he whispered, drawing up and away from her, staring down at her tight abdomen and soft skin. Groaning low in his throat he squeezed his eyes shut for a few heart-stopping moments, and when he finally lifted his eyelids again, the passion burning so brightly in his gaze had died. "What're you doing to me?"

He rolled away from her and sat with his back to her, his rigid arms supporting him as he drew in deep, ragged breaths. "Damn it. Why can't you just leave me alone?" His voice was rough, the hand he plowed through his hair trembling.

"I didn't start this, Gavin."

"Well, you sure as hell didn't stop it!"

Humiliated, Melanie sat up and started working on her clothes. "This wasn't my fault," she said, still buttoning her blouse.

"Wasn't it?" he flung back at her, glancing over his shoulder before pushing himself upright. His features twisted in pain for just a second as he strained his ankle.

"Of course not!" she declared hotly. "And I'm tired of you always throwing the blame at my feet!"

"Maybe that's where it belongs."

She swept in a long breath. "You can really be a bastard when you want to be."

"Yeah, well, you don't seem to mind sometimes."

"Maybe that's because sometimes, when you're not trying out for boor of the year, you're wonderful."

He stopped, his eyes locking with hers. Time stood still. His throat worked, and his face gentled for just a second. Warring emotions strained his features. "You're dreaming! Living in a past that didn't exist."

"Gavin—"

Swearing roundly under his breath, he hobbled toward the bookcase. He opened an upper cabinet, withdrew a bottle and glass, then poured himself a quick drink. "Why didn't you leave a couple hours ago?" he asked suddenly. "What were you doing hanging around?"

"I wasn't finished sorting through the pictures."

He tossed back half his drink and stood rigidly near the windows. "Or you were waiting for me—because of that," he said, cocking his head toward the now ruined snapshot of the two of them.

"No, I just stumbled across it. But don't worry, I'm leaving now."

"Not quite yet," he said, slowly drawing the back of his hand across his mouth, as if he were wiping off excess whiskey—or the feel of her kiss.

Furious with him, she grabbed her camera bag and slung the strap over her shoulder.

Gavin set his unfinished drink on the window ledge and closed the distance between them. "There's something I have to know," he said quietly, though his anger was still evident in his uncompromising expression.

"It's too late for this discussion."

"Just one thing," he said again, his features set.

"What?"

"Why did you marry a bastard like Brooks?"

"It's none of your business," she lied.

"Like hell. Why, Melanie?" he thundered.

She slowly counted to ten. There were reasons, but they wouldn't come to mind. Melanie grappled with the truth, wishing she could just tell him about the baby they'd never shared.

"I'm waiting," he said, his voice low. "Was it because of his money? Is that what you found so attractive?"

"No!"

"God, I hope not," he muttered, shaking his head. "But I can't help wondering why you're hanging around here, lingering in my room, more than willing to seduce me."

"What?" she gasped. "I wasn't lingering and I had no intention of seducing anyone!"

"You could've left."

"I told you, I wasn't finished."

"Well, you are now."

"You got that right." She grabbed her purse and swung

toward the door, but one of Gavin's arms snaked out and surrounded her waist.

"You haven't answered my question yet."

There was nothing she could say to change the past. With a sinking sensation, she realized that telling Gavin the truth about the baby would only increase the tension between them, making it impossible for her to work with him. "I don't think your question merits an answer."

"You walked out on me—"

"No, Gavin. You did the walking—or to be more precise, the skiing," she charged, unable to hide the bitterness in her tone. "You just skied your way out of my life and I fell in love with someone else."

The corners of his mouth twitched, as if he found her reason bordering on the ridiculous. "You loved Brooks? After me?"

"Yes."

His eyes narrowed. "Save that for someone who'll believe it. You sold out, Melanie, to the almighty dollar."

Without thinking, she slapped him with a smack that echoed through the room. Gavin's teeth set, and he clamped both hands over her arms. "Don't ever do that again."

"I'll try never to get that close!" Her voice shook with anger.

"Then you'd better stay out of my bedroom."

"You're what? Oh, God, Gavin, don't flatter yourself!"

His eyes blazed, and his fingers dug into her flesh. For a few seconds they glared at each other, breathing deeply, fury and other, more dangerous, emotions tangling between them.

Gavin sighed finally. "You make me crazy," he admitted.

"Same here. It's a bad combination."

Something flickered in his gaze, and then his mouth crashed down on hers. She wanted to fight him, to stop this insanity, but when his lips molded over hers intimately, she couldn't resist.

Closing her eyes, Melanie willed herself not to respond.

Though her heart was thudding wildly, her blood on fire, she set her jaw and acted as if she could barely endure the kiss.

But Gavin didn't give up. His lips coaxed, his hands moved magically across her back, and at last she gave into her weak knees and leaned against him.

"Why do we always have to hurt each other?" he whispered raggedly.

"I don't know." Her heart felt as if it might break all over again. Slowly Gavin released her.

"I don't believe you ever loved Neil Brooks," he said quietly.

"It doesn't matter what you believe," she lied. Reaching behind her, she found the door handle and yanked it open. As quickly as her legs would carry her, she walked through the dark lodge and outside, where she took in deep breaths of fresh air.

Her legs were unsteady as she walked to her car, but she held her chin up and decided that Gavin Doel, damn his black-hearted soul, was going to be harder to deal with than she'd ever imagined.

She tried to start her car, but it stalled. Slowly counting to ten, she tried again. This time the old engine sputtered and caught. She didn't waste any time. Shoving the Volkswagen into first, she barely noticed the battered old pickup that pulled into the lot. She had other things on her mind.

"Don't be a fool, Mel," she told herself as she turned on her headlights, but she had the sinking sensation that she was falling in love with him all over again.

Gavin grabbed his drink, almost tossed it back but at the last second chucked the whiskey down the drain. He didn't usually drink—at least, not the way he had in the past few weeks. Having lived with an alcoholic father, he had always been careful with liquor.

Until he'd seen Melanie again. Just being with her, gazing into her intelligent eyes, seeing glimpses of her sense of humor, touching the slope of her jaw or burying his face into the clean scent of her hair, made him crazy.

"Get a grip on yourself," he said, knowing that alcohol didn't solve any problems. He twisted the cap on the bottle just as he heard footsteps in the outer lobby.

He froze. Melanie? Back? God, how was he ever going to keep his hands off her? He'd intended to kiss her to prove that he could kiss her without his emotions getting in the way, to prove that he really didn't care about her—

"Gavin?" a rough male voice called out.

"In here," he replied. So his old man had made it back to Taylor's Crossing. Ignoring his cane, Gavin crossed the room and held open the door, letting the light from his apartment spill into the hallway.

"Oh, there you are! This place is a goddamn maze!" Jim Doel, tall and gaunt, his hair snow-white, strode down the hallway to Gavin's apartment.

"It just takes a while to get to know your way around."

Casting a critical eye on the rooms his son now called home, Jim took a seat on the raised hearth of the fireplace. "Quite a comedown from what you're used to, isn't it?"

"It's all right."

"And you're already fixin' it up. I saw the rigging." He rubbed his hands on the faded knees of his jeans.

"It should be finished by the time ski season opens."

"That's not so far away." Jim noticed the bottle of whiskey on the table and glanced meaningfully at Gavin. "I saw you had a visitor."

Gavin braced himself.

"That Walker girl still sniffin' around?"

"She's a photographer for the paper."

"So what was she doin' here so late?"

"Rich hired her to do some publicity for us. Brochures, maps, that sort of thing."

Jim raised an interested eyebrow. "And where is Rich?"

"In Portland."

"Convenient." Jim reached into his pocket for a pack of cigarettes.

Gavin thought about protesting, but decided the grand opening was months away, and instead of upsetting his father, he could open a couple windows once he was alone again.

"I think it'll work out."

"You thought that before," Jim observed. He lit up and clicked his lighter shut.

"What're you trying to say, Dad?"

"Nothin', nothin'." Jim drew hard on his cigarette. Gavin waited as his father blew smoke to the ceiling, "I'm just a little concerned, that's all. That girl hurt you once before."

"Water under the bridge," Gavin lied.

"Is it, now? I wonder. But then, I guess I don't have to point out to you that she didn't bother to wait for you when you took off for Colorado. No siree, she just up and married Neil Brooks within weeks after you left."

"What're you getting at?"

"She's fickle, that one. First you, then the minute you're gone, she puts the richest boy in town in her sights, marries him, then when she gets bored, divorces him. Now she's back here, making herself available because you're back in town— and now you're probably the richest man in town."

"Not by a long shot."

Jim shrugged. "Well, she does seem to be developin' a pattern, doesn't she?"

"What do you know about her marriage?"

"Nothing except it was short. Six years or so, I think, and then she comes back when her dad gets sick." Jim's face grew tense. "I never did like old Adam Walker, you know. He never forgave me for what happened to his wife."

"That was a long time ago," Gavin said, hoping to ease some of his father's pain.

Jim sighed. "But it's something that'll stick with me until the day I die." He cleared his throat and tossed his cigarette into the grate. "You don't know how many times I prayed I could've changed things."

"Probably just about as many times as I did," Gavin admitted.

Scowling, Jim looked his son straight in the eye. "Don't get mixed up with Melanie. She'll only hurt you again."

Gavin bristled. "I survived."

"If that's what you call it."

"Look, I can make my own decisions. Now tell me, what else is on your mind?"

"I thought maybe you'd give your old man a job." Seeing that Gavin was about to protest, he held up one hand. "Hey, you've been good to me. If it hadn't been for you, I probably never would've dried out. And for that I owe you. But I'm tired of being a charity case. This time I want a job—a real, bona fide job. I'm not old enough to be sent out to pasture yet, and I'm handy with a hammer and nails. What d'ya say?"

# CHAPTER EIGHT

The next three weeks went by in a blur. Indian summer waned, and the air turned brisk and chilly. Gray clouds lingered over the Cascades, promising early snow.

Melanie barely had time to notice the change in the weather, let alone eat or sleep. When she wasn't at the newspaper office, she was working in her studio or at the lodge, where she tried to keep her distance from Gavin. She wasn't always successful.

Fortunately, he, too, was working day and night. They spoke to each other only when absolutely necessary. She dealt primarily with Rich Johanson, unless he was out of town, and somehow managed to keep her relationship with Gavin strictly professional.

She was friendly, businesslike and cheerful, hiding her innermost feelings. Gavin was cordial but reserved, and glared at her suspiciously whenever she seemed in a particularly good mood.

The tension hovered between them, gnawing at her insides while all the time she plastered a smile on her face.

She was lucky on one count. Gavin and Rich had no

trouble agreeing on pictures for the brochure. When she showed them her favorite shots, they weeded out the ones that didn't fit their image of the resort.

Rich slipped the good shots he needed into an envelope and said he'd take them, along with the copy he'd written for the brochure, to a printer in Portland.

Gavin handed Melanie a sealed envelope with a check inside and said, "Good job."

The words sounded hollow, and Melanie, despite her fake smile, was miserable. She couldn't wait to get through the charade and regretted taking the job.

As for the resort, the renovation of Ridge Lodge was on schedule, and the parking lot, lodge and lifts teemed with construction workers. A handful of employees had already been hired for the operation of the lodge and lifts, and a chef, a doctor, building supervisor and an equipment manager were already on staff.

Jim Doel, who had recently returned to Taylor's Crossing, had been hired as a handyman, and Melanie had kept her distance from him as well as from his son. Though Jim was never openly hostile, Melanie sensed his animosity whenever she dealt with him. And she, too, hadn't resolved all her feelings toward him. As much as she wanted to rise above it, the simple fact was that he'd killed her mother and robbed her of a normal childhood. Maybe that was Adam Walker's fault. Her father had spent years bad-mouthing the man.

"So, how're things going up at the lodge?" Jan asked late one Friday afternoon as Melanie handed her some pictures of people gathered at a city council meeting in city hall.

"I think everything's on schedule."

"Good. I've got another interview with our friend Mr. Doel next week and I wanted to be prepared. If there's any trouble at the lodge, I'd like to know about it. But everything's okay, right?" Jan asked, perching on the corner of Melanie's desk.

"No trouble," Melanie replied, carrying the pictures to the

layout editor's desk. "In fact, when you go up to the lodge, I think you'll be surprised how smoothly everything's running."

"Oh really?" Jan's eyebrows drew together, and she made a point of studying her nails.

"Uh-huh. Looks as if the resort will be a huge success," Melanie added, wondering why she felt compelled to defend Gavin.

Constance, who had overheard the tail end of the conversation, made her way to the coffeepot and asked, "So, do you know who'll be invited to the grand opening?"

Jan mumbled, "I wish."

Melanie shook her head. "I haven't the foggiest. I'm on the inside, you know, just doing some freelance work for the resort."

Constance sighed. "I'd give my right arm for a look at that guest list."

"Why don't you just ask?"

"I have. I got Doel on the phone yesterday, but he told me very succinctly that it was none of my business. I just thought maybe you had some idea."

"Not a clue," Melanie replied.

"Well, I'm going up there Monday and I'll have a look around," Jan said, filled with confidence as usual. "Maybe I can convince Mr. Doel that a copy of the list would add public interest. He might just sell a few more lift tickets if people thought some celebrities were staying at the lodge."

"I wouldn't bet on getting anything more from him," Melanie said.

Constance agreed. Refilling her coffee cup, she said, "He's impossible. It's almost as if he resents the free publicity we're handing him."

"You were the one who pointed out that he was publicity shy," Melanie observed as Constance's phone jangled loudly from her desk.

With a dramatic sigh, Constance, said, "Jan, see what you

can do." She hurried back to her desk. "Beg, borrow or steal that guest list."

"I doubt if I'll burglarize Gavin Doel's office all for the sake of a few names."

"Not just any names. We're talking names of the famous," Constance reminded her as the phone rang impatiently. "There's a difference. A big difference." Frowning, she picked up the receiver and plopped down at her desk, immediately absorbed in the conversation.

Jan turned her attention back to Melanie. "What do you think her chances are of getting the names of the invited?"

"From Gavin? Zero. From Rich Johanson?" Melanie lifted her hand and tilted it side to side, "About fifty-fifty."

Jan nodded. "Yeah, Johanson's always been more interested in publicity than Doel. And speaking of our local infamous professional skier, how're things going with you two?"

"Fine, I guess. We work together. That's it."

"That's it? Really?" Jan arched a skeptical brow. "Come on, Melanie, you can talk to me. I saw how he looked at you, and you said yourself that you'd been serious with him."

"I think I said I'd dated him."

"You said you were serious."

"Did I? Well, if 1 did, I meant I was serious for seventeen." Dear Lord, why had she ever brought it up?

"I know, but I read between the lines," Jan replied. "You two act as if you've never gotten over each other."

"That's ridiculous!"

"Is it?"

"Of course," Melanie said, pretending to study an enlarged photograph of wheat fields to the south of town. "Gavin's not interested in me," she added tightly.

Jan laughed. "Yeah, right, and I'm the Queen of England! Don't try to convince me that you can't see the signs. That man is interested—whether he wants to be or not."

Melanie didn't comment and went back to work when Brian called Jan into his office.

The rest of the day she heard snatches of conversation in the office and most of it centered around Gavin. As she drove home, she wondered if there was any way to escape from him.

Unfortunately, Taylor's Crossing was a small town and Gavin was highly visible and extremely gossip-worthy. She heard about him and the lodge everywhere she went. And it didn't end when she stopped by her Uncle Bart's and Aunt Lila's house that evening.

"The weather service predicts snow in the mountains by Friday," Bart said, squinting through his kitchen window to the night-blackened sky. Melanie dropped into a chair near the table, and Bart followed suit. "That should be good news for Doel."

Melanie, tired of all the talk about Gavin, took a swallow from the steaming mug of coffee Aunt Lila handed her.

"Now, Bart," her aunt said, "you quit fishing."

"Is that what I'm doing?" Bart asked, one side of his mouth lifting at the corner.

"Of course it is. She's barely been here ten minutes and you've brought up Gavin twice."

Bart lifted a foot and placed it on an empty chair. "I was just making an observation about the weather."

"Sure."

"And it wouldn't kill me to know how Melanie and Gavin are doing working so close together."

"You're worse than a gossiping old woman," Lila muttered, but smiled good-naturedly.

"Oh, for God's sake, I am not. I'm just interested in Melanie's welfare, that's all."

"She's old enough to make her own decisions without any help from you."

Melanie couldn't help but grin. Lila and Bart's light-hearted banter had always been a source of amusement to her, and since she'd lost her mother at a young age, Aunt Lila had stepped in and filled a very deep void. "Well, if you must know," Melanie said, deciding to end the speculation about Gavin once and for all, "Gavin and I get along all right. We don't see a lot of each other, though. I deal primarily with Rich Johanson."

"That stuffed shirt!" Bart muttered.

"He's okay," Melanie said. "In fact, I like him. He keeps Gavin in line."

Bart smoothed his white hair with the flat of his hand. His faded eyes twinkled. "Does he need keeping in line?"

"All the time," Melanie said.

"And I heard he hired his old man, too."

This was dangerous ground. Melanie felt her equilibrium slipping a little. "That's right. Jim does fix-it jobs for the resort—things that the general contractor didn't bid on, I guess."

"How long is he staying on?"

"I don't know," Melanie said honestly. "We don't talk much."

"I'll bet," Bart said. "But Gavin can't be all bad if he takes care of his kin."

For once Aunt Lila agreed. "He's helped Jim more than any son should have to." Then, as if realizing she'd said too much, she added, "You're staying for dinner, aren't you?"

Melanie finished her coffee. "Another time. I've got an appointment later tonight. Cynthia Anderson is coming over to choose some pictures I took of her boys a few weeks ago, but I had something I wanted to give you." She reached into her purse and pulled out a small package wrapped in tissue paper.

"What's this?" Bart asked as she handed it to him.

"Open it and see," Lila prodded.

Bart didn't need any further encouragement. He unfolded the paper and exposed a framed picture of himself and Big Money taken on the day of the fair over a month before. Bart was grinning proudly, while the nervous colt tugged hard on his lead and tried to rear.

"Melanie," Bart whispered, touched, "you didn't need to—"

"I know, but I wanted to. This was my favorite shot, but my editor preferred the one that ended up in the paper. I picked it out weeks ago, but it took a while to find the right frame."

"I have just the place for this," Lila said, eyeing the picture lovingly. "Thank you."

Melanie felt a lump in her throat as she finished her coffee and pushed back her chair. "You're welcome. Now I'd better run home before the Anderson boys show up and terrorize Sassafras."

Uncle Bart walked with her out the back door. Rain had started to fall, but the temperature had dropped. Goose bumps rose on Melanie's arms.

"Despite what your aunt said in there," Bart said, squaring an old Stetson on his head, "you know she thinks the world of Gavin. He used to do odd jobs around here, you know, and Lila's pretty soft where he's concerned."

Melanie eyed him in the darkness. "You already told me I should be chasing after him."

"I didn't say that." Bart's teeth flashed and his breath fogged. "But if he decides to do the chasing, I wouldn't run too fast if I were you."

"I'll remember that," she said dryly as she slid into the car.

Bart slammed the door shut for her, then paused on the step to light a cigarette. Melanie waved as she drove away. So now everyone thought she should try to start a new romance with Gavin. Jan, Uncle Bart and even Aunt Lila. It was enough to make a body sick.

And yet, falling in love with Gavin again held a distinct appeal. "You're hopeless," she told herself as she wheeled into her driveway and recognized Cynthia Anderson's gray van parked in front of the house. "And you're late."

As she climbed out of her own car, the side door of the van flew open and the boisterous Anderson brood, dressed in blue and white soccer outfits, scrambled out.

Cynthia herded them toward the front porch. "I know I didn't say anything when I made this appointment," she said quickly, "but do you have time to take a couple of shots of them in their soccer gear?"

Groaning inwardly, Melanie nodded. "I suppose."

"Good, good. Because Gerald would just love a picture of them like this—oh, but, boys, we mustn't tell Daddy, okay? It'll be a surprise. For Christmas."

Melanie wondered how the four boys could keep a secret for ten minutes let alone two months. "Let's get started."

"Oh, thanks, Melanie," Cynthia said, whipping her comb from her purse and pouncing on the youngest one. "Okay, Tim, hold still while I fix your hair."

"No!" the boy howled. "No, no, no!"

"Aw, knock it off, Mom," Sean, the oldest, chided. "We look good enough. Besides, I'm freezin' my tail off out here. Let's go inside!"

Steeling herself, Melanie opened the front door, the boys thundered down the hall and Sassafras bolted outside, splashing through puddles as he headed around the corner of the house.

Melanie followed the Andersons through the door and hung her coat on the hall tree near the stairs. She didn't have time to think about Gavin for the rest of the evening.

The first snow arrived on a Saturday in early November. Large powdery flakes, driven by gusty winds, fell from a leaden sky. Storm warnings had been posted, but Melanie decided to chance the storm, hoping that it would hold off for a few hours. She tossed her chains into her car and carefully placed five huge portfolios in her car.

The drive was tedious. Already tired from spending most of the previous night getting the coloration on the prints just right, and she was anxious to take the pictures to the lodge and finish that part of her employment.

*Because you want to see Gavin again,* her mind tormented, but she pushed that unpleasant thought aside and ignored the fact that her heart was beating much too quickly as she drove through a fine layer of snow to Mount Prosperity.

Aside from half a dozen cars and a few trucks marked GAMBLE CONSTRUCTION and the snowplow, the freshly plowed parking lot was relatively empty.

Melanie drove straight to the lodge, and because she wanted to protect the prints as well as her car, she pulled into a parking shed that connected with the side entrance to the lodge. Grabbing her largest portfolio, she steeled herself for another cool meeting with Gavin. *You can handle this,* she told herself as she trudged up the stairs and opened the door.

Inside, the lodge was quiet. The screaming saws, pounding hammers and country music were gone. Only the few workers finishing the molding remained.

Most of the renovation was complete. The high wood ceilings had been polished, the oak floors refinished and new recessed lighting installed in the lobby and bar. Two snack bars boasted gleaming new equipment, and the restaurant had been recarpeted.

Fresh paint gleamed, and new blinds were fitted to the windows. An Oriental rug had been stretched in front of the fireplace, and several couches and lamps had been placed strategically around the room.

Melanie propped her portfolio against a post and eyed the renovations. Tugging off her gloves, she walked over to the bar to admire the polished, inlaid brass.

"Something I can do for you?"

She nearly jumped out of her skin at the sound of Jim Doels, voice. She whipped around. Tall and lined, Jim settled a cap on his head and waited, his face tense, his eyes never wavering.

She and Gavin's father had never gotten along. Working at the lodge together hadn't made things any easier. She pointed to her portfolio. "I'm here to meet Rich. I have those old pictures he was interested in."

"He's busy."

"Then Gavin."

The older man's lips tightened. "He's busy, too."

"Are they here?"

Nodding, he motioned toward the back of the lodge. "Got some bigwigs with them. Don't know when they'll be through."

"It's okay," she said, forcing a smile. "I'll wait in the north wing."

"It may be awhile."

"I've got plenty of time," she replied, not letting him dissuade her. Jim Doel had never said why he didn't like her, but she assumed it was a combination of feelings—guilt for the death of her mother and anger that she, at least in Gavin's father's opinion, had betrayed his only son. He'd never know the truth, so she would have to get used to his glacial glances and furrowed frowns until she was finished with her job here.

Inching her chin up a fraction, she hauled her heavy portfolio off the floor and said, "Please let Rich know where he can find me."

Jim nodded grudgingly, and Melanie, rather than ask for his help, made two more trips to the car to pick up the bulky pictures. It took nearly half an hour to carry them into the north wing, and as she paused to catch her breath on her final trip, she heard the sound of voices coming from the banquet room.

The door was ajar, and her curiosity got the better of her. She looked into the crack and caught a glimpse of several men, all dressed in crisp business suits, clustered around the huge, round table. Smoke rose in a gentle cloud to the ceiling.

Gavin sat across from the door, and he looked bored to tears. His hair was combed neatly and he was wearing a blue suit, but his gaze lacked its usual life and he tugged at his tie and stuck his fingers under his collar.

Melanie couldn't help but grin. Where were the beat-up leather jacket and aviator glasses? she wondered, wishing she dared linger and watch him a little longer. She'd never thought of him as an entrepreneur, and she found it amusing to catch a glimpse of him in a starched white shirt and crisp tie, dealing with lawyers or accountants or investors or whoever the other men happened to be.

She made her way to the end of the hall and the north wing. As wide as the lodge itself, the huge room was vacant, aside from some chairs stacked in a corner and a few tables shoved against the windows.

Melanie shrugged out of her coat, then began setting out the photographs that she'd selected for the sepia-colored pictures that were to decorate the main lobby. There were pictures of miners with pickaxes, wagon trains and mule teams, crusty old-timers panning for gold and younger men gathered around a mineshaft. There was a shot of a steaming locomotive and another of a nineteenth-century picnic by a river. She laid them out carefully, proud of her work.

She didn't hear Gavin walk into the room, nor did she notice when he stopped short and sucked in his breath.

Gavin hadn't expected to find her here, leaning over the table, her hips thrust in his direction and her black glossy hair braided into a rope that was pinned tightly to the back of her head.

Her lips were pursed, her eyebrows knitted in concentration, and her hips, beneath her denim skirt, shifted seductively as she arranged photograph after photograph on the table.

As if feeling the weight of his gaze, she glanced over her shoulder, and for a fleeting second her eyes warmed and her lips moved into a ghost of a smile.

Gavin's breath caught in his lungs for a heart-stopping moment, and he had trouble finding his voice. "Are you waiting for Rich?"

He noticed her shoulders tighten. Turning, she eyed him suspiciously. "Isn't he here?"

"Not now. He had business in Portland."

Her lips turned down. "But I just saw him—"

"I know. He got a call. There's some emergency with a case of his. He just took off."

"Well, that's great," Melanie said, motioning to the windows. "I hoped to get out of here before the storm really hit."

"What's keeping you?" he baited, and saw a spark flash in her eyes.

"My job. We have a contract, remember?"

"Rich's idea."

"Well, it doesn't matter whose idea it was, does it? Because, like it or not, you and I are stuck with it."

"You could always leave," he suggested, and the look she shot him was positively murderous.

"I came here to do a job, Gavin, and I intend to finish it. The sooner it's done, the sooner I'm out of here." She placed her hands on her hips.

"Then let's get to it."

"Okay, first you need to figure out exactly where you want these hung. For what it's worth, I think you should hang them in chronological sequence—" Impatiently he listened as she explained about each of the pictures and how each shot had a particular meaning to the forty-niner theme of the lodge. Though she spoke with enthusiasm, he had trouble concentrating and was constantly distracted by the slope of her cheek, the way her teeth flashed as she spoke, or how her sweater stretched across her breasts.

". . . and that picnic, it's my favorite," she was saying. "It took place at the base of Mount Prosperity sometime in the eighteen-eighties, I think, much later than forty-nine, but it still has a certain flavor." Her voice drifted off, and her face angled up to his. "You haven't heard a word I've said, have you?" she charged, lips pursing angrily.

"Does it matter?"

Her eyes flashed. "I suppose it doesn't. I just thought since you're the owner of this place, you might be interested. I guess I was wrong."

"Go on," he suggested. His thoughts had taken him far from the photographs on the table. He knew that he and Melanie were virtually alone in the lodge. Rich had left with the accountant and investors, the workers had the day off, the carpenters who had come in were now gone, and even his father, after gruffly announcing that someone was waiting for Rich in the north wing, had left the premises.

Vexed, she placed her hands on her hips and tilted her head to the ceiling. "I don't know why I try," she muttered as if conversing with the rafters in the vault high overhead.

Gavin motioned impatiently at the table. "Look, they're all fine. You just tell me where to hang them and we'll do it."

"You and me?" she asked.

He felt one side of his lip curve up. "Face it, Melanie, we're stuck with each other."

She paled slightly. "But you're still laid up—"

"My ankle's fine."

"And you don't mind risking breaking it by falling off a ladder?" she said, sarcasm tainting her words.

"Won't happen," he replied, noticing how anger intensified the streaks of jade in her eyes. "Just give me a minute to change."

She didn't have time to protest. He dashed off, leaving her with the photographs. *Don't argue with him,* she told herself. *Take advantage of his good mood.* But she glanced through the windows to see the snow begin to drift around the lodge. Most of the mountain was now obscured from her view. They'd have to work fast. The railing of the deck showed three inches of new snow, and the wind had begun to pick up. Maybe she should just forget this and come back when the storm had passed.

Not yet, she decided. She had too much to do to let a little snow bother her. She'd grown up around here and she knew how to drive in the snow. She'd be fine. She hazarded another glance outside and decided she didn't have any time to lose.

By the time she'd hauled the photographs back to the main lobby, placing each matted print on the floor near the appropriate wall space, Gavin reappeared, tucking the tail of his blue cambric shirt into faded jeans. He strode quickly, without the use of a cane, to the huge fireplace on the far wall. Bending on one knee, he began stacking logs on the huge grate.

"Do we really need a fire?" she asked, glancing at her watch.

"Probably not."

"It'll go to waste."

Ignoring her, he struck a match. The dry kindling ignited quickly, sizzling and popping as yellow flames discovered moss-laden oak. His injury didn't seem to bother him, and when he straightened and surveyed his work, he nodded to himself.

"Now that we're all cozy," she mocked, hoping to sound put out, "let's get started."

"You're the boss," he quipped, gesturing to the stack of prints she had started positioning around the main lobby.

"Remember that," she teased back.

"Always." His eyelids dropped a little, and Melanie's breath caught in her throat as he stared at her.

Clearing her throat, she pointed to a picture of a grizzled old miner and two burros. "You can start with this one," she said. "It should go near the door. And then, I think, the picture of the locomotive on the trestle. Then the mine shaft . . ." She walked around the large, cavernous room, shuffling and reshuffling the prints. Gavin was with her every step of the way, and her nerves were stretched tight. She felt the weight of his gaze, smelled the musky scent of his aftershave and saw the set angle of his jaw. *Dear God, help me get through this.*

When she finally decided on the placement of each picture, he took off in search of a ladder. Melanie sank against the windows and felt the cold panes against her back. *Just a few more hours.* She glanced anxiously through the window and noticed the storm had turned worse. The higher branches of the pines surrounding the lodge danced wildly in the wind, and the snow was blowing in sheets.

When Gavin returned with the ladder, his face was grim. "I just listened to the weather report," he informed her. "The storm isn't going to let up for hours."

Melanie's heart sank. Nervously, she shoved her bangs from her eyes. "Then I should leave now."

"No way."

"What?" She looked up sharply.

"It's nearly a whiteout, Mel. Winds are being measured over forty miles an hour. I'm not going to let you leave until it's safe."

"It's safe now. Not that you have a whole lot of say in the matter."

"Just wait. We've got a lot of work to do. Maybe by the time we're done, the winds will have died down."

"Is that what the weather service said?"

Tiny brackets surrounded his mouth, and he shook his head. "Afraid not. In fact, they predict it'll last through the night."

"Then I've got to leave now!"

"Hold on," he said firmly, one hand clamping over her arm. "If there's a lull, I'll drive you out of here in one of the trucks with four-wheel drive."

"I've got my car here. I'll—"

"You'll stay put!" he said, his eyes gleaming with determination. "Until it's safe."

"Oh, so now you're the one giving orders."

"While you're up here in my lodge, you're my responsibility," he said quietly.

"I'm my own person. I don't need you or anyone else telling me what to do!"

A muscle worked in his jaw. "Then use your head, Melanie. You know how dangerous a storm like this can be. Just wait it out. We can finish here."

"And then what?"

"I don't know," he admitted, "but at least you won't be in a ditch somewhere, freezing to death."

"No, I'll just be suffocating in here while you keep ordering me around."

He couldn't help but smile. "Is that what I'm doing?"

"Damn right!"

He laughed then, and Melanie was taken aback at the richness of the sound. "So be it," he muttered. "Now, come on, quit complaining and let's get to work."

She hated to give in to him, but the thought of driving out in a near blizzard wasn't all that inviting. "All right," she finally agreed, "but I'm leaving the minute the winds die down."

He didn't comment, just started up the ladder. She was afraid his ankle wouldn't support him, but he didn't once lose his balance, and slowly, as they hung picture after picture, the rust-tone prints began to add flavor to the lobby.

As she watched him adjust a picture of oxen pulling a covered wagon, she noticed how quiet the lodge had become. The only sounds were the scrape of the ladder, their soft conversation and the whistle of the wind outside. "Where is everyone?" she asked.

"Gone." he replied, glancing down at her from the top of the ladder.

"Gone?"

"Yeah. It's just you and me."

He was still staring down at her as she shifted uncomfortably from one foot to the other.

"Does that bother you?" he asked, one foot lower on the ladder than the other, his denim-clad legs at her eye level.

"Nope," she lied. "As long as I've got one self-centered egotistical male bossing me around, I'm happy as a clam."

"Good." Gavin struggled to keep from smiling. He stepped up, and she tried not to watch the way his buttocks moved beneath the tight denim. "I figured the sooner this was done—"

"The sooner I'd be out of your hair."

He made a disgusted sound. "I was going to say, the sooner you'd be happy. If that's possible."

She didn't bother responding. And she tried to drag her gaze away from him to keep from noticing the way his shirt pulled across his broad shoulders and the lean lines of his waist as he reached upward. His hips, too, under tight jeans, moved easily as he shifted his weight from one rung to the next.

Without warning, the lights in the lodge flickered.

Gavin froze on the ladder. "What's going on . . ." But before he could say anything else, the only illumination in the entire building came from the fireplace. "Son of a bitch!" He shoved his hands through his hair, then climbed down the final rungs of the ladder. "Stay here," he ordered. "We've got an emergency generator, but I don't think it's operational yet." He started down the hall, his footsteps echoing through the huge old building.

Melanie watched him disappear into the darkness, then walked anxiously to a window. Snow, driven by a gusty wind, fell from the black sky to blanket the mountain. It peppered against the window in icy flakes.

Now what? she wondered, shivering. Rubbing her arms, she walked back to the fireplace and checked her watch in the firelight. Gavin had been gone nearly fifteen minutes.

The old empty lodge seemed larger in the darkness. The windows rose to cathedral spires and reflected gold in the firelight, and the ceilings were so high overhead they were lost in the darkness.

She heard the clip of Gavin's footsteps and saw the bob of a flashlight. "Well, so much for the generator," he said, his lips thin in frustration.

"What's wrong with it?"

"Nothing that some new parts won't fix, but that's not the bad news. We have a ham radio in the back, and I listened for a few minutes while I found these." He held up several kerosene lamps and a couple of flashlights. "The storm is worse than they expected. High winds have knocked down power poles and some of the roads are impassable."

With a mounting sense of dread, Melanie said, "Then I'd better leave now, before things get worse."

"Too late," he replied. "The road to the lodge is closed. I called the highway department. A falling tree took out several electricity poles and has the road blocked. This storm is more than the electric company can handle right now. The sheriff's department and state police are asking everyone to stay inside. The weather service now seems to think that this storm won't let up until sometime tomorrow at the earliest."

Her stomach dropped. "You mean—"

"I mean it looks like you and I are stuck here for the night, maybe longer."

"But I can't be. I've got work and my dog's locked in the house and . . ." Her voice drifted off as she saw the glint of determination in his eyes.

"You're staying here, Melanie," he said, his voice edged in steel. "You don't have any choice."

# CHAPTER NINE

"I can't spend the night here," Melanie stated, stunned.
"That's a crazy idea."

"You have a better one?" Anger crept into his voice. So he didn't like the arrangements any better than she did. Good.

"No, but—"

"I don't have time to stand around and argue with you. Since we don't have any power, I've got to make sure the pipes don't freeze, that the building is secure and that you and I find a way to keep warm tonight."

"But—"

"Listen, Melanie, we just have to accept this," he said, his fingers gripping her shoulder.

"I can't."

He muttered an oath, "Can I count on you to help me, or are you going to spend the rest of the night complaining?"

She started to argue but clamped her mouth shut.

"That's better."

"I just want to go on record as being opposed to this."

"Fine. Consider it duly recorded. Now let's get on to business, okay?"

Ignoring the hackles rising on the back of her neck, she silently counted to ten. He did have a point, she grudgingly admitted to herself. There wasn't much she could do but make the best of the situation. Even if it killed her. "Okay," she finally agreed. "Let's start by being practical. Are the phone lines still working?"

"They were fifteen minutes ago."

"Good." She pushed her hair from her face and ignored the fact that he was staring at her. "I need to call someone to check on Sassafras and I'd better let Bart and Lila know where I am."

"You sure that's a good idea?" he asked, his face a hard mask.

She bristled. "Would you rather they send out a search party? No one knows I'm up here, and believe me, I'd like to keep it that way, but I can't."

Gavin crossed to the bar, yanked the phone from underneath and slammed it onto the polished mahogany. "Suit yourself."

Ignoring his temper, Melanie picked up the receiver and dialed. "Come on, come on," she whispered as the phone rang and Gavin, blast him, stared at her in the mirror's reflection. Finally Aunt Lila picked up on the sixth ring.

"Mellie!" the older woman exclaimed, her voice crackly with the bad connection. "I was worried to death! Bart went over to check on you and brought Sassafras over here, but we didn't know where you were."

Melanie squirmed. She caught Gavin's tawny gaze in the mirror and turned her back on his image. "I brought the photographs for the lodge up to the resort," she said, trying to concentrate on anything other than the man glowering at her in the glass. Quickly, she explained how she'd lost track of time and the storm had turned so wild. "I just should have paid more attention and left before it got so bad outside."

"Well, thank goodness you're safe. Now, you just stay put until the roads are clear."

"That could be several days," Melanie said.

"I know, but at least you're safe."

*Safe?* Melanie doubted it. She cast a sidelong glance at Gavin. His features were pulled into a thoughtful scowl, his lips thin.

She hung up and let out a long breath. "Okay, get a grip on yourself," she muttered.

"What?"

She shook her head. "Nothing."

He was standing at the end of the bar, lighting the wicks of several kerosene lanterns. He glanced up at her and nearly burned his fingers. "That's the first sign that you're losing it."

"I always talk to myself."

"I know," he said quietly. "I remember." He looked up at her again, his eyes warm in the firelight, the angles of his face highlighted by the flame of the lantern. Melanie's heart turned over, and she looked away quickly, before her gaze betrayed her.

He cleared his throat. "I'll go check on the pipes and you can see if there's anything for us to eat in the kitchen."

"Is that what I'm reduced to—cook?"

Gavin smiled. "Gee, and I figured that was a promotion."

"You little—"

"I've heard it all before," he said, striding down the hall.

"Cook, eh?" Indignantly, she grabbed a lantern and headed past the bar to the restaurant and the kitchen beyond.

Stainless steel gleamed in the light of the lantern. The refrigerators, freezers and pantry weren't completely stocked for the season, but there were enough staples to get through several meals. They might not dine on gourmet cuisine, but they wouldn't starve. And if she didn't decide to poison Gavin, he might be in for a rude awakening!

She found a thermos and saved the rest of the coffee, then pulled a bottle of wine from the wine cellar. *This is dangerous,* she thought, eyeing the bottle of claret. Wine had been known to go to her head, and tonight, she knew instinctively, she should keep her wits about her. But what the hell? She intended to show Gavin up, and if a little claret could help, why not?

She couldn't resist the temptation and placed the wine and thermos on a serving cart along with a huge copper-bottomed pot and some utensils.

Water presented another problem. Without electricity, the pumps wouldn't work. No problem, Melanie thought, refusing to come up with any excuses. She'd prove to Gavin that she could bloody well take care of herself—and him, if need be.

Melanie threw on her jacket and gloves and braved the elements long enough to scoop up snow in several huge soup kettles. She gritted her teeth against the wind that ripped through her clothes and pressed icy snowflakes against her cheeks. Even through her gloves, her fingers felt frozen as she lugged the filled kettles into the kitchen and placed them on the cart.

She pushed the cart to the lobby and placed the kettles in the huge fireplace, then headed back to the kitchen, where she grabbed spices, bouillon mix, tomato juice and all the vegetables she could find. Thinking ahead, she added bowls, utensils and a loaf of bread. She'd never considered herself a great cook—in fact, Neil had thought she was "hopeless," but she figured, as she shoved the cart back to the lobby, it really didn't matter. Haute cuisine wasn't the issue. Survival was— and, of course, showing Gavin up.

Once she was back in the lobby, she poured the juice into a huge pot, added bouillon and canned vegetables, then peeled and cut potatoes. She tossed the thick chunks into the simmering mixture and kept warm by staying close to the fire.

When Gavin returned half-frozen an hour later, he was greeted by the scent of hot soup heating on the grate. Candles and lanterns flickered on nearby tables.

He brushed the snow from the shoulders of his sheepskin jacket and warmed his hands by the fire. His eyes narrowed at the sight of the simmering pots. "What's this?"

"Oh, just a little something I whipped up," she tossed back.

"Sure."

He lifted a lid, and scented steam rose to greet the suspicious expression on his face. "You outdid yourself."

"I just aim to please, sir," she replied, smiling falsely.

"Okay, Melanie—what's up?"

"Oh, Mr. Doel, sir, I hope you're pleased," she said, her lips twitching at the way his eyebrows drew together. Served him right! "Here, take this." She handed him a cup of coffee, and he wrapped his chilled fingers around the warm ceramic and sipped. "What's your game?"

"Game? No game."

"Oh, sure. Right."

She couldn't keep a straight face. "I just got tired of you barking commands at me and telling me what to do."

"As if you've ever listened." He frowned into his cup.

"I listen."

One of his brows lifted skeptically. "You do a lot of things, Melanie. And," he acknowledged, pointing to the kettles in the fire, "most of them very well. But listening isn't high on the list."

"And how would you know?"

"I remember more than the mere fact that you talk to yourself, Mel." He paused, looking deep into her eyes. "In fact, I remember too much."

Her throat suddenly started to ache. She swallowed hard and whispered, "We'd better eat now."

Ladling the soup into bowls, she tried to ignore him. But she saw the snowflakes melting in his hair, the nervous way one fist clenched and opened, the manner in which he tugged thoughtfully on his full lower lip.

They ate in silence, both lost in their own thoughts as they sat on the floor in front of the fire. Melanie pretended interest in her soup and coffee, wishing she was anywhere but here, alone with the one man who could ignite her temper with a single word, the man who could turn her inside out with a mere look.

*It's only for a few hours,* she told herself, but the wind continued to moan and mock her.

It seemed to take her forever to finish her soup. She set her bowl aside, then, sipping her coffee, slid a glance at Gavin from the corner of her eye. She wondered what would have happened if, all those years ago, she'd told him the truth about the baby, if they had married, if their child had survived.

"What's this?" he asked, spying the bottle of claret for the first time.

"A mistake," she said.

"Oh?" He picked the bottle up by its neck, found the cork on the cart and slid her a knowing look. "Don't tell me, you were planning to get me tipsy, then, when I wasn't thinking properly, you were going to strip off all my clothes and have your way with me."

Blanching, she could barely speak. But when she found her tongue, she threw back at him, "Sure. That's exactly what I planned. Right after we both took a midnight swim in the pool, then ran naked through the blizzard."

His eyes darkened, and her throat closed. "There are worse fantasies."

"Well, that's not my fantasy."

"Isn't it?"

"You're giving yourself way too much credit."

"Am I?"

"Yes!" she cried, the sound strangled. *Don't let him get to you,* she told herself, but couldn't stop the knocking of her heart.

"If you say so."

Good Lord, was there a more frustrating person in the world?

He poured them each a glass of wine, then clicked the rim of his to hers. "To blizzards," he mocked.

She laughed. "Blizzards?"

"And running naked through the snow."

Melanie's pulse leaped, but she tried to appear calm. "Hah. Yeah."

His mouth twisted wryly, but his eyes gleamed, and as he swallowed his wine, Melanie couldn't help but notice the way his throat worked.

The fire hissed and popped as a chunk of wood split. Outside, the storm raged, and Melanie, drinking slowly, caught alone in the lodge with Gavin, found that life outside the lodge seemed remote.

*Don't let the night get to you.* . . . But Gavin was so close, pouring more of the clear red claret, his hand touching hers as he steadied her glass, his gaze lingering on her mouth as she licked a drop on her lips. She remembered him as he used to be—loving and kind. Their love had been simple and pure . . . and doomed.

"It's been a long time," he said quietly, his thoughts apparently taking the same path as hers.

"We were kids."

He shook his head. "I don't think so." His eyes held hers, and in that instant, she knew he intended to kiss her.

"Gavin, I don't—"

His mouth silenced the rest of her words, and her blood heated slowly. He tasted of wine, and the feelings he evoked were as violent as they had been years before. A thrill of excitement crept up her spine. Her heart began to pound, and she parted her lips willingly, moving close to him, feeling the contour of his body against hers.

"You don't what?" he asked, lifting his head and regarding her with slumberous golden eyes.

"I don't want to make love to you."

"Good. Because I don't want to make love to you." But his lips found hers again, and she yielded.

Gentle at first but more insistent as he felt her respond, his mouth moved over hers. Melanie's blood burned like wildfire as he clasped a hand around her neck, lacing his fingers in the loose knot pinned to the back of her head.

His heart thudded a rapid cadence, matched only by her own. She felt the pins slip from her hair, one by one, to fall on the floor as his kiss intensified and his tongue slipped familiarly through her teeth.

His weight carried them both to the carpet in front of the fire. Melanie's breasts pressed against the hard wall of his chest, and her arms circled his neck.

"Melanie," he whispered against the shell of her ear, and she shivered in anticipation. He pulled the final pin from her hair, and her thick braid fell over her shoulder.

Gavin touched the dark curls, his fingers grazing her breast. Beneath her sweater her nipples grew taut, and heat began to swirl deep inside.

Melanie knew the wine was going to her head, and even worse, the intoxication of being close to him was creating havoc with her self-control. She should stop him now, while she could still think, but the words couldn't fight their way past her tongue.

When he reached beneath her sweater and his hand touched her skin, the same old warning bells went off in her mind, but she didn't listen.

Instead she moaned and curved her spine, fitting herself perfectly against him. His breathing grew ragged as he lifted the sweater from over her head and gazed down at her.

"This is crazy," he muttered, as if his self-control, too, had been stripped from him.

He placed the flat of his hand between her breasts, his long, warm fingers feeling her heartbeat. His eyes closed for a second. "I want you, Melanie," he said, as if the words caused him pain. "I want you as much as I've ever wanted a woman."

Melanie's throat went dry.

"But this could be dangerous."

More than dangerous, she thought, gazing up at his powerful features and focusing on the sensual line of his lips held tight with failing self-restraint. Making love to him was an emotional maelstrom. "I—I know."

"I don't want to hurt you."

"Hurt me?"

"By getting you pregnant."

Tears threatened the corners of her eyes. "It's okay. . . ."

"You're safe?"

"Neil and I couldn't have children."

He stared down at her for a long second.

Her throat ached, and she blinked as he lowered his head and kissed her with all the passion that had fired his blood years before.

Melanie lifted her hands, her fingers nimbly unbuttoning his shirt, her hands impatient as she shoved the fabric over his shoulders. In the glow from the fire, his skin took on a golden hue.

Her fingers swirled around his nipple, and he sucked in his breath, his abdomen concaving, his muscles a sexy washboard beneath his tight skin. Sweat dotted his brow, and she wondered vaguely if he was arguing with himself, listening to voices of denial screaming in his head.

She touched his waistband, and his eyes leaped with an inner fire. "You always could make me go out of my mind." Then his lips crashed down on hers, and gone was any trace of hesitation. His tongue pushed into her mouth, parrying and thrusting, exploring and claiming.

Melanie wrapped her arms around him, felt the fluid movement of his muscles as he shifted, lowering his lips down the slope of her cheeks, brushing across her skin. He kissed her eyes, her cheeks, her ears and lower, to her neck and the small circle of bones at her throat. His tongue tickled the pulse that was thundering in that hollow, and one hand moved in delicious circles on her abdomen.

Her breasts ached, and she moved impatiently.

"Slow down, Mel," he whispered hoarsely. "We've got all night."

His promise should have been a final signal for her to stop, before it was too late. But Melanie was well past turning back. And when he slid the strap of her bra over her shoulder, she moaned, her nipples strained upward, and he stared down at her. "God, I missed you," he admitted as he tugged on the ribbon and her breast spilled out of its lacy bonds, the dark nipple puckering under his perusal.

Melanie writhed at the sweet torture, wanting more, aching deep inside as he cupped her breast and kissed the hard nipple.

His tongue caressed her as his mouth closed over her. His arms wrapped around her torso, and his fingers splayed across the small of her back, pulling her urgently against him.

He kissed her again. Melanie exploded in her mind, memories of love and trust, passion and promises.

Quickly, he removed her bra and skirt, then kicked off his jeans and lay next to her, his naked body, bronze in the firelight, pressed intimately to hers. No words were spoken as he lay upon her, finding a path he'd forged long ago. Their bodies joined and fit, moving rhythmically, heating together, fusing into one.

Melanie gazed up at him, and her heart, pounding a thousand times a minute, swelled. His tempo increased, and she dug her fingers into the sleek muscles of his back, her body arching, her mind spinning out of control. She could feel him pulsing inside of her, and tilted her head back and closed her eyes, lost in her own pleasure.

Gavin cried hoarsely as the earth shattered into a million

fragments of light. She felt him complete himself as wave after wave of euphoria took over her body.

Her nerves were tingling as he collapsed against her. She clung to him, holding on to this special moment, feeling his weight as a welcome burden as afterglow enveloped them.

*I love you* stuck in her throat, but she didn't say the words, nor did she hear them. The only sounds in the darkness were the gentle hiss of the fire and the moan of the wind outside.

When he finally rose on one elbow, looking down at her through warm tawny eyes, one side of his mouth lifted and white teeth flashed against his skin. "You know," he said, tracing the slope of her jaw with one finger, "I think we'd better go."

"Go? Where?" she said dazedly. Shoving her hair from her eyes, she wondered what she was doing here, naked, still feeling the warmth of afterglow invade her.

"To my suite." He glanced to the shadowed rafters and sighed. "There's no way I can keep this room warm—not until the power comes back on. There's just too much space. But we'd be warm in my room."

*And in your bed,* Melanie thought. The thought of sleeping with Gavin, waking up in his arms, was inviting—but dangerous. Falling victim to him spontaneously was one thing; making love to him again was just plain foolish. "I don't think this is such a good idea."

"I know it isn't, but I'll be damned if I'm going to sleep alone tonight. We'd both freeze."

"Oh, so this is just a matter of convenience."

"No—pleasure."

"Stop this," she cried as he started to carry her. "Gavin, your leg!"

"My leg's fine."

"No, I mean it." She started to squirm out of his arms, then realized that she was probably doing more damage than good. "I'm perfectly capable of walking."

He chuckled deep in his throat. "Believe me, I'm not underestimating your capabilities."

"And I could carry things."

"We don't need anything."

"But the flashlight and the lanterns—"

"Unnecessary," he replied, carrying her down the dark hallway without once stumbling. He kicked open the door to his room. Red embers glowed from the fireplace, and a lantern, flickering quietly, had been placed on a bedside table.

"You planned this," she accused as he laid her onto the bed. The sheets were cold against her bare skin.

"No . . . well, maybe." He covered her with an antique quilt and crawled into bed with her.

"You devil!" she rasped, wishing she had the strength to climb off his bed and stomp back to the lobby.

"Absolutely."

"And beyond redemption."

"God, I hope so."

"And—"

His mouth found hers, and his hands wrapped around her waist, drawing her naked body to his. It was incredible, he thought, how perfectly she fit against him, how her curves molded to his muscles, how she seemed to melt into him. He'd stupidly thought that making love to her would purge her from his system, but he'd never been more wrong in his life.

It had been only minutes since they'd joined and he'd felt the wonder of her flesh wrapped around his, and yet he was ready again, his body fevered, his mouth hungry.

And she responded. Her breasts felt heavy in his hands, her nipples willing buds that he brushed with his thumbs. And when he took her into his mouth, tracing those dark points with his tongue, she moaned, her body arching up to his, her moist heat enveloping him.

He rolled her onto him and was lost to pleasure as she

slowly descended upon his length. Suckling at her breasts, his hand firm on her buttocks as she started to grind against him. She was in the driver's seat this time, as the windows rattled with the wind, and he thought vaguely that he hoped the storm would never end.

With the morning came regret. What had she been thinking about? Making love to Gavin was asking for trouble. Yet, lying in his arms, she found it impossible to roll away from him and pretend that a one-night stand with him meant nothing to her.

*Once a fool, always a fool,* she thought, a willing prisoner in Gavin's arms. The storm had subsided, and the day promised to be clear and cold. Soon she would have to leave him.

She rested her cheek against his chest and fell back into a dreamless sleep.

Gavin, however, was very much awake. As he lay in the bed, gazing through the window, watching the sunrise blaze against the snow-covered mountain, the bedside phone rang loudly.

He groaned, unwilling to move. Melanie's cheek rested on his chest, and one of her arms was flung around his abdomen. Her skin was creamy white, her tousled black hair in sharp contrast to the white pillowcase and sheets. His heart warmed at the sight of her tucked so close and lovingly beside him.

He wanted to protect her and cherish her and love her—

The phone rang again, and she stirred, lifting her head and shaking the hair from her slumberous eyes.

"Uh-oh," Gavin growled. "Looks like someone found us."

"Bound to happen sooner or later," she said, yawning through a smile.

"I suppose. Go back to sleep." He grabbed the jangling

receiver with his left hand while still holding Melanie with his right.

"Ridge Lodge."

"About time you answered! I've been trying to reach you all night," Rich grumbled.

"I've been here."

"Well, you didn't answer!"

"The phones must've been out," Gavin replied, not really interested. "And you know cell reception is spotty at best up here."

"What's going on up there? No, don't tell me. You've probably got some beautiful woman waiting for you in bed."

"Get real, Rich," Gavin replied, smothering a smile. "The electricity has been out since last night."

"What about the backup generator?"

"Not yet fully operational."

"Oh, God," Rich groaned. "Any damage?"

"Nothing severe." Gavin stretched lazily. For the first time since he'd agreed to this project, he wasn't really interested in the resort.

"Listen, we've got a million things to do. Now that there's snow, we're wasting big bucks every day we're not open. So I called all our suppliers and the trucks will deliver as soon as the roads are clear. Get ready. Make sure the lot is plowed and that Erik and some of the other boys are there when the shipment of rental gear arrives." He rattled on and on, giving instructions, though he expected—and got—no answers, Gavin just grinned, and when Melanie tried to roll out of bed, he pinned her hard against him. He hadn't felt this good in years and he wasn't about to give it up.

He harbored no illusions that he and Melanie could ever get back together. She hadn't wanted him when he was dirt poor and she probably didn't want him now. But while they were locked away from the rest of the world, he was going to spend every second with her. She was warm, willing and . . . damn it, the one woman who could make love to him as no other had ever . . .

"So I've called the ski patrol, and a group of would-be instructors will be at the lodge as soon as they can get through. Take their applications, talk to them, and for God's sake, make sure you see them on a pair of skis. Put them through their paces."

"I'll handle it," Gavin said, glancing down as Melanie looked up at him through the sweep of dark lashes.

"Right. And check on the—"

Gavin dropped the receiver back in its cradle and rolled over, giving her the full attention she deserved.

"Problems?" she asked.

"Nothing that won't wait." He fingered a strand of black hair that curled deliciously around her face, neck and breasts. Her eyes flashed silvery green in coy delight.

The phone began to ring again, and Gavin reached to the bottom of the bed and yanked on the cord. There was still a faint jangle from the phones in the lobby and bar, but Gavin didn't pay any attention. Instead, he wrapped his arms around her. "I think we have more important things to think about."

"More important than opening the lodge?"

"Mmm." He nuzzled her neck. "Definitely more important." And, kissing her, he proved it.

Later, while Gavin was working elsewhere in the lodge, Melanie dialed the newspaper.

The receptionist answered on the second ring. "Taylor's Crossing *Tribune*."

"Hi, Molly, it's Melanie."

"Melanie! Where've you been?" Molly asked, her voice breathless. "Brian's been looking everywhere for you!"

"I got stuck up at Ridge Lodge when the storm hit last night," Melanie said, feeling more than a trifle guilty as she glanced at the still-rumpled bed. "The road's been closed. Is Brian there?"

"Yeah, I'll connect you."

Molly clicked off, and a few seconds later, Brian Michaels's voice boomed over the wires. "Where the hell are you?"

"Ridge Lodge," she said, repeating everything she'd just told Molly.

"And you were up there all night?" Brian asked.

"That's right."

"Melanie, I need you down here! We need pictures of the downed lines and the road crews and God only knows what else."

"I'll be there as soon as the roads are clear," she promised. "And I've got some great shots of the lodge."

"Good, good. According to the state police and the highway department, the road to the lodge will be open this afternoon."

A twinge of regret tugged at Melanie's heart. "I'll make a beeline to the office." she promised.

"Good. I'll be in all afternoon." His voice lowered. "And, since you're up on the hill anyway, there's something I'd like you to check into for me."

The hairs on the back of Melanie's neck rose. "What's that?"

"I want you to nose around. See if the resort is experiencing any financial trouble."

"Financial trouble," she repeated, her temper starting to rise.

"Right. There's a rumor circulating that an investor is backing out, that Doel's sunk all his personal fortune into this place and unless it opens and opens big, he's in trouble."

"I doubt it," Melanie replied tightly.

"Where there's smoke there's fire."

"I think that depends on who set up the smoke screen." She kept her voice low, hoping Gavin wouldn't walk in on her.

Clenching her fingers around the receiver, she felt trapped. To think she'd defended Brian to Gavin!

"Well, Rich Johanson spends a hell of a lot of time in Portland trying to keep that legal practice of his alive."

"So what?"

"Seems strange to me."

"You're fishing, Brian."

"Maybe, but you keep looking around. As long as you're there, you may as well keep your eyes and ears open."

"Listen, Brian, I'm the photographer for the *Tribune*. I'll take all the pictures you need, but that's as far as it goes! I'm not going to run around here trying to ferret out some dirt."

She hung up and slowly counted to ten. She'd gotten only as far as seven when the door to the apartment opened and Gavin strode in.

"Road crews are already working between here and Taylor's Crossing."

"So I heard," she admitted, motioning to the telephone. "I just called the office."

A lazy, self-deprecating grin stretched across Gavin's jaw. "And what did good old Brian have to say?"

"He misses me."

Gavin lifted a lofty brow. "Anything else?"

"Well, he did mention that I should poke around here and find out if you were financially stable."

"You're kidding." Gavin swore loudly.

"Nope."

"Then he was"

"I don't think so."

Gavin shoved his hands into his back pockets. "Michaels will stoop to anything," he said, disgusted. "The financial situation at the lodge is none of his business. You know, I wouldn't be surprised if he sent you up here just to find out what was going on."

Melanie hardly dared breathe. He wasn't serious, was he? Here, in this room, the bed still warm from lovemaking—how could he even say anything so cruel? "Brian didn't send me, Gavin."

"Of course he didn't," Gavin agreed. "But I wouldn't put it past him."

"And me?"

He snorted contemptuously. "I don't think you sleep with men to get the kind of story or pictures or whatever it is you want from them."

"I don't sleep with men, period. Except for you," She picked up a pen from the table and twisted it nervously.

His face lost all expression. "What about Neil?"

"Only while we were married."

He blanched.

"And there's something I should explain about that," she said quietly, her voice shaking as she struggled for the right words. "I married Neil because of the baby."

The room went still. Melanie heard her own heart thud painfully. She lifted her eyes to meet the questions in Gavin's gaze.

"I thought you said you didn't sleep with Neil until you were married."

"I didn't."

"And just last night—you told me you couldn't get pregnant?"

"I couldn't—I mean, I can't, not now, not with Neil—I mean. . . ." Her hands were shaking and her throat was cotton dry. She forced herself to stare straight into his eyes. "What I'm trying to say, Gavin, is that the reason I married Neil was because I was pregnant." She couldn't help the tears clogging her throat. It was all she could do to stand there, keeping her knees from buckling.

The air in the room was suddenly hot, the glare in Gavin's

# CHAPTER TEN

"Mine? What?" he whispered hoarsely, his face devoid of color, his lips bloodless.

"I was pregnant when you left, but I didn't know it. When I found out you were already trying out for the ski team and—"

"Lies!"

"No! Gavin, why would I lie?" she cried.

"I don't know," he growled, stepping forward, his eyes gleaming menacingly. "But you must have a reason."

"I just thought you'd want to know."

"Now? After eight years?" His voice was so low and threatening that her skin crawled. "When it's so convenient? How stupid do you think I am?"

"I don't—"

He grabbed her upper arm, his fingers digging deep. "Just last night you told me you couldn't conceive. That's right, isn't it? Or has that story changed, too?"

She didn't blame him for being angry, but the explosion of emotion on his face scared her. She tried to jerk her arm away but he clamped down all the harder.

gaze positively murderous. "Pregnant?" he rep
quietly.

"Yes."

"But you said . . ."

She squeezed her eyes shut. "I know what I said.
get pregnant once, Gavin. And the baby was yours."

"I'm not lying, Gavin."

"Oh, no? So where's the kid? Hmm? The son—or daughter—that I fathered?"

She crumbled inside. "Oh, God, Gavin, don't. Can't you see how hard this is for me?"

"I see that you lied eight years ago and you're doing it still."

"No—please, you've got to believe me."

"Why?"

"Because it's the truth!" she cried, desperation ringing in her voice.

"You don't know the meaning of the word!"

"How would you know? You never stuck around long enough to find out!"

He winced. "All right, Melanie. If you want to go on spinning your little tale, go right ahead." He released her suddenly, as if the mere touch of her made him ill. Crossing his arms over his chest, he muttered, "Go on. I'm all ears!"

Melanie lifted her chin and fought the tears that kept threatening to spill. "I was pregnant with your child, and my father talked me into not telling you."

"Wonderful guy."

"He was thinking of you."

"Sure."

"He said you weren't ready to be burdened with a wife and child, that you'd only grow to resent me because you'd have to give up your dream."

"Are you expecting me to buy any of this?"

"Only if you remember how much I loved you," she said, fighting fire with fire. His eyes betrayed him. Emotions, long hidden and tortured, showed for one instant, and he was again the vulnerable boy from the wrong side of the tracks. Her heart felt as if it were breaking into a thousand pieces. "I loved you. All I thought about was loving you and living with you for the rest of my life. I—I didn't mean to get pregnant. It just happened."

"So you married another man. And Neil was more than happy to play daddy to my kid. Oh, come on, Melanie. This just doesn't wash."

"Why else would I marry a man I didn't love?"

"Money," he said cruelly, his voice filled with conviction.

"I didn't care about money. But I wanted a good life for the baby."

"The baby." He lifted his hands. "Where is he?"

She swallowed the hot, painful lump in her throat, "I miscarried. Six weeks after I married Neil."

"Now didn't that work out fine and dandy?" he mocked, his words cutting to the bone.

She shook her head at the memory. "It was awful—"

"It was a lie. Either you're lying to me now, or Neil Brooks is a bigger fool than I am for believing you."

"You think I made this up?"

"I don't know what to think, Melanie. But you just told me yourself that you couldn't get pregnant. How do you expect me to believe something as outrageous as this?"

"I didn't lie. Neil and I couldn't have children. I—we— after I lost the baby, we never used birth control. And, even though we hoped, there never was another baby."

"And how does medical science explain this incredible phenomenon?"

"It doesn't. Neil wouldn't go to the doctor and . . . well, I didn't bother. Things started falling apart, and we started sleeping in different rooms."

"So you're expecting me to believe that I got you pregnant and you, out of some convoluted sense of nobility, refused to tell me about it but you convinced Neil to marry you and raise another man's child as his own. Only, lo and behold, before the blessed event occurs, you lose the baby and never, ever conceive again?"

She fought the urge to snap back at him. Instead, curling her fists, she blinked against tears of frustration. "Yes."

"Well, Melanie, you missed your calling. You shouldn't have become a photographer. You should be an actress. You've just given one helluva performance!"

Melanie's temper exploded. How could he have become so cruel? So callous? So jaded?

She thought of their recent lovemaking; the scent still lingered in the air. He'd been tender and kind—and now, so heartless. Sick inside, she knew she had to leave. Now. Before whatever they'd shared turned ugly. Without a word, she started gathering her things.

"What're you doing?"

"Leaving."

"You can't leave."

"Watch me."

"But it's freezing, the roads are blocked and—"

"I don't give a damn about the roads or the weather!" she flung out as she found her camera and purse.

"You're angry."

"I'm fucking *furious!*"

"Just because I didn't believe your story."

"Forget it." She started for the door, but he grabbed her arm, spinning her around.

"You can't leave," he said again.

"Let go of me, Gavin."

"Your car won't make it."

"What do you care?" She peeled his fingers from her arm. "I'll walk if I have to."

"Melanie—"

She ran out the door and through the now familiar hallways.

The lodge was empty; her footsteps rang on the hardwood. She heard Gavin behind her, but she shoved open the front doors and was blasted with the rush of bitterly cold air.

Snow glistened and still fell in tiny flakes. She nearly

slipped on the icy front steps and he caught up with her. "Melanie, listen, I'm sorry."

"No reason to be!" she snapped, plowing through the snow that nearly hit her at the knees. "You think I'm a liar. Fine. At least I know where I stand." She plunged on, determined to find a way to leave him.

"For crying out loud, Melanie . . ."

Her Volkswagen, even parked under cover, was under a pile of snow. Ignoring the wind, she brushed the icy flakes from the windshield, climbed into the car and turned the key. The engine ground slowly as she pumped on the gas. "Come on, come on," she whispered, sending up a silent prayer. She couldn't stay here a minute longer—she wouldn't!

Gavin opened the car door as the engine sputtered, coughed and died. "Now, just a minute—"

"Drop dead!"

"Look, I didn't mean to ridicule you."

"Well, you did!"

"It's just that your story is so unbelievable."

"So you said!" She stomped on the accelerator and twisted the key again. "Come on, come on," she muttered to the car. *Oh, please start! Please!*

His jaw worked. He was obviously struggling with his own temper. "Come back into the lodge. I'll make some coffee and we can talk this over."

"Just leave me alone! That's what you're good at—leaving!"

His lips tightened. "I'm trying, Melanie. Now the least you can do is meet me halfway."

"After what you said to me? After being accused of being a liar?" She turned furious hazel eyes up to him. "You know me, Gavin. You know I wouldn't lie about something like this. What would be the point?"

"I thought you needed an excuse for marrying Neil. Something I might understand."

The car gave a last sickening cough and died. When she turned the key again, all she heard was a series of clicks. Gavin's hand touched her shoulder. She shrank away.

"I'll buy you a cup of coffee and I'll listen to what you have to say. Besides, this car isn't going anywhere. Even if it did start, you'd never make it through the lot."

He was right about that. The lot was covered with nearly two feet of snow. The Volkswagen wouldn't get out of the shed before stopping dead—that was, if she ever could get it started.

"Come on, Mel," he insisted.

"Forget it! You won't believe me."

"I'll try." His voice turned gentle. "You threw me for a helluva loop."

"Then you believe me?" she asked, her features tormented.

He glanced up at the sky, and snow collected in his hair and on his collar. Lines bracketed his mouth and eyes. "I don't know what to believe."

"Fine." She yanked hard on the door, but he wedged himself between the handle and the interior.

"As I said before, you're not going anywhere in this," he ordered tautly, taking hold of her and hauling her from the car.

She tried to climb back inside, but he pulled her out, carrying her back to the lodge.

She wriggled and kicked, trying desperately to get back on her feet and find her rapidly escaping dignity. "Put me down! You'll slip and ruin your ankle and—"

"Be quiet!" he growled, trudging through the snow, following the trail she'd broken only minutes before. "We're going back inside and you're going to start over, slowly, from the beginning."

"If you think I'm going through this again, you're out of your mind!"

"Probably," he said. "But I think you owe it to me to—"

"*I owe you?* Give me a break. I owe you nothing! I shouldn't have opened my mouth in the first place."

"But you did," he reminded her, slowly climbing the steps and kicking open the front door. He didn't stop until he'd carried her all the way into his apartment. Plopping her onto the couch, he said, "Now let's start over."

"I've told you everything."

"A little late, isn't it?"

"I explained that I didn't want to burden you."

"So very noble of you," he mocked, trying and failing to keep his temper under control. "So you, pregnant with my child, married Neil Brooks?"

"Yes."

"And he agreed to go along with your scheme?" he asked dubiously.

"It wasn't a scheme!"

He shoved shaking hands through his hair. "What I don't understand, Melanie, is, if this is true, why you didn't at least have the courage to tell me about it. Didn't you think I'd want to know?"

"I didn't want you to feel trapped," she said, her hands curling into fists of frustration.

"But if I was the father—"

"You know you were!"

"Then the child was my responsibility."

"A child you didn't want."

"It was nice of you to make that decision for me." He crossed to the window, and anger fairly radiated from him. "If the baby had lived, would you have ever told me the truth?"

She opened her mouth, closed it again and struggled with the truth. When her words came, they sounded strangled. "I—I don't think so."

"And why the hell not?" He whirled, facing her again, his temper skyrocketing. His nostrils flared and his eyes blazed.

"Because I wouldn't want a scene like this one!"

Something flickered in his eyes, something dark and dangerous. "Or because I wasn't good enough for you?"

"What?"

"Is that why you ran to Neil instead of me? Because you wanted to raise your child—our child—by a rich man instead of the son of the town drunk?"

She couldn't believe it. Not now. Not after he'd sworn that he would listen to her. "I don't have to listen to this, Gavin. I loved you. I loved you so much I was out of my mind with wanting you. But I didn't want to make you hate me for the rest of your life!"

"So you married Brooks in order to pass off my child as his," he said, disgust heavy in his voice.

"No!"

"This is one for the books—"

"You said you'd listen!"

The sound of footsteps rang through the hall. Someone had made it up to the lodge. The roads were clear! She could leave.

"Mr. Doel? Are you here? Mr. Doel?" Erik Link's voice echoed through the corridors, and Gavin's lips pursed.

He muttered an oath, then called over his shoulder, "In here."

The door flew open. "I just wanted to say that the roads are clear and—" Erik's voice fell away at the sight of Melanie, and she realized how she must look, her hair in tangles, her cheeks burning, her chin thrust forward like a recalcitrant child getting the lecture of her life. "I—uh, didn't mean to interrupt."

"You didn't," Melanie informed him. She jumped to her feet and grabbed her things. "In fact, I'd really appreciate it if you'd give me a ride back to town. My car's dead."

"Sure." Erik's gaze moved from Melanie to Gavin.

"I'll drive you home," Gavin said. "If the roads are passable—"

Melanie tossed her hair over her shoulder. "Oh, I wouldn't want to bother you, Mr. Doel. You must have a thousand and one things to do before the resort opens."

"That's right, and the first one is to get you safely home." He grabbed his keys from a hook near the door, gave Erik quick instructions about plowing the lot and keeping the lodge warm, then followed Melanie, who was walking briskly toward the back lot.

"You shouldn't have bothered," she shot at him when they were once again outside.

"I'd feel better about this if I made sure you were all right."

"I can handle myself. I don't need you bossing me around," she flung back, wishing she could hurt him as he'd hurt her. All his horrid accusations filled her head and she ached inside. Well, she'd done her duty, told him the truth. Now she couldn't wait to get away from him, from the lodge— from Taylor's Crossing if she had to!

They walked to the garage, and she climbed into a huge four-wheel-drive truck and waited while he slid behind the wheel and turned the ignition. The engine caught immediately. Melanie didn't so much as glance in his direction. But he didn't shift out of park. Instead, he drummed his fingers impatiently on the steering wheel, jaw set, as if struggling for just the right words.

Well, she wasn't about to help him. He'd been wretched and he deserved to squirm.

He sighed, shifting uncomfortably, and the bench seat moved beneath her. If she could only get through this. . . .

The cab of the truck was warm, the windows fogged, and Melanie, against her best judgment, sneaked a glance his way. He was staring at her, lips tight, eyes narrowed, as if he were trying to size her up. One wayward strand of honey-blond hair fell over his forehead.

The air between them fairly crackled.

Melanie broke the silence first. "I just wish you'd remember that you trusted me once," she said.

"That's the problem. I remember all too well."

"And you think I betrayed you."

"You did."

"Fine. Think what you want. Can we go now?"

He shoved the truck into gear and let the wheels grab. The truck lurched, and he tromped on the accelerator, plowing through the unbroken snow until he was on the path that Erik's truck had broken through the parking lot.

The trip down the mountain took nearly an hour. Melanie turned an ostracizing shoulder to Gavin and stared out the window at the aftermath of the storm. Pine boughs drooped under a blanket of thick snow. The sky was gray, the clouds high, the air frosty and clean.

But inside the truck the atmosphere was thick. The miles rolled slowly by. At the sight of a road crew, Melanie yanked her camera out of its case and, asking Gavin to slow down, clicked off several shots of workers sawing through fallen trees and restringing electrical cable.

She didn't say another word until he reached her house. It took all of her willpower not to throw open the door and run up the front steps.

He ground the truck to a stop. "Melanie—"

She didn't want to hear it. Opening the door, she climbed out. "Thanks for the ride and all the hospitality," she said, her tone scathing. "Believe me, I won't ever forget this morning."

*And neither will I,* Gavin thought as she slammed the door of the truck shut and stomped through the snow to the back door. He waited a few seconds, until he was sure she was inside, then he threw the truck in reverse.

He wanted to believe her. In his heart he desperately wished he could trust her again. But how could he? And this cock-and-bull story about the baby. . . . Why the hell would she lie? Why now? It would have been easier for her to keep quiet.

There was obviously some truth to the tale. He knew her well enough to recognize her pain. And her private agony was matched by his when he thought about a child he would never know, a child he'd helped create.

His hands gripped the wheel tightly, and an angry horn blared as the truck moved too close to the centerline. Teeth clenched, he focused on his driving, but a thousand emotions tore at his soul.

He could have been a father—the father of a seven-year-old. For God's sake, he didn't even know what a seven-year-old was like!

And Melanie could have been his wife—not Neil's. If only she'd been honest with him way back when.

What kind of life could he have given her? Would he have given up his chances for glory on the Olympic team? Would he have forced Melanie and the kid to travel from one ski resort to the next while he tried to scratch out a living as a pro? Without the catapult to fame from the Olympics, would he have had the backing to race professionally, to get on his feet? Or would he have returned to Taylor's Crossing and become a ranch hand or a logger or given lessons to children during the weekends at Ridge Resort?

*But there was no baby.* An unfamiliar pain, raw and cutting, seared straight to his soul. If he'd stayed in Taylor's Crossing and married Melanie, would the child have survived? Hell, he didn't even know why a woman miscarried, but he felt tremendous guilt that he hadn't been around to offer support and comfort to Melanie for a child they would never share.

"Son of a bitch," he muttered, driving straight to the lodge. He parked near Erik's truck and noticed that several other vehicles had arrived. Two plows were working to clear the lot. Rich must have gotten through to the crew.

He walked into the lodge and made a beeline for the bar. Ignoring the looks cast his way by some of the workers, he grabbed a bottle of Scotch, twisted open the cap and took a long swig right from the bottle. It burned like hell.

"What's eatin' you?" his father asked. He glanced up, and in the mirror over the bar he saw Jim Doel's florid, lined face, an older version of his own.

"You wouldn't believe it."

"Try me."

Gavin shook his head and took another tug on the bottle.

His father approached and, laying an arm over Gavin's shoulders, said, "I don't know what you're fightin', son, but believe me, this—" he touched the bottle with his free hand "—isn't gonna help."

"Nothing will," Gavin agreed.

"It's that Walker woman again, isn't it?" his father guessed. "Don't you know it's time you got her out of your blood once and for all?"

"I wish I could," Gavin admitted. "But I don't think it's possible."

"Anything's possible."

"What I don't need right now is a lecture," Gavin grumbled.

"No. What you need is another woman."

Scenes of lovemaking filled Gavin's mind. He remembered Melanie snuggled tight against him, her hair brushing his bare skin. "I don't think another woman's the answer."

"'Course it is," his father countered. "I know that model has called you."

"Not interested."

"Well, maybe you should be." His father's eyes met his in the glass. "There's no reason for this girl to tear you apart."

Gavin clenched his teeth. What he felt for Melanie went way beyond the bonds of reason.

"So the lost lamb has found her way back to the field," Guy remarked when Melanie shoved open the door and walked briskly past his desk.

Melanie, in no mood for humor, replied, "Since when was I a lamb?"

Guy held up his hands in surrender. "Only a figure of speech."

She unwrapped her scarf, shrugged out of her coat and hung them both in the employee closet. "Was I the only one who didn't make it in?"

"Are you kidding? The county was literally shut down. Constance and Molly were both out yesterday." He retrieved Melanie's Garfield mug from her desk, rinsed it out and poured her a cup of fresh coffee. "Even Brian's place lost power for a few hours. He came in late yesterday, and boy, was he fit to be tied."

"So things were just like usual," Melanie remarked.

Guy grinned. "I guess. Anyway, he's on a real kick to sell more papers."

"What's new?"

"Yeah," Guy muttered, fidgeting with his watch and avoiding her eyes. "But this is different. I don't know what happened, but my guess is he got the word from the powers that be to increase circulation or—" Guy rotated his palms to the ceiling "—*sayonara!*"

At that moment Brian Michaels himself burst into the newsroom. His face was flushed from the cold, and he saw Melanie instantly. "So you're back," he said, yanking off his gloves and hanging his hat in the closet near the front door. "Good. We've got work to do. Come into my office."

"Be right there." Melanie grabbed a notebook from the top

of her desk and, ignoring Guy's worried glance, followed Brian into his private office. "Now listen," Brian said before she'd even had a chance to sit down, "I'm serious about the rumors about the lodge being in financial trouble. I want to know all about it. You were up there—what's going on?"

"Nothing out of the ordinary. Because of the storm, they're hoping to open early."

"That's it?" he asked skeptically.

"That's it." She eased into one of the uncomfortable chairs near his desk.

Brian's brow furrowed, and he reached into his top drawer for a stress ball. "No sign of any financial difficulty?"

"None. They were expecting delivery of the supplies and equipment as soon as the roads were clear."

"You wouldn't keep anything from me, would you, Melanie?"

"No."

"But if you thought I was prying into someone's personal life, especially if that person happened to be someone you cared about, you wouldn't give up private information easily."

She felt heat climb up her back. "You're right. I wouldn't."

"Not even if it was news?"

"No."

Squeezing the ball harder, he continued. "This job's important to me, Melanie. We owe it to our readers to report the truth, no matter how . . . uncomfortable . . . it might be."

"I didn't see anything at the lodge. As a matter of fact, I've been there when Rich Johanson has been paying bills." She leaned across his desk as he lit his cigarette and snapped his lighter closed. "I think you're barking up the wrong tree. The lodge looks solid as a rock. And if they can open earlier than planned, I would think there's a better chance than ever that they'll make it work."

"How long were you at the lodge?"

"Less than twenty-four hours," she said uneasily. "I got there just before the storm hit."

"Who else was there?"

"Just Gavin Doel."

"Just Doel?" One sharp eyebrow arched. "How was that?"

"Cold," she lied. "The lodge lost power."

"And phone lines?"

"They were down—at least for a while in the middle of the night."

"So what did you and Doel do all that time?" he asked.

Was he suggesting something? She couldn't be sure. With effort she kept her voice steady. "We tried to keep the pipes from freezing, attempted to start the backup generator . . . that sort of thing."

"And in all that time Doel never once said anything that might indicate that things weren't running smoothly at the lodge?"

"Well, he wasn't too pleased about the lack of electricity."

"I mean financially."

"No." She leaned back in her chair. "What's this all about?"

"Just a rumor I heard."

"From whom?"

He grinned. "You know I won't reveal my sources."

"Well, I think your sources are yanking your chain."

"But you won't mind checking into it when you're back up at the lodge doing whatever it is you do there."

Melanie's temper snapped. "Of course I'll mind!" she said, standing and glaring down at him as if he'd lost his mind. "I can't go creeping around spying on Gavin and Rich, and I wouldn't even if I could. I don't know why it is that all of a sudden you want to do some big smear campaign against Ridge Lodge, but I won't be a part of it!"

"This isn't a smear campaign. Think of it as investigative journalism."

Melanie's sound of disgust eloquently voiced her feelings.

"You don't have a choice," Brian added calmly.

"Of course I do. . . ."

But his meaning was clear, and his face had hardened. "Not if you want to keep your job. Let's be straight with each other. Circulation hasn't picked up and I've got to make some cuts in expenses around here. I'm going to trim some people from the staff."

"Are you saying you're going to fire me?"

"Not yet, but I expect you to be a team player. Now, why don't you upload the shots you've already taken up there, then go up with Jan and find out what's going on at the lodge?"

His intercom buzzed, and Melanie walked out of the office. She couldn't afford to lose this job, not yet. She still had debts to pay off from her father's illness and the addition to her house. But she'd be damned if she was going to help Brian ruin Ridge Lodge or Gavin Doel.

Brian watched as Melanie marched stiffly back to her desk and pulled out the connecting wires for her camera. Something had happened to her while she was up at the lodge, and his reporter's instincts told him she'd gotten herself mixed up with Doel.

Now *that* was interesting. Gavin Doel, internationally famous athlete, involved with a local woman?

For the first time all week, Brian smiled to himself. Maybe he was going for the wrong angle on Doel. Sure the man was newsworthy, but the readers just might be more interested in his love life than his lodge.

And Melanie Walker was beautiful as well as spirited. Exactly what was going on?

Jan had mentioned that Doel and Melanie had known each other way back when. Brian wondered just how well.

It wouldn't take much to find out. He had microfiche and old newspapers that went clear back to the fifties. There was also a town library filled with high school yearbooks and a lot of people who had lived here all their lives.

Surely someone would remember if Gavin and Melanie were involved before. Maybe it was nothing, just a passing friendship—or maybe not even that. But Brian wasn't convinced.

No, there was a spark that leaped to life in Melanie's eyes every time Doel's name was mentioned. He could see through her feigned nonchalance. And she'd been defensive as hell.

Oh, yes, it was time to do some checking on Gavin Doel. And this time, he'd put Jan on the story. Jan didn't have the same overrated sense of values that Melanie clung to.

In fact, he might even do some digging himself. He'd never liked Gavin Doel. Doel had once cost him his job, and from that point on, his career had gone downhill until he'd landed in this two-bit town. Well, maybe now Gavin Doel was his ticket out.

The guy had everything, Brian thought jealously. It was time Doel was knocked down a few pegs, even if it cost Melanie Walker.

It was too bad about Melanie. Brian liked her. She worked hard, was nice to look at and was smart. Except when it came to Gavin Doel. Yep, it was too bad about Melanie. Brian felt an abnormal twinge of conscience and hoped she didn't get hurt—at least, not too badly.

But if she did, it was her fault. She was better off without an arrogant bastard like Gavin Doel. The sooner she knew it, the better for everyone.

# CHAPTER ELEVEN

Melanie returned to Ridge Lodge, determined that the next story in the *Tribune* would reflect the excitement of reopening the resort.

As she parked in the lot, she realized that the story would nearly write itself—if Jan would let it.

Ridge Lodge was frenetic.

Delivery trucks brought skis, boots, fashion skiwear, food, snacks, light fixtures, paper products, tourist information, utensils, medical supplies, souvenirs and on and on.

The ski patrol had already started checking the runs, and an area had been cleared near the Nugget Rope Tow for the ski school to meet, Chairs and gondolas moved up the hill as the newly named lifts became operational. Grooming machines chugged up the snow-covered slopes, while snowplows kept the parking lot clear.

A rainbow of triangular flags snapped in the wind, and the snow continued to fall, bringing with it hopes for a long and prosperous season.

Inside, the lodge was hectic. Employees manned the phones as the resort geared up for an early season. Others were briefed on the way the lodge worked, dishes were stacked, beds were made in the rooms, the bar was stocked and a new sound system was turned on.

Melanie smiled as she saw her sepia-toned pictures hanging near mining equipment, adding to the Gold Rush atmosphere of the lobby.

In the huge stone fireplace a fire crackled and burned invitingly. Workers arranged furniture in the bar and lobby, and the Oriental rug where she and Gavin had made love was still stretched across the floor. A pang of regret tore through her.

Her smile disappeared. Hadn't she learned anything? Chiding herself for being a fool, she pulled out her camera and made her way past the bustling workers.

"Well, how do you like this?" Jan asked, breezing in the front door and stamping the snow from her boots.

"What—oh, the lodge?" Melanie glanced around. "Looks a little different, doesn't it?"

"*Very* different." Tucking her gloves in her purse, Jan eyed the walls. "Those your pictures?" she asked, moving closer to a print of miners panning for gold.

"Yes."

"They're not bad."

"Thanks."

Jan's mouth tightened. "You know I hate this, don't you?"

"Hate what?"

"Being the bad guy. I wouldn't be surprised if Doel and Johanson tried to kick me out of here."

Melanie was skeptical. "Would you blame them? You keep asking all sorts of personal questions."

She lifted a shoulder. "Brian wants a more personal story. I try to give him one." Jan's eyes clouded a minute. "Melanie, I think I should warn you . . ." She let the sentence trail off.

"Warn me about what?" Melanie demanded, then understood. "About Gavin?" When Jan didn't reply, she added,

"Come on, Jan. Weren't you the one who thought I should chase after him?"

"Maybe that wasn't such a hot idea," Jan replied nervously. She looked as if she were about to say something else when she spotted Rich Johanson. "Look, just be careful," she said cryptically. "Don't do anything foolish."

*Too late for that,* Melanie thought as Jan, following Rich, took off in search of her story.

Melanie wandered down a long corridor to the shops. Mannequins were already dressed in neon and black jumpsuits. Sweatshirts, imprinted with the resort's logo or simply saying "Ski the Ridge!", were displayed in a window case.

All around her, employees chatted and laughed, stocking the shelves or waxing skis or adjusting bindings on rental skis.

In the exercise room machines stood ready, and nearby, steam rose from the aquamarine water in the pool. Yes, Ridge Lodge was nearly ready for its guests. Despite Brian Michaels's arguments to the contrary, Ridge Lodge was destined to be a success. She could feel it. And the photographs she snapped reflected that success—smiling employees, gleaming equipment, well stocked shops.

She worked her way outside and changed lenses. Then she clicked off shot after shot of the moving lifts, a group of instructors in matching gold jackets as they practiced together, an operator in the cage at the bottom of Daredevil run, and above it all, Mount Prosperity stood proudly, a regal giant in a mantle of white.

She didn't notice Gavin for nearly two hours, then, as she trained her lens on a group of instructors making their way through the moguls at the bottom of Rocky Ridge run, she spied him in the lead, blond hair flying, skis so close together they nearly touched, his form perfect.

Her throat went dry as she camera zoomed in for a closer shot. She noticed the concentration in his face, the natural grace with which he planted his poles, the way he turned effortlessly, as if he'd never been injured.

"The man is awesome," Jan said as she stepped through the snow to reach Melanie. Her eyes were trained on Gavin, as well. "Looks like he's good as new."

"I suppose." Melanie turned her camera on another instructor, a woman who was gamely trying to keep up with Gavin and losing ground with every turn.

"I wonder if he'll race again."

"I hope so," Melanie muttered, still adjusting the focus.

"You do?" Jan said. "Why?"

"Because he loves it. It's his life. He's not happy unless he's tearing down some mountain at breakneck speed."

Jan sighed wistfully as Gavin, flying over the last of the moguls, twisted in midair, tucked his skis together and cut into the hillside, stopping quickly and sending a spray of snow to one side.

"So you think once this lodge is up and running, he'll take off for the ski circuit?"

Melanie stiffened. "I don't know," she said honestly. "You'll have to ask him."

"Don't worry, that's on the agenda." Jan's eyes darkened thoughtfully. "There's a lot more I'd like to know about Mr. Doel."

At that moment Gavin looked up. His gaze scanned the lodge before landing on Melanie. Through the lens, Melanie noticed his jaw tighten.

With a quick word to the instructors, he planted his poles and skied, using his arms and a skating motion with his legs, as he crossed the relatively flat terrain from the base of the run to the lodge.

Melanie's stomach knotted.

"Well, if it isn't the *Tribune*'s finest," he said, eyeing Melanie's camera and Jan's ever-present notebook.

Melanie ignored the jab and decided to try her damnedest

to be professional. She would put what happened between Gavin and her behind her if it took all of her willpower. "You agreed to the series of articles, remember?"

"Yeah," he said flatly, but his lips twisted. "What's the angle—isn't that what you call it?—for this week's edition?"

"Financial impact," Jan said as Gavin leaned over and shoved on his bindings with the heel of his hand. With a snap, he was free of his skis. "The *Trib*'s interested in the economic impact on the community, as well as how you keep a lodge resort this size out of the red."

"It takes some doing," he replied.

"I'll bet."

"But we have backing."

"Investors?"

He straightened, his expression menacing. "Where're you heading with this?"

"Nowhere," Jan said guilelessly, but Melanie decided to step in.

"I thought I already mentioned that there've been rumors that the resort is failing financially," she said, warning Gavin.

Gavin's jaw set. His eyes turned as cool as the early winter day. "And I thought I explained that there are no problems, financial or otherwise."

"Then none of your investors are bowing out?" Jan asked.

Gavin whirled on her. "Not unless you know something I don't." His eyes narrowed threateningly. "Oh, I get it. Michaels is fishing again. Well, give him a reminder for me, will you? If he prints anything the least bit libelous about this lodge or me, I'll sue. Now, if you don't mind, I'd like to speak with Melanie. In private. And don't print that!" Lips compressed angrily, he took hold of Melanie's arm and, without a backward glance at the reporter, propelled Melanie up the few steps to the back deck.

"What the hell's going on?" he demanded once they were out of earshot.

"You know as much as I do," she replied, glancing over his shoulder. Fortunately, Jan, after casting them a questioning look, had turned back toward the main lobby.

"What's Brian's game?"

Melanie yanked her arm away from him. "All I know is he's looking for dirt. Any kind of dirt."

"On me?"

"Yes. Or the lodge."

"Then that brings him right back to you, doesn't it?" he countered, his expression hard. "Does he know about you and me?"

Melanie caught her breath. How could Gavin talk about their past without so much as a hint of emotion? "No," she replied levelly.

"You're sure?"

"Positive. A few weeks ago he asked me to look into your past—you know, dig through the files—and I told him I came up empty, that you walked the straight and narrow while you lived in Taylor's Crossing."

The lines near his mouth tightened, and he muttered a nearly inaudible oath. "And he doesn't know about Dad?"

Melanie shook her head, thinking about the pictures she'd lifted from the file cabinet. "There isn't a file on your father—at least, not at the *Trib*."

Gavin's brows shot up. "But—"

"Don't ask. Just don't worry about your father."

He studied her face for a second, and her breath seemed trapped in her lungs.

With all the effort she could muster, she inched her chin up a fraction. "Is that all you want? Because I've got work to do—"

He exploded, pounding a gloved fist on the top rail of the deck. "No, damn it." His voice lowered, and he grappled for control of his emotions. "It's not all I want."

"I don't think I want to hear this—"

"Just listen. I've been thinking. A lot." His gaze touched hers, and she quivered inside. It took all her grit to hide the fact that he was getting to her. "Look, I know I came on a little strong the other day."

"A little strong? You mean your impersonation of Genghis Khan? Is that what you call a little strong?"

He shook his head and let out an exasperated sigh. "You shocked me, Melanie. And you threw me for a helluva loop!"

"I didn't mean to. I just thought you should know the truth."

"It came a little late."

Melanie had heard enough. She tried to storm away, but he grabbed her arms again and his face became tender. "Let me go, Gavin," she insisted, "before we cause a scene we'll both regret."

He ignored her. "How did you expect me to act?"

*As if you cared. As if you remembered how much we loved each other.* "I didn't expect anything, Gavin. I still don't."

"I'm sorry," he said softly, his gloved hands still gripping her arms. "Really. But you dropped a bomb on me the other day, and it's all I've thought about ever since. I made some mistakes. We both did. I'm just sorry you thought I was too irresponsible to handle fatherhood."

"Not irresponsible," she said tightly. "But I just didn't want to be the one to destroy your dreams."

He dropped his hand and yanked off his gloves. "You don't understand, do you? Eight years ago you were part of that dream," he admitted, his eyes narrowing on her. "The skiing was great, don't get me wrong. But it wasn't the same after you married Neil."

Melanie froze. She could hardly believe him. Though the pain etched across his face seemed real enough, she didn't trust him. "Believe it or not, Gavin, I just tried to do the right thing."

"But it wasn't right, was it?" he said softly.

"I don't think there was a right or wrong."

His eyes searched her face. She thought he might kiss her. His gaze centered on her lips for a heartbeat, but, as if he had a sixth sense, he glanced over his shoulder and furrows lined his brow. "Great," he grumbled.

Melanie looked past him and spied Jan heading for the deck.

Gavin touched her shoulder. "You and I need to talk somewhere quiet, somewhere without your friend." His mouth curved down as Jan climbed onto the deck.

"I don't mean to interrupt," she said, eyeing them with interest, "but I do have a few more questions and a deadline."

"Just a minute." He turned back to Melanie. "When things slow down here, I'll call."

Melanie shook her head. "You don't have to."

"I know. But I want to."

Their gazes held for just a second, and Melanie melted inside. Quickly, she squared her shoulders. "I'll be waiting on pins and needles," she quipped.

Gavin cleared his throat, took in a deep breath and, folding his arms over his chest, turned his full attention back to Jan. "All right, Ms. Freemont. What is it you want to know?"

Melanie didn't stick around for the rest of the interview. She took a couple more shots of the staff busily at work, then, trying to forget that Gavin wanted to see her again, returned to the office.

Two days later, all hell broke loose.

Melanie caught her first glance of page one of the *Tribune*. With a sinking heart, she read the headline that screamed: FINANCIAL PROBLEMS PLAGUE RIDGE RESORT.

"This is outrageous!" she sputtered, skimming the article and feeling sick. How could Jan have reported anything so blatantly false? The article stated that Gavin himself was in serious financial trouble, that since his injury he'd become a recluse, not giving any ski clinics, not endorsing any skiwear, not making a dime.

He'd sunk his personal fortune, according to the story, into Ridge Lodge, and when he and his partner had run out of money, they'd sought private funds from investors, who were rumored to be upset with the way their money was handled.

By the time Melanie finished reading the article, her insides were in shreds.

The pictures she'd taken of the workers readying for the opening of the resort were sadly missing. The shots that were included were some she'd shoved aside—a worried profile of Gavin, a picture of an empty lift, another shot of chairs stacked on tables in the empty bar, a photograph of Rich and Gavin talking, their faces set and grim.

Anger burned her cheeks, and her fingers clenched the thin newsprint. "That bastard," she hissed.

Guy Reardon looked up from his desk. He seemed paler than usual. "I was afraid of something like this." He dropped his pencil and sighed. "I think it's only going to get worse."

"How can it get worse?"

Guy's eyes were troubled. "Believe me, it can."

"Do you know something I don't?" she asked.

He lifted a shoulder but avoided her gaze. "It's just a feeling I've got."

"Well, it's got to stop!" Brandishing the newspaper as if it were a sword, she walked swiftly between the desks to the editor's door. She didn't even bother knocking but shoved open the door and cornered Brian. He was just hanging up the phone.

"I can't believe you published this!" she said, tossing the paper onto his cluttered desk. The headline fairly leaped from the page.

"Why not?"

"Because it's not true! I've been up to the resort!" She

thumped her fingers on the front page. "There's not a shred of truth in that story!"

"Maybe you're biased."

"What?"

"Close the door, Melanie," Brian said, lowering his voice. Her skin crawled, but she yanked the door shut and stood glowering down at him while he lit a cigarette. "Let's not pull any punches, okay?" he suggested.

"Fine with me. Why the smear job on the lodge?"

"Reader interest."

"And if readers are interested in gossip, in pure speculation, in anything no matter how damaging or incorrect, the *Trib* will print it, right?"

"This has never bothered you before."

"Because it hasn't happened before. I thought this newspaper had some pride, some integrity, some sound journalism behind it!" Melanie's blood was beginning to boil. "And what about libel? Aren't you afraid of being sued?"

He thought about that and shook his head. "I think you're too personally involved."

*"What?"*

His eyes behind his glasses squinted. "I know about you and Doel, Melanie. I know you dated him in high school." He reached into the top drawer of his desk and withdrew an envelope.

Melanie's stomach turned over as Brian dumped the contents of the envelope onto the newspaper she'd dropped on his desk. She recognized her own face as well as Gavin's in the black-and-white shots. They were younger, obviously in love, and seated together at Ridge Lodge long before it closed. Eight years ago.

"Where did you get these?" she whispered.

"I had Jan dig through the files. When she came up empty, I had her look through the high school records and check with people around town." He shook his head. "It seems that all the

*Tribune*'s personal history on Gavin Doel is missing. As for Gavin's old man, Jim Doel, he doesn't even have a file here. Isn't that strange?"

"Not so strange. I took them, Brian."

"Big surprise. You know that's stealing, don't you?"

"I was just trying to protect my personal life."

He waved off her explanation and pointed to the prints on the desk. "It doesn't matter, does it?"

Her insides shredding, she said, "I just don't think any of our readers would be interested in this."

"And I think you're wrong. I think the readers will find everything about your . . . well, for lack of a better word, *affair* with Gavin Doel interesting reading."

"No!" she said vehemently.

"It'll be great. The angle will be 'The Girl He Left Behind But Never Forgot'."

"It'll never sell, Brian. Too much schmaltz."

"I don't think so."

Desperate, she whispered, "You can't be serious,"

Brian frowned. "Look, Melanie, I've got a problem. If I don't increase circulation, I'm out of a job. Now, from my experience, I can tell you what will sell papers."

"My life?"

"Not yours. Doel's."

"My private life is none of your business, none of the readers' business."

"Unless you're involved with a celebrity."

"Not even then!"

"Anyway, I know, for whatever reason, you broke off with Doel and married your ex."

Melanie's face drained of color. Sweat dotted her back. He couldn't know about the baby—could he? Her knees were suddenly weak, but she forced herself to stand, her fists tightening, her fingernails pressing painfully into her palms. "My life is not open for inspection," she said quietly. "And neither is Gavin's!"

"You know, this can work to our advantage. Mine, yours and the *Tribune*'s."

"How's that?" she asked suspiciously, not entirely sure she wanted to hear his rationale.

"I want you to get close to Doel again, see what you can find out."

"You're not serious," she whispered.

"Why not?"

Her eyes narrowed on the man she had once respected. "If you don't know, I'm not about to tell you."

"Hey, this is business—"

"Not to me, Brian. This is bullshit. I quit!"

His eyes grew round. "You don't know what you're saying."

"Yes, I do," Melanie flung back with newfound conviction. "And you know what? It feels good. I should've done this the first time you suggested I dig up some dirt on Gavin."

"I'm just doing my job, Melanie."

"Well, you can do it without my help!" With all the dignity she could muster, she turned on her heel and marched out of the office, letting the door bang closed behind her. More than one interested glance was cast in her direction, but she was too angry to meet anyone's eyes. She crossed the room to her desk. Grabbing her purse, briefcase, mug, computer, camera case and coat, she took one final look at the newspaper office and started for the doors.

"What happened?" Constance asked, biting on her lower lip nervously.

"Ask Brian."

"You're leaving?"

"For good."

"But . . ." Constance glanced quickly to Brian's glassed-in office. "I'll call you."

"Do that."

As she headed through the front doors, Melanie ran into Jan and couldn't help saying, "I don't think Barbara Walters has too much to worry about."

"What?"

"Your story, Jan. It's garbage."

"You're the one who was holding out," Jan reminded her. "You knew a lot about Doel and then you took the damned files—"

"Wouldn't you, if you were in my shoes?" With that Melanie swung outside, not feeling the cold wind as it blew from the east.

"I told you that girl was trouble!" Jim Doel flung a copy of the *Tribune* onto the empty bench in the weight room.

"What girl?" Gavin, working on strengthening his thigh muscles, let the weights drop with a clang.

"You know which one." Jim's face was rigid, his mouth a firm, uncompromising line.

"You must be talking about Melanie."

"That's right."

Grabbing a towel, Gavin wiped the sweat from his face and ignored the churning in his gut. "What happened?"

"See for yourself!" Jim growled, motioning toward the newspaper.

The headline nearly jumped off the front page. "Son of a . . ." He bit off the oath as he saw that the article was written by Jan Freemont. "How do you know Melanie's involved?"

"She works for that rag, doesn't she?"

"Yeah, but she already told me that Brian Michaels was up to something. I doubt that she would tip me off, then be a part of it."

"Why not? That way she looks innocent."

"She *is* innocent," he retorted vehemently, wanting to believe his own words, instantly defending her.

"If you ask me, you've got it all wrong. If she works for the paper, she's part of the problem." Jim sank onto the empty bench, lifted his wool cap and scratched his head. "I know you've always been soft when it comes to Melanie," he said quietly, "but it seems to me she causes you nothing but grief."

*If you only knew,* Gavin thought, reading the article and slowly seething. Though no concrete evidence was given, the story suggested that Ridge Lodge would close soon after it opened, leaving its investors, and anyone foolish enough to pay in advance for lift tickets and lodging, high and dry.

Gavin stripped the towel from his neck. "This is probably my fault," he admitted.

"Your fault?"

"For not playing the game."

"What game?"

"Years ago I met Brian Michaels. He was a reporter with the paper in Colorado. He wanted dirt on the ski team and then personal stuff on me and my teammates. I not only told him to get lost, I called the paper he worked for and complained. So did my coach. Michaels lost his job."

"And you think he'd hold a grudge?"

A corner of Gavin's lip lifted cynically. "I don't think he'd chase me down to get back at me, but since it's convenient, I'd bet he can't resist a chance to get even."

"And so he's payin' you back?"

"Not for long," he muttered, his eyes narrowing. He wasn't about to take all the bad publicity lying down. Rich was a lawyer; he could deal with the legalities of libel. As for Michaels, he intended to talk to the owners of the paper.

But first he had to deal with Melanie.

Leaving his father sitting on the bench, Gavin walked through the shower, then threw on a pair of jeans, a sweater and a battered pair of running shoes. On his way out of the lodge, he spied the manager and left some quick instructions.

He couldn't wait to hear Melanie's side of the story.

Newspaper tucked under his arm, he shouldered open the door of the lodge. A blast of cold mountain air swirled in. Outside, dusk was settling around the mountain, shading the snow-covered landscape in shades of lavender and blue. He barely noticed.

As he climbed into his truck, Gavin told himself that Melanie wasn't involved in this—she wouldn't have used him for a story. But he couldn't ignore the seeds of doubt his father had planted.

After all, hadn't she lied to him, kept the secret of their child from him? If there really had been a pregnancy. His lips pursed in a grim line as he shoved the truck into gear and accelerated. The pickup lurched forward. She wouldn't have lied about the baby. There was no reason. No, he decided, his jaw clamped, her story was genuine—at least to a point. He still wasn't convinced that she'd kept the secret for altruistic purposes. No, she probably wanted to snag rich Neil Brooks all along.

Or had the baby been Neil's? Was there a chance she'd been sleeping with Neil at the same time she was seeing him? That made more sense. Neil would much rather claim his own child than a bastard of Gavin's.

"Stop it," he ground out, his fingers tight on the wheel.

His chest constricted, but he forced his thoughts back eight years to the hayloft where they had met, to the moonlight that had streamed through the window to cast her black hair in a silver sheen, to the look of sweet, vulnerable innocence that had lingered in her eyes.

No, he couldn't believe that she had lain with him one night and the next with Neil Brooks. No matter what had happened between them, he wouldn't believe that she was that emotionally cold and calculating. "Get over it," he growled at himself as he cranked the wheel. The truck skidded around the corner, then straightened.

In the distance, through the pines, the city lights of Taylor's Crossing winked in the darkness. It would take twenty minutes to get to Melanie's house. He only hoped that she was home—and alone.

# CHAPTER TWELVE

Melanie finished touching up some photographs in her studio, responded to a couple voicemails and tentatively planned two portrait shoots for the next couple of days. Since she was officially out of a job, she needed all the work she could get—and that included working at Ridge Lodge. With Gavin.

She dialed the resort's number and was told by a foreman that Gavin and Rich were out.

"Terrific!" she muttered, wondering about their reaction to the article as she fixed herself a meager dinner made from leftover chicken, vegetables and gravy. "Use your imagination, Mel," she told herself as she rolled premixed pie dough and laid it over the top of a casserole dish. Gavin would be furious—and hell-bent to avenge the article. "Well this is going to be fun," she muttered sarcastically, switching on the radio and adjusting the volume. The disk jockey reported that another storm was about to hit the central Oregon Cascades. More snow for the lodge, she thought. At least some news was positive.

Sassafras, hoping for a morsel of chicken, stood at attention near the stove. "Later," she promised, then eyed her creation. "We'll both have some—to celebrate."

Though not working for the *Tribune* created a score of financial problems, she felt a sense of relief.

Shoving the dish of chicken potpie into the oven, she winked at the old dog. "Tonight, we dine like kings," she announced, then wrinkled her nose. "Well, not really kings, maybe more like dukes or squires or . . . well, peasants would probably be more appropriate. But we're celebrating nonetheless."

To prove her point, she pulled out the bottle of champagne she'd had in the refrigerator since her birthday and popped the cork. She found a glass high in the cupboard over the stove.

"Here's to freedom," she said, pouring the champagne. It frothed over the side of the glass, and she laughed. "I guess I won't get a job pouring drinks down at the Peg and Platter, hmm?"

Sassafras whined and lowered his head between his paws, still staring up at her with wide brown eyes as the doorbell pealed.

With a loud growl, the dog leaped to his feet and raced, toenails clicking on the old hardwood floor, to the front door. Melanie set her glass on the counter and followed.

Through the narrow window near the front door, she saw Gavin, collar turned against the wind, blond hair dark and wet, snow on the shoulders of his leather jacket, jaw set and stern.

A newspaper was folded neatly under his arm. Today's edition of the *Tribune*.

"Give me strength," she whispered prayerfully as she unlocked the door and swung it open.

"What the hell is this?" he demanded, shaking the paper in front of her nose.

"It's good to see you, too," she tossed back at him, the hackles on the back of her neck instantly rising.

He strode in without an invitation. "Whose smear job is this?"

Melanie closed the door behind him and braced herself. "Brian Michaels's."

"And what did you have to do with it?"

"Nothing."

His sensual lips compressed. "You're sure?"

"Absolutely. I didn't see the front page until this morning."

"Helluva way to bring tourists into town." He flung the newspaper onto a nearby table.

"Did you come over here to accuse me of something?" Melanie asked, unable to keep the irritation out of her voice. "Because if you did, let's get down to it."

"What would I accuse you of?"

"I don't know. It sounds like you think I was part of some conspiracy."

"No, I don't believe that," he said quietly, though he was still angry. White lines bracketed his mouth, and his jaw was clenched so hard a muscle worked beneath his cheek.

"Oh, so this is just a social call," she said, unable to resist baiting him.

"I just want to know what's going on. You work for the paper—"

"Worked. As in past tense."

His eyes narrowed. "What happened?"

She motioned to the newspaper. "That happened and . . . well, it's probably going to get worse."

"How?"

"Brian's not about to let up. Come on into the kitchen. I've got something in the oven and I've got to keep my eye on it." He followed her through the hallway by the stairs. The scent of stewing chicken and warm spices wafted through the air. "Join me?" she asked, holding onto the neck of the champagne bottle.

He lifted a shoulder.

"I'll take that as a yes." She poured his glass and handed it to him. "I'm celebrating."

Lifting an eyebrow, he took a sip from his glass. "Celebrating what?"

"My emancipation. I quit the *Tribune*."

He frowned. "You said things would get worse."

"They will. Brian found out that we dated in high school, Gavin. He plans to use it. He even asked me to get close to you again, get you to confide in me."

"Great guy, your boss."

"Ex-boss," she reminded him. "That's when I quit."

"How much does he know?"

She shook her head. "I don't know."

"The baby?"

His words sliced through the air like a sharp knife. "I don't think so," she replied, shivering.

"Who does?"

Shaking her head, she frowned. "My dad did and Uncle Bart and Aunt Lila." She closed her eyes and rubbed her temple. "And of course Neil and the doctor."

"No one else?"

"I don't think so." Drawing in a shuddering breath she opened her eyes again and, grateful for something to do with her hands, lifted the glass to her lips. "I lost the baby before I'd started to show—before Neil or I had said anything to our friends."

Gavin's nostrils flared. "And you didn't mention it to your 'friend' Jan?"

"Of course not!" Melanie replied guiltily. She knew now that she should never have confided anything to Jan. "I told her we dated so she'd stop asking questions. I didn't think it would backfire." She finished her drink in one gulp.

"When reporters can't find news, they create it."

"Not usually," Melanie replied, noticing that Gavin's glass had been drained. She poured them each another glass and asked, "So why does Brian have it in for you?"

"You think he does?"

She nodded. "Don't you?"

"Probably. I met him a long time ago in Colorado. He started sticking his nose in where it didn't belong, and I complained. He was fired shortly thereafter."

"He never mentioned it," Melanie said thoughtfully. "When your name was first linked with the lodge, Brian was pretty interested, but I don't think it was because he wanted to dig up some scandal. At least, I hope not." She sipped from her glass again and stared over the rim at Gavin.

He was tense, his features hard, the muscles beneath his shirt bunched, but his gaze, when it touched her, was warm and seductive. His tawny eyes were as they had always been, erotic and knowing.

Her mouth grew dry, and she quickly finished her second glass of champagne.

He stood near the windows of the nook, one shoulder resting on the doorframe, large fingers wrapped around the slim stem of his fragile champagne flute.

The soft noises in the house filled the room—the slow tick of the clock in the front hall, the steady rumble of the furnace, the muted strains of a love song from the radio, a creak of ancient timbers and the old collie's whispering breath as he slept under the table.

"So what're we going to do about this?" he finally said, his eyes searching her face.

"About what?"

"Us."

That single word caused her heart to start thumping. "I don't know if there is an 'us.' I'm not sure there ever was."

"Sure there was," he said easily, finishing his champagne and setting the empty glass on the counter.

"It was a long time ago."

"What about last week, when you were up at the lodge?"

*Yes. What about those precious hours we spent together?* "As I remember, it didn't end well."

"You shocked me." He let out a long, slow breath, but his gaze never wavered. "If I'd known about the baby . . ."

"What would you have done?"

"Come home."

Her heart wrenched. "But that would have been no good," she whispered, her words difficult. "You didn't stay for me. You couldn't come back for a baby. You would've felt trapped." She saw the denial in his lips and held up a palm. "You would have, Gavin. Someday, sometime. You would have wondered, 'what if?'"

"And you weren't willing to gamble that I would decide it didn't matter?"

"No."

He crossed the room slowly, his gaze moving deliberately from her eyes to her lips. "You didn't give me enough credit, Mel."

"I just wanted you to be happy—"

Wrapping strong arms around her waist, he drew her against him. "Happiness is elusive," he whispered before he kissed her, his lips molding over hers. He smelled of snow-flakes and tasted of champagne.

Knowing she shouldn't give in, Melanie closed her eyes and leaned against him, content to feel his hands splayed possessively against her back. She welcomed the feel of his tongue as it slid easily between her teeth, his hard body pressed so intimately to hers. His thighs moved, pinning her legs to his. Her pulse leaped, and her heart thundered.

When at last he lifted his head, his eyes were glazed. He touched her wet lips with one finger, tracing her pout, his gaze searching hers. "I thought that if I ever saw you again, it wouldn't matter," he confessed. "I told myself that I was over you, that you'd been a boyhood fascination, nothing more." Disgust filtered through his words. "Obviously I was wrong."

The timer on the stove buzzed so loudly Melanie jumped.

"What's that?" Gavin asked.

"Dinner."

"It'll wait." In a quick motion, he turned off the stove and the buzzer. Noticing the coat rack near the back door, he tossed a long winter coat in her direction, grabbed her hand and tugged, pulling her outside.

"Hey, what're you doing?" she said, laughing as he led her down the back steps and through the snow. "I'm not dressed for this."

"Don't worry about your clothes," he said, sliding a hard look over his shoulder.

"Gavin . . . ?"

He didn't answer but just tugged on her arm, leading her across the yard. The sky had turned black, in stark contrast to the white earth. Snow covered tree branches, roofs, eaves and ground, drifting against the fence and piling onto the stack of wood near the barn.

*The barn.*

The air was suddenly trapped in her lungs.

With a tingling sense of deja vu, she knew where he was taking her. Her throat went dry, and time seemed to spin backward.

He tugged on the handle of the door, and it slid to the side on rusted rollers, creaking and groaning. Inside, the dark interior smelled of dust and old hay. There were no more cattle or horses, and the barn itself was in sad need of repair.

Melanie balked. Her breath fogged. "You're not seriously thinking of—"

"Let's go," he insisted, leaving the barn door open, letting in a pale stream of illumination from the security lamp near the garage and the silvery reflection of the snow.

He paused at the bottom of the ladder to the hayloft, and Melanie stopped, yanking her hand from his. "They say you can never go back, Gavin."

"I'm not going back."

"This might not be a good idea."

"Why not?"

"It's been eight years for a reason."

His arms surrounded her, and his mouth closed over hers. Memories rushed through her mind, yet they paled to the here and now, to the rough feel of his jacket against her cheek, the smell of his cologne mingling with the dust, the warmth of his hand pressing hard against the small of her back. She'd been kidding herself, she realized, when she'd made love to him before and thought she could remain emotionally detached.

Groaning, he half pushed her up toward the loft. Melanie's throat went dry, but a thrill of anticipation skittered up her spine and she stepped onto the ladder.

With each rung, she wondered if she were making a mistake she would never be able to undo, but she kept climbing, one step at a time, until she stood in the cold, darkened loft and Gavin was beside her, his breath stirring her hair as he slid the coat from her shoulders and tossed it onto the old straw. Then, holding her chin between both his palms, he molded a kiss against her lips that made her shiver from head to toe.

A tremor passed through Melanie, and she was sure he could feel it as his tongue pressed insistently against her teeth and into her mouth, searching, tasting, plundering.

His hands held her tight against him, his thighs pressing against hers, her breasts crushed to his chest.

"I never forgot you Melanie," he admitted, his voice rough. "Never." His hands slid lower, cupping her buttocks, pulling her against him. Through their clothes, she felt the hardness between his legs, the urgency in his touch.

"I tried. God, I tried. And there were other women—women I hoped would make me forget."

"Shh," she whispered, the breath torn from her lungs. She touched his lips with the tip of one finger. "I don't want to hear about them."

He drew her finger into his mouth and sucked, his tongue playing havoc with her nerve endings as it tickled and toyed.

Melanie's abdomen tightened. Liquid heat scorched her veins, and she couldn't stop the moan that slipped through her lips.

Kissing her again, he pulled her closer, forcing one of her legs to move upward and rest against his hip. Her head lolled backward, and her arms wrapped around his neck as they fell to the hay. Her old coat was a meager blanket against the cold air and the rough hay, but Melanie didn't notice. She was on fire inside, and the scratch of the straw only heightened her already tingling senses.

Gavin's mouth found hers again. Hot, anxious lips pressed hard against hers in a kiss that was as punishing as it was filled with promise.

"Gavin," she cried wantonly. She arched upward, closer, closer. He stripped away her sweater and took both lace-covered breasts in his hands. Burying his head between the mounds, he kissed the skin over her breasts as he pulled her bra away. The stubble on his chin was rough, his lips and tongue wet and wild and wonderful as his hot breath whispered across her nipples and caused a fire to burn deep within.

He teased her. His tongue grazed a nipple, parrying and thrusting, wetting the tight bud until Melanie was wild with desire.

An ache stole through her, and she cradled his head to her breast. He suckled long and hard, and Melanie grasped his hair in her hands, her fingers tangling in his thick blond locks.

He began to move against her, and she felt his rhythm, still holding him close as he struggled out of his clothes and kicked his jeans away. Lord, she wanted him. She could barely think for the desire rippling deep within.

His eyes were gold and glowing with a passion matched only by her own as he discarded her clothes quickly. And then they were naked. Again in the barn, but this time the love between them was a savage, forceful desire that stripped them bare. "You make me crazy," he muttered, as if trying to get a grip on his exploding passion.

Was he going to stop? Now? Oh, God, no! "Gavin . . . please . . ." Writhing, she lifted her hips, and he ran his hand along her inner thigh, touching the apex of her legs, and groaning in satisfaction at the evidence of her desire.

"Melanie . . ." he whispered, his breath fanning her skin, his tongue wetting a trail against her leg.

His hands once again found her buttocks, and she moved closer to him, trembling with desire as he found her, pleasuring her until she could stand the sensual teasing no longer.

"Gavin, oh, please . . ." She reached for him, drawing him up along her body, her hands forcing his head to hers, and she kissed him with all the desire flooding through her veins. Touching the flat nipples in his mat of golden hair, she sucked on his lower lip and he lost control.

"What do you want from me?" he rasped, his voice echoing off the old beams.

"Everything."

Shifting, he lifted her legs in the air, leaning her smooth legs against his chest.

"Oh really?" she said, biting her bottom lip sensually as he moved his body against her in this new position.

"This one gives me such a nice view," Gavin responded, smiling slyly.

Slowly, she could feel him enter her and they both reveled in the sensation. First with shallow thrusts, and as things heated, Gavin took control. He plunged deep and she arched upward, meeting the fervor of his thrusts anxiously, closing around him again and again, their bodies fusing in savage fury.

Her senses were on fire as he massaged her breasts while he entered and withdrew, pushing her to the edge of rapture. Her fingers dug into the supple flesh of his arms and at the sound of his primal cry, she shuddered, dropping her legs and convulsing against him, a thousand sparks igniting and sizzling.

With a dry gasp, he collapsed atop her, crushing her breasts and pressing her hard against the rough coat. Perspiration fused their bodies, and his curling chest hair tickled her sensitive bare skin.

"Melanie," he whispered, his voice raw and hoarse. "What am I going to do with you?"

*And what am I going to do with you?* Wrapping her arms around him, she closed her eyes and tried to slow the still-rapid beating of her heart. She wasn't going to fall apart now, to weep for what might have been. But she held him tightly, as if afraid he might disappear.

When he slowly rolled to his side, she reluctantly released him.

"This is insane," he said. "Just plain crazy." He plucked a piece of straw from her hair and sighed loudly.

"So what're we going to do about it?"

"I wish I knew," he muttered.

# CHAPTER THIRTEEN

"I think it would be best if we went low profile," Gavin stated, finishing his second helping of slightly burned chicken potpie. As if the passion that had exploded between them less than an hour before had been forgotten.

"Low profile?" Melanie repeated, unable to touch her food.

"If Michaels is really serious about making us the lead story in his next issue, we should diffuse it."

"By not being together?" Why did it hurt so much?

As if noticing her pain, he reached across the table and wrapped warm fingers around her palm. His thumb slowly rubbed the back of her hand. "I just don't want the focus of attention shifted from the lodge to us." He offered her a patient smile. "It's only for a little while, 'til the lodge gets on its feet. And believe me," he added with a devilish twinkle in his eyes, "it'll be as hard on me as it is on you."

"You think so?"

"I know it." With a sigh, he scraped his chair back and reached for his coat. "I've got to get back, but I'll see you at the resort, right. Rich says you've got some pictures on consignment in the ski shop?"

"That's right."

"And you'll be there for the grand opening?"

She nodded, though her throat was tight as she walked with him to the back door. "You bet."

"Bring your ski gear. Maybe we could take a few runs together."

"You'll be too busy."

"Then come up sometime before." He reached for the handle of the door.

"I thought we were going low profile," she teased, though she didn't feel much like joking.

"We will. I doubt if Michaels will catch us on Devil's Ridge or West Canyon." He smiled as he mentioned two of the toughest runs on the mountain.

"It's a date," she said as he drew her outside and swept her into his arms. His lips caressed hers in a kiss that was full of promise and pain.

When he lifted his head again, he groaned. "We've got to do something about this," he whispered, his voice rough as he rested his chin against her crown and held her close. Wrapped in the smell and feel of him, she hated to let go.

When at last he released her, she stood on the porch and watched as he ran across the yard and climbed into his truck. With a roar the engine caught, and as the pickup backed out of the drive, the beams of his headlights flashed against the old barn and the trunks of the trees in the backyard. As the light receded, she noticed the huge ponderosa with the gash in its bark, the ugly cut her father had made when he'd first learned she was pregnant all those years ago.

She closed her eyes for a second and wondered where she and Gavin would go from here. Would the future be bright and filled with happiness, or black with the loss of a love that was never meant to be?

"Don't even think about it," she told herself as she walked back into the house.

* * *

"I've got good news," Dr. Hodges said as he switched on the light and illuminated an X-ray of Gavin's leg.

"I could use some." Gavin eyed the X-ray but couldn't make head nor tail of it. He hadn't seen Melanie in days, and was irritable. The lodge was opening the day after tomorrow, and he was up to his eyeballs in preparations. But he really didn't give a damn. He just wanted to be with her.

"The fracture's healed." Hodges studied the X-ray again, narrowing his eyes, looking for some sign of the flaw that had sidelined Gavin.

Gavin felt a slow smile spread across his face as he thought about the season ahead. "I can race again."

"Well," Hodges said, his lips protruding thoughtfully, "there's no physical reason why you can't, at least not in your ankle. But if I were you, I'd give it a year before I raced competitively again."

"So you're releasing me?"

Hodges smiled a boyish grin. "For the time being. But if you have any pain—any at all—I want you back here, pronto."

"You got it." Gavin stood and shook Hodges's hand. He felt as if a ton of bricks had been lifted from his shoulders and he wanted to celebrate. With Melanie. This afternoon . . .

Melanie was miserable. The past few days without Gavin she'd been cranky and upset and her stomach had been queasy. "All because of one man," she chided herself stepped out of her studio and walked into the kitchen.

"About time you finished in there."

Melanie nearly Jumped out of her skin. Gavin was there, half-kneeling, scratching Sassafras behind his ears.

"How'd you get in?" she asked, drinking in the sight of him. Dressed in gray slacks and a pullover sweater, his skin tanned and his hair unruly, he was as handsome as ever. He glanced up at her and her heart turned over.

"Breach in security. The front door was unlocked. I heard you in there and I didn't want to bother you." He straightened and his eyes sparkled. "Come on, get your gear."

"My gear?" she repeated as his arms surrounded her.

"We're going skiing."

"Now? But I have work—"

"Who has time for that? We're celebrating!" Wrapping strong arms around her waist, he spun her off the floor.

"Wait. Your leg!" she cried, though it was her stomach that lurched.

"That's what we're celebrating," he said, dropping her back to her feet and planting a kiss against her forehead. "I'm invincible again."

"You're not making any sense."

He winked. "The doctor's released me. Given me the okay to race again!"

She felt her face drain of color. "This season?"

"As soon as I can pull it off. I'm rusty, of course, and older than most of the guys on the circuit. It'll take some intense training, but I can work out at the lodge. And once Ridge Lodge is up and running, Rich and the manager can handle the rest."

So he was leaving, again. All her private hopes disintegrated. Her father was right. Gavin's first love was and would always be the thrill of downhill racing.

"Are you all right?" he asked, his eyes suddenly serious.

"I'm fine," she lied, forcing a smile that felt as fake as a three-dollar bill. "Just let me get my things." Wriggling out of his embrace, she ran out of the kitchen and upstairs. Her head was pounding, and when she looked in the mirror she noticed that her face had turned ashen. "Great, Melanie—you're a real trooper," she chided, changing into a black turtleneck and her new jumpsuit, a purple and sea-green one-piece that she'd found in a local shop before she'd quit working for the *Tribune*.

She found her skis, poles and boots and packed a small bag for her goggles, gloves, sunglasses and an extra set of clothes. Then, before she went back downstairs, she splashed water on her face and fought a sudden attack of nausea.

"Hang in there," she said angrily, furious with herself for overreacting to the news that he was leaving. A little blush and lipstick helped, and when she hurried downstairs, she'd pushed all thoughts of life without Gavin from her mind. They still had a little time together, and she was determined to make the best of it.

They drove to the lodge, and while Gavin changed, Melanie waited for him outside. The sky was blue and clear, and other skiers tackled the runs, gliding gracefully down the slopes or, in the case of the less experienced skiers, grappled with their balance as they snowplowed on the gradual hills.

Melanie smiled as she heard the crunch of boots behind her. Turning, she expected to find Gavin but was disappointed. Jim Doel was walking toward her, and his face was firm and set.

"I'm surprised to see you here," he said.

Nervously, she replied, "Gavin and I decided to ski together before the crowd hits this weekend."

Jim frowned. "Look, I don't see any reason to beat around the bush."

Melanie braced herself.

"A lot of things have happened between your family and mine, and Lord knows if I could change things I would. I'm the reason you grew up without a mother and I've lived with that for eighteen years. I've also lived with the fact that I wasn't much of a father to Gavin, but he made it on his own. Became one of the best skiers in the whole damned country."

"You should be proud," Melanie said icily.

"Of some things. All I'm saying is that I'm sorry for the accident. If I could've traded places with your ma, I would've."

"If you're expecting me to forgive you—"

"Nope. What I expect is for you to leave Gavin alone. You've messed with his mind enough." He raised faded eyes to hers. "He's got a second chance, you know. Most people don't get another one. And he loves racing."

"I know."

"So let him go."

She inched her chin up a fraction. "Why would I take away something he loves so much? I'm not going to stop him from racing."

He didn't look as if he believed her, but she didn't care. She had something else she had to get off her chest. And, though a part of her longed to blame him for the tragedy, she knew it was unfair. He'd paid for it with every day of his life. "As for my mother's death, it was a long time ago," she said, offering a slight smile. "I hope you can put it in the past where it belongs. I have."

His jaw worked.

"And, though I doubt you and I will ever be close, regardless of how we feel about Gavin, I'd like for us to try to be fair with each other."

His lips compressed. "All I want from you is a promise that you won't interfere in his life."

"How Gavin lives his life is Gavin's business."

"Glad you see things my way."

"But I do care about him very much."

"Then do what's best for him." With that, he strode toward the machine shed, and Melanie let out her breath slowly. She watched as Jim disappeared inside the shed, then she headed toward the lift. She wondered if she and Jim Doel could ever be comfortable around each other. Probably not.

Frowning, she adjusted her bindings and practiced skiing on the flat area behind the lodge.

"Hey! Let's go!" Gavin, already on skis, was making his way to the Daredevil lift. Wearing a royal blue jacket and black ski pants, he planted his poles and she followed. Her heart soared at the sight of him, and she shoved his father from her thoughts. Today she was going to enjoy being with the man she loved.

The lift carried them over snow-covered runs, thick stands of pine and a frozen creek. Gavin rested one arm over the back of the chair, and they laughed and talked as they were swept up the mountainside.

Cool air brushed her cheeks and caught in her hair. Gavin touched her cheek and she smiled, happy to be alone with him. At the top of the lift, they slid down the ramp.

"Follow me," Gavin urged, his voice excited, and Melanie only hoped she could keep up with him.

Melanie's ski legs were better than she remembered, and she flew down the mountainside, snow spraying, hair whipping in the wind. Gavin, far ahead of her now, skied effortlessly. His movements were sure and strong, and as he glided from one plateau to the next, he waited for her.

At one plateau, she didn't stop to catch her breath but flew past him, her laughter trailing in her wake. Gavin gave chase and breezed past her along a narrow trail that sliced through the trees.

Exhilaration pushed her onward, and the wind rushed against her face, stinging her eyes and tangling her hair. She rounded a bend and found Gavin stopped dead in his tracks, flagging her down.

"Giving up?" she quipped as she dug in her skis and stopped near him. She was breathing hard, her chest rising and falling rapidly.

"No, I just thought you could use a rest." To her amazement, he pressed hard on his bindings, releasing his skis from his boots.

"Me?" she mocked, still gulping breaths of fresh air. "I could do this for hours! You're just wimping out on me."

"Psh. Don't kid yourself." He glanced up, and his smile slashed his tanned skin. "Well," he drawled, "I did have an ulterior motive."

"And what's that?"

"I wanted to get you alone up here."

For the first time she realized that they had skied away from the major runs and that the lifts were far in the distance. The area was secluded, trees surrounding the trail and the frozen creek that peeked from beneath drifts of snow.

Gavin reached down and unfastened her bindings as well.

A thrill raced up Melanie's spine. "And what did you plan to do with me?"

"Just this," he said, taking her into his arms and pressing ice-cold lips to hers. They tumbled together in the snow and laughed as the icy powder tickled their noses and caught in their hair.

"Someone could come along at any minute," she protested.

"Let them." He kissed her again, and his lips warmed hers, heating her blood, easing the chill from her body.

Melanie's heart knocked loudly, her pulse leaped and she wished she could stay here forever, locked in his arms, the pristine stillness of the snow-covered forest surrounding them.

When he reluctantly drew back, his gold-colored eyes gleamed and he smiled at her as if they'd been lovers for years, as if all the pain and twisted truths of the past had never existed. "I love you, Melanie," he said, and tears tickled the corners of her eyes. She could hardly believe her ears. Gavin loved her? If only she could believe it was true.

"Well?" he asked.

"You know I love you, Gavin. I hate to admit it, but I probably always have."

He laughed. "What're we going to do about that?"

"I don't know," she replied honestly.

"Well, I do." He kissed her again and, pulling her against him, lay with her in the snow. Warmth invaded her body, and she closed her eyes, remembering how much she'd loved him. That love seemed to pale compared to the emotions that tore at her now.

Shouts and hoots interrupted the stillness, and Gavin, with a groan, struggled to his feet. He pulled her upright just as two teenagers swished past them, spraying snow and hollering loudly.

"Come on," Gavin said, eying the retreating figures. "Let's get in a couple more runs before I lose control completely."

"Or I do," Melanie thought aloud, stepping into her skis.

They spent the rest of the afternoon on the mountain, laughing and talking.

Finally, after dark, Gavin drove her home. He lingered on the doorstep, holding her close and pressing urgent lips to hers.

"You could stay," she offered, surprised at her sudden boldness.

"I have to be at the lodge."

"Tonight?"

"I should be."

She grinned up at him. "What would it take to change your mind?" she asked coyly, her fingers crawling up his chest

He grabbed her hands. "Don't get me excited."

"Why not?"

He kissed her again, harder this time, his lips sealing over hers, trapping the breath in her lungs. When he finally lifted his head, his eyes had darkened. "Oh, the hell with it! Since when was I responsible?"

Lifting her off her feet, he carried her inside, slammed and locked the door with one hand and hauled her upstairs, where he dropped her unceremoniously onto the bed.

A second later he was beside her, kissing her and removing their clothes, anxious to love her. And Melanie didn't stop him. Sighing, she wound her arms around his neck, tangled her fingers in his hair and pulled his head to hers.

*Tonight,* she thought. *I'll just think about tonight.*

She woke early the next morning. It was still dark outside, but Gavin was staring down at her, his hand moving slowly against the smooth texture of her shoulder. She could see his face in the half-light from the moon sifting through the window.

"I've got to go," he whispered.

"Already?" She clung to him, his body warm as it molded to hers.

"No choice. The grand opening is tomorrow."

"At least let me make you breakfast."

He brushed a wayward strand of hair from her eyes. "You don't have to."

"I know I don't," she said crankily, unhappy he was leaving her, "but I want to."

"Sure you do." He laughed as she climbed out of bed and, slipping into her bathrobe, struggled with the belt.

Downstairs, she started the coffee, opened the back door for Sassafras, then decided to get the paper. Donning a ski jacket over her robe, she hurried to the mailbox, grabbed the paper with near-frozen fingers and returned to the warmth of the kitchen.

She tossed the paper onto the table and returned the coat to the rack, then set about making waffles and sausage, suppressing a yawn and listening to the sound of water running as Gavin showered.

How right this all felt, she thought dreamily, wondering what it would be like to be married to him.

Within minutes Gavin hurried downstairs, his hair combed and wet, his expression positively devilish. "Well, aren't you the domestic one," he joked, wrapping strong arms around her waist and standing behind her.

"Watch it," she warned, lifting her spatula. "I'm armed."

He laughed, his breath stirring her hair. "I'm shaking in my boots."

"Sit," she ordered good-naturedly, pointing with the spatula to the table. "You're the one who had to get up at this ridiculous hour."

He did as he was told, and as Melanie plucked the first waffle from the iron, Gavin snapped open the paper. Melanie placed the waffle and a couple of sizzling sausage links onto a plate, turned and set the plate on the table. As she did, Gavin's hand grabbed her wrist.

She giggled, thinking he was still playing, but when she caught his glance, she realized that something was horribly wrong. His eyes were hard, his nostrils flared and his mouth a grim, hard line.

"What—what's wrong?"

"Everything!"

"I don't understand."

Confused, she looked down at the table, then stood frozen, reading the headlines of the front page of the *Tribune*: GAVIN DOEL RETURNS TO TAYLOR'S CROSSING FOR LONG LOST LOVE.

"Oh, God," she whispered.

"It just gets better and better," he said, his lips tight.

Swallowing hard, she read the article, written by Jan, which detailed their romance and the feud between the two families. There was a picture of her and Gavin at the lodge, obviously young and in love, and a picture of Jim Doel, the man who went to jail for negligently killing Melanie's mother.

"You've got to be kidding me," she whispered, reading on and feeling sick to her stomach. There was nothing written about the baby, just Melanie's quick change of heart and short marriage to Neil Brooks.

"It could be worse," he muttered, "and it probably will be."

"What do you mean?"

"Just that Michaels isn't about to let up. Each week he's going to find something to dredge up. Again and again."

"The baby?" she whispered.

"Eventually."

She sank into the nearest chair and told herself to be strong, that there was nothing more to worry about. She reached for Gavin's hand, but he stood slowly and impaled her with angry eyes.

"I think I'd better leave."

"Why?"

"Because I've got things to do." His face darkened with determination. "And I can't be sure that some reporter or hot-shot photographer isn't camped outside your back door." There wasn't the least spark of friendliness—or love—in his eyes. His expression was murderous.

"You—you think I was a part of this?" she whispered, disbelieving.

His jaw clamped together. "I don't know, Melanie. Were you?"

"Are you *serious?* You know I wouldn't do anything . . ." But she could see it in his eyes—all the past lies and accusations surfacing again. Her world tilted, and her fantasy shattered. "You're right, you'd better leave," she said, standing on legs that shook and threatened to buckle.

He hesitated just a moment as a glimmer of love glinted in his eyes, but he grabbed his jacket and stormed out of the house, letting the door bang behind him.

"And good riddance!" she said, tossing his uneaten break-fast into the trash before she collapsed and slid down the cabinets to the floor. Tears flooded her eyes, and she tried to fight them back.

Pounding an impotent fist against the cabinets, she hic-cupped and sobbed, and then her stomach, already on edge, rumbled nauseously. She scrambled to her feet, dashed to the bathroom and promptly threw up.

When she was finished, she sluiced cold water on her face and looked at her white-faced reflection in the mirror. *You've really got it bad,* she thought sadly. She hadn't wretched in years. The last time had been—

Time stopped. The world spun crazily.

With numbing disbelief Melanie realized that the last time she'd been so ill had been eight years ago, when she'd been pregnant with Gavin's child.

# CHAPTER FOURTEEN

Melanie stared in disbelief at the blue stick from the pregnancy test. There it was—physical proof that her monthly calendar wasn't inaccurate. She was pregnant. With Gavin's child. Again.

Ecstasy mingled with pain. What could she do? Sitting on a corner of the bed, she weighed her options and decided not to make the same mistake twice. She had to tell Gavin and she had to tell him soon.

Sighing, she shoved her hair from her eyes. She had to confide in him—there was no question of that. But she didn't have to marry him. In fact, she'd be more than willing to raise his child alone.

No longer a frightened girl of seventeen, she could handle the demands of a child and a career—if she ever got her career going again. Never again would she turn to another man. Marrying Neil had been a mistake she would never repeat. If and when she married, it would be for love.

And she couldn't imagine loving anyone but Gavin.

"You're hopeless," she told herself, but couldn't ignore the elation that she was pregnant.

Suddenly she wondered how she'd be able to speak with Gavin alone tonight—opening night. She thought about avoiding the party but knew that both Gavin and Rich expected her to attend. As official photographer for the lodge, she could hardly beg out now.

She spent the day wondering how she would tell him. There was no easy way.

Finally, that evening, she took an hour getting ready for the formal party that would officially kick off the season and reopen Ridge Lodge. Tomorrow there would be races, sleigh rides, an outdoor barbecue and snowboarding and skiing demonstrations, but tonight the lodge would be ready for dancing and hobnobbing.

Not in a party mood, Melanie stepped into her one nice dress, a mid-thigh royal blue silk sheath with high neckline and long sleeves, then added a slim silver necklace and matching bracelet. She brushed her hair and let it fall in curls that swept past her shoulders.

Slipping into a pair of heels, she muttered, "Here goes nothing," to Sassafras as she petted him on the head while grabbing her coat.

She drove carefully to the lodge, joining a procession of cars up the steep grade and smiling to herself as snowflakes landed on the windshield. If Gavin's lodge failed, it wouldn't be for lack of snow.

The lodge was ablaze with lights. Torches were lit outside and every room cast golden rays from the windows and dormers. Melanie parked near a back entrance and, squaring her shoulders, walked through the main doors, where her pictures were now highlighted by concealed lamps.

Guests, employees, caterers and musicians already filled the lobby. In one corner a piano player and backup band were playing soft rock. In another a linen-covered table was arranged with silver platters of appetizers, and behind the bar two bartenders were busy refilling glasses. Waiter and caterers hurried through a throng of bejeweled guests.

Smoke and laughter floated up the three stories to the ceiling, and Melanie wished she was just about anywhere else on earth. She spotted some local celebrities and a couple of famous skiers and their wives, as well as some of the more prominent townspeople.

She mingled with the crowd, searching for Gavin, wondering how she could break the news.

"Well, what do you think?" a male voice whispered in her ear. She turned to find a beaming Rich Johanson surveying the crowd.

"Looks like a success."

"I think so," he agreed anxiously. "And Gavin was worried!"

"That's what he does best."

"I—um, sorry about the article in the paper," Rich said. "I had no idea—"

"None of us did," she said. Then her heart thumped painfully. Behind Rich, through the crowd, stood Gavin, tall and lean, impeccably dressed in a black tuxedo. At his side, her arm threaded through his, was the most beautiful redhead Melanie had ever seen. With a sinking heart she realized the woman was Aimee LaRoux.

Rich, following her gaze, frowned. "Surprise guest," he said with a shrug.

"She wasn't invited?"

"Not by me."

But by *Gavin*. Melanie cast the unhappy thought aside. She trusted Gavin, and he had told Melanie he loved her, hadn't he?

"If you'll excuse me," she said, wending her way through the guests to Gavin. He hadn't seen her yet—his head was bent as he listened to Aimee—but when he raised his eyes and found her standing in front of him, he managed a tight smile.

Melanie returned with one of her own. "Congratulations, Gavin," she said. "The party looks like a big hit."

"Thanks."

"Oh, this resort is just fabulous!" Aimee said, bubbling. "But everything Gavin touches turns to gold."

"Not quite," Gavin said.

Melanie drew on her courage. "When you've got a minute—not now—I'd like to talk with you."

"Alone?"

She nodded. "Yeah."

Gavin glanced at his watch, whispered something to Aimee, then, taking Melanie's arm, propelled her quickly to the back hall. "Hey, wait, you've got guests," she protested.

"Doesn't matter." He strode quickly to his private suite and locked the door behind them.

"There's something you should know—"

"Mr. Doel?" A loud knock thudded against the door.

Gavin, swearing, opened it quickly. "What?"

The caterer, a tall man of thirty or so, stood fist in the air, poised to knock again. "I'm sorry to bother you, but the champagne is running low—"

"Open another case—there's more in the refrigerators near the back door," Gavin said, unable to keep the irritation from his voice. "And if you have any other questions, talk to Mr. Johanson."

"Yes, sir," the caterer replied.

Gavin closed and locked the door again. "Now—what's so all-fired important?" he demanded.

Her stomach, already knotted, twisted painfully. "You left the other morning in a hurry," she said, reaching for the back of a chair to brace herself. "And I didn't get a chance to say goodbye."

"Goodbye?" he repeated, frowning. He folded his arms over his chest and waited.

Her palms began to sweat. "Aren't you leaving soon . . . to rejoin the racing circuit?"

"I don't know. I haven't made definite plans. It all depends on what happens here." He crossed the room and stood only inches from her. "What's going on, Melanie?"

She cleared her throat. "I'm pregnant," she whispered, facing him and seeing the shock and disbelief cross his features.

"You're what?"

"Pregnant." When he paled, she added, "Of course, the baby's yours."

"But you said—I thought you couldn't have children."

"I couldn't—not with Neil."

"You're sure about this?" he said, still not making a move to touch her, his suspicious gaze drilling into hers.

"I took a pregnancy test this morning, but no, I haven't seen a doctor. I'm late and I've been throwing up and I haven't felt this way since the last time." Her fingers were digging into the back of the chair, and she felt herself begin to shake.

"We'll get married," he said without a second thought.

"No."

His head snapped up, and he regarded her in disbelief. "What do you mean, 'no'?"

"I'm not going to trap you, Gavin. You have your life and it doesn't include me or a baby. You won't be happy unless you're racing headlong down a mountain as fast as you can."

"And so what do you plan to do? Marry another man?"

She sucked in a swift breath. "No. I'm going to raise this baby alone, the way I should have the first time. And I'm going to love it and—"

"You lost the first one."

The words crackled through the air, burning deep in her heart. "I won't lose this one," she vowed, "no matter what."

"You're right about that," he said, his disbelief giving way to a new emotion. His lips twisted, and his eyes turned thoughtful. "I won't let you," he said softly, kicking the chair from her hands and throwing his arms around her.

"Mr. Doel?" Pounding erupted on the door again.

"Let's get out of here," he whispered against her ear.

"But . . ." She cast a worried glance at the door.

"Come on!" Taking her hand, he opened the back door and hustled her down the steps of his private deck.

"Where're we going?" she asked, and his answer was a ripple of laughter.

When her high-heeled shoes sank into the deep drifts, Gavin lifted her easily into his arms and carried her toward the base of Rocky Ridge, where a gondola sat.

"You're not serious . . ." she whispered, but he was. He started the lift and ushered Melanie inside the gondola. The operator, recognizing Gavin, took instructions, and within seconds Melanie and Gavin were moving quickly uphill, the night dark around them.

"You're insane," she chided.

"Crazy. The word is crazy and I'm crazy about you." When the gondola was at the top of the lift, it stopped suddenly.

Melanie gasped. "What's going on?"

"Tony's giving us half an hour of privacy." Gavin drew her tightly into the circle of his arms. "And in those thirty minutes, I'm going to convince you to marry me."

"Gavin, you don't have to—"

His mouth closed over hers, and his tongue slipped intimately between her teeth.

Melanie's knees sagged, and he propped her up against the side of the car. "Marry me, Melanie."

"But I can't—"

He kissed her again, and this time she gave in, kissing him with all the fire that raced through her blood. She closed her eyes, unaware of the view of the lodge or the surrounding night-darkened hills.

Groaning, he lifted his head. "Well?"

"OK," she said, her lips breaking into a smile.

"Just 'OK'? Tough crowd."

"Yes! I'd love to spend my life with you."

His grin slanted white in the darkness, and he reached into the pocket of his tuxedo. Taking her hand, he placed a soft velvet box in her palm.

Breathless, she opened it to discover a large solitary diamond ring nestled in a tuft of black velvet. He slipped the ring on her finger, and it fit perfectly.

"You had this planned," she whispered.

"That's why the operator was standing by at the base of the lift," he admitted sheepishly. "I was going to wait until the party had wound down a little, but I had already decided I wanted to marry you and I wasn't going to take no for an answer."

"You did?" she asked incredulously. "But what about the *Tribune?* You accused me of—"

"I know. But we don't have to worry about the *Tribune* anymore."

"Why not?"

"I bought it yesterday."

"You did what?" She stared up at him, sure that he was teasing her, but his face was dead serious.

"Remember, I told you I had things to do. When I left your place I called the owners of the paper, made them a more than generous offer and bought them out. As for Brian Michaels— he's already packing, along with Jan."

Melanie could hardly believe it.

"Yesterday I decided that it was time to set a few things straight. So—if you want it, you can have your old job back, with a raise."

"And what about you?"

"I've decided that I don't need to race in Europe, unless my family needs a vacation."

"Will you be happy living here?" she asked.

"Only with you."

"But what about your dad?"

"Oh, I straightened him out. And it seems that you two had a chat the other day. Dad's decided maybe he was wrong about you."

Melanie could hardly believe her ears. "So why did you put me through all this—this confession? Why didn't you propose *before* I told you about the baby?"

He took her into his arms again and pressed a kiss to her forehead. "Because I wanted to hear what you had to say—I had no idea you were pregnant. And then I wanted to make sure that you really wanted our child."

"Oh, Gavin, did you doubt that?"

"Not for a minute, love," he said, grinning ear to ear. "But I had to know that you were marrying me because you wanted to, not because you wanted the baby to have a father."

"That's convoluted thinking."

"No more than yours." He kissed her again, and she snuggled against him. "I can see it all now—the headline in the next edition of the *Trib*: DOEL MARRIES GIRL OF HIS DREAMS."

Melanie laughed and glanced down at the diamond on her left hand. "It's my dream, you know. I've dreamed about this for so long."

"It's our dream," he replied, his voice tight with emotion. "A dream that will last forever."

# D IS FOR DANI'S BABY

*June 28*

*Dear Baby,*

   *This is the hardest letter I've ever written, the hardest I will ever write.*

   *First and foremost I want you to know that I love you with all of my heart and I will never let a day go by without thinking about you and wondering where you are, what you're doing and how you're feeling.*

   *Today I gave you birth. It was the most miraculous experience of my life, but also the saddest. For though I held you in my arms for ten minutes and stared into your little, beautiful face so that I'd never forget it, I had to let you go—you, my precious son.*

   *I don't want to give you up. If I could, I'd hold on to you forever and never let go. I'd see you take your first steps, say your first words, hit your first baseball. I'd watch as you trundled off to the school bus with a lunch pail and a pair of gym shoes and I'd teach you to ride horses like the wind.*

   *But I can't. Because I love you too much. I'm eighteen and single. The sacrifices you would have to make to stay with me would be too great. So I'm letting someone else adopt you—a married couple who will care for you better than I could have, who want you as desperately as I do and who have the means to see that you'll grow up happy and strong. You'll never want for anything. I only hope that when you think of me you'll know that I love you more than anything in the world.*

*As I said, this is the hardest thing I've ever done. I love you, baby. I always will. I pray that some day we'll meet and I can hold you once again.*

> *Your loving mother,*
> Danielle Patrice Donahue

# CHAPTER ONE

"Stop it!" Dani sniffed loudly and glared at her reflection in the dusty mirror of her bureau. Her eyes were red and swimming in tears, her cheeks flushed, her hair scraped back in a ponytail. "You're a fool, Dani Stewart," she chided, slapping the unshed tears from her eyes and squaring her shoulders. For eleven years she'd been strong. She wasn't going to fall apart now. But the letter in her fingers quivered.

"Damn it all." She wadded the yellowed pages in her fist. Why now? Why did she have to find this damned letter tucked away in the pages of her old high school annual? A lump filled her throat as she remembered packing the letter away along with the faded flowers from a corsage and a few ribbons she'd won barrel racing. For years she'd tried to repress all the memories of that time in her life—that wonderful, horrid, painful time.

A summer breeze teased at the curtains of the open window, and fading sunlight slid into the room. The smells of dry grass and freshly mown hay chased away the must that had collected in the tattered box. Her black-and-white cat, Solomon, sunned himself on the windowsill.

Through the glass she watched the brood mares pick at the sparse, dry blades of the stubble that had once been lush grass. She loved this place as much as if she'd truly owned it.

And she was going to lose it.

Unless she worked fast.

"Dream on," she chided, biting her lower lip.

She needed to win the lottery to buy the old Macgruder spread. Instead, she'd have to settle for subleasing it and that's why she'd found the yellowed box with her high school memorabilia in it. She was packing because she was being forced to move from the main house in hopes that a new tenant would rent what had once been her home.

Blowing her bangs out of her eyes, she pulled herself together. No time to waste being maudlin. No reason to dwell on ancient, painful memories. At least not now. She eyed the hot room and sighed. The bedroom was a mess—clothes everywhere, boxes half-packed, suitcases lying open. She'd been at this for hours. Maybe she needed a break. Ramming the letter into the back pocket of her jeans, she walked determinedly through the house to the back porch, where her favorite pair of boots was propped against the screen door.

Yellow jackets and flies crawled up the inside of the mesh, searching for escape, and the sweet scent of honeysuckle floated on the breeze. A rabbit, startled by the sound of the back door slamming shut, scooted across the yard to burrow deep in the brambles near the woodshed. Dani slid her feet into the battered, familiar leather of her boots and ran across the yard to the stables, where a hot rush of air and the odors of sweat, urine and horseflesh greeted her. Horseflies buzzed at the windows, and despite Solomon's presence, mice skittered through the holes in the feed bins.

Sliding a bridle from its peg, Dani hurried through a maze of gates to the back paddock, where her favorite mount, a game sorrel mare named Typhoon, was grazing.

Dani whistled softly and Typhoon's red ears flicked slightly, but she didn't move.

"Oh, come on, lazybones," Dani said, approaching the horse. "This is gonna be fun."

Typhoon lifted her head and snorted. For a second, Dani thought the mare might revert back to her ways as a stubborn filly and bolt at the sight of the bridle. Instead, Typhoon nickered, tossed her head, then ambled over to Dani and searched Dani's outstretched hand for a treat. Soft lips and warm breath brushed over her open palm. "That's a girl," Dani whispered, patting the mare fondly. She slid the bridle over Typhoon's head, adjusted the chin strap and, clucking her tongue, led the mare to the gate that opened to the fields.

Once the gate was latched behind her, she climbed onto the mare's bare back. "Let's go," she said, leaning forward, and Typhoon, true to her nature, broke into a loping gallop. Within seconds, she picked up speed and the ground sped by in a blur, horse and rider's shadow racing alongside the fleet animal. Wind tore through Dani's hair and caused fresh tears to stream from her eyes.

This time she didn't care. She thought of her baby—her son, now eleven—and wondered where he was. Alive? Healthy? An athlete? The fleeting glimpse she'd had of her baby was forever imprinted in her brain and she knew that he had his father's coloring—dark skin, black hair, big hands. How could one impression stay with her so long?

"Hiya!" she yelled and aimed Typhoon at a fallen oak tree that had been uprooted in the last windstorm. Twisted roots, tangled with dirt clods and rocks, reached upward at one end, while the crushed branches with dead leaves were on the other. In the middle, the long trunk of the tree formed a formidable barrier. "You can do it," Dani encouraged. The mare gathered herself as the trunk loomed in her path. Muscles bunched then stretched as Typhoon leaped, soaring over the sun-bleached bark to land with a thud that jarred Dani's bones.

"Good girl," Dani said with a smile as she patted Typhoon's thick neck, and once again they were racing over the dry fields. Grasshoppers and pheasants flew out of their path in a panicked whir of wings.

Despite her melancholy, Dani's heart swelled. Riding had always been her passion, horses her first love. Whenever her life became too complicated or too mundane, Dani found solace in the steady drum of hoofbeats, the feel of a thousand pounds of horseflesh carrying her forward, the elation of the wind tangling her hair. Freedom. Each time she was astride.

In those first few painful years after giving up the baby, Dani had spent more time riding and training horses than she had with her family, and then later, when her marriage to Jeff Stewart had begun to crumble, she'd spent hours in the saddle, working through the pain, trying to straighten out her mind and her life.

Now, she pulled on the reins and turned toward the brook that cut through the north end of the spread. Wildcat Creek was dry now, barely a trickle of water winding over smooth stones in a narrow ravine, but that would change with the coming winter.

Typhoon slowed to a walk and Dani caught her breath. What had happened to her baby? That question had followed her like a dark shadow, forever with her, never far from her thoughts. Over the years, she'd expected to have other children and had hoped that during her marriage to Jeff they would start a family. Maybe then, the pain of knowing her only child was out there—somewhere with strangers—would lessen. But Jeff hadn't wanted kids—at least not right away—and eventually he really hadn't wanted her, either. The marriage had been doomed. There was a chance, she knew, that she might never have another child, might never meet the son whom she'd borne eleven years earlier. A familiar ache settled deep in her heart.

*Find him.*

The voice in her brain, the one she'd ignored for over eleven years, seemed to scream at her.

*He's your son, your flesh and blood. It's your destiny and your right to know where he is if he's healthy and safe. Find him.*

She wasn't one to believe in fate; didn't take much stock in kismet or even good luck. But today she felt different and a chill stole up her spine even though the temperature had to be pushing ninety degrees. Something was different. It wasn't just the fact that she'd stumbled onto the letter she'd burrowed away; there was something else. She could feel it in her bones, the way her grandfather had often predicted a summer storm on a cloudless day.

She glanced at the sky and saw a hawk circling overhead. Wasn't that supposed to be a good luck sign or something?

Smiling, she shook her head. "You're losing it," she told herself. "Losing it big time." Pulling on the reins, she clucked her tongue.

*Find him, Dani. What have you got to lose?*

There it was again, that damned voice she'd been able to quell for so long.

She pressed her knees into Typhoon's ribs and felt the rush of wind against her face as the mare galloped across dry acres that rolled ever upward to mountains topped by knuckles of red rimrock.

*Jeff can't tell you what to do anymore.*

That much was true. For the duration of their marriage, Jeff had adamantly refused to help her look for the baby she'd given up for adoption. He'd seen no reason to dig up the past, had no understanding of Dani's concerns.

"You've got to give this up," he'd said, squinting against oncoming headlights as he'd driven home through a snow-storm when she'd mentioned trying to find her son. They'd been driving the big truck and pulling a trailer of horses. Tires slid on the icy asphalt and Jeff swore loudly, as if she were to blame for the blizzard.

She hadn't been deterred. Worrying her gloved hands, she'd said, "I just think I should try to find the baby—just to see that he's okay."

"Oh, yeah, Dani, great idea," Jeff had mocked. "Jeez, get a life, would you? First of all, he's not a baby anymore. He's nearly what—eight or nine and probably hell on wheels. Trust me, kiddo, you're better off not knowing anything about him. And he's better not knowing about you. Hell, you don't even know if his folks, *his folks*—the ones who adopted him legally, remember—you don't even know if they've told him about you. He may even think they're his real, biological parents." The truck shimmied and Jeff swore again, squinting into the night. "Damn, it's a bitch tonight."

She'd leaned against the passenger window, arms crossed over her chest as she'd tried to fight a deep-seated anger that swarmed through her each time Jeff tried to dictate to her. A car sped by, washing the interior of the truck with harsh light.

He slanted her a dark look. "Okay, so you're not buying this, right? Well, let's just say you were—by some miracle—able to locate the kid. What then? What good would it do?"

"It would make me feel better."

"You. Make *you* feel better. Listen to yourself. Quit being so selfish. For God's sake, Dani, think about what you're suggesting." He reached into the console, found a tin of snuff and managed to open the can and place a pinch of tobacco behind his lower lip. "If you found him, you'd only screw up his life, his parents' lives and our lives!"

"I wouldn't. I just want to know if he's okay."

"He's fine, for crying out loud. Forget him, will ya? What the hell is it with you?" He sniffed loudly and shot her a glance without a trace of understanding. The truck slid around the next corner until the tires grabbed hold of the slick pavement. Another blue streak of foul words. "Look, if you want a kid, we'll have one, but just not now, okay?"

"I have to know," she'd argued, and Jeff had glowered at her before snapping on the radio. The cab was filled with Willie Nelson's voice. Snowflakes, driven by an arctic wind, froze on the windshield before being slapped away by the rhythmic wipers.

"You're better off not knowin'."

"It's something I have to do."

"Hell, Dani, if you really loved me, you wouldn't want another man's kid." He rolled down the window and shot a stream of tobacco juice into the night.

"He's my kid, Jeff. *Mine*." She hooked her thumb at her chest in agitation. "I just want to know that he's all right."

"You should have thought of that years ago—like before he was born."

"I did."

He braked for the turn into the ranch. The truck glided on a sheet of black ice. "Son of a—hold on!" Dani braced herself. With a groan, the rig made the corner, the trailer side swiping one of the gateposts. Horses squealed. Jeff let out a stream of oaths that wouldn't quit. Dani seethed.

As the truck rambled through the snowdrifts piled on the lane, Jeff hazarded a glance at his wife. She wouldn't back down. Not this time. Mutinously, she inched up her chin a fraction. Lately they'd fought. A lot. She couldn't help but notice the resentment harbored in his brown eyes, the fierce displeasure etched in the corners of his mouth.

"Face it, Dani. He's not your boy any longer. You took care of that, gave up all your rights as a mother—every last one of them—when you signed those papers. You're out of luck on this one, babe. Besides, how would he feel if he met you?

Knew you gave him away? Knew that his old man was a bastard who knocked you up then split?"

"But—"

At the stables, Jeff eased on the brakes and the truck shuddered, tires spinning against wet snow as the pickup and trailer slid to a stop.

"I don't want to hear any more of this talk."

"You can't tell me what to do."

"Of course I can." He offered her a smile without the slightest trace of warmth. Tobacco flecked his teeth. "I'm your damned husband. Remember?"

Irritation crawled up her spine. "That's not the same as lord and master."

"It is in my book." He raked frustrated fingers through his thick butterscotch-colored hair. "Look, I'm not trying to come off like Attila the Hun here, but you're driving me nuts with all this talk. You know that, don't you?"

"I'm not trying to."

"Like hell. The next thing I know, you'll want to find a private investigator, then an expensive big-city lawyer so you can get custody."

"I'd never do that. He has parents, probably good ones. I just want . . ." *I just want to see him, to know that he's all right.* But was that really enough, or was Jeff right? Would she want to talk to him, to try to explain, to hold him and kiss away his tears . . . Damn it all, her own eyes were starting to fill.

"What's going on with you, Dani?" Jeff asked, his voice so low it could barely be heard over the whistle of the wind. He studied his wife huddled against the door, as much distance as possible between their bodies. With a long-suffering sigh, he turned off the ignition and let the keys dangle from his fingers. "Don't tell me you're still hung up on the kid's father?"

"Of course not."

He ignored her denial and tapped his fingers on the steering column. "It's strange, you know. The way you've never told a soul who the bastard was who did this to you. You haven't even confided in me and I'm your husband."

"It's not important."

"Isn't it?" He pocketed his keys. "I've always wondered about him—what kind of a yahoo he was."

"Doesn't matter." She wanted to squirm. True, she'd never told anyone about the baby's father and she had her reasons.

"Better not," he said with a humorless smile. "'Cause you're mine, damn it. Until I say otherwise."

"Or I do."

Condensation was collecting on the windows. Jeff opened the door and a blast of wind as raw as the Yukon swept into the cab. "Sometimes I can't remember why I bothered to marry you."

She thought the same thing. He'd been kinder in the beginning, more understanding, and they'd wanted the same things in life, or so she'd thought. A carefree man, he'd had an easy smile, and though his tongue had been sharp, it hadn't been aimed at her until two years into the marriage. But their dreams—a ranch of their own, horses, cattle and children— had become a burden.

His philandering and cutting remarks had hurt. That night of the blizzard his comments had penetrated deep into her heart, but she had learned to ignore the hateful little barbs, just as she'd turned her eyes away from the fact that he'd been cheating on her. She'd guessed that there were other women from the start, but she'd never had any proof, didn't want any. She'd kept the marriage together—the dream—because she believed in the "until death do you part" section of the marriage vows. In fact, she believed in all of them, but eventually there had just been no reason to continue. Their life together

was a sham; everyone in town knew it. Jeff wanted out. So
they'd divorced and split their meager assets. Dani had clung
on to this ranch as if it were her own, refusing to give up the
lease, working from dawn to dusk trying to make enough
money to save this little scrap of land tucked under the rimrock because it was all she had left.

She'd never considered giving up. Stubborn Donahue
pride, her mother had often suggested. After the divorce, Dani
had lost weight, hadn't been able to sleep nights, and worried
herself sick about the future. She'd even bought her first pack
of cigarettes in years, enjoying the calming smoke. In the
darkness of her room, she had shed her share of tears over yet
another failure in her life, but during the day, she'd worn an
I-don't-give-a-damn smile that she'd pasted onto her face for
everyone to see.

Most of the pain was in the past now. The fact that Jeff was
living with Wanda Tulley, a waitress at the Black Anvil who
was four months' pregnant, bothered her, but it wasn't the
same dull ache she'd experienced for months after giving up
her baby. No, this ache was simpler. Her pride was bruised.
Any love she'd felt for Jeff had died a long, long time before.

Now, as she rode up the final slope toward the ranch
house, she was determined not to fail again. But fate seemed
against her. Despite her best efforts, she couldn't afford to
keep up the payments on the ranch and her mother's words
rang in her ears. "Running a ranch isn't a job for a single
woman, Danielle."

Dani's cocky reply had been something to the effect that
she didn't plan on doing it by herself. But it was as if she'd
been cursed on that day, and now, true to her mother's worries,
she was scrambling to make ends meet. Alone. Trying to save
a ranch she didn't even own.

She'd worked a deal with the owner of the property and
planned to sublease the main house. She could live over the
garage in a small apartment. If only she found the right person

to rent the place. She'd left the actual leasing and subleasing and all that legal mumbo jumbo to her brother-in-law, Max, who was a lawyer and whose company, McKee Enterprises, owned a good share of all the buildings in the small town of Rimrock. Max would find the perfect tenant with the right credit rating. All Dani had to do was move out by the first of July and she was just about ready.

"Let's go," she said to the horse. The sun had disappeared over the western ridge of mountains and dusk was settling through the valley. A sliver of moon appeared in the deepening sky as Typhoon crested the final hill and the heart of the Macgruder ranch came into view. Outbuildings, ranch house, stables and a network of interlocking paddocks were a familiar and welcome sight.

Home.

For as long as she could keep it.

Clucking to the mare, Dani saw a movement beneath the pine tree near the garage. Parked next to her old Ford Bronco was Max McKee's new Chevy pickup.

Urging Typhoon into a faster gait, she waved, recognizing Max from a distance. Tall and broad shouldered with brown hair streaked by the sun, her brother-in-law stood in the lengthening shadows beside another man, a man she didn't recognize. He, too, was over six feet and had ink black hair and dark skin. His head was bent in conversation and she couldn't see his features clearly, but her heart gave a little kick. Maybe this was the new tenant, the man who would help her hold on to the ranch. Smiling inwardly, she hoped that he had a wife and a couple of kids to fill up the empty house she'd shared with Jeff—the house she'd hoped to pack with her own children. She'd always loved kids and had envisioned a passel of them running through the fields, splashing in the creek, chasing after the barn cats, laughing and talking and asking her to show them how to ride bareback.

Her heart ached.

*Someday,* she told herself. *It's still not too late. And someday you'll have your own, or at the very least, find the one you've already had.*

And no one would be able to stop her. No one. From this day forward, she was a woman with a purpose. Single-minded and determined.

Clearing a suddenly thick throat, she dug her heels into Typhoon's dusty sides and charged forward, determined to face whatever God had in mind for her.

# CHAPTER TWO

Life seemed to have a way of turning things around. Just when you thought you knew what you wanted, you found out you were wrong, or so it seemed to Brandon Scarlotti as he took in the panorama that was the Macgruder homestead. The very things that had driven him from this part of Oregon—weathered buildings bleached from the harsh sun in the summer and driving snow in the winter, acre upon acre of dry grass and windswept plateaus, a slow pace and friendly people who knew not only their business but yours, as well—had been reasons enough to climb onto his motorcycle and bum up the road to Southern California.

He studied the man who had taken the time to show him the place. Max McKee was tall, straight shouldered and seemed to shoot from the hip—a far cry from the spoiled rich boy Brandon remembered. "You've got yourself a deal, McKee." Brandon extended his hand and strong fingers clasped his open palm.

"I think you'll like it here."

"Plan to," he said, thinking that the place was perfect, just what he was looking for. Peace and quiet, a sense of solitude, and yet close enough to Elkhorn Lake to oversee the job site, and a ranch where his half brother Chris could stretch his legs, explore, maybe even learn to ride. For the first time in over ten years he wouldn't be battling traffic, on the road for hours, concerned about earthquakes, mud slides, freeways that could pass for parking lots, wild fires and gang violence. Crowded city life was behind him. It was time to return, time to take things in slower stride. L.A. had been good to him and he'd loved the sunny days, elegant palm trees, calming Pacific Ocean and miles of white beaches, but for the past couple of years he'd felt the nagging urge to move on—or back here. Home to Oregon.

He had some old business here that needed to be finished, and of course there was his family to consider—what little family he had. His jaw grew so tight it ached when he considered how he'd grown up and what he'd lacked. No father. No money. A mother who loved a glass of wine more than her son. His gut still burned at the memories, but the chip on his shoulder had disappeared over the years as he'd learned how to cope, how to make a name for himself, how to become successful on his own. Why he still felt hollow inside, he didn't understand, assumed it was just a character flaw inherent in him.

He surveyed the dry acres that he would call home—golden fields dotted with the dark shapes of cattle and horses. The sigh of the wind, low moans of the cattle and the ever-present choir of crickets as the night beckoned would replace the sound of traffic. Steep, rimrock-topped cliffs guarded this valley, casting deep shadows over the land. His new home. At least for a while.

When he'd left this part of the country, he thought he'd never return, but here he was, pumping hands with a man he'd known long ago, a man he'd despised. Max McKee, first-born son of the richest man in the county had worn his wealth easily, as if it had been written somewhere in the stars that he was destined to be born with a silver spoon wedged firmly between his teeth. Brandon, from a distance, had detested the rich kid. Max had always been too perfect, molded too much in his old man's image, doing whatever old Jonah had wanted. Well, almost. Things had changed over the years and Max McKee had mellowed, learned that his father wasn't the god he'd pretended to be, and eventually Max had become his own man while suffering a few tragedies of his own. All in all, McKee seemed a decent sort now, made of tougher, more independent stuff these days, and old Jonah was dead, killed by someone he crossed in one of his shady dealings.

Good riddance.

"You think I'll be able to move in by the weekend?" he asked, taking off his sunglasses as night brought a dark cloak to the land.

"Sooner, probably." Max flashed a quick, confident McKee smile—the kind that once had gotten on Brand's nerves. "My sister-in-law is anxious to sublet and from the looks of it—" he motioned to the boxes stacked on the front porch "—she's nearly cleared out of the house." Fingering a corner of one of the crates, he said, "The deal is that the place is just too much for her alone. She and her husband ran the ranch together, but then . . . well, I won't bore you with the sordid details, but Jeff split." Max's mouth thinned slightly, as if he was trying to keep a lid on an anger that just kept boiling inside him. "She doesn't talk about it much and I guess I respect her decision to try to make it on her own, but just the same, I for one will feel better knowing that someone's in the main house—that there's a man on the place."

Brand felt suddenly cornered. He hesitated as he clicked his pen. The one part of the deal he didn't like was that his new landlord would be living so closely to him in an apartment over the garage. He valued his privacy and didn't want some busybody woman peering through her blinds at him. Nor did he want to hold her hand. He'd gotten the impression from Max earlier that this wouldn't happen, that he'd have as much solitude as he needed. Now he wasn't so sure. "You don't expect me to play some kind of baby-sitter or bodyguard, do you?"

Max barked out a laugh and his face, so recently serious, was animated once again. The idea of Brand trying to take care of the woman who lived here seemed to amuse him. "You don't have to worry about that. My sister-in-law, well, she's not exactly meek. She can rope a steer, ride a runaway horse bareback, climb mountains and knows her way around a rifle—supposedly can shoot the head off a dandelion, or probably a squirrel, at a hundred yards."

"Superwoman," Brand said dryly.

"Not exactly. She can't cook and she's not all that excited about keeping house. She won't be showing up on your doorstep with a batch of freshly baked cookies to welcome you, if you know what I mean. You'll be lucky to get an offer for some of the worst coffee brewed in the state."

Brand couldn't help but smile. "Won't bother me."

"Good." Max slid a glance toward the house. "She's a stubborn thing and arguing with her is like tangling with a wildcat." He flexed his hand nervously. "I was afraid that the divorce might kill her, but she's pulled herself up by the bootstraps, and other than being unable to keep this place in the black all by herself, she's done all right. She's independent, not looking for husband number two, and proud of it."

Satisfied that the woman wouldn't be showing up on his doorstep with flimsy excuses to get to know him or spy on him and that she wouldn't be peering through the curtains of her apartment to keep track of what he was doing, Brand held the lease against the rough cedar walls of the house and scrawled his name on the bottom line. The other spot was blank, the typed name reading Danielle Stewart.

*Danielle.* For a moment his throat closed, then he gave himself a swift mental kick. It was a common enough name, especially when fathers hoped their firstborn would be sons and sometimes tagged them with manlike names to get even. He'd known several girls named Danielle in his lifetime. Nonetheless, he felt a premonition, a sense that he might be making a mistake, that somehow this ranch might be connected with a girl he'd known a long time ago, a girl who had messed with his mind and toyed with his heart.

But that was crazy. Just because he was back in eastern Oregon, he seemed to be caught in this time warp. Ever since crossing the mountains, he'd experienced a few pleasant, though disturbing thoughts. Of her. He shoved those sensual, better-left-locked-away memories out of his head. So he'd known a girl named Dani a long time ago. What were the chances that his landlord was one and the same woman? And even if she was, so what? He wanted this place. He'd been shown other ranches and houses in town that weren't suited to him either in terms of the lease, location or amenities. This spread, the old Macgruder homestead located between Dawson City and Rimrock, seemed perfect.

True, Max hadn't explained much about the mysterious woman who lived here, just that his sister-in-law was divorced, saddled with a lot of debt and anxious to sublet the house and part of the property to a new tenant. But the less he knew of her, the better off he was.

"Dani will probably give you a wide enough berth."

"Dani?" he repeated, and that strange feeling, something akin to déjà vu, crawled through his innards again.

"My sister-in-law."

Danielle Stewart. Not an unusual name. "She from around here?" he asked casually. No reason not to know what he was up against.

"Lived here all her life. Here she comes now." Max hitched his chin in the direction of a lone rider on a muscular red horse. The animal was racing flat out over the windswept fields, hooves thundering, legs flashing. The woman, tucked low over her mount's straining neck, tanned legs gripping the beast's sweating ribs, rode bareback, as if she'd been born on a horse. Streaming behind her was a banner of red-gold hair, tangling wildly in the wind. For a second, Brandon's stomach dropped. He remembered a younger girl, surly and sexy as hell, with a devil-may-care attitude, pouty lips and laughter that was as clear as a June morning. Her hair had been the same brilliant shade.

His throat tightened as she reined in and their gazes met. Instant recognition flared in her eyes. The color drained from a pretty face flushed from a breathless ride.

"Well, I'll be damned," he said under his breath.

"Brand." Her voice was soft and low, like a prairie wind. Shoving the tangled mass of curls from her face, she slid to the ground. There wasn't the hint of a smile on her sweat-streaked face, not so much as a glimmer of relief to see him again. "Well, well, well." Silently appraising him with the rebellious gaze that had always cut straight to his soul, she wrapped the reins of her mount around the top rail of the fence and walked with quick, determined strides through the gate. "What're you doing here?"

Max, glancing from Brand to his sister-in-law, scratched his chin with the pen. "You two know each other?"

"Yeah. A long time ago." Brandon was fascinated by her. Her figure, though still slim, had filled out a little and there was a maturity in her face that he didn't remember. She'd aged well and he imagined she was probably one of those women who just looked better and better as the years wore on. Too bad. He didn't need her kind of distraction. Even in faded, dusty cutoff jeans that frayed around her thighs and a sleeveless blouse that had seen better days and stretched a little too tightly over her breasts, she was earthy and beautiful in a way that touched him deep in a dark spot of his soul he usually didn't admit existed.

Max was right about one thing, Brand decided as she glared at him with an expression about as warm as the bottom of Macgruder's old well in the middle of winter: Dani wouldn't be showing up on his doorstep with a platter of freshly baked cookies, unless, maybe, they were laced with strychnine.

"We barely knew each other," Dani clarified, and Brandon kept his mouth shut though he couldn't resist lifting an eyebrow in silent mockery at the baldness of her lie.

*Barely knew each other?* Who was she kidding? Their lovemaking still burned in his mind and seared his guts. He wondered what it would have been like if she'd really known him. A smile twitched at the corner of his mouth, but he kept it resolutely at bay. If she had secrets to keep, he wouldn't be the one to betray them.

Her spine was straight as a board, her face tense. She was sweating, but it could have been from the exhilaration of the fast-paced ride. "You didn't answer my question." Folding her arms over her chest, she continued to stare at him with those soul-searching whiskey-colored eyes. "What are you doing here?" Was there a thread of dread running through her question? She seemed to be asking it while already guessing the answer.

"Brandon's renting the house," Max said, his gaze thinning as if he was thinking hard, putting two and two together and coming up with five.

"No way." A flush stole up her neck. Her fingers curled into fists of frustration.

"There's a problem?" Max looked from one to the other.

"Don't think so," Brand drawled, enjoying watching her squirm, though why he didn't understand. There was and always had been something about Dani Donahue—make that Dani Stewart—that brought out the devil in him. "My credit should be good."

Max cleared his throat and handed her the paperwork. "Credit's not a problem."

Dani was frantic, her heart beating as wildly as the wings

of a bird suddenly trapped in a small dark cage. Brandon? Here? Wanting to rent her house? Of all the bum luck! Brandon Scarlotti was the last person she wanted to lease the place to. Anyone, *anyone* else would be better. She caught her brother-in-law's scrutinizing gaze and couldn't stop her tongue. "I thought I told you I wanted a family—" She stopped short. She didn't know anything about this man anymore. Maybe Brandon wasn't single. For all she knew he could have a wife and a dozen kids tucked away somewhere.

She turned her gaze on his ringless left hand and suddenly felt like a fool. What did it matter? He was here wanting the place and had the cash to make the deal work. A check for several thousand dollars was clipped to the lease, flapping in the honeysuckle-laced breeze, mocking her. First and last month's rent, security deposit, cleaning deposit, the works. She was running out of time and options. He provided the resources for her to hold on to her dream. That was all and it certainly wasn't a crime. In fact, if she wasn't such an emotional wreck today, she might realize that he was a blessing in disguise.

A blessing? Oh, sure! She made a deprecating noise in the back of her mouth and both men stared at her. Brandon Scarlotti may have been a lot of things, but a blessing? Was she suddenly out of her mind? She licked her lips, conscious of the time ticking by and the tension running in deep, noiseless undercurrents through the air. All she had to do was collect his rent each month and be civil to him. Nothing more. No strings attached. Squaring her shoulders, she shook her hair out of her face and cleared her throat. "Fine," she muttered, forcing a smile she didn't feel. Somehow she managed not to sound breathless. "I, um, I just thought—"

"You didn't expect to ever set eyes on me again." Brand's voice touched a hidden place in her heart, a place she'd nearly forgotten, a place she'd rather not acknowledge.

She slid her hands into the back pockets of her cutoffs and nodded. "Yeah. Something like that." Her fingertips brushed the edge of the letter she'd written so long ago and her throat clogged. Brandon had never known about the baby. Few had. She'd spent a few months away from Rimrock, out of sight, so that no one—aside from her mother, Jonah McKee, in whom her mother, Irene, confided, and the hospital staff in a small, private hospital—could say for certain that she'd been pregnant.

His hair was still the color of ebony—not a trace of gray showed in the thick strands. His eyes were clear and blue and only a few lines from spending hours in the sun had altered his face, stealing away the traces of the boy she'd once known. He looked harder edged, honed to a more ruthless man than she remembered. A shame. "Yep," he drawled evenly, his gaze warm as it touched hers, "I'm back."

"So it seems." She could hardly believe this was happening—on the very day she'd discovered the letter she'd written eleven years before. Was it kismet? Fate? Destiny? Or just plain bad luck? "For how long?" she heard herself ask, hoping she didn't sound as anxious as she felt. "Permanently?"

He lifted a shoulder. "Eight to ten months at least. That's about as permanent as I get."

This was her out and she grabbed for it. "But I wanted a tenant for a minimum of a year."

Max thumped a finger on one paragraph of the agreement. The check flapped in the breeze. "Brandon's signed for a year."

Dani's heart sank. How could she possibly live this close to Brandon for the next three hundred and sixty-five days? The distance between her apartment over the garage and the main house was less than twenty yards.

*Because you have to. You have no choice. Be thankful it's not a leap year!*

If she didn't rent to Brandon, she'd have to find another tenant, or give up the ranch and all the money she'd put into it, or borrow cash from her sister. Not that Skye hadn't offered. But Dani had spent too many years growing up poor and dependent upon the charity of others—first with her mother and their choking reliance on Jonah McKee with whom Irene had been half in love, then with Jeff who had always been pushing her to borrow from Skye and "tap into the McKee money." She still remembered his skewed reasoning. "Hell, they can't spend it all in a million years! We have a right to it, Dani. Why should we suffer?" Jeff's words still stung. Fortunately, she'd never listened to him. She'd always had too much pride to accept any offer of a loan, even from her older sister.

But Dani was running out of time. It was now or never and she couldn't look a gift horse in the mouth, even one that came with extra emotional baggage. Like it or not, she had to accept Brand as her tenant. "Then I guess there's nothing more for me to do but sign on the dotted line," she said, forcing that practiced smile that felt so fake—the one she donned whenever someone asked her how she was getting along now that she was single. Propping the document against the side of the house, she inked her signature on the appropriate line, pushing hard as the forms were in triplicate. "You can move in tomorrow," she said to Brandon as she clicked the pen closed.

"Good." Brandon's gaze held hers for a second too long. "I'm looking forward to it."

Her stomach seemed to drop to the dusty ground.

"I've only got a few things," he said. "Believe in traveling light. I'll bring them by in a couple of days."

"I didn't think you were ever coming back," she blurted out, unable to stop herself.

"Me, neither." His voice lost some of its warmth.

For years she had envisioned him wandering the globe, a

man running from his past, uncertain about his future. Now, she realized, she'd been wrong—so very wrong. Brandon Scarlotti wasn't the hard-luck boy from the wrong side of the tracks any longer. No, in his expensive slacks and crisp white shirt, he looked confident and assured and she doubted that he was afraid of anything. Even his tie, loosened and casual, reeked of good taste.

*Oh, Brandon, what happened to you?*

His gaze found hers briefly and his blue eyes landed long enough to suck some of the breath from her lungs before he looked quickly away.

"So what brings you back to Rimrock?" She surprised herself with her calm voice that belied the perspiration collecting on her palms and the urge to scream the truth at him. The letter in her pocket seemed to scald through her jeans and panties to her skin.

His lips tightened almost imperceptibly. "A project."

"Project?"

"Brandon's in charge of building the new resort on Elkhorn Lake," Max interjected, his blue eyes twinkling with an unlikely amusement.

"You?" she said, disbelieving.

"My company," he clarified. "S & J Limited."

"You must be the S," she reasoned, surprised that she'd never heard his name in connection with the resort that the townspeople had been gossiping about for months. After years of red tape, the project had finally been given the go-ahead by all the state and local agencies involved.

"Yep. A friend of mine, Mitch Jones, was the J, but I bought him out last year. Didn't seem reasonable to change the company name. We'd just ordered more letterhead," he said, teasing, of course, though she didn't smile at his attempt to lighten the mood. Too many unchecked emotions were raging through her system, too many fears. Dear God, how could she live this close to him without telling him the truth?

"But that project—it will take longer than six months. . . ."

"Two, maybe three years."

"You said—"

His face was suddenly grim. "I said I'll be here for a minimum of six months. After that I might have to move closer to the lake."

Relief drizzled through her blood, but she still found it impossible to believe that he was back. Dear Lord, now what?

He checked his watch and scowled. "I've got to get back— I'm expecting a phone call." When he lifted his head, he stared straight at Dani. "Maybe you could give me a tour of the place tomorrow. Max showed me the house, at least through the windows, since that's all I'm really leasing, but I'd like a look around the place. That is, if you don't mind."

"'Course not," she responded with as much enthusiasm as she could muster. He may as well have asked her to visit the graveyard at midnight, for all the joy she found in his request. She couldn't imagine spending even a second alone with him, but she nodded. After all, they were going to be neighbors. Close neighbors.

"Late afternoon?"

"Fine." She lifted both shoulders as if it didn't matter in the least, as if they'd never shared a look, a touch, a kiss before. As if she hadn't lain naked in his arms, her body bathed in sweat, his ragged breathing warm against her ear. Everything had happened so long ago. What could it matter? "What about your family? Will they be coming—?"

The muscles in his face turned to stone. "Just me. Don't you remember, Dani?" His hair caught in a breeze that had suddenly kicked up and his nostrils flared just a little. "Things haven't changed all that much. I'm still not a family man. No wife. No kids. No strings attached."

Max watched the exchange and said nothing, but Dani read the interest in his eyes he tried so vainly to veil. If she and Brandon weren't careful, Max would guess the truth. And she wasn't ready for that. Not yet.

"You can take possession tomorrow," she said stiffly as she studied Brandon's face—a face she was sure, at seventeen, she'd loved with all of her naive heart. Silly girl.

His smile was older than she remembered; his eyes had seen far more than they had when he'd left Rimrock so many years ago. "I'm looking forward to it," he said and her heart did a silly little flip. There was a moment when their gazes touched that she remembered just why she'd found him so irresistible.

With a wave he climbed into Max's truck, and as the pickup left behind a thin cloud of dust, Dani leaned against the post that supported the roof of the porch.

What was it about Brand that had touched her? Why was he different from a dozen other boys who had been interested in her so long ago? Why had she let him near her?

Because of his wild irreverence? Because she'd seen a spark of nobility hidden deep in his blue, blue eyes? Or because she'd been a foolish young rebel herself, hell-bent to live her life her own way despite her mother's worries and her older sister's concerns?

Her throat grew thick and memories swirled through her mind like a whirlpool, moving rapidly, blurring, carrying her on a spinning tide, but getting nowhere.


The first time she'd seen Brandon Scarlotti she'd been barely seventeen, full of life and wanting to break free of the shackles of her tedious existence. She was tired of doing what was right, tired of being poor, tired of her mother's incessant warnings and tired of living in her older sister's shadow.

She'd been driving home from work in her mother's rattle-trap of a car when the engine had sputtered twice and died. "Oh, God, no," she'd whispered, silently cursing and looking out at the highway. "Not now. You can't quit on me now!" It was nearly midnight, she was alone, and another car might not come along for a while. Even if one did come by, who was to say it would stop or that it would be driven by a Good Samaritan? At this time of night, chances were whoever was behind the wheel might be drunk or looking for trouble. "Great!" she muttered, slapping the steering wheel and trying once again to start the old brown sedan.

"Come on, come on," she encouraged as the engine fired only to die again. All her mother's warnings came back to haunt her. Not knowing what else to do, she waited, then tried to start the car several times but to no avail. Eventually the damned engine wouldn't even turn over.

"Oh, save me!" she muttered, flinging herself back against the seat. She was dead tired after a full day of school followed by an eight-hour shift waiting tables at the diner of the Dawson City Truck Stop, five miles out of town. She reached in her purse, dug around and unearthed a pack of cigarettes, not yet opened, the pack she'd picked up from the vending machine on her way through the lobby of the diner. She opened the pack, found some matches and lit up, inhaling deeply, hoping the smoke would calm her nerves.

"Think, Dani, think," she muttered as she released a white cloud. In five minutes, no car had appeared, so she brushed aside maps and napkins and a pair of sunglasses in the glove compartment until she felt the ribbed handle of a flashlight. Climbing out of the car, she squashed her cigarette, looked up and down the winding, desolate stretch of road and felt an utter sense of defeat. She was in the mountains between Rimrock and Dawson City, but the main highway was far enough away that it could be a long time before someone came along. She switched on the dim beam of the flashlight, located the latch and managed to prop the hood open.

Knowing it was a waste of time, she swept the beam of the flashlight over the grimy metal contraption that was the engine, but she didn't know enough about cars to have the first idea what was wrong with her mother's old lemon. There seemed to be an excess of oil, steam rose from the radiator, and corrosion had settled over the battery posts.

To be honest, it looked like the car was ready for the junkyard. "Not yet," she said, adjusting some wires, burning her fingers in the process and getting nowhere. "Perfect," she said on a sigh. "Just perfect."

The car breaking down was a fitting end to the worst day of her life. She'd already been referred to the principal's office when she'd been caught smoking during lunch, then she'd been fired from her job at the truck stop. One of the other waitresses, Brandy Barlow, had accused her of stealing tips and another girl had said she'd seen Dani skim some of the bills off one of Brandy's tables. Though the story was pure fabrication—concocted by two girls who didn't know how to smile and wink and ease a little extra cash out of the truckers' wallets—Dani was let go. Her boss regretted the decision, but he was tired of the bickering between his crew and it seemed strange to him that Dani's tips were always twice what the other girls were making.

*Guilty until proven innocent.* Dani had learned a long time ago that life wasn't fair. Truth to tell, she hated her job at the diner. It wasn't so much the work as being cooped up inside. She didn't mind flirting a little and listening to a few wolf whistles or compliments, but some of the patrons thought that for an extra couple of dollars they could make lewd remarks or paw at her and that's where she drew the line. She'd rather work with animals anyway and was only saving the money she earned at the all-night diner so she could buy a horse that she'd been eyeing for the past few years. The mare, a fleet brown five-year-old, was owned by Glenn Stewart and he was finally willing to sell her. For the right price. Dani nearly had enough money to buy the horse and board her at the stables just outside of town.

But she was still a couple of hundred dollars short. "Thanks a lot, Brandy," she muttered, leaning her hips against the fender of her mother's car and tapping her fingernails nervously on the dull finish. Walk or wait? Even though she was dead tired, she was far too restless to sit idly, hoping some kind stranger would show up. She'd just decided to hike to the nearest farmhouse, pound on the door, wake up the poor farmer and call her mother. Irene, in turn, could call a friend and have the car towed. Dani cringed at the thought of how much hauling the dead auto would cost. Her mother was already on overload, worried about her wayward daughter.

Blowing her bangs from her eyes, Dani heard the distant whine of a motorcycle racing through the mountains. She listened hard, holding her breath, trying to determine which direction the rider was moving—closer or farther away? She crossed her fingers and hoped that the biker was riding in this direction and was a decent man who would give her a lift home.

Inwardly Dani winced when she imagined explaining all this to her mother who, along with raising two daughters single-handedly, held down a job at McKee Enterprises as Jonah McKee's secretary. Oftentimes, Irene Donahue worked overtime, her hours stretching long into the night. Dani wished, as she had all her years growing up, that she'd had a father. At times like this, she needed a man who would know what to do.

But Tom Donahue was dead, killed in a logging accident while working for Jonah McKee. Dani didn't even remember her dad. She'd seen snapshots, of course, photographs of a strapping blond man with a muscular build, shaggy mustache and daredevil smile.

"Yeah, well, if wishes were horses, beggars would ride," she told herself, spouting the words her mother often quoted. So she didn't have a father—big deal. She was getting along. She kicked at a tire of the car and stopped to listen. The motorcycle was getting closer. Maybe she could flag down the midnight rider.

*And what if he's a pervert? A rapist? A murderer? Drunk or loaded on drugs?* Her fingers curled more tightly around the flashlight. Small weapon. Even smaller consolation.

Ignoring the drumming of her heart, she waited while the motorcycle roared through the mountains, gears whining as the rider put the bike through its paces. "I hope you're a good guy," she said as the beam of a single headlight became visible, just a speck at first and then brighter and brighter, a luminescent disk boring down on her. "Please be a good guy."

Swallowing back any trace of fear, Dani stood by the car, one arm thrown up to shield her eyes from the blinding light as she waved wildly.

She heard the engine slowing as the driver noticed her. The hairs on the back of her neck rose. The bike—a big Harley— slid to a stop only a few feet away. Dani pushed herself upright. All her nerve endings were aroused, the metallic taste of fear in her throat.

A man, dressed in black leather from head to toe, straddled his bike. The huge machine thrummed between his legs. Crossing her fingers again and swallowing against a suddenly dry throat, she prayed that he wasn't part of some kind of wild motorcycle gang, the kind she'd seen in the movies.

"Car trouble?" he yelled. A tough, deep voice.

"'Fraid so."

"Humph." He ran a hand through hair that was unruly, hair that hadn't been trapped beneath a helmet. "Don't know if I can help much, but I'd be glad to take a look if ya want."

"Thanks . . . I, um, appreciate it." Her palm was so sweaty she nearly dropped the flashlight.

He rolled the bike onto the shoulder, cut the engine and swung a leg over the seat. "Okay, let's see what's going on."

"I can tell you what. Nothing." She didn't know his name, wasn't sure that she could trust him. Unfortunately, on this star-studded night, alone on the highway with mountains looming on either side of the road, she was stranded and had no choice but to place her life in the hands of this stranger.

She held her breath.

Whether he guessed it or not, this man she'd never met before was about to change the course of her life forever . . . .

# CHAPTER THREE

"Shine that light over here."

He was already peering under the hood, reaching into his back pocket for a rag and poking around.

Nervous as a cat, Dani pointed the weak beam over the engine. Who was this guy—a Good Samaritan or a thug? He seemed safe enough as he scrutinized the old engine, but still she glanced anxiously down the empty road and realized how alone she was. How vulnerable. "Tell me what happened," he asked, his voice muffled.

"It just died on me. I was on my way home from work— I'm a, well, I was a waitress at the Dawson City Truck Stop. My shift was over at midnight and I live in Rimrock. I started driving and all of a sudden everything gave out." She handed him the flashlight and he glanced in her direction for just a second. She caught a glimpse of deep blue eyes. He didn't respond, just turned back to the car. Not a whole lot older than she, he seemed to know what he was doing. At least she hoped so. Her fingers raking nervously through her hair, she added, "Now the darned thing won't even turn over—I just hear a clicking sound whenever I try to start it."

"Probably the battery."

"But why would it give out in the middle of a trip? I was driving along just fine and then . . . nothing."

He shrugged. "The car's old."

She felt the sting of heat wash up the back of her neck. It seemed she was always being reminded of the painful fact that there was never enough money to go around. While some families such as the McKees were incredibly wealthy, others were destined to always struggle to make ends meet. Such seemed to be her mother's lot in life. Dani swore she'd never let the same thing happen to her. Somehow, someway, she was going to be able to take care of herself and her family, and it wasn't going to be by relying on some rich guy's charity like her mother did with Jonah McKee, who had been Irene's emotional and financial support since her husband died. No way. She intended to make it on her own. She might even end up rich, if things worked out right. But these were her private thoughts, her secret dreams. She shared them with no one, especially a stranger she'd barely met.

"Old parts wear out." He handed her the flashlight and wiped his hands on the white rag now streaked with black grease.

"The car's really not that old," she protested, her spine stiffening with false pride.

"Got a lot of miles on it, though. Right?" He focused his attention back under the hood and began poking around again, pulling out dipsticks, pushing on wires, looking at hoses as she shined the failing beam on the radiator and the battery. "No problems before tonight?"

She couldn't lie. "There are always problems. Sometimes it won't start, especially in the morning if it's cold outside, and sometimes it needs a little oil or transmission fluid, but it's never stopped dead in its tracks before."

He climbed behind the steering wheel and tried the ignition. For all his efforts he heard a series of clicks, nothing more. He instructed her to try to start the car while he watched the engine. In the end he shrugged. "My guess is still the battery," he said with a slow shake of his head. "This car's not going anywhere."

Her heart sank. Not that she hadn't expected the news, but she'd hoped someone with a little more mechanical know-how than she could get it started.

"We can get another car or truck, come back here and jump-start it with cables, but that'll take time. Otherwise you'll have to call and have it towed."

"How much will that cost?" she asked, mentally counting the money in her pocket. She had her tips for the night and nothing more—probably less than twenty dollars.

"Couldn't guess."

She bit her lower lip and thought as he slid a glance her way. For a second, she imagined she saw a flicker of pity in his eyes, but it was dark and she couldn't be sure. Her vertebrae snapped to attention. She didn't want his sympathy.

"You said you were going home to Rimrock, right?"

She nodded miserably. She didn't want to leave the car. Nor was she happy at the prospect of leaving him, and that seemed to be where his questions were leading.

"Listen, the best I can do is give you a ride." Still wiping his hands, he started toward his bike.

"But you were going the other way." She didn't want to inconvenience him any more than she already had and she wasn't comfortable jumping on a huge motorcycle in the middle of the night with someone she didn't know. True, so far he'd been nothing but helpful but she didn't even know his name.

"Rimrock's not that far," he reasoned, flashing her a smile that slashed white against the dark night.

Sweat was gathering on her palms. She told herself that she was being silly, but the guy made her nervous. "Maybe someone will come along who's heading that way."

"And maybe they won't stop."

"Maybe they will." Why he brought out the argumentative side in her, she didn't understand. "You did."

"Yeah, but I'm just that kind of guy," he said, turning on his thousand-watt smile again. She could hardly resist. "This time of night the next guy might have stopped off at a bar and had a few too many."

No argument there. She'd seen too many well-meaning guys who, after working all day, spent the next few hours un-winding with several drinks, only to nearly lose their balance when they stood up from their stools. Oftentimes, Smitty, the owner of the diner, caught them and called a cab, but a few slipped past his watchful gaze.

"Or the guy could be worse than a drunk," he added, echo-ing her very own thoughts. "There are all sorts of nuts out at night. Even here, in the middle of nowhere. I wouldn't trust anyone if I were you."

"I might not have a choice."

His lips clamped together and he muttered something about hardheaded females under his breath. "Come on."

She planted her heels in the gravel. If there was anything she hated, it was playing the part of the helpless woman. It galled her to think that she had to rely on this guy or anyone else for that matter. "How do I know I can trust you?"

A hard-edged smile stretched across his face and he glanced up at the stars as if seeking divine intervention. "As you so aptly put it, you don't have much of a choice." Reach-ing forward, he took her hand. His fingers were warm and strong. "Okay. Maybe we got off on the wrong foot and should start over. I'm Brandon Scarlotti."

Her heart plummeted. Brandon Scarlotti? Her throat turned to sand. Though Scarlotti lived in Dawson City, she'd heard of him, whispers from her girlfriends about a boy—a very sexy boy—who was nothing but trouble. Rumor had it that he was a bastard who'd never met his father and wore a chip on his shoulder like a badge of honor. He'd been caught drunk and thrown into juvenile detention more than once. He'd been accused of stealing everything from cars to stereo equipment to motorcycle parts. He'd been found in bed with the police chief's underage daughter but then he'd been underage himself, so no charges had been pressed.

Somehow he'd survived every scrape, avoided doing serious jail time, but was the scourge of Dawson City, the cocksure, I-don't-give-a-damn boy who sent chills into every father's heart and caused most girls to want to tame him. Even Dani's mother knew of him. She'd heard about him from Bess Jamison, a friend who lived near the Scarlottis. Brandon had been blamed for everything from stealing money and liquor to breaking Bess's daughter's heart.

And now he was here. Waiting. Staring at her with eyes so intense she felt her skin heat. "Well?"

"I'm . . . I'm Dani Donahue."

"Okay, Dani Donahue, hop on the bike."

"But—"

"I don't have time to argue, okay? You need help, I'm offering and—" his gaze found hers in the pale light from the stars "—you can trust me."

Considering all the rumors surrounding him, she doubted it. But then, they were just rumors. Idle gossip.

"I don't think . . . I mean . . ."

His lips twisted downward as if he'd read her mind. "Despite what you've heard about me, I don't bite. Nor do I make it a practice of kidnapping girls I've never met before. You're safe with me, darlin', and from the looks of it, you're lucky I came along." When she still hesitated, he swore under his breath, revved the engine of the bike and shook his head. "Damn it, Dani, climb on the bike, and do it now. I've had a helluva day, I'm dead tired and I'm sick of arguing with you. Got it?"

She ground her back teeth together, but nodded tersely. He had a point. She didn't have many options.

"Good. For crying out loud, I'm not going to hurt you!"

Biting her lip, she swung a leg over the seat, wrapped her arms around his waist and scooted close enough so that her breasts were crushed against his broad back. He flexed, let out the clutch, and the motorcycle took off with a screech of tires and burst of gravel. The back end shimmied a bit. With a roar the metal beast leaped forward. Involuntarily, her arms tightened around him and she rested her head between his shoulders. He smelled of old leather and tobacco, soap and smoke. The air whistled in her ears and tore at her hair as the pavement slid beneath them at a dizzying speed.

She'd always loved speed, ridden horses all her life, thrilled to the feel of a swift beast racing as if the devil himself were on its tail. The motorcycle was different, a powerful machine that whined loudly as it ripped through each gear, wheels spinning smoothly over the road.

Dani hung on tight as they skimmed along the asphalt, weaving through the valleys and hills until the lights of Rimrock shone in the night sky. Her heart was a snare drum, but she couldn't help but smile. She was riding through the mountains with Brandon Scarlotti, the wild one himself. The rebellious part of her reveled in the excitement of it all; the cautious side of her nature was scared spitless.

"Where to?" he asked as they passed the city limits. He slowed at an intersection where a service station was already locked up for the night.

"Home, I guess. Pine Street." She directed him down the avenue lined with trees and vintage houses that were beginning to show signs of aging—peeling paint and weathered steps. "There—third house on the left," she said, pointing to her mother's yellow bungalow with its never-need-paint aluminum siding, the only house Dani had ever lived in. A porch light was blazing, attracting moths and casting harsh illumination over the old swing near the front door. Brandon pulled into the driveway and Dani swung off the bike. "Thanks," she said, feeling suddenly awkward. "You're a lifesaver."

"Your car's still out there." The engine of his Harley idled, throbbing in the warm night air.

"I know, but I'll find a way to get it in the morning." She slid her hands into the front pockets of her jeans and rocked back on the worn heels of her boots. If only there was some way to prolong the evening, she thought, surprising herself. She didn't want him to leave, at least not yet. She was beginning to trust him and found him fascinating and disturbing. Her arms still tingled from holding tight to him and feeling, beneath the soft, worn leather, hard, lean muscles. He was staring at her with those deep-set, intense eyes that cut into the depths of her soul.

"Would . . . would you like to come in for some soda or something?" she blurted, then felt like a foolish schoolgirl.

He hesitated, his gaze touching hers for just a second more before he looked away. For a silly little instant, she thought he might agree. He stared at the pulse point thundering in her throat. "Another time. It's late. I'd better get going." His voice sounded rougher than she remembered and he twisted on the accelerator, revving the engine.

Disappointment drilled a hole in her heart. "Oh. Well. Sure. Uh, thanks again." She sounded like a blathering idiot. She, Dani Donahue, the master of the quick comeback was reduced to a mumbling, blushing girl of twelve.

"Anytime," he said before favoring her with one last smile and rolling the motorcycle out of the driveway.

"If I can ever return the favor . . ." Jeez, did she really say that? How stupid!

"I'll call," he promised as the big machine roared away. She stood with the dry weeds brushing her ankles, her gaze glued to the plume of blue exhaust left in his wake.

"Dani?" Her mother's sharp voice caught her off guard.

Dani froze. Did her mother recognize Brandon?

"What happened? Where's the car?" She stepped from the open doorway and onto the porch and Dani wondered how much of the conversation she'd overheard. Irene Donahue's hair was hidden beneath a pink hair net and a cigarette burned in her hand.

"The beast broke down."

"What? What do you mean 'broke down'?"

"One minute I was driving and the car was going along just fine, the next minute it quit on me. Wouldn't start no matter what I did. I got a ride home."

"From a boy on a motorcycle?" her mother asked, unable to hide the suspicion in her voice as she stared after the retreating taillight.

"Yes."

"Someone you know, I hope." Her brow creased in worry.

"No—I, um, didn't even get his name." She felt horrible lying about him and yet if her mother even suspected her of having anything to do with Brandon Scarlotti, she'd flip. Guilt riddled, Dani held her tongue.

Taking a deep drag from her cigarette, Irene turned her attention back to her younger daughter and Dani knew what she was thinking—that Dani had always been more of a problem than her older sister, Skye and that if she could, Irene would try to rein in Dani and mold her into Skye's pristine image. "So where exactly is 'the beast'?" she asked.

"About halfway to Dawson City at the final hill in the mountains." Dani's words came out in a rush, tumbling over each other, as if by speaking rapidly she could stem the sense of disappointment that seemed to be settling on her mother's thin shoulders. "I didn't have a choice, Mom. I had to leave it. But it's parked off the road far enough on the shoulder where it shouldn't get hit. I tried to start it about a million times and then the guy on the motorcycle looked under the hood and tried, but it just wouldn't do anything. I—I think it'll be all right." She crossed her fingers.

"I hope so." Irene took a drag on her cigarette. The tip glowed brightly—orange coals in a black night. "Lordy, what next?" she said on a long-suffering sigh. Smoke filtered from her nostrils. "I suppose I can walk to work in the morning." She seemed older in the harsh glare of the porch light.

"I'll call and have it towed."

Irene shook her head. "That would cost a fortune. You just come on in the house and go to bed. I'll worry about the car."

Dani was too tired to argue. She entered the house and walked down a short hallway to the bedroom she'd shared with her sister until Skye had moved out. Kicking off her jeans, Dani closed her eyes and heard her mother lock the front door and sigh wearily.

Still thinking about Brandon, wondering if all the scandalous tales about him could be believed, Dani peeled off the rest of her clothes, threw a nightgown over her head and tossed back the covers of her twin bed.

"I know it's late and I hate to bother you . . ." Irene's voice, barely a whisper, drifted through the bedroom door Dani had left ajar. "I wouldn't have called, but I didn't know who else to turn to."

*Jonah McKee.* Dani's heart seemed to nosedive through the mattress to the floor. She didn't have to hear his name to know who was on the other end of the line. As always, whenever there was a problem, Irene Donahue called the old bastard even though it was the middle of the night and he was probably in bed with his wife.

Dani squeezed her eyes shut and tried not to listen, but bits of the one-sided conversation drifted into the room on a cloud of smoke from Irene's cigarette. "I know. I know," she was saying. "Well, it's old and it needs new brakes and battery . . . Yes, while she was driving home . . . I don't know really—someone happened by on a motorcycle and brought her home . . . What? . . . I don't know. She didn't know him, either, though. I don't think she even asked him his name. I know, I know, it's dangerous, but she didn't have much of a choice . . . Yes, some stranger. Thank God it wasn't someone who would kidnap her or . . . well, you know."

There was a soft, sad laugh. "Yep, she's always been a handful, ever since she was a little girl . . . A lot like her father . . . I hated to call, but I knew you'd understand. I hope I didn't wake Virginia . . . Thanks. I will . . . Really . . . I don't know how to thank you—you've been so kind already . . ." The words were soft, filled with adoration. They made Dani sick.

She fought tears, but hot and bitter they filled her eyes and ran down the sides of her head to dampen her pillow. She could never live up to her mother's impossible expectations. Never. Why even try? Whatever she did, it wasn't good enough. She swallowed back a sob.

For a long while, she'd guessed that Irene Donahue was in love with her employer. Jonah McKee was a god on earth in Irene's estimation—his children perfect, all three of them. Max, the oldest, did everything ever expected of him, excelled at anything he tried. Jenner, second born, was more trouble and rebellious, but handsome and cocky. And Casey, the youngest, was Jonah's little princess. He spoiled her and was proud of it.

Again Dani felt like a failure and it hurt her to know that her mother was in love with and possibly having an affair with Jonah McKee, the man who had taken care of the Donahue family ever since the accident that had claimed Tom's life. Their house was paid off and kept up with McKee money. Irene had a decent job with McKee Enterprises, and whenever there was trouble, she turned to Jonah. Dani was mortified that her mother was so dependent upon him and she couldn't help but wonder if Jonah, in his own twisted way, liked to keep Irene under his all-encompassing thumb.

Speculation ran high in a town the size of Rimrock, with

the wealthiest man so visible. Gossip swept through the narrow streets as quickly as a prairie fire fueled by a hot summer wind. Rumor had it that Jonah liked women—all kinds. His marriage vows were loosely kept, though his wife, Virginia, never seemed to doubt him. No matter what the scandal, Virginia McKee stood by her man, not in the spotlight but just to his side, ever smiling, ever suffering. Dani loathed her.

Several women in town were rumored to have been Jonah's mistresses at one time or another. Virginia never wavered in her abject faith and loyalty. What a fool! In Dani's estimation, love shouldn't come at the expense of respect. Nor could it be bought. She didn't care how much money the old creep had; she believed that marriage vows were meant to be upheld—by both parties.

A soft click indicated that her mother had hung up and Dani closed her eyes, refusing to think about Irene or Jonah or their unhappy situation. Instead, she let her thoughts run in different circles and conjured up the face of Brandon Scarlotti—dark, intense and devastating. She wondered if she'd ever hear from him again. He promised he'd call. What then? Would he ask her out? Probably not, and even if he did, her mother would refuse to let her go. She could hear it now. "You want to go riding with that boy? Oh, honey, why? When there are so many nice boys like one of the McKees or Dale Bateman? Scarlotti's bad news, let me tell you. I've heard it all from Bess and she's not one to gossip idly . . ." Dani would never hear the end of it if she openly saw Brandon. Not that she had to worry about it. Most likely she'd never see him again.

Brandon rode back to Dawson City and pushed the speed limit. The night-shaded countryside flashed by, but he barely noticed because he was thinking about Dani—a girl he'd never met before, a girl who seemed lodged in his mind. He usually didn't go for the damsel-in-distress types, but even considering the circumstances, he knew instinctively that Dani Donahue wasn't a weak female. The defiant tilt of her jaw and the flash of intelligence and humor in her eyes got to him, and though he was loath to admit it, he could still imagine the feel of her arms surrounding his chest and the soft pressure of her breasts against his back. The scent of her perfume still clung to him and he didn't want it to dissipate.

"Idiot," he growled, shifting again. The night screamed past him and he passed Dani's mother's car, still intact on the shoulder of the county road. It would probably be safe for the night, and if not, it wasn't a huge loss. The car was ready for the junkyard.

He drove through the hills until the lights of Dawson City winked at him, but instead of welcoming beacons leading him home, he thought of them as huge security lamps—the kind that rise from a prison wall, illuminating the cold ground in their harsh glare. All his life he'd felt as if he was locked away, imprisoned by responsibility.

He tried to shake off the feeling as he wheeled into the old subdivision where his mother had lived for what seemed to Brandon to be a thousand years. Nothing ever changed here. Nothing ever got better. Things might not have been so bleak if his old man had hung around, but when Jake Kendall had learned that Venitia was pregnant, he'd taken a permanent hike, never once meeting the son he'd sired.

An A number-one jerk.

Brandon parked his bike near his mother's old Ford. The lights in the house were blazing as he walked up the back steps and let himself in. "Ma?" he called, not expecting an answer and not getting one.

A cold feeling spread through him and he wondered why, after all these years, he wasn't numb, why he still cared.

Because she tried her best. It wasn't good enough, but damn it, she tried her best!

"Ma?"

Nothing. Just the sound of the clock ticking on the mantel and the low rumble of the television. He rounded the corner to the living room and found her curled in a corner of the couch, her head propped up by a shiny overstuffed arm, her wineglass empty on a nearby table, the bottle lying on its side half-under the couch.

"Why?" he whispered, trying to stem the anger that usually overtook him when he found her like this. A cigarette was smoldering in the overflowing ashtray and he knew why he stayed, why he hadn't moved out, though inside he was screaming to leave. She needed him. It was that simple. And that hard. "Come on, Ma," he said, hauling her into his arms. She was thin, almost waiflike, and her eyes fluttered open just long enough for her to smile—still a beautiful smile—as she touched the side of his face with cool fingers.

"Brand. You know you're a good boy, don' ya . . ." Anything else she said was lost as he carried her into her bedroom and gently folded back the old chenille spread. She made smacking noises with her lips then returned to a semi-fetal position as he turned out the light.

"Night, Ma," he whispered and knew she wouldn't answer. The weight of responsibility, as heavy as a ton of bricks, slumped his shoulders. He snapped out the lights and stopped in the living room to extinguish the burning cigarette before dumping the entire contents of the overflowing ashtray into the fireplace.

Once the house was dark, he stared past the streetlights to the dark hills surrounding the town and knew that he'd never leave—not until he was certain she could take care of herself. And that, he realized with an air of fatality, might be never. Even if she did end up marrying Alvin Cunningham, a sawmill worker who'd been sniffing around for the past year or so.

Though Venitia talked about leaving Dawson City, about marrying Alvin, Brand didn't believe it; he didn't want to believe it. Because he was certain that she could do better. She certainly deserved it.

"I didn't catch the name of the guy who gave you a ride the other night," Irene said as she picked the clothes out of the hamper and frowned at the filthy state of Dani's jeans and blouse.

Dani was washing up, standing at the bathroom sink in her bra and panties as she wiped the dust and grime off her body from hours in the saddle. She hesitated, decided she didn't want to worry her mother any further, and lied. "I thought I told you that I didn't ask who he was. He didn't say." What good would it do for her mother to know that she'd clung to Brandon Scarlotti and never wanted to let go?

"Odd, don't you think? You rode all those miles and didn't exchange names?" Irene was obviously dubious. Her gaze said as much in the mirror's reflection.

"It was confusing and a little scary—leaving the car and getting on the bike. I . . . I just didn't think about it." With a shrug, Dani lathered her arms and face with soap. "It—it was kind of a crazy night. I was worried about the car."

"I know, but surely—"

"I didn't tell him my name, he didn't tell me his, okay? He was just a decent guy who went out of his way to bring me here. I didn't ask to see any of his ID and it was so dark I doubt that I would know him if I tripped over him." Boy, she was getting good at lying. It scared her a little.

"I hope you thanked him."

"Of course I did."

"But you didn't recognize him?"

"How many times do I have to tell you?" Dani demanded. "He was a stranger. I'm sorry that I didn't put him through the third degree." She kept the edge in her voice in the frail hope that her mother might take the hint and back off.

Irene didn't look convinced, but Dani ignored her, rinsed the soap from her skin, turned off the water and buried her face in a thin towel. She dabbed the moisture from her face and arms, and when she was finished, her mother had disappeared, along with the dirty laundry from the bathroom. The truth of the matter was that Dani was disappointed. She'd hoped that Brandon would call, though she didn't really understand why. She dated a lot of boys, never tied herself down, promised herself that she wouldn't fall into the same trap as her mother by becoming so dependent on one man. So why did she think about Brandon Scarlotti night and day?

Probably because it was safe to fantasize about him. He was off-limits. A little older than she, he ran with a faster crowd and wouldn't be interested in a senior in high school.

She changed into clean shorts and a sleeveless blouse that she tied under her breasts. Twisting her hair into a ponytail, she walked into the living room, where her mother, seated near the window, was sorting through the mail. A letter from the high school was lying open on the couch beside her. "You were nearly suspended last week for being caught with cigarettes in your purse," Irene accused.

"Yeah, it fell open and the pack slid under Martin Olson's desk in health class." Smiling, Dani thought of the expression on the face of her teacher, Miss Vann, as the cigarettes spilled onto the shiny linoleum. Her lecture that day had been on lung cancer, heart disease and the hazards of smoking.

"You didn't tell me."

Dani flopped into her favorite old rocker and tucked her legs beneath her, poised for the lecture that was sure to come. "It slipped my mind—"

"No, Danielle, it didn't. You hoped I wouldn't find out."

Scooting low on her back, Dani countered, "It wasn't a big deal."

"You're too young to smoke," Irene said, then looked guiltily at the steel ashtray shaped like a horseshoe that sat prominently in a corner of the coffee table.

"How old were you when you started?"

"We're not talking about me."

"How old?"

"Back then we didn't know better, didn't realize all the health hazards. When I started, there weren't all the warning labels or all this brouhaha over secondhand smoke or low birth weight in babies . . ." Irene's back stiffened and she looked very much like she wanted a cigarette. "I was never suspended from school."

"Neither was I."

"Not yet."

"Mom? How old?"

Sighing, Irene slid her reading glasses off the end of her nose. "Okay, not that it matters, but I was fifteen. My cousin, Nick, swiped a pack from his father's store and we each tried a couple."

"I'm seventeen."

"I know, but I wish I'd never started. Every day I wish I could quit."

"I can quit any time I want."

Irene pinned her daughter with her knowing glare. "You just don't want to, is that it?"

"Yeah, that's it."

"Then you're not as smart as I think you are."

"That's the problem, Mom. I'm not smart. Not like Skye."

Irene stacked the mail on a side table and sighed sadly. Removing her glasses, she rubbed her temple as if staving off a headache. "You don't have to be like Skye, Dani. How many times do I have to tell you? You're different and smart in other ways."

"Other ways?" Dani repeated. "You mean other than school."

"You don't apply yourself in school."

"I *hate* school."

"No, you don't—"

"Yeah, Mom, I do. And I won't be a Goody Two-shoes like Skye, so none of the teachers like me. They're all full of—"

"Don't even think it!" Closing her eyes wearily, Irene slowly shook her head. For the first time, Dani noticed the streaks of gray that had begun to thread through her mother's hair. "I don't know what's gotten into you lately."

"Neither do I," Dani said, then felt like a heel. She didn't want to make her mother's life more difficult; she just wanted to live her own. Her way. By her rules. "Hey, I'm sorry—"

Irene waved off her apology.

"How's the car?" she finally asked, guilt climbing up to sit on her shoulders.

"I get it back tomorrow, but Jonah thinks I should sell it. Even with a new battery and brakes, it needs help. The transmission's going and there's something about a problem with the driveline."

"That's what *Jonah* says?" Dani couldn't hide the sarcasm that stole through her voice.

"He's a smart man, Dani. He wouldn't have made his fortune if he didn't understand business."

"He inherited money."

"And made a whole lot more. Besides, he checked with his mechanic. The car won't make it through the winter."

Dani felt a pang of sympathy for her mother. Being single wasn't easy; loving a married man who would never return her feelings had to be hell.

"Jonah found a used Buick. Four years old, one owner, not many miles. He thinks I should buy it."

"*He* picked out a car for you? And you let him?"

"I just asked his advice."

Dani couldn't hide her dismay. "Jeez, Mom, can't you find your own car—"

"You don't understand," Irene snapped, standing quickly and scattering the mail on the floor. "Oh, Lordy, now look what you made me do! Someday you'll figure out, Danielle, that a person can't bulldoze through life all by herself. That she needs assistance, that sometimes it's better to ask for help than to try to fix things on her own. You're a good example of that! What would you have done without the help of that boy on the motorcycle the other night?"

"It's not the same." Dani reached down and handed her mother a stack of envelopes, all bills. Again she felt the stranglehold of guilt. Who was she to complain about her mother's choices when deep down she knew that Irene was doing the best she could, all because she wanted her daughters to have easier lives than she'd had.

"No, you're right. It's not the same—not exactly. But believe me, it just doesn't get any easier. Now, if you're smart, you'll quit smoking, study hard and hope we can find a way to send you to college. That money you're saving for a horse would be well spent on classes at the community college." She straightened and marched to the kitchen.

Dani bit back a hot retort. Her mother had never understood her fascination with horses. Growing up in San Francisco and never having ridden, Irene hadn't experienced the blast of freedom that Dani felt every time she was astride a fleet horse, how her heart seemed to beat in tandem with the rhythm of thundering hoofbeats, how sometimes she felt that animals understood her better than any human being ever could.

The phone rang and Dani unfolded her legs as Irene answered

in the kitchen. "Just a minute," she heard her mother tell the caller before yelling toward the living room. "It's for you."

For the millionth time, Dani wished for another extension, but she pushed herself upright, walked down the short hallway and took the receiver from her mother's hand. "Hello?"

"Hi."

Her heart kicked a little and she licked her lips. *Brandon*. Though she'd only met him once, she'd recognize his voice even if he were calling from Timbuktu.

"It's Brand."

"Yeah, I know." Winding the cord through her fingers, she turned her back to her mother, avoiding Irene's curious stare.

"I thought we should see each other again."

Her heart soared before quickly falling to earth and crashing on the cold stones of reality. Her mother would never let her go out with him, especially not now after the note from the school about her nearly being suspended. "Sure," she said brightly, the wheels spinning in her mind as she fabricated an excuse to get out of the house. It wasn't a lie—well, not a big one, and besides, this was her chance to be with Brand.

"How about tonight?"

"Okay." She licked her lips nervously. How was she going to pull this off?

"I'll be over about—"

"I'll meet you there," she said quickly. "In the library. Second floor."

"The library . . . what is this?" he asked.

"That would be great." She forced a smile and faced her mother even though she felt as if her insides were in a vise that was slowly being tightened. "See you in a little while, about seven."

"Oh, I get it—you're in some kind of trouble. Grounded?"

"Right."

"And you don't want your folks to know that you're going out?"

"I'll be at a table near the back window."

"I don't like sneaking around," he said bluntly, and her fingers curled over the receiver until her knuckles showed white.

"Neither do I. But it's the way it's got to be." She hung up, her heart pumping wildly. His words scorched through her brain and her hands were shaking so badly she shoved them into the back pockets of her shorts. Her mother, leaning against the counter, eyed her suspiciously.

Dani usually wasn't one to lie but recently she'd been coming up with stories nearly every time she turned around.

"You're going to the library?" Irene asked as she began emptying dishes out of the portable dishwasher.

"That's right. I'll take care of these." Grabbing a couple of glasses, Dani began stacking them in the cupboard.

"Why the library?"

"Big government test on Friday."

"Who're you meeting"

Dani thought fast as she slid plates into their spot in the old cupboard. "Russ Kellogg and probably Mandy Groves. Maybe a few others. Everyone's worried about the test. It's half our semester grade."

"Is it?" Irene reached into the drawer for her cigarettes, thought better of it and rubbed the side of her neck. "You've never studied with anyone before."

"I know, but we thought it might help. Lots of kids work in study groups. That was Russ on the phone. If he doesn't pass this test, his grade could slip and he'd be off the football team." Dear God, the lies were tripping so easily from her tongue she was certain to get caught. "Look, Mom, I'm really sorry for messing up at school." At least that wasn't stretching the truth. Dani hated hurting her mother.

"All right, but just be back early," Irene said, her eyes narrowing and her jaw sliding to the side, as if she didn't quite believe what she was hearing.

"I will. Promise." Guilt crept after her as she grabbed her books. Why didn't she just tell her mother the truth, that Brandon was the boy who had given her a ride home when the car had broken down and that she was meeting him tonight?

Because no matter how kind or thoughtful or noble Brandon had been that night, Irene wouldn't approve.

Because Irene wouldn't allow Dani to see him. Hadn't she already concocted a list of boys—troublemakers—that Dani wasn't supposed to date? Brandon Scarlotti was near the top of the list.

And because Dani had discovered that she'd do just about anything to see him again.

"That's stupid," she told herself. She'd always prided herself on keeping her cool and never letting a boy get too near to her. And she'd never had to resort to lying to be with one before.

She felt a headache coming on as she walked past the park and playground, but she fought it. So she lied. Big deal. What was done was done and she wasn't going to beat herself up over it. In fact, she was going to ignore her guilt and have a good time.

With renewed determination she walked into the library and dashed upstairs to a table by the window.

Keyed up, she opened her government book and notebook and tried to study, but her concentration failed her. She read the same page over three times and kept glancing at her watch while listening for the thrum of a motorcycle engine.

She heard nothing, just the whisper of pages being turned and the soft hum of the computers. Somewhere on the other side of the stacks, someone was softly reading a children's book out loud. Every once in a while, the kid boomed forth a question and Dani jumped. Now, drumming her fingers in distraction, she shifted in her chair. She read the first boring paragraph on the justice system one more time.

"As I said I don't like lying and sneaking around." Brand's

voice, a whisper, was just audible enough for her to hear him. She looked up sharply as he approached, and her throat caught. Under the fluorescent lights, his skin was dark and tanned, his black hair gleamed and his eyes were sharp electric blue.

"Neither . . . neither do I," she admitted, having trouble finding her voice.

So furious he seemed to radiate anger, he glared at her as he slid into the chair on the opposite side of the small, scarred blond table.

"Then what is it? You ashamed to be seen with me?"

She swallowed hard. "No, that's not it."

His look was scathing.

"I don't usually lie, but if I hadn't, my mother wouldn't have let me see you, okay? She's got this thing against guys who've been in trouble with the law. You've made quite a reputation for yourself, you know, and my mom's heard all about it. She and Bess Jamison are good friends."

His lips thinned into a hard, unyielding line. "Bess Jamison is a gossip who should keep her nose in her own business. She makes a habit out of jumping to conclusions."

"Probably, but Mom doesn't know that. So she believes her."

"And I'm dirt." A tic started beneath his eye.

"No, not dirt—just a . . . a—"

"Criminal."

"Well, not quite. But near enough."

He scraped back his chair. "Nice knowin' ya."

He was leaving? She couldn't believe it, but he'd turned his back and started walking to the stairs. "Brandon!" she whispered, gathering her books and backpack. "Wait!"

She ran past the stacks and hurried down the stairs but she was too late. He had already crossed the lobby and was shouldering his way through the front door. "Damn it," she muttered under her breath as she ran after him. First she'd lied, then she'd provoked an argument, now she was chasing after him, making a fool of herself.

Though it was after seven, it was still light, and a hot breeze blew through the town, creating a whirlwind that tossed a few dry leaves into the air.

Dani caught up with Brandon in the parking lot. He was already astride his motorcycle, a pair of sunglasses covering his eyes.

"Wait!" She clutched at his arm, her fingers tightening over the worn leather of his jacket.

Impatience hardened his features. "Why?"

"I—I'm sorry. I guess I fouled this up. I didn't mean to. I wanted to see you again, but—"

"But you were too ashamed to let anyone know." His jaw showed white. "Don't worry about it, Dani."

"Not ashamed. Just concerned."

"Let's just forget it." He revved the engine.

"No, Brandon, please, just listen—"

But he was off. The motorcycle screamed out of the parking lot and he didn't look back. Not once.

"Fool!" she growled at herself and kicked a pebble across the nearly empty lot. It landed with a clink against the hubcap of a new BMW. Letting out her breath, Dani stood, squinting after him, smelling exhaust, hearing the motorcycle's engine blend with the noise of the other traffic moving slowly through town. So that was it. Over before it began.

Probably for the best, she told herself as she glared into the lowering sun. "Good riddance. I don't need this kind of grief."

But deep in her heart, she didn't believe a word of it.

# CHAPTER FOUR

"It's official," Venitia announced, dropping a basket of laundry onto the top of the dryer as Brandon hung his jacket on a peg near the back door of the closed-in porch.

"What?" He braced himself. His mother was always pulling something. But at least she was sober as she turned on the washing machine; the roar of water filled the small room.

Grinning widely, she waggled her fingers in front of her son's face, and he noticed the ring, a gold band with a tiny diamond sparkling merrily on the fourth finger of her left hand. "Al and I are going to get married."

He'd been expecting it, of course, but still Brandon felt as if he'd been kicked in the gut. Suddenly the smells of hot water, detergent and mildew were overpowering. "You know how I feel about it."

Traces of sadness edged her smile. "I don't know why you want to ruin my happiness." She opened the lid of the washing machine and tossed in a cup's worth of detergent.

"Al won't make you happy." He was blunt and he knew it, but this time she couldn't be coddled. Al Cunningham was a louse, and Venitia, despite everything she claimed, didn't love him.

"Of course he will."

"Ma, really—"

"And he'll make my life easier," she said, her brow puckering as it always did whenever she fought tears. Quickly tossing in the sheets and white towels, she scanned the counter near the sink. "Now, where's my bleach?"

Brandon found the white bottle, stuck on a shelf behind some boxes and a can of floor wax.

"Thanks," she said as he handed her the bleach. She unscrewed the cap and fumes of chlorine filled the small room, burning the insides of Brandon's nostrils. She measured out a cup before adding it to a dispenser in the machine. "I don't know what you have against Al. He's rock steady and Lord knows that's exactly what I need."

"He'll bore you to tears."

"He's got a good job."

"With Jonah McKee's mill. You know how things are in the logging business right now. McKee's already sold off two mills and one of his logging camps. People are let go all the time." Uncomfortable in his role of marital advisor, he rubbed the back of his neck. Why was his mother so damned naive? Sometimes he felt as if their roles were reversed and he was the parent, she the child. "Don't marry Al for the security, Ma."

"You don't understand. Al's taken a job with another mill where they make chipboard. In Everett, Washington. He'll make more money than he does here and I can give up my job with the janitorial service. But that's not what matters, Brand. I want you to know I'm marrying Al because I love him." She inched up her chin despite the telltale blush climbing up her neck. She'd always been a lousy liar. "I can't pine after your father forever." She slammed down the lid of the washer.

Brandon didn't want to be reminded of his old man. The

jerk had bailed out before he was born, and the irresponsible creep hadn't even bothered marrying his mother. It had been nearly twenty years, for God's sake. He never once remembered his mother pining for Jake Kendall, a cowboy and drifter who pulled up stakes when he found out he was going to be a father. No, Venitia hadn't cried too many tears for the son of a bitch and he didn't blame her. Brandon suspected her of loving someone else, someone inaccessible and from a distance, though he had no proof. It was just a gut feeling— that his mother was the victim of unrequited love. "There have been other guys," he reminded her as gently as he could.

Bending over, she yanked faded jeans and sweatshirts from the dryer. "Yeah, well, they weren't the marrying kind."

"Is that so important?"

She didn't answer, just grabbed her wicker basket and turned a stiff back to her son as she stalked out of the room. He knew it had been hard, raising a baby without the benefits, support and respect that a husband provided. He'd heard the whispers and taunts, been the butt of a hundred jokes himself. No wonder she grasped the chance to become respectable. He couldn't fault her there. But marrying Al Cunningham? The guy was so boring he probably put himself to sleep.

Brandon followed her into the kitchen where she was folding towels on the scarred Formica tabletop. "Think it through, okay?" He pulled an old pair of Levi's from the basket and snapped them briskly, as he had a thousand times. From the age of seven, he'd helped with the laundry and other household chores. He used to mind and as a thirteen-year-old he'd thought all housework was for women, but slowly he'd learned that it was all part of living.

"I have thought about it," she said stubbornly. "And I'm going to get married, Brandon. I'm forty-three—I think it's time. The wedding's already planned for next month and then, well, after we tie up a few loose ends around here, we'll be putting this house on the market and moving."

"To Everett?" He didn't hide his skepticism.

"That's right."

"Where you don't know a soul."

"I'll make new friends. Come on, baby," she said, her eyes suddenly soft. "Can't you be happy for me?"

"I'm trying, Ma," he said, though for the life of him he couldn't find an iota of joy in the situation. He should have been ecstatic, buoyed by the sense that he would finally be free. His mother would be married off and would have a husband to look after her—to worry about her and tuck her into bed when she'd had too much to drink. But he wasn't. He felt that she was settling, giving up on her dreams, and she deserved so much better than Al Cunningham.

"My only worry is you," she said, smoothing a once-thick sweatshirt and folding the arms into the middle. "If you want to stay here, I don't have to sell the house right away—"

"No," he cut in swiftly, though he wouldn't tell her that the tiny cottage didn't hold many happy memories for him. After all, she'd tried. Done her best. "Rent it. Sell it, or whatever. I don't want it."

"You wouldn't mind?" Was there just a tiny crack of disappointment in her voice?

"Not at all." How could he explain that he'd only stayed on because he'd felt duty bound, that he hadn't moved out long ago for fear that she'd be incredibly lonely? "I planned to go to California come winter. You know that."

"A pipe dream." Her fingers fluttered in the air as if she were brushing the ridiculous idea aside. "You should move in with us. Maybe take some classes at the community college. Make some new friends."

Inexplicably he thought of Dani. But then he'd thought of her a lot these days, more than was healthy. "I don't think so."

"But it would be a chance for you to make a clean start."

"I can do that in L.A."

She frowned, unable to let him go. "Al says there are plenty of jobs up there and—"

Tired of dancing around the subject, he snapped. Grabbing her by the arms, he held on tight. The worn T-shirt she'd been folding drifted to the floor and he tried to control the anger that swept through his blood. She'd been laying a guilt trip on him for too long, a trip that wouldn't work if she was serious about marrying Cunningham. "I don't care what Al says. It's past time for me to leave. We both know it."

Worry clouded her eyes. "I don't see why you can't accept Al."

He held up his hands and backed out of the room. "Look, it doesn't matter what I say. You're going to marry Al and I hope to God that you're happy. Really. What I think doesn't matter. Whether you marry him or not, I'm outta here. Shoulda left a long time ago." He stalked back to the porch and reached for his jacket.

"You could have the decency to wish me good luck," she said, her shoes clicking against the yellowed linoleum.

"Good luck," he retorted, unable to keep the sarcasm from his words. *You'll need it.*

He was out the back door when her voice reached him again. "Brand?"

"What?" He didn't stop striding toward his bike.

"I was hoping you'd give me away."

He stopped dead in his tracks. Slowly he turned to face her then and found her standing in the doorway, a proud woman who'd spent the best years of her life trying to provide for him. "Oh, God, Mom, you're not serious."

Her back stiffened as if it had been starched. "More serious than I've ever been in my life." She was down the steps and across the uneven yard within seconds. As she ducked under the clothesline, her chin wobbled a bit and it got to him, even though he knew it was probably just an act.

"Don't ask me."

"I already have, Brand." She placed a hand on his sleeve, a warm, motherly hand meant to remind him of all the things she'd done for him, all the sacrifices she'd so willingly made. "Please, if you don't do another thing for me the rest of my life, walk me down the aisle."

An ache settled deep in his heart, but he steeled himself. Yanking his arm away, he swung onto his cycle. "If it's what you want, okay. But that's it. After the ceremony, I'm gone."

She bit her lip. "You're all I have, you know."

"Not anymore, Mom," he reminded her, his voice more savage than kind. "You've got Al now." It sounded so final. He ignored the tears shimmering in his mother's eyes and tried to forget the guilt that was pounding at his temples. He should have been thrilled to finally be free. But as he put his bike through its paces, speeding toward the city limits, he felt the breath of disaster hot against the back of his neck.

If she didn't watch herself, she'd end up just like her mother, Dani thought grimly as she sat on the old log that had fallen across Wildcat Creek and formed a natural bridge. She spent nearly every waking hour thinking of Brand. Ever since their argument in the library, she'd jumped each time the phone rang, considered calling him and found excuses to drive into Dawson City. "Pathetic," she said, dragging her bare toes through the shaded waters. "Just plain pathetic. He doesn't even know you're alive."

Frowning, she knew she should make her way back home. It was nearly dusk and she'd sought solace in this private place just as she had every time she'd been troubled during her growing-up years when it just didn't seem right to burden her mother or older sister with her problems. She often exercised horses for free when she was upset, but since she couldn't today, she'd come to this shady little grove. She'd never seen another living soul in this place, except during hunting season, when an avid rifleman had ignored the posted No Hunting signs and searched the woods for signs of game.

A few times, Dani had brought her friends with her, but usually she walked to the outskirts of town, climbed a couple of fences and hiked down an old deer trail to the creek. The property belonged to somebody, but no one seemed to know who actually held the deed.

Jonah McKee was a name that came readily to mind and it bothered her to think that the old man might own this private little spot as well as most everything else in Rimrock.

Ignoring her mother's comments from the other day, she reached into her pocket, found the last cigarette in her pack and lit up. Drawing the smoke deep into her lungs, she nearly coughed at the sound of another voice.

"Those things'll kill ya."

Brand! Her heart leaped as she looked over her shoulder. Miraculously, as if appearing out of the shadows, he was leaning against the bark of a scraggly old pine tree.

"I'm not kidding. Maybe not right away, but eventually, in the next thirty to sixty years, they'll do you in."

She ground out her cigarette in the bark of the tree she was sitting on. "Did you come by just to give me an update on the surgeon general's latest findings?" He laughed and the deep sound rumbled over the small ravine and echoed in her heart. She suddenly felt self-conscious, as if he could read in her eyes how much she'd missed him, how desperate she'd been to see him again. "Wh-what are you doing here?" she asked, trying to sound as if she didn't care, as if the drumming in her heart was a normal state for her.

"Looking for you." He said it bluntly, a simple statement of fact.

Her heart nearly stopped. She swallowed hard. "But how'd you find me?" No one ever came to this little bend in the creek just outside of town.

He pushed himself upright and edged down the overgrown embankment to the creek. "I followed you."

"You what?" She was flabbergasted. "But why?"

"I didn't want to risk calling or stopping by because I thought you might catch hell from your mother if I started hanging around."

"That's always a possibility," she admitted, feeling more than a little embarrassed. "It's not you she doesn't approve of, just your reputation."

"And I've spent so much time cultivating it," he dead-panned.

"Very funny," she mocked, but laughed at his sarcasm. "My mother thinks I should hang out with a different crowd."

"Such as?"

"I guess I could start with the McKees—though she's a little concerned about the younger brother. He's a wild one."

"Jenner's the only decent one of the lot. You could go chasing after him, I suppose, but he's hard to catch." Brand's blue eyes flared with amusement, and Dani, smothering a smile, drew back her leg, dragging her toes through the water, then kicked forward to send a spray of water to the bank, splashing him. "Hey!"

She giggled and did it again.

"Cut that out!" But he was grinning, revenge twinkling in his eyes as water dripped from his face, down his neck and T-shirt. "You're asking for it," he warned.

"For what?" Playfully she angled her chin up at him.

"Trouble," he said, climbing onto the log.

She scrambled to her feet. "I'm not afraid of a little trouble," she said, cocking a brow in silent challenge, though she was braced to run.

"How about big trouble?"

"Oh, I can handle that, too." She knew she was baiting him but couldn't help herself. He walked forward, without looking down, his boots not slipping a fraction. His eyes were intense, his thin lips turned into a crooked smile that caused her pulse to beat out of control. "Why were you looking for me?"

"Good question." He stopped just inches from her, and the sounds of this thicket near the creek, the slap of water over smooth stones, the drone of insects, the whisper of wind through the boughs overhead, seemed to mute until all she could hear was the pounding of her heart and her own shallow breathing.

"I—I thought you were mad at me."

His eyebrows arched slightly. "Oh, I am," he said.

"You are?"

"Furious. Can't you tell?"

Her throat turned to dust.

"So why did you come here?"

His eyes sparked. "Guess."

"To scare me?"

"Nah." A quick shake of his head and she felt her body tingle.

"Punish me?"

He hesitated. She caught her breath. If she didn't trust him so much, she might have considered him menacing. Reaching forward, he slid work-roughened fingers under her jaw. "I don't believe in punishment." His face was so close to hers that she noticed how thick and black his eyelashes were. His gaze narrowed, centering on her lips. "Besides, you didn't do anything wrong, did you?"

She flushed from guilt or his heat, she didn't know which. "I lied to my mother and—"

"Because you wanted to see me." His fingers touched the underside of her chin, and her knees threatened to give way.

"Yes."

"Why did you want to be with me so badly?"

"I wish I knew," she whispered while his finger stroked her throat.

"So do I." He stared at her long and hard, as if he was

measuring what he was about to do. Then he lowered his head and slanted his lips over hers.

In one quick motion his arms surrounded her. He drew her close and kissed her with lips that were hot and hard and demanding. Dani's eyes closed, her heart thundered, and places deep inside her started to melt. She sagged against him, opening her mouth to the warm, insistent pressure of his tongue.

Lifting his head, he held her close, cradling her, holding her so that her forehead fitted against his chest. "I knew it would be like this with you."

She didn't respond. She'd never felt like this before, never felt so completely undone, so empty inside, so wanting. Although she had a reputation as a party girl, deep down she thought she might be a prude. Oh, she liked kissing, found it pleasurable, but never like this, and she'd never let a boy so much as touch her breasts.

One time after a date with Martin Olson, he'd kissed her in the car. His hands had found the hem of her sweater and his fingers had slipped underneath, grazing her abdomen before quickly clamping over her bra. He'd been breathing heavily, his hands sweaty and anxious as he'd pawed at her. She'd stiffened, trying to relax, but couldn't. Some of her girlfriends had told her how they'd trembled with desire when their boyfriends touched them in private places, but all that Dani had felt with Martin had been sick revulsion.

She'd tried to slip away but he'd become more insistent.

"Oh, Dani, let me," he'd pleaded into her open mouth as his hands tried to unhook her bra. "You're so beautiful. I know they're beautiful, too. So beautiful." He'd licked his lips and kissed her sloppily, his entire body pressing urgently to hers as he tried, fumbling, to find her nipple beneath her cotton bra. "I just want to look at them, to touch them, to feel them in my mouth."

"No way!" She'd pulled away, reaching for the door handle of his old Ford.

"But I love you."

"You do not." Her fingers had encountered the cold metal. "Dani, don't. Come on, what does it hurt—"

She'd fought her way out of the sedan, slammed the car door shut and raced up the driveway, more scared than she'd ever been in her life. What had been wrong with her? She'd liked Martin; he was a decent guy and he honestly seemed to care about her. But his fascination with her breasts had turned her off. She'd squeezed back tears thinking she was frigid, unlike her friends, Alison and Terry, who couldn't wait to "do it" with their boyfriends.

Now, she knew differently. Brand kissed her again so soundly that she clung to him, her body limp. For the first time in her life, she understood how passion could rob a person of her senses, could make her blind and wanting, aching inside. She realized that she was normal in her desire to touch and explore, that, with Brandon, she wanted more.

"Hell," Brand whispered as he released her and shoved both hands through his hair. Without his support, she nearly toppled off the log, and he caught her arm, quickly drawing her close. His face was full of wonder, as if the lightning that had sizzled between them was new to him. "This could be dangerous."

"It already is."

He chuckled and she sighed happily, her breath spreading over his chest, her arms wrapped loosely around his waist. The lean, hard muscles felt good to her and it seemed as if she belonged here—forever in his embrace. But that was silly, wasn't it? Brandon Scarlotti wasn't a forever kind of guy.

"Come on, Dani. We'd better get out of here before we do something we'll both regret."

"And what would that be?" she asked saucily.

"You wouldn't want to know."

She smiled, because she already knew that, whether they planned it or not, it was only a matter of time before she kissed him again. Her throat dry as cotton, she realized that she might make love to him. But that was crazy—her fantasies were running away with her, her mind spinning in wild, new directions. What was she thinking? Blushing to the roots of her hair, she scurried off the log.

Sandals dangling from the fingers of one hand, she walked barefoot across the field, the stubble of grass pricking the bottoms of her feet, grasshoppers flying ahead of them. Brand held her other hand firmly in his, as if he expected her to bolt and run from him, until they reached the old, dilapidated gate with the rusted metal No Trespassing sign that they'd ignored. On the other side, parked on a packed-dirt road, was his motorcycle. He helped her over the gate, and as she landed on the far side, his hands slid up her waist and held tight to her ribs. "You're something else," he whispered.

"Oh, yeah? Good or bad?" she teased.

"Bad. Definitely bad, Miss Donahue."

"I've got news for you. So are you."

"Old news," he said, his eyes searching hers as if looking for the key that he could use to unlock her secrets one by one.

She licked her lips nervously and he groaned, then he drew her to him and kissed her hard, his lips seeming to sear into her skin, to brand her forever. Again she melted and a yearning, deep and dangerous, awakened in her. His fingers seemed to leave impressions on her skin.

Quickly, muttering something about leaving while he still could, he let her go, slanted her an I-don't-believe-this-is-happening-to-me look and strode to his bike. "See ya," he said.

"Yeah." *I hope so!*

His big motorcycle glinted in the sunlight as he took off, and her heart followed after him, riding on a blue cloud of exhaust.

* * *

Brand couldn't quit thinking about her. During the day, at work, while he was helping out with the construction crew, she invaded his mind. He worked for Red Ingstrom, a burly man with muscular arms that looked nearly out of proportion to the rest of his body. "You remind me of myself when I was a kid," Red had told him when he'd applied for the job of general construction apprentice. "Hell on wheels." He'd moved a glob of tobacco from one side of his mouth to the other. "A guy gave me a break and I ended up okay—settled down and worked hard, raised two no-good sons and three daughters and I've made more than my share of money. You can have the job, long as I know that you'll give me a hundred and fifty percent."

Brand had agreed and worked for Red ever since, learning the trade, listening and watching as Red's company renovated old buildings as well as built new. Everything from houses to shopping malls. No job was too big or too small. "That's the key," Red had confided in him. "Do a good job for a decent price and make a little money at a time. Forget about the big score—like as not all you'll end up doing is losing your shirt."

Red had treated him fairly, given him raises when he deserved them and lectured when Brand had fouled up. Red had even helped get him out of jail a time or two—at least Brand assumed that his unknown benefactor had been his boss, though Red steadfastly claimed that he hadn't done anything. "You land in the big house, it's your problem, believe me." But Brand had never believed him. Who else would have had the time, money or inclination to get him off? Red Ingstrom was the closest thing to a father Brandon had ever known.

And right now Red was mad. Smoke-breathing, vein-popping mad. "What the hell's the matter with you?" Red demanded, his face flushed and sweaty. He swiped it with a scarlet-patterned handkerchief. "That makes twice today that you've misread the blueprints. The window's on the south side of the house, for crying out loud."

"You're right," Brand said, feeling like a fool—a complete novice.

"You've never screwed up like this since I hired you." Red shoved his face close to Brand, though he had to angle his head upward. Sweat was visible in Red's crew cut. "Got a problem I should know about?"

"No problems."

Red snorted and slammed his hard hat back on his head. "Nothing to do with a woman, right?"

"No way."

"Good. Just be careful, okay?"

For the rest of the day, Red, whenever he was around, was double-checking Brand's work, grunting in satisfaction when the job was done right. Brandon could have kicked himself. He'd always been professional on the job. No matter what else happened in his personal life, he was able to keep the two separate. Until now. Until Dani Donahue.

For no reason he could name, that girl had him tied in knots. Not only during the day, but at night, alone, when he tried to sleep, her image would come to him. And though he was determined to will her away, she stayed in his mind, messing him up and making him so hard he ached. He dreamed of her. Naked and hot, writhing under him, screaming his name, he saw her in his mind's eye and he'd wake up sweaty and tangled in his sheets, lust pounding in his temples and throbbing in his loins. He'd managed to see her a couple of times since he'd found her down by the creek. She'd always seemed glad to see him and flashed him a breathtaking smile before kissing him as he'd never been kissed in his life. Kisses that kept him begging for more.

He was meeting her after work at the Kellogg farm outside of Rimrock. Old Cyrus was out of town for three weeks and Dani had agreed to exercise his horses. She'd asked Brand to join her, and though he had no affinity for long-legged beasts with minds of their own, he couldn't wait to see her again.

\* \* \*

Dani bit her lower lip and waited. She'd already run two of Kellogg's horses, letting them stretch their legs. Now Bourbon, a tall dun gelding, and Kimo, a feisty white mare, were saddled and waiting, their tails switching and hides twitching against the ever-present flies. The reins of their bridles were looped over the top fence rail and the horses pulled, hoping to stretch the leather so that they could graze on a few dry blades of grass near the fence. She probably shouldn't have asked Brandon to meet her here, but she'd wanted to see him so badly that she'd thrown caution to the wind. Sneaking around was getting to her, though. Every time she walked out of the house and didn't tell Irene she was planning to meet Brand, she felt guilty and foolish

On the other hand, her mother had no right to be so prejudiced against him. Several times, Dani had brought up his name, careful to include names of other kids, as well, and her mother had started on a tirade.

"I don't know why you pick such a sorry lot of kids to hang out with," Irene had raged just yesterday. "Alison's giving her parents fits, let me tell you. She's so wrapped up in her boyfriend, there's going to be trouble, you mark my words. And I'm surprised you even know that Scarlotti boy. Stay away from him, y'hear. That one's nothing but trouble."

"He seems all right to me," Dani had argued.

"If you call being a juvenile delinquent all right. He's always—and I mean *always*—getting into trouble with the law. Lordy! It's amazing that he hasn't been put in some kind of home for wayward boys."

"He helps his mother—"

"Venitia," Irene said, her lips curling into a deep scowl. "She's the real problem. Had that kid out of wedlock and held her head upright, which I guess you can't blame her for. She got herself mixed up with the wrong kind of guy, and that's why I'm telling you to stay away from her son. He's messed up—grew up without knowing his father—"

"Like I did?"

Irene stopped and just stared at Dani. "You at least knew of him, knew that he was a decent man, that we were married when you kids were conceived. Your father died, Dani. He didn't take off because he didn't want to be tied down with kids."

"That's not Brandon's fault."

"No, but let's just say he's always been wild. Venitia's never had the strength or know-how to keep him in line. It's a shame really, but none of our concern. You stay away from that boy, and believe me, you'll save yourself a mountain of grief."

"I swear, Mom, he's not as bad as everyone makes out," Dani said defensively. Her mother might have been more concerned except that Dani had a reputation for picking the side of the underdog. Hard on the outside, Dani had a soft interior and she was a sucker for stray dogs and cats, lost kids or anyone who got a raw deal in life.

Now she drummed her fingers on the split-rail fence and smiled when she heard his motorcycle. So he had come after all.

He wheeled into the graveled area that served as a parking lot and climbed off his bike. Dressed in a T-shirt and sun-bleached jeans, his hair wild from the wind, he strode up to her with a look so intense Dani's heart started knocking crazily.

"I thought you might chicken out," she teased, tossing her hair over one shoulder.

"Me?" He eyed the horses and sighed. "To tell you the truth, I thought about it. Horses and I don't get along all that well."

"Maybe it's time to change all that."

She reached for the reins, but a strong hand covered hers. Before she could move, he drew her close to him and kissed her with a passion that trapped her breath in her lungs. The sunlit day seemed to spin around them before he lifted his head. Amusement flickered in his eyes.

"Let's get one thing straight," he said, pressing her back against the fence rails so that his hips fitted snugly into the V of her legs, his hardness firm against her mound. Even through the denim of both their jeans, she could feel the throbbing down there, the pressure building, the lust that burned through the frail cloth. "I didn't come here because of some mangy beasts."

"They're not mangy," she said, gasping. "They're incredible. I feel about them the way you feel about your bike."

"My bike doesn't kick or bite and the garage doesn't have to be shoveled out all the time."

"By the end of the day, you'll love riding," she said, unwrapping the reins and trying to ignore the fact that she was tingling all over, that her skin was more alive than ever.

"Don't count on it."

"Sourpuss," she muttered under her breath while she held the gate open for him.

"Careful, lady," he warned, one dark eyebrow arching as he surveyed the horses.

"They're docile. Really. This is Bourbon." She handed Brand the reins. "I have a feeling you two are going to be fast friends."

"Don't bet on it."

They climbed into the saddles and Dani led the way through a series of gates to the single big pasture. The hay had been mowed a while ago and the stubble that remained was the color of winter wheat.

Brand didn't seem as unfamiliar in the saddle as he'd proclaimed. When Dani urged Kimo into a trot, Brand, astride Bourbon, kept up. And as she changed pace first into a slow lope, then into a gallop, Brand clucked his tongue and followed suit. The two horses took off over the soft hills, stride for stride.

Dani squinted against the lowering sun and breathed deeply of the hot, dry air. The wind tangled her hair and she felt the same sense of elation, that wild thrill that she always experienced astride a swift horse. They ran until she knew that her mount was tiring, then she drew up on the reins and slowed Kimo into a walk. The mare was blowing and tossing her head, and as Bourbon approached, she turned quickly and nipped at the dun's rump.

"Hey, what's this?"

Laughing, Dani pulled back hard and forced Kimo's head away from the taller horse's flank. "She's a little mean spirited."

"Now you tell me."

"But he's as gentle as a lamb." She hitched her chin toward Brand's mount. "Not that it matters. You've ridden before," she said, and Brand held up both hands, letting the reins, already knotted, fall onto Bourbon's neck.

"Guilty as charged."

"Then why'd you let me believe that this was your first time?"

"I didn't say that. You just assumed."

They drew up beneath a cottonwood tree hugging the shores of a creek that was nearly dry. "Where'd you learn to ride?" she asked as they let the horses graze on the dry grass and weeds.

"A friend of mine. Bobby Grayhawk's family had a lot of horses before they moved. He and I used to ride them bareback, pretend we were his ancestors. He claimed to be the great-great-grandson of some big-shot Nez Percé chief, I think, but then Bobby's imagination had a way of always running away with him. Anyway," he said, walking to the shade of the tree and leaning against a low branch, "that was a long time ago. Bobby moved when we were in the seventh grade."

"So why all the bad-mouthing about horses?" She walked up to him, close enough that he slipped a strong arm around her waist.

"I guess I grew out of horses and into cars and motorcycles."

"You were just giving me a hard time."

"Trying," he admitted, slanting her a devilish smile that melted her heart.

"And I fell for it."

"Hook, line and sinker." He pulled her closer so that his breath was warm against her face and moved the strands of her hair. One of the horses nickered softly as Brand lowered his head and his lips pressed intimately to hers. Inside she quivered and opened her mouth willingly to the sweet pressure of his tongue. Her hands reached upward to clutch steely shoulders as he kissed her and pulled her snug against him. Big hands, strong fingers, hot skin rubbed her lower back in sweet, seductive circles. She moaned as his fingertips skimmed her rump, then clutched both cheeks hard.

Hot desire stirred her blood. The kiss deepened and she closed her eyes, feeling as if she'd been swept away on some delicious tide of passion. She couldn't think, could barely breathe, and though warning bells clanged through her mind, she ignored them.

Together they tumbled to the ground, and Brand, as if some keeper had set him free, began undressing her. Hot, feverish hands unbuttoned her blouse and touched the lacy edge of her bra. "Dani," he whispered, his breath warm through the scanty cloth. They'd never gone this far, but she couldn't stop him—didn't want to.

He kissed her eyes, her cheeks, her neck, before moving lower and pressing wet lips to her sternum.

Trembling, she cradled his head, holding him close, her insides raging with forbidden fires as he cupped her breast then kissed it. She gasped, her nipple puckering anxiously, wanting more, so much more. He unhooked her bra, letting her breast fall free, kissing the white skin, rimming her dark circle with his tongue. She bucked on the ground, forcing his head closer, and he rolled her on top of him so that he could receive more, so that he could suckle freely while his hands worked with the zipper of her jeans.

"I want you," he said when at last he looked up at her. His face was flushed and sweaty, his eyes dark with desire.

"I want you, too."

"You don't know what you're saying."

"Yes, I do. Oh, Brand, yes, I do," she said, straddling him and sliding her crotch over the bulge in his jeans. All her doubts and reservations had fled and now desire pumped through her blood, controlled her mind. She moved as if she'd done it a hundred times, though no one had ever touched her. The power of his body, the heat of his skin, made her do things that were new, but felt so right. So natural.

"Dani, listen," he said, then sighed loudly as he saw her breasts swinging freely above him. With a raw groan he suckled again and his hands struggled with her jeans. Soon she was dressed only in white lace panties and she felt him shift beneath her, his hot lips moving anxiously, lower and lower still. His tongue rimmed her navel and she felt a tremor slide over her as he rubbed her panties with his hands, forcing her legs farther apart. She cried out when one of his fingers slipped beneath the elastic and probed gently but firmly. Hot wax seemed to melt inside her. "That's a girl," he whispered against her thigh and she writhed with an ache so deep she felt near to tears. Slowly he moved, expanding her, another finger joining the first.

"Brand, oh, Brand," she cried, from ecstasy or torment she didn't know.

"Be patient, darlin'."

Another finger touched a special spot and she rocked forward. He stripped her of her underwear and then his face, warm and beloved, was between her legs, his breath sweet and hot in her curls. Perspiration sheened across her skin and the world seemed to slip away.

"Wh-what—oh, oh . . ."

The tip of his tongue tickled her and she opened up, feeling him enter her, his hands gripping her buttocks as he kissed her and touched her where no man had dared. Sweet juices flowed and he groaned. She moved against him, rocking, the world splintering as he moved upward, rolled her on her back. And as his lips crashed down on hers, he entered her, thrusting deep, breaking the barrier that was her virginity. She cried out and he withdrew only to thrust again, pushing harder, deeper. Her mind spun in spectacular whirlpools and she moved with him, feeling their bodies join. His tempo increased, faster and faster, and she was with him, clinging to him, screaming his name, a wild thing who knew no bounds.

"Brand, oh, Brand—"

"Love me, Dani, just love me!" He threw back his head and let out a primal yell.

"I do! Ooooh—" She shuddered, the earth moving, the skies exploding as he fell gasping against her, crushing her breasts, his hands tangling in her hair.

She held him as if she would never let go. Slowly her breathing returned to normal and she realized that she was no longer a girl. For now and forever, Brandon Scarlotti had made her a woman.

# CHAPTER FIVE

"You should have told me," he said as they lay entwined together staring at the silvery leaves of the cottonwood tree that were turning in the wind.

"Told you?" she repeated, letting out a sigh of contentment.

"You were a virgin."

One side of her mouth lifted. "Okay, I was a virgin!"

"Jeez, Dani . . ."

She levered up on one elbow and her naked breast touched his chest. "Would it have mattered?"

"Yes . . . no . . . hell, how would I know?" He ran stiff fingers through his hair.

"I take it you weren't."

"Oh, for cryin' out loud!" He wanted to be angry with her or himself or anyone, but he couldn't. Seeing the spark of life in her amber eyes and the smile that twitched at the corners of her mouth, his fury dissipated into the summer-sweet air. The white horse snorted and pawed at the earth as if impatient. "I just assumed that—"

"That I'd done it?" she cut in. "Stupid, Brand. I think you were the one who told me not to assume anything."

He ignored her nipple brushing the inside of his arm. "Then I don't suppose you're on the Pill."

"Why would I be?" she asked, then the color drained from her face. With a self-deprecating laugh, she shook her head and picked a wildflower, twirled the stem, making the white petals blur like the blades of a helicopter. "I never thought I'd ever have to worry about getting pregnant."

"I think you . . . we should worry about it now."

She sighed and bit her lip. "What would you do if it happened—if I was going to have a baby?"

"Marry you," he said without a second's hesitation.

"You would?" For a moment, the light of anticipation shone in her eyes.

"I'd never leave my kid," he said flatly, "regardless of how I felt about his mother."

"Even if you didn't love her?"

"Wouldn't matter," he admitted, thinking of his own up-bringing. "A kid needs a name, a picture, a face to recognize the man who sired him."

Dani touched his arm. "What if the girl refused to marry you?"

"That wouldn't be an option." He stared at her long and hard. "Love doesn't matter." Then, as if tired of the conversation, he rolled her onto her back and held her hands over her head. "Now, let's forget about all that for now. The damage has already been done, right?"

"Right," she said, and he watched her pulse begin to throb as he raked his gaze down her body, seeing past her fading tan lines, where her bathing-suit top had covered her breasts, and looking at those luscious brown disks. He kissed her nipple and watched her respond, her pelvis tilting upward, her nest of blond curls still dewy from their last encounter. He grew hard again and knew in that instant that he was lost. No matter how much he tried, he wouldn't be able to get Dani Donahue out of his system. He could make love to her for hours and only end up hungering for more.

Closing his mind to thoughts of pregnancy, he delved into her delicious warmth again and intended to love her until he couldn't drag in another breath.

A week later, Brand drove home after an unholy day at work and spied an expensive car pulling out of the driveway. A white Mercedes. Brand's stomach lurched. As far as he knew, there was only one white Benz in the whole damned valley and that particular car belonged in Jonah McKee's vast fleet. Teeth on edge, Brand parked his bike and strode through the back door. "Ma?" he yelled, his boot heels ringing as he swept through the covered porch and kitchen. "Ma, you home? What the hell was Jonah McKee doing here?"

He found her in the living room, standing at the window, staring outside. She'd been drinking; a half-filled bottle of wine stood near her empty glass—only one. Apparently, McKee hadn't been here for a taste of cheap zinfandel.

"What's going on?" Brand asked when she let out a long sigh.

"Jonah owns this house."

"What?" Brand just stared at her. He knew that she paid a mortgage every month, but she'd never let him see the payments nor the bank statements; she'd been private about her money or lack of it for as long as he could remember. He just assumed that the house was mortgaged by the bank. "I don't get it. You have a mortgage . . ."

"I bought this place on contract—a private contract with Jonah McKee. It was all handled through the bank. For a small fee each month they do the paperwork."

Stunned, Brand just stood in the archway separating the

living room from the foyer. "I didn't even know you knew McKee."

A nostalgic smile played upon her lips. "Who doesn't know him around here?"

"But to buy the house from him . . ." Brandon was having trouble keeping up, making sense of all this.

"It's what he does, Brand. He's in the business of renting, leasing, selling and buying property. Anyway, the house isn't paid off yet. He heard through the grapevine that I'm getting married and planning to move, possibly selling, and he wanted to make sure I understood the terms of our agreement."

The hairs on the back of Brandon's neck began to rise. Somehow his mother was going to get the raw end of the deal again; he could feel it. Well, not if he had anything to say in the matter. "Terms? What terms?"

"Sell-back terms. There's a clause in the contract that says I can't sell the property to anyone else without first contacting McKee Enterprises. They—well, really Jonah—have first option or something to purchase at, and I quote, 'fair market value.'"

"Which is?" Brandon asked.

She waved as if to brush his concerns away. "Oh, he'll take care of that."

"I just bet he will."

"He's got appraisers on his payroll who'll come up with a fair price."

"I'd double-check that if I were you, Ma. Anyone on McKee's payroll will be looking out for his best interests. You should have your own appraisal."

She sighed heavily. "That's what Al says."

"For once we agree."

She looked out the window one last time, then snapped the blinds shut. "Don't worry about it. You're going to California anyway, so what does it matter?"

"Right," he said, unable to shake the feeling of impending

doom. Jonah McKee only looked out for himself. He didn't give a damn about a woman who had spent her life raising a bastard son. One way or another, the old man was going to try to fleece Venitia out of her money. "I just don't trust McKee. He's only interested in number one."

Deep furrows cut across her brow. "You don't even know him."

"Just of him."

"Careful now," she warned. "Sometimes, because of gossip, people are slapped with names they haven't earned."

The remark hit deep and close to home. His own tarnished reputation was about half truth and half the imagination of the good citizens of Dawson City and Rimrock.

She found her bottle of wine and slowly refilled her glass. "So how come you didn't tell me you knew McKee?"

"I never wanted to bother you with business or money matters."

"Has he ever been here before?"

She hesitated and her fingers seemed to clamp so hard around the stem of her glass, Brandon thought it might shatter. "A couple of times—when there were questions with the property taxes and when the house next door was being added on to." Taking a sip of her wine, she closed her eyes. "Why?"

"Because I think it's strange," he said. "Why bother with this himself? Why not send a flunky? A big shot like him, he must have a dozen on his payroll."

"I don't know, but it doesn't matter."

Brandon fingered a framed photo that was proudly displayed on a shelf in the living room. It had been taken years ago, when he was about seven. Only one front tooth had come in and Venitia was still young and pretty in a seductive, voluptuous way—a way Brand never liked to think of his mother. She and Brand were both grinning into the camera and the ocean stretched out behind them—a vast sea of gray-green complete with thundering waves crashing against the rocky shore. The photo had been taken on one of their rare vacations, this one to Cannon Beach. He set the photo aside. "Maybe you shouldn't sell the place."

"What? So now you're nostalgic?" she said with a laugh as she downed more wine.

"Nah, but . . . I know I thought you should get rid of it, but now I'm not so sure." The thought that McKee wanted this old house made Brand think it had more value than he'd first guessed. "You know, what if things don't work out with Al?"

"They'll work out," she said firmly, her eyes snapping suddenly at her son's insolence.

"You don't know that, Ma. You could keep this place, rent it to someone, maybe make a couple of hundred bucks a month. Make Al buy the new house in Washington."

"But we agreed—"

"I know, I know." He held up a hand, cutting off further argument. "Just talk to him about it and think about the future, okay? If something happens to Al—maybe he gets injured, or laid off or even dies—"

"Brand!"

"Well, or you guys split up, you'd still have the house. By that time, even the mortgage to McKee might be paid off."

Swirling the wine in her glass, she seemed to consider his line of reasoning. "I'll think about it," she finally agreed, her huge eyes meeting his. "I'll check the mortgage, see if it's possible, and if it isn't, I'll talk to Jonah . . . if Al agrees."

"Good." He felt as if he'd made a little progress.

"So, where have you been?" she finally asked as she finished her glass and set it down.

"Out." Since Dani wasn't telling her mother about their relationship, Brand had decided to keep it quiet on his end. No telling what that old busybody, Bess Jamison, might hear from Venitia and pass along to Dani's mother.

Venitia straightened a stack of magazines, then dumped the ashtray into the fireplace. "You're 'out' a lot these days."

Slanting him a knowing glance, she added, "My guess is you're involved with a girl again."

Brandon didn't answer.

"Well, just be careful, all right?"

He ignored the jab, knowing she was referring to Miranda, the police chief's daughter, and their hot, short-lived affair. He didn't want to think about that mess again. "I'm always careful," he said, lying a little. With Dani he'd been more reckless than he should have, letting his passion cloud his judgment, giving in to the pure ecstasy of loving her without thinking of the consequences.

"I guess I won't have to worry about you."

"Never should. I can handle myself," he said tightly.

"Good. And I guess this new girl doesn't mind you moving away?" She eyed her son as she wiped the ashtray with a tissue and placed the dish back on the table.

"Guess not," he said, but continued to hold his tongue because he hadn't yet told Dani of his plans. She'd changed everything. He'd thought he could leave Dawson City and never look over his shoulder, but then she'd come into his life and brought light into an otherwise dark existence. For the first time since he could remember, he doubted the wisdom of saying goodbye to this part of the country. All because of one whiskey-eyed strawberry blond woman who could touch his soul.

Dani hadn't planned on an affair; didn't know how to handle one. It wasn't anything she'd ever expected to happen to her and she was torn inside—guilt eating at her on one hand, the thrill of being with Brand on the other hand. She kept her secret to herself and didn't tell anyone about Brand. In the beginning she hadn't wanted her mother to guess that she was seeing him, but now, since they'd made love, things had become more intense. The thought of another person suspecting that she and Brand were lovers seemed a violation of their privacy and would have cheapened what was so beautiful.

Irene was suspicious, of course, because of all of Dani's prolonged absences. "If I didn't know better I'd say you were meeting some boy somewhere," Irene grumbled one Saturday morning. "You're never here when I get home from work and you spend a lot of hours studying at other kids' houses."

"I thought you wanted me to get good grades," Dani retorted. Sooner or later she'd have to tell her mother about Brand, but she didn't want to rock the boat just yet. It was too important that she keep seeing Brand and she didn't want her mother to lay down some law about avoiding him. Because Dani would have to break whatever rules Irene imposed—no matter what, she wasn't about to give up Brand. For the first time in her life, Dani Donahue was in love—head over heels in wild, passionate love.

The truth of the matter was that she *had* started studying. She couldn't very well lie about doing all this homework and then end up flunking all her courses. So she was burning the candle at both ends—going to school during the day, working with the Kellogg horses, seeing Brand on the sly, then staying up until one in the morning cracking the books. She even managed to ace the government test that she'd lied to her mother about, earning her first A in years. She should have felt good about it, instead she just felt empty.

"I knew you could do it," Irene said, retrieving the graded test when it slid out of Dani's notebook and dropped beneath the dining-room table where Dani had stacked her books. "All it takes is a little work. Look at Skye—"

Dani's smile froze on her face. She'd been looking up to Skye all her life, hoping that some of her older sister's brilliance would rub off on her. "I'm not her," she said sullenly as she dropped her backpack onto a side chair and headed into the kitchen. What would her mother think if she came to understand that Dani was only studying hard to maintain her alibi? This was getting awfully complicated.

"I know, I know," Irene said hastily. "I'm sorry. I shouldn't have compared you to your sister and I didn't mean to. Oh, Lordy, I've really done it this time, haven't I?" She followed Dani into the kitchen and tucked a strand of hair behind her ear, her hands moving nervously. "All these years I've tried to tell you how special you are, how unique, but you won't listen. You think I'm just talking through my hat, trying to bolster your self-esteem or something. I guess I am, but more than that, I'm just letting you know that I wouldn't trade you for a dozen more Skyes."

"I know." Dani grabbed a diet soda and twisted off the cap. She took a long drink and tried not to get into another argument with her mother. What was the point?

"I just want you to succeed, Danielle. At whatever it is you want to do."

"I want to train horses, Mom. That's all I've ever wanted to do. Someday I'm going to have my own ranch, and getting all the A's in the world won't help me!" She saw her mother's face fall though Irene bravely tried not to show her reaction. "I know it's not as grand as wanting to be a doctor like Skye . . . but it's what I like. What I'm good at." Another swallow of cola. If she could just get out of here.

Her mind, with a will of its own, twisted back to Brandon. Always to Brandon. Midnight walks when she sneaked out of her room, wild rides on his motorcycle with the moon shining down, racing the Kellogg horses only to end up laughing and tumbling to the ground and making love beneath the cottonwood tree where Brandon had carved their initials in a crude heart. He'd climbed up nearly to the top and done the deed, saying he wanted someone to know how he felt even if it was only God and the bravest of the Kellogg grandkids who might scale the branches and eventually see his work.

Irene licked her lips. "Getting good grades never hurts, no

matter what you end up doing in life. Even running a ranch, you've got to keep books and track of feed and animals and taxes and oh, Lordy, Dani, so many things. Owning that much land takes patience, money and hours of hard work and . . . well, honey, to be honest, you need a man to help you. It's not a job for a woman alone."

"Who says I'm going to be stupid enough to try to do it by myself?" Dani asked, then felt a cold hand clamp over her heart when she saw her mother's face turn the color of chalk.

Clearing her throat, Irene twisted her ring, a silver wedding band with a few scattered diamond chips, the ring she'd transferred to her right hand the day of Thomas Donahue's funeral some fourteen years before. "Sometimes we can't predict what will happen to us. I never thought I'd lose Tom or not remarry . . ." Her voice trailed off and Dani swallowed back a huge lump in her throat. She should never have said anything. Irene reached for a towel and absently wiped the counter. "Lucky for all of us, Jonah was there."

"Lucky?" Dani cringed at the man's name. Jonah McKee, richest man in the eastern part of the state, a man who doled out his money and his affection in well-measured sums, was a first-class bastard. He acted as if he didn't know that Irene, his secretary for ages, was half in love with him, and though he made sure that her car ran and her house was paid for, he never offered her an ounce of emotional support. But how could he? He was married. And not to Irene Donahue.

"He's been good to me. To you," Irene insisted.

Dani hesitated, took a long, bracing drink from her diet soda, then whispered, "Are you in love with him?" There. She'd asked the question that had lingered in the air for years, hanging between them, never asked, never answered.

"Of course not," her mother responded. "Don't be silly Jonah's married."

"That doesn't matter. You can love someone who's married to someone else or . . . someone who doesn't love you."

Irene's shoulders stiffened slightly and the rag stopped its smooth, circular movements. "No, Dani. I wouldn't waste my time on a man I couldn't have." The towel started moving again and Dani knew that her mother was lying for the sake of her pride.

Dani didn't blame her. Wasn't she doing exactly the same thing, hiding the fact that she was in love, denying it to everyone but herself and Brand? *Dear God, please don't let me make the same mistake.* Her insides froze at the thought. But her love with Brandon was different, wasn't it? Brandon loved her. Though he hadn't said it, he'd carved their initials in the cottonwood, made love to her so passionately that she thought she might die from ecstasy. Yes, it had to be different from her mother's pathetic love for a man who acted as if she was nothing more than a hardworking employee—a woman he took care of as a matter of obligation because her husband had died in a logging accident while working for him.

Dani finished her drink as her mother folded the towel over a stainless-steel bar screwed into the inside cupboard door, then lit a cigarette with fingers that shook a little. "Your accusations are entirely out of line."

"I didn't accuse, just asked."

"Well, I won't have you dragging Jonah's name through the mud, or mine, either, for that matter. He's a good man. A kind man. A decent man who's helped me when I needed it." She struck a match and lit up. Sucking deeply, she inhaled the smoke into her lungs as if she could calm her nerves in a single throat-scorching breath.

"He's not any of those things, Mom," Dani said, feeling that it was time to clear the air. "That's why I think you're in love with him, because you can't see him for what he really is."

"Which is?"

Dani opened her mouth. It was on the tip of her tongue to call Jonah McKee a meddling old skinflint who ruled his family with an iron fist and shackled his wife with golden handcuffs, but what did it matter? Why inflict more pain? "I don't know, Mom, I just . . . I just want you to be happy," she finally admitted upon seeing the silent agony in her mother's face. "You deserve it."

"Don't we all?" Irene said, staring out the window, one arm surrounding her waist as if to protect herself, while she held her other hand close to her head where the cigarette burned, smoke curling up to the ceiling.

She seemed so sad and Dani knew it was her fault. Why couldn't she just have taken the praise for her damned government grade and kept the conversation light? Why was it in her nature to always keep pushing?

"I just hope for your sake, Danielle, you're luckier than I was."

*Please, God, don't let her hurt anymore,* Dani silently prayed as the walls seemed suddenly to be closing in, suffocating her. The conversation was too heavy and she needed to find a way out of the house.

The phone rang and Irene answered it. Dani waited to find out if it was for her, then as Irene lowered her voice, deep in a conversation she didn't want Dani to overhear, Dani waved, grabbed her jacket and hurried out the front door. "I'll be back later."

"Dani? Wait!" Irene's voice trailed after her as she raced down the steps. "Danielle? Oh, Lordy, what now? You be back soon or call me, you hear?"

"I will. Don't worry!" Dani sang back as she tossed the jacket over her shoulders and buried her hands deep in the pockets. It was still warm outside, but Dani felt a chill settle deep in her bones.

She couldn't worry about her mother any longer; she had her own life to live. Yet, deep in the bottom of her heart, she knew she was lying to herself. For too many years, Irene, Skye and Dani had relied on no one but each other. Oh, sure, Jonah McKee had helped out along the way, but the three women had fought with each other, held each other, banded together when things got rough. Only now, with Skye gone and Dani's need for independence rearing its ugly head, it seemed as if the family had become fragmented to the point where she could lie so easily to her mother. About Brandon. Maybe it was time to come clean, tell her how she felt and hope for the best.

Taking the same path she'd used hundreds of times as a kid heading to the candy store or soda shop, she zigzagged through the familiar streets and vacant lots to the Shady Grove Café, an A-frame restaurant that had become a hangout for the locals and a Rimrock institution.

A help-wanted poster was plastered on the front door and Dani, after ordering a Coke and fries, talked to the head waitress about the job. Cyrus Kellogg was due back at his ranch in a couple of days, and unfortunately, Dani hadn't found another job doing what she loved best—working with horses.

"It's weekends," Barbara Kingsley said, straightening the hem of her apron. "Fridays from five 'til closing, same with Saturdays. One night during the middle of the week, maybe two, depending upon the other gals' shifts, and once in a while on Sundays." Barbara, a woman with a shelf of a bosom and gray wig that never looked quite natural, eyed Dani speculatively. "Would cut the heck out of dating time."

Dani thought of her moments with Brand, stolen as they were. Since they didn't openly date and met each other at secret times when no one suspected, there would still be time to see him. Smiling, she lifted a shoulder and said, "I can handle it." The bottom line was that she needed the money.

"Good." Barbara seemed pleased. "Just fill out the application and I'll give it to Joe. He'll call you in a couple of days."

Dani found a pen in the bottom of her purse and started filling out the form. Though she'd rather work outside with animals, or kids, or doing anything else, waitressing was a means to an end and she liked having her own money, which she used on clothes, gas for the car and her savings. Carefully she filled in all the blanks on the application and gave it back to Barbara when the waitress brought her basket of fries. This job would be better than the one in Dawson City. She'd probably make less in tips, but it was closer to home and sharing the car with her mother would be easier. She wasn't much for going to football games or school dances, so Friday nights weren't a big deal.

The door opened and a bell overhead tinkled loudly. "Hey, Dani!" Alison Marchant's voice chirped above the wheeze of the overloaded air-conditioning system. Alison, a cheery, happy-go-lucky girl with the most gorgeous red hair Dani had ever seen and an overbite that needed correcting, plopped down on the other side of the booth. She wiggled a French fry out of Dani's basket and pointed it at her friend. "What are you doing here?"

"What does it look like? I just filled out an application for the weekend waitress job."

Alison wrinkled her nose. "Weekends? Oooh. Bad idea, Dani." She glanced around the old building. The booths were sagging, the interior paneling dark with years of smoke and grease, the floor dingy where countless mops had shoved wax into forgotten corners. Glancing at the few other patrons, Alison leaned over the table. "I meant, what are you doing here when there's going to be a party at the lake?"

"Tonight?"

"Hmm." Alison's eyes sparkled. "A kegger."

"Where?"

"At the old Mason place. No one's been there for years and it's out of town so no cops will show up."

"I don't think so." Ever since becoming involved with Brandon, Dani had avoided parties and ignored her friends. She felt a little jab of guilt because she and Alison had been friends since second grade when Alison's parents had split up.

Both girls had grown up without a father figure in the house, though Alison still saw her dad on most weekends.

"Say you're staying over at my house," Alison persuaded. She leaned closer and snagged another French fry. "Besides, if you start working here, your social life as you know it will be over. May as well have one last fling just in case you're unlucky enough to land the job."

"I don't know," Dani hedged. But why not? Brandon was working overtime this evening and she probably wouldn't see him. That thought depressed her. Also, though she hated to admit it, she knew that something was bothering Brandon. Maybe it was his mother's upcoming marriage. From what she could glean, he didn't approve of the guy. But Brandon was a private person and rarely opened up to her. For a second, she thought that he might want to break up with her and her heart glitched. The thought of a future without him scared her to death and Dani didn't scare easily. She hated the feeling and a shadow slid ghostlike through her mind—what if she ended up like her mother? She swallowed hard.

Alison was going blithely on, stealing French fries and dipping them in catsup. ". . . so I figured, why not? A lot of kids will be there. Some from here, some from Dawson City."

"Is that so?" Brand's face came to mind, but she tucked the image away. He was working tonight; he'd said so. He wouldn't end up at a party without her. Or would he? Furious with herself for her doubts, she took a long, calming swallow of soda.

"I'll give you a ride."

"I don't know."

"Come on, Dani. What've you got to lose? A few hours with the books? What's gotten into you? We could have fun. You do remember what that is, don't you?"

"Of course, but—"

"It's probably the last party at the lake since it's already October and the nights are cooling off a little."

"All right," Dani said, dreading the party the minute the words passed her lips. But why not? Alison was right. She couldn't sit around and wait for Brandon to call, nor could she spend another minute studying the United States Government or calculus. Talk about boring. So she'd go to the party. What could it possibly hurt?

The Mason place had seen better times. The driveway was little more than two deep ruts through dry grass and spindly weeds. The old homestead had collapsed on itself leaving a mere skeleton of sun-bleached wood and a tumbling rock chimney. A worn rocking chair had fallen off what was left of the porch, the seat eaten away by time, one of the legs twisted away. There was an ancient pump that no longer brought up water and brush had grown through the thin stands of pine. Cars and pickups were parked at odd angles along the lane, but nowhere did Dani see Brand's motorcycle.

Relief washed over her. *Fool,* she silently chided herself for doubting him. But she'd never been in love before, never cared deeply. She'd had her share of boys interested in her and she'd never let herself fall in love with any of them. She was just too damned practical. Until now. Brand had changed all her firmly held views on life and love.

"What's eating you?" Alison asked as she parked her mother's car beneath the scraggly branches of a pine tree planted close to a creaking aluminum gate. Someone had sprung the rusted lock and left the chain to coil on the ground like a sleeping snake.

"Nothing," Dani said. "Just worried about getting the job, I guess."

"What's to worry? If you don't get the one at the Shady Grove, you'll find another." Alison flashed Dani one of her upbeat smiles. "Tonight, we're not gonna worry about jobs and school, okay? We're gonna party."

Dani was far from the partying mood. In fact, the few parties she'd been invited to hadn't been all that great. The two girls followed the sound of music and laughter drifting in the crisp Indian-summer air. Though the days were still hot and dry, the nights had become cool with the promise of autumn. Dry leaves crackled beneath Dani's thongs, and weeds, once supple, now gone to seed, brushed against her calves. The sun was just setting and the water was on fire, reflecting a brilliant sky of orange and pink. A rocky beach was littered with blankets, and a few of the braver souls had found an old rope tied to the branch of a crooked pine tree. They swung out over the water, let loose a scream and dropped into the frigid depths.

"Alison—hey, where's your suit?" Billy Crawford yelled and shook his head as he climbed out of the lake. He sprayed pellets of water on a couple of girls, who shrieked and nearly dropped their cups of beer.

"Hey, watch it!" one cried.

Her friend danced out of the way. "Billlly! For crying out loud, stop!"

Ignoring the girls' protests, he ran up to Alison and Dani. He was six foot three and skinny, with a few hairs on his chest and hands big enough to palm a basketball. He twirled Alison off her feet as easily as if she weighed less than a feather. "I wondered if you'd show up."

"Said I would," she teased, flirting outrageously. She and Billy had gone together since eighth grade, and though they fought as often as not, continually breaking up and getting back together, Dani assumed that someday, soon after high school, they would marry. Billy was insanely jealous of any boy who even glanced Alison's way and she was nearly as bad.

"Hi, Dani." Billy was always friendly, except when he drank too much or when another boy gave Alison too much attention. "Wanna beer?"

"Sure," Alison said with a wicked grin.

Dani shook her head. "Later."

Billy loped off to the keg and waited his turn in line with some kids Dani didn't recognize. She looked around and wondered why she'd agreed to come.

"He's so damned sexy," Alison said, eyeing Billy's buttocks and the way his swim trunks hung beneath his tan line.

Sexy wasn't the word Dani would use to describe Billy, but she didn't say it. He was big and gawky with a crooked grin and a hearty laugh. But sexy? No way. Ah, well, to each his own.

"I can't say no to him." Alison bit her lower lip and for once her smile disappeared. "You know what I mean?"

Dani knew exactly what she meant, but she didn't admit to it; if she did, Alison would start asking questions. Billy returned, balancing three plastic cups of beer. His smile was wide. "I thought you needed one," he explained, handing Dani her drink. Foam, smelling of malt and yeast, slopped over the side. "If you don't drink it, I will." His grin was guileless. He'd never been much of a student, but then Dani had that distinction herself. On the basketball court, however, Billy Crawford was pure magic, just as she was on horseback. "Cheers," he said, touching his cup to hers and slinging his free hand around Alison's tiny waist.

"Cheers."

Dani took a sip and watched as Billy guzzled his to the bottom. Alison took a gulp and licked the froth from her mouth. "Hey, that's my job," Billy said, his eyes already slightly glazed. He bent down and kissed Alison hard on the lips, one big hand still holding his empty cup, the other sliding down to grab one side of Alison's rump. Alison's spine curved easily as she arched her body and pressed against him.

Dani, embarrassed, turned away. She knew what Alison was feeling but believed that lovemaking was a private act between the two people involved. Carrying her unwanted cup, she walked to the edge of the lake, sat down, kicked off her thongs and wiggled her toes in the clear water. Ice-cold, it lapped at the bottom of her feet. An eagle swooped low over the lake as fish rose to the surface. Dani sighed. Listening to the drone of insects coming alive with the night, she propped her drink on a rock, wrapped her arms around her knees and wondered how she could get home. She could walk, she supposed, but it was over five miles to town and she was wearing thongs. Great.

She really wasn't much of a party girl, she realized as she scanned the knots of kids talking, laughing, drinking and smoking. Someone turned up the music. A couple of girls began dancing in the empty bed of a pickup parked near the ramshackle old house. Boys hooted.

She didn't belong here. That seemed to be the biggest problem in her life—the not belonging. Though she had a mother who loved her and an older sister who would do anything for her, Dani felt out of step with her small family, just as she felt out of place here. She picked up a rock and sent it skimming over the water; it skipped on the glassy surface, sending out ever-expanding ripples.

Then she heard it, the unmistakable rumble of a motorcycle engine. Scrambling to her feet, she saw the beam of a single headlight flashing behind the thin stands of pines. *Brandon!* She crossed her fingers and held her breath, realizing for the first time that she'd come here with the express hope of seeing him again.

Her breath caught in her throat as she watched him stop the bike and take in the party. His stare was hard and sure and landed with heart-stopping intensity directly on her. Climbing off his bike, he ignored greetings from his friends.

"Hey, Scarlotti, where ya been?"

"How about a beer?"

"Hell, I'd given you up for dead."

Brand didn't even glance in the direction of the shouts, swore under his breath and strode over the mashed-down grass to Dani. "What do you think you're doing here?" he demanded, his voice a harsh whisper.

"I just—I mean Alison invited me to—" She saw the fury in his eyes and stopped. "Well, what did you expect me to do, Brand, just sit around and wait for you?"

"No, but I didn't expect this."

"It's not like we ever go out—"

He stopped dead in his tracks, whirled and brought his face to within inches of hers. Glaring at her, he growled, "And whose idea was that, hmm?" His lips barely moved. "Who didn't want anyone to know we were seeing each other?"

"But—"

"Come on," he said, dragging her with him.

"You've been to dozens of parties."

Again he swore and his lips thinned. "Yeah, and I've been hauled into j.d. court more times than I want to remember. All the trouble I ever got into started out as innocent fun." His grip tightened around her arm. "Let's go."

"You can't tell me what to do!"

"Like hell, Dani. This is for your own good." Then as if hearing himself, he stopped, placed his hands firmly on his hips and drew in a long, calming breath. When he faced her again, some of his hostility had fled. "You want to stay here or come with me?" he asked, his fingers slowly straightening as he released her. They were standing in what had once been a rose garden. Most of the bushes had died long ago and only a couple of hardy, untrimmed plants had survived to trail thorny vines that clutched at her legs and shorts.

"I want to go with you . . . you know I do. But I don't like to be manhandled or told what to do or treated like a child."

A tic developed near his eye. "I didn't mean—oh, damn it all anyway." He gazed at her then and offered her a sad, knowing smile. "I think we should leave before the cops come and crash this party."

"And go where?"

Sighing, he glanced at the darkening sky. "I wish I knew," he said under his breath, before rubbing the back of his neck in frustration. "Look . . . I need to talk to you. Alone." For the first time, she noticed the shadows in his eyes, as if he was hiding something from her, carrying some unspeakable burden.

"Then let's not waste any more time," she said, taking his hand and walking quickly toward his motorcycle. His fingers, usually so warm, felt cold despite the heat of the evening. His jaw was clamped so hard, the bone showed through on his chin. Lines of tension framed his mouth. "What's wrong?" she asked, dread beginning to drip into her bloodstream.

"Everything." In the distance, she heard the distinctive wail of sirens. Brandon spewed out an oath and pulled her hard toward his motorcycle. "Hell," he grated. "I knew it! Come on!" She didn't need any further urging and slid onto the bike behind him.

The sirens screamed closer. Several other kids heard them.

"Son of a bitch!"

"Clear out, everybody! Cops!"

"Leave the damned keg!"

Footsteps pounded. Engines fired and roared. Tires screeched over the oaths and panicked warnings of the party-goers.

Brandon wound up the Harley and headed, not back down the lane toward the main highway and the approaching police cars, but through the grass past the old house to a strip of beach rimming the lake. "Where are we going?" she yelled, tears blurring her vision as the bike screamed through the night.

"Anywhere!"

The cycle skimmed the lake as the sirens drowned out every other sound. Dani wrapped her arms around his waist, pressed her cheek against his broad back, held on tight and wondered why he'd come for her, how he'd known where she was. Not that it mattered.

Red, blue and white lights strobed the night as Brand twisted hard on the handlebars. The bike turned sharply to the right, headed deep into the forest. The back wheel nearly spun out, dirt spraying, but then they were riding on a dusty trail, overgrown with weeds and barely wide enough for the Harley. Branches slapped at their faces. Dani closed her eyes and clung to him as the path wound ever upward toward Elkhorn Ridge.

Suddenly he slowed. Nearly at the highway, Brandon stopped, turned off the bike's headlight and waited. In the distance, a voice crackled over a bullhorn as the police rounded up the kids unlucky enough to have been caught. Tickets for minor in possession would be slapped on the partygoers and they'd all be hauled into jail.

It wouldn't be the end of the world, but still, Dani was thankful that she'd avoided the humiliation and embarrassment of calling her mother from the county jail.

Eventually, the music was turned off, the voice on the bullhorn faded away, and the noise of engines being started carried up to the ridge. Soon, even the sounds of cars leaving the old Mason place gave way to the gentle stillness of the night.

They didn't move, but stayed astride the bike, hearts pounding. Dani could barely breathe. A bat flew overhead and an owl hooted softly before Brandon, satisfied that they wouldn't be overheard, climbed off the bike. He walked to the edge of the ridge and looked at the quiet waters of Elkhorn Lake, shimmering with the reflection of thousands of stars.

"I thought you were smarter than that," he finally said as he kicked a pebble over the cliff edge and listened to it tumble ever downward, bouncing along the ledges of rock and dirt.

"Than what?"

"Than me." He closed his eyes a second. "Whatever you do, Dani, don't make the same mistakes I did."

"You survived."

"I was lucky."

She held back the fear that something horribly wrong was happening, that he was working up to something more devastating than being caught at a party. Though she didn't want to know, she'd always been a person who faced trouble straight on. "What's wrong?" she asked, her voice shaking a little. "Brand?"

He came to her then and kissed her long and hard, his body flexing against hers in desperation, his hands tangling in her hair. "Dani, Dani, Dani," he whispered as his lips molded over hers. "Oh, Dani, I love you."

She tingled at the words and all her reservations fled. She kissed him back with a renewed hunger, wanting to give, hoping to take, feeling his fingers against her skin, anxious and strong, as they tugged off her clothes. Kissing, touching, caressing, while the night breeze skimmed her bare skin. He kicked off his boots as she tore at his clothes. He pressed hot lips against her neck, her breasts, her legs, and she writhed in anticipation, his fever infecting her as they finally joined, his hard body thrusting into her moistness, penetrating her body and soul, lifting her above the pine trees to the starry night where the constellations seemed to blur and dance behind her eyes. Clinging to him, moving to his wild, desperate rhythm, she felt the world spin off its axis and her body convulse against his. He fell against her, breathing hard, whispering words of love, holding her as if he'd never let go.

"I love you, Dani. Believe me," he said, gasping as he rolled over on his back onto a rough bed of pine needles. He cradled her head next to his, his muscles strident, his fingers gently caressing her chin.

"I love you, too, Brand," she said, happier than she'd been in all her life. She gazed up at the moon and smiled.

He hesitated, then his arms around her tightened. "And that's what makes this so difficult."

"Difficult?" she repeated, fear drumming in her heart. "What?"

He hesitated, then blurted, "I have to leave."

"Leave? Now? Where?" she asked, laughing, though her nerves were suddenly stretched thin. She heard the sound of doom in his voice. "You mean go home, right?"

"I mean leave Oregon. For good."

"And go where?" she asked, panic taking over. Surely he was just kidding her, but the pain on his face convinced her that something was very, very wrong.

"California. L.A. I've been offered a job."

"But you have a job here—"

"A dead-end job, Dani. I need to start somewhere new."

"No!" She tried to pull away from him, but he held tight, anticipating her reaction. "No! No! No!"

"Shhh. Just listen."

"That's why you had to come and find me, that's why you had to drag me up here and . . . and make love to me one last time?"

"I didn't mean—"

"Bull!" She struggled, writhing like a wounded snake, but the hands around her were steel manacles, holding her fast. "You knew this was going to happen! You knew and you let me fall in love with you!" Anger shot through her and she wanted to scream, to kick, to curse the fates, to pound his chest in frustration.

"I didn't count on falling in love with you."

"Love? You love me?" She flung her hair out of her eyes. "If you loved me, you wouldn't leave me!"

He swallowed hard and his eyes shimmered in the darkness. She was lying atop him, her hair falling around her face in tangled waves, her naked chest heaving with each painful breath. "I don't have a choice, Dani. What do you expect me to do? Stay here, a bastard known by everyone in the county, work for Red the rest of my life, barely scratch out a decent wage because no one else will give me a break?"

"You don't have to—"

"Can't you understand that I have to start over and make something of myself, something better than being Venitia Scarlotti's mistake?"

She gasped. "You're not a mistake. You're wonderful. You're everything—"

"Stop it, Dani. Don't," he begged, and his voice, already hoarse, cracked. "Don't you know how hard this is for me?"

"Oh, please, no," she whispered, trembling, cold from the inside out. Somewhere in the back of her mind, she heard a voice telling her that if she loved him, really loved him, she would let him go. Love held no one prisoner and she had too much pride to beg—even for Brandon. A roar filled her head, a desperate roar not unlike surf crashing against cliffs. "Then go," she heard herself saying as she tried to roll off him. "Just leave."

"Not this way."

"Brand, please, if you have to go, just do it." Tears were running down her face and she fought against breaking down altogether. "Please. Don't drag it out."

"You're right," he said, but kissed her one last time. That was her undoing. Her throat closed in on itself. They made love all night long in the forest above the shores of Elkhorn Lake. Tenderly. Desperately. Knowing that it was over.

She watched him leave in the gray light of dawn and suffered her mother's pained expression and lecture for making her worry. And she never told him she was pregnant, nor did she ever breathe his name to another living soul. She would never tie him down, never force him into a life he didn't want.

She took extra credits, graduated early, left Rimrock for a

while, and with the ever-present help of Jonah McKee, gave up Brand's baby to a nameless couple who, she was assured, would give him everything he needed or wanted in life—especially a loving mother and father.

Gifts she could never provide.

And she never expected to see Brandon Scarlotti again.

# CHAPTER SIX

So now Brand had returned, acting as if nothing had happened between them, literally planting himself on her doorstep. Dani glanced down at the rental agreement and the check in her hands. She could tear them both up, tell Max she'd changed her mind and Brand to take a hike, but what good would that do?

He couldn't hurt her again. Or could he?

*If you let him, Dani. Only if you let him.*

When he'd left Dawson City, she'd been bereft. Heart-broken. Certain that he'd write or call. She'd planned to take off after him, once he settled down. But as the weeks passed and she hadn't heard a word from him, she'd finally faced the painful fact that it was over, even though she'd been pregnant with his child.

She'd been scared, her life turned inside out. Her mother had been shocked, her knees nearly giving way when Dani, stuttering, had confided in her.

"What—oh, God, no," she'd whispered, tears starring her lashes. "Dani, are you certain?"

From that point on, Irene had been a pillar of strength, but

Dani had been forced to rely on her mother and Jonah McKee to make everything work.

Giving up her son had been the most difficult task she'd ever faced. No amount of telling herself it was for the best ever chased away the guilt. But from the point that a nurse had taken away her son and left her with suddenly empty arms, Dani had become determined and strong, her own person. She planned to get on with her life and try to close her mind to the past, never letting another man near her. Until Jeff. A good-time cowboy type with an easy smile and a carefree live-for-the-moment attitude, he'd been the antithesis of Brandon, a man who wasn't the least bit threatening.

On a whim, they'd married. But their quick elopement to Reno had been the start of the deterioration of their relationship. Jeff hadn't been suited to married life. The responsibilities were too heavy and Dani's need for children scared him. He found other women and she divorced him. They left on speaking terms, and once again she promised herself that she'd never get involved with another man. She'd dedicate her life to the ranch, and as soon as she was on her feet, she'd adopt a child, if not a baby, then an older boy or girl. It didn't matter. And she'd locate her own boy, wherever he was.

But she hadn't counted on seeing Brand again nor had she ever thought they'd be next-door neighbors. "Oh, Lordy," she whispered, borrowing a phrase her mother used whenever a situation seemed too complicated to deal with.

Well, she wasn't the rebel seventeen-year-old girl he'd left; she was a full-grown woman now with some measure of maturity. Not that he seemed to care. In their meeting at the ranch she'd acted as if they'd only been casual acquaintances. His agreement hurt a little, but she wasn't going to let it bother her. She and Brand were ancient history. "So stop beating yourself up about it," she told herself as she tucked the deed and check into her back pocket and turned her attention back to Typhoon. "Sorry," she said, scratching the horse between her eyes. "You've been awful patient." Pushing all thoughts of Brandon out of her mind, she unwound the reins from the top rail and led her horse to the stables. No matter what, she wasn't going to let a man, *any* man get the better of her again. Especially Brandon Scarlotti.

Dani tossed the currycomb into a bucket, unclasped Typhoon's bridle and watched as the mare took off with a snort, galloping wildly over the packed dirt near the stables to join up with the rest of Dani's small herd. Mares and foals picked at the stubble, tails switching, ears flicking.

In another field, the cattle were all lying in the bleached grass, their dusty hides black, gray, dun and red. She and Jeff had experimented, crossing black Angus with white-faced Herefords and even Brahmans. The lazy beasts lay in the shade, flies collecting on their faces as they slowly chewed their cuds.

She wasn't much of a cattlewoman; the bovine part of the ranch had been Jeff's domain, of which, she found out later, he knew little. She would sell off most of the herd this year, but if she could afford to, she'd keep a few head because a part of her enjoyed the lumbering, seemingly docile cattle. Though they could be startled or even dangerous, they appeared slow and lovably dim-witted when compared to her feisty, high-spirited horses corralled in neighboring fields. "You're all right," she assured them, as if they could hear or understand her.

Carrying the bucket to the stables, she worked the kinks from her neck and tried not to think about Brandon or the fact that she was going to be living next door to him for the next three hundred and sixty-five days.

"One day at a time," she muttered as she eyed the sacks of grain and mentally calculated how long they'd last—probably until the first of the year. Now that Brand was paying the lion's share of the rent, she would be able to survive here. But for how long? She knew that the owner of the property,

Seth Macgruder, would like to sell the place to her. Seth and his wife, Katherine, had lived here for forty years before Katherine had died of a stroke and Seth, due to arthritis, had been forced to move to a retirement center.

Dani had always dreamed of having a small working ranch—nothing fancy, just a place of her own. The old Macgruder homestead had seemed perfect.

Now she had to share it. With Brandon Scarlotti. The father of the baby she had given up for adoption eleven years earlier. She'd balmed her conscience over the years, convincing herself that it was right not to tell him about the baby. After all, he'd taken off for California without a backward glance.

*But what about now? Doesn't he deserve to know the truth, now that he's here? Not saying anything is pretty close to lying and you swore off lying a long time ago.*

"Damn it all anyway!" Why did he have to come back now?

Dropping the bucket on the back porch, she kicked off her boots and marched into the kitchen. She'd have to tell him that he was a father; it was the only decent thing to do. "Great. Just great." How would he react to the notion that he had an eleven-year-old son who was probably just starting to latch onto a major growth spurt? Her throat felt suddenly dry. Biting down on her lip, she opened the refrigerator and grimaced at the few items stocked on the wire shelves. A pitcher of iced tea, yesterday's soup still in the saucepan and a head of lettuce that had seen crisper days. She'd never been much of a cook or a housekeeper and had preferred working outdoors to spending any time inside.

Sighing, she poured herself a glass of tea, searched for a lemon that didn't exist and contented herself by opening the drawer near the door and finding her pack of cigarettes. As she stared out the window to the paddock where several pregnant mares were grazing, she lit up and drew the smoke deep into her lungs. "For old times' sake," she said, exhaling a soft white cloud. She saw her reflection in the glass and frowned.

Is this what just seeing Brandon again could do? Disgusted, she squashed out her cigarette and crumpled the pack in her fist. After giving up the habit years before, she'd started smoking when Jeff had moved out; now it was time to stop again. She was over Jeff, over the pain of the divorce and ready to make it on her own. She didn't need a man and she certainly didn't need nicotine to see her through. By God, Brandon was *not* going to change all that!

But as she sipped her iced tea and leaned against the edge of the table, she felt the letter in the back pocket of her jeans, reminding her that a part of her life was unfinished. She'd never registered herself as a mother looking for a child, never tried to make contact because of Jeff. Besides, she'd always figured that she'd made a decision that couldn't be changed. Jonah McKee had promised her that the boy had been placed with a loving couple who would give her boy everything he needed.

Now, of course, she and the rest of the county knew that Jonah had been a liar. She drained her glass. Jonah McKee was dead—murdered—and by his death, all the secrets of his life had come to light. Jonah McKee had made his own rules, played his own game. To Jonah, the law had been meant to be broken. So why should she trust his word that he had indeed placed her son with a loving, well-to-do family? For all she knew, Jonah could have given or sold the boy to anyone.

"Oh, God," she whispered, denying the horrid fears that had been with her ever since she'd handed her son back to the nurse in the hospital. She should have demanded to meet the couple, checked to see that they were real. She watched the mares nuzzle their spindle-legged foals and a huge lump filled her throat. It was time to find out. After eleven years of second-guessing herself, Dani needed to find her baby, assure herself that he was being well taken care of.

She wondered what he looked like—fair like the Dona-hues or dark-skinned like his father? The few seconds she'd held him, he'd been red and wailing and she'd thought he looked like the man who had sired him, but what had she known? The baby had only been minutes old and she'd been a kid herself. A kid who just kept making mistakes.

Her first mistake had been getting involved with Brandon Scarlotti, the second had been becoming pregnant, the third losing contact with her son.

It was time to rectify a few things.

Dani considered herself a practical woman not prone to flights of whimsy. She believed in God, but didn't attend church, was convinced that a person made her own way in the world, rarely catching a break, and that people created their own destinies. She didn't believe in fate or kismet or great epiphanies, but she couldn't fight the feeling that some greater force was playing with her life today. Why else would she discover the letter to her newborn baby on the very day that she was going to start life living next door to Brandon?

*Destiny.*

"More like disaster," she told herself as she pulled the letter from her back pocket, scanned it once more, then struck a match and burned the damned thing, letting the dark ashes fall into the sink.

Maybe it was time to stop letting the world spin around her. Maybe it was time to be in control of her own future. Her own life. Her child's. She had rights.

Fingers trembling, she opened the cupboard and pulled out an address book she'd had for years. Flipping the pages, she found the number for Sloan Redhawk, a private investigator who had recently married Casey McKee, Max's younger sister.

Casey and Sloan lived outside of Warm Springs now and his office was in their small ranch house. Swallowing back the doubts of over eleven years, Dani dialed, closed her eyes and waited. After four rings, the phone was answered by a machine, with Sloan's voice giving instructions.

As the taped message played and she waited for the beep,

she cleared her throat. "Hi. This is Dani Stewart, Sloan, and I want to hire you. There's someone I want you to locate for me—"

The telephone clicked and Sloan answered. "Just walked in," he said. "What's up?"

Dani's voice sounded strangled and her heart was thudding wildly. "I, um, I need your help."

"Name it."

She could barely breathe. Her palms were slick with sweat "I don't know if you had any idea, but I had a baby a long time ago. Eleven years. And . . . and I've lost all contact with him. The adoption was handled by Jonah McKee and I was hoping—" she crossed her fingers and took a deep breath "—I was hoping that you would help me find my son."


"How do you know Dani?" Max asked Brand as he guided his truck along the smooth county road that rimmed Wildcat Creek.

Settled low on his back, Brand glared out the window and barely heard the question.

"You grew up in Dawson City, didn't you?" Max was nothing if not persistent.

"Yeah." Brand rubbed his chin, feeling a day's worth of stubble and wishing to high heaven that he'd never set eyes on Dani Donahue again. She brought back too many memories of a time he'd tried desperately to forget. Though he'd known there was a chance he'd see her again, a high probability that she'd never moved away from her family, he hadn't expected to be living next door to her; nor had he anticipated the rush of emotion that had swept over him. Hell, one look at her and he was a randy teenager again. What a dumb reaction. "We ran with the same crowd for a while." No reason to lie.

"She never mentioned it." Max downshifted as the truck started climbing toward the summit of Elkhorn Ridge. Max's brows drew together in strict concentration, as if he was trying to figure out a puzzle but didn't have all the pieces.

"She didn't, eh? Well, it wasn't that big of a deal," Brand lied, his chest constricting a bit, the memories he'd tried to suppress for years rising from the back of his mind like the morning mist on Elkhorn Lake. Near this very canyon, he and Dani had spent their last night together, making love until the sun had painted the sky a pale golden hue. Guts churning, he willed away the memories that he'd managed to bury without too much trouble. All those years in California, he'd forced himself not to pine for her, had been determined not to think about her after the first few months. Their lives had been on different courses and he'd told himself that their affair was just the passionate throes of youth. So why, with just one glance from her amber eyes, did she manage to awaken all those ghosts of the past? With a single look, nearly twelve years seemed stripped away.

He studied the countryside. The road was narrow at the summit, and far below, the creek sliced through Stardust Canyon.

He realized that Max was still waiting for more of an explanation, more specifics to explain his sister-in-law's reticence to lease to Brand. "As I said, I knew Dani a long time ago, just before my mother got married and I took off for California."

"She didn't seem to want to lease to you."

"She didn't, did she?" Brand acknowledged with a bitter smile. "Well, I was always getting into trouble."

"You ever date?"

"No," Brand said quickly. It was the truth. "We just ran into each other at parties. That kind of thing." He found his sunglasses and settled them onto the bridge of his nose, and Max, for the moment, seemed appeased. He grew quiet, nearly brooding, and for a minute, Brand thought that he was digesting everything he'd learned this afternoon until Brand realized where they were—the very spot where Jonah McKee had died.

Max's gaze drifted from the ribbon of asphalt to the steep canyon walls. Brand guessed from the gossip he'd heard that Max was thinking of his bastard of a father, who had been driving this stretch of road when Ned Jansen, a man he'd swindled, had taken the law into his own hands and forced Jonah's Jeep off the road. Jonah McKee had met a sudden and brutal death in the swift waters of Wildcat Creek at the bottom of the ravine. A fitting end, Brand thought, feeling not a drop of remorse for the man.

"You know Dani well?"

"Well enough," Brand said. The Jeep was getting hot. Too close. He loosened his tie. He didn't want to remember Dani, the girl he'd left behind when he'd started over. It had been best for both of them. They'd been on a collision course ever since they'd first met. "But like I said, it was ages ago."

"There it is," Max said, the shimmering waters of Elkhorn Lake visible through the trees.

Brand felt a small grain of satisfaction. This was his new project. Long ago he'd decided that Elkhorn Lake, nearly a mile wide and several miles long, would be a perfect place for a new resort. Already the clear waters were a haven for speedboats, water-skiers, fishing craft and even houseboats. Several farmers had sold adjoining properties on the north end of the lake and the deal was coming together. That part of his life seemed to be working, but it was the only part. He had his mother and half brother to deal with, and now there was Dani. Beautiful, independent Dani.

He was still brooding about her when the town of Rimrock came into view. As they turned onto River Drive, Max slowed for the speed limit. He glanced at Brand. "I think you should know something about Dani."

"What's that?" Brand braced himself.

"She was married."

"So I gathered."

"It didn't work out. The guy turned out to be an irresponsible bastard who ran around on her."

Brand held on to his temper, but the term "bastard" always set his teeth on edge and the thought of a man cheating on Dani only made it worse.

"Well, it's over now," Max went on. "The divorce was final six or eight months ago. She's tough as nails on the outside but . . . well, she's still picking up the pieces."

"Oh."

"She doesn't need someone messing with her mind." Max glared at Brand as if he knew his darkest secrets.

"Someone? Meaning me?"

"Meaning anyone. She's working like hell to get back on her feet and I don't want to see her knocked down again."

"Sounds like a warning."

"Just a piece of advice. Look, Scarlotti, I'm not blind. I saw the way she reacted when she saw you. I don't know what happened between you two and I don't want to. Besides, it's none of my business."

"You got that right."

"Just be careful, okay? Tread softly."

"I'm not interested, okay? We were friends a long time ago, got into a little trouble—drinking under age, that kind of thing—but that was all."

Max wasn't buying it. His expression clouded. "Whatever you say, Scarlotti. I just wanted you to know the ground rules."

He parked in a reserved spot in the lot for McKee Enterprises. They shook hands, and Brandon, with his new lease tucked into his briefcase, climbed into his car—a new midnight blue Mercedes—and drove to the Lucky Star Motel a few blocks away. There, he wedged his car between a rattletrap of a pickup and a dirty station wagon that sported one door held closed with bailing twine and a hand-scratched plea—Wash Me—scrawled on the back window. So much for blending in. His gleaming luxury car stood out like the proverbial sore thumb.

The Mercedes would have to go. It worked in Southern California, where it was almost a necessity to make bankers, investors and rivals understand you meant business, but here, where everyone drove four-wheel-drive rigs and pulled horse trailers, the car would be a hindrance. People wouldn't be in awe so much as envy. Brand was a practical man. The Mercedes would go and he'd buy a Jeep—one that was three or four years old at that.

He pocketed his keys and climbed the outside stairs of the shoddy motel. He could afford better, but this one had had the first vacancy sign he'd seen when he drove into town yesterday. He hadn't bothered to move to fancier quarters and he had no intention of staying with his mother and half brother. She begrudgingly had taken his advice and kept the house, and when her marriage to Al had disintegrated, she and her son, Chris, had moved back to Dawson City. Brand wasn't anxious to be constantly reminded of his youth, so he'd found his own place.

"Great, so you moved in next door to Dani Donahue." He unlocked the door and stepped into the room. It smelled of stale cigarette smoke and some kind of rug deodorizer that was supposed to be fragrant. Cracking open a window, he muttered, "Stewart. Dani *Stewart*. She was married. Remember that, okay? She's probably still hung up on the guy." He slung his tie over the back of a chair and unbuttoned his shirt. What was Max's warning all about? How much did he know about Brandon's affair with Dani? Hell, it had been ten—no—nearly twelve years ago. Ancient history.

But it was still there. That sizzle. He'd felt it when she'd raised her golden eyes to his and notched her chin up a degree in silent defiance. She might have settled down, become a model citizen, but lurking in the amber depths of her eyes was the spirit of a rebel, the girl who had straddled his Harley and, without a lesson, driven off; leaving him stranded one night when they were alone together. The girl who had laughed at his ambitions to make something of himself. The girl who had told him that it didn't matter if you were rich or poor. The girl who had skipped school to spend the afternoon in a field making love with him, the girl who had willingly given him her virginity and adoration. The girl he'd purposely left behind.

A headache began at the base of his skull where his neck muscles were clenched into tight knots. He didn't need to remember her small breasts pointing upward to a cloud-scattered sky. He didn't want to think about the long, supple legs and the thatch of red-blond curls at their apex. It wasn't smart to concentrate on how her spine had arched off the carpet of grass and wildflowers, how her whole body had jolted every time he'd entered her, how her legs had wrapped around his naked torso, how she'd smiled upward, breathing rapidly, her hair fanned out on the grass as she'd clung to him, her sweat-slickened body melding so perfectly to his.

He'd spent every waking hour trying to find ways to be with her, making love to her in fields, barns, in the back seat of his mother's old Ford, in the river while skinny-dipping. Wherever he could.

And she'd let him—she'd reveled in his lovemaking, enjoying it as much as he.

"Damn, what a mess." He shouldn't have signed the lease. It would be impossible living next to her and not remembering. He stripped off his shirt, poured himself a drink and walked onto the balcony, where he stared across the railroad tracks and watched a half-starved dog nudging through the garbage. Brandon whistled and the beast took off, running and ducking through the shadows as if he'd been beaten a hundred times before. Brand felt an immediate kinship with the dog—a setter of some kind. He knew what it felt

like to be beaten down so far you never thought you'd climb
up again.

He took a sip of his liquor and scowled as it burned a path
down his throat. He didn't drink all that much—usually considered it a crutch. With an oath he poured the Scotch onto the
bleached barkdust two stories below. Things had changed
since he'd been here last. He'd left town at the bottom and
come back on top.

Everything would be just fine, except that he didn't know
what the hell he was going to do about Dani.

"I was wonderin' when you'd show up," Venitia said,
reaching for her glass as Brand walked through the front door.
The smell of stale smoke, cheap perfume, cleaning solvent
and grease hung in the air just as it always had. If he'd crossed
the threshold with his eyes closed, he would have recognized
the odors of the home where he'd spent his youth. Even
though there had been several years when Venitia hadn't lived
in the house while she and Al were living in Washington,
those years when Brand had rarely seen her, the little bungalow hadn't changed.

"I had business in Rimrock." Striding into the living room,
he felt the same cloying feeling he'd experienced as a teenager that the dingy wallpapered walls were about to close in
on him.

His mother was sitting in a corner of the couch, one foot
propped on an ottoman, the television turned down low. A
talk show was in progress. Newspapers were spread on the
coffee table and a half-worked crossword puzzle had been
transformed into a coaster for her glass. One of her menagerie
of cats wandered across the back of the couch, a second was
seated on the window sill, tail switching as he stared through
the glass at birds fluttering around a feeder.

The phone rang and she answered it quickly. "Hello . . .

No, he's not here right now. Can I take a message or tell him who called? . . . I'm not sure, any time now . . . all right, then." She hung up and sighed. "Your brother. Not even twelve and the girls are calling. Just like you."

"I don't remember the girls calling."

"They did," she said with a wistful smile. "Night and day for a while."

"I was older."

"Times were different."

He hadn't come here to discuss his adolescence; in fact, he'd been reminded of that painful time of his life too much lately. *Get used to it. Living next door to Dani is only going to make it worse.* Settling onto one of the overstuffed arms of the couch, he asked, "How're you feeling?"

The corners of her mouth tightened. "I'm fine."

"That's not what the doctor told me."

"He shouldn't have told you anything." She reached for her glass and took a long swallow.

He cringed inside knowing that every drink was killing her bit by bit. Her liver was already damaged and she wasn't doing it any favors. Cirrhosis was in her future if she didn't abstain. But her dependence upon "a couple of glasses of wine" hadn't diminished over the years. How many times had he come home from school to find her passed out on the couch? How many times had he cooked dinner himself— usually canned spaghetti or macaroni and cheese or peanut butter sandwiches? He wondered if his kid brother did the same and felt guilty for not doing something about the situation earlier. He'd tried, right after Venitia's divorce from Al, but she'd shunned all his attempts at help.

"I thought you gave that up." He tried not to sound as if he were standing behind a pulpit as he motioned toward the glass in her hand.

"And I thought you agreed not to lecture me."

"I'm just concerned about your health."

"My health. Not yours."

"What about Chris?"

She finished her drink. "He's doin' okay."

Brand sat down on the edge of the sofa. "He's not doing okay. He wrote me a letter. Said he was worried about you."

"I'm—we're both doin' fine." A calico cat crawled across her lap and settled in, purring softly. Venitia absently patted the animal's head. "I know you think you can come in here and wave your money around and make things better, but you can't."

"You could move. I found a house closer in—"

"I don't want to move. I like it here. You're the one who talked me into keeping it," she reminded him with a smile. "And you were right. It's bought and paid for now."

"But you could have a newer place with a garage and a sun porch and—"

"And strings attached. No more. I had enough of that when I owed Jonah," she said with a sad shake of her head. "No thank you, son. I know that your intentions are probably for the best, and I appreciate your concern, but just leave me alone."

"Maybe you've been alone too much."

"I've got Chris. So what if Al turned into a jerk and left us behind?" She found an empty pack of cigarettes, crumpled it and tossed it into a brown paper bag she used as a waste-basket. Her lips pursed. "Never had much luck with men," she said reflectively as a hummingbird flitted to a feeder near the front window. "Your pa took off without even botherin' to marry me and then there was Al." Clucking her tongue, she shook her head. "He couldn't stick around, either. I know you think I should move. Start over. But this is my home, Brand. It may not be the fanciest house in town, but it's mine and I feel safe here. Comfortable."

They'd been over this ground a hundred times. "Okay, but at least let me fix it up for you. Weatherstrip the doors, put in double-paned windows, shore up the porch, that sort of thing."

Sighing, she pushed herself to her feet. "You don't owe me anything."

"I know that."

"You already pay most of my bills."

"I can afford it."

"It's not right, a son taking care of his mother. Should be the other way around." She crossed to a secretary pushed into one corner, opened a drawer and found a fresh pack of cigarettes.

"You did take care of me."

"Not very well."

"The best you could, Ma. Now I'm able to afford to help you out a little."

She tapped the pack on the desktop before opening it. "I don't like taking handouts, even from my own son."

He wasn't going to argue with her. "The bottom line is that this is your decision. Just don't think of it as charity."

Footsteps clomped on the front porch. The door swung open and banged hard against the wall. "Sounds like your brother's home," Venitia said as she lit up. Relief crossed her eyes and Brand realized that Chris was giving her the same worries that she'd been through with him.

His half brother thundered into the room. He was a skinny kid, tall for his age, with dark brown hair, green eyes and the hint of what would someday be a mustache. Though only eleven, he could easily pass for fourteen. "Hey, Brand!"

"Hey."

"Is that *your* car?" he asked, eyes round as saucers.

"'Fraid so."

"Cool!"

"Want a ride?"

"Are you kiddin'?" He was practically bouncing off the walls. The kid was energy in motion. Though it was eight degrees outside, he wore long baggy jeans, a long-sleeved flannel shirt tossed over a ratty T-shirt and a baseball cap turned backward.

"Oh, Lord," Venitia whispered.

Brand tossed Chris the keys. "I'll be right there." Chris, all arms and legs, sprinted out the door.

Venitia sighed, a soft cloud of smoke trailing from her mouth. "I'm afraid he's a little out of control. He didn't take Al's leaving very well, and he's discovering girls or they're discovering him—they call all the time."

"Does he call them back?"

"Not really. He'd rather be skateboarding or in-line skating, but he's beginning to show some interest."

"He's too young."

"You were twelve."

"No way—"

"Polly Henzler started calling you in the seventh grade."

"She was just a kid."

"You didn't think so at the time." Venitia peered through the window. "Uh-oh, he's in the driver's seat. That's a dangerous sign."

Brand started for the door. "We'll be back in an hour or two. You need anything from town?"

"A jug of milk and a bottle of—" She cut herself off and smiled slightly. "Milk'll do."

He walked on the porch just as he heard the engine rev. Vaulting over the rail and a row of withering petunias, he raced to the car and convinced his half brother to slide into the passenger seat.

"This is one kickin' car," Chris said, his dirty fingers caressing the leather interior gently. "How much did it cost?"

"Too much." Brand looked over his shoulder and reversed out of the two gravel ruts that were his mother's driveway.

"Are you rich?" Chris angled his head upward, his eyes squinting against the sun.

"I do all right."

"Are you a millionaire?"

"What kind of a question is that?"

"An easy one."

"Don't you know it's rude to—"

"Are you a millionaire?" Chris insisted, playing with the electronic windows.

Brand slid the kid a look and slipped the car into drive. "None of your business."

"A billionaire?"

"No."

"So you are a millionaire!" Chris let out a long, low whistle. "When I grow up, I'm gonna be just like you instead of a loser like my old man."

"Al's not a loser." Brand forced himself not to wince.

Chris's smile fell away from his face and he looked suddenly older than his years. His jaw jutted forward defiantly and his lips were pulled hard against his teeth. "Yeah? Well, what do you call a bastard who leaves his wife and kid?"

"Maybe he was just—"

"A loser." Chris slid down in his seat and stared out the windshield. "I don't want to talk about him."

Brand understood. He'd never met his own father, never seen a picture of the old man. Kendall had had enough of a conscience to send money orders every other month or so— no letter included. Venitia had never heard from him again, but she'd decided to have her baby alone despite the fact that her parents had disowned her and her sister, good old Aunt Roma, had never spoken to her since.

Frowning at the dark turn of his thoughts, Brandon drove Chris to McDonald's for a burger and soda.

"Someday I'm gonna have a car just like this," Chris said around a mouthful of his cheeseburger as they drove home.

"What kind of car you drive doesn't make a difference."

"Sure it does," Chris argued and Brand held his tongue. He

remembered once thinking that if he was as rich as Max McKee and had a dad who bought him expensive cars and boats, he'd have the world by the tail.

"I'm selling it."

"No way!" Chris's face fell. For the moment, he forgot his cheeseburger. Incredulous, he asked, "Why would you do that?"

"I need something a little . . ." Less flashy. Not quite so ostentatious. Unlike L.A. ". . . more rugged."

"Jeez, Brand, don't do it for a while, okay?"

"You can come and help me pick out something else."

Chris's infectious smile returned. "A Ferrari or a Porsche or—"

"A Jeep."

Chris chewed slowly. "Will it be jacked up with big tires and have a CD player and fog lights and—"

"We'll see," Brand said.

"It could be good. Not as good as a Benz, but—"

"Better."

Chris slid a French fry past his lips and waved wildly when Brand passed a group of kids on in-line skates, bikes and skateboards.

"Friends?"

"Nah. Some jerks from the eighth grade."

Boys he wanted to impress. Brand's insides grew cold. He remembered how important it was. How he hated to be considered poor, though that wasn't the worst of it. There were quite a few of his classmates who didn't have much money, others who grew up without one of their parents in the picture, but he was the only kid he knew who had never laid eyes on his father. The only one who was truly "a bastard," or "illegitimate." Words that still cut him to the bone. When and if he ever came face-to-face with good ol' Jake Kendall, he'd . . . what? Spit in the guy's face? Call him a coward? Rant and rave at all the injustices and pain Brand and his mother had suffered? What if the guy were dead, or seriously ill or just scratching out a living and feeding his six kids?

Years ago, Brandon had sworn he'd beat the living tar out of the man, pound him with his fists to let Jake know the rage and agony he'd suffered. But now Brand had mellowed, made his place in the world, and though he suspected that he'd spent the past twelve years trying to prove to himself and everyone around him that he was as good as the next guy, he no longer felt the need to use his fists to show how tough he was.

He slid a glance at Chris, who had devoured all his food, put the scraps and garbage into the bag and was drinking the remainder of his soda while eyeing the side streets and parking lots, hoping to see someone he knew, someone he could impress just by riding in a damned car.

Brand turned onto the street where he'd grown up. The trees that were planted too close to the sidewalk had caused it to buckle, and weeds were as common as flowers in the yards. His mother's was distinctive. Along with the overgrown flower beds that were the norm for the neighborhood, she had flower boxes and hanging pots with trailing blooms on the front porch. Birdbaths and bird feeders stood high over the unmown grass. An old-fashioned swing, in sad need of detergent and water, sat on the porch with three cats curled on its lumpy cushions. "Just how many cats does Mom have now?" he asked Chris as he cut the engine.

"Eight . . . no, seven. Inky died a couple of weeks ago. Got hit by a car."

"Seven? But why so many?"

"They just end up at our house," Chris said with a shrug. "She feeds 'em, posts notices that she found 'em and eventually keeps 'em if no one else'll take 'em. They're all neutered."

"Good. Otherwise she'd have a couple of hundred."

The cats were a new obsession with Venitia. She'd always had one or two hanging around, but when a stray had shown up, she'd found a home for it. Now it seemed that the cat just settled in with the rest of the family.

Chris opened the door and climbed out of the car. "I kinda think they're cool. Especially Lazarus. He's the one she found and gave up for dead—had feline leukemia or somethin'."

"But he made it." Brand locked the door.

"Yep. He's part Siamese and tough as nails, that's what Ma said." Chris bounded up the steps and Brand followed, eyeing the dandelions that dared grow between the cracks in the sidewalk and the thin layer of barkdust that had bleached in the sun. Venitia had always taken pride in her yard. Until Al left and she'd been forced to move back here. Then she'd started letting things slide.

Brand walked up the front steps, making a mental note that the bottom one was loose and that the gutter needed replacing. He was keeping a list, and whether his mother wanted his help or not, he was going to improve the house—add smoke detectors, insulation, a new roof and windows. If she wanted a little bit of remodeling, he'd even throw that in, but if she didn't, he'd back off once he knew that the building was safe.

He touched the molding near the window and watched as the caulking crumbled. Yep, the place needed a lot of work, but he had the time and the means and he'd convince his stubborn mother to let him help her.

He opened the screen door and caught Chris sifting through the mail stacked on the old lace cloth covering the dining-room table. The letters and bills slipped through his fingers and his eyes darkened with pain. He glanced at Brand and his chin slid forward defiantly. "Did I get any mail?" he yelled toward the back of the house.

No. answer.

Brackets showed near the corners of his mouth making him look older than he was. With a pang, Brand was reminded of himself and the chip he'd carried on his shoulder at that age.

"Just lookin' for some CD's I ordered through this company. You get six for a penny a piece."

"Didn't come, eh?" Brand said with a smile, as if he bought the kid's story, even though there wasn't any doubt in his mind that Chris had been looking for a letter from his father. A part of Brandon ached for Chris. He knew what it was like to be rejected, to live with false hope.

However, if Brand had anything to say about it, Chris wasn't going to live the rest of his life thinking his dad didn't love him. Brand was going to call that useless son of a bitch and convince Al to show some interest in his own kid. He thought for a second and decided that while he was at it, maybe it was time to try to find out if his own useless father was still alive.

Chris escaped to his room at the back of the house and Brand walked into the living room where his mother was propped up on the couch, a forgotten glass of wine sitting on the table, the ashtray filled with half-smoked cigarettes. She was snoring softly, blissfully unaware of all the emotional turmoil in her two sons.

"Come on, Mom," he said, gently lifting her off the couch. It was barely seven o'clock, hours away from nightfall. "Let's get you into bed." Then, as he had since he was twelve, he hauled his mother into the bedroom, laid her on the bed, drew the covers to her chin and closed the door softly behind him.

"She's pathetic, isn't she?" Chris's voice was thick, filled with unreleased sobs. He stood in the shadows of the hallway, his hair falling into his eyes.

"No, she's—"

"Just don't tell me she's sick, okay? That's what that neighbor lady, Ida Kemp, is always telling me, but I'm not a baby anymore. I know the score. Mom's drunk. Just like always."

"She's got a problem."

"I'll say. She can't go one day without a drink."

"It's deeper than that."

"Bull!" Chris ran into the living room, snatched up the wineglass and hurled it against the window. Birds perched on the feeder on the other side of the glass squawked and flew off, feathers fluttering, a cat near the window slunk behind the couch and blood-red stains ran down the old panes. Chris's rage wasn't spent. "She's a drunk, Brand, and everyone in town knows about it! Some lady from social services has been out a few times, and no one says it but I think . . . I think they're going to take me away from her!" His chin wobbled before he sniffed loudly, wiped his nose with his sleeve and fought tears. "Maybe it would be good," he muttered, disgust twisting his face.

"No, Chris—"

"You don't know how it is!"

He did. Oh, God, he knew. The lies, the hidden bottles, the numbing fear that he'd find her dead instead of just passed out, the ever-present knowledge that he might be taken away from her. "I know it's tough."

"Do you?" Chris challenged, then ran from the room. He slammed his door shut, just as Brandon had a hundred times before.

A lock clicked as Brand walked down the hall and rapped with one knuckle on the stained paint of the door to the room he used to sleep in. "I think we should talk."

"Nothin' to talk about."

"Sure there is."

"Go 'way." A minute later, heavy-metal music of some kind thrummed through the wood panels.

"I'll be in the living room."

No answer, just the nasal wail of a singer and the thick beat of bass guitars.

Brand wanted to break the door down, to try to talk some sense into the boy when there was no sense to be made. But maybe the kid needed to cool off. Everyone was strung tight, much too tight.

Brand would wait on the couch, all night if he had to, then he'd set down some rules. This might be his mother's house but if she didn't pull herself together, she'd lose her younger son. Her older one would see to it.

Dani dropped the last box onto the end of the old couch and rubbed the kinks from the middle of her back. Her stomach rumbled, sweat dripped down her face and back and a headache was building behind her eyes. Every muscle in her body ached from packing crates and hauling them up the stairs. She'd barely slept four hours last night, tossing and turning and staring out the window at the moonlight-drenched fields or the hours on her digital clock radio. Thinking of Brandon and the baby. Rotating her neck, she winced as she walked to the sink and turned on the water. Creaking pipes and a rush of water the color of rust greeted her. "Oh, great," she muttered, waiting until the water was clearer before splashing some on her face. In her rush to move out before Brandon landed permanently, she'd forgotten that these pipes needed replacing.

She wasn't worried about getting the job done—she'd become an ace plumber and electrician ever since she'd been on her own—but she hadn't had the time.

"Add another job to the list," she told herself and found a diet cola in the refrigerator. She'd have to live on bottled water until she could find the time to replace the pipes and faucets in both the kitchen and bath. "The joys of being single." She popped the top off her can of orange soda and gulped down half of it. And now she'd have to deal with Brandon Scarlotti and all the emotional baggage he brought with him.

Of all the people to lease the place—why Brandon?

*Destiny.*

She let out a brittle laugh and reminded herself she didn't believe in that kind of hogwash. She flopped on the couch, an old one made up of rawhide-covered cushions tossed over a scratched maple frame. A basket of laundry, not yet folded, rested near a wagon-wheel coffee table. She rifled through the clean clothes looking for a handkerchief or towel and settled for a clean sock to mop the sweat from her forehead. She was used to hard work—hours in the saddle, wrestling a calf to the ground, shoveling manure or fixing broken pipes—but this move was different, emotionally draining as well as physically exhausting.

She'd promised herself that she'd never be dependent upon a man again. But she'd never learned how to forget—or how to face the past, which she would have to do every time she looked into Brandon's blue eyes.

"Damn it all," she muttered, staring wretchedly at her surroundings. Her other furnishings consisted of a small end table, two chairs, braided rug, one free-standing lamp and a table with drawers that served as her desk. Behind a screen was her bed and a mirror, the bureau near the front door. There was a bathroom big enough for one person to stand in and a kitchen complete with two-burner stove, midget refrigerator and sink tucked behind folding doors.

She searched vainly for a bottle of aspirin and ended up walking to an open window, where she leaned against the sill and listened to the sounds of the evening—crickets beginning to chirp, a saw shrieking in the far distance and somewhere a dog barking. Dusk was laying dark shadows over the land and she saw a star glimmering in the lavender sky.

> *Star light, star bright*
> *First star I see tonight . . .*

How many nights had she seen the evening star and whispered those words? How many times had she thought about the child she'd borne? Her child. Brandon's child. A nameless, faceless couple's child.

Headlights caught her attention and the smooth purr of an engine cut through the night. Her heart squeezed as she trained her eyes on the dark blue car streaming down the lane, leaving a plume of dust in its wake. She forced all thoughts of her baby from her mind. She couldn't be maudlin or emotional, not now.

Because, like it or not, Brand was back.

# CHAPTER SEVEN

The slacks, tie and jacket were gone, replaced by sun-faded Levi's and a loose-fitting shirt with the sleeves shoved up to Brandon's elbows. His hair was mussed and he didn't seem to care as he strode to the front door of the house and pounded loudly.

"Go on in." Dani stood at the top of the stairs that angled up the side of the garage to the front door of her apartment. She felt grimy even though she'd quickly washed her face and hands after she'd spied his car in the driveway. "It's not locked."

At the sound of her voice he turned, tilting his head up to look at her. Incredibly, though it had been years since he'd kissed her, her silly heart fluttered. "Thought you were going to give me the grand tour."

"It's almost dark."

"Not quite." His back to the door, he stood, legs apart, looking too much like a perfect specimen of a man. Broad shoulders, lean hips, black hair falling over a strong forehead. Blue eyes stared up at her from a face that was tanned and sharp featured. "Seems to me when I leased this place, it came with electricity."

"Very funny," she muttered as she hurried down the steps, though she didn't want to show him that she was the least bit amused. His sense of humor wouldn't catch her off guard, wouldn't fascinate her or remind her of their few happy weeks together. No way. She'd be immune to him, even if it killed her.

Determination setting her jaw, she swept by him and shouldered open the door. "Here we go." Her boots rang on the old plank floors, recently oiled and gleaming, as she switched on the lights. "Thought you already saw this."

"Just peeked in the windows." He walked a few steps behind her, viewing the empty house that smelled of cleaning solvent and polish. "I didn't want to intrude."

"If you only knew," she whispered, trying not to notice the faint scent of soap that clung to him or the way the denim of his jeans stretched taut as he bent over to examine the antique andirons in the old river-rock fireplace. Muscles worked in his forearms, strong arms that were dusted with dark hair.

"Knew what? That I intrude?"

She caught her breath, surprised that he'd heard her.

Dusting his hands, he straightened, leaned his shoulders on the old mantel and crossed his arms over his chest. His eyes bored into her. "Okay. Out with it. Something's bugging the hell out of you—something about me—and since we're going to be neighbors for the next year or so, we'd better clear the air right here and now."

"Year or so?" she repeated. "Last I heard, you were committed to about six months even though the lease runs for twice that time."

"I just don't know how on schedule the project will be."

"Isn't that your job?"

His smile was downright devastating. "Yeah, well, a lot can go wrong. I like to give myself a little leeway. Is that a problem?"

"Not unless you plan to overstay the lease."

"It's only day one. We'll renegotiate later, okay?"

Blast the man, he had the audacity to smile as if he enjoyed sparring with her. Great. Just what she needed.

His eyes held hers and he didn't give an inch, just stood there, waiting. What could she say? She felt like a fool and a dirty one at that. She hadn't even had time to wash up properly before he showed up. Not that it mattered, she reminded herself. What did he care if she smelled of horsehide and sweat?

"It's because you and I slept together, isn't it?" His words seemed to echo in the room and in her heart.

She glanced up sharply. "Pardon me—"

"You're this way—"

"What way?"

"Prickly, because we slept together."

She wanted to look anywhere but at his face, but the magnetism of his gaze held her fast. "You really don't believe in beating around the bush, do you?"

"Do you?" He craned a dark brow.

"No, I guess not, and to be perfectly honest, yes, I thought the past might get in our way."

"Not a chance."

A silly flicker of hope—that he still cared, that when he walked away from her there had been some regret—died a quick and excruciating death. "Oh."

"Is it a problem for you?"

She could lie, but what was the point. "Maybe."

"Why?" The question hung in the air. When she didn't answer, he pushed it. "Because I left you?"

She felt as if a horse had kicked her in the stomach. Honesty was one thing. Being out-and-out blunt was altogether different. "That has a lot to do with it, I suppose."

"Still? It's been what—twelve years?" She nodded and was horrified when she saw the ghost of a smile play upon his lips—that same devilish smile that had coaxed her into foolishly believing in happy-ever-afters. "Don't tell me I made that much of an impression on you."

"It—it was an impressionable age." She stood her ground, crossing her arms under her breasts, wishing she could level him with the news that he was a father. But that was just anger and one-upmanship talking; she'd never do anything so cruel for shock value.

"I remember." Something flickered in his eyes, something very much alive and exceedingly dangerous, but it quickly disappeared as if it had been willed away, and she told herself that she was imagining things; what had happened between them was long over.

"I'll show you the rest of the house. It was one of the original settlements around here, you know." Lovingly she touched the smooth log walls, walking him through the kitchen, dining room and three bedrooms, all of which had been added on to the original homestead cabin during various stages of remodeling. "I thought it was strange that you didn't want to see inside before you signed the lease."

"As I said, I looked through the windows. It seemed to fill the bill."

"Which was?"

"Privacy, I guess. Room to set up an office. Close enough to the project to get there in half an hour, far enough away so I can relax. An extra room for my kid brother to come and visit if he wants."

"You have a brother?"

"Half brother," Brand said, shaking his head. "From what Ma says, he's hell on wheels already and not yet twelve." Dani nearly missed a step, hearing him speak of a boy about the same age as their son. Brand walked to the center of one of the bedrooms, his eyes scanning the walls for electrical outlets and closets. "Girls keep calling him and he's got a screwed-up sense of values. Thinks owning an expensive car will solve all his problems."

"And you don't?" she asked. He took in a swift breath.

"Not anymore."

"Good. I guess you'll have to straighten your brother out."

"I plan to," he said solemnly. "But it won't be easy. Chris is a handful."

"I'm surprised I haven't heard of him."

"Why would you? Mom only moved back to Dawson City two—no, closer to three—years ago, and unless you have some connection over there, how would you know a kid by the name of Christopher Cunningham?"

"I give weekly lessons to my niece—well, Skye's stepdaughter—who lives in Dawson City with her mother part of the time. Hillary's pretty gregarious and she knows a lot of kids. I thought she might mention him."

"Chris is in junior high."

Of course he was. What was she thinking? The kid was nearly twelve, almost a teenager. Just like her son. "That explains it," she said, showing him the bathroom with its claw-footed tub, which was probably original, and the glass-and-cedar shower, which wasn't. "Hillary's in elementary school—she'll be in first grade this year, I think."

As she showed him the rest of the house, they made small talk, discussing telephone hookups, electricity and gas connections, satellite dishes and mail delivery. He wanted to convert the third bedroom into an office with a computer, fax capabilities and all sorts of electronic gear that would have to be wired and installed.

"So you want a ranch away from it all, then you want to bring it all back to the ranch," she said as they passed through the kitchen and he glanced at the scarred wooden countertops, old wood stove and newer appliances.

"Something like that." He chuckled softly.

"You must be some kind of big wheel."

"Not that big."

She threw out a hip and shook her head. "Don't start in

with the false modesty bit. You went to California to prove something, to make it on your own, and it looks to me like you did it. Big time."

"Who would have guessed?" he said, his voice suddenly harsh, his words filled with an anger that burned deep.

"What?"

"That's what you're thinking, isn't it—that no one would have thought it possible?"

"That's where you're wrong, Brand," she said, stung. Honesty controlled her tongue. "I always knew that you'd accomplish anything you set out to do." His gaze sharpened on her and Dani looked away, afraid he might notice the emotions she knew were surfacing in her eyes. She crossed the room and opened the back door, where she motioned past the torn screen to the porch. "My washer and dryer are out here and there's no room in the apartment, so I thought I'd leave them here. We could both use them . . . unless you have your own."

"Yours'll be fine."

"Good. And as I said, the phone company is supposed to come out next week and install a phone in my apartment. I have the name of a serviceman who can probably install yours at the same time. It's—" she walked over to the counter where the phone and answering machine sat and tore off the top piece of a notepad "—Sam Burton."

"Thanks," he said, his voice low as he took the paper and followed her back to the entry hall. The front door was still ajar and a moth had slipped through the crack to flutter near the light. Brandon cleared his throat. "Most of my stuff will be here tomorrow. If I'm not here, will you let the movers in?"

She reached into the front pocket of her jeans, withdrew a small ring of keys and slid one off. "Here—you can do it yourself if you want." She handed him the key. "It works both the front and back doors, but sticks a little on the back one. I also kept a second one hanging by the light on the back porch, in case I ever got locked out. The only other one is with the owner."

"One should be enough."

"You don't have a . . ."

"Girlfriend?" He shook his head and rubbed the side of his jaw. "Never found the right woman I guess."

"So you've never had any children?" she returned, unable to resist bringing up the subject.

He frowned as he walked outside. Dani snapped out the lights and waited as he locked the door. Darkness had fallen and his face was in shadow as he slid the house key onto a ring that jangled. "I've never had time for children. And I don't believe in having any unless you're married. I know that sounds old-fashioned, probably even archaic, but that's the way it is. All these women having babies on their own— maybe it sounds great but then when the kid reaches eleven or twelve . . ." His voice drifted off.

*If you only knew,* she thought, condemning herself for never telling him the truth.

"I would probably have been better off, less determined to raise hell, I think, if my old man had stuck around."

"You don't know that," Dani said defensively as she, too, had grown up without a father. How would she ever be able to tell him about her child—his child, *their* child?

"I think it would have been easier for me. For my mother." He sat on the rail of the porch and stared up at her with eyes that had seen so many different things. "I left Dawson City and everyone thought I'd end up in jail."

"Not everyone," she said softly. The wind had died down and the air was still. From the hillside, a horse neighed softly. "I knew you'd do all right. Don't get me wrong. I didn't expect you to be quite so—" she glanced at the Mercedes shining against the split-rail fence and gravel, sparkling like a diamond in the sand "—well, so L.A."

"Neither did I." He slanted her a smile that bordered on

humility. "I just wanted out of this place. Away. I guess I had something to prove."

"What was that?"

His grin faded and he rubbed his palms on the denim covering his thighs. "That I was good enough, I suppose. That even though I was raised poor, that I didn't have a dad, I was as good as everyone else."

"Of course you were," she said. "Better."

His hands stopped moving, and when he looked up at her again, his eyes searched hers as if looking for flaws, or a lie that he could uncover. "I . . ." He cleared his throat and sighed. "I suppose I owe you an explanation."

She stiffened. "You don't owe me anything. We were just a couple of kids."

"Were we?" He reached out, his strong fingers clasping over hers. "Then why did I get the feeling when I showed up here yesterday that you'd just as soon strangle me as talk to me?"

She blinked rapidly. "I want to—" The honesty in his eyes stopped her from lying, "Okay, I was hurt. I expected you to call, to write, to . . ." She let the sentence trail off. What was the point?

"To what?" he persisted, his voice suddenly louder. "Send for you?"

She lifted a shoulder and yanked her hand away. She didn't need to be reminded of the power of his touch, the feel of his skin rough and warm against hers. "You just left me with nothing."

"You were in high school."

"So you acted like I was dead."

"I didn't have anything to offer you," he said as he stood.

"Did I ask for anything?" Her throat was thickening, her stomach churning, and this was getting them both nowhere fast. "Look, let's not talk about it now, okay? It's over, we were a couple of kids experimenting with sex, and that's that.

Now, do you want to see the rest of the place?" Without waiting for an answer, she walked down the two porch steps and across the yard.

Her blood was pounding in her ears. What would he do if he knew that he was a father, that she didn't even know the name of the parents who had adopted their son? What would he think? Would he blame her? But that was ridiculous. She hadn't conceived the baby alone.

"This way." She walked stiffly, her legs rigid, her insides feeling like jelly. Maybe she should tell him the truth now and get it over with; or maybe she should keep her secret forever.

The stable door creaked open and she flipped on the light. The smell of old leather, fresh hay and dust lingered in the air and the sounds of mice scurrying behind the oat barrels met their ears.

"No horses?" he asked, looking down the row of empty stalls.

"It's summer—they'd rather be outside. They come in for food when I give them grain or hay, but they're range horses, not hothouse flowers." She showed him the room where she kept the tack and an emergency medical kit, then pointed out the water spigots, grain barrels and the interlocking system of stalls that led to the wide back doors, which were left open if any of the animals wanted to wander inside.

He didn't say much, but observed it all. Dani walked in front of him and felt the weight of his gaze, knew that he was staring at her.

"We can go this way," she said, leading him outside. The moon, climbing in the sky, was about half-full and shedding enough light to wash the roof of the stables in a soft, silvery light. "The pump house is on the other side of the garage, there's a shed for the large equipment, and then there's the windmill and an old chicken coop, where we store some barbed wire and metal posts for any fence that needs to be fixed. The cattle are rarely in the barn, but we have hay in the loft and park the extra tractor on the ground floor. Other than that, you've seen the place."

He seemed larger in the darkness, and she talked fast, to make sure there weren't any lapses in the conversation. As the wind picked up, catching in her hair, they walked back to his Mercedes. "I won't need much space, just the house, some room in the garage and storage shed."

"The lease gives you access to some of the acreage."

"I know. Don't need it." Leaning his hips against a glossy fender, he said, "It's funny, kind of. When I left here, I thought I'd never look back. Couldn't wait to get to California. And here I am."

She couldn't help asking, "What was in L.A.?"

"Opportunities. Millions of them."

"You liked it."

"At first. I started working on projects as an apprentice carpenter, learned the business, took some night classes and spent as much time as I could on the beach. Even learned to surf though I never got very good at it." His smile was self-deprecating, a cynical slash of white in the warm night. "Yep, thought I was gonna live the Southern California dream. At first it looked that way. I saved as much money as I could, worked overtime any chance I got, eventually caught a couple of breaks and had the chance to buy into a construction company that was in trouble. That's when I quit surfing— quit everything. Once I was in business for myself, I worked twice as hard and started remodeling houses I bought, then turned around and sold for a tidy profit. One thing led to another. The company grew, expanding into commercial properties. When the market started to turn sour, I bailed out of California."

"So here you are."

"Back where I started."

"Still ride a motorcycle?"

He let out a harsh breath. "I did until I laid it down."

"You—what?"

"Wrecked. First time. I was going too fast, took a corner and there was a semi parked in the middle of the road. I tried to stop, couldn't, swerved and hit gravel. The bike slipped out from under me and we skidded a long ways." He made a sound of deprecation in the back of his throat. "Have the scars to prove it. But I still have the bike."

"You ride it?"

"Nope. It's just there to remind me how close I came to meeting Saint Peter." Glancing at his watch, he scowled. "I'd better shove off." His gaze centered for a second on her lips and Dani didn't dare move. She watched his Adam's apple as he swallowed then bit his lip. For a breathless second, she was certain he was going to kiss her, and damn it, she would have let him. Then he turned quickly away, unlocked his car and climbed inside.

"See ya," he said as the engine turned over.

"Right." Heart in her throat, Dani shoved her hands into her pockets and stared after the car until its taillights disappeared down the lane.

"So how do you know this guy?" Skye, eight months pregnant, poured them each a cup of coffee. Though she'd gained nearly thirty pounds, Skye was tall and carried the baby back far enough that she didn't look ungainly. Since she was happier than she'd ever been in her life, she fairly glowed. For so many years, Skye had been convinced that she couldn't conceive and now it was only a matter of weeks before she would become a mother. Her blond hair was swept into a haphazard bun at the top of her head, and even without makeup and what she described as a "hellish night's sleep," she looked simply radiant.

The back door was open and the sun streamed through the house that Max, Skye and oftentimes Hillary shared. Their dog, Atlas, a Border collie, lay on the top step, eyeing the lane and whining when he caught sight of a squirrel in a nearby thicket of trees.

Skye carried a tray with two cups and a small pitcher of cream to the table where Dani was seated, waiting for Hillary to don riding gear for their lesson. "You didn't answer me. Max said you knew the guy who rented your house— Brandon something or other."

"Scarlotti."

"A hotshot developer from California."

"But he lived here a long time ago," Dani said, not wanting to divulge too much. She'd never confided in Skye about her baby's father and wasn't about to start now—not until she told Brandon. If she ever did. "I met him in high school." She poured cream into her cup. Watching the clouds roll upward in her coffee, she avoided Skye's penetrating stare and pretended interest in her sister's notoriously weak, decaffeinated brew.

"Max said you turned white as a sheet when you saw him." Obviously Skye wasn't going to give up.

"Max's imagination was working overtime."

Skye settled her considerable bulk into a chair. "Not usually."

Dani sighed and blew across her coffee cup. Leaning back in her chair, she said, "Brand lived in Dawson City and we hung out with the same crowd for a while."

"So how come I never heard about him?"

"You were in college."

Skye's brows pulled together in a small pout as if she had a question on the tip of her tongue but didn't quite know how to ask it.

Dani didn't help her out. "Anyway, Brandon took off for California and none of us who stayed around here ever saw or heard from him again. His mom remarried and moved away, just came back a few years ago."

"You've never said a word about him."

"Why would I?" Dani tried to sound nonchalant. "He was in trouble a lot back then and Mom heard about him from a friend she had in Dawson City—" She snapped her fingers trying to remember the busybody's name. "You know who I'm talking about. Betty or Beth . . . no . . . that's not right. Bess something or other."

"Jamison?"

"Bess Jamison. Right. Anyway, Bess was kind of a gossip and she filled Mom's head with all sorts of stories about the Scarlottis. Especially Brandon. Some were true, some weren't, but Mom didn't think it was a good idea that I be anywhere near him."

"Mom was worried about you."

"I know," Dani said, biting on her lower lip. Should she tell Skye about the baby—that she was trying to locate her son? Surely her sister who had wanted a child for so many years would understand her need to know that he was okay. Or would she?

"Oh!" Skye chuckled, her attention diverted. "This one—" she pointed a long finger at her protruding belly "—is going to be a live wire. He's kicking all the time."

"He?"

"Well, I'd like to think it's a girl, but Max would like a boy and . . . oh, we'll be happy with whatever it is." Her eyes positively shone. Skye, though a doctor, seemed to believe that a miracle had happened when she'd conceived. Smiling slightly, she rubbed her abdomen as if caressing her child.

Dani's throat grew tight. It was ironic, she thought. For years, Skye, who knew about Dani's pregnancy, had envied her the ability to have children, and now the tables were turned.

"Ready?" Hillary clumped noisily down the stairs. She was wearing new jeans, little boots and a rawhide vest decorated with tooled silver disks.

"You spoil her," Dani mouthed.

"Can't help it." Skye's attention was on her dimpled stepdaughter.

Hillary's springy curls had been clamped back in a pony-tail, the sides fastened by pink barrettes. Her eyes were bright, her cheeks rosy.

"Oh, honey, you look beautiful."

Hillary's face broke into a smile. "Do I?"

"Mmmm."

Hillary faced Dani, eyebrows aloft, silently asking her opinion.

"Yes," Dani agreed. "Definitely beautiful."

With a giggle, Hillary twirled on her tiptoes, her arms spread wide. "Daddy thinks I dress too fussy."

"Oh, what does he know?" With a wink, Skye ruffled Hillary's hair and a few wild curls sprang from their bonds.

"You tell Skye that your dad knows everything," Max said, sauntering into the room. With a smile for his daughter and a glance that fairly sizzled for his wife, he picked up Hillary and nuzzled her little neck. "Now you remember, if anyone ever asks, Daddy knows everything."

"Save me," Skye said. "Coffee?" She started to stand, but he waved her back to her chair.

"I'll get it." As he poured a cup and balanced Hillary on one hip, he asked, "What's this, another riding lesson?"

Hillary nodded. "Dani's gonna show me how to jump today."

"Jump?" Max eyed his sister-in-law. "Jump what?"

"I brought some things," Dani replied. "Don't worry."

"I'm a good rider, Daddy."

"'Course you are." He kissed her cheek as she squirmed to the ground. "But you still have to be careful."

"Let's go!" With a clatter of new boots, Hillary was out

the back door. Atlas bounded to his feet and woofed before chasing after her.

Finishing her coffee, Dani stretched out of her chair. Some of her muscles were still sore from all the lifting and packing she'd done the day before. "Duty calls. I'll have her back in a couple of hours." As she placed her cup on the table, Skye's hand covered hers.

"Is there something you're not telling me about Brandon?" she asked softly.

Dani could barely breathe. The room seemed to spin a little. Max pretended interest in his coffee cup. She swallowed back denial. "You want to know if he was the one." Her voice was barely a whisper.

Max shifted, still avoiding her eyes, but Skye's fingers tightened over her sister's wrist. "I don't mean to pry."

"I know." Dani's throat worked. Skye was and always had been good to her, though years ago when they were both teenagers and Skye had sailed through school on a cloud of popularity, Dani hadn't known how much Skye had cared for her. "Look, I gotta go—"

"If you want to talk, you know where to find me."

Dani blinked back her tears and glanced pointedly at Skye's protruding abdomen. "You have enough to worry about," she said.

"I always have time for you."

"Tell me that when the baby's here, you haven't had two hours' stretch of sleep in weeks, and some doctor at the clinic wants you to fill in for him."

Skye laughed. "You paint a wicked picture."

The horn of Dani's truck blasted. "I think your daughter's calling," she said and raced outside. Hillary was frowning, pounding impatiently on the horn and Atlas was jumping and barking at the commotion. "Hold your horses, I'm coming!"

Dani said as she slid behind the wheel and jammed a key into the ignition.

"You're late!"

"And you're precocious."

Hillary's little nose wrinkled distastefully. "What's that mean?"

Letting out the clutch, Dani eased the truck backward, then shoved it into first. "It means that someone should tell you no once in a while."

Hillary crossed her chubby arms over her chest. "Daddy does all the time."

"Sure." Dani didn't believe it. Max positively doted on his only little girl. It was a good thing Hillary was going to have a little brother or sister to vie for her father's attention, otherwise she'd soon be impossible to live with. Whenever she stayed with Max, she was spoiled mercilessly, though, Dani suspected, when she was at her mother's place, Hillary had to battle for attention. With her other children, Colleen Wheeler didn't have a lot of time for her firstborn. Max, on the other hand, had been singularly devoted to his daughter, spoiling her without a second's regret. Ever since the fire in the McKee stables, when he'd nearly lost Hillary, Max had decided that she could do no wrong. Dani felt he needed another child just to balance things out a bit.

"So are you ready to do some jumps today?" Dani asked as the truck bounded down the lane. "Hey—put on your seat belt."

Hillary shot her a glance but buckled up. "Jumps on Cambridge?"

"He's your horse." Dani turned onto the main road that curved around the McKee ranch.

"I know. Daddy gave him to me. I like him a lot, but he's kinda lazy. I think for jumps I should ride Hellcat."

"Oh, right," Dani said, unable to hide her sarcasm. Hellcat, as his name suggested, was a feisty three-year-old bay gelding with a mean temper that Max sometimes rode. "I don't think so."

"Please, Aunt Dani?"

"Not today, pumpkin."

"Please, please, please." Hillary's begging was hard to resist, but resist she did.

"No way. Now, if you don't stop this, we won't have a lesson at all."

Hillary's lower lip protruded into a well-practiced pout. "You're mean."

"Not as mean as Hellcat," Dani muttered and was grateful the argument was over. She turned into the long, tree-lined drive of the Rocking M, the McKee ranch where Max's mother and grandmother still lived. The house was a sprawling, single-storied building with a wide porch. Across the yard were several outbuildings, including newly constructed stables to replace the ones that had burned nearly a year ago. Painted a gleaming white, the building was a harsh reminder of the trauma they'd all gone through.

Hillary unbuckled her seat belt, scrambled out of the truck as soon as it was parked and raced straight for the stables. If nothing else, the little girl was eager. Dani wondered about her own boy again. So far she hadn't heard a word from Sloan about locating him, but the wheels were in motion.

It was only a matter of time.

*Then what?* she wondered as she followed her niece. Her heart tore a little. Her son was too young to understand about giving up a baby for adoption, about unplanned pregnancies, about lying awake nights and wondering about him, hoping he was all right, wishing he was with her. She'd have to wait. Years. And in the meantime, she'd have to find a way to tell his father the truth.

"God help me," she whispered.

# CHAPTER EIGHT

As the moving van rumbled away from the ranch, Dani walked into the house—once hers, now his. It seemed strange to view his things—to know that he'd be living where she had.

Rotating the kinks out of her neck, she walked into the living room. She'd spent part of her day rounding up calves that had wandered over to the Newman place after finding a spot in the fence where the old barbed wire had frayed away from the post. Bawling and lost, the calves couldn't seem to find their way home, so Dani had driven the four strays back into the field, then took the rest of the morning to repair the fence. Later she'd given a couple of riding lessons, fed the stock and used the remaining hours of the afternoon trying to rearrange her apartment so that she didn't trip over boxes every time she tried to walk from one end to the other. She wasn't completely settled in, but by the end of the week she expected to have the apartment in some kind of shape.

Now, Dani surveyed Brand's things. Boxes were set against walls in every room, and furniture was placed haphazardly wherever the movers had determined the pieces should go.

Brand, after giving the men instructions, had taken off for some kind of business meeting, or so he'd told Dani when she'd driven home after one of the lessons. As far as she could tell, he hadn't come back.

She ran her fingers over the curved back of a forest green leather couch. A matching side chair and ottoman were complemented by two high-backed chairs in a plaid of the same forest green, burgundy and ivory. A rectangular carpet, ivory trimmed with burgundy, lay beneath a glass-topped table. Brass lamps, a light oak bookcase with matching end tables and some pictures not yet hung finished off the room. All the work of an interior decorator, it seemed. Far too sophisticated for this old ranch house. Far too sophisticated for the bad boy from Dawson City.

She walked into the kitchen and turned on the answering machine. "Dani? It's Jack. If ya want, I can help with the plumbing and the stock tomorrow. Give me a call." She smiled. Jack Fairmont was an old friend, a guy who did odd jobs in the spring, summer and fall so that he could ski all winter. Since her divorce, he'd helped Dani out whenever she'd needed it. She made a mental note to phone him.

The next two messages were about riding lessons and Dani wrote down the numbers before listening to the final recording. "Dani? I hope you get this. It's Brand." As if she wouldn't recognize his voice. Her heart raced a little. "Look, I took the liberty of giving out this number to a couple of subcontractors who'll be calling. I hope you don't mind. Just leave the messages on the tape—this'll be all straightened out next week but in the meantime, I decided you wouldn't mind." She bit her lip. What did she care? "And look, I'm gonna be hung up in town later than I thought, so if you could lock up after the movers, I'd owe ya one—well, two, really, considering the phone deal. Anyway, I appreciate it. Thanks." He clicked off and she tried to erase his voice from her mind.

She'd have to find a way to keep her pulse from leaping

every time she was near him. "Listen to the tape, dummy," she chided. "He thinks of you as a housekeeper or a secretary. Nothing more." That realization hurt, but she supposed it was for the best. It was bad enough that she couldn't look at him without remembering the past; at least he'd had the good sense to get on with his life and forget what had happened between them. But, of course, he didn't know about their son. Guilt, needle sharp, pricked at her conscience again. "Oh, get over it," she growled, picking up the receiver.

She returned Jack's call and he promised to come by the next day to help her separate some calves and replace the pipes. It galled her to have to hire someone, but at least the job would be finished and she'd be able to wash the dishes, her body, her hair and have a drink of water straight out of the tap for a change. But she wouldn't be able to settle into a bathtub and soak her muscles as she liked to after a long day. No more baths by candlelight while sipping wine and listening to her favorite CD. Nope, she'd have to settle for a quick wash in a tiny metal shower stall for at least the next year, maybe longer.

"So live with it. At least you'll be clean and the bills will be paid." But a part of her wasn't ready to relinquish her one little indulgence at the end of the day.

She heated a frozen chicken pot pie, poured herself a diet Coke and stared out the window. It was dusk and Brandon still hadn't returned. But then he'd said he'd be late, which probably meant he had a dinner meeting that might stretch on for hours. He might not be home until midnight or later.

Though she loathed herself for it, she watched the lane while she ate. No headlights. No Mercedes rolling into the yard. The idea she hadn't been able to nudge from her mind earlier took hold. She stripped out of her dirty clothes and slipped her arms through the sleeves of her bathrobe. Telling herself she had every right to use his bathtub—her tub, really—she packed candles, lotion, bath-oil beads, soap and shampoo along with clean underwear into a big canvas beach bag, which she flung onto the top of her laundry basket. Carrying everything down the steps and across the yard, she felt a little like a sneak thief, but shook off the feeling. Brand would never know, and even if he did, he wouldn't care. On the back porch, she threw in a load of jeans, and while the washer was filling, walked through the house to the bathroom.

She lit two candles, placed them in the window, shoved the plug into place and turned on the faucet. Adding a couple of scented bath-oil beads and a capful of bubble bath to the water, she tossed her robe over a hook on the door and slid into the tub. Warm water caressed her skin and soothed the tension from her overworked muscles. Steam rose and she cracked the window open slightly, watching the flames of her candles flicker with the whisper of a breeze. No wine, no music, but she didn't care. She shampooed her hair, rinsed it, then leaned her head back on the rim of the tub and closed her eyes. She'd just soak for a few minutes, get rid of the grime and aches of the day, then swab out the tub in time to throw her clean clothes into the dryer. No one would be the wiser. Besides, didn't Brand say he owed her a couple of favors? This bath was payback number one.

Brand parked in the garage and tried to quiet the pounding in his head. The meeting with the architects and engineers was supposed to have ended hours ago, but had stretched out, and he was reminded of L.A. and some of the reasons he'd left the rat race of the city. The trouble was that he seemed to have brought the rat race back to this sleepy part of Oregon.

He climbed out of the car, grabbed his briefcase and noticed that the lights in Dani's apartment were glowing softly. He wondered what she was doing and if it would be appropriate to climb up the stairs and offer her a drink or a cup of coffee. The urge to see her again, to hear her voice, to sit next to her, was overpowering and he wondered what was the matter with him. It wasn't as if she was his wife, or even his girlfriend, for God's sake. He didn't even know her anymore. But still there was a tug and he clenched his jaw tight to avoid making a fool of himself by climbing those stairs.

"Get a grip, Scarlotti," he muttered as he headed for his front door. He noticed the flickering light through the slightly open window of his bathroom. Strange. As if pulled by an invisible force, he made his way to the glass and, like a voyeur, peeked into his own house.

His breath held still in his lungs when he saw her, asleep in the tub, water lapping around her body, a few last foaming bubbles lying on the water. The scents of jasmine and heather floated to him, probably from the candles burning in the window.

Something inside him snapped as he stared at her, blond hair twisted away from her face, eyes closed, her usually tense face now peaceful as the sweep of her lashes caressed cheeks flushed from the warm water. Knowing it was a violation, he let his eyes wander down her body to her tanned limbs and white torso. Her breasts were larger than he remembered and the nipples, rosy disks that poked above the remaining foam, seemed bigger, as well. Her waist was tiny, her abdomen flat, the skin stretched tight and her legs long and lean and meeting at that sweet cluster of red-gold curls that seemed forever seared in his memory.

His throat tightened at the memories of her, soft and supple and loving. There was a time when he couldn't get enough of her and yet he'd found the guts to leave her. Had it been a mistake? Was his empty life in L.A. and all the dollars he'd made worth it? Was her unhappy marriage the direct result of his rejection? Whatever he'd told himself he'd done, however noble his intentions, he'd hurt her, brutally and callously. And now he was standing and gawking at her through the window like some damned pervert.

After one last look, he headed toward the front door, made as much noise as possible clomping up the stairs and across the floorboards, then fumbled for several minutes with his key and the lock. By the time he finally entered the house, she'd had enough of a warning.

He was hanging up his jacket in the front hall when Dani, dressed in a thick pink robe, peeked sheepishly around the corner. "Brand?" she whispered, a new flush climbing up her gorgeous neck.

"What? Oh, Dani," he said, hoping to sound surprised when he knew he was a lousy actor. "What are you doing here?"

Her belt was cinched tight but the neckline of the robe was a deep V, showing off some of her cleavage. He doubted if she was wearing a stitch beneath the soft cloth and the thought caused a quickening of his pulse. His throat was suddenly as dry as a desert wind.

"I—I used your tub because my shower isn't quite working yet and . . . well, I should have asked, but you weren't around and I thought I'd be done before you got home."

"It's no problem," he said gruffly.

"I'll just gather my things and go—"

"Don't." He said it so sharply she jumped. "I mean I'd like you to stay, have some coffee with me. I have this feeling that we got off on the wrong foot the other day and I'd like to start over. . . ."

She looked at him with those wide amber eyes, eyes that stripped him bare. "It's too late, Brand. Too late for a lot of things."

"I just meant that—"

"I know what you meant," she said, cutting him off as if she was unable to listen to another word. "But, really, it's not a good idea. I shouldn't have intruded and it won't happen again."

"You didn't intrude and any time you like you can use—"

"Don't worry about it," she snapped, hurrying back to the bathroom and emerging with a beige canvas bag filled with all sorts of bottles. The scent of fresh flowers trailed after her. "As soon as my phone is hooked up in my apartment, I won't have any reason to be in here."

"Unless you want to see me."

She stopped dead in her tracks, her hand poised over the back doorknob, her pulse throbbing just below her ear. "We'll probably be seeing enough of each other."

"Will we?" He walked closer and she turned the knob. The door opened. He shut it with the flat of his hand. The lock clicked resolutely into place. "We don't have to be enemies, Dani."

"We're not."

"Then how come I feel like I live in some damned war zone?"

"Because you're imagining things." Her gaze dropped to his lips and she swallowed. Brand watched the motion and an ache so hot it threatened to boil his blood caught hold of him.

"I don't think it's impossible to live next door to each other."

"I hope not." Her voice was breathy, rushed. "Otherwise it's going to be an incredibly long year."

Telling himself he was making the single worst mistake of his life, he lifted her chin with one finger and slowly lowered his head to kiss her. Their lips brushed. She quivered. His lungs could hardly inflate. Damn it, he was scared! Of what he didn't know. Complications to his already crowded life? The fear that her kiss wouldn't be as passionate as he remembered? Or that it would? Slowly he applied pressure, his tongue rimming her mouth as his arms surrounded her. She seemed to sag as he kissed her harder, pressing her against the door, fitting his body intimately against hers.

The robe gaped. As he closed his eyes he saw the dusky

hollow between her breasts. Fire swept through him and he ran his tongue along the seam of her lips, asking, taking, demanding. With a moan she opened her mouth and his tongue found hers, flirting, dancing, embracing. His blood thundered and the fingers of one hand twined in her damp curls. She kissed him back, her arms lifting to encircle his neck, her breasts pushing against him. His heart pounded wildly. The canvas bag slipped to the floor, its contents spilling across the worn linoleum. He didn't care. Whatever had frightened him was long gone and he was lost in her. So lost.

Her breath came in quick, short gasps, and when he slid a hand along the V of her robe, she didn't stop him but let him slip his palm inside to the warmth. The softness of her breast filled his palm. Her nipple was stiff, ready. Eager. He touched it and felt an electrical impulse that caused his loins to heat and the hardness there to throb.

"Dani, sweet, sweet Dani," he whispered into her open mouth as he massaged her breast and felt its glorious weight. "You're so good."

Closing her eyes, she let go, just felt. Sensation after glorious sensation soared through her and she felt the knot of her robe loosen, the fabric part as Brand slid lower to his knees, kissing her, touching her, catching her skin on fire. "Brand," she said, her voice the barest of whispers. His tongue touched her nipple and she arched forward, holding his head as he began to suckle. Tears formed, from happiness or regret, she didn't know. This was how it was supposed to be, how it should feel with a man—the father of the child who had never known her breast.

A cry broke from her lungs, pained, the howl of a wounded animal, but he must have mistaken it for passion because his hands splayed on the small of her bare back, pulling her closer as he slid downward and kissed her naked abdomen, rimming her navel with his tongue, kissing her everywhere.

He kissed her damp curls and she thought she might crawl out of her skin. His hands gently prodded her legs apart, running along the inside and out, teasing her as she writhed against the door. His lips and breath came closer.

*Ring!*

The phone startled them both. "Ignore it," Brand said, kissing her inner thigh. A shudder of anticipation raced through her body.

*Ring!*

Dani tried to reach for it but Brand kissed her and she couldn't move, could only feel. Heat, warm and wild and thick as honey, moved inside her most private regions.

*Ring!*

"Oh, Brand, please . . ." But he wouldn't stop his ministrations, only kissed her harder, his tongue touching her inside. Sweat soaked her brow and the ache inside her pulsed, yearning to be relieved.

*Ring! Click!* Dani's voice filled her ears, instructing the caller to leave a message.

Brand lifted one of her legs, placing it over his shoulder, and she drifted far away on the wings of passion, her heart thudding, her body throbbing with a need only he could fill. She let out a long low moan as he kissed her so intimately, so gently, her heart threatened to break.

"Hi, Dani, it's Sloan." The words cut through the passion. "Look, so far I've been hitting a brick wall—"

Her eyes flew open. "What?" *Oh, no! No! No! No!* She scrambled away from Brand, nearly tripping over the candles that had fallen and were rolling on the floor.

"Hey!" Brand cried. "Dani, what the hell—"

Sloan's voice continued to fill the room as Dani reached for the receiver. "I've been checking on birth certificates and—"

She picked up the phone quickly, her mind spinning in crazy circles. Brand stared up at her, passion still glazing his eyes, his shirttail out of his pants, an unmistakable bulge at his crotch.

Dani dragged her eyes away and tried not to sound as breathless as if she'd been running a thousand miles an hour. "Hi, Sloan, I'm here. Just walked in and heard your voice," she said, wondering how she was going to explain this to Brand. "I'm sorry, what were you saying?"

Brand straightened and came up to her, his arms slipping around her waist, his hands cupping her breasts. Oh, no, what was she going to do? If he overheard the conversation . . .

"I've checked all the records—hospital, court—and can't locate a certificate."

"What? But there had to be one—" She almost added that she was certain she'd signed one, but bit her lip as Brand was still touching her, nuzzling her neck, listening.

"Well, don't give up. I've just started. Sometimes it takes a while. Look, I'm still checking. Knowing my father-in-law, there's a good chance that he had all the documents altered."

"But why? How?" She was having trouble concentrating with Brand kissing her neck and fondling her breasts, but she couldn't just push him away or he'd become suspicious. Besides, the sensations rolling through her were so good she could barely stand.

"I don't know, but I've just started digging. I'll keep you posted."

"I appreciate it. Thanks."

She replaced the phone with trembling hands. Brand was still holding her and she didn't care about anything other than his strong arms around her. Her worst fears were confirmed. Jonah McKee had lied to her. Tears filled her throat. *Dear God, where was her child? Was he alive? Safe? Would she ever know?* Squeezing her eyes against the terror, she clung to Brand, and as if he sensed her change of mood, he stopped rubbing her and held her as she fought the urge to break down and sob on the shoulders of her son's father.

"Bad news?" he asked, his voice tender.

"Yes." She sniffed loudly.

"Want to talk about it?"

She shook her head and slowly leaned back, keeping him at arm's length. She suddenly felt cold and alone. "No, I, uh, can't. It's personal." Then, realizing her state of undress and that she would have willingly made love to Brand again had the phone not interrupted them, she pulled away from him. "Oh, my," she whispered, reality chasing away any hint of lingering passion. "We can't . . . I mean I can't . . ." Wrapping her robe around her and pretending it was a suit of armor, she said, "I've made a couple of big mistakes here tonight. I had no right to barge into your house and make myself at home in your bathtub and I . . . I don't want you to think that I . . . For the love of heaven . . . I don't want this . . . us . . . it can't work." She cinched her belt around her, knotted it and double-knotted it, as if in so doing she would be safe from his erotic eyes and wonderful hands.

Brand's jaw was tight, his eyes a fierce shade of blue. "Neither one of us planned it, Dani." His lips flattened into a hard, uncompromising line. "I had no intention of seducing you, if that's what you're thinking."

"I know, I know, but—" Her fingers fluttered in the air, as if looking for something solid to hang on to. "Things got out of hand . . . way out of hand. If we're going to live here this close, well, even if we weren't . . . This can't happen."

He rubbed the back of his neck, as if he were trying to erase his anger. "Who called?"

"What?" She was already bending down to pick up her shampoo bottle, the candles, the bath-oil beads, everything that had spilled from her bag.

"Who called?"

"What does it matter?" Not now. She couldn't tell him now. Not while she was emotionally turned inside out. One candle holder had rolled beneath the counter. She picked it up and straightened.

"Whoever was on the other end of that phone was like a bucket of cold water for you," he said. "So, was he a friend?"

"Yes, I guess he's a friend."

"Someone you're in love with?"

"Oh, for Pete's sake. You think that I . . . that I'm involved with someone? How could you even suggest . . . when you and I . . ." She couldn't believe her ears.

"Who, damn it!"

"You heard him. It was Sloan. Sloan Redhawk. He's married to Casey McKee."

His eyes were thunderous, and deep ravines scarred his forehead. Dani shook her head. If this wasn't so damned tragic, it would be downright funny.

"Sloan and Casey have only been married a few months and he's absolutely one hundred percent devoted to her."

"Then why'd he call?"

She slung the strap of her bag over her arm. "Not that it's any of your business, but he's a private investigator. I need him to do some work for me."

Brand's eyes narrowed. "What kind of work?"

"As I said, it's personal."

"Something to do with your ex?" Why the thought of Jeff Stewart caused his guts to twist he didn't know. But the sick idea that Dani's husband had mistreated her and run around on her made him want to strangle the stupid son of a bitch. *And you're any better, Scarlotti? Didn't you run out on her when you knew she loved you—when you loved her? Who're you to sit in judgment?*

"This isn't about Jeff," she said, reaching for her bag.

"Then who?"

"Brand, don't push it." This time she opened the door all the way. "I think it's time I went home." She stepped onto the porch, swore and didn't bother to transfer the load of laundry from the washer to the dryer. She couldn't trust herself with him. Running down the steps and along the path, her robe flowing open to show off her long, perfect legs, she flew up the stairs to her apartment.

Brand closed his eyes and willed away the vision of her. She was right about one thing: they couldn't live this close together if he was forever hoping to get her into his bed and, damn it, that's exactly what he wanted.

"You had your chance," he growled at himself and then spied the answering machine, red light blinking. Knowing he was intruding where he wasn't wanted, he played back the messages to the last one—the entire conversation between Dani and Sloan Redhawk. Then he played it again. Why was Dani interested in birth certificates? Who was she trying to find? Gnawing on his lip, he drummed his fingers on the counter. It was none of his business, plain and simple, and yet anything Dani did fascinated him.

It seemed to be his personal curse.


"You can't be serious!" Skye's eyes were wide, her color high as she stared at her sister.

"I can and I am," Dani said, wondering if confiding in her older sister had been a mistake of grand proportions. "Watch this," she said, pointing to the corral where Hillary was atop Cambridge, the palomino gelding her father had bought her. The horse approached the jump at a smooth lope, then sailed over the white rails of a two-foot-high fence. If one hoof hit either of the rails, the fence would topple. It wasn't much of a jump, but it was a start and Hillary executed it perfectly.

"I did it! I did it!" Hillary crowed proudly.

"Good girl," Skye said with a bright smile, though her fingers were digging into the top rail of the fence to hide the case of nerves that Dani had already seen.

"She's a natural," Dani said.

"Wanna see again?"

"Sure." Skye nodded and smiled but her fingers never relaxed their death grip on the fence.

"Now, remember, Hillary, talk to Cambridge through the reins. Let him know what you want by the feel of the bit in his mouth and your position on the saddle. You're in charge."

"I know all that," Hillary said.

"Shouldn't she be wearing a crash helmet?"

"And a seat belt, but watch."

As Hillary repositioned Cambridge at the far end of the field, Skye placed a hand on Dani's arm. "Why have you decided to look for your son now?"

"Because I have to know. It's time, Skye. I always told myself that I'd do it someday, but for one reason or another put it off. I can't any longer. It's driving me crazy."

"Because of Brandon?" Skye asked as Hillary aimed Cambridge at the jump and leaned over his shoulders. The horse shot forward, loping easily, approaching the jump before his muscles bunched and he soared again, carrying Hillary easily over the rails.

"Whether he came back or not, I wanted to find out."

"Have you talked to him about it?"

"I haven't talked to anyone except Sloan. And now you. Maybe that was a mistake, but I thought you might need some information in case Sloan wants to go through some of Jonah's personal papers. He might also need access to some of the old hospital records in The Dalles where I had the baby. Since you're a doctor—"

"Forget it. What you're suggesting isn't just unethical. I think it's illegal."

"This is something I have to do."

"But what happens if you do find your baby?" Skye demanded, her eyes worried. "He's what—ten years old now?"

"Eleven."

"Eleven! Do you know what it would do to a boy that age

to find out that his biological mother is around? What if his adoptive parents haven't told him the truth? What if he thinks he's their biological child? What about his siblings? What about his folks—the ones who've nurtured him?"

"I'm not going to try to take him away," she cut in. "I just want to find out if he's okay."

"That's what you say now, Dani, but you're playing with fire here." Skye shook her head.

"You know what it's like to want a child."

"So now you want him?"

"No—I don't know. I just have to find out if he's okay."

"Oh, God, Dani, this could turn into a disaster," she whispered.

Hillary rode to the fence, and Cambridge, stretching his neck, shoved his soft nose into Dani's chest. "Are you fighting?" she asked her stepmother as her proud smile faded.

"No, honey, just having one of those heavy discussions."

"Well, don't, 'cause my mommy says you're not supposed to fight with your sisters."

"That's because you pick on the twins."

"Do not, they pick on me!"

"And you fight with your cousin Cody."

"That's different—he's a boy. A mean boy."

Dani laughed. "How can a three-year-old be mean?"

"He's Jenner's son," Skye said with a wink. "That should be explanation enough. So, Hillie-girl, are you all done here?"

"That's it for today. She just has to help put Cambridge away."

"Yuk!" Hillary muttered.

"Hey, he worked hard. He deserves a little special treatment. It'll only take a minute." Hillary's lower lip protruded, but Dani ignored it. "Take him inside. I'll be right there."

Skye sighed as Hillary turned the reins and the good-natured gelding ambled away. "I hope you know what you're doing by looking for your son," she said, worry shadowing her eyes. "I hope to God you know what you're doing."

*So do I,* Dani thought as she slid through the gate and started disassembling the jump. *So do I.*

Venitia stared at her son as if he'd just said he'd come from Mars. "I've told you all I know about your father," she said, reaching for the glass of wine on the kitchen counter. The warm odors of peanut butter and cinnamon scented the air. The timer clicked loudly as one batch of cookies cooled on a rack near the window. Venitia made a big show of scooping spoonfuls of dough and plopping them onto a baking sheet that was black from years of use.

"You haven't told me squat. All I've got is a name, Ma. Just a damned name. No memories, no photographs, just some vague ideas of who he was supposed to be."

Her hands paused over the mixing bowl for a second. "Oh, Brand, for the love of Saint Mary, just leave it alone. Your father was useless, okay? Just plain useless. But we survived without him."

"If that's what you call it."

"That's the way it was." She dropped the last of the dough on the sheet and shooed a cat out of the open window. After a long swallow of wine, she picked up a fork and made prints on each new cookie. She acted as if the conversation was over, just as she always did.

This time Brand kept on pushing. "He sent you money until I turned eighteen. You must have had some idea where he was."

"I never paid any attention."

"I don't believe you."

"It doesn't matter what you believe."

He couldn't stop a cruel smile from sliding across his face. "Now that's where you and I differ, Ma. I think it matters a lot what a kid thinks, especially when it comes to things about his old man. And besides, I'm not a kid anymore."

"I know that," she said softly.

"Just tell me a little bit more about Kendall. "Where was he from?"

"Oklahoma."

"I know, but *where* in Oklahoma. It's a big state."

"I don't know."

"What about his parents—my grandparents? Or sisters or brothers or cousins or—"

She shook her head and her gaze was glued to the nearly empty bowl of cookie dough. "We've been over this before. A hundred times at least. I don't know anything more today than I did ten years ago or twenty or thirty. He sent me money orders."

"Like clockwork."

"Yes."

"From all across the United States and Canada—you never missed a check. Always came on the first. At least you told me he drifted around the country."

"He did. That's right."

"It's odd, Ma. Don't you see? The mail isn't that dependable especially when you're talking about the entire continent, and what about the guy, huh? A drifter who won't even stick around to meet his kid and yet makes sure, makes damned sure, that the check gets there on time."

"What're you saying, that I'm lying to you?" she asked, her voice lifeless.

"Just that it's unusual, really unusual." He studied the lines on her face and hated himself for wounding her. "I'm gonna find him, Ma."

"No! Oh, Brandon. What would be the point?" she objected, licking her lips nervously. "He could be dead—he quit paying support when you turned eighteen."

"The month I turned eighteen. The very month. Like he

remembered. Never sent a birthday card, no note, never talked to you or wrote you and yet, damn it, he knew the minute I hit eighteen. Kinda makes you wonder, doesn't it?"

"Wonder what?" she asked in the same flat tone. She reached for her wineglass and held it with trembling fingers.

"If he was keeping track. Somehow. Some way."

"No—"

"Too many things don't add up, Ma, and someday I might settle down, get married, have a kid of my own. I would like to know a little family background—medical history as well as the usual things—where the family settled, how long we've been in America, which side we were on in the Civil War, who the damned black sheep are!"

His voice had risen to the point where it thundered through the kitchen, then, seeing the shimmer of tears in his mother's eyes, he swore under his breath and placed both hands on the kitchen counter. His shoulders were so tight they ached.

"Look, this is something I've thought about for a long time, okay? I was never ready to face him before, I guess, not until I was ready, until I knew that . . ." That what? He wouldn't be disappointed? Brand knew that he'd never felt strong enough to face the man who had sired him until now, until he'd become successful—until he'd been able to afford the damned Mercedes.

Feeling like a hypocrite, he closed his eyes and mentally started counting to ten. He was at seven when he heard metal wheels sliding across concrete. A second later, Chris dropped his skateboard on the back porch and swaggered into the house.

He shot a glance at Brand. "Thought you moved out," he grumbled as he snagged a cookie from the cooling rack.

"I did."

"Yeah, so what're you doing hanging around here?" Green eyes glared up at him defiantly and Brand realized for the first time that the kid thought he was abandoning him again.

Even though he hadn't been around much in all Chris's growing-up years, suddenly the boy, just starting adolescence, wanted to be with him, which was probably good considering that Chris was already getting into his share of trouble.

He'd had his first run-in with the law a year ago—at the Fourth of July parade when he'd set firecrackers off too near one of the horses and it had reared, throwing its rider before rampaging through the crowd. Luckily no one had been hurt. Then there was the incident when Chris had been caught with his dad's old shotgun and had been accused of peppering road signs with buckshot. Yep, he was on the fast track to no place good.

"I thought you'd like to come and see the ranch," Brand invited.

Chris shrugged as if he couldn't care less, held the cookie in his mouth and swung the refrigerator door open. He poured himself a monstrous glass of milk and ignored Brandon's remark.

"Where've you been?" Venitia asked, obviously relieved that the conversation about Brand's father had been forced to a close.

"Hangin'."

"Hangin' where?" his mother persisted as the timer buzzed. She pulled a sheet of cookies from the oven using a pot holder that had been scorched around the corners for years.

"Down at Bigg's."

Bigg's was a convenience store similar to the franchised minimarkets but locally owned by the Bigg sisters, Zelda and Connie, both divorced and raising young children. They had taken back their maiden name, bought the mom-and-pop operation from their ailing father and tried to make a go of it. Everything in the store was oversize to keep people reminded of their name. Teens and preteens hung out in the parking lot, usually just to get together but sometimes causing trouble.

"Who were you with?"

"Just some kids."

"Who?"

"Sean," he said, his voice edged in belligerence.

Venitia stiffened. "You know how I feel about him."

"He's not a bad guy," Chris said, defending his friend just as Brandan had done years before.

"Then why is there always trouble when Sean's around? Hmmm? I don't like you hanging out with him. He's been in trouble with the law already. Got caught sneaking into the Jamison place just last week. Bess Jamison raised holy— well, anyway, she was fit to be tied."

"She's always fit to be tied," Chris sneered. Brand agreed, but held his tongue. "So what's the big deal?"

"The big deal is that what Sean did is called breaking and entering and trespassing and who knows what else. He's broken the law. If anything comes up missing, he'll be blamed."

"Ma's right," Brandan said.

"You don't even know Sean."

"No, but I was him."

"What?"

"I was the kid all the parents didn't like—the guy who was always in trouble. It got me nowhere. Believe me."

Chris took a big swallow of his milk. "Looks like you did okay to me."

"I got lucky."

"Well, so will I," he said cockily.

Venitia sighed wearily. "Not if you hang out with that Sean."

"Sean didn't steal anything, okay? He just looked around. And besides, what's it to you? You're half-crocked most of the time!"

"Chris!" Brandon roared, and his mother seemed to crumple in on herself. "That's enough."

"It's true. You know it's true."

"This isn't about Ma."

"Well, it should be."

Venitia's back stiffened.

This was going nowhere fast. Brand clapped the boy on his shoulder. It was time they had a heart-to-heart. "Why don't you come and hang out with me this weekend," he said. "I can get you riding lessons."

"On a horse?" Chris said as if he'd tasted something bad. "*Girls* like horses."

"I know a woman who could give you lessons."

"Big deal."

"Not just any woman," Brandon said. "This one trains rodeo stock. She used to barrel race and do tricks."

"Tricks?" Chris asked, chewing on his cookie as the timer went off again. Venitia, still pale, pulled out the final batch.

"Yeah, I think she could stand up in the saddle, do a handstand and lean over so far that she could pick up a hand-kerchief with her teeth—all this while the horse was running at top speed."

"Sure," Chris said nonchalantly, totally unimpressed.

"It's true."

"Who was that?" Venitia asked, and Brandon noticed that somehow, while he was talking with Chris, she'd poured her-self another glass of wine. Two cats—one black, one gray striped—shot through the room hissing and spitting. "Shag, Pfeffer, you stop that!"

"Dani Donahue—uh, Stewart. The woman I'm renting from."

"Stewart?" Venitia repeated, shaking her head. "Never heard of her, but the Donahue name's familiar."

"Her older sister, Skye, is a doctor in Rimrock. Married Max McKee last Christmas. Dani was married to Jeff Stewart."

"Was?" Venetia asked.

"Divorced now. She lives in an apartment over the garage, rents out the main house to me, manages the ranch, owns some stock and gives riding lessons on the side."

"Busy lady," Venitia said as she finished removing the cookies from the sheet. Her hands were still shaking and Brandon wished somehow this family would quit wounding each other.

"That she is," Brandon said as an image of Dani, warm and fragrant from her bath, her hair damp, her skin so soft, entered his head. What had he been thinking about, kissing her so passionately? If the phone hadn't rung, they might have ended up in his bed, and that thought, though pleasant, scared the hell out of him. From past experience, he knew that if he made love to Dani, he'd never want to stop.

"Okay," Chris said suddenly, his green eyes assessing.

"Okay what?"

"I'll spend the weekend with you and ride a horse. Even though I know you're just trying to change the subject from Mom's drinking."

"Oh, Lord," Venitia whispered, sagging against the counter.

"You got a problem, Mom. We all know it." His eyes drilled into Brand's. "Don't we?"

"This isn't the time or place."

"It never is."

Brand looked at his mother. "We'll talk about this later."

"I don't want to—"

"Ma, we have to. I'll make an appointment with—"

"Don't you dare, Brand. This is my life we're talking about. *Mine!*" She hooked her thumb at her chest.

"And Chris's."

"I've managed to take care of him for eleven years."

Chris snorted.

"They'll take him away," Brand said flatly, knowing he was wounding her. "We'll talk, Ma, and when we do, we'll make some decisions."

Her voice quivered in indignation. "You have no right—"

"You can come to the ranch, too."

She closed her eyes. "I don't think so."

"Ma—"

"Forget it—she won't," Chris said angrily.

Venitia forced a strained smile and, as she always did, pretended that the conversation hadn't been tense, that everything was fine. "You two have a good weekend and I'll stay home and relax—enjoy the peace and quiet. The house could use a good cleaning and I'll bury myself in a book or rent one of those relationship movies that Chris hates so much."

Chris glowered.

Venitia took a swallow from her glass. "He wouldn't watch one with me if I paid him."

"Depends on how much you paid," Chris said, his jaw set and hard.

"Forget it." She seemed relieved to have some free time and Brandon realized that for as long as he could remember and probably longer, she'd been worried about one son or the other and how to make ends meet. With him, there had been the check from his father and she'd had Al to help her raise Chris, at least for a few years, but for most of her adult life, Venitia Scarlotti Cunningham had been scrimping, saving and worrying about her boys. And drinking. The lines on her face were testament to her concern. She needed a break from the stress—longer than a weekend.

Brand glanced at the wine bottle, then looked away. She'd be all right, he supposed. It was only a couple of days. "I'll pick you up after school tomorrow," he said to Chris.

"Cool," Chris responded without too much enthusiasm and Brand walked to the front door, his mother following him like a shadow.

"Workmen should be here next week," he said. "They'll fix anything you want. I already told them about the porch and windows and linoleum in the kitchen—you'd better pick out some new stuff for the floor and countertops and what about the bathroom? Looks like you could use a new shower stall."

"You don't have to do anything to the house, Brand."

"I want to, Ma." He shoved his hands through his hair. "And while the house is torn up, I think you should go to the hospital, have those tests done on your liver."

"I don't need to—"

"I talked to the doctor, Ma."

"Hospitals are expensive."

"Yeah, and death is permanent. Don't worry about the bills, okay?"

She bit her lip and he knew what she was thinking. She'd get another lecture about the evils of drink, the way the wine was destroying her liver and health, how it was affecting her mind. There would be suggestions to seek help through counselors and programs.

"I'll think about it," she promised, glancing back toward the kitchen, as if expecting her younger son to be eavesdropping.

"Good. Do it for Chris."

She swallowed, blinked hard and touched him lightly on the arm. "I didn't mean to belittle your need to find your father." Brand's stomach tightened at the mention of Kendall. She hesitated then swallowed. "It's just that . . . he wasn't a very decent man."

"Meaning what?" he asked, stiffening.

"Meaning that there are some things better left just as they are."

"Family secrets that wouldn't stand the light of day?"

"I just don't want to see you disappointed, that's all."

"I won't be, Ma," he said, then walked out the door. He felt her stare at his back. She was lying about his father; it was something he'd suspected for years, but now he was certain. Venitia knew where Jake Kendall was, or at least where some of his relatives were, but there was something so painful to her, or so vile about him, that she was protecting Brandon.

But from what?

Brandon waved at the calico cat resting on the hood of his car and the cat scrambled down, leaving a trail of footprints on the glossy paint job. Brand didn't mind. He just wanted some answers.

He remembered playing the tape of Dani's conversation with Sloan Redhawk. She'd hired a P. I. to find someone; maybe he should do the same. He was getting nowhere with his mother. He drove away from the small house where he'd grown up and headed out of town to the house that he leased from Dani.

Funny, he'd been there less than a week, and it was already starting to feel like home. For the past three days, he'd avoided Dani, deciding it was best to keep his distance, but he hadn't been able to shove her completely from his mind. Not only did he remember their lovemaking in every delicious detail, he also couldn't shake the memory of her phone call to Sloan Redhawk. Who, he wondered, for the dozenth time, was she trying to track down?

# CHAPTER NINE

"Jonah McKee was a bastard. He did things his own way. Played by his own rules." Sloan's voice sounded as if he were in the next room rather than miles away at his ranch near Warm Springs.

Dani blew her bangs out of her eyes and sighed. Wrapping the telephone cord around her hand, she leaned against the wall. "Jonah's dead now. It's time to fix things."

"I know. I'm checking on a couple of leads, but they may turn out to be nothing. That private hospital has been sold two times, and now is part of a huge conglomerate. The doctor's retired, living up on some lake in Canada near Banff somewhere, and the lawyer who handled the adoption is practicing in Detroit—corporate stuff. Since I can't find a birth certificate listing you as the mother, I'm checking all boys born around that date, but I've got to tell you, there isn't even an admitting record with your name on it."

Dani's heart turned to stone. "I was there, damn it, and I had my baby twelve hours later."

"I know. I'm still checking with the staff, but there's been a tremendous turnover in the past eleven years."

"Great."

"If you can come up with some names—the nurses that took care of you or the baby—"

"I can't remember any," she said, closing her eyes and conjuring up the faces of the two women who were in the delivery room. A large, buxom nurse took the baby to the scales and cleaned him off, and another one, a petite woman with a cap and black hair had held Dani's hand, kept encouraging her during the delivery. Dani had never noticed their names. "It was so long ago," she said, feeling defeated. "I was just a kid."

"Keep working on it."

"I will," she said.

"And I'll keep you posted."

"Thanks." Dani hung up her new telephone and dropped into a chair. She was dead tired and Sloan's call only deflated her. After eleven years of waiting, she was suddenly impatient, anxious to find her missing son. She'd already listed her name with the various social agencies; now she had to wait until one of them contacted her—if they were so inclined—or until Sloan dug up more information.

She grabbed the glass of lemonade she'd poured. Ice cubes clinked as she pressed the glass to her head in hopes of warding off another headache. Every muscle in her body ached and now she was depressed. Jonah McKee had covered his tracks, and her baby's tracks, as well.

"You won't beat me," she vowed as if Jonah could hear her, as if she had to make him understand her determination to find her child. "This is just a setback, that's all," she told herself. "What did you expect?"

She heard the sound of a truck pull into the yard and turned to look out the window. She half expected Jack to stop by, but the rig parked near the stables wasn't Jack's old pickup.

A Jeep of some sort—a couple of years old from the looks of it—backed into Brand's spot in the garage below Dani's apartment. A minute later, Brand, wearing sunglasses, his jacket slung over his shoulder, an overnight bag in one hand, emerged. Along with him was a gawky kid who looked somewhere around thirteen.

The boy was lanky, with shorts that brushed his knees, coffee brown hair that flopped around his ears and features that were too big for his face. He swaggered as he walked and carried a skateboard with him. A kid with an attitude. She smiled; he reminded her a little of Brand as a boy and she realized that this must be his brother.

To her horror, they mounted the steps to her apartment. Within seconds, there was a series of loud raps on her door.

Great. Just what she needed. It was difficult enough to deal with Brand, a man she couldn't look at without feeling her pulse jump. Somehow she had to get over this fascination. But then her thoughts turned back to the night in his kitchen, her bathrobe gaping open, his mouth touching her intimately, and her insides turned to jelly.

"Coming," she yelled as Solomon, startled from a nap on top of her desk, bolted across the room. Dani opened the door to find Brandon standing on the landing. His easy smile was in place, his gaze as blue as the summer sky. The boy hung back suspiciously, staring at her through a shank of long hair that hid his eyes.

"This is my brother, Chris," Brand said as she stepped out of the way, silently inviting them inside. "Chris—Dani Stewart. She's my landlord."

"Hi," the boy mumbled, not bothering to meet her gaze.

"Hi." Dani waved to her small kitchen. "I was just having some lemonade. How about you?"

The kid glanced at Brand. "Nah. Thanks." He looked as if he'd rather be any place on earth than her cramped quarters.

"Sure?" Maybe he was just being polite. "I've got a pitcher already made." She turned her attention to Brand and steadfastly pushed aside all memories of their night together. "How about you?" God, her face felt tight, her smile plastic.

"Sounds good. Thanks."

Dani poured another couple of glasses. "Here ya go." She smothered a smile when Chris swallowed half his down in one long gulp.

Brand, amused, caught her gaze over the rim of his glass as the boy finished his drink. Without a word, Dani refilled it.

"Chris is gonna be staying with me for a few days," Brand explained. "I promised him that if you had the time, I'd buy him some riding lessons."

Dani managed to hide her surprise. Boys this kid's age weren't usually interested in riding horses—they were already primed for cars. "Oh, well, sure. I, um, could do it tomorrow," she said, mentally checking her schedule. "In the afternoon, around three?"

"You're sure?"

"Absolutely."

Chris studied the floor, then he tossed his hair from his eyes and Dani's breath caught for a second. He looked so much like his brother. Only the eyes were different. Chris's were a hazel green and not quite so deep set as Brandon's, his face a little rounder, his chin not so square but time would file off the softer edges. "I think horses are a pain," he grumbled.

Dani shot Brandon a look. "So why do you want to ride?" she asked the boy.

"It was his idea." He hitched his chin toward Brandon.

"Oh," What was going on here?

A smile tugged at Brandon's lips. "I told him you were a hotshot rodeo rider."

"That was a long time ago."

The kid, who had just the hint of peach fuzz on his upper

lip seemed suddenly defiant. "Brandon says you used to race horses and do tricks on them."

"Brandon remembers a lot," she said, curiously eyeing the pair. While she and Brandon were seeing each other, she hadn't competed in one rodeo. She'd stopped when she was about sixteen, at a time when she'd become more interested in boys than horses and when she'd realized that she couldn't count on prize money if she didn't win and she needed a steady job with wages she could depend upon. That's when she'd begun to wait tables and collect tips.

"Can you really stand on your head in the saddle?" Finishing his drink, he sucked on an ice cube, then cracked it with his back teeth.

She laughed and shook her head. "No."

"What about picking up a handkerchief with your teeth while the horse is running?" The ice cube crunched loudly.

"Oh, Lord, no." She pinned Brandon with a knowing glance. "Is that what you've been telling him?"

"Just repeating what I heard."

"And embellishing a bit, I'll bet." She sent Chris a chagrined smile. "I just raced and trained horses. I could sit backward and get up on my knees, but that's about it. Everything else your brother's been pitching to you has been a big stretch of the imagination."

Chris rolled his eyes as if to say "big deal." He shifted from one foot to the other and studied her carefully. Dani was painfully aware of her appearance—dirty and sweaty clothes, her hair pulled back, her face probably streaked with dust, without a hint of makeup. What had Brandon thought he would accomplish by bringing him here?

"I don't like horses," Chris stated baldly.

"Why not?"

"They're stupid."

Dani saw instant red. She thought of all the horses she'd worked with over the years, all the soft noses, liquid eyes and quick hooves. "Horses are incredibly bright creatures," she said, hating the sound of her voice—almost preachy, it was. "They're loyal, courageous, and will, if you treat them well, do anything for you. And that," she said with a crisp smile, "is a lot more than you can say for most people."

Chris made a sound of disgust in the back of his throat.

"Now, I'll admit that some of them can be royal pains, a few are mean spirited, and some aren't as bright as others, but in general, they're as smart as they need to be."

"Right." Sarcasm dripped off his words.

Brandon sent him a look that could melt lead. "He'll be ready tomorrow at three." He placed his empty glass in the sink and Chris followed suit. "Thanks, Dani."

"No problem," she said, though it was a lie. Everything with Brandon was a problem. Within seconds, they were gone, out the door and down the steps.

Dani should have been relieved. Instead, she felt disheartened. The apartment seemed strangely empty without Brandon and his cocky half brother.

"I guess I should warn you about Chris." Brand's voice caught her off guard. She'd just closed the stable door and the soft chorus of crickets whispered through the night. No quiet cough or sound of gravel crunching under boots had signaled his approach. He was waiting for her, sitting on the top rail of the fence, his hands braced around the old wood on either side of him. The moon, not quite full, rode high in the sky and cast its silvery glow over the landscape.

"What's to know?" she asked, walking closer to him and seeing the starlight catch in his eyes. Her heart did a silly little flip and began to pound.

"He might be here a lot."

"Fine with me," she said, wrapping her arms around her waist. "I like kids."

"He's trouble."

"Weren't we all?"

Brand chuckled softly. "I blamed my . . . well, trouble with the law on the fact that I didn't have a dad hanging around pointing me in the right direction, though my mother tried her best. But I probably would've been hell on wheels even if old Kendall had been in the picture. Chris was with his dad for quite a while, but he's still starting to rebel."

"It's all part of growing up. Besides, Chris seems older than eleven."

"Always has," Brand said, then frowned. "I didn't know him much when he was a little kid—didn't even see my ma all the while she was pregnant or the first couple years of Chris's life—too caught up in my own, I guess, and I never cared much for Al Cunningham. Still don't." His skin seemed to tighten over his face. "He sure doesn't seem to give two cents for a kid he helped bring into the world."

"Not all men are cut out to be fathers," she said, the pain in her voice evident.

"Then they shouldn't be," he said flatly, and she died a little inside. "Anyway, Chris is okay. I didn't mean to stick you with him. I just thought he should find some different outlets for all that restless energy." He paused, looked down at her, then toward the house where lights were glowing in warm patches. "Yeah, he seems older than he is—more like thirteen or fourteen. The girls are already calling." His smile was infectious—a cocky white slash in the darkness—and Dani couldn't help but respond.

"He's cute, in that awkward preteen way. I bet the phone calls don't stop."

"Ma's worried."

"Why? Didn't they call you when you were Chris's age?"

Brand rubbed his chin. "I don't remember it that way, but Ma seems to think so."

"She probably knows."

He hopped down from the fence and dusted his hands on his jeans. "Yeah, I suppose." The levity had left his voice and he was so close to her, she could feel his heat. Arms folded over his chest, he leaned over the top rail while eyeing the moon-drenched fields where the animals still grazed lazily, dark shapes against the hillside.

"So this is it, isn't it? Your dream."

"Yeah," she admitted, thinking that owning the ranch was only part of her dream. The other included finding her son. "I've wanted it for a long time."

He placed an arm around her shoulders and it seemed only natural to rest her head against his chest. She heard the soft, steady thump of his heart, almost an echo of her own. "You'll get it," he said with quiet encouragement. "You're the kind of woman who gets what she wants."

Her heart nearly broke. If only he knew the truth of her life; if only he could see past the lies. She felt moved and gazed for a while at the sky while wondering if this was the right time to tell him they had a son.

Turning, he slid a hand to her face, and with his hand on her throat, gently tipped her chin upward, forcing her to stare into his eyes. Slowly, as if searching her face for answers, he kissed her, his lips bold as they claimed hers, his muted groan an answer to the soft cry in her throat.

Closing her eyes, she felt his arms clamp more tightly around her, drowned in the smell and touch of him. His tongue slipped between her teeth and she opened to him, kissing him fiercely, letting the wonder of the moment lock them together as if for all eternity.

"Dani," he whispered hoarsely as one of his hands rounded over her bottom and rubbed against the worn denim, drawing her close between his legs where she could feel the hard bulge in his crotch. Desire thundered through her blood. "Damn it, Dani, you make me crazy."

"Me?" she whispered.

"You. Everything I thought I believed in is turned upside down and inside out when I'm with you and all I want to do is carry you into the house and throw you on my bed."

She pressed a finger to his lips. "Don't even say it."

"Why not? It's the truth." To prove his point, he took her finger into his mouth and gently sucked.

Her insides turned to liquid fire and she wanted to give in to the passion that roared through her. Delicious, seductive sensations curled through her body until she pulled her finger away and took a step backward. "This can't happen," she said. "I—I think I said it before."

"And I think it's inevitable."

"No way, Brand." Shaking her head, she drew in a deep, mind-clearing breath. "I don't want to get involved with you . . . with anyone. Not now. Maybe not ever."

He barked out a laugh. "You're pretty young to make that kind of a statement."

"It's the truth."

"Because of Jeff?" he asked, and a quiet fury flashed in his eyes.

*Because of you!* "Partly."

"And the other part?"

"I just want to be my own woman, okay? I don't need a man in my life. Not as a lover and certainly not as a husband."

"No one said anything about marriage," he returned. And Dani felt some little ray of hope wither and die within her.

"Good thing, 'cause I'm not interested. Nor do I play house. Look, I'm not trying to be a prude or one of those . . . what do they call them, born-again virgins or something. I just don't want to get into anything that would be a mess to get out of." She tried to step back, but his arms tightened around her waist.

"We're going to be living next to each other for a long time," he said slowly, his breath whispering over his face. "Do you honestly think we can ignore what's happening here?"

"I sure hope we can," she replied, "because I'm not into replaying the mistakes of my youth."

"You and I were a mistake?" he asked, one dark brow arching in challenge.

"The biggest," she lied and worked her way out of his uneasy embrace.

"Why was that?"

*Because you broke my heart, you bastard.* "Because it didn't work out," she said, turning on her heel and hurrying to the garage. She ran up the stairs, flew through the door and locked it behind her. Then she laughed. What was she afraid of? That he would chase her, catch up with her, throw her on the bed and make love to her until dawn? That she would be a ravaged, satiated woman in the morning? That she'd wake up to find Brandon, the dark shadow of his beard coloring his jaw, staring down at her, ready to make love again? Her knees went weak at the thought. Good grief, she was a fool.

She started unbuttoning her blouse and walked into the bathroom. Ignoring the stained shower stall, she turned the water on full blast, shrieked as the cold jets stung her body and waited until the water would do the trick, freeze her blood, shrivel up her desire and set her free from wickedly wanton thoughts of Brandon Scarlotti.

He wasn't even the same man she remembered. He'd traded in his Harley for a Mercedes—no, now a Jeep, she reminded herself—and given up his battered denim vests for designer leather jackets and expensive suits. "Heaven help me," she whispered. Placing both palms on the side of the stall, she faced the pathetic stream of icy water and ducked her head under the frigid spray. Right now, Brandon Scarlotti reeked of money and power and wasn't the same man who'd ridden out of her life twelve years ago. She'd loved a wild boy who spit in the face of authority. She couldn't be attracted to the new Brandon, all clean and upright, a man used to riding in corporate jets and having his orders obeyed. He was just too damned polished these days.

Dani lathered up, turned on the warm water and told herself she would never again be played for a fool. And certainly not by the same man. She was living life by her rules and come hell or high water, Brandon Scarlotti wasn't going to waltz back into her life and foul it all up for her. She just plain wouldn't let him. Even if it killed her.

The kid wasn't too good on a horse. Oh, he managed to stay in the saddle, but when asked to turn the animal to the right or left, Chris was all thumbs.

"A bike or a board is easier," he complained when his mount stood in the middle of the corral refusing to move. He pulled on one rein, then the other. "They don't have minds of their own."

"I know. That's what's so great about animals," Dani said, walking forward and showing Chris how to hold the reins in one hand and lay the leather straps alongside the gelding's neck. "Now, cluck your tongue and give him a little nudge with your knees or heels, but nothing too hard."

Chris made some feeble attempts at tongue clucking and the horse, a bay named Gilder, ambled to the left. "Hey, how about that!" Chris laughed. "Does he go any faster?"

"Lots, but first let's get some basics down, like how to make him turn or stop. Then we'll talk about second gear." Dani worked with him in the paddock for about forty-five minutes and Chris, a quick learner, showed more interest than she had anticipated. A few times when he was especially excited, she got a glimpse of the little boy he had once been, instead of the attitude he wore like some kind of medal. Though loath to admit it, he seemed to enjoy riding Gilder, who had a sweet temperament but, upon command, could explode into a gallop that would take a boy's breath away.

"Can't we go out in the fields, make him run?" Chris asked after nearly two hours of instruction about care of the animal, tack and general signals to the horse.

"Not until I know that you'll think of him more as a partner than a machine."

"Yeah, sure," he said, rolling his big mischievous eyes. "Come on, *partner*, let's show her what we can really do."

"Time enough for that later," Dani said.

"When?"

"How about tomorrow?" She mentally calculated. Chris wasn't a natural in the saddle, but he was learning. And he was quick—sharp as the proverbial tack. But he still wouldn't let go of his cocky I'm-sooo-cool attitude that would eventually get in his way. He seemed to like to show off or prove himself.

"When?"

"I could make a picnic lunch—although I'm not much of a cook, but I think I might be able to put a couple of sandwiches together and find a Coke or two. We could ride up to the bluff—from there you can see across the valley—and catch a glimpse of Elkhorn Lake, where your brother is building his resort."

"Cool," Chris said with more enthusiasm than she expected. He even went so far as to let a ghost of a smile play upon his lips before he turned surly again.

Dani showed the boy how to cool off his mount, how much water should be given after a long ride, how to remove the saddle and bridle, where the blankets were kept, how to brush a horse and avoid getting kicked. By the time they were finished, Brandon drove into the yard, his Jeep sporting a film of dust.

"How'd the lesson go?" Brandon asked as Dani and Chris washed off at the old pump near the back porch, a relic from the days before indoor plumbing.

"A snap," Chris replied. "I'm ready for racing."

"Well, almost," Dani said wryly. "We still have a few bugs to work out."

"Tomorrow we're going up to the bluff for a picnic," Chris said. "Wanna come?"

"On a horse?" Brandon glanced skeptically at Dani.

Chris's eyes sharpened. "What? You don't ride?"

"Not for a long time."

"It's just like a bike," Dani observed. "Once you learn, you never forget."

"Right. You'll remind my horse of that?" he said.

She grinned widely, forgetting for a moment that she was supposed to avoid him whatever the cost. "All part of the package deal."

"How can I pass it up?"

"You can't," Chris said, and Dani wondered what she was getting herself into with Brandon and his devil-be-damned half brother. She had problems enough, she reminded herself, without getting involved with them. But then she just couldn't help herself and why should she? A day up at the bluff would be pleasant, and in her mind she was already figuring out what to pack for lunch—something heartier than her usual fare of crackers, an apple and a can of diet pop. "Come on, Brand," Chris said, shoving a baseball cap on his head backward. "We'll have a blast."

With Dani in the lead, they rode along a dusty trail that wound upward through the pines to the highest ridge of rimrock. Dani always found the view breathtaking, the sky so close she was certain God was nearby.

A few wispy clouds dared shift across the blue sky, and far below, in the valley that stretched for miles, was a view of one corner of Elkhorn Lake. Deep, clear water reflected the azure summer sky.

"So that's where you're gonna build the resort?" Chris asked as he eyed the sun-dappled waters.

"On the north end," Brand replied. For someone who had acted as if riding a horse was about as appealing as catching rattlesnakes with his bare hands, he'd done a fair job of riding—just as he had all those years ago.

Chris, after a slow start yesterday, had taken to riding as easily as an eaglet takes to soaring in the sky. He'd never shown an inch of fear today, and even when his horse, Gilder, had been spooked by a pheasant rising out of the dry grass, Chris had maintained control, calming the flighty bay with steady hands and a soothing voice that cracked occasionally and caused a red flush to steal up his neck.

They spread a blanket on the ground and pulled out a lunch of cold chicken, potato salad, sourdough biscuits and honey, grapes and applesauce cake from a knapsack packed especially by Kiki, the cook for the McKees. When Skye had learned of Dani's plans, she'd enlisted Kiki's help. The old cook, complaining all the while according to Skye, had been secretly flattered and outdone herself. Plaid napkins and silverware had been included, as had a bottle of chilled wine, which had been stowed in an insulated saddle pack and retained its cool temperature.

"Gourmet fare," Brandon remarked as Dani opened plastic containers of goodies and handed him a corkscrew. "How'd you manage this?"

She laughed and squinted against the sun, watching as Chris tethered the horses beneath a couple of scrawny pine trees. "I'd like to lie and tell you that this was all my doing, that I had hidden talents, but the truth of the matter is that I'm pretty much a lousy cook, and my sister, hearing my plans, was horrified enough to enlist the help of a professional."

Brandon watched as she set out the paper plates on the blanket. "So you're a fake. Is that what you're telling me?"

"Not quite. I'm just admitting that I'm lacking a little when it comes to being domestic."

"Hard to believe," he said, working the cork out of the bottle.

"Ask my ex," she quipped, then quickly regretted bringing Jeff into the conversation. Jeff was a part of her life she never wanted to discuss, especially not with Brandon. Clamping her mouth shut, she handed him two plastic glasses.

"I wouldn't ask him anything," Brandon said as he poured. "The man's got to be a fool."

"Why's that?" Dani couldn't resist asking.

"He let you go, didn't he?"

*So did you, Brand. So did you.* The air was suddenly still. Dani's throat tightened, seemed clogged with unshed tears. One of the horses neighed softly. "Yes, well," she said, barely able to speak, "it was a mutual decision." She busied herself with napkins and silverware, but Brand's hand captured her wrist.

"I would never make that mistake."

"You already did," she countered.

"We were kids and we weren't married."

She cleared her throat and looked away, afraid her eyes would give her feelings away. "Why are you telling me this? Why now?"

The tips of his fingers rubbed the inside of her wrist and he muttered, "I'll be damned if I know." It wasn't a lie. Why did he feel suddenly compelled to offer her something, anything, to chase away the sadness in her eyes? Why did he think he had to keep telling her that he'd cared, when it was obvious from the way he'd run out on her years before that he hadn't loved her enough. He couldn't atone for his past sins, so why was he bound and determined to play the knight-in-shining-armor routine? Sure, she attracted him. Hell, if he could, he'd make love to her until they were both sweating and gasping for air, but that was a purely physical dream—the heat of his body wanting to meld with hers. But on an emotional level, he knew he was being ridiculous, even fatalistic.

The moment was awkward and he dropped her hand just as Chris ran up and flung himself down on the blanket. "What's for lunch?"

"What isn't?" Brand asked, looking at the spread.

"Well, what are we waiting for?" Chris demanded, and Dani, as if anxious for a distraction, began helping him fill a plate.

Brand leaned back and sipped his wine, wondering why he felt more content than he had in years. The restless edge that had been with him during his adolescence and early years of manhood seemed to have suddenly vanished and he enjoyed watching the shadows from the few trees play upon the ground. He'd been running so long, he'd barely had time to catch his breath, but here, up in the mountains and away from the roar of the city, his voracious ambition—his overwhelming need to prove himself—had all but disappeared. He watched as Dani and Chris piled plates, handing him one and laughing together until Chris spied the wine bottle.

"You don't need that," Chris said, jabbing at the half-empty bottle with his uneaten chicken leg. Deep furrows etched his forehead.

Dani looked from one brother to the other and took hold of the situation. "You're absolutely right, Chris. We don't." Dani sipped from her glass anyway. "But it's a nice touch. Kiki outdid herself."

Chris scowled and chewed on his chicken leg.

"This is a picnic, not a fancy banquet." Tossing out the rest of his chardonnay, Brand realized that to Chris, alcohol, especially wine, was the enemy.

Dani's mouth dropped open, but as if she understood, she didn't say a word and corked the bottle. They ate the rest of the meal slowly, listening as Chris did impressions of his friends and teachers from his past year in school, feeling the sun warm on their crowns, leaving the cares of the rest of the world behind.

A hawk circled above them and far away a jet dared slice across the blue sky. Dani's laughter filled the air and Chris, too, seemed to relax.

Brandon picked a long blade of grass and chewed on the end as he watched the sunlight gild Dani's hair. Her gaze touched his, and in a heart-stopping instant, he knew that he'd never ceased loving her. That silly boyhood passion that he'd buried for so long was still in his heart.

He smiled and let out his breath. For the first time in his life, Brandon Scarlotti felt as if he belonged.

# CHAPTER TEN

"I don't get it. Why're you changing the tire by yourself?" Chris plopped onto the seat of the tractor and eyed Dani speculatively, as if he'd never seen a woman do this kind of physical labor.

"Who else is going to do it?" she asked, yanking the tire from the car and eyeing the bare patch where the black rubber had fallen off to reveal the steel belt beneath.

"I don't know. A ranch hand maybe."

"Don't have one."

"What about that guy, Jack?"

"He only works here part-time. The tire needs to be fixed now."

"Well, your husband or boyfriend should do it," he said, squinting a little and watching her intently.

"Out of those, as well." She straightened and rubbed her back. Sweat collected around her forehead and drizzled down her spine. The day was hot, the work dirty, and she felt grimy and gritty far beneath her skin. At times like these, she almost envied women who relied on some big strong man to do their dirty work. Almost—but not quite. She'd rather be independent, even if it did make things a little tougher.

Swiping the sweat from her forehead, she reached for the spare and lined it up.

Chris hopped from the tractor seat and was right beside her, peering over her shoulder. "Brandon could help you."

"He's got enough to do, don't you think?" she said.

"But—"

"It's all right, really. I can manage."

"Maybe I could help out around here," he offered earnestly. He reached into the hubcap and picked up a lug nut, then flipped it into the air and caught it deftly.

"Don't lose those."

"I won't." He flipped it again like a coin and it turned end over end before landing back in his palm. "You were married."

She felt her chest constrict. "That's right."

"But you got a divorce."

"Mmmm—hand me that nut here, would you?" She took it from his outstretched palm and spun it onto the lug.

"You got any kids?"

The ground seemed to shift beneath her feet. "Kids? Well, you don't see any, do you?"

"Thought maybe they live with their dad."

She shook her head and hardly dared breathe. "Nope."

"You should. You like 'em."

"That's true enough," she admitted. Rocking back on her heels, she looked into his earnest hazel green eyes and didn't have the heart to tell him that she loved her independence and guarded it fiercely. She turned the subject back to his wanting to work. "Look, if you want to help out around here, you can, but only under the condition that I pay you."

"But I thought you didn't have any money. That's what Brandon says. That's why he's living in the big house and you're in the apartment."

Humiliation singed through her veins. The last thing she

ever wanted anyone to think was that she was some kind of
charity case. She twirled a lug nut into place, then reached for
another. "It's true," she said slowly, wishing she could give
Brandon a piece of her mind. "I don't have a lot of money
right now. I'm hoping to buy this ranch and I've got to save
everything I can. Besides, now that I'm living alone, I don't
really need all the space of the house—the apartment will suit
me just fine."

"Brandon lives alone."

"Unless you come to visit." She reached for her wrench
and Chris slapped it into her open palm like a nurse handing
a surgeon his scalpel in the operating room. "Which I suppose
will be fairly often." She tightened one nut, then worked on
the one on the opposite side of the wheel.

"Depends."

"On what?" She glanced up at him and noticed that his lips
had formed a hard, unhappy line.

"Ma, I guess. Brandon's worried about her."

"Oh?" When he didn't elaborate, Dani let the subject drop.
"Well, anyway, I'm going to pay you for helping out, either in
dollars and cents or a trade for riding lessons. Whichever you
want."

"Really?" He seemed to consider.

"Your choice."

"Okay, I'll take the cash."

"Smart boy." He stuck out his hand and Dani shook it
firmly.

From that moment on, he was her shadow, following her
around the ranch, learning the ropes, catching on quickly as
Dani sorted calves, repaired fences and vaccinated some of
the horses. Eventually, when Dani began cleaning out the
stables, he tired of the work, and she gave him hammer, nails,
saw and plywood so that he could construct a jump for his
skateboarding. He was a good kid, she thought as he walked
back toward the house, even though he had a restlessness

about him that reminded her of Brandon. His hands and feet were too big for the rest of his body, his arms and legs lanky, his shoulders just beginning to broaden. An early bloomer. No wonder the girls were calling and chasing after him. She leaned on the end of her shovel, her hands burrowed inside rawhide work gloves, and stared after him.

Her son would be about the same age, she thought, aching inside. Would he be so big, so close to being a man? She'd already missed so much of his life. A huge, dark hand reached around her heart and squeezed hard. She had to fight off an onslaught of tears. She wasn't going to cry; she'd shed all her tears in a previous lifetime and now she was going to be strong and in control of her life—no longer would she be the victim.

All she had to do to end this pain was find her son.


A backhoe lifted its giant jaw of a shovel and dug deep into the dry earth, chewing at rocks and dirt, spewing black smoke into the cloudless sky.

Brandon, eyes protected from the bright sunlight by dark glasses, watched as the ground was broken for his resort. Though now it was just a gaping hole a quarter of a mile away from the shores of the lake, soon a concrete crew would come in to pour the foundation, and a week or so later the framers would follow. Elkhorn Lodge would become more than an idea drawn on blueprints.

He imagined the swimming pool, tennis courts and weight room. Farther away there would be stables, an eighteen-hole golf course flanking the river, private airstrip and acres upon acres of biking and hiking trails. The park by the lake would have a private moorage for sailboats and speed craft, even a dock for the houseboats that lumbered through the water. A vacation paradise, all near his own hometown. He thought that his mother could move here, have her own quarters with maid and room service along with a separate minisuite for Chris. But first he had to get her to the doctor and into some kind of treatment program.

Squinting as the first truckload of dirt rolled away on the crushed-rock road, he picked up a handful of soil and let the dry earth drift through his fingers. This project felt good—better than any he'd done before. Because he was home. Because he was close to his family. Because of Dani.

Yep, he could see the building already taking shape before his eyes, even though nothing yet existed. He was getting away from himself. It would take over a year to construct the lodge, longer yet for the rest of the project. He planned to finish it in three stages and he'd be around a long time.

Close to Dani.

After the lodge was finished, he had planned to move into his own suite and leave Dani's ranch to her. Strangely, he experienced a tug on his heart and told himself he was being a nostalgic fool.

"Brand!" His foreman, Syd Crane, a bowlegged man of fifty, sauntered up. He was looking at a map and scowling.

"What's up?"

"Nothin' good, let me tell you." Syd shot a stream of tobacco juice onto the ground. "We got ourselves some problems."

"Don't we always?"

Syd snorted, unamused.

"Okay, let's hear it." Brand straightened and dusted his hands on his jeans. He wasn't worried by Syd's concerns; his entire life consisted of solving problems that Syd, worrier that he was, despaired of fixing. Syd was a good man, an industrious man, the hardest worker Brand had ever met, but he wasn't long on imagination.

Syd chewed on a lower lip flecked with pieces of tobacco. "Looks like the northwest corner of the property has some significance to a local tribe of Indians."

"The northwest? We bought that from Gib Wilkins, right?" Brandon asked, trying to remember all the details. "Wilkins sold us his farm . . . been in the family since the first Wilkins pioneer came over on the wagon train into Baker City, right?"

"Yeah, but apparently a few acres of the land were part of an Indian burial ground and there was some agreement between the original Wilkins—Ezra, I think his name was—and the chief. This part of the land wasn't to be disturbed. Gib claims he doesn't know anything about it, but the attorney for the tribe, a woman named Janice something-or-other, has the original deed or whatever it is and it looks valid." He rubbed the back of his weathered neck furiously. "So now we're thinking about putting a par five on this strip of holy land or some damned thing and the Native Americans aren't too happy. I took the call in the trailer from your lawyer, who's been in contact with some legal representative of the tribe."

"I'll handle it," Brand said, willing to make concessions. As a bastard who had no roots of his own, he respected the ancestors of others. "Anything else?"

"Well, there's a threat of a strike involving the drivers of the dump trucks."

"Great."

"Also, a fella called about waste management. With the Department of Environmental Quality." Once Syd got started with his complaints and worries, he didn't give up.

Brand offered Syd a grin. "Been a full morning, hasn't it?"

"I guess. Then there's the problem with the plumbing company we hired. They can't get some of the pipe, trouble with the IRS or something, and Ed Banks, the engineer in charge of the sewage system, broke his leg in two places last night playing soccer like he was some young kid or something. Had to have surgery and pins and plates and all sorts of things, so he'll be out of the Portland office of his firm for a couple of weeks. If we have any problems we're supposed to talk to his assistant, a junior engineer." Disgusted, Syd spit another stream of tobacco juice onto the dust, startling a lizard that darted quickly away. "Other than that, everything's right on schedule."

Brandon winked as he clapped Syd on the shoulder. "That's what I like about this job," he said. "Everything is always so easy." They walked back to the office—a trailer parked on the site—that was divided into two rooms with a small kitchen and bathroom separating them. Syd shared his office with a secretary, Rinda Todd. Brandon's desk was in the back and included a small closet and sofa bed that he could use if he had to work late. Though they were located in a remote part of Oregon, they were linked by phone and computers to Portland and Bend. "At least we've broken ground," he told the worried foreman. "These other things'll work out. I'll talk to the law firm about the Native Americans and the union and I'll put in a call to the engineers. Relax, Syd, we're still ahead of schedule."

"Yeah, but winter will be here before you know it and it's damn cold over here. Not like California."

"Anyone ever tell you that you worry too much?" Brandon asked, with a knowing smile.

"Nope," Syd deadpanned. "Everyone thinks I'm a regular optimist."

Brandon laughed as he climbed the two steps into the trailer and settled into his chair. A stack of messages littered one corner of his desk, a computer monitor glowed on the other and he realized that he'd been away from the job longer than he'd planned. For the first time in years, he'd taken the weekend off and spent it with his brother and Dani. A smile played upon his lips and he looked forward to going home, not because he was a homebody at heart, but because he knew that he'd probably see her. And damn it, much as he didn't want to, he liked knowing that Dani, with her wide gold eyes, mutinous little chin and hot-tempered determination, was nearby. Just a stone's throw away.

* * *

Dani's fingers tightened over the receiver and her heart nearly stopped for a second.

"I've got a line on a nurse at the hospital," Sloan admitted, though there was a trace of reluctance in his voice, as if he was afraid of raising her hopes just to dash them.

"Who is she?" Dani, seated at her small table, was in the middle of paying bills. Now, all her pressing debts were forgotten. Her throat was dry with anticipation and she tapped her pen nervously on the table's edge.

"Her name is Bobbi Ragsdale and she was an R.N. who worked in the delivery room when you were admitted." He hesitated for a second and Dani's teeth sank into her lower lip. "Look, Dani, this may not pan out. I wouldn't have even mentioned it, but I wanted you to know that I'm still working on it. This nurse is the first person associated with that private hospital who might remember seeing McKee at that time. Everyone else seems to think he was on the board of directors but never showed his face at the hospital. Nurse Ragsdale was on duty the night you delivered, though she doesn't remember your name, just that an unwed mother was giving birth."

"No?"

"Could you have been admitted under an alias?"

"I don't think so—"

"You weren't eighteen, right?"

"No, not quite."

"And your mother was with you?"

"Yes, she filled out all the forms because of the insurance and all and Estelle was there."

"The woman you were staying with, Estelle Getwright."

"Uh-huh."

"Too bad she's gone," Sloan said.

Dani leaned back in her chair. Estelle, who ran a small home for unwed mothers, had been good to her, taking her in, helping her through those last final weeks when she'd felt so alone in the world. Prematurely gray, with a nervous smile and a heart of gold, Estelle had been a godsend. A lump came to Dani's throat as she remembered the kindly middle-aged woman with her sharp birdlike eyes and brittle chortle whenever she laughed.

"Your mother was working for Jonah McKee at the time, right? The insurance payment would have been from the policy for his company."

"I—I think so, but I don't know. No, wait, there was something about my medical expenses being paid by the couple who adopted the baby. I don't think an insurance company was involved. I'm sorry, that part's pretty hazy. I was just a kid and didn't think about the cost of things. I guess I thought that Mom or maybe Jonah McKee had taken care of the bills."

"Yeah, I know," he said, and she could almost hear the wheels turning in his mind. "Why would he care?"

Dani tossed her hair over her shoulder and stretched the phone line tight. She clicked her pen nervously. "I've asked myself that same question about a million times. The only thing I can figure is that he somehow felt obligated to my mom. Dad was killed while working for him when I was just a little kid and ever since then Jonah seemed to step in whenever there was a family problem. My pregnancy was just one more."

"You think?"

"I've always wondered why. I just don't know," she admitted, wishing now that she'd approached the old man while he was alive, that she'd demanded answers, that she'd found out what had happened to her baby and the couple who'd adopted him, that she'd stared into Jonah McKee's eyes and asked him why he'd cared what had happened to her child.

"Okay, look, I'll talk to this Ragsdale woman and let you know if it comes to anything."

"Thanks," she said, hanging up and ignoring the bills on

the table in front of her. Leaning her head in her hands, she closed her eyes. That night was a blur. She'd woken up because of the labor. Pain so intense she could barely breathe shot through her abdomen. When it passed and she tried to roll out of bed, her water broke, gushing all over the sheets and floor.

Another girl ran for Estelle who, in pin curls and flannel nightgown, hurried to her bedside. In complete control, Estelle helped her get dressed, telling her not to worry about the mess, all that mattered was that the baby was healthy. Estelle threw on a robe, made a couple of hasty phone calls to the hospital and to Dani's mother—or had one been to Jonah McKee?—and Dani was bundled into Estelle's old sedan that coughed and sputtered as she backed out of the driveway of the old house that was home to several mothers to be. The pains came quickly and Estelle kept talking to Dani while pushing the speed limit, driving through the streets of The Dalles to the hospital, located about ten miles past the city limits.

"Breathe shallow and fast," Estelle kept telling her as they drove through the night. "You're doing fine."

With each stabbing pain, Dani felt as if her entire insides were shredding, tearing apart. She held her arms around the bulge that was her middle, fought back tears of fear and reminded herself that this was what she wanted. When she'd found out she was pregnant, she'd told her mother, and Irene hadn't wasted any time in finding a solution to her daughter's "situation." Dani had been firm on the abortion issue; she wasn't going to get rid of Brand's baby. She desperately wanted to keep and raise the child, but her mother—probably following Jonah's advice—was convinced that she was doing the baby, herself and Brand a favor by giving the infant to a loving couple.

It had been the hardest decision of her life and, she was certain, the best. Jonah McKee was integral. He'd found

Estelle, a kind woman who, Dani was told, had herself been a child given up for adoption years before. Once Estelle's husband had died and her own children were grown, she boarded girls in trouble, helping them through the last stage of their pregnancy, providing moral support and a place to live in relative anonymity.

Then Dani was in the hospital, to spend hours in labor before being wheeled to a delivery room. Wearing masks and matching green hospital scrubs, the doctor and two nurses were in the room. They lifted her from the gurney and onto the delivery table, talking rapidly, telling her the baby was prone and would have to be turned, probably with forceps.

Frightened, she'd agreed to anything, assured that they knew far more than she when it came to delivering babies into the world. She was told to push, had no choice because her baby was coming, and suddenly under the blinding lights, her son had been born. She'd seen him only briefly before he'd been whisked away, presumably to meet his new parents.

Now, Dani blinked hard and stared at the telephone.

Even then, she hadn't completely trusted Jonah McKee and had blamed him for forcing her into a situation she wasn't comfortable with. All her mother's counseling had been at the suggestion of Jonah once Irene had confided in him. And the convenient way of dealing with the problem—of sending Dani to another town, finding a woman who would look after her, provide for the bills that were racking up—was Jonah's doing, as well.

Irene considered the man a god on earth, but Dani had decided long ago that he was only interested in helping himself. So why had he taken charge when he'd acted as if she barely existed, would have done anything to make sure that his older son didn't marry Dani's sister, Skye? Just to help Irene? Or were there deeper reasons? Dani had always wondered. Now that she was actively searching for her boy, and Jonah, curse him, was dead, her curiosity burned deeper than ever. What was Jonah's involvement?

Somehow, she'd find out. No matter how painful the truth might be, it had to be better than not knowing.

"Hey, Dani!" A voice cracked as it yelled up at her. She threw open the window and spied Chris in the yard. The strap of an overnight bag was slung over his shoulder and he held one hand to his forehead to shield his eyes from the sun as he looked up to the roof of the garage.

She poked her head out the open window of one of the dormers. "Hey! What're you doing here?"

"Another visit," Brandon said, emerging from the garage with a couple of bags of groceries tucked under his arms. "We're celebrating."

"Big deal," Chris grumbled.

"It is."

Chris shrugged, and for the first time, Dani noticed the cast on his arm, hidden beneath the long sleeves of a flannel shirt that was several sizes too big.

"What happened to you?" she asked. After slanting a glance at his brother, Chris scowled.

"Nothin'."

"Looks like somethin' to me. Are you okay?"

"Fine," he grumbled.

"I take it we're not celebrating the fact that you've been to the emergency room."

"Nah. Brand's ticked about that" He almost smiled as if he'd won some kind of victory, then quickly ducked into the house.

Dani's gaze followed him, then landed back on Brand, who was scowling darkly. "What happened?" she asked.

"A long story. I'll let him tell you."

Dani's curiosity got the better of her. "Okay, I'll wait. So what are you celebrating?"

"We broke ground on the lodge this week." His head was

tilted back, the throat of his shirt open, his skin bronzed from the sun, and she experienced that same familiar little catch in her breath. So male. So sexy. So wrong.

"Congratulations."

"So, you'll join us?"

She glanced at the house, dying to know what had happened to Chris. Despite his arrogant attitude, she liked the boy. But then, she liked all kids. The more rebellious, the better. Still, she hedged. She couldn't trust herself around Brand. "I've got work—"

"We'll wait," he said, a grin stretching wide on his beard-darkened jaw.

"No, go ahead. I'll just fix something here."

"Dani." His voice was louder, more commanding. "Please. Chris asked specifically if you'd come."

Her throat tightened and she forced a smile. She and the boy were becoming close; there wasn't any reason to disappoint him. And she had to find out how he'd hurt himself. Once again her thwarted maternal instincts were working overtime. "Okay."

"Just show up whenever it's convenient." Brand disappeared under the eaves and she told herself it was just a simple little dinner. No big deal. The kid wanted to see her, and damn it, she wanted to see him. Almost as much as she wanted to be with Brand.

"It's happening again, Dani," she told herself, but didn't listen to the warning.


". . . and so when Kent insulted me, I popped him one," Chris said as he pronged a piece of steak and began chewing. Not only was his wrist broken, but he was sporting a black eye and cut lip. "Bam, a right hook across the jaw."

"And that's how you broke your wrist?"

Chris slid a glance to his half brother, but Brand didn't

help him out, just sat across the table from him and waited, as did Dani. They were seated in the kitchen at a round, bleached wooden table. Brand had barbecued steaks and thrown together a Caesar salad that came in a sack, along with heating baked potatoes and garlic bread.

Chris dunked his steak in a dollop of sauce. "I broke my wrist when Kent nailed me and I went down. Tried to break my fall."

"So this isn't a you-should-see-the-other-guy story?"

Some of Chris's bravado left him. "Nah. He's okay. Just a swollen jaw."

"What were you fighting about?"

Chris stared down at his plate and didn't answer.

"He insulted our mother," Brand explained.

"So you were defending her honor?"

With a sound of disgust in the back of his throat, the boy pushed away from the table. "She doesn't have any honor."

"Chris!" Brand said sharply.

"It's true. You know it, I know it. The whole damned town knows it." His face was twisted in pain, and he sniffed loudly, fighting back tears.

"I said I'd handle it."

"Sure," Chris said, standing. "You've said it before and she's just as bad as ever. Worse. Damn it, Brandon—"

"Enough!" Brandon was on his feet in an instant. "Don't put Ma down, not when she's done the best she could for you and for me. And keep your language clean."

"You can't tell me what to do!" Chris's nostrils flared. "Damn, damn, damn!" he yelled as he ran out the back door.

Brand started after him, but Dani caught his wrist. "Let him go."

"After that?"

"He needs to blow off steam."

"He can blow it off without swearing and without insulting Ma."

"He will. But let him cool down. He doesn't mean it—he's just frustrated. I don't know what happened, but you and I, we've both been where he is now."

Brand didn't seem convinced and glared out the open door to where Chris, with some difficulty, had scrambled up to the top rail of the fence and, brooding, stared off to the hills.

"Come on, tell me about the lodge."

Slowly he relaxed and together they cleared the dishes, cleaned the kitchen and made coffee. It seemed strange, yet right, that they were together in this old house. Brand told her his expectations for the resort and avoided the subject of his mother; Dani explained about her plans for the ranch, how she hoped to own it and train horses at the same time. They discussed livestock for the stables and Brand offered to buy the horses from her—even give her a job organizing trail rides for the tenderfeet who would come to vacation on the shores of Elkhorn Lake.

Eventually Brandon, calmer, approached his brother. As Dani watched from the porch, she saw Brand say something to the boy. Chris didn't move; if he responded, Dani couldn't hear him. Whatever his brother's reaction, Brand didn't give up, but climbed onto the fence with him, his head bent toward the boy as he listened to him. There were words spoken on both sides, then a burst of Brand's laughter before he clapped Chris on the shoulder and encouraged a smile from him. Dani's heart tore as she sipped her cold coffee and watched the two brothers.

Brand, she thought, would have been a wonderful father.

Within a few minutes they returned, Chris mumbling an apology for being rude and Brandon smothering a smile. Night descended slowly, the pale sky darkening to show off a million stars. Dani had always loved the ranch at night once the chores were done and the day had seeped away; then she could feel a cooling breeze against her face and listen to the howl of a lonely coyote.

Chris was in the house, in a room Brand had set up with him that was complete with bed, television, video games and phone.

"He'll never want to go home," Dani accused as they walked along the path leading to the garage. "You spoil him."

"Someone needs to."

"I think that's your mom's job."

"Or his dad's," Brandon said. "I've called Al a couple of times, left messages for him, but he never phones back. Helluva father he turned out to be."

"So you're trying to fill his shoes?"

Brand raked stiff fingers through his hair. "I don't know what I'm doing, but the kid needs an anchor of some kind. Al's not interested and Ma . . . well, she has problems." The muscles in his face pulled into a frown that Dani wished she could wipe away.

"It's not easy raising a child alone, I suppose," she said wistfully. Maybe she should have tried.

"No and Ma's done it twice." They stopped at the bottom of the steps leading to her apartment.

"A strong woman."

"Sometimes," he said, then let his thoughts wander away as he stared into the distance. "I've been meaning to ask you about something."

She felt it then, an undercurrent in the air warning her that she should be careful. "About?"

"Well, I've decided it's time I tracked down my old man, find out more about him and that part of my family that I don't know a thing about. My mother's not very cooperative on the subject. It's like Jake Kendall is some deep, dark secret and I think I have the right to know something about him, even try to reach him if I can."

"I understand," she said. "If my father were still alive, I'd want to see him, too." *Just as I'd want to meet my son.* Her throat tightened.

"So, I heard you on the phone the other night with Sloan Redhawk."

Her heart nearly stopped beating and she felt the color drain from her face.

"I thought I'd give him a call, see if he can help me."

"Oh, well—"

He touched the underside of her jaw, forcing her eyes to meet his. "Who is it you're trying to track down."

"Track down?" she whispered, her voice hoarse.

"The message—I heard all of it. You're trying to find someone, aren't you?"

She couldn't lie. Trapped, she stared into the magnetism of his eyes and nodded. Her heart was pounding, thundering in her brain. *Tell him. Tell him now.*

"A long-lost relative?"

"Yes," she said, her mouth so dry she could barely speak.

"Have you found him . . . or her yet?"

"No, but we're still looking." Every muscle in her body was strung so tight she thought she might explode.

"So," he asked. "Who is it?"

# CHAPTER ELEVEN

Brand scowled as he drove to his mother's home. A foul mood clung to him as he stared through the windshield peppered with rain. His day at work had been a complete bust and he'd barked at poor Rinda when she'd asked him for the umpteenth time where a set of blueprints was located. Syd had come with his daily set of problems and Brandon had dealt with them without his usual dose of humor—something he'd lacked since this past weekend when Dani had all but avoided him.

After he'd asked her about the mysterious phone call to Sloan Redhawk, she'd gotten all tongue-tied and serious, as if she were going to lay the weight of the world on him. He'd half expected to hear some horrible tale about her life, but when he'd pressed her, she'd held her tongue, and for the next two days he'd barely seen her. She'd given Chris a couple of riding lessons and been more than civil to him, but whenever Brand was around she'd been busy. Always with that Jack character—some ranch hand who worked for her part of the time, then took off in the winter to be a ski bum. With his tanned skin, sun-streaked blond hair and easy smile, Jack had been more than attentive, helping Dani put in new pipes in the bathroom of her apartment and checking over all the equipment—baler, plow, tractor, seed drill, you name it, Jack checked it out.

Brand's fingers tightened over the wheel. He wasn't a man prone to jealousy; thought the emotion was downright stupid. But when it came to Dani, his thinking wasn't straight at all. Never had been. She managed to get under his skin like no other woman ever had.

"Hell," he grated as he drove past the city limits of Dawson City and angled the nose of his Jeep toward his mother's house. He switched on the wipers and dirt streaked the rain-splattered windshield. Venitia was another problem. A big one. He'd gotten a panicked call from Chris just this morning; the social worker had been out, poking around, asking questions, staring at Chris with pity in her eyes. Venitia was digging her own grave.

Gritting his teeth, he knew he was in for the battle of his life—and hers. But it had been coming for a long time. She, probably unsuspecting, would be home from work by now as it was nearly five, and he wanted to catch her before she'd gotten too far gone. He'd called a treatment center early this morning and made a reservation for her; now all he had to do was talk her into drying out. "Good luck," he muttered to himself and caught a glimpse of his reflection in the rearview mirror. His mouth was firm and set, white lines around the edges, his eyes hidden by reflective glasses against the glare of a sun partially hidden by gray clouds. He looked more like a prison warden in an old B-movie than a concerned son.

"Get a grip, Scarlotti," he growled, parking next to the curb. Several cats were hiding in the bushes, avoiding the rain that fell from the sky intermittently. He noticed that some of his crew had been out. A new unpainted post shored up the porch and old gutters had been ripped away to be replaced by newer prepainted downspouts and pipes. Even the sagging step had been fixed. The windows hadn't been changed yet but first things first; the men who'd done the work here had managed to wedge it between their other jobs.

Stuffing his sunglasses into his breast pocket, he knocked lightly on the screen door, then let himself in. He found her in the living room, curled near the arm of the sofa, her feet tucked beneath her. For once he didn't spy a bottle of any kind in the room.

"I've been expecting you," she said, her colorless lips compressed, no hint of makeup on her face. She looked older than she was and Brandon felt like a heel.

"Why?"

Wrapping her arms around her chest, as if to ward off a chill in the warm room, she glared up at him with wounded eyes. "I got a call today. From a Dr. Kelly Bush, a friendly woman who seems to think I'll be admitting myself into some place called the Blue Haven Clinic." Her fingers drummed on the shiny arm of the couch. "I assume this is your doing?" It wasn't really a question. More like an accusation.

"Guilty as charged." He sat on the other arm, hands clasped loosely between his knees, one foot swinging, as he told himself not to let her talk him out of this. Sure, he felt like a damned heel. Who wouldn't? But if someone didn't intervene, she'd lose everything she held dear. Including her second-born son. "Chris is worried, Ma, and so am I."

"Chris is just a kid."

"Doesn't mean he can't worry."

She made a sound of disgust in her throat. "I suppose he told you about the social worker." Staring through the window, Venitia tried hard to keep her chin from trembling.

"This is hard on him, Ma."

She blinked and swallowed. "And what about me? Isn't it hard on me, too?"

"Of course it is," he said in his most soothing tone as a tear tracked from the corner of her eye.

With agitation, she motioned in the air. "What's supposed

to happen to Chris while I'm away—while I'm in treatment, huh? What about him? I will not, *will not,* have him go into some foster home and Al—" She bit her lip and closed her eyes. "Al doesn't want him."

*"What?"* Brandon was on his feet in an instant. Fury roared through his blood. "Doesn't want him," he repeated, his lips curling. "He should have thought of that before he fathered the boy!"

"Oh, Brandon, if you only knew," she said on a heavy sigh.

"I do know, Ma," he said, hooking his thumb at his chest. Leaning close enough, to smell the cigarette smoke still clinging to her hair, he said, "I was treated the same way, remember?"

"You don't understand."

"And I never will!" he roared. "When a man becomes a father, he'd better take responsibility or risk fouling that kid up forever."

Tortured eyes met his. "What if he can't afford a child? What if he really didn't love the woman involved? What if the baby was just a mistake?"

"Nothing that can't be fixed," Brand muttered, then it hit him. She wasn't talking about Chris any longer. "What're you trying to say, Ma?" he demanded.

"That . . . oh, God, Brandon, if you only knew how much I loved you, how I adored you, how full you made my life. Would a father have made any difference?"

"A helluva lot." Crossing the room, he tried to gain control of his temper, which always shot into the stratosphere when the subject of fatherhood was brought up. Turning, he pinned his mother with a furious stare. "Tell me everything you can about Jake Kendall."

"I—I already have," she said, her voice faltering, her eyes sliding away.

"But you've told me nothing."

She took in a tremulous breath, looked up at her son, then back to the floor.

"Why don't I know a damned thing about him?"

"Because he doesn't exist, Brand. Doesn't now, didn't then."

"What?" he snarled. Fear, dark and foreboding, spun through his mind, and it occurred to him, not for the first time, that she might not know who'd sired her bastard; maybe she played fast and loose those days and there were lots of men who could have been the one who . . . A dull ache throbbed relentlessly at the base of his skull. "What do you mean?" His voice was low and hoarse.

She licked her lips nervously. "Jake Kendall was a figment of my imagination, a name you could cling to, a . . . an excuse for your father not to be around."

"So who was the real guy?" Dread thudded through his brain.

"I swore that I'd never admit the truth," she hedged. "That was the agreement—he'd pay child support and help out and I'd keep his name out of it."

His heart was pumping. "So you do know him. It wasn't because there were too many men—"

"Brandon!" she cried, wounded to the depths of her soul. She stood on shaking legs, staring at her son, fighting tears that seemed determined to run from the corners of her eyes. "I didn't tell you because I promised and it would only have made things worse, but of course I know who he is—was—and I probably should have told you sooner so you could have met him as son to father."

"Could have?" he whispered, his fists clenching in frustration. "What happened? Is he dead?"

"He was killed, Brandon. Just last summer."

"Killed?"

"Ned Jansen ran him off the road at Elkhorn Ridge."

The earth seemed to split open. "You don't mean—"

"I do, Brand," she said wearily, tears streaming down her cheeks in rivers. "Jonah McKee was your father."

"No!" he bellowed, hearing the sound like that of a wounded calf as his cry hit the walls of the old house and bounced back at him.

"Brand, just listen—"

"I can't believe it, Ma!" he said, then felt like a fool.

"Why would I lie?"

"Why have you lied for the past thirty years?"

"I had a pact."

"Oh, for the love of Jesus! Don't tell me about pacts or deals or honor, for God's sake! You're telling me that Jonah McKee was my father and I'm supposed to just sit here and take it and *understand?* Do you know what you're saying? Do you?" he asked, aching inside, his emotions severed and frayed. "That my whole life has been a lie. That my father lived a stone's throw from me but never once, *never once, damn it,* so much as looked in my direction. He never spoke to me. He never—"

"He did what he could," she said, her shoulders quivering. "And you can't blame just him. I was there, too. I got involved with him, knowing full well that he was married."

"This is sick, Ma. Sick! You're telling me that Max McKee is my half brother?"

"And Jenner. Casey's your—"

"I know what she is! I can figure it out. My legitimate half sister, right? Favored daughter, while I was a secret to be swept under the damned rug! Holy Mother of God, I can't believe this," he whispered savagely, trying to gain control of his raging emotions. He felt as if he'd been mentally drawn, quartered and disemboweled. Everything that he'd known, all he'd believed in for over thirty years had been a lie! A twisted ugly lie that had grown with each passing year.

Was it true? Could he possibly be a McKee? *A McKee?*

bad taste rose up the back of his throat as he thought of all the years of envying Max McKee and his brother and sister for their wealth, for their stability, for their loving parents. Even that was a lie. Jonah, his father—his damned father—had been a philanderer and a cheat.

Nausea roiled in his stomach and he didn't want to believe the truth. It was so much easier to think that his father was a low-life drifter, an ambitionless man who had no time to step into the role of fatherhood. But to know that his old man was the richest damned son of a bitch in the county, a family man devoted to seeing that his precious children got the best—always the best—ripped a hole in his already-bruised heart. While Jonah's legitimate children, his pride and joy, had been showered with gifts and money, and groomed to inherit Jonah's vast empire, Brandon, the *bastard,* the boy without his name, had been completely ignored, never once spoken to, never once praised, never once reprimanded. Aside from the monthly checks—hush money—he was treated as if he didn't exist, because there was no room in Jonah McKee's well-laid-out life for a bastard.

Brandon squeezed his eyes shut and listened to the dull, mocking roar inside his head—the silent screams that he refused to utter.

"Brand?" Venitia whispered.

"I don't believe it, Ma," he said, but the defeat in his voice must have given his true feelings away. The truth explained so much, yet left twice as many holes in his life.

"I shouldn't have told you."

"No, Ma, you're wrong. You should have told me years ago and the old man should have come forward." He drew in a deep breath. "So how did it happen, huh?"

"You don't want to know."

"Like hell!" He walked to the couch and leaned down to see her. "Were you in love with him?"

"Oh, God, Brand, don't—"

"Were you?"

"No!"

The truth slammed through him like a runaway freight train. He nearly stumbled. "No?" he repeated, feeling disgust gnaw at his insides.

"No." She drew in an unsteady breath. "It would be easy to lie and say I was seduced by his power, his wealth and his money. That I was young and naive enough to believe that he loved me or we loved each other or some such nonsense. The truth of it is we happened to meet at a political rally. I was . . . well, more involved than I am now. It was held in Bend at one of the hotels on the Deschutes. Anyway, the candidate whom Jonah had backed won and we all partied."

She ran a trembling hand over her forehead. "The truth of the matter is that I got drunk and woke up in Jonah McKee's hotel room." She shook her head at the thought. "I didn't know much about him, but I did realize that he had a lot of money and a wife and kids. I was horrified at what I'd done— I'd never been with a man before, never . . ." Her voice broke and Brandon, transfixed, wished he could turn the wheels of time backward, that he could ease away her pain.

"Anyway I turned up pregnant and even though . . . even though I didn't love Jonah, didn't really know him, I wanted the baby. I had no one in my life and a baby . . ." She blinked rapidly and let out a shuddering sigh. "I know you didn't have a lot growing up, I know it hurt you that you never knew your father, and I know that you're wounded now because I lied, but believe me, Brandon," she said, grabbing hold of his arm in a surprisingly strong grip, "I did everything because I love you. From the day I found out I was pregnant, I loved you!"

His throat closed in on itself. "And Jonah?"

"He . . . he wasn't happy with my decision, but was decent enough to take care of me financially. He was a lousy father to you, I'll admit that much—"

"He wasn't a father at all."

"I know, but he did take some responsibility."

Brandon needed to spit. The foul taste in his mouth wouldn't go away. "He could have talked to me."

"He probably would have, son. He didn't expect to die—"

"We all die, Ma. That's no excuse." Gazing down on her, he saw all the pain she'd endured, all the humiliation because of him. His anger was misdirected if he leveled it at her and yet the rage burning so white-hot inside him couldn't be extinguished with a few calming words. "Look, I just need some time to digest all this."

"I know."

He rubbed his face, as if massaging the tense muscles would erase some of the pain. It didn't work. "Let's not talk about it anymore."

Her eyes shone with tears and defeat. "You'd rather discuss putting me away."

"Not away, Ma. Think of it as a vacation."

Her gaze cut right through him. "A vacation?" she snapped. "Oh, Brandon, don't act like I'm that stupid." Squaring her shoulders, she stood. "Okay, I'll go give the clinic a whirl, but promise me that you'll take care of Chris. I can't stand the thought of some do-gooder social worker taking him away."

"You know I will, Ma."

"Good." She seemed about to say something more, to unburden yet another secret from her heavily laden soul, but she held her tongue. "My bags are already packed. Chris is at Larry Hargraves' house. He's spending the night—it's already arranged. He knows that I might be leaving for a while, but I didn't fill him in on all the details. This was your idea, so I figured you could do it," she added bitterly, then before he could say a word, rushed on. "The Hargraveses' phone number and address are tacked to the bulletin board. I told them you'd probably be picking him up around eight in the morning. If that doesn't work out, give them a call. They're reasonable and easygoing, so whatever works for you will probably work for them, as well."

"I'm glad you accepted this," he admitted, relieved that there wasn't more of a fight.

"I haven't accepted anything, Brand. This is a prison sentence. You and I both know it. You just haven't given me any choice in the matter."


"You miserable low-life scum," Brandon growled as darkness settled over the land and he stared at the grave of Jonah McKee. The air smelled fresh from the recent rain and the wind blew steadily from the east. Stars twinkled above, and the headstone, an imposing slab of marble engraved with all sorts of sentiments, stood nearly as tall as the man who rested six feet below the earth. Fresh flowers, brought weekly, filled vases at the head of the grave. Jonah's wife, Virginia, was nothing if not loyal. Even her husband's death didn't end her loyalty. Even knowing that her husband was a class-A cheating bastard. Brandon laughed at the irony of it. Who was really the bastard?

"You should have talked to me," Brand said, emotion clogging his throat. "You should have told me, let me know, explained what it was that you couldn't accept! Hell, McKee, the least you could have done was own up to it."

He looked across the grassy knoll. Anger clutched his stomach and he nearly threw up all over his pathetic father's grave. "And Ma. She deserved a helluva lot more than a check each month. God, she still thinks you're some sort of saint because you doled out a little change to her, but I know you for the black-hearted son of a bitch that you are!"

Sneering, he wanted to spit on Jonah McKee's grave, but he didn't want the old man to have any satisfaction—even in death—of seeing his pain. So he strode back to his Jeep and decided that the night was just damned perfect to get drunk. Not just tipsy, but fall-down-on-your-face, stumbling drunk.

As he climbed into the rig, he thought of Dani. Wouldn't she get a laugh out of this? Because of Skye, Dani was an in-law to the McKees, practically in the family, and now he was Jonah's damned bastard.

So convenient. So tidy. So sick.

There was an old half-full bottle of whiskey in the kitchen cupboard. Brand twisted on the ignition and the engine fired. Easing off the clutch, he drove through the open cemetery gates, engine roaring, gravel spinning beneath his tires.

"Good riddance, McKee," he growled under his breath. "I hope you rot in hell."

Restless, Dani had walked through the fields surrounding the house, checking the fence line, thinking of Brandon, knowing that she had to tell him about their son. Sloan had tracked down the nurse who'd been working in the hospital the night her baby was born and he thought he'd come up with some answers soon. Whether she wanted to or not, Dani would have to tell Brand the truth. He'd be furious with her, probably never speak to her again, but she had no choice. Her conscience wouldn't let her lie any longer.

Sighing, she felt the cool breath of night against her back and listened to the crickets beginning to stir. Somewhere nearby, a horse nickered softly and was answered by the plaintive hoot of an owl. The moon was full—a perfect silver disk that rode high in the sky and was surrounded by thousands of stars, winking jewel-like in the night-black sky.

As she turned toward the house, Dani saw the lights burning in the ranch house and noticed smoke curling from the river-rock chimney. Though it was the dead of summer, Brandon had built a fire. The thought of cheery coals glowing in the old grate warmed her heart and she was tempted to visit him.

"Don't," she warned herself. She'd avoided him in the evenings, preferring to have their short conversations in the light of day when the surroundings were less intimate, when her defenses were less likely to be overcome.

She'd stepped through the gate when she saw him, propped against the support for the porch and watching her intently.

"Evenin'," he drawled like some kind of cowboy.

"Hi."

"Thought you might want to come in for a drink."

"A drink? I don't think so," she said without much conviction. Truth to tell, she wanted very much to be with him, never mind the drink. Standing there, one shoulder braced against the beam, his arms folded over his chest, he looked all male in his faded jeans and open-throated work shirt. Its sleeves rolled to his elbows, the shirt stretched tautly over muscles that were evident even in the darkness. His jeans rode low on his hips.

Involuntarily, her pulse beat a little more quickly.

"Suit yourself. How 'bout some conversation then?"

"You want to talk?"

"Need to, is more like it." There was a thread of steel in his voice, a determination that usually wasn't so evident. "Come on in."

She was aware of her heart pounding as she crossed the gravel yard, her boots crunching on the sharp stones. *This is a mistake,* an inner voice warned. *An irreversible mistake.*

He held the screen door open for her and she noticed a gleam in his eye—something was definitely on his mind—and the set of his jaw, as if he'd been provoked way too far. *He knows,* she thought frantically. *He found out about the baby and now he knows! Why didn't you tell him earlier? It would have been so much better for the news to come from you!*

Misery slid through her insides, like a snake coiling, getting ready to strike. How could he have found out? No one, not even her own mother, knew that he was the father of her child.

Suddenly chilled, she walked into the living room where the fire crackled merrily against dry, pitchy chunks of pine. Though her insides were as cold as ice, she began to sweat and didn't argue when he poured her a chilled glass of Chablis. Anxiously she twirled the stem of her glass between her fingers. No lights were on; just the hazy red glow from the fire illuminated the room.

He was drinking whiskey and this wasn't his first shot, she suspected as she stared at him. He leaned against the window and the ticking of the clock resting on the carved fir mantel was in sharp counterpoint to the pounding of her own heart.

"Wh-what is it you want to talk about?" she asked, deciding two could play this game—whatever it was. Standing next to the couch, she watched the play of emotions on his face; repressed rage caused a muscle to tic beneath his eye.

Darkness settled in his eyes.

*Here it comes,* she thought with fatalistic certainty and steadied herself against the back of the couch ready for the blow that was sure to hit and hit hard.

"Well," he said. "I learned a lot this afternoon."

*Oh, God.* "You did?" She took a sip of wine. It slid cold and easy down her throat.

"Yep. Things that happened a long while ago."

*Give me strength.* "Oh?"

"I was in the dark about a lot."

Knees threatening to buckle, she waited, holding her breath, ready for the one-two kick, a drone beginning in her head.

"Believe it or not, Dani, you and I, we have a lot in common."

Her throat was as dry and scratchy as cotton.

"Yes, sirree. Here you are an in-law to the old McKees and you probably never guessed that I was one of 'em."

"Wh-what?" she stammered, hardly daring to believe her ears, or maybe she'd misunderstood his words over the buzz echoing through her brain.

"That's right. Old Jonah had a fling with Ma. I'm the result. There is not and never was a Jake Kendall." Pain and quiet fury etched the brave lines of his face, but there was something more, something deeper as he gazed at her.

"Oh, Lord," she whispered. "How did you find out?"

"Ma. She told me. Just before I took her to a clinic in Bend."

"A clinic?" He was talking in circles. "Is she ill?"

"Yes, but the first disease we're tackling is her addiction to alcohol."

Dani flushed as she looked down at her own glass of wine.

Brand offered a twisted smile. "I know. Ironic isn't it?" he said, staring into the amber liquor in his tumbler. Then, as if repulsed, he tossed the rest of his drink, ice and all, into the fire. In a violent hiss, flames shot upward. "Damn it all to hell anyway," he growled, slamming the empty glass onto the mantel and striding over to Dani. As if to drive away the demons in his head, he vaulted the couch, stood in front of her and stared straight into her eyes. "I've made more than my share of mistakes in this life," he said, taking her wrist in his. Her wineglass rolled gently to the floor. "Walking out on you was one of them. I think it's time to change things."

"Change?"

"Take care of past mistakes."

"But—"

"Right here. Right now."

"Oh, Brand, don't. You've been drinking and—"

"I've thought about this a long time, lady," he said, his blue eyes unwavering. "I want you. And not just for now."

The words were simple and straightforward. They seemed

to pulse in the semidark room. And there was a thread of tenderness in his voice that touched a dark corner of her heart.

"Wanting isn't enough."

"But I want you forever." His voice was low and seductive and he moved closer so that she stepped around the couch trying to keep a few inches of distance between the heat of their bodies. "It's time we made up for all the years we lost. The years I threw away."

"What?" Her heart was a drum. "You don't—"

"I do. Marry me, Dani."

The words she'd waited so long to hear were now hollow. She couldn't marry him, not with so many obstacles in the way. "No, Brand, you don't know what you're asking."

"I sure as hell do. Marry me."

"I can't."

He jerked on her wrists, pulling her roughly to him, slanting his mouth over hers in a kiss that was rough and gentle, hard and persuasive. The room seemed to spin and Dani's legs began to give way, but she couldn't make promises she couldn't keep. If and when he found out about the baby . . .

He tasted of whiskey and the scent of his soap mingled with the smell of burning wood. Her mind quit arguing as he touched her lips with his tongue, applying pressure. Sweet, sweet pressure.

Her insides quivered, and as if he felt her resistance fading, he kissed her harder and his tongue gained purchase, sliding over her teeth, flicking against the roof of her mouth, exploring and plundering, causing her senses to reel.

It felt so right. His body melded close to hers, as if there were no clothes separating them, as if they belonged together, as if they were destined to fuse.

"Brand—" she murmured.

"Don't tell me no." He touched her breast, his fingers scorching her skin, though cotton fabric held them at bay.

"I—I won't," she whispered and gave up the battle as desire, deep and dark and wanton, seared through her blood. Her arms circled his neck and she kissed him back.

"Dani, love," he said softly, his voice hoarse.

Her heart ached for the little boy who hadn't known his father and the man who now did.

His hands tracked down her ribs. His weight forced her backward and they tumbled onto the couch. Brand, still kissing her, deftly worked the buttons of her blouse, parting the fabric then edging the lace of her bra with one long finger.

Dani quivered inside as his finger grazed her nipple. Her breast swelled and the nipple seemed to ripen, jutting hard against its lacy barricade. With a groan, he unhooked her bra and her breast fell into his open hand. Dani's eyes fluttered closed and she was lost in the powerful feelings that this one special man evoked in her. He loved her. Hadn't he said as much? He wanted to marry her.

A small cry crossed her tongue. She couldn't marry him now—not until she told him the truth about their baby. She opened her mouth to speak, but he captured it with his again and his hands moved anxiously against her skin, ridding her of blouse and bra, then dipping seductively under the waistband of her jeans. She didn't stop him, didn't try. Liquid fire was building deep within her, flowing slowly as her jeans popped open and he slid them lovingly over her hips.

She unbuttoned his shirt, and gazing at the hard muscles of his chest, she laid a finger on one nipple. He groaned and the flat disk hardened beneath a swirl of dark hair.

"You're asking for trouble," he warned and she, with a smile, asked again by touching his other nipple, then slid her fingers down the washboard of his abdomen, tracing the hard muscles, watching him suck in his breath as she opened his fly and slipped her hands inside his jeans to touch his buttocks. Firm and supple, they flexed beneath her fingers.

He kissed her hard then, his lips fitting fiercely over hers, his hands tangling in her hair. Her body trembled, hot from the inside out. His fingers and lips were everywhere, touching her intimately, kissing her, stroking her, adding fuel to the fire that was already consuming her.

Moaning, she writhed beneath him, and he removed her panties and kissed her in the most intimate of places before shucking off his own jeans and briefs. Closing her eyes, she felt the world quake as he slowly brought up his head and dragged his body between her legs. "I've waited forever for this," he said, his voice hoarse and low. Firelight flickered in his eyes and gilded his skin as he poised over her, gazed into her eyes and whispered, "I love you."

The words were like a bucket of ice water thrown over her. She couldn't. Not yet. Not until she told him the truth. "Brand, there's something you should know—"

With a primal groan, he thrust into her, and her willing body arched up to join with his. Her worries, so vivid a second before, fled in the heat that he created as his arms surrounded her and his body moved over hers. She found his tempo, caught it and felt the earth shift again. Faster and hotter, as if trapped in a wildfire, Brand moved. Dani's breath was short and fast, her heart pounding, her mind spinning.

"Dani!" his voice was raw, his head thrown back.

Her soul was ripped from her flesh in that instant when their bodies and the stars collided.

Her own throat was raw from her cries.

He collapsed against her and her arms held him close, waiting as his breathing slowed, feeling the soft fingers of afterglow cuddle them both.

One hand lazily stroked her hair, his other arm was wrapped securely around her waist. As he gazed down at her, he smiled and some of the pain had left his eyes. "What about it?" he finally asked in the near darkness. "What do you say, Dani? Will you marry me?"

A lump grew in her throat and tears starred her lashes. "I—I can't," she whispered, then bit her lip.

"Why not?"

She took in a long, slow breath and tried not to break down, but her voice failed her, and when she spoke it was the barest of whispers. "Because," she said, staring into his blue, blue eyes, hoping her words and courage wouldn't fail her, "because . . . because somewhere—and I don't know where yet—somewhere you and I have an eleven-year-old son."

# CHAPTER TWELVE

"We have *what?*" Brand's eyes so recently glazed in afterglow were now sharp and burned as brightly as the coals in the grate. He rolled off the couch, swept up his jeans and yanked them on in a quick, angry motion.

"A son," she said, swallowing hard.

Emotions from rage to awe transformed his face. "A son. My God, are you serious?"

"He's . . . he's the person I'm looking for. Our baby—well, child now. Oh, God, Brand, I wanted to tell you earlier—"

"This had better be your idea of a sick joke." He hitched his jeans up.

"You think I would joke about this?"

"I don't know. Would you?"

"For heaven's sake, I'm telling you that when you left I was pregnant!" She climbed to her knees and reached forward, catching his hand, but he stared down at her with damning eyes.

"I can't believe it," he said, peeling off her fingers as if her touch revolted him. His gaze raked over her body and she'd never felt so naked, so vulnerable in all her life.

"Look, I've been meaning to tell you—"

"When?" he asked, snapping shut his fly, then leveled his gaze at her again, *"When, damn it!"*

"There was never a right time—"

"In eleven years? In eleven damned years?" He threw his hands over his head and turned away from her. She watched the smooth muscles of his back flex as he swore roundly over and over again. "Do you know what this means, Dani?" he asked, rotating swiftly, his nostrils flaring as he suddenly smelled something hideous. Striding up to her, he glared deep into her eyes. "Do you?"

"That—"

"That *I* have a son whom I've ignored. For eleven damned years. Just like my louse of an old man!"

"No—"

"Why didn't you call or write or—"

"Why didn't *you?*" she demanded, her anger getting the better of her. She was breathing rapidly, her breasts rising and falling each time she gulped air. He glanced at her nipples, proud little points, and then looked quickly away.

"It's not the same."

"No, of course not. But do you honestly think I would've tried to find you, to chase you down, just because I was pregnant? Why? So I could get some kind of halfhearted proposal, so that you in all your nobility would have offered to be my husband? Well, sorry. If you wanted me because you loved me, that was one thing. My being pregnant had nothing to do with it!"

"Like hell."

"Did you call even once?" she demanded, a flush heating her body. "Even so much as sit down to write a letter?" She shook her head. "No. Because, face it, Brandon, you didn't want to be tied down and it was the last thing, the very last thing I would have done to you." Shaking, she reached for her clothes and tried to make her fumbling fingers work as she started dressing.

"You knew how I felt about being a responsible parent."

"And you knew how I felt about you!" she retorted, her fingers unable to fasten her bra. Suddenly the dimly lighted room was too close and she just wanted out.

"And you gave him away."

"Yes!" The bra was finally hooked and she found her blouse.

"Why?"

"Because I couldn't raise him alone." Stuffing her arms through her sleeves, she stared angrily at him. "And don't you dare lecture me about not having the guts to do it. I gave him up, Brandon, willingly, thinking it was the best thing for everyone, and there hasn't been a day, not one single day in the past eleven years, that I haven't worried about him, wondering where he was, how he was doing."

"At least you knew about him."

"At least you were spared over a decade of heartache!"

He advanced on her as she stepped into her jeans. "So where is he?"

"I don't know."

"You never kept track?"

"I couldn't."

"Tell me what happened." Strong hands gripped her shoulders, fingers digging into her muscles.

She zipped up her jeans and tilted her face up to him. "You want all the grisly details?"

"Every last one."

"Okay, but you don't have to manhandle me to get the truth," she said, and he, as if realizing how hard he was clutching her, suddenly let go and stepped away.

Dani found her glass on the floor and poured herself a gulp of wine. She swallowed and leaned on the mantel, her fingers sliding along the varnished wood, her thoughts rolling back

in time. Inside she was shaking, but she tried to appear calm
and in control.

"I didn't know about the baby until after you'd left," she
said, blinking against tears. She couldn't break down.
Wouldn't! "And when I realized I was pregnant, I was scared.
Damned scared. I didn't tell anyone until I was starting to
show and then I confided in my mother. She . . . well, she was
devastated at first, and between her and Jonah McKee they
convinced me—"

"McKee?" Brand bellowed, a new rage contorting his features. That slimy son of a bitch. "What the hell did he have to
do with this?"

"My mother worked for him, you know, and he'd always
helped out. I . . . I think she was in love with him."

Brand snorted. "Looks like we have more in common than
I thought. He rested his hips on the end of the couch, then
nodded. "Go on." His lips were still hard and flat, the corners
of his mouth bracketed in white lines of fury, but he seemed
to have control of his emotions as he sat, without his shirt, the
firelight throwing gold shadows over his skin.

Slowly, Dani told him the rest of the story, about Estelle
and the hospital, about keeping his name a secret and her
newly found frustration of trying to locate the boy.

All the while, Brand sat there, watching her intently, as if
looking for a flaw, a lie that he could latch on to. When she
was finished, he rubbed his chin. His voice was flat and cold,
without any inflection whatsoever. "What will you do when
you find him?"

"Nothing. I'll just be happy to know that he's okay."

"Will you?"

"Yes."

"And what about me? What is my role in all this? Don't
you know this is my worst nightmare—to know that I fathered
a son and abandoned him?" He cleared his throat and Dani
fought the hot tears that slid from her eyes.

"I . . . I'm sorry. I didn't think I'd ever see you again and then you showed up here. I wanted to tell you then, but the timing never seemed to be right." She dashed away any trace of her tears and stiffened her spine, her chin angled in defiance, as if daring him to hit her with another emotional blow. "So now you know."

And a silent thought passed between them; they'd made love again. They already could have started the same chain of events as before. Neither of them had given any thought to protection, even against any possible disease. Passion had ruled over sanity. Brand mentally kicked himself. How could he have been such a fool as to not protect her?

"I'm going to find him," he said, reaching for his shirt.

"No—"

"And when I do, I'm going to go through the courts and do whatever it takes to exercise my rights as a father—"

"Stop! Brand, for the love of God, listen to yourself. You can't bust in on an eleven-year-old boy's life and turn it upside down." She repeated the same warnings her sister had said to her. "You don't know what will happen, but all you'll cause is heartache for you, me, the boy and his parents."

"*I'm* his damned parent."

"No." She shook her head miserably, knowing full well that she couldn't have wounded him any more than if she'd stabbed him in the heart. "I took that right away from you." She watched the look of defeat enter his eyes. "I've said I'm sorry and I'd say it a million times over if it would do any good, but it won't. I can't change what happened, nor can you. The best thing we can do for our son is to let him grow up healthy and happy and secure with the family he has."

"Oh, God, Dani, listen, will you? We have to—I have to find out about this." He stood near the door, his shirt open, his shoulders so tight they looked brittle, his spine ramrod stiff. "I think you should go."

She didn't need his invitation; she knew that whatever they'd shared was over. The expression in his eyes was condemning, the set of his jaw grimly determined. Whatever they'd recaptured, even fleetingly, was gone. "I'll tell Sloan about you, in case you want to work with him."

"What I want to know is why would Jonah McKee give two cents about your kid?"

"I don't know," she admitted. "I've never understood his relationship to my mother or us." Shivering from a cold deep within, she swept past him and tried not to notice the scent of his skin or the weight of his gaze. With as much pride as she could muster, she walked out of the house and out of his life.

"You're mad, aren't you?" Chris asked as he followed Dani out to the vegetable garden. She was toting a hoe over her shoulder and walking with strides so fast he had to jog to keep up with her.

"Mad? No. Angry? Well . . . no, not really." She offered the kid a smile. Ever since he'd moved in with Brand two weeks earlier, he'd been puppy-dogging after her, following her around and helping out. He was still cocky, but for the most part, he seemed to enjoy life on the ranch and was learning fast with the horses. Aside from his complaints about the lack of a dog at the ranch, he seemed happy with life. If he was worried about Venitia, he kept it to himself.

Though Chris was always underfoot, Dani hadn't seen much of Brand since she'd confessed to him about the baby. The few times they'd run into each other, he was barely civil, hiding behind aviator glasses that shielded his eyes as well as guarded his expression.

"Wanna help?" She tossed Chris the hoe.

"Nah. I hate weeding."

"Don't think of it as work, but more like . . . character building."

"I think I got enough character."

She couldn't help but grin as she stared at him with his untied shoes, hat turned backward and peach fuzz on his upper lip. "Yeah, maybe you do."

He didn't seem concerned that his mother was, as he put it, "drying out." His attitude was more of relief. But Dani thought it strange that his father never called or wrote or visited the boy. Brand was right on that score. Al Cunningham was a zero of a dad. Seemed to run in the family. Jonah McKee had been less than zero.

She hadn't said anything to Skye or Max about Jonah being Brand's father. They had their own worries as Skye was due to deliver her own baby any day. Why get them all worked up about Jonah's illegitimate son? Besides, that was Brandon's call and deep down she hoped that the word never got out—for the sake of the McKee family. Jonah may have been a louse, but his wife didn't need to be reminded of it.

Chris handed her the hoe before trotting off to the garage where he was working on a skateboard ramp.

Dani, frustrated, attacked the rows of squash and green beans with a vengeance, slicing at weeds with her hoe and wishing that life hadn't become more complicated than it already was. Finally her finances were in decent, if not great, shape and now she had the emotional, gut-wrenching problem of dealing with Brand. Or not dealing with him.

Sweat dripped on the ground and she wrapped a handkerchief around her forehead to catch the drops before they trickled into her eyes. The old windmill blades rattled occasionally, but the air was fairly still and searing.

She felt Brand's gaze before she saw him. Steeling herself, she glanced over her shoulder to find him standing in the shade of an apple tree, resting his elbows on the rickety split-rail fence between the garage and the garden.

"I thought we should talk."

"What about?"

"The other night."

"I think we said enough."

"Not quite." He vaulted the fence and walked down the dusty rows of bush beans, looking cool and hard, his face set, no trace of a smile. She was tired of his cold determination and the disapproval in his eyes.

"The answer is still no."

"Answer?" he asked cautiously.

"I still won't marry you and nothing you can say will change my mind."

He almost smiled. Not quite, but almost. "Brassy, aren't you?"

"Bossy, aren't you?"

At that, he caught hold of her wrist, forcing the hoe to drop with a thud to the hard ground. "Enough, Dani. We can't spend the next eleven months sniping at each other."

"So what do you *propose?*" she asked, emphasizing the last word.

His jaw clenched as he gazed at her with piercing eyes. "You're a hard woman."

Her stupid pulse was jumping again; he could probably see it throbbing at her neck or feel it beneath his fingertips wrapped around the inside of her wrist. "Not half as hard as you are." She yanked her arm away and picked up the hoe. "I've got work to do." She started down a row of corn, now as high as her shoulder.

"We've got to think about Chris."

Stopping short, she turned and wanted to scream at him, wanted to shout at him that over the past two icy weeks she'd come to realize how much she cared for him, how much she missed the soft rumbling sound of his laughter, how she'd come to wait for him each night, hoping to see him, how she loved him. Damn it, that was the crux of the problem: she loved him. Biting down on her lip, she grabbed hold of her runaway thoughts. "You're right. Chris doesn't need to see us acting like children." Leaning against the hoe, she yanked off her work gloves. "So what do you suggest, some kind of truce?"

There was a slight lift of one of his powerful shoulders. "If that's what you want to call it."

"We can't very well go back to the way we were," she observed, leaving the hoe planted and sauntering up to him. Squinting against the sun, she angled her face to his. "Okay, Scarlotti," she said, extending her hand, "you've got yourself a deal." He squeezed her fingers briefly and that same wonderful, hateful jolt that always occurred whenever he touched her sizzled up her arm.

Dropping her hand and looking decidedly disgruntled, he took a step away. "Okay. So that's it."

"Not quite," she said, deciding to clear the air. "Sloan called today—I think he contacted you, too."

"Faxed me a note. Said he did some more digging and found the lawyer who handled the adoption. Sloan called and must have pressured him, because the attorney threatened to sue if he pushed any harder."

"Can he do that?"

"People sue for anything these days."

Dani untied her handkerchief and mopped her face. "I don't think Sloan's too worried about a little lawsuit. He's pretty persistent."

"Good." Brand watched her wipe the sweat from her forehead and neck, her blouse gaping slightly to reveal the swell of her breasts, and he was suddenly aware of how difficult it was to breathe. The air was cloying, and the thought of Dani swimming naked in the cool waters of the creek or taking a bath in his old tub, or a shower in the new stall, made him so hard he had to shift to keep a bulge from being apparent in his crotch. "I need a favor," he said.

"Oh, so that's what all this friendly stuff is about."

"No, I—" Then he saw that she was teasing. "Can you stay

here with Chris? It's Ma's two-week anniversary or whatever
the hell you call it at the clinic and . . . well, she wants me, just
me, to visit. Tonight at seven."

"Sure," she said with a smile. "I was just giving you a little
guff earlier. I'll stay with Chris anytime. Maybe I'll even take
him to a movie."

Brand's heart tore a little. How he'd like to be a part of that
little expedition. "Good. Thanks." He turned and walked out
of the garden while a ground squirrel jeered at him from the
top of the woodpile and Dani's cat, still as death, watched
from a clump of tall grass. This place was becoming familiar,
so damned familiar. He wondered if, when the lodge was
finished, he'd ever want to leave.


The cigarette was nearly steady in Venitia's hands and she
forced a smile. When he'd first greeted his mother, he'd seen
her improvement, noticed that she was calmer than usual.
They'd spied other patients sitting in groups, smoking and
talking, laughing and playing cards or watching television.
They were allowed, his mother explained, during the free hour
and a half after dinner. Then it was back to routine—strict diet
and exercise, counseling sessions, group and private.

They walked through a sun-room of the old Victorian
house. Grape arbors and fruit trees that reached to the sky
graced the backyard. Plastic tables and chairs were grouped
near a fish pond or beneath shade trees. Scenting the air, a
rose garden added splashes of pink, yellow, red and white.

"How's Chris?" she asked as they sat near the pond, where
brightly colored tropical fish were swimming beneath wide
lily pads.

"He's great. He misses you, of course, but he's glad that
you're getting some help."

"Not easy when you think your mom's a drunk."

"He never said—"

"Sure he did, Brand." She took a shaky drag on her cigarette, then let the smoke curl from her nostrils. "They're big on being truthful here, you know. No matter how much it hurts."

"I think that's good."

"Sometimes the truth can hurt."

He thought of Dani and her admission that she'd borne him a son. "I know."

"Sometimes it can drive people away."

Again his thoughts fled to Dani. His heart swelled when he thought of her, so strong, so independent, so damned proud of finally making it on her own. He'd been half in love with her as a feisty, rebellious teen, but now he was completely smitten by the strong woman she'd become. True, her tongue was still sharp, but she could be kind, as well, and a truer person he'd never met. The fact that she was beautiful was only the proverbial icing on the cake. "I know it can, Ma," he said, his hands clasped between his knees. "So tell me, how're they treating you?"

She smiled sadly, told him a little about her days, and to his surprise, seemed somewhat serene. She wasn't so calm, she assured him, during the first few days. As she stubbed out her cigarette, they made small talk which eventually petered out. Finally she asked about Dani.

"She's fine," Brandon said, wondering where this was leading.

"Getting along with Chris?"

"Seems to adore the kid. She's with him tonight, taking him to the movies."

"Good. That's good," Venitia whispered, watching as a sparrow flitted from one branch of a cherry tree to another. "As I said, the people here think it's always wise to tell the truth and unburden yourself of lies."

"Does this have something to do with Dani?" he asked, his mind spinning ahead. What was Venitia hinting at?

"Yes. And you."

His heart started to thump. "What, Ma?" he said, but his brain was already clicking ahead, putting the pieces of a worrisome puzzle together. "Oh, no."

"It's Chris."

His mouth lost all moisture. He couldn't move.

"He's your son, Brandon," she said, biting on her lip to keep from breaking down. "Your son and Dani's."

"God, Ma," he whispered. "Why?" This was too much to digest, way too much. And yet, it all made sense—in a strange way. He'd never seen his mother pregnant and Chris resembled him. And this explained Al's lack of interest in the boy. He felt as if he'd been slugged in the gut.

"Jonah thought it would be best."

"Jonah?" he repeated, shocked all over again. "What did he have to do with it?"

"Well—"

"He didn't want anyone to find out that his bastard had sired a bastard?" he said, standing up swiftly and kicking the table so hard it went flying.

"Mrs. Cunningham?" one of the attendants called, concerned.

Venitia held up a hand. "It's all right."

"The hell it is," Brand said, then looked at his mother, his pitiful, sick mother. Once she was through with this clinic she was faced with medical tests on her liver; He held his tongue, waved off the attendant who wouldn't quit hovering nearby and stood at the edge of the pond, staring down at the fat orange and black fish swimming lazily in the cold water. "Why, Ma?"

"I didn't know what to do. Jonah told me about the baby. He knew you were seeing Dani, how I don't know, probably from some of your friends—there was something about the two of you running away from some party that the police raided. Jonah had connections, remember, with the police and sheriff's department and practically every county judge on the bench. Your names must have come up as being together and Jonah put two and two together when he heard the story from one of his friends in the department. These friends kept you from ever being charged with anything."

"Jonah bailed me out?" he asked, thunderstruck. No wonder. He'd never questioned his not being charged, but now it all made sense.

"And bought you off."

"Oh, God." His insides were ice, his blood frozen. He'd never guessed, not once, not even when Dani admitted that they'd borne a son, that Chris . . . his half brother, for crying out loud, was really his boy.

"Jonah did care about you, Brand, in his own misguided way."

"So he told you I was going to have a son."

"Yes. You were already in California, making a new life, and I was married to Al, living in Everett. We'd just moved to a small town and I didn't want your son farmed out to strangers. So . . . I convinced Al that we should adopt him. Al wasn't happy about the idea, but Jonah wanted to keep tabs on his first grandson and offered us some money."

"Oh, Ma, no . . ." he said, shaking his head.

"I couldn't stand not knowing where Chris would be, so we adopted him. I'm not sure it was perfectly legal, but Jonah pulled some strings and . . . well . . . Chris was mine." She was openly crying now, tears raining from her eyes, her shoulders quivering with sobs.

Brand took her into his arms and fought the urge to scream and yell. She'd done what she thought was best, and though it burned a hole in his gut to think that for eleven years he hadn't known, had not one clue that he'd been a father, now he could set things straight. It wasn't too late.

"You can't tell him now, you know."

Brand closed his eyes and rocked his mother. She'd given up her youth for him twice—once as his mother, then again as the adoptive mother to his son. "I know. In time."

"Yes, in time. When he's old enough to understand. Oh, God, I've messed things up, haven't I?"

"Nah, Ma, you did what you thought best. That's all anyone can ask," he said, though rage gnawed at his soul. That old bastard, Jonah McKee, was the manipulator, the main puppeteer while all the others were his playthings, his marionettes. "But I have to tell Dani."

"Oh, Brand . . ." she said, clinging to his shirt. "Don't. Please—"

"It's her right, Ma. Hers and mine. She's been looking for her child for a long, long time."


Chris was asleep in the car. Barely eight o'clock and the kid had conked out. They'd driven into Dawson City, eaten at a local burger joint and watched an action movie that in Dani's opinion was much too violent, peppered with too much foul language and sexual innuendo, but Chris had loved it. Now, as he lay with his head propped against the passenger window, she was struck by how much the boy was like his brother.

Brand.

Just the thought of him brought fresh pain to her heart. She loved him and once again that love was thwarted. "You're an independent woman," she reminded herself, but the thought of running the ranch alone, without him coming home each evening, cut a hole through her middle as wide as Stardust Canyon.

As she slowed near the mailbox to pick up the letters, magazines and daily paper, Chris woke up and stretched. Yawning, he reminded her again of Brand; even his temperament was close to his older half brother's. Nonchalantly he sorted through the envelopes as Dani drove down the lane to the house.

"Great," he grumbled when she slid to a stop and the last envelope was dropped onto the dash.

"Lookin' for something?"

His eyes flashed in defiance. "Nah." Chewing nervously on his thumbnail, he looked out the bug-spattered windshield. "Who cares anyway?"

Dani touched his arm, understanding that he was hoping to hear from Al. "Your dad's probably busy."

"Yeah and he never wanted me, okay?" Sudden color rushed into his face. "I heard him and Ma arguing, right before the divorce. They didn't know I was standing outside their open bedroom window looking for a cat that had crawled under the house. They were screaming at each other and Dad said something crazy, like he didn't ever want me or I wasn't his kid or something! It was all just for money."

"He was just angry."

"No, Dani, it was more than that." He swallowed hard and gulped in air. "He hates me. I don't know why, I don't know what I did, but he hates me."

"Oh, honey." She tried to touch him, but he threw off her arm, opened the door and flung himself out of the Bronco. Dani knew she should give him time to cool off, but she couldn't. Heart breaking, she ran after him and caught up with him at the porch. "Look, Chris, I can't speak for your father. God knows he hasn't treated you decently, but you have to remember that we all love you. Your mother, Brand and I, we think you're a terrific kid."

"Yeah, well, what else can you say?" he charged, eyes flashing, nose beginning to run. He swiped at it with his sleeve.

"I don't have to like you, you know. I don't have to want to

be around you. It's not like you're . . . like you're my . . ." She
let the words fall away.

"Your what?"

"Well, my son." She saw the resemblance then, the shape
of his mouth, the little bump on the bridge of his nose, the
few freckles that seemed out of place on his olive skin. Her
heart jolted. He couldn't be. Just because he was the spitting image of Brand except for the few traits that belonged
to her family . . . No. Her imagination was running away with
her. "But . . . but I care about you anyway."

"Because of Brand?"

"He has nothing to do with this." Or did he? Did he have
everything to do with it? Could it be? Her feet felt leaden, her
mind was spinning way out of control. She was letting her emotions play havoc with her rational thinking. "Come on upstairs
and I'll buy you a Coke."

He hesitated, then his gaze slid away and he tried to hide
the fact that he dashed away tears. "In a minute, okay?"

"Okay."

On wooden legs, she walked up the stairs, her heart thundering in her chest, her fingers suddenly cold. Inside the
apartment she walked to the sink, splashed water over her
face, then saw the message light flashing on her answering
machine.

Without thinking, she pressed the play button and Sloan
Redhawk's voice filled the room. "I think we found our
couple, but they're divorced," he said, and she braced herself
against the table. "Your boy was adopted by—hold on to
your hat, I've already sent Brandon a Fax—Venitia and Al
Cunningham."

She closed her eyes. "Dear God."

"His name is Chris, but you probably know him. You might
want to give me a call . . ."

There was a gasp from the doorway and she turned to find
Chris standing on the threshold. He had on a clean flannel

shirt, his hair was wet as if he, too, had thrown some water over his eyes and forehead and his face was a pasty shade of white. "What?" he croaked, his voice cracking on the single pain-filled word. "What did that guy say?"

"Oh, Lord, Chris, I didn't know. I had no idea that—"

"That what? That I'm your son? Yours and . . . and Brand's? Who is that guy?" he demanded, poking his finger at the machine. "Who?" His face twisted in revulsion. "It's lies, right? All lies?"

"I don't know—"

"No!" She took a step toward him but it was too late. "No! No! No!" He flew down the stairs, nearly tripping, his shirt-tails flying. "You're not my mother, you're not!" He ran to the old windmill and she followed him across the field, through the door and up the rickety old steps. At the top, he was waiting, his eyes hollow and filled with rage. "I hate you."

"You don't."

"Yes, I do." He spit the words out, as if they tasted vile. "How could you? How?"

"If you'll just listen . . ." He was crying openly now, his face twisted in an agony so deep it tore at her soul. Dani hurt for him, for the boy she'd known as Brand's brother, for her son. "I love you."

"That's why you gave me up! 'Cause you *loved* me?"

"Yes."

"That's sick! Twisted! Perverted!"

"Chris, just listen, okay? That's all I can ask you to do. After that, if you still hate me . . . well, I can't change that."

"You're one poor excuse for a mother."

"I know. That's why I gave you up. I was young and scared and your dad had already gone to California. I didn't know where he was. I . . . I had hoped we'd get married . . . but then things changed."

"You mean after he screwed you, he took off."

"It wasn't like that," she snapped. "If you'll just listen, I'll tell you what happened."


Brand felt as if he were about to explode. Emotions, old and new, ripped through him and he couldn't get home fast enough. He only stopped once, at a corner where a kid was giving away puppies. He didn't understand the sudden need for a dog, but he stopped by instinct and handed the ragtag boy a twenty-dollar bill even though the puppy was free—the last of the litter, a runty little tyke that was supposed to be half Lab and half greyhound. Not the cutest puppy in the world, but a dog nonetheless. Chris had been wanting a dog.

Dani's Bronco was parked in its usual spot, but no lights shone from any of the windows. Dog in hand, he searched the house and the apartment, hurrying, hoping to find her, to explain that he'd found their son. Worry clutched at his heart because the front door to her apartment was standing wide open. He called out but didn't hear a response.

The groan of gears caught his attention and he glanced at the old windmill. On the upper level, he saw a spot of blue through the window.

Chris was probably holed up there, sneaking cigarettes or something. Dani might be in the stables. "Come on, you," he said to the pup and hurried across the expanse of dry grass. As he walked through the open door, he heard voices drifting down the stairs and Dani's voice, soft and gentle, filtered down to him.

". . . so you can't blame your father, he never even knew about you."

His heart stopped. She was telling Chris? No!

"I felt as if I had no other choice, but I hated myself for i and I thought about you every day."

"Oh sure!" Chris said. "So you made it with Brand and g knocked up."

"I loved him and I think he loved me. We were just too young to do the right thing."

"You *loved* him?" Brand heard the sneer in Chris's voice.

"Yes," she said passionately.

"But you married someone else."

"I know." Her voice shook. "I thought it was over with Brand, that I'd never see him, or you, again. I wanted to start over, to have a new life, but it didn't work out."

"'Cause you're a loser!"

"Is that what you think?"

"Hell, I don't know what to think, Dani!" he cried and Brandon's heart nearly broke. "What about Brandon? What about him? Do you still love him?"

"Yes," she said without a second's hesitation.

"Are you gonna marry him?"

"If he asks me." *Again,* she added silently.

"Why don't you ask him?"

She hesitated. "To tell you the truth, I was thinking about it," she admitted, and Brand sent up a silent prayer of thanks.

"So what about me?"

"I don't know, Chris," she said honestly. "I just found out about you today. But, of course, I would want you to live with me and Brand and your grandma."

"This is way too heavy. Way too heavy."

"I know."

"I don't want to believe it."

"I don't blame you, but I want you to know something. I love you now and I loved you before I knew you were my son. I also loved that little baby I gave up eleven years ago—differently, of course, but believe me, no one will ever love you more."

"Bull!" Brand mounted the stairs, his boots ringing on the old wood. "That is bull," he said as he climbed into the loft. "Because I love you, too. Every bit as much."

"Brand, I didn't know—" Dani flushed. "Do you know, did you hear—"

"That's what Ma wanted to talk to me about."

"She's a liar!" Chris said, pointing an angry finger at Dani. "And Ma—she's lying, too."

"She just wanted to protect you."

Chris wasn't convinced and the glare he sent Brandon was pure hatred. Brand wouldn't give up. He set the pup on the dusty floorboards and the poor little dog whimpered.

"Who's this?" Dani asked.

"Our new dog."

"Our?"

"This family needs a pet."

"Family?" she repeated, her throat catching.

"Yes. I know I've asked you once before but I'm asking again. I want you to marry me, I want Ma to live with us and I want us to start raising our son."

"No way!" Chris yelled. "You can't just—"

"Listen to me, Chris. I never knew until a few days ago that I even had a son. Then today I find out *you're* my son. Believe what you want, but here's the way it is. I'd go through hell to claim you as my own."

"Bull—"

"Don't even say it," Brandon warned. "I've lived all my life not knowing my dad's identity and I'm not going to let it happen to my kid. Your mother and I . . . we made mistakes. Hell, we're human, but I hope she'll marry me and we can start fixing everything right away."

"You can't fix this!"

"It'll take time."

Chris sniffed, dashed the tears from his eyes and tried not to notice that the puppy, a golden bundle of fluff, was nosing his leg.

"And it'll take counseling. We'll all see a family counselor including Ma."

Chris shook his head. "I don't know——"

"You want to talk to Al?"

Chris's face curled in on itself. "No way. He hated me."

"Well, I don't. I love you, son," Brand said, tears standing in his eyes. Dani felt hot trickles run down her cheeks.

"So do I," she whispered.

Brand reached forward and offered Chris his hand. Hesitantly the boy stretched out his fingers. As their hands touched, Brand pulled hard, slamming Chris against him. "I'll never leave," he vowed, his voice husky. Then, with his free hand, he grabbed Dani in a fierce grip that promised he'd never let go. "And I won't leave you ever. No matter what happens." His gaze held hers and she believed him.

Openly sobbing, her arms surrounding Chris and Brand, Dani felt a surge of happiness well from deep inside her. They were together—a family. Finally. No more wondering, no more worrying, just a future filled with love. "Of course I'll marry you," she said, smiling through her tears. She tilted her face up and brushed a kiss across his lips. "It's what I've wanted for twelve years."

"So now it's your turn," Skye said, grinning widely whil she cradled her new son, all of three months old, i her arms.

"Yeah." Dani smiled and rubbed her abdomen. She an Brand would be parents again early in June. Chris would hav a brother or sister.

"How about that?" Skye whispered to her son. "You' going to have another cousin, Charlie." The baby yawned, o little fist curled near his face. "And things are working o with Chris?"

"As well as can be expected," Dani said, turning her atte tion to her son, who was braced against the lead rope as tried to train a particularly stubborn black colt. The pup, ha grown and all legs, yipped at his heels and danced around t paddock. Together they were going to counseling sessions a Chris seemed to finally understand how much Brand and D loved him and why he'd been raised by his grandmother, a accept that he would always be with them.

Life had settled down. The McKee children and gra children were growing in number. Beth and Jenner were proud parents of a daughter and Casey was pregnant with twins.

Now, leaves, dry and brittle, swept across the yard. Autumn was in the air.

"And Venitia?"

"She's doing well," Dani said. Venitia, after her treatment at the clinic, refused to move in with Brand and Dani, preferring her own house and cats. So far she was sober and, as she said, "taking one day at a time."

Dani had never told her sister that Brand was Jonah's bastard. She and Brand saw no point, at least not for a while.

The baby let out a squawk as he opened his eyes—blue McKee eyes—and squinted against the harsh sunlight.

"Gotta run," Skye whispered, "before my milk lets down and I embarrass myself and Charlie all over the place." She snapped the baby into his car seat and drove away, honking at Brand, who was just driving in.

Dani's grin widened as she spied her husband and waved. He shot her a look that made her heart flutter. He stopped by the corral, talked to Chris for a few minutes, then strode up to her. "You're a sight for sore eyes," he said, twirling her off her feet.

"My, my, my, aren't you in a good mood?" she teased, straightening his tie.

"Always with you."

"Not true, husband dear. Your black moods are legendary round here."

He let out a laugh and his eyes twinkled. "I have something for you," he whispered.

"Something naughty?" she teased.

"You're a wicked woman."

"Only with you, love."

"Let's keep it that way, okay?" He reached into his pocket and withdrew a letter. "Read it," he said, yanking off his and tossing his jacket over the top rail of the fence.

"Now?"

"Now." He climbed over the rails and hopped onto the ground in the paddock. "Hush!" he yelled to the pup, who barked wildly and jumped up on him.

Dani opened the letter and read. Tears of joy filled her eyes. Never would she have believed she could be so happy, but now, thanks to Brand and Chris, her life was complete, her destiny as shining as the sun that warmed this valley. She touched her abdomen again and swore she felt the baby kick as she reread the letter that touched her heart.

*Dearest wife*

*On this, our two-month anniversary, I want to tell you how happy you've made me. How complete. After years of searching, I feel as if I've finally come home. To you. Chris. To our unborn child.*

*I can't promise you that our life together will always be perfect, but I pledge that I'll move heaven and earth to try to make it so.*

*I love you, Dani. I always have and I always will. You can count on it.*

> *Forever Your Loving Husband,*
> *Brand.*